KET**LEY ALLI**SON
DARK & SPICY ROMANCE

Rival

One

"YOU'RE GOING, Callie. That's final."

My stepfather gestures at his new wife to pass the potatoes, but he's fixated on me.

The New Wife, a.k.a. Lynda *with a Y*, lifts the platter of potato gratin before adding her opinion. "I can't understand why you would object to attending an exclusive academy for your final year of high school."

"Lynda worked hard to get you accepted, honey," Dad continues. "You should be grateful."

Pete Spencer may be my stepdad, but since I've known him longer than Lynda, I begrudgingly call him by a baby's first word. New parents pray for the day their child calls them by that name. It signifies growth, recognition, *love.*

For me, it doesn't mean much.

"Because," I say, pushing my dinner around with my fork to buy time and think of an excuse. I don't have friends to keep me here anymore. I lost them a few months ago. And the one remaining person I could count as family isn't even at this table. "Because I've grown up in the city. I've laid down roots, and I don't want to"—*leave my mom*—"leave here. Ever."

Dad lifts a forkful of Sunday night's roast to his mouth and chews. "Well, it's not like we're giving you an option. You're under my guardianship now, and I'm responsible for what's best for you."

His tone doesn't soften as he lays his claim on me. It contains nothing of his love for my mother, or what we had, or how it was taken away so brutally.

My fork lands against the china with a clatter. I glance up from my plate. "You mean *Lynda's* decided what's best, and that's whisking me away to Rhode Island, so she can start fresh with an untarnished family."

Across the table, Lynda tilts her head, her hand resting gently on the barest bump of her belly. "Callie, that's not fair."

3

Her tone is kind, but her hand is possessive.

"Why not? It's true," I say, blinking hard. I can't let them see me cry.

"That's not even close to accurate," Dad barks. "Apologize to Lynda. She's thinking of your future, Cal, as am I. You're better served at a school that has a direct path to the college of your choice. Your grades were excellent. Before..."

"Before what, Dad?" I sit straighter in my chair. "Go on. Say it."

His lips thin into bloodless slits while his cheeks splotch with red, like the very words are chasing the heat away from his mouth. His eyes shine under the chandelier, but it's an indeterminable glimmer. Dad could be internally raging. He could be howling. He could be wishing I'd just disappear already.

"I'm not going to ruin this dinner further by opining on your behavior this last year," he grits out. "Suffice it to say, the one hurdle stopping you from getting an education of that stature was—"

"Money," I cut in, and I make sure my sidelong glance at Lynda is noticeable. "I'm aware."

Dad shoves another bite into his mouth and falls back against his chair, his jaw muscles bulging as he chews. Although, it's not his chair, is it? Pete Spencer hit the jackpot when he attended a banquet whose attendees paid $25,000 a head to sit in the Metropolitan Museum of Art and eat canapés. Dad used his connections—he's always had those, even when he possessed empty pockets—and there he met Lynda Meyer, granddaughter of *the* Meyers line of department stores. Six months later, they were wed in a whirlwind multi-million-dollar wedding before moving into a historical monument on the Upper West Side, depositing me along with them as an afterthought.

If I ever had any doubts I was a ride-along, those are long dissipated as I sit in a ridiculous ballroom for a dining room and listen to how they're sending me away to boarding school for my senior year.

He might as well hold a trumpet while announcing I'm not his real daughter.

"Apologize, Callie," my dad says again.

I cross my arms, my appetite and my patience departing this room a long time ago.

"That's how you're going to play this?" he asks, his dark brows forming into two eclipsed moons.

"How else should I?" I ask, proud my voice isn't trembling like it wants. But my eyes emote what my voice can't. *Please tell me to stay. Confess that you love me and want to keep me. Please, Dad.*

Dad reaches a hand over the pristine white linen and perfectly aligned table settings.

My stomach lifts, as if pulled up by my heart, and I raise mine to—

Lynda clasps his hand, and they squeeze their fingers together.

"Your train departs early tomorrow morning," Dad says to me. "If this is how you'd prefer to end your dinner with us, then by all means, be my guest. I've long ago tired of your antics."

"*Antics?*" I echo shrilly. "Mom's isn't even cold in the—"

"If you're not going to eat the prime rib Sophia slaved all afternoon in the kitchen to prepare for us," Lynda says, her pale blue eyes a pair of icicles sharp enough to pierce my chest. "Then you can kindly go upstairs and spend your final evening in your room."

"That's not my room," I spit. I throw my napkin over my untouched meal despite the mild *pang* in my chest that the one person who's been nice to me in this house, Sophia, actually did slave over this food. Lynda's never lifted a chef's knife in her life. "And it isn't my bed. My home, my *life,* is on Broome and Allen Street, a place I thought you loved, too, Dad."

Dad shakes his head. "Honey, you've got to let go. This is a better life for you, don't you understand?"

"Plenty," I say, pushing to my feet.

"Wherever you're going," Dad warns, knowing full well I won't be headed upstairs, "you better be back in time for Clifton to drive you to the station. You're seventeen, Callie, and therefore my ward. You'll be attending Briarcliff Academy by this time tomorrow, do you hear me?"

A server laden with a full plate of the dessert course scuttles aside as I head to the giant oak doors and proceed into the expansive foyer.

It's all so elegant. So unfamiliar. If I'd had the chance to tell Mom about how Dad would remarry a trust-fund billionairess and we'd live in a mansion with a private grooming room for a single mini-poodle named Frans, she would've laughed her head off, then told me to finish my chow mien or she'd eat it.

Then I would've confessed to her how lonely I'd be in such empty spaces, and she would've pulled me into a hug, rubbed my back, and kissed my head, telling me there can be no loneliness when a mother loves you this much.

Tears prick, and I rub my eyes with the heels of my palms to keep them at bay.

"So help me, Callie," Dad calls down the hallway. "You will be on that train!"

As my answer, I slam the front door on a father who can't be bothered to drive me to the station after deciding to ship me off.

Two

I WON'T ADMIT IT, but going to a new school makes me squeamish.

I clutch my duffel tighter in my lap, the rest of my luggage resting in a private section of the train a couple of cars back.

The sun hadn't even cracked open its eye when I departed Meyer House this morning. I managed dig out my mom's college tee—old, ratty and softened by wear from the trash bag Lynda filled to send to Goodwill—and paired it with my comfy jeans, worn and naturally ripped in various spots.

My phone goes off in my purse, and I pull it out. When I see who's calling, a thin smile breaks through the scowl I'd been deploying out of the train car's window. "Hey."

"Hey, kiddo," Ahmar says on the other end. "Sorry I missed you this morning. And at dinner yesterday." His voice sounds pained. "I was called away."

"It's okay. I left pretty early."

Ahmar Kazmi, my mom's former partner in the NYPD, reads me better than most. He sighs and then adds in a quiet tone, "Your momma would've wanted you to go."

I frown as I tip my head back in the seat and close my eyes. "You knew I was leaving?"

"You and I text a bunch, and I love getting your daily download, but sometimes I like to check in with the big man Pete and make sure you're treated right."

My heart twinges. The meaning of "Dad" should be given to Ahmar. I've known him since I was a toddler. He rode along with Mom and me to my first day at elementary school. Then middle school. Ahmar was there during my first break-up at twelve, and my first heartbreak at fourteen.

Ahmar was just … there. For hugs. For sarcasm. To be taken advantage of when I wanted to win an argument against Mom.

"It's true," Ahmar says. "You can't get that kind of diploma just anywhere. Definitely not at that sham of a school you were attending here. You gotta go. Make your momma proud."

"Yeah. I'm on the train." There's little point in arguing with Ahmar, just like it wasn't worth the effort to fight with Dad and Lynda this morning. All of them stopped being able to handle me a year ago when Mom died.

This isn't the first time they've banded together in an attempt to "fix" me. I guess they get props for not surrounding me with white walls and a locked door this time.

As if sensing my inner monologue, Ahmar says, "You deserve to look forward to the future. You can turn this situation into something that can better your life. You fucking *got* this, kid. Shit..." he mutters, pulling away from the phone.

"It's okay," I say when he comes back on. "You can go." At his breathy hesitation, I add, "I'll be fine. Promise."

"You text me. Or call me. Every damn day, I don't care. I got your back."

Just like he had my mother's.

"Okay," I say. But the urge bubbles up, and I'm unable to swallow it. "Ahmar?"

"Yeah, kiddo?"

"You'll catch the guy who killed her, right?"

Static crackles between us for a few seconds. "Sweetheart," he says. "I ain't ever gonna stop."

I hold the beaten in, faded duffel bag closer to my chest as the train slows to a stop at Briarcliff Station.

My luggage Lynda packed while I was out last night follows me as I step down the train's stairs, a staffer rolling them toward me between the rows of seats. Unused to such treatment, I stutter out a thank you while lifting the suitcases onto the platform.

He lifts his attention from second suitcase as I grab it. "You a Briarcliff student?"

After a second of hesitation, I nod, lifting my the case before the train bell rings for its imminent departure. "Yeah."

"Well, shit," the guy says. "You're going to be eaten alive, young pup."

He ducks his head in just as the train's doors slide shut.

Frowning, I hitch my duffel higher on my shoulder and push forward, rolling my suitcases with one in each hand.

"Callie Ryan?"

I straighten.

"Over here," the voice says.

A man in a full suit stands at the curb. A girl stands with him in school uniform, propping up a sign with a weak wrist, while using the rest of her energy to hold her phone to her face. I squint, since the girl doesn't seem particularly helpful in angling the sign toward me, but eventually see my name scrawled in lazy cursive.

"That's me," I say as I make my way over. He busies himself lifting my luggage and carrying them over to a town car parked on the street.

The girl is wearing Briarcliff's colors of maroon, black, and white, with her plaid skirt hiked up well past her knees and shirt unbuttoned one button too low. Her long, straight hair is held back from her face with a simple black-lacquered headband, and her blazer is thrown over her arm as she gives me her profile and scrolls through her texts.

I try for polite. "Um, hi?"

Her jaw moves, but not to talk. It's to grind down on the piece of gum in her mouth. Her thumb moves across her screen at warp speed, and she's still holding up that damn sign with the help of her elbow leaning into her thin frame.

Maybe she's hearing challenged, I think as I set my own jaw. I stick my hand out. "I'm Callie."

Pop goes the bubble she's formed. "I know."

"Okay."

I decide to turn to the person who has actually acknowledged me as he approaches.

"You ready to go?" he asks.

"I think so. You're here to take me to Briarcliff Academy?"

The girl snorts, as if I've just blurted out the dumbest thing imaginable.

"I am." The man has kind eyes, softened at the edges from age. "I'm one of the school's most requested drivers, Yael."

Piper gives another snort.

Yael's proud smile falters. "If you'll come with us."

My feet don't move. I glare at the girl. "I'm gonna blame your snot nose on allergies, since you can't possibly be insulting the man who drives your ass all around town while you make out with your phone."

It's enough to get the girl to peer over her screen. "Excuse me?"

I shrug. "Or maybe you're working on your Tinder profile so you can learn about human connection. I mean, I doubt your phone works as a proper dildo." I raise my brows. "Even with the vibrate function."

Her lips peel back in disgust, but I notice Yael's subtle grin behind her as he motions to the car. The girl spins on her heel and waltzes to the passenger side door he's left open, impressively walking a straight line despite her eyes never leaving her phone's screen. The sign falls to the pavement as she steps into the vehicle with a *swish* of unimportance.

Yael follows after her, hastily picking up my discarded name and tossing it in the nearby trash can.

I don't debate whether that's a sign of things to come.

I slide in after the girl, the car's air conditioning a cool refreshment against the surprising late August heat. Gusts from the vents blow back the girl's pin-straight strands around her shoulder like her own subtle wind machine.

That same air makes my kinky brunette waves stick to my lip gloss. I pull my sunglasses from my bag and perch them on my head, scraping my hair back. This impossible doll of a human has the right idea with her headband.

Yael starts the car, and soon we're motoring off.

"What's your name?" I ask the girl.

She tongues one side of her cheek. The word "Piper" leaves her lips, and her participation surprises me enough to ask a follow-up question. "Are you a senior, too?"

She sighs. "Yes."

I purse my lips. "And you're my welcoming committee?"

She looks at me sidelong. "Lucky me."

"Awesome. Are all the new kids fortunate enough to have you be their escort?"

Piper takes a longer study of me. Her eyes are bright blue and in stark, beautiful contrast to her skin and hair.

She smiles, and it's like rays of sunshine stream into this car and rest their beams strictly on her.

With a dying star behind them.

"Oh, dear. Have I shirked my duties? Welcome to Briarcliff Academy." Piper arches a sculpted brow. "Callie, is it?"

"That's what the sign you were holding says, so yep, that's me."

Piper doesn't enjoy my wit. "Okay, *Callie*. You're coming in seventy-five percent of the way through Briarcliff's four-year attendance requirement. That type of thing happens to two types of students—charity cases and unfair connections. I assume you're—"

"The latter."

"—both," she finishes, drawing out the word.

"Look, I'm not here by choice. My ... parents ... decided it would be best to finish high school at Briarcliff. If I had it my way, I'd be back at my old school, believe me."

"Did I forget to mention there's a third type of student?" Piper smiles. "Those that are entirely ungrateful for the opportunity they've been given by getting a spot here."

Piper turns back to her phone in obvious dismissal.

I settle into my seat and stare straight ahead, Yael's unassuming form a mere shadow in my periphery as he drives us to my new place of doom.

He has the right idea in becoming a peripheral blur. It's how I survived in public school, and I guess it's a method to stay alive here, too.

"Don't despair, Callie," Piper says to me, even though she's back to texting. "The third option is what we all are. You'll fit right in." She lifts her head for a smile, which to me, resembles a silent vow of entrapment. "Promise."

9

Three

WE PASS through the sleepy seaside town of Briarcliff, its coast boasting the high, jagged rocks of its name. The mix of green and stone blend its beauty into the dark blue of the Atlantic, the white crests of waves smoothing the sharp, fatal crevices below.

It's a mix of allure and destruction. I press my fingers to the car's window as we drive, utterly struck by the vision.

The picturesque Main Street gives way to a thin road with thick clusters of trees and lazy curls of fog on either side. If it weren't for the rolled-up window, I'd smell the woodsy, musky scent of peeling bark and pine needles. The lifting fog gives way to a private road, and as we draw nearer, an exquisite bronze sign peeks through the trees.

Welcome Briarcliff Academy
Home of the Wolves
resurgemus corroborari

I'd skimmed Briarcliff facts on my phone during my trip here. *Resurgemus corrobarori* is Latin for "rise with might." And the wolves are ... well ... I glance over at Piper.

We pull into a circular pavilion rimmed with expertly pruned hedges. At the center is a gray-stoned structure, two stories high and U-shaped with its wings projecting forward on each side.

I exit the car with graceful awe. The pictures I'd trolled online did *not* do this place justice.

Above the main double doors is Briarcliff's crest, carved out of stained glass, the multitude of colors set off by the early afternoon sun.

Those doors open as Piper slides out and smooths her skirt. She makes a humming sound when she notices the figure descending toward us and hastily buttons up her shirt, clips a maroon crosstie around her collar, then throws on her black blazer.

I arch a brow at her Transformer-like speed.

"Welcome to Briarcliff, Miss Ryan. I'm Headmaster Marron."

The man stops at the base of the steps, dressed in a tailored navy suit. His salt-and-pepper hair flows back in sprayed-down waves, away from his face, and shrewd gray eyes, as if the school shines through the back of his head and into his stare, regard me.

"Um ... thank you," I reply, since I can't think of anything else.

Marron's focus glides from me to Piper, but in those last seconds of study, he's catalogued all my parts, from my scuffed Converse sneakers to my unkempt, free-flowing hair.

Yet, none of his thoughts are in his expression when he fixes his cuffs and says, "Miss Harrington, thank you for your assistance today."

"It was nothing, Headmaster." Piper pastes on a wide smile. "Now that Miss Ryan's safely on school grounds, may I be excused?"

"Not just yet," Marron says. "If you'll both come with me to my office."

"But—"

"Now, Miss Harrington."

Casting a glare my way as if I'm the one responsible for Marron's decision, Piper falls into step behind him.

I turn to the car, thinking I should grab my things, but the trunk is open and empty, with Yael nowhere in sight.

I hastily catch up to Piper and Headmaster Marron at the top stair, my duffel bouncing against my thigh, and fall into step beside Piper as Marron strides into the foyer with us close behind. The floor is white marble tiles threaded with black stone.

There's a sound above, and I glance up, past the hanging chandelier and onto an indoor balcony overlooking the foyer.

Four boys stand near the wooden railing, splayed out in relaxed, yet calculated, poses. They're all in school uniform. Even from a distance, their body language exudes insolent gorgeousness, like it's *definitely* their fault they're this pretty.

Their skin is flawless. Their hair perfectly barbered. Their bodies ... *not* made for high school, and instead sculpted for some pre-ordained future.

It's the one in the middle who catches my eye, the golden sun from the large window behind him casting its rays against his thick, blond hair, run-through and textured. He's too high to see the color of his eyes, but our distance doesn't conceal the savagery of his stare.

He's not scanning the ground floor like the rest. His head follows ... me.

His fingers drum against the polished wood as we pass underneath their perch, and the prickles on the back of my neck don't stop until he's out of view.

I shiver, but it's unclear if the chills are from being at the end of someone's rope, or the sheer deep freeze of the air conditioning pumping its heart out to cool such a vast space.

We turn into a wide hallway with shining, lemon-scented wooden cases housing trophies in glass displays, as well as the grim portraits of alumni, professors, and headmasters.

Marron continues his lithe stride, turning us down a large hallway with a domed, church-like ceiling.

A second display catches my eye, outside of Marron's office. He moves inside, but I linger, frowning at the iron crest nestled circumspectly between graduating class photos, sports team portraits, and trophies. It's not Briarcliff's, but it's familiar to me somehow.

The hammered circle with a raven at the center, spreading its wings in flight, nudges at my memories. The Latin script *altum volare in tenebris* is carved underneath. With the way my index finger hovers on the glass above it, it's like I'm *supposed* to know what it means.

"What is this?" I ask, assuming Piper is nearby.

A hand slams against the glass in front of my face. I squeal, stumbling back.

"None of your business," a low voice responds.

My hand knots against my shirt.

Luxurious bronze-colored eyes meet mine. On an average person, they'd just be brown. But I'm not ... *he's* not ... normal.

He's god-like. Beautiful.

His presence sucks all the air out of this cavernous hallway. Heat prickles along my exposed skin, my T-shirt feeling rough and uncomfortable against my nipples, a thin sports bra barely managing to keep them under wraps.

High cheekbones frame his continued, unadulterated study, a carved curvature that hugs the corners of his sharp, Cupid's bow lips.

"I, um..." I clear my throat. "What?"

He arches a blond brow, but thick, inky lashes border his unwavering stare. "I said, none of your damned business, new girl."

Blinking, I say, "I, uh..." Then, because I can think of nothing better, "You were on top."

He was the blond guy in the middle on the balcony, observing me as I stepped onto Briarcliff turf.

"Exactly how I prefer it." His eyes narrow momentarily on my face before reassuming a cold veneer. "We call it the Wolf's Den. Are you my next lamb?"

"Callie?" Piper pops her head out of Headmaster Marron's office. "Did you get lost in the five steps it took to—oh, hey, baby."

Piper peels off the doorframe to drape herself over him. She kisses him on the cheek, but his head doesn't move in her direction. His eyes don't roam to hers.

Piper asks, "What are you talking to the new girl for?"

"I'm not," he says with a lingering, hypnotic tone. "And I don't care to."

The undeserved insult, one that's been uttered in my company and out of it during the entire summer at Lynda's many societal parties, snaps me from my stupor.

"Then let me do you the honor of exiting the *public* hallway that you approached me in, and get out of your highness's way," I say.

His brow tics up again. "Do that."

My upper lip lifts in a mirroring sneer, and I whirl into Marron's office.

"Chase," I hear Piper titter, "Don't be rude."

Chase? Ugh, even the guy's name sounds douchey and unacceptable.

I take a seat across from Marron who holds court behind his desk, impatiently waiting for his charges to sit.

Piper drifts in, mentioning that Chase needed an answer to a prudent question, and Marron's face relaxes. "Chase Stone has a big year ahead of him."

Every part of my frontal lobe wants me to dismiss all factoids about Chase, and this school, but the iron raven haunts my thoughts, and I wonder why Chase used a horror-level movie introduction to scare me away from it.

"Big year for him?" I echo.

"Hardly your concern," Piper says as she crosses her legs. The pleated skirt hitches just a bit higher.

"We have the top crew in the nation," Marron supplies. He interlocks his fingers. "And Mr. Stone is both the captain and the stroke for our boys' eight."

I nod politely as if I know what he's referring to.

"Not that Miss Harrington here is to be outdone," Marron says, "She's an excellent athlete herself. Perhaps she can introduce you to the crew team once she finishes giving you a tour of the school grounds. I assume that's where Mr. Stone's headed?" he asks Piper.

Piper nods. "I plan on going to the boathouse as soon as this meeting's concluded."

She doesn't mention anything about agreeing to a tour, and I get stuck on the word *boathouse*. What other resort-like amenities will I find during my stay here?

"Ah, yes," Marron says, his expression brightening. "Onto the reason you're both in my office."

He turns to his computer, his fingers moving across the keyboard. "Calla Lily Ryan, do I have that correct?"

Piper doesn't stifle her laughter behind her hand. "That's your full name?"

I clench my jaw. "Aren't you named after a dude who leads a bunch of rats out of town?"

Piper gasps.

"Ladies," Marron warns. Then says to me, "Miss Ryan, I'd like you to apologize," Marron says. "Miss Harrington was merely voicing her intrigue over such a unique name. Weren't you, dear?"

"Of *course*," Piper simpers. She even throws in a few eyelash bats. "While we're on the topic, I also forgive Callie for suggesting I use my phone as a dildo when we first met."

Damn. She got me. And in front of the headmaster, too.

Marron coughs behind a fisted hand.

"Briarcliff students pride themselves on decorum," Marron says to me. "I'd advise against the use of such terms while on campus."

I turn to Piper and say through a toothy smile, "I whole-heartedly apologize for my attempt to stage an intervention."

Piper glares.

"Very good," Marron says, then sounds out deft strokes against his keyboard. When he's finished, he pushes back against the desk. "Because, Miss Harrington, Miss Ryan, you two will be roommates for the rest of the school year."

One beat passes.

We both exclaim, "*What?*"

Four

"HEADMASTER, SURELY YOU'RE MISTAKEN," Piper says. "Can't Callie stay with the underprivileged kids?"

I'm not even insulted. "She's right. There has to be a mix-up."

Marron responds, "Miss Ryan's family has paid the entire tuition up front, and Miss Harrington, you're the only girl left without a roommate. I must insist that you—"

"My parents *ensured* I would have a room to myself," Piper says.

"They did, but I also explained to them, if there were any enrollees, your private room was subject to change. Now, at the time," Marron continues, holding up a hand to stop whatever is coming next out of Piper's mouth, "there were no additional students meant to attend. Miss Ryan is a last-minute addition, and I do apologize, but the Meyers insisted she be given a position here. And they also *ensured* as such."

There's a different conversation going on behind Piper and Marron's eyes as they continue to politely spar. It contains a world so outside my depth, I'm closed-mouthed and confident that I'm about to share a room with this expertly disguised she-demon.

"But, Headmaster…"

"It's settled. I expect both of you to be living comfortably in the dormitory after Miss Ryan's school tour is completed. Have I made myself clear?"

Piper nods, and I follow suit.

"Wonderful." Marron stands. "I have a conference in ten minutes, so if you two will kindly busy yourselves elsewhere."

"Sure thing," I say tiredly, and throw my duffel's strap over my shoulder as I rise.

Marron smiles, and I'm surprised it's directed at me. "Miss Harrington will direct you to Thorne House. You are the recipient of a rare position in this school, Miss Ryan. I hope you enjoy your time here."

Those words have never sounded so ominous coming from such a silver wolf's lips.

Outside the headmaster's office, I ask Piper, "So, which way is—"

"I have somewhere to be," Piper clips out.

She strides down the hallway, her footsteps echoing louder the farther she retreats.

"Hey!" I call. "I'm not expecting a grand tour, but you could at least tell me to turn left or right out of this hallway!"

Piper's arm snaps out, indicating a right turn at the end of the corridor.

"Thanks bunches," I mumble, then begin my personal school tour.

I turn right, as directed, but stall halfway.

Chase waits on the opposite side, where Piper turned. She's wrapped around him again, but Chase's face—notably, his expression—lifts from her shoulder and finds me.

This boy's focus should be giving me the creepy-crawlies, but instead, it's causing the bursting-bubble kind of tingles, an effervescent buzz that ignites my blood.

Chase smiles like a skilled sorcerer cursing his victim, his grin lethal. Poisonous. Alluring.

Piper, clueless to the exchange, murmurs something in his ear. His hand dips low in response, cupping her ass through her skirt. His unblinking gaze doesn't leave mine.

I'm breathing heavier. My cheeks feel warmer. Sweat forms under my arms.

Guys like him don't exist where I'm from. I know this deep in my soul.

And so, like the skittish elk I am, I bolt in the opposite direction, and it leads me to a wood-paneled door at the end, bringing me back outside.

I burst through, blinking against the sudden brightness of the sun. I scan the lush, landscaped grounds, then sigh, hitching my bag higher on my shoulder and following the thin, paved walkway, hoping to hit something or someone that will point me in the right direction.

No students seem to be around, and no one dots the horizon. The day bursts bright and beautiful, but there isn't anyone outside to enjoy it, almost as if this small section of the world, with its old-century buildings and perfectly blossoming hedges and trees, has been enchanted into silence.

When two structures appear once I'm over a modest hill, I mutter, "This has to be right," and walk faster, my hurried footsteps the only sound. Ideally, my bags will be where I end up, too.

I get within reading distance and notice each building's placard. One states, ROSE HOUSE in bronze lettering, and the other, THORNE HOUSE.

I do a silent fist bump, glad I'm where I aimed for. Then, I glance up at the rows of windows on either side, hoping I didn't just geek out in front of the entire student body.

I pull at the double-doors leading into Thorne House, experiencing another blast of air conditioning that floats curly strands of my hair until I'm over the threshold.

There's a desk at the entrance and a girl in a basic tee and jeans chilling on the chair behind it, her feet settled on the desk's surface as she spreads out in her seat and flicks through her phone.

Great, I think. *Another one.*

"Hi," I say as I approach.

The girl looks up, her azure gaze getting wider as I come closer.

"The new girl!" she exclaims.

"Yeah," I say with a tentative smile.

The girl stands and throws out her hand. "Pleased to meet you. I'm Ivara Alling. But you can call me Ivy."

I find her smile infectious. "I'm Calla Lily Ryan, but you can call me Callie."

Ivy laughs. "Weird names unite. You and I now have a special bond because our parents were probably high when they named us. Welcome. Do you know where the powers-that-be have stored you here?"

"Uh..." I shake my head. "I haven't gotten a chance to familiarize myself with the place. My supposed Student Guide ditched the crap out of me in order to hang out with her hot boyfriend."

Ivy laughs again, and this time it encompasses the entire room. My own lips widen in response.

"I see you've met Piper Harrington and Chase Stone," she says. She tucks a strand of white-blonde hair behind her ear as she rounds the desk. "Briarcliff's benevolent rulers."

"Yeah. They're super nice."

Ivy responds with a knowing smile, then peers at my bag. "Did you get any sort of class roster or pamphlet or ... anything to help me guide you to your room?"

"If I did, Piper has it all and she's not about to give it up." I reluctantly add, "I'm her new roommate."

Ivy gasps, and it's so sudden and visceral that I laugh. "She's as bad as I think she is, isn't she?"

"Worse," Ivy whispers, but she manages to collect herself. "But that at least tells me your room number. C'mon. I'll show you."

I follow Ivy to the inlaid brass elevators. At this point, I should be used to the luxury afforded to these high school students, but who knows if I'll ever be.

Ivy steps in, and I note she's pressed the third floor—the top.

"Do you live here, too?" I ask.

"Nah. I'm what they call a 'charity case.' I live with the free rides and in a modest dorm down the road. Richardson Place."

I raise my brows. "You're here on scholarship."

"Yeah." Ivy's gaze narrows. "Is that a problem?"

I lift my hands. "Nope. I'm impressed. It must take sizable brains to get a scholarship to a school like this."

Ivy's expression softens, and she sighs as the doors open to the third floor and we step out. "You don't know the half of it. But don't fret," Ivy says, "I only had to sacrifice *two* young goats and one human baby to the ruling class in order to do it."

At my stunned silence, Ivy adds, "Too dark?"

"No," I say with a chuckle. "You're weird. I like it."

Ivy spins around and starts walking backward. One corner of her mouth lifts when she says, "I just might like you, too."

There's a sudden bounce in my step, led by this girl with fairy-light hair, dusky eyes, and a tinkling laugh. We share a smile, and I follow her, thinking I might've just made a new friend at this peculiar, intimidating new school.

Five

IVY STOPS at a wooden door with a brass number plate marked 303.

"This is you," Ivy says, sweeping her arm out like a game show hostess.

Then she blinks at me. Waiting.

I roll to the balls of my feet. "I ... don't have a key."

Ivy balks. "Let me get this straight. Headmaster Marron told you to room with Piper but gave you no instruction? No key?"

"I guess he assumed Piper would do all that." I let my bag's strap slide off my shoulder. "I can wait around until she gets back, maybe in the sitting room I saw downstairs." I pause, an unwanted image of Piper wrapped around Chase—this time, he's naked—burrowing into my mind's eye. "She has to come back at some point, right?"

Ivy purses her lips. "Jury's out on that one."

I hate where my mind goes, picturing Piper doing dirty things with Chase. I also hate that I'm responding to that image with everything but disgust.

Chase is sexy, so what? He's also crude. And mean.

Ugh. *Why* do I also find that hot?

"You okay in there?" Ivy asks, tapping my temple for emphasis.

I exhale, hoping that any lingering sexual images of Chase blow out, too. "It's been a long day."

"I get it." Ivy's forehead smooths in understanding. "As a front desk clerk, I'm not supposed to do this, but you have an honest face."

Ivy pulls out a keycard, black and inlaid with a golden Briarcliff crest.

"You're letting me into a student's room without proof I'm allowed?"

Ivy laughs, the sound carrying down the hallway.

"Your face has been the talk of the school since we heard that a new kid was coming on such short notice. These people? They grow up together as soon as they're out of the womb. Attend the same daycares. Go to each other's parties. *Screw* each other. When fresh blood drips into their water, the sharks are alerted, believe me. You've been Googled, Facebooked, Instagrammed—all the things."

"Err, I'm conflicted about that."

That boulder in my gut twists its jagged edges at the thought that someone could've read about my mother.

"Like your feelings make a difference," Ivy says, poking me with her elbow. Then she stills and takes a deeper look at me. "Your skin has lost a bit of color. Are you okay? I didn't mean to offend. Me and my big mouth."

"No, no, it's fine." I try on an assuring smile. "I'm just not used to data scrapes on my life."

"I wish I could say you have nothing to worry about." But Ivy collects herself, then bounces on her toes with a grin. "Good news is, I recognize your face and have full confidence that you're rooming with Piper, since she's the only girl left without one."

Ivy presses the master keycard into the card reader above the doorknob. She doesn't knock before she swings the door open, which makes me question how often Piper is even around.

Hopefully never.

"Here you are," Ivy says, then steps aside.

I lift my bag and walk forward.

My bag drops again, this time with a heavier thud.

It's one large room with a shared bathroom and two bedrooms on either side. A twin bed sits in Piper's, just out of view. There's also a desk with attached book-shelves, a six-drawer dresser with a vanity mirror, but clothing is squished into every available space, dresses and skirts and shoes spilling out into the center room.

Despite the clutter, the rest of the space is insanely big—larger than anything I've ever lived in before my stepdad married Lynda. But that's not what's so disconcerting.

It's when I turn to what's supposed to be my room.

"Sheesh, we've been in school for a week. It looks like she's lived here for years," Ivy says behind me, eyeing supposed "shared" couch and all the clothing draped over it. She comes to a stop beside me in my bedroom doorway. "Huh. Where's all your innards?"

"I was hoping you could answer that."

My bedroom has identical furniture to Piper's—a desk, a dresser, a bed, a closet. Problem is, there aren't any drawers in the dresser or the desk, and I'm staring at an empty, wooden bed frame.

"I don't see my luggage. Or a mattress." I spin to face Ivy. Maybe I should've listened harder to Lynda about what she said I needed to pack for a rich school. "They didn't expect me to bring a mattress, did they?"

"Heck no," Ivy says, but her furrowed brow is telling me different. "I mean, no one does, unless they want their familiar six-k remote control mattress from home. Now that I think about it, there are quite a few of those..." Ivy frowns and stares up at the ceiling.

"Ivy, stay with me here," I say. "I'm not the kind of kid who brings their own bed to school."

"Then I dunno what to tell you, dude. Your half should be outfitted."

And there's my *aha* moment. "Piper."

Ivy's realization follows suit. "She must've stolen everything."

"But how? I just saw her, and the walk took me fifteen minutes."

Ivy grows serious. "Don't underestimate the power of Piper and her minions. She got on her phone the minute your back was turned. Her younger sister waltzed into Thorne House just before you, with some of her friends. I assumed it was to steal the coffee from the cart offered to seniors." Ivy grimaces. "Guess I was wrong."

I spin in a circle. "Piper got people to remove my *shelves*? Seriously?"

"You ain't seen nothing yet," Ivy mutters, but before I can comment, she pulls her phone out and starts typing. "I'll find it for you, don't worry."

I nod and pace around the room, my bag swinging at my side. I park it on the wooden slats of my bed frame.

"Look on the bright side," Ivy says. "Because you're on the top floor, you get the highest ceilings."

I look up at the wooden beams, with two hanging light fixtures, and blink back tears.

Piper's brief spurt of immaturity is nothing. I should be used to the feelings of an outsider by now.

I say to Ivy, lowering my chin once I've willed the tears away, "I think I'll wait in the sitting room downstairs until my luggage gets here."

"Good idea."

"Yeah, assuming Piper hasn't redirected it to the trash or something."

"Probably a—oh, crikey." Ivy breathes out. "That might be where it is."

I ask after a resigned sigh, "Where's the school dump?"

Ivy answers, but I'm wandering and don't catch it. A shimmer on the kitchenette's counter draws my attention. A black envelope rests there, embossed in gold and torn open. An unfolded letter sits near it, also matte black. It's so at odds with the messy rainbow of colors of Piper that I'm drawn to it, my arm lifting of its own accord.

The letter begins with, ***Altum volare in tenebris...***

"You won't go it alone," Ivy says, hooking my elbow in gentle understanding, "I'll show you where the coffee cart is so we can be caffeinated while we explore the dump."

We turn for the door, but stop when a voice says, "You seriously have a death wish, new girl."

Six

PIPER STANDS in the doorway with Chase's shadow looming behind her. Before I can speak, she storms over to where I am, eyes blazing, and rips the letter from my hands.

She shrieks, "Who the hell do you think you are to go through my things, you perv?"

Though my heart's pounding at being caught, I respond mildly, "I'm the person whose *things* you dumped in the trash." I flick pages of the letter Piper's now holding. "Tit for tat."

Piper bares her teeth. "You little whore—"

"Now, now," a mild, low voice interjects. Chase comes up behind Piper, his head angled, his eyes sharp. "There's no need to start a fight, is there, new girl?"

"I haven't started anything," I say, but I direct my answer to Piper, since Chase's stare is causing goosebumps to spread down my neck. "All my stuff's been taken. Including my damn bookcase."

"Then there must be a mistake." Chase settles his hand on Piper's shoulder, drawing her to his chest while using his other hand to pluck the letter from Piper's hand and smoothly pocket it. Piper maintains her glare, but her body relaxes against him, and she gives me a closed-mouthed smile, as if she's won something I never had a chance of challenging her for.

"Your things got delayed at the airport, or, I don't know..." Chase gives an exaggerated eye-roll, "...the additional car carrying your luggage was caught in traffic. I hear there was a horrible accident on 95." Chase lowers his chin to address Piper, a slow, awful grin drifting across his mouth. "Terrible tragedy. Didn't you hear, babe?"

Piper settles against Chase and smiles. "Totally."

I glance between the two of them. "You expect me to buy that? There's no extra car, and I didn't come here on a plane."

Chase's grin fades, and a preternatural calm takes its place. "You must not have heard me, new girl. Your things got delayed. They'll be along shortly." Chase darts a glance at Ivy, who squeaks and drops the phone she was probably texting an SOS on. Then he centers back on me. "There's no need to report anything missing."

"But—"

"I'm telling you nicely," Chase says, "to shut up."

"And I'm *demanding* you return my things." I cross my arms. "Or I'll have Marron up here so fast—"

"Sweet, sweet new girl." Chase reaches over Piper and tucks a strand of hair behind my ear. I jerk back, my expression hopefully communicating repulsion and not giving away the scary-fast heat that shot to my core the instant he touched me. "You have so much to learn."

That scary-heat is now an inferno. I clear my throat, hoping I don't choke on the intensity.

"Enough of this shit," Piper says. "You're trespassing. Get off my half of the room and go live in the hovel that is yours."

"Bring me my stuff," I retort.

"Find and collect it yourself," she says.

"Callie, let's just go," Ivy says, pulling at my arm. "I can help you bring everything back up here."

Piper laughs. "Enter the squeaky little church mouse. You're always so helpful, aren't you, Freebie?"

Ivy's lips thin, but she doesn't clap back, which is odd, considering the Ivy I've been conversing with is the complete opposite.

"Let's go, Callie," Ivy says again.

I don't want to. These people don't know that my whole life is packed up in those two suitcases. They don't care, and it's with a frustrated growl that I tear my attention away from them and follow Ivy out the door.

"Don't be a Karen," Chase says as I pass. "That is, if you're hoping to survive more than a day here."

I whirl, sweeping my arm in the direction of my room. "You two immature assholes can have your win. I've survived a lot worse than you."

"Aw," Piper says, faking a trembling lip. "Are you gonna cry, babe?"

"It's so cute that you think we care about your life," Chase adds, cocking his head.

My mouth works, but Ivy gets to me first. She grabs me by the elbow and drags me out.

"I'm saving you," she says as we stumble into the hallway. "Before you get under their skin."

The word *fury* doesn't come close to describing what's crawling under mine. "I don't care."

"Callie." Ivy holds my shoulders and leans in close. "You do care. Do not get on their bad side, okay? Let them bat you around a little and get bored with you. It's the only way."

Ivy pulls me down the hallway toward the elevators, but when I risk a glance over my shoulder, I see Chase moving to stand in the center of the hallway, watching us, his hands tucked in his pockets, and his blazer flared out behind.

He catches my eye and winks.

Seven

WE FIND my missing furniture exactly where I feared.

The Dumpster behind the dorms.

Automatic sprinklers from the neighboring acre of lawn cast their spray across the mattress propped against the giant, stinking canister, soaking the material to the point that when it dries, it will forever smell like mildew. My drawers are stacked haphazardly beside it, some cracked, others missing knobs because of all the manhandling they experienced during their brief travel from the third floor to here.

But that's not the worst part.

Garbage bags were ripped, and their contents poured over my things. Spoiled food, rotten milk, used tampons, and the flat slugs of condoms drape over the contents of my suitcases, unzipped for all the putrid detritus to slip in.

"Christ on a cracker," Ivy whispers beside me.

I run a hand through my hair, clenching my fingers against my scalp as I take stock of the scene.

What Piper—and Ivy—don't know is, I'm not above searching through trash. There was a time I Dumpster-dived behind restaurants to collect their cast-off food when my mom was between jobs. It's amazing, the fresh, untouched meals one can find in an NYC trash bin, but something tells me these girls would never understand. My eyes grow hot with warning, but I bite down on the inside of my cheek, redirecting the pain.

"How are clothes cleaned around here?" I ask, hoping my voice is steady.

Ivy's expression becomes pained. "At Thorne House, they put their laundry in special fabric bags and leave it outside their door to be picked up and returned."

I can't imagine packing all my soiled clothes into a bag to have someone else pick through the mess, brimming with terrible hygiene.

I point at the pile of my shit. Literally. "Safe to say, my special Briarcliff laundry bag is in there somewhere."

"Yikes." Ivy bites down on her lower lip. "I guess that means your school uniform's in there, too."

"Yep." My lips pop against the *p*.

"Off-campus laundry is Thorne and Rose House policy," Ivy says. "At Richardson Place, we're normal folk. We have a laundry room with washers and dryers. Coin operated, even."

I breathe in deep. "I guess that's where I'm headed, then."

Ivy nods, and I sense her study of me. I won't buckle beneath her gaze. I don't want to see the pity there.

After a moment, where it's only the sound of the sprinklers between us, she says, "I'll get the luggage caddy. It's around here somewhere. Then we can start stacking."

A tug of guilt grows tight in my belly. "Ivy, thank you, but you don't have to. You probably have class or somewhere to be. I can handle this."

"Can you?" Ivy props her hands against her hips. "Because as a human being, I can't leave you to this mess. Besides, I have free period the rest of the afternoon, hence why I took a shift at Thorne House."

"Shouldn't you be out front, then? I don't want you to get fired because you're helping me."

"I'm absolutely positive the Briarcliff girls will be able to get themselves into their apartments without any help from me. I'm more of a mascot, anyway. Or a zoo animal. 'Look at the charity case, working at a job just like the hired help. How cute and interesting to watch. Look at the way she signs people in and out. What a unique way to use one's hand.'"

I can't help but smile. "Thank you, Ivy."

"Not a problem." Ivy throws an arm around my shoulders, which is somewhat awkward considering she's half a head shorter than me. But the comfort works. "I'll also track down Darren. He's the custodian around here. We are *definitely* gonna need some gloves."

"And maybe some bleach."

I lean into her shoulder. Despite the knowledge that the rest of my afternoon will be knee-deep in garbage, I don't feel so alone.

"That's the last of it," Ivy says, lowering the hose from the drawers.

Darren ended up being super helpful and provided us with goggles, forearm-length cleaning gloves, disinfectant, and directed us to the attached hose to wash down the furniture.

We also made three trips to Ivy's dorm with the rolling luggage caddy like you see at hotels, my suitcases dripping unidentifiable goo onto the walkway as we traveled, and we took over three washers and two industrial-sized dryers to try and salvage my clothes.

Evening has fallen, and I take one glove off and swipe the back of my hand against my forehead. "Good, because I think I've gone nose blind."

"Consider that a gift," Ivy says, then drops the hose to the ground and checks her watch. "My stomach's grown a giant hunger-monster. You ready for dinner?"

I glance down at my clothes, the front of my mom's old shirt dampened with water and ... brown liquid. My jeans haven't fared much better, either. "Does this place have room service?"

Ivy laughs. "That's where the luxury ends. We all have to eat at the dining hall regardless of status. We'll shower in my dorm, and I can lend you some clothes until yours are dry. If we hurry, we'll catch the last bell."

"Bell, huh?" I say as we begin our trek from Thorne House to Richardson House.

"Not a cowbell, if that's where your peasant mind is going." She says it as a joke, then points to the east. "See the bell tower? It'll ring at seven PM."

I pause and stare at the brick laid tower, at least five stories high, with an open, white-beamed cube at the top and a large brass bell in the middle.

"Is there an actual person that goes up there and rings it?" I ask.

"Ha, no. Briarcliff isn't hiding a hunchback. They've embraced the technology to build an electronic lever up there that moves the bell at specified times."

"Wow. Cool," I say, then rush to catch up when Ivy starts walking again.

"While I'm your tour guide, I might as well point out the line of trees over there. See?"

I do. It's sort of like a manmade forest at the end of our flattened landscape on the west, lining the school grounds for privacy rather than promoting nature. But it's thick, and I can't see through it.

As if she reads my thoughts, Ivy continues, "There's a huge cliff on the other side, called Lovers' Leap. We aren't supposed to go anywhere near it, but schoolkids are always hopping the gate. Certain people are known to go there. Those of us who haven't made use of it call it Fuckboys' Leap."

I find myself staring long and hard through the trees. Chase comes unbidden into my thoughts, his haughty, handsome face like a physical alarm for my body. "People like Chase?"

"How astute of you." Ivy elbows me as we dawdle. "Him and his crew, yeah. And Piper and hers. There's plenty of intermingling, if you know what I mean."

I remember the group of guys that were with Chase on the upper balcony when I entered Briarcliff.

"I can point them out to you in the dining hall," Ivy says with a secret smile, and this time I elbow her.

"I have zero interest in that clique," I say, and I'm half-honest, at least. I want nothing to do with Piper and her band of merry thieves. "Can I ask you something?"

"Sure."

We're drawing close to Richardson Place, so I make it quick. "Has anyone ever stood up to those assholes and won?"

Ivy's step slow. "Those people are bad for you. I hope you know that. They're alluring and have a ton of charm, but none of it is real."

I frown. "Did something happen to you? With them?"

Her throat bobs. "Something happens to everyone who comes across that group."

I whisper, "Like what?"

But Ivy blinks out of whatever memory she fell into. "My advice ... don't think too hard on it. Piper and her followers, they're drawn to shiny new things. But just like fickle, overly-groomed house cats, they'll get bored and move on to the next sparkly object."

"I may not be here by choice, but now that I am, it's to get into a good college, that's all. Not get caught up in a bunch of drama."

"That's a great attitude to have," Ivy says with a wide smile. But her lips are too stretched, and it doesn't reach her eyes. "I hope you can keep it going."

Eight

IVY'S DORM, Richardson Place, is a one-story brick building stretched wide to hold about ten apartments.

Ivy unlocks door 5, smack in the middle, and she mutters about neighbors against both walls as she strolls inside.

I follow suit, and I can't say I'm shocked, but...

"Whoa," I say.

Ivy tosses her backpack onto her bed. "What?"

"This place is *nice*." And I mean it.

While not the opulence of Piper's dorm (which I refuse to call mine, too) with Persian carpeting, high ceilings, and an en suite bathroom, Ivy's apartment is still way better than any of the places my mom and I rented before she found a stable career.

Two twin beds have headboards with built-in shelving measuring all the way to the ceiling. Two nightstands with drawers are also attached and nestled between both beds. A pair of desks stand against the opposite wall.

"You think Briarcliff gets their furniture custom made?" I ask as my finger drifts across Ivy's desk. It seems to fit perfectly in its spot.

Ivy snorts. "I wouldn't put it past some alumni putting in funds for it. You know, Piper's family owns the furniture conglomerate Comfy-At-Home. I bet it's them."

"Huh," I muse. "How nice for them, helping out the less fortunate."

Ivy snorts again. "Communal bathrooms are through that door there, and down the back hallway at the end. You can borrow a towel and some clothes until your stuff is dry."

"Thanks. I appreciate you helping me out."

"Have you found another orphan, Ivy?"

Said door widens to reveal a girl with long, damp hair, ample bosom wrapped into a towel, and a scowl.

"Callie, meet my roommate, Eden." With her back turned to Eden, Ivy adds an eye roll.

"So, you're the fresh blood, huh?" Eden looks me up and down.

"I guess," I say. "I had no idea I was this interesting."

"You're not," Eden says. "The bobbleheads around here are simply bored."

"Bobbleheads?"

"You know, the yes-men. And women," Eden says. She pulls on a drawer and starts rifling through. "That's all anyone is around here. I assume you're no different. Just like Ivy Dearest, over here."

I raise a brow. "You've known me for two seconds."

Eden raises her eyes from her underwear to meet mine. "I'm great at what I do. Watch out for Ivy. She may seem like an outsider, but she's not."

"*Anyway*," Ivy says, coming up beside me and holding a folded towel with some clothes on top. "You remember where I said the bathrooms are?"

"Yeah. Thanks." I take the stack from Ivy.

"It's just a plain T-shirt and leggings. Hope you don't mind. We have to wear our uniforms for breakfast and lunch. The one restriction at dinner is no jeans or flip-flops."

"Am I going to my school dining hall, or a formal restaurant?" I say with a smile.

"You're going into the wolves' den." Eden says it without cracking a smile, and my stomach flutters with the kismet of using the same comparison Chase did.

"I thought it was referred to as the Wolf's Den," I say.

"Off you go, Callie," Ivy says to me. "I'll put Eden back on her leash to keep her from biting."

Eden bares her teeth at Ivy but manages to do it without moving any other muscle on her face.

While it looks like *so* much fun having Eden as a roommate—about as enjoyable as being paired with Piper—I do what Ivy suggests and step into the hallway.

I find the showers, pleased they're deserted, and I clean and change within fifteen minutes. Ivy eventually joins me in the bathroom, and we make some friendly talk as we get ready and Ivy applies some fresh make-up. Asking Ivy to borrow some is overkill, since we just met, so I resign myself to going barefaced and wet-haired to my first dining hall experience.

I'm glad for the spare hair tie I always keep around my wrist, and finger-comb my brown strands until they're so fed up, they surrender into a top knot.

Ivy and I venture to the central building but use a side door. I admire the ease in which she floats from building to building, using side doors and shortcuts, and I hope to emulate it soon. They look like easy escape routes.

We cut through the foyer, and, as if my eyes are tugged on by an unseen force, I glance up. This time, no boys peer over the balcony's railing and into my soul.

"Is the Wolf's Den for all students?" I ask Ivy as we pass under it. "Or just the popular kids?"

"Technically, it's a lounge area for seniors, but the only seniors that tend to use it have connections to either Chase or Piper."

I snort. "You're telling me Chase calls dibs like a school bully on a playground?"

Ivy chuckles. "Still got a mind toward Chase, huh?"

"Ew. No," I say. "I saw him up there when I came in with Headmaster Marron and Piper."

I deliberately fail to mention how his stare bolted through me like lightning, so much so that my heart was singed upon contact.

I rationalize that this was *before* I truly met him and saw him with Piper. I can't help how my body reacts to a gorgeous guy, but I can certainly have my mind rein in my hormones once he proves what a jackoff he is.

Ivy pulls one side of large, mahogany double doors, saying, "You'll come to learn that Chase gets ample privileges compared to the rest of us seniors."

"Why?" I ask, but either Ivy doesn't hear me or chooses not to answer, because the moment we step into the dining hall, she gestures to the left. "There they are."

Across the multitude of tables, some seating six, others four, and the ones around the edges two, I find who Ivy's talking about. Four guys are clustered around a far table, the ones from the Wolf's Den, but an invisible magnet pulls me to the one in the center.

Damn it. Chase.

"From left to right, you have Riordan Hughes, Tempest Callahan, the infamous Chase Stone, and James Windsor. Commit those names to memory so you can avoid them at all costs."

"Ah, you lost me at Tempest."

Ivy gets my joke, because she laughs. "And you thought *your* name was extra. Let's go."

Ivy draws me to the side where a trussed-up buffet with a bunch of silver platters awaits us.

The dining hall is decorated with pure, unadulterated church-like excess. Four chandeliers hang in a row, centered in the arched, two-story high ceiling. Massive stone columns frame the stained glass-windows, but I don't linger on the details for too long, because people keep looking at me funny as we pass.

Maybe it's my sensitivity and hyperawareness at being the new girl. I suppose it's interesting to these people when a stranger walks onto territory they've been trampling since they were in diapers.

I'm ogling the table-side pasta bar containing noodles I've never even heard of when I hear my name whispered behind me. I throw a look over my shoulder just in time to see a girl turn back to her plate, with her five friends dipping their heads low to hear her better.

Hesitating, I swivel to the pasta bar and ask the chef for spaghetti Bolognese. He nods and gets to work.

"Ivy," I mutter. She's deciding between a Caesar or garden salad beside me. "Is something going on?"

"Other than Spaghetti Monday, my favorite dinner day?" Ivy picks up a premade Caesar and places it on her tray. "No, why?"

"Because ... people keep staring at me."

My instincts whisper their caution, and I lift my chin, searching for the source of that warning.

Chase.

He stares back, draped across a chair angled to see me better. His tie's askew, but that's because Piper is twisting it around her hand as she leans her hip against the table and tries to win his attention. His friends blur in my periphery, but I take note that Piper's entourage has also joined the table and made it a party of eight.

"Yep," Ivy says once she follows where my attention's landed. "And there we have the four witches of Briarcliff. Piper, Falyn Clemonte, Violet Tobias-Hayes, and Willow Reyes."

I purse my lips. "It's fitting there's four of them, you know, to round out the evil coupling."

Ivy smiles, then nudges me to accept the plate of hot pasta the chef's holding out. "You're not wrong. Emma Loughrey used to make it five, but she left a few years ago."

"Left ... as in dropped out?" I ask as I rebalance my tray, laden with too many fancy food items I couldn't resist. "Why?"

"You're always asking that question as if I have some kind of dark and stormy response," Ivy says, laughing.

Chase won't take his eyes off me, and curiously, the others stare me down, too.

"Can you blame me?" I say as we navigate to the scholarship table.

As we turn, I catch Piper's snake-like smile. She holds up her phone, waving it like she has a carrot on a stick. She gestures with her chin for Ivy to check hers.

"Maybe not," Ivy answers me, then, while balancing her tray with one arm, she cautiously pulls out her phone. "Emma ... left. There was drama. Nothing I should tell you on your first day, though. But ... oh, yikes."

Ivy's eyes pop wide as she stares at her phone's screen.

"What?" I ask, and when I get no immediate answer, I twist so I can see the screen, too.

"*Fuck,*" I whisper-yell.

It's a picture of me plundering Thorne House's dump, my lower legs encased in two trash bags and tied with shoelaces so I wouldn't ruin my sneakers. My hair's in a messy top-knot. I'm wearing protective goggles and blue sanitary gloves, and there are streaks of ... glop ... on my exposed arms and chest as I'm stepping up to the dumpster to look inside.

Did I mention I'm also holding up a thong? My panties, found at the top of the pile.

It doesn't end there. I've been made into a meme, and underneath my beautifully stinky self are the words, **TRASH BITCH.**

Ivy swipes left to a .gif of an opossum screaming and baring its teeth inside a dumpster. Blinking scroll text reads, **MAKE YOURSELF AT HOME, TRASH BITCH.**

Nine

"GOOD LORD, SHE'S LAME," Ivy says as she blacks out her screen. Likely for my benefit.

I rub my lips together and look up. Phones that aren't switched to vibrate start going off. After reading their phones, heads pop up like groundhogs and beady eyes stare at me before students start laughing.

"Oh, God," I say, my stomach swinging dangerously.

"Forget it." Ivy presses her hand to my back and pushes me forward. "Just a stupid prank."

Ivy may be able to direct my feet, but she can't force my head forward. I glance back at Piper, who's got a hand to her chest and laughing. Chase, however, is unfazed, almost bored.

"Sit," Ivy says, and when I don't, she plants a hand on my shoulder and shoves. I land in my seat with a smack.

Ivy sits beside me, and though I feel like I'm as red as the spaghetti sauce I'm staring at, I can tell she's landed warning looks on each and every person at this table.

"The only trash bitch in this room is her," I hear someone mutter across from me.

It's Eden, Ivy's roommate.

"Eat your food," Ivy says, patting my hand. My arms have gone limp around my tray. "You win by ignoring it."

I blink. Swallow. Straighten my spine. If I can get through my mom's death, I can get through this shit, shit, *shit* of a first day. I just have to turn my luck around.

I say to Ivy while attempting a smile, "There's no way I can leave without eating the five-star cuisine in front of me."

Ivy raises her fork in salute. "That's the spirit!"

Smiling, I cheers my fork with hers and dig in, refusing to look behind me and at that table *ever* again. Like Ivy keeps reminding, no good can come from gaining their interest.

But Ivy isn't done talking. "Callie, meet the rest of my crew. You've met Eden, but this is Paul, Luke, Mercy, and—"

Someone's tray, filled with dirty dishes and smeared food, lands on our table.

I jump back at the sound, and Ivy flies against her chair.

"Seriously, dude?" she says to the student who did it. He just smirks and keeps walking.

Blinking rapidly, Ivy says to me, "What the heck was th—"

Bang.

A second tray lands on the original, used silverware and flat soda spilling onto our plates.

Mercy, a cute blonde with ringlets, jolts to a stand, hands raised as cola drips from her skirt. "Callie, what did you *do* to them?"

My mouth opens and closes. "Who? Chase? Piper? I've been here half a day—!"

Crash. More trays. More plates. More glasses.

This time, they're coming from a line of students, some cutting in and throwing their tray at us before scampering away.

"Screw this, I'm out," Paul says, and Luke throws his napkin down and follows suit.

"Thanks, *guys*," Ivy calls after them, but says to me, "They have the right idea. We need to leave."

I glance furtively at the table, noticing Eden is already long gone. During Ivy's and my brief exchange, Mercy and the girl I never got the name of left as well.

Throwing a sad, mental farewell to the delicious food I can no longer eat, I start to rise, but something heavy and wet forces me back down.

I yell. My eyes burn, and I rub at them, realizing warm liquid drips down my face. Something else falls from my head to my back with a wet, sucking sound.

"Piper!" I hear Ivy yell, but before she can follow that up with anything else, I stand, whirl, and shove my palms into the closest chest.

Piper laughs at my feeble, half-blind attempt to push her. "No need to get so angry, Callie. I'm putting my trash where it belongs."

"What's going on here?" an authoritative voice booms out.

I scrunch my eyes, trying to see better, then feel a napkin forced into my hands. I swipe my face, squinting through all the red sauce.

A teacher storms forward, his face lined with fury. "Girls! What is all this?"

"Nothing, Professor Dawson," Piper says. "Callie just had an accident and slipped and fell while holding her tray. Didn't you, Callie?"

Appalled, I answer, "No, I fucking did not."

"Language, Miss Ryan," the teacher says. "And in case it's not clear, that kind of rudeness is not the way to properly introduce yourself to faculty members."

Piper says to him, "It's all a misunderstanding, sir. I swear."

"Then explain the pile of trays on this table," I say, close to shrieking. I glance around frantically, searching for Ivy, for *someone*, to back me up.

But Ivy's held back by one of Chase's boys, his grip tight on her arm. The straw-

34

berry blond one, the one named James. Her eyes are steady on mine, but pleading. Her lips are a thin, white line.

The students who haven't exited the dining hall with tray-throwing flare don't bother with pretense and abandon their food, ogling in silence.

"Oh, in case you didn't know, Callie," Piper flaps her hand. "At the end of the evening, one table is selected to help clear and clean the dining hall. It's a way for students to appreciate our custodial staff. This table was selected for tonight, was it not, Professor Dawson?" Piper's question rises with innocence at the end. "Miss Ryan isn't yet aware of how things work around here. Are you, Callie?"

The double entendre isn't hard to miss. Except for this Dawson, who still has yet to choose a side while he studies the trays in grim silence. "Well, yes, Miss Harrington, but usually students are a lot neater than this."

"We're in a big rush, sir," Piper says. "What with the night run that's happening tonight."

"Mm." Dawson nods, resting an infuriating finger on his chin as he listens to this bitch.

"That's not even sort of true," I say. "Piper *threw*—"

"—I'm here to help with clean up," she cuts in.

"You're out of your mind!" I say, still wiping droplets of red sauce from my eyes.

"Callie," I hear Ivy whisper close by. "Stop."

"I saw it all," another girl says as she sidles up to Piper. Is it Violet? Falyn? The evil little sister? Who the hell cares.

"More importantly," this girl says, "Piper's been Callie's Student Guide all day, so it makes sense that Callie learn the kitchen rules from her."

Piper squeezes the girl's hand. "Thanks, Addy."

My eyes are close to bugging out. What I say is being twisted.

"Ivy saw it, too. Right, Ivy?" Piper asks.

Dawson asks Ivy, "Is this true, Miss Alling?"

Ivy's throat moves. I wait for her response, *certain* she'll have my back...

"Yes," she says. Then follows up, in a dull tone, with "Callie tripped. The students were in a rush to see the race and the table got overcrowded. It ... got out of hand."

Ivy's name bursts from my lungs, but she can't look at me. Or won't.

"Okay, then." Dawson smacks the sides of his legs. "Problem solved."

My jaw goes slack, and I'm ready to unhinge it when he adds, "It means you'll also be wonderful at showing Callie the rules of detention, of which you'll be joining her for two weeks' worth."

Piper's face blotches, her voice taking on the notes of an out-of-tune flute. "But Professor!"

I smile.

"I can fall for your stunts only so many times, Miss Harrington," Professor Dawson drawls. "As for the rest of you, you'd better hurry. Mr. Stone, aren't you leading the boats this evening?"

Ugh. I'm not surprised to see Chase on the fringes of this gathered group, observing from afar.

"Hell, yes," he responds.

"That settles it. Miss Ryan, you can be exempt from assisting in dining hall clean up tonight considering your ... appearance, but don't make this a habit, okay?"

I have no words. But what I lack in syllables, Piper makes up for with a blubbering defensive argument, appalled she's made to clean up the mess *she* instigated.

I leave her to it, storming through the gathered group and pass Ivy along the way.

"Callie..." she says, but my answer is my shoulder hitting her on the way out.

I'm a fool. I shouldn't have been so trusting, so fast. So *clingy*. Ivy's been here a lot longer than me, and she has her own motives to make a priority. They all do.

I push through the doors and into the cool, empty air of the hallway, lights dimmed for the night. Trophy displays cast their glow onto the marbled floor, but I fly past them.

"Hey," I hear a voice say behind me. I don't stop.

"New girl," it says again, and my molars clench.

I throw a "fuck off" over my shoulder.

"Is that any way to thank a guy for bringing you a towel?"

My steps slow, but I keep moving. Unfortunately, Chase has much longer legs than I do, and he comes up beside me with smooth precision. "Here."

I bat the towel away. "I don't want your help."

"Aw, don't be such a *Carrie*."

I halt and spin so fast, red droplets scatter, some hitting Chase's perfectly pressed polo shirt. I'm glad for it. "What part of *fuck off* don't you understand?"

"Hmm. I understand the 'fuck' part well enough," he responds, a slow grin creeping across his face.

I raise my upper lip in disgust. "I don't want anything from you. Or anyone else in there. I just want to be left alone."

"Not gonna happen."

"Why? What did I do to piss you all off so much?"

"You're new." He shrugs. "And somewhat easy prey. Frankly, Piper's becoming lazy. I don't condone what she did in there."

"Yeah, right." I scoff. "If you for one second consider yourself a white knight, you can take your piss-poor armor and shove it up your dick. You didn't do anything to help back there. You just *looked* and enjoyed. Like the rest of them." Then I laugh. "You know, when I met Piper, I asked if she led a bunch of rats around." I give Chase the once-over, ignoring the twinges and pulls in my belly at the sheer length of him and the amount of muscle bunching underneath his shirt. "Guess I was right."

"So, what am I then, new girl? A dickless knight, a useless bystander, or a rat? Choose one analogy, at least, if you're determined to insult me for offering you a towel."

"It's not just the towel," I spit. "It's that you do nothing. You just stand by and *watch*."

"That's where you have it wrong." Chase lowers his head, shadows from the hallway forming a tarnished demon over the angelic curvatures of his face. "I'm merely waiting my turn."

He moves before I can clock it. In an instant, Chase stands close, his nose inches from mine. I'm shocked to feel his finger trailing down my cheek, leaving sparks in its wake. My lips part of their own accord, and I'm drowning in the chocolate depths of his eyes, dark and bitterly sweet.

"For the record," he murmurs, angling his lips close, "you look nothing like a possum."

The word—the memory of the graphic image—snaps me from the reverie. Horrified, I harden my features, rip the towel from his grip, and continue stalking toward the exit.

His laughter follows me all the way outside.

Ten

IT'S when I hit the pavilion out front that I realize I have nowhere to go.

I'm in clothes that aren't mine, in a place I've never been before, and in less than a day, managed to attract the derision of the entire school.

Great job, Callie. I wish proving to Dad and Lynda I don't belong here didn't have to hurt so much.

As I walk in the dark, with tall, electric lanterns providing minuscule light, my phone illuminates in the thigh pocket of my borrowed leggings. I pull it out, thinking that at least my phone has survived this hell-pit.

Ahmar: How was your first day?

I stop in the middle of the walkway. The crashing waves half a mile from here are amplified in the silence.

Ahmar's been a shoulder I've often cried on, but there's not much comfort he can provide from New York City. I could call him and whine about my circumstances, but I've already done that. This is where I am now. Accept it and move on. Despite drawing Piper's inexplicable ire, I'm still a student at a world-class school, and my classes start tomorrow.

Great, I text back, the screen of my phone smearing with garlicky red sauce from my thumbs.

Ahmar: I love hearing that. Call me anytime, ok?

Sure! I text.

I've never been so fake with Ahmar. Ever. But what are my options? Tell him I'm currently standing outside, my things destroyed, kicked out of my dorm, and have no friends to speak of? Then ask him to please come over and arrest the bitch who started it all?

A smile spreads across my lips as I advance forward, picturing Piper screeching in handcuffs as Ahmar plops a hand on her flat-ironed head and pushes her into a police car.

I reach Richardson Place and file that fantasy away for a later date. I knock on Ivy's door. Eden answers with a frown.

"Ivy's not here," Eden says.

"I know. I'd just like to get my stuff from the laundry room."

Eden looks me up and down, refusing to move from the doorway. Just as I'm about to appeal my case, she mutters, "You need to use the showers again, too."

"Yeah," I say.

Eden steps aside, her expression unreadable.

I cut through the room, but pause at the back door when a sharp, humiliating realization hits.

"What now?" Eden says as she resumes sitting at her desk, a lamp lighting the textbook she's been highlighting.

"My luggage was destroyed. The bags, I mean." I can't even look at her as I say this.

"That sucks. But how's that my problem?"

"I, uh..." I close my eyes for this part. "Do you have some garbage bags I can put my clean clothes in?"

Silence.

I wait for the laughter, or maybe a highlighter to hit my head. I know nothing about Eden, other than she's overtly rude, whereas Piper hides her distaste until the minute she can wield it. And Ivy ... Ivy isn't who I thought she was.

Eden says, "Fine."

Her chair creaks as she moves, and I hear the rustle of plastic bags she's pulled from somewhere. "Here."

I turn to grab them—quickly, so maybe the humiliation will end faster—but also latch on to cushy-soft fabric.

"What's this?" I ask.

"A sleeping bag." Eden shrugs. "I hear things."

It wasn't even said that nicely, but the gesture makes my eyes sting with tears.

"Eden, I..." Oh, please, don't break down and cry. "Thank you."

Eden clicks her tongue as she waits for me to regain control. "You might want to use the back walkway behind this building that leads to yours. Since you'll be carrying trash bags and all, I doubt you're aiming to be photographed."

"That's true," I say. "Thank y—"

"Go away now."

I sniff. Nod. Then head to the bathrooms. Again.

I'm spinning my hair into a wet top knot when the sound of the bathroom door draws my head up.

An ice-blonde head appears. It's Ivy. "Hey," she says.

I meet her eyes through the mirror.

She fidgets with her hands at her sides, then continues, "I'm sorry about dinner and how I didn't help."

"It's fine." My hair tie snaps into place. "We just met. You don't owe me anything."

"Callie, I—"

I bend to grab my two garbage bags and swing both over each shoulder. "You helped out today. I'm grateful that you picked through trash with me. But what I most appreciate is how you educated me on the class system here."

Ivy's eyes soften. "Callie, I'm so sorry. I wish I could make you understand, but I..."

"You don't have to. Like I said, we're not even friends. I have no idea how you interact with those guys—"

"The Nobles," she whispers. "They're called the Nobles."

"Uh-huh," I say, staring at her sidelong. "I have no idea how you interact with guys who deem themselves royalty from centuries ago. God, it's like they've replaced compensating their tiny dicks with fancy cars to using royal titles instead."

One corner of Ivy's lips tics up. "They still have those fancy cars."

I resist warming to her smile, but it's harder than I thought. "Point is, you *did* help me today. You've been nice when you didn't have to. So, it's okay. I've got it from here."

I step closer, indicating that I need the space to get around her, but Ivy doesn't move. "Do you?"

"Sure." I put extra pep in my tone. "Avoid them at all costs. Keep my nose in the books. Literally. Survive two semesters here, then go to college like my mom always wanted. Easy peasy."

"They're bad," Ivy says, and I don't need to ask who. "Like really harsh. This could just be the beginning for you."

I lick my lips. "Then at least now I'll know to expect it. Excuse me."

"Where will you go tonight?" Ivy asks, remaining in place.

"I don't know," I say honestly. "But it'll come to me. I refuse to go to Piper's room."

"I could—you could stay with us."

I think of Eden and how much it pained her to even share garbage bags. She did provide me with a sleeping bag, but I doubt her kindness extends to a third room-mate. Then I think of Ivy, and how she showed me just how easy it is to be super-kind, then super-silent, in just five hours.

"Thanks, but I'll be fine."

Ivy hesitates. When I don't show any indication of wavering, she steps aside.

"I hope we can be friends," she says.

I stop with my hand on the door. "I think we will be." I muster up a smile to toss over my shoulder. "Just give me the chance to survive twenty-four hours."

Ivy's answering smile is sad and hopeful, but it doesn't distract from the fear in her eyes before the door swings shut behind me.

Eleven

THE BACK WALKWAY Eden suggested is better titled the *hidden* walkway.

Richardson Place is at the bottom of Briarcliff's sprawling hill, flush against the trees lining Briarcliff's property. The paved stones cut through a miniature forest as I trek along, aiming for the main building at the top and hoping I don't get eaten by a wolf.

Real or fake.

The crashing waves nearby are extra loud. I keep on the pavement, since I'm so unfamiliar with the layout and worried about wandering off track and ending at the bottom of an unexpected cliff. I'm one of those people who goes blind when night falls.

Electric streetlamps are scattered throughout, so I do have some light as my footsteps pad silently forward. I keep my eyes straight ahead, ignoring the random snaps of twigs and rustle of leaves.

It's not a wolf. It's not a bad man. It's just the wind.

Saliva builds in my mouth, and I swallow, the trash bags making squishing sounds against my back as they swing with my movements.

I'm lulled into a hypnotic pace and warm up to the sounds of the forest. I've almost convinced myself the echoing snaps and crackles and pops aren't a threat and just the former mascots of puffed rice cereal screwing with me like little elves.

It's why when I hear a whisper, I halt.

I set my jaw, searching the area with my feeble vision, positive I heard a human voice.

Over here.

My head snaps in the direction of the hushed speech. It's to the right, where the forest becomes deeper and the cliffs get closer.

Are they calling to me?

If so, are they living under a rock? I'm not about to follow some faceless asshole into the woods after having trash slung at me all afternoon.

Something flits across my vision, and I'm careful not to yelp.

It was a person, running, with something flowing behind them.

Oh, fuck. It's another prank.

I readjust my bags and start running, bending my head to go faster—I'd rather run into a tree than face whatever they have planned next.

As I run, panting and following the curves of the walkway, spurts of fire draw my attention, flickering higher the closer I get.

I slow to a hesitant jog, then to a creep, when I realize my poor vision's brought me deeper into the woods instead of its fringes. The forest bed is soft, fallen leaves and soil obscuring my sounds. I squint at the little fires ahead, formed into a circle with hands cupping their stems. Faces are obscured by shadows layered with the dark of night. I have no sense of whether they're twisted in glee or tense with wait as their prey—i.e., me—scampers around the edges.

Slowly, I set the two bags on the ground. Then I move, bending low, into a denser thicket of trees.

These people are in cloaks. Like, Red Riding Hood cloaks with the hoods pulled up and their voices murmuring in a low chant as they surround a bonfire.

I tilt my ear so I can hear better.

"*Altum volare in tenebris, altum volare in tenebris, altum volare in tenebris...*"

What the *what*?

I study harder, blinking just in case I'm seeing things, but the spooky imagery doesn't go away.

Some cloaks are black. Others are a color I can't tell in the firelight. Gold? White? Come to think of it, the black could be a dark purple or deep blue...

Ugh. Colors don't matter. What's important is that I get the hell out of here as fast as my sneakered feet can carry me.

I straighten to escape at a low run, but of course, hook my toe on an exposed root and faceplant into damp leaves.

Excellent, Callie. Now you can add rotting leaves to your rotten day.

I land with a muffled "*oof*," but stay on the ground, refusing to move until I'm sure I haven't been heard.

The chanting stops.

Crap.

"Rise," a voice booms, and I cower against the decaying leaves until my brain logic figures out it's not me he's screaming at.

"And honor," the voice continues. I keep still, one half of my face pressed against the slimy, rotting fronds. The sharp, distinct smell of soil, ripped leaves and damp wood makes me want to sneeze. I pray no creepy crawlies come along to add to this nightmare.

"You have been chosen. Our two chapters are gathered here for the inaugural initiation," the low, male voice says, "as extended by exclusive invite. Show your papers, and let the fire eat the truth."

I hear the spit and crackle of fire as something's thrown in.

"Now, lower your torches and let the fire of ambition grow."

A waft of heat hits my exposed skin.

"Are we ready for this year?" the voice asks.

"Yes," come a chorus of voices, both male and female. "We are ready. We await."

"Then let the sacrifice begin..."

Oh, man. I don't want to be present when whatever's being sacrificed shows up.

I scoot onto my elbows and knees, crawling through the underbrush as chanting begins anew. I jam my fingers on exposed roots, and my knees catch on some over-turned stones as I move, but the pain doesn't hit my throat until I'm back on paved ground and I wheeze out a relieved breath.

Pushing upright, I grab my bags and run.

I'm in full-on sprinting mode, even though I've never joined a track and field team in my life, bags swinging as my arms pump side-to-side.

Unfortunately, my untrained gait, coupled with my poor night-vision, makes me plow into a firm, insanely hard, wall of a person.

"Ack—" I gasp, tripping back and landing on my butt.

A cloaked form stands above me, his face overcast by the large hood, but I'm sensing his study of me. I say it's a guy, since I did not fracture my face on soft boobs.

"I—sorry," I blurt. The form doesn't move. "I'm just—I'm going. Gone. I'm gone."

I right myself, with no help from this immovable figure, lift my bags, and skirt around him.

I don't look back to see if he's following me, and instead half-limp, half-walk the rest of the pathway and up to the academy.

Using the side door Ivy showed me earlier, I stumble in, dropping the bags and then spreading a hand across my chest as I pant.

I couldn't tell who was behind the hood, but he certainly saw me. I wonder how much time I have until he tells his friends and they come back to toss me into their cauldron.

What did I just see? Devil worship?

I wouldn't put it past the demons wearing human skin in this school to engage in nightly rites and rituals. Piper is probably in there somewhere.

Stairs to the Wolf's Den loom before me, its structure cast in the dim glow provided by the stained-glass windows, and I trod over, dragging my bags along. The balcony will be the safest place tonight. I can sleep, then live to fight tomorrow.

Once up top, I scope the loft-like space for a place to hunker down. Two couches are angled in the center, with a low table in the middle. The skeletal shapes of high-top tables perch against the back wall. There's a coffee cart, too, with an emptied-out pastry station neighboring it.

Sighing, I search through my belongings until I find my makeup bag, dry from being hosed down. I had to pick through a profuse amount of garbage to locate what was inside, but I ended up finding most of it. I tear at a pack of travel wipes and swipe the fragrant, damp cloth around my face to remove the rest of the Briarcliff woods from my cheeks.

In the silent gloom, I unroll Eden's sleeping bag (smelling suspiciously of weed) onto the couch and burrow in, bone heavy and tired.

My mind isn't ready to shut down. Instead, I lift my phone, bathed in its blue light as I scroll through Instagram, a place where I never post but always creep.

As soon as I tap on the app, my notifications *ping*. I've been tagged multiple times —bordering on over a hundred—and my thumb hovers over the heart icon. Most of me knows what I'll find, and I'm right.

Hashtag after hashtag of #trashbitch and #trashbitchgohome is tagged to my handle. I don't look at the images.

That's not why I'm creeping, anyway. I planned to scroll through the posts of my friends back home and shift my mindset toward what kinship feels like instead of whatever I just witnessed in the forest. Except ... they're not my friends anymore. When my mom died, I'd become a different person, and Sylvie and Matt had difficulty keeping up. Sylvie especially. After what happened during our last night together, their parents got involved, and I'm lucky Sylvie's mom and dad didn't press charges.

I'm on Sylvie's account, and I suck in a breath when her pictures load. She's unblocked me.

I don't hold onto that hope for more than a second. Our friendship is over, but I'm thankful I can see slices of her life, and that she's okay. Her summer consisted of a greater number of pictures of her and Matt. Arms slung around their shoulders, linking hands in front of the Coney Island Ferris Wheel, sharing a Salty Pimp from the Big Gay Ice Cream shop ... and kissing. Lots of tongue action boomerangs.

I lower my phone until it's flat against my chest and stare at the ceiling until the sad smile drains from my lips, and I feel nothing. A fan *whirrs* its blades above.

The soft sound lulls me into a doze, and I close my eyes, trying hard to fall sleep, but familiar bodies keep forming, using the backs of my eyelids to come alive.

They're not my old friends. They wear hoods and move in a circle around a large fire.

Then, one turns.

He steps closer, and my heart kicks into an erratic beat.

His cloak is velvety soft and shifting with his long strides, changing shades in the moonlight, until he lifts it and settles the heavy fabric over my face.

And I go blind. All I see is darkness, black as a raven's feathers.

Twelve

THE PUNGENT SCENT of coffee hits my nostrils, and I scrunch my nose, snorting at the smell.

I mumble, turn over, and plant my face straight into fabric that rubs the wrong way against my skin.

It's velvet. A cloak. *No*, my waking brain tells my racing heart. *Suede*.

I pry one eye open and cautiously twist until I'm not facing the back of the couch. Then, in an instant, the when, where, and how, all hit me.

I bolt upright.

"Shit, where's my phone?"

I'd set an alarm before falling asleep so this wouldn't happen. I frantically search around, within the folds my sleeping bag, in the cracks of the couch—

Someone chuckles.

Someone else clucks their tongue. "Looks like a bag lady broke in and tried to sleep it off. Fuck, she stinks."

I hold my breath and peer through the strands of my hair, noting the two figures idling near the balcony's overhang.

"Your phone's on the coffee table," one says.

I tuck my hair behind my ears. As soon as it's clear who's speaking, I sneer, then snatch my phone off the table and frantically tap against the screen as I register the time.

Son of a bitch.

No wonder I never heard my alarm. It's been turned off.

The horror must read in my expression, because the second voice laughs.

"Why the hell did you do this?" I ask Chase, ignoring the laughter of his friend, who I think is the one named Tempest.

Tempest's hair is as dark as the promise of his name, cut at an angled chop where some strands fall across his brow. His eyes are a bright green and at odds with his thin, jaded lips. He's laughing, but I'm certain his happiness will never match the natural spark in his irises.

"I believe you're on my turf, therefore, I can do what I want," Chase answers. He leans back on his elbows, resting against the railing behind him, exactly like the playground bully I predicted he'd be.

I have the vapid wish for the wood to buckle. Chase is too handsome for 7:30 in the morning, showered and groomed. His scent cuts through the freshly ground coffee beans in the air, a freshwater mix of pine and sage.

Like he's been tramping through the woods, my mind whispers.

"What, destroying my furniture wasn't enough?" I ask. "Soiling my clothes and trashing my uniform didn't give you the jollies you were searching for?" I throw off the sleeping bag and shift until my feet touch the floor. "Now you make me late for class, too?"

I swipe my make-up bag off the coffee table and scrounge through it, finding a compact. Flipping it, I check to see that these twerps didn't draw a Sharpie penis on my face while I was sleeping.

"I'm not the one who chose to trespass up here," he responds, the brown of his eyes shining amber from the stained-glass sun above.

"Then why are *you* up here? The both of you."

Chase pushes off the banister. "We've acquired the privilege."

"Damn it," I mutter, deciding to ignore the boys. I'm late, my uniform is somewhere and wrinkled, and I was hoping to get up at five so I could secretly use the gym showers and get ready. Now, I'll be lucky if I make it to class with my hair brushed.

In an effort to do that much, I start packing up my things.

"Are we too much?" Chase mocks. "Is your phone charged enough to call Daddy to come save you?"

I glance up from tossing my sleeping bag and necessities in a garbage bag. "Have you not left yet?"

"She has a point," Tempest adds, retaining his spot near the railing. He lifts his chin, as if to smell the air around him. "I thought we came to take her garbage and put it out in the rain to putrefy further. If we're not doing that, why are we here?"

I glare at him while pulling my bags full of clothes closer. "I don't have time for this. Or you."

"We make the time, not you," Chase corrects. "And if your aim is to make it to history before the bell, you'd better scoot that ass of yours out of here."

"Yeah, so we can get our caffeine buzz without a homeless chick shaking her cup for change," Tempest adds.

"You've used that insult twice in ten minutes," I snap. "I guess Briarcliff's best and brightest requirements don't include creativity."

"I don't need creativity to make you cry, Trash Bitch." Tempest cocks a brow. "Today's going to be so fun for you."

"Run along, Calla Lily," Chase adds, while he idly pours himself a cup of coffee.

I'm ready to oblige. It's unnerving they've been up here long enough to start a brew, fuck with my phone, and watch me while I slept.

And it's incredibly disconcerting to hear Chase say my full name. Where did he get that tidbit of trivia? Piper?

"Gladly," I say. "But first…" I storm over to the coffee cart and shove in front of Chase. He responds to the contact with a low chuckle.

I refuse to back down, so I let him press up against me—so hard, so firm, so *male* —as I pour the carafe into a to-go cup, dump in some cream, find a lid, then twist out of his unsettling hold.

When I turn, my front molds with his, the bumps and ridges of his muscular chest pressing against my chest.

His gaze drops, and I pretend I don't feel the length of him. Or how it's made my lower half stir with awareness.

There is not one soft spot on this guy.

My breathing quickens, but my stare holds steady, exuding an arrogance I don't feel. There are places—the wicked ones, the ones that delight in sinful pleasure—on my body that come alive with his presence, sending their request for more by setting off electric waves across my skin, goosepimpling my flesh.

Chase's pupils dilate, but his lips cut through the passion, cold as a steel knife. He says, "The coffee up here is for members only."

I point to my two bags, now containing my entire sorry life at this school. "Consider it an *earned* privilege. Now, if you'll excuse me."

Chase makes a low rumble in his throat but stands aside. He's backed me up against a wall, and it's cold where his body once was.

"It'd be in your best interest to run, not walk," he says. "Because once I give the go-ahead, the Den'll be crowded within minutes. Wouldn't want you caught with your garbage bags hanging out."

He glances down at my chest, appraising, before drifting over to Tempest.

My throat's tight, and I exhale to loosen the muscles.

"See ya, trash possum," Tempest says as I hitch both my bags over one shoulder, clutch my coffee, and head toward the stairs. He's munching on a cinnamon roll that I swear he must've pulled from his pocket, but it smells *divine*.

Chase must hear my stomach rumble, because he says as I hit the staircase, "Breakfast is over. Classes start in twenty minutes."

"I'm aware," I say, and start my descent.

"Piper keeps granola bars in the shared kitchen cabinet."

I pause. Chase sips his coffee with an expression that is anything but innocent.

"Why would I care about that?" I ask.

"Come on, little possum. You can't scurry around forever. Go to your room." Chase follows up with a feral smile. "Don't be afraid. Piper's not there. She's finishing up training at the boathouse."

"I'm not scared of her. Or you."

It's infuriating, but Chase is right. I can't sleep in the Wolf's Den forever now that *he* knows I'm here.

My feet pound down the stairs, but just as I break through into the foyer, Chase leans over the railing and calls, "Be glad I got to you first, new girl. I'm the only nice face you'll see today."

"I'm doomed," I mutter, and dash through a smattering of students out front, fat raindrops splattering both the plastic and my head.

Thirteen

I STROLL through the public areas of Thorne House with my damp head held high, only a hundred snickers and whispered *trash bitch* insults trailing behind. No one offers to help.

A girl is at the front desk area, and she doesn't question me when I tell her my name and that I need a key to my room.

She hands it over without comment, but I don't miss the rush to her phone as soon as I head to the elevators and her snide glances at me as she texts.

Great. Trash Bitch lives in infamy.

My lips flutter with my exhale as I ascend to the third floor, and once the doors slide apart, I don't dawdle.

The key works on the first try, and I step inside with dread stretching its wings inside my chest, but I won't let them release to full mast until I know what lies in wait.

Lucky for me, it's blissful silence.

Chase was telling the truth. Piper isn't here, though she's left a heavy cloud of gardenia perfume (otherwise known as overly sweet entitlement) in her wake.

To be safe, I call, "Piper?" but the doorknob to her room doesn't move. Nor do I hear any scuffing sounds behind it.

Good.

I turn into my room, discarding my empty coffee cup in the kitchen bin along the way.

During my entire walk in the misting rain, I mulled over how I was going to dress for class, when despite multiple attempts at washing and ironing yesterday, I couldn't get my uniform to the pristine condition it once was, or for it to stop smelling like raccoon piss.

God, I'm so screwed.

My wet bags land on the floorboards of my room with a thud. On a positive note, the plastic is waterproof, and my clothes missed a second fate. I stare down at them, preparing myself for a thorough, desperate search, when—

Holy shit.

My attention centers on my bedroom, and I'm either wishing so hard that I'm hallucinating, or my room is fully furnished.

My desk has drawers. My nightstand has drawers. My dresser has drawers! I touch it all, the wood grain running up against the pads of my fingers as I glide them over the surfaces.

A thorough inspection confirms my suspicions—these aren't the drawers Ivy and I spent over an hour washing yesterday. They're too flawless, too unstained to have come from the dump. After receiving such a heavy dose of water, they'd be warped and hard to fit into their shelving, but these open and shut with ease, the movement bringing with it the sharp scent of freshly sanded wood.

Twirling, I move to my mattress, as white as the day it was wrapped up at the factory.

It can't be. None of this is mine. I haven't had the chance to report the missing furniture to Marron. There's no way the faculty could've known.

"What the..." I scan my surroundings, half-expecting Piper in full Briarcliff attire to leap from my closet and launch red paint on everything while she cackles.

Yet, the room is silent.

"Snap out of it, Callie," I whisper to myself. "You can solve this shit later. Get to class."

As I'm bending to sort through my belongings, something swinging on a hanger catches my eye through the crack of my closet door.

There it is, I think grimly. *The hidden snake.*

I pad over anyway and open the door further. Then step back in surprise.

A pressed uniform hangs from the railing, including a white button-down, maroon cardigan, black blazer, and a tri-color plaid skirt. White knee socks are thrown over the hanger, and my fingers slowly sift against the cashmere and cotton fabrics.

I lift the hanger, inspecting the uniform closely for hidden traps, but find nothing until I flip it around. I almost drop the clothes to the floor, but the instinctual clench of my grip prevents the immaculate outfit from puddling to the ground.

"Are you serious...?" I murmur, pulling the uniform closer.

A long-stemmed rose, its petals stained with black ink, is pinned between the shoulders of the blazer, tied with a golden ribbon.

No note.

Just a goddamned rose.

What am I supposed to do with that? Other than wear this uniform—which fits me perfectly, by the way—instead of the wrinkled and stained one on my first day of school?

There's no time to determine whether this is Piper's next curse in petaled disguise, or if this flower has something to do with the cloaks of last night.

I don't want to think about that last part, though. I did *not* attract the attention of weird ritualists in the deep reaches of the Briarcliff woods. Nuh-*uh*.

Before scampering out of my room, I throw the textbooks I'll need into my backpack, along with my laptop that survived the Dumpster delegation because it was nestled comfortably in my duffel I carried yesterday. Since phones aren't allowed in classrooms, I leave mine on my bed.

My wet hair is combed and thrown back in a ponytail, I've applied some cheek and lip stain and a coat of mascara, and my perfume of choice is *eau de raindrops*, because that's all I have time for before shutting my door—and locking it.

A benefit to these keycards is that they're specific to your identity. I can only lock and unlock my room, not Piper's, and vice versa, yet we can both access the front door to our apartment.

I have to admit, the added level of security against Piper is assuring, and I focus on that barricade instead of wondering how someone else redecorated my room last night.

It's with a full sprint under an umbrella (I need to send Lynda a thank-you text; she thought of everything when ejecting me from Meyer House) that I make it to the Briarcliff building, the clocktower tolling the start of class. I'm proud to only have gotten lost on the ground floor twice. I'm not counting the third time when I caved and asked a passing student where History with Dr. Luke was.

"That way," he said, pointing to the East Wing, and I fly past closed classroom doors until I find Classroom 110.

I stop in front of the door, staring at the frosted glass for a full minute before I twist the doorknob.

"—so you'll come to appreciate the importance of our roots before extending to the U.S. as a whole—Ah. I see we have a straggler."

"S-sorry," I say, clutching my backpack's strap hanging off one of my shoulders. "I got lost."

What feels like a stadium's worth of eyeballs shift in my direction, but I keep my focus on the teacher, Dr. Luke, and not on the growing grins and whispers spreading like a virus from the desks.

"You must be Miss Ryan," Dr. Luke says. He's perched on the front of his desk in slacks and a white button-down, with his blazer thrown over his chair.

What draws me to him is that he's young, but not trying to be hip. Shaggy caramel hair partially obscures his light eyes, and he sports a bit of scruff on his sun-aged face. He's handsome, disarmingly so, in that California surfer-by-morning, teacher-by-afternoon kind of way. I'm beginning to wonder if there's something in the water here that makes people at Briarcliff either stunningly gorgeous, or sinfully hot.

"Try not to make this a regular thing," Dr. Luke says, then gestures to the class. "Take a seat."

"Yes, sir," I say, and for some reason, that causes a wave of giggles.

Dr. Luke smiles. "You'll come to learn I'm not like the professors here. You don't need to call me 'sir' or stand when I walk into the classroom. Okay, history buffs." Dr. Luke claps his hands. "Let's get back to it. Briarcliff Academy has its own deliciously evil past..."

Thoroughly dismissed, I pick my way through the closest line of desks, scanning for an available seat. I briefly land on Piper two rows in, then glance away. It's when I do that I almost trip over a set of legs splayed out in the aisle.

I stop before I stumble, and I wait for the feet to move and let me by.

They don't.

They're crossed at the ankle, and they're comfortable staying where they are.

I sigh. Chase is attached to these damn feet, his arms crossed, and he arches his brows over his heavy lids, daring me to say something.

Move, I mouth, as Dr. Luke drones on behind me.

A grin drifts across his face. His lips part. *Nope.*

Fine. I step over his obnoxious kneecaps and continue down my path, working hard to ignore the muffled *trash bitch, possum breath*, and *rabies and scabies* comments. I reach an empty seat and collapse into it.

"You okay there, Miss Ryan?"

I nod without looking up.

"You sure?" Dr. Luke eyeballs the students in my immediate periphery. "Because I swear I heard detention-worthy slang uttered in this vicinity."

I resist, vehemently shaking my head. Chase, Tempest, and James surround me on one side, with Piper and her friends manning the opposite.

My first day of school already includes my first detention with Piper. I'd prefer that *none* of these people join us.

"All good," I say to Dr. Luke with too much enthusiasm.

"If you insist," he says. "But if I hear one more peep outta you peckers, instant lunch detention. I'll even add an additional two-thousand-word essay as a bonus, due at the end of the day. Got it?"

There's mumbled assent at Dr. Luke's threat. Satisfied, he goes back to his lecture, but as soon as his attention's away, acerbic glares turn in my direction.

All except for Chase. He maintains deep interest in what Dr. Luke has to say and traces his thumb along his jaw in thought.

I follow the trail over his sharp, clean curves, his thumb hitting his full lips and staying there. I swallow, thinking of how it would've been to wake up in the Wolf's Den to that thumb tracing my face, then landing on my lips.

Someone snorts.

I blink, then put my head down and take out my textbook, pretending like I didn't just ogle Chase Stone in plain sight.

I might as well just gift Piper a box of ammo to fill her pariah pellet gun.

But my attention won't stay on blocks of paragraphs. I'm all too aware of the shifting bodies and angled profiles of my fellow classmates, and whether or not they're for me or against me. I've been here less than a day, and already I feel like Piper's condemned my two semesters into loser status. If I wanted to make more than one friend during my stay, I'm screwed.

In search of a friendly face, I look for Ivy's with a nervous, agitated sweep. Being thrown into a full class of jerks and jerk-followers has made me rethink the whole being strong and leaving Ivy behind angle I had going on yesterday.

I don't find her, and my stomach sinks.

"Briarcliff has skeletons I want each of you to unearth," Dr. Luke continues. I start listening. "You were divided into groups of three and given a founder to study and write an essay on in hopes that the twenty-one of you will leave here with some local history under your belts. I know, I know, it's not the epic battle of the Civil War or the grotesque effects of the Spanish Flu, but let's see if I can't hold your interest with some small-town lore, hmm? Ah. Wait a sec. There's now twenty-*two* of you. Hello again, Miss Ryan."

Dr. Luke's focus is nothing but friendly, so I tentatively smile in response.

"Therein lies a problem." Dr. Luke raises his finger. "Any mathletes want to take a shot on what that is?"

"Sure, Dr. Luke," a low voice purrs. "Twenty-two doesn't make for even threes."

"And they say you get by on looks alone, Mr. Stone," Dr. Luke says. "Well done."

The skin under Chase's eye tics dangerously at the veiled insult, and this time, my smile is true.

"What a pickle!" Dr. Luke proclaims, and he lifts his tablet from the desk. "I assigned this topic yesterday, so breaking up a triangle shouldn't be a problem. Miss Harrington."

My stomach dips. Scratch that—my stomach finds the cliff called Fuckboys' Leap and throws itself off it.

"You can work with Miss Ryan," Dr. Luke says.

Piper's shoulders stiffen into sharp angles. "You can't possibly want me to work with her."

"Oh, but I possibly do." Dr. Luke's eyes twinkle, like he knows the exact kind of fuckery he's creating. "You're roommates. You're in the best position to explain the assignment to her as well as my best practices. And hey," Dr. Luke includes me, "you may even let Miss Ryan in on the rules all her professors want her to aspire to. First and foremost: being on time."

I give a stiff nod. I have trouble speaking when in the spotlight. Namely, Chase's, and how I can't shake the sensation that he's memorizing my face, searching for any flinch of weakness.

I am strong. I am my mother's child.

I sit straighter in my seat.

"Can't you divide the entire class into pairs?" Piper asks. She won't give up. "There's an even number now, and—"

"Sadly, that will not do," Dr. Luke says, his expression grave.

"Why not?"

"Uh, because that gives me more papers to grade." Dr. Luke tosses his tablet back on the desk. "The pairing's done, Miss Harrington. As you cool kids say, deal with it. Moving on."

Dr. Luke begins his lecture, and heads turn to him. I relax in my seat, content to get through the rest of class with as little a peep as possible.

Piper's eyes slide over to mine, turning into slits the instant she hooks my attention.

She mouths the word, *trash*, and I commit further into pretending she doesn't exist, well aware that throwing food in my face was a mere introduction to our newfound enemy status.

Fourteen

THANK God the rest of my morning classes don't contain Piper or Chase. English literature even manages to catch my attention for the entire period. So much so, that I stop thinking about either of them for the whole hour.

When the clocktower tolls, I collect my things off my desk and dump them in my backpack. I'm not looking forward to lunch, but I suppose I chose my destiny when I shoved Piper into a dining hall table yesterday.

I wish I'd pushed harder. Then, maybe, detention would've been worth it despite how unfair it feels.

Trudging out of English, I study the Briarcliff brochure, its corners already becoming worn. It's the only map I've found of the school grounds, discovered at the bottom reaches of my backpack where I'd carelessly shoved it before leaving Dad and Lynda. Since my roommate and student guide—I use both terms loosely—is nowhere in sight, I'm trying my damnedest not to be late by using it as a directory.

"Callie. Hey."

I glance up from the brochure, my shoulder brushing against the stone wall as I find my balance. I'd been sticking to the edges of the hallway, so I don't bash into anyone while I figure out where the hell I'm going.

Ivy stops in front of me, clutching textbooks to her chest.

"Hi," I say, carefulness lacing my tone.

"So ... how's your day?"

I fold the brochure. "Shitty."

Ivy winces, and guilt creeps its way into my throat. I add in a softer tone, "I'm surviving."

"I didn't see you at the night regatta yesterday," Ivy says, perking up.

"I ... don't understand the words coming out of your mouth."

"Oh." Ivy laughs. "Sometimes I forget that people have lives outside of this school. Outside of *crew*."

"Uh-huh." I'm still not getting it.

"Briarcliff lives for its athletes, the rowing team especially," Ivy explains. "Even though it's off-season, the boys' and girls' teams still train stupid-hard. The Night Ride is the anticipated opening head race. It kicks off the school year in the manmade lake, down through the south woods. The guys' and girls' eights are what everybody wants to see."

I purse my lips and nod. "I think I understood most of that."

"You didn't go," Ivy surmises. "I mean, I understand why, but it's too bad." A shy smile crosses Ivy's face. "You could've seen me whoop Chase's ass."

I give her an answering grin. "What's more badass? That you're on the rowing team, or that you kicked Chase where it hurts?"

"Well, okay. Maybe I didn't hurt him *too* much." Ivy grimaces. "He's good. And super strong."

I don't doubt it. But I say to her sincerely, "I'm sorry I missed it. You row in this eight that you speak of?"

Ivy nods. "Eight girls in a boat. One coxswain to direct us. You should come to practice. You're tall. Somewhat graceful." Ivy's stare rakes me from head to toe. "I bet you could make the team."

A peal of laughter escapes me. "No, thanks. I'm not a sports person."

"But that's the best part! It's a team vibe. If you fail or suck or whatever, the rest of us lift you up. It's amazing. I think you might like it, too."

"I, uh, I can't."

"Look, I know yesterday sucked." God, Ivy's relentless. "But I'd love the chance to show you the sweeter sides of Briarcliff. You know, the parts without mean rich kids and terrible roommates."

"Ivy, I can't."

"The good exists, I promise. If you open up to it, it starts with crew."

"I'm sorry, but it's just not for me."

"You won't even try? Callie—"

"Ivy, no."

"But—"

"I can't swim!" I yell, then lower my voice as soon as I attract the attention of passing students. "So, thank you, but no."

Ivy's staring at me like I've just been gang-banged by a passing alien ship. "You ... can't swim?"

I sigh. "I grew up in Manhattan. There aren't a lot of pools around, not where I lived. Never mind manmade lakes in our backyard. Hell, I can't even ride a bike."

"You *can't ride a bike?*"

"Would you stop?" I smack her in the arm. "You're the one friendly face I have here. Don't ruin it by judging my lack of a suburban childhood."

"Shoot. I'm sorry." Ivy shakes herself out of it. "I'm the last person who should be judging. My parents are Danish and like to watch me hitting the cat out of the barrel at Fastelavn."

I can't help but laugh with her. "All right, a compromise. I'll be at the next practice and take a look at you slicing waves through the water so long as you don't ask me to join crew again."

Ivy bats her eyes at me like I'm the cutest thing, then loops an arm through mine.

"Slicing waves ... that's not a crew term, is it," I say.

"Not even kinda." We settle into a comfortable walk. "Thank you for forgiving me."

She says it so faintly, I have trouble catching it. Once I do, she changes the subject.

"Where are you headed?" she asks. "I promise I'm way better than an outdated flyer."

"Shit!" I screech to a halt in the foyer. "Detention!"

"I see you've yet to embrace the term *prompt*," Dr. Luke says as I knock on today's assigned detention classroom.

I grimace. "I'm—"

"Sorry. I'm well aware."

Dr. Luke is propped in a chair with his feet crossed on top of the teacher's desk, a paperback spread open on his lap.

Piper's seated in front of him, reading a textbook by standing it vertically on the desk and hunching behind it.

We're the only two students here.

"Listen, being the new kid sucks," Dr. Luke says. "Winning over your classmates is hard. Try not to piss off your professors, too, all right?"

Nodding, I step inside. I'm all for friendly teachers, but it's ultra-weird when that teacher is ridiculously hot and close enough to my age that I want him to like me.

"I drew the short straw and got stuck with detention duty all week," he adds as I plop myself into a front-facing desk—the farthest one from Piper. "Take it from me. Don't be the short straw."

I nod again, avoiding his assessment by pulling out my English homework. From my vantage point, I notice that Piper's using the textbook as a wall to hide the smuggled phone she's texting on.

"Normally, this is a silent hour where you contemplate all the wrongs you've done to Briarcliff Academy," Dr. Luke says as I straighten. "But, since it's just the two of you, and I'm your detention proctor, why don't you guys start the history assignment? You have the added bonus of having me all to yourselves to answer any questions that might pop up."

"Can't," Piper says without looking up. Her thumbs are nothing but a blur over her phone.

Amazing. It's hard to believe Piper's so unaffected by Dr. Luke's looks *and* his unintended proposition of having him all to ourselves. Is that what it's like when you're that pretty? To have the problem of so many prospects that even teachers with movie-star jawlines don't keep your attention?

You dummy. She doesn't need to fantasize about Dr. Luke. She already has a god under her hands. She's had Chase.

The thought of Chase sprawled against her bed sheets, bare-chested and groaning under Piper's hands as they scrape down his pecs and abs, has me feeling uncomfortably bothered.

I clear my throat, forcing myself to think about Jane Austen.

"I have science homework," Piper says.

"Uh-huh. And what type of science would that be, Miss Harrington?" Dr. Luke asks.

"Chemistry."

"Then why do you have your math book open? Are the strange symbols helping you with new emojis to text your friends?"

My eyes widen at his flippant candor. Piper glares at Dr. Luke over the edge of her text. The phone drops to her desk with an obvious and pissed off clatter. She doesn't break eye contact with him when she does it.

"I could confiscate that, you know," Dr. Luke says.

"I dare you," Piper says with a devilish grin.

"Don't tempt me, Miss Harrington."

Their glares clash across the room. I should creep out of here and leave them to it. But Piper is the first to interrupt their silent war. She stands.

"Dr. Luke." She smiles coyly. "You and I both know my parents pay Headmaster Marron *way* too much money to be associated with such silly drama like lunchroom misunderstandings. Callie and I both consider it ridiculous we're even here. We made up, like, yesterday."

I may be mute for the moment, but I'm not dumb. I purse my lips at Piper.

"Is that so?" Dr. Luke crosses his arms. "Miss Ryan? Care to add to this dog-and-pony show?"

"I'd like to focus on my studies," I say. If I side with Piper, I'm an idiot, but if I side with Dr. Luke, I'm a brownnoser. Either way, I can't win.

Piper makes a sound of disgust. "I'm telling you to leave, too, Callie."

"What about the all-important chemistry homework?" Dr. Luke asks Piper. As he says it, his expression goes back to what I've come to recognize as his usual sexy and relaxed self.

"Take it up with Headmaster Marron." Piper swings her bag over her shoulder and sashays to the door, her short skirt covering her ass-cheeks by half an inch.

"Do not push me, Miss Harrington," Dr. Luke warns, but Piper keeps on striding.

Dr. Luke stares at Piper while she leaves, but it's not at the hem of her flapping, plaid skirt, like most red-blooded males would. It's directed at her shoulder blades.

I'm not as focused, and I hitch in a breath when I notice who's waiting for Piper at the doorway.

Chase.

He's not watching Piper saunter over. His attention is on me, unwavering, cat-like, *wild*.

It's like he's the magnet, and I'm the poor piece of broken metal that can't move out of his pull. His utter charisma creeps into my bones, and his expressionless face seems to have memorized every twitch, every blink, every heartbeat I emit.

I feel, deep in my bones, I'm supposed to recognize what he's communicating, but for the life of me, I can't grasp his request.

It's unnerving and ... hot.

Boys don't pay attention to me like this. Normally, they don't look twice, unless you count my old friend Matt's and my brief, drunken sexual encounter when sneaking into his dad's closed bodega last Halloween.

That was amateur fumbling compared to Chase's scrutiny. I've never felt *hunted* like this, but it's not like the physical target Piper's painted on my back. I can't say I hate the way Chase's lips part every time he lays eyes on me.

Piper glances over as she passes by, and once she notices where my attention is, she slams the door behind her, ensuring Chase's hardened, calculating features disappear behind the frosted glass.

Fifteen

MY FINAL PERIOD is independent study, and I use those minutes to get caught up on the day I missed, hoping to get out in front of the lengthy assignments and high expectations of each professor I come across.

Once finished, I head back to my dorm for some quiet before dinner. My gut feeling is that Piper's not there. She's too popular and involved in sports to be in her room much, even if she's determined to claim both bedrooms as her own.

Ivy isn't at the front desk when I arrive, and I'm coming to learn that during school hours, it's usually a hired employee—or a nearby college student hoping to make some quick and easy cash while they keep our dorms "secure" and study their own shit.

On a quick flash of my keycard and ID that the girl doesn't lift her eyes from her textbook for, I enter the elevators and let out a *whoosh* of air.

I did it. I made it. First day of school: check. And there's not one deliberately inflicted stain on my uniform, either. Bonus!

My backpack is heavy on my shoulders as I traverse the hallway to my new home. I don't trust using the student lockers available at the school yet, since it's on a combination lock attached to the door, therefore, anyone fluent in bribery can access the code.

My card *beeps* its entry, and I step into the central room, the beige sectional calling my name. Now that the adrenaline from constantly looking over my shoulder has faded, my bedroom seems too far away. And ... the rose is still there, on my nightstand, asking its unanswerable questions as to how it got here.

My bag lands by my feet with a thump, and I fall onto the couch, arms spread, and face the ceiling. I let out a long sigh.

"Ugh. You're here."

I slow-blink at the ceiling, having no urge to allow my head to fall forward and find the statement's source.

"It's my space, too," I say to Piper.

I hear Piper walk into the room through the door I must've accidentally left open. Clangs and rattles sound out as she fishes through our kitchenette.

"I need coffee," she mumbles. I'm not about to believe she'll offer me any.

"Rough day?" I ask, my voice full of sarcasm.

"No more than usual," Piper says on a sigh.

My head lowers. Is Piper initiating small talk?

I decide to take advantage. "Hey, do you know anything about the new furniture in my room?"

"You have new furniture?" Piper asks it with the flat tone of someone who Does. Not. Care.

"Yeah ... someone came into our apartment and set it up. I figured you'd be aware of it."

"Nope." Piper flips her hair off her shoulder. "I just assumed you whined to your daddy about all the mean girls and got him to shell out for new shit."

The way she baby-voices the word *daddy* sets my teeth on edge. She can't know about my lack of one, or how the one I'm unrelated to couldn't wait to be rid of me and start fresh with a baby.

In response, I'm desperate to shout, *you are such an ignorant, superficial bitch.*

Yikes. Even the logical part of my brain is shocked at my vitriol.

Instead, I latch to Piper's mistake. "I thought you said you didn't know about any delivery?"

Piper's expression freezes for a fraction of a second before she sculpts it back to her uppity mockery. "I don't. But if you're talking about a new bedroom set, then obviously someone had to pay for it. That someone must be your father. Or heck, your mom." Piper shrugs. "I'm all for boss bitches. Maybe she holds all the cash and your dad has to beg for it."

My teeth scrape together. "You are something else, you know that?"

The Nespresso machine gurgles to life behind Piper as she faces me.

"Are we gonna do this assignment, or what?" she asks.

I'm pissed, so I say nothing.

"It has to get done some time," she continues, "which means I have to acknowledge your existence. Can we get this part over with so I can get back to the people who matter?"

"Wow." I raise both brows. "What a proposition."

"They're your grades, too."

"True," I say, shaking off the clinging animosity. Piper has a point. "How do suggest we go about this?"

Piper pulls her fresh cup of coffee out from under the machine, grabs her backpack, then wanders over and perches on the other end of the couch.

A waft of cologne comes with her, a mix of cedar and an indeterminable musk. I squirm when I realize what it could mean.

Sex.

Recent sex.

Recent sex with Chase.

For a veritable host of reasons, I *do not* want that image in my head, but Chase comes uninvited anyway, sculpted torso and all.

I grunt and rub at my eyes, hoping to erase what my imagination's conjuring up in front of the one person I don't want to give any evidence to.

Piper stills beside me, and I open one eye to find her staring at me. "You look more and more like a possum each hour that goes by," she says in awe, shaking her head.

"I have a headache," I snap. "And I'm in total agreement with you—let's get this over with so we can retreat to our designated sides of the apartment."

"Yes. Let's," Piper says tartly, then pulls out her laptop and gestures at me to do the same.

Once she wakes up her computer, she adds, "I suggest we do our paper on Rose Briar, Thorne Briar's wife.

"Waaaaait a second, a couple named Rose and Thorne founded Briarcliff?"

Piper blinks at me. "Yeah, why?"

My mouth falls open. "Can you not picture the shipping that would happen in this day and age with those names?"

"Oh-em-god." Piper rolls her eyes. "You are *such* a sad weirdo. They're not the *only* founders. Thorne Briar had two brothers, Richard and Theodore, and they had wives, too. Sophia and Martha."

"Not nearly as shippable," I observe while bringing up a blank document on my screen.

"We can't write our paper on the popularity of combining couple names, Callie."

"I'm aware," I say. "Which is why I'm looking up Rose Briar."

"Don't bother, I already have a whole list of bookmarked pages I can email to you. When I was paired with Violet and Falyn, I suggested Rose Briar, but they wanted Thorne, since his photo is hot." Piper shrugs. "For an old, dead guy, he is kinda cute."

I say, straight-faced, "And *I'm* the weird possum in this scenario."

Piper shrugs me off. "I'll send you what I've found."

"While I wait with bated breath, why don't you give me the Cliff Note's version of why we should profile her."

At this, Piper turns to me, eyes gleaming. I'm so thrown by the sudden activity to her usually resting bitch face that I recoil.

"I'm *obsessed* with this story. Have you ever wanted to know why the cliff nearest to us is called Lover's Leap?" she asks.

"No...?"

I mean, I assume it's because of all the co-eds banging there, but since I'm including Piper in that assumption, I don't want to say it out loud and risk offending her. I still smell like red sauce from "stealing" her dorm room.

"Rose was full of telenovela issues," Piper continues. "She was always fragile, sick as a child, and you know what that's like in the nineteen-hundreds."

"Not personally."

"*Obviously*, Callie. Jesus. So, she marries Thorne young—I have a theory it's arranged. Then, they try to have a baby. Throughout her entire life, all Rose wanted was a child."

"Oh," I say, and I have the heavy feeling I know where this is going.

"They couldn't conceive. Not initially. Then, when she managed to get pregnant, she miscarried. Six times..." Piper pauses for dramatic effect, then adds, "some at a later term than others."

"That's terrible." I'm so appalled, I can't even type notes as Piper speaks.

"One stormy night—and I'm talking brutal, with rolling thunder and insane flooding and blinding rain, Rose disappears. It's said that she jumped off the cliff."

"God," I say.

Piper nods, then flaps her hand. "In between all that, Thorne was accused of having an affair and further disintegrating his wife's mental state, but let's focus on the mystery. On the leap, if you will. There's something so cruelly romantic about it, don't you think? Like, why jump? Why not take a vial of poison or slit your wrists? Personally, I think she was *pushed*."

"You are darker and more twisty than I ever gave you credit for," I say. "And I gave you a bunch of credit."

"Well, it's way better than a hot, dead guy who died of a boring heart attack, isn't it?"

"I guess," I say. And because I haven't researched any founders to argue my case with, and the paper's due too soon, I suppose this is what we'll write about. "Why do you think it was murder and not suicide?"

"I've been looking forward to this paper since, like, last week. I found these old notes in the library that point to a completely different story than Rose's official obituary. Don't you get it? There's a piece of history the school doesn't want revealed, and it's a big one. Briarcliff Academy is hiding a scandal, and out of every professor at this stuffy library of a prison, Dr. Luke is the most open to out-of-the-box theories. I'm practically guaranteeing us an A. He wants to unearth some skeletons? We have one. So, listen close. I think Rose might've had a—hang on."

A buzzing sounds from Piper's bag, and she pulls it out. Her lips pull up when she reads the notification, then she sucks her lower lip under her teeth as she responds.

"Unless you're video chatting," I say dryly, "No one can see your Come-Fuck-Me face but me."

Piper ignores my remark, finishes her text, then drops her phone in her bag. "I'll take the mystery and questions surrounding Rose's death. You can do Rose's biography."

Piper smacks her laptop closed and stands.

"Wait a sec," I say. "According to you, we're about to write a scandalous exposé on Briarcliff Academy, and you're giving me the vanilla?"

"Oh, like you care that much, Callie. Rose Briar's background will be a breeze compared to the rest of the student load you didn't have the summer to prep for, and I don't need some new girl screwing up my life *and* my GPA. Got it?"

She doesn't wait for my answer and strides toward her bedroom.

I don't stop her. Piper's given me the easiest and most boring part of the paper, yes, and while it won't get me five stars from Dr. Luke, it keeps me away from tragedy and gore, something that's all too real in my flashbacks.

I decide to let Piper walk out of neutral ground and into her territory, thinking she's won.

"Don't breathe in my direction for the next hour, okay?" Piper says. "I have to prepare. There's somewhere I need to be."

When Piper shuts her bedroom door, I fixate on the wood paneling, my grip tight on my laptop. Piper can dissect poor Rose's sordid past all she wants.

Especially if it distracts her enough to never get to mine.

Sixteen

FALLING asleep in a foreign room is hard.

I would've thought bunking in the Wolf's Den was worse, but I slept better there. The echoing sounds and ricocheting creaks were easily attributed to the cavernous space, yet the enclosed air felt fresh, the ceilings untouchable, the walls less likely to shrink in.

This morning, I greet my ceiling, hands behind my head, wondering if I blinked enough times last night for it to be considered sleep.

I skipped dinner in the dining hall yesterday, opting to sneak one of Piper's granola bars instead. After, I had a quick shower and debated starting my research on Rose Briar but opted for bed. Unfortunately, I was too attuned to Piper's noises once she came back from wherever she went, showering, then padding around for what I supposed was a midnight snack. Each shuffle made me afraid of my knob turning, of Piper and her friends filling my doorway, armed with their next attack.

Then, as the night grew darker, I worried about the people in cloaks and whether they were students who saw me, and if they wanted to make me pay for witnessing such a secret ritual.

Rolling over, I check my phone for the time, noting the missed text messages from Ivy asking where I was at dinner last night.

My phone feels hot in my hand, but it's not real heat. It's more because it lay close to a mysterious, hidden object all night.

I'd shoved the rose in the drawer of my nightstand, having nowhere else to put it. I didn't want to display it in a makeshift vase, nor could I throw it out. It's shrouded in too much mystery to toss it aside without understanding its origins.

I'd rather leave it to wilt in the closed-off walls of my drawer than have it be discovered by Piper. Why I don't want her to see it, I'm not too sure, so I chock up the passing chills on my skin to not wanting Piper to ever see anything of mine.

I slip out of bed, fixing my wrinkled, oversized tee, then unlock my door with a yawn.

My yawn turns abruptly into a choke.

"Morning, sunshine."

Chase lounges on the couch, bare except for his briefs.

I cover my mouth, swallowing, but it does nothing to control where my eyes go, straight to his morning wood.

Which I swear he makes twitch once he notices my attention.

Chase smiles, his blond hair in disarray, one muscular arm behind his head, and glasses on his nose. He's holding a book in the other hand.

He's sexy. So, so sexy, and I hate it.

"What are you doing here?" I ask, hovering in my doorway.

Chase cocks his head. "Nice stems, Calla Lily."

My bare thighs instantly clench together. "This is a girls' only dorm," is the one stupid thing I think to say.

A low quiet laugh sounds in his throat. "I'm known to work around that rule."

And sleep with Piper.

The thought doesn't sit well, so I busy myself by veering into the kitchenette and making a cup of coffee. I don't cover myself, since he's already seen me half-naked and isn't overly concerned about the erection between us.

I am, though. Oh *boy*, I am, because he's … large in that department.

"I'll take one, too, new girl."

"Whatever," I mumble, then make a mental note to leave campus at some point and buy groceries. "Since I'm your unofficial butler today, does your girlfriend want one, too? Where is she, by the way?"

Chase's answering smile is slow and indecent. "I take mine with a splash of milk. And Piper isn't my girlfriend, and she's in the shower."

I can't ignore the strange leap of faith in my stomach before I smash it with a stern, *what the fuck is wrong with you, Callie?*

It shouldn't matter whether or not Chase is taken, because I refuse to be a girl who's taken in by him.

But, now that he mentions it, I hear the soft spray of the shower behind the closed bathroom door. I'm unable to fight the instant questions my mind flings at me —is Chase's hair wet? His body damp with steam? Was he in there with her?

He's not close enough to tell.

I say, "Does your fuck buddy want a coffee, then? It is her stash, after all."

"Such crass language from such a delicate flower." Chase moves to a sit, setting the book beside him.

I'm drawn to the movement, but we both hear the faucet shut off. He lifts his hand to his chin, holding a finger to his mouth. "*Shh.*"

As if we're doing something wicked behind Piper's back.

I'm oddly disturbed and turned on by the thought of getting into trouble with him, so I turn my back to Chase and finish the coffees. I make one for Piper, too, since it is her stash and it looks better for me if I steal and give at the same time.

I say, as airily as I can, "I don't care what you're up to over there, or if Piper'll be mad at you for it."

Chase's stare holds steady, and even though I can't see him, my body responds to his focus, growing achy and nervous.

"Aren't you curious as to what I'm reading?" Chase says behind me.

My spoon clanks against a mug as I stir. "Your notes for the history project?"

Chase's laugh becomes a growl: predatory and deep. "You could say it's historic."

"Well, it's nothing of mine, so I can't say I'm intrigued."

Chase considers this. "Does that mean you might have something I want?"

He says it with such a sexy curvature to his words that my kneecaps melt before I can yell at them to keep stiff as soldiers. "It's a toss-up on what's worse. Piper's in-my-face despising, or this whole mystery façade you have going on that you think is so sexy."

It's so sexy.

"Aren't you curious about what I think of you?" he asks, but the question mark lags, like he already knows the answer.

"Pretty sure I'm already aware."

"I wonder how I'm progressing in your head," he muses as if I haven't spoken. "Piper puts on a show, you know, that's completely unlike who she truly is. We've known each other a long time. Her opinion of you isn't what you think."

Damn him for piquing my curiosity. I disguise it by handing him his coffee. "You're not getting anywhere near my head, and the private thoughts of Piper sound like my personal nightmare."

Chase's finger curls against mine on the coffee mug's handle, its stroke so light and delicate, my breath follows its touch. I can't seem to pull my grip away.

"There are some things between Piper and me that go unspoken," he says, his finger still curved against my skin. "And there are ... operations ... at this school you will never understand. I'm looking out for her."

At my frown, Chase adds, "And I can't seem but to want to look out for you, too. I wonder why that is?"

His index finger moves, tracing my knuckle. Once my eyes meet his, he bites his lower lip. My attention drifts to his perfect Cupid's bow.

"Fine." I pull my hand away, breaking his strange, hypnotic connection. "Have whatever kind of obsession you want. I'm gonna be late."

I turn before he can notice how pert my nipples are, how exposed and aching they've become without a bra to protect them.

"How's your new furniture?" Chase asks.

Whirling to face him, I say, "How did you—?"

The bathroom doorknob turns. "God, my head." Piper sniffs as she steps out with a towel wrapped around her torso. Upon closer inspection, her eyes are swollen and rimmed red—like she's been crying. "I need coff—Chase, what the hell? You're supposed to leave before the rest of the dorm wakes up!"

Chase shrugs, and with that movement, he deftly knocks back the full cup of hot coffee. He lowers the mug, entirely unaffected by the burning, caffeinated flames that must've flared up in his mouth. "Relax. No one will care."

"That's not the point," Piper says. Her eyes snap to mine. "What the hell are you standing there for? This is none of your damn business. Scurry back to your room, rodent."

Her crabbiness sets me straight. I take one final look at Chase, but he ignores my silent prompt to answer my previous question just as easily as he dismisses Piper's name-calling.

"Thanks for *looking out*," I say to him, then force a fake smile for the both of them. "Have a nice day, you two."

I ease into my room, but I'm saddled with more questions, hormones, and *want* than any woman should have to experience before 7 AM.

Seventeen

BY THE TIME the clocktower tolls its bell for lunch, my shoulders ache so badly from carrying a backpack laden with books that I'm close to crawling the rest of the way to the dining hall.

I tread through the hallways, thinking, *This is it. This is the literal straw that broke Callie's back.*

And there's only one solution: use my assigned locker.

I'm no dummy. A student's locker is open season for their enemies, and there's no reason to think it'd be any different at a private school. Maybe it's worse here, since these kids have nothing to worry about outside of their cushy, padded future. It allows boredom to take over, and with monotony comes the devil's work.

I heft my bag higher on my shoulders and dip into the West Wing, happy that by my third day here, I've come to know the school grounds better.

Locker 4323 is harder to find than I imagined, as the long, dark mahogany lockers (yes—they're fancy wood), don't vertically line the hallway. Instead, they're formed into 3/4 squares, much like you see in fitness center changing rooms. I peer into five of them before finding mine, nestled in one corner.

On the outside, my locker appears unharmed and lemony fresh. Not one scratch mars any of these doors. I doubt I'm in the type of area where students tag lockers with spray paint. No, these kids are crafty.

I'd unintentionally memorized my locker combination when I received the Briarcliff Incoming Student Paperwork, having inherited a knack for numbers from my biological dad—according to my mom, since she insisted there was no way it could've come from her.

My lips pull down in a wry twist. To this day, I'm stuck on the fact that Mom never gave me a name for him, but she gave me his penchant for numbers.

"It's not worth it, Calla," Mom's ghostly voice whispers in my head. "It was a one-night-stand. I don't remember him, and he doesn't remember me. Heck, I never told him I was pregnant..."

Mom never hid the fact that nineteen-year-old Meredith Ryan didn't make the best decisions in life.

I shake off the sad reminder, spinning the combination. It unlocks with an innocent click.

These lockers are much wider and taller than public school issued tin cans, and the door is heavy with quality as I pull.

If you could see me now, Mom, with a walk-in closet for schoolwork storage—

I scream as a wet, furry *stink* engulfs me.

Passing students freeze at my distress. The ones at their lockers around me jump and scatter back.

"Get them off, get them *off*!" I yell, but no one wants to touch me.

Dancing backward, arms flailing, I fall into someone's chest before I stop writhing. Strong arms wrap tight, and as I struggle, I think I hear, "Calm down, Callie. You're fine."

I fight against the hold, freeing myself and spinning around.

"I'm not fine!" I shout. "Someone put fucking dead rats in my locker!"

I catch my breath and realize I'm shouting at Chase. He's the one who caught me. The one who held me and murmured words of comfort.

He also could be the one that did this. Or knows who's behind it.

Piper.

Chase's face hardens as he takes in the scene. He snaps his fingers at the dawdlers, some laughing, others retching in horror.

"Get the fuck out of here," he says, so faint there's no way they'd hear.

But they do. And like proper, terrified sycophants, they scatter to the wind upon Chase's command.

I trip back, my heel landing on something squishy, and I yelp.

"This is so overboard." I can't stop gasping. "You people are so fucked up in the head, you know that?"

And I was too lost in the haunting of my lifeless mother to remember any caution when unlocking my damned locker. A mind-fuck of its own accord.

"I didn't do this." Chase's voice doesn't rise in tone.

"I don't care," I seethe. "We both know who the mastermind is. I'm reporting her to Headmaster Marron so *she* can be the one to clean up these corpses—"

Chase hooks my arm in an iron grip as I attempt to pass. "Don't."

"Like I'm going to listen to you," I hiss. "This has gone too far. There's ... God ... there's like seven dead rats here."

"Ten," Chase says, his eyes flicking back and forth as he counts in his head.

I wrench my arm away. "Is that supposed to mean something?"

"Not to you," he murmurs, his attention still on the poor rodents on the ground.

"Piper needs to pay for this," I say.

He shakes his head. "It wasn't her."

"Oh, no?" I'm on a roll now. "Do you know anyone else who's chosen to make my life hell? Any other girl who's thrown trash over my head, destroyed my room, and given me the name of a rodent? Anyone? Come *on*, Chase, even you can't be this dense."

He crosses his arms, meeting my stare. "Piper wouldn't touch a rat, even if she had one of those grabber tools for old people."

I'm about to argue, but sadly, in my brief time of knowing Piper, I can believe that much. "Then who did?"

Chase's chin lifts, his intense scrutiny changing to one of languid survey. "Don't know. Don't care. All I can say is, it's a mistake to report her to Marron." Before he turns to leave, he says over his shoulder, "This is me looking out for you, by the way."

"Leaving me among a bunch of rat bodies?" I say. "Yeah, that sounds about right."

Chase's strides don't slow as I launch my retort. I don't expect them to.

Sighing, I turn back to my locker, pinching my nose at the smell. I use the back of one of my books to usher the rest of the tiny, mauled bodies out, and decide to leave my locker door open and empty so the stench can dissipate.

"Gross," I mutter to myself. "Gross, gross, gross."

Once the last of the furries leaves my space, something shadowed and bunched up in the bottom back corner catches my eye.

I lean back—not in—just in case it's alive. When I don't see additional movement, I tentatively reach in and bat it out, just in case it *really* is alive.

A rose falls onto the marbled flooring. Wilted white petals hang off a stem tied with an ebony bow.

"Miss Ryan?" a voice asks from behind, and I startle to attention.

Dr. Luke strides toward me, his stare roaming across the tiny, rotting bodies scattered on the floor.

I step forward. "It wasn't—" but can't finish my sentence. Something wet squelches under my sole, and I yelp before leaping into his arms while kicking the corpse away.

Dr. Luke's arms tighten to catch me, then release as soon as my forehead hits his chest.

"I'm—I'm sorry," I stutter, but he's shaking his head.

He says softly, "Don't bother with detention today. Go to the headmaster's office. *Now*."

I don't argue.

How can I, when there are a bunch of rotting rats at my feet?

I do as Dr. Luke asks, but not before grabbing the rose and hiding it my bag.

"If that heinous shrew wants me out of here," I say, slamming my lunch tray onto the table. Ivy and the scholarship kids jump. Eden doesn't react. "She needs to do better than becoming Briarcliff's pest control Employee of the Month."

"I heard," Ivy says as I slump down across from her.

"Judging by the stares and pinched noses as I passed the dining hall's tables, *everyone's* heard the latest," I say.

"That was some twisted shit," Mercy says beside me. "The whole school's buzzing about it."

Eden lifts her attention from her food, her expression bland as she picks at her truffled mac and cheese. "Any idea who it was?"

"Piper," I spit. "It had to be her. Or her minions."

I don't mention the rose, its presence the one uncertainty in an otherwise flawless argument. Piper may not have wanted to touch poisoned rats from the basement cellars, but one of Chase's guys would. My money's on Tempest, the one most likely to have killed kittens as a toddler.

I twist in my chair and observe Chase and his buddies—these Nobles Ivy speaks of, lounging and belly-laughing as they enjoy their lunch, content in their own, isolated world. Thinking they're better. Royals among peasants.

Chase must've let his royal court out to play, because he's strangely absent from the scene. Piper's also gone, probably finishing detention with Dr. Luke, while I was given a reprieve from it by Headmaster Marron. He considered being reamed by him out a suitable substitute.

"They think they're invincible." I seethe through my teeth. "Someone, at some point, needs to do to them what they do to us."

"Callie..." Ivy pleads, eyes wide when I turn back to her. "It's in your best interest to just ride the wave until they get bored."

Mercy, Paul, and another person I can't remember the name of, nod their agreement.

Eden murmurs her dissent. She says, "Wake that inner beast, Callie."

I say, "I was threatened with expulsion because of them."

Ivy gasps. "But you've only been here three days!"

"I had to sit through an entire twenty minutes of Marron's tirade." I gesture with my fork. "When he stopped yelling to take a breath, I managed to convince him I had trouble remembering where my locker was, never mind where the pest traps are in this building—oh, and the slight logical problem of me vandalizing my own locker with rat corpses."

"To put it simply, Miss Ryan, we've never experienced a vileness of this sort in all our one hundred and seventy years of education," Marron had said. *"By process of elimination, you're the single variable we've added recently, and these 'injustices,' as you see them, keep happening to you, and you alone."*

Injustices, I realized, when Marron's computer went to screensaver mode and I saw the photo, that Marron will never believe Piper and her cohorts are behind.

On the pixelated screen, Marron had his arm slung around Willow's shoulders while holding a fishing pole. Willow grinned widely at him, strands of her auburn hair flying into her face from the wind. Sections of an expensive, white yacht and an exquisite, foreign coastline painted their background with white and turquoise dream colors.

Willow must be his kid or a close relative, since she doesn't have his last name. Either way, she's besties with Piper. There's little chance Marron would side with me over those two. I'm the unchartered variable within this mess.

So why the hell am I targeted with these roses?

"Ivy," I say, "Did you know Willow Reyes is related to Headmaster Marron?"

Ivy starts at the statement. She swallows then sets down her fork. "Shit, I didn't think it'd matter, but yeah, she's his daughter."

"That settles it." I slouch against my chair, folding my arms. "I'm screwed. They can do whatever they want to me without any consequence. God, that *pisses* me off."

"From my perspective," Eden says, keeping focus on her plate. Her hair becomes a curtain around both sides of her pockmarked face. "That also means you can do whatever you want without getting in trouble. Black ops were invented for a reason."

I blink at her. "You're right. I can be as devious as them."

"Now, now," Ivy says, placing her hand on the table between Eden and me. "I don't think escalating this war is the answer. I swear to you, Callie, Piper has the attention span of an indoor Persian cat. She'll move on as soon as you stop reacting."

"Do you know what cats do to their prey?" I ask. "They bat them around, flaying them with their claws and teeth until their prey can't strike back. Then, the cat shakes the animal until they break their neck. And the poor thing isn't even dead yet."

After a beat of silence, Eden says, with her mouth full, "I'm gonna like you."

Mercy's plate scrapes as she low-key shuffles her chair away. I ignore her, because if Mercy's offended by my grotesque description of a cat's meal, then she'll have a hell of a time surviving outside of this preppy-ass school when she graduates.

"I don't want to be Piper's mouse, Ivy," I say.

Ivy holds up her hands. "Fair enough."

I've lost my appetite and push my lunch away. Maybe I should've just let Marron expel me. Then I'd be able to go back to my old school and my old friends ... who want nothing to do with me and are now #couplegoals on Instagram. Not to mention, I'd leave here with no luggage and a big, bold EXPULSION written on my transcript.

If my aim is to go to a good college, then staying here and weathering this garbage storm is my only choice. With *them*.

"I'll be in my room until classes start again," I grumble, and push to a stand.

"Don't go, Callie," Ivy says. Her face grows serious as she thinks. "I know ... let me take you on a tour of the boathouse down at the lake." When she sees me wince toward a *no*, she adds, "It's a nice day. You can shake off some of that negative energy before afternoon classes."

I waver at her words. Should I stew at the injustice in my room, or enjoy a gorgeous walk of the school grounds, something I've yet to make time for?

"You win," I say.

Beaming, Ivy stands. "Excellent! Plus, there's the added bonus of fresh air, beautiful landscaping, a bright sun in a cloudless, early September sky—"

"Relax, Ivy," I say, laughing as she rounds the lunch table toward me. "You had me at 'cooling off.'"

"Let's go," she says and weaves her hand around my arm to pull me through the aisle. "Before you change your mind. Bye, guys!"

I offer a weak wave to my table of sort-of-but-not-really friends, but it's Eden I notice, watching us closely as we leave.

Eighteen

THE SUN IS out in full when Ivy and I step out, the September air bringing cool ribbons of wind to help dissipate the remaining summer heat.

I sniff, my nostrils tingling with salt.

"The eastern breeze must be bringing some ocean with it," Ivy observes as we head down the staircase.

"Is there any way down the rocks to see the ocean?" I ask. "Like, a cliff walk or something?"

Ivy shakes her head. "Not that I know of."

"Too bad."

On the rare weekends my mom took off, sometimes we'd head upstate in pursuit of hiking trails. We'd never stay overnight in the woods—we laughed that we weren't *that* boho chic—but would book an overnight at a local bed and breakfast, then hit the trails. After, we'd try the popular restaurant in whatever small town we chose that weekend, trying out the local fare.

And, to be honest, I was more about the eating part than the trekking one.

The memory brings expectant sadness, which I push away by using the subject to ask Ivy, "Is there a bus or anything that takes us into town?"

Ivy turns us left, skirting around the massive school building and bringing us closer to the ring of trees at the bottom of the hill.

"Nah," Ivy says. "Nobody goes into town."

"But what if somebody wanted to?"

"Like you?"

Ivy's question isn't judgmental, but it's definitely flabbergasted.

I respond cautiously. "Yeah. I need groceries. Piper will have my head if she realizes a rodent's been gnawing at her food. It'd be cool to also explore the town—"

"We get our groceries delivered," Ivy cuts in, then motions for me to veer left with her.

73

My chest tightens when I realize the path we're taking, but Ivy doesn't give me time to peer through the trees and see if remnants of the bonfire are still there, or maybe a discarded cloak stuck in the branches and flapping in the wind.

The memory of the man under a cloak, standing above me as I fell to the ground without offering a hand, comes to the forefront, the hood's folds obscuring his face...

"All you have to do," Ivy says, unaware that I've craned my neck around her to better look through the copse of trees, "is fill out an online shopping cart on Briarcliff's website. Groceries are taken out of your stipend and delivered Saturday mornings."

Her information makes me glance back at her. "So, no one leaves campus, like ever?"

"Well, I didn't say *that*." Ivy's shoulders shake with indulgent laughter. "I've yet to tell you about the parties."

"Parties?" I echo.

"Being on the fringe of the social ladder, I don't go to many, but we all know the types of parties Chase and his friends throw. Sometimes at the cliff, other times at the lake houses owned by various rich parents nearby. Usually on Fridays, but any day of the week is fair game."

I hum in acknowledgment, but given my current situation, joining their fun and games doesn't seem too fun for me.

"It's just through here," Ivy says, and I'm forced to walk behind her as we take a thin, dirt path through the trees.

"Are you sure there's a boathouse and not a labyrinth at the end of this?" I ask through stiff lips, since my focus has gone to avoiding errant branches. I'm forced to dig up long-ago buried memories of exploring trails with Mom in order to navigate foreign terrain without face-planting.

"You should try doing this at five in the morning," Ivy says over her shoulder, "during season when training is in full effect."

"Please tell me flashlights are involved." *And you don't encircle a campfire.*

Ivy laughs. "Some use the flashlight on their phones, but I could navigate this in my sleep."

"I bet," I say as she nimbly avoids exposed roots in the trail.

I'm so focused on scattered stones and slippery, damp leaves blown onto our path that I almost stumble into Ivy's back when she stops.

I lift my head to notice we've reached a clearing with a sparkling, flat lake in front of us. It's *unbelievable* that this is manmade, a special body of water created for Briarcliff's wealthy and elite. Adding to the glamour is what most people would think is a lake house for the rich and fabulous.

Those people would almost be right.

"Welcome to Briarcliff Boathouse," Ivy says cheerily, and grabs my hand to pull me closer. "A gift from former crew alumni." Ivy notices how I'm catching flies, and adds, "Rowing has been a dedicated sport of Briarcliff since it debuted in 1820. As you can imagine, there's been some sizable alumni wallets passing through."

I'm in awe of the size and architecture. If I thought Briarcliff's campus resembled a gothic church, this mere house perched on a lake is like a ski resort mansion without the snow and laid with brick and wood three stories high. Four or five garage-like doors face the water, with wooden docks sprouting from each.

I'm not fluent in boat-talk, so all I can say to Ivy is, "Hot damn."

"Shoot," Ivy mutters. "You see him, too. Jeez, he trains any chance he gets. I hope he hasn't spotted us."

That grabs my attention. "Who?"

But Ivy doesn't have to answer. I notice Chase lifting himself from a thin, vertical boat, pushing onto the dock with his arms, then deftly landing on his feet. He lays his two oars aside, then pulls the boat from the lake, twists it effortlessly, and balances it above his head.

With a frickin' boat for a head, Chase strides from the docks and into the boathouse, his body's profile in full, detailed effect. He's wearing some sort of maroon and black spandex short-and-tank combo, so tight I admire the perfect melons of his ass-cheeks and the sculpted muscles sprouting underneath. The shorts stop at the knees, and after that, it's just golden skin covering bulging calf muscles as he walks.

"Is he carrying an entire boat?" I whisper, and Ivy elbows me at the waist, stopping me from ogling. "And what is he *wearing*?"

"That boat is a scull—it's what they call single shells when we're out training on our own. And he's wearing a unisuit," Ivy informs. We start toward the boathouse again. "The mean girl version of a uniform. You have a flaw? It'll show it."

"Got it," I say, and blink rapidly before my vixen mind can show me what Chase's front must look like.

Ivy pushes on a red, wooden door at the side of the building. I follow her inside while she drones on about the boathouse, surprised Ivy has to turn on the lights, since Chase came in before us.

"Where'd he go?" I ask.

"Probably the showers," Ivy says offhand.

Her tone clues me in to shut up. I shouldn't care what Chase is doing or where he is, and Ivy will start to think I care if I keep at it.

"If he's here, then Coach is in her office upstairs," Ivy says, "I've got to talk to her for a sec. Go that way." Ivy points to one of the boat bays overlooking the water, where shells are stored on racks bolted to the walls. "The view's insane if you step out onto the dock."

"I, uh..." I say, but Ivy's already dashed to the back, her motion flickering on the overhead lights as she passes by. When she opens a door, I inwardly shrink at the sight of water tanks. They are goddamned giant fish tanks with eight-person rowing machines in the middle of them. Getting stuck in one would be my worst nightmare come to life.

As soon as the door shuts behind Ivy, my vision clears, and I wander far away from them and through the sitting room of the giant space—the Club Room, Ivy called it— with fabric-covered patio furniture in Briarcliff's colors—white, black, and maroon. There is a line of windows overlooking the lake, showcasing the wild forest across the water.

As if on instinct, I'm drawn into the sunlight instead of the shadows. I step through one of the four boat bays lined parallel to the water, my hand trailing across one of the "shells" hung up at waist-level. It's wet, and I assume it's Chase's boat. My fingers touch the seat inside, still warm to the touch.

I walk across the thin platform to the dock outside, attuned to the lapping water below. I assure myself that an expensive structure like this would be safe and sturdy. I'll just stay away from the edges.

My shoes make hollow sounds as I pass over the floorboards. I pull at the hem of my skirt when I look down and see spaces between the wood, the water flowing underneath.

Why did I let Ivy bring me here again?

"For God's sake, Callie," I mutter. "You're in a mansion they call a boathouse. You're fine."

A noise sounds out, and I startle at the echoing clang.

It's just Ivy, I reason. *Or Chase, skulking around in the corners—*

"The fuck are you doing here?"

I cry out when the voice registers at my shoulder, then whirl, my hands up in defense. The movement sends my feet in a tangle, and I topple sideways—

Strong arms hold on and drag me to the safety of the dock.

"Christ, new girl," Chase says as we disentangle.

Gasping, my throat tight with stress at the mere thought of my lungs filling with lake water, I stare up at Chase, whose relaxed pose is the complete opposite of a boy who just saved a girl from certain death. He smirks.

"I was..." I gulp. "I mean, I was exploring." I catch my breath, but my hand stays at my throat.

Sunlight beams onto Chase's head like a fallen angel's unearned halo.

Droplets of sweat shimmer on the exposed parts of Chase's chest, lifting rhythmically as he breathes. When he'd grabbed me, and I held on, his arms were damp and sticky, but the scent of him, though similar to the boathouse, wasn't as cloying. It was ... indescribably addicting.

Conscious of how obvious I must look, I tear my gaze from his torso and meet his calculating, metallic eyes.

Chase's golden glow doesn't meet his intentions. He asks, "You interested in crew?"

Chase looks me up and down. I feel naked, even though I'm dressed in Briarcliff uniform. The sun warms me, but I shiver.

He continues, "Because you need more grace than that."

"I'm—that's the last thing I want," I say, and move closer to him, if only to get farther away from the dock's edge. "Ivy said something about the view being nice..."

"You like what you see?"

My back is to this allegedly epic view, and I'm focused solely on the boy in front of me, who looks nothing like the boys my mother would want me to get to know.

And yeah, the front of him is precisely what I pictured it'd be in the unisuit.

In an effort to release this ridiculous hold Chase has, I say, "What I don't like is what your girlfriend's doing to me."

Chase's cheek tics. "I told you, she's not my girlfriend."

"Then whatever she is, tell her to stop. This morning was epically fucked up."

"Ah yes, the famous rat infestation." Chase raises a brow. "What makes you think she was behind it?"

"Because she has all of you," I spit. "You asshole Nobles who think you can *hurt* people the way you do and think there won't be conseq—"

"What did you just say?"

Chase closes the space between us with such viper-quick movement, I'm caught off-guard. My heels scrape back, dangerously close to the edge.

I sense where the dock ends and the depthless water begins, so I cling to his arms for balance. Chase's eyes tunnel into mine. There's no savior here now, fallen or otherwise.

My fingers dig into his bare arms, his muscles hardening beneath, yet he doesn't shake me off.

I respond, keeping my voice level, "I said, you Nobles are assholes."

Thunder rumbles in Chase's chest. "I'll ask you one more time. How do you know that name?"

I've rankled him, and I decide to keep going. "Isn't that what your immediate fanbase calls you? What about the girls you sleep with? Don't you let them in on your cool clubhouse name—?"

"Shut up."

He says it with such succinct poison that my teeth clank together.

Chase lowers his head so we're nose-to-nose. I can smell his breath—spearmint— I can smell *him*, sweat and freshwater sweetness.

I refuse to buckle, but my hands don't leave his arms. I doubt they'll do it of their own volition until I'm well off this fucking floating wood.

He says, "Don't mention that name again, to anyone. You understand?"

My brows smush together. "Why? You'd think you'd be proud of the title. I was positive it's what you and your buddies put in front of your name when you present your dicks."

Chase snarls, but it only brings our lips closer together. Electricity sparks between us, a tingling spread that will dissipate if one of us backs away.

Neither of us does.

I stop breathing, and Chase takes my air as his own.

He rasps, "And you wonder why there were dead rats in your locker. Your big fucking mouth'll get you in trouble. Consider this your one warning."

I resist the temptation to grasp the back of his neck and ram my mouth against his, the craving to taste him unlike *anything* I've been brought up to do with a boy.

"So, you jerks did have something to do with it," I snarl.

Chase backs off, his upper lip lifting in a half-cocked grin. "We don't dabble in pest control."

"But you dabble in something," I persist. "Does it involve cloaks and roses?"

Chase steps away, leaving my hands bereft as I'm left to face my vertigo on my own. He turns on his heel and starts down the dock, leaving behind no clues as to whether I'm right.

"Chase!" I call. "What the hell? We were having a conversation!"

"No, we weren't," Chase says, his voice fading with the additional distance he's putting between us. "And I never saw you here, either."

"What the...?"

But Chase disappears into one of the boat bays, and that's the last I see of him.

Lake water *glugs* against the dock, the noise of the waves making me scurry into the boathouse, oddly chilled despite being greeted by the warm September sun when I got here.

"Sorry, Callie, but I've never heard of this craziness you're talking about."

I decide to fill Ivy in on my secret roses on our way back to campus, our school-issued shoes plodding along the dirt trail as we walk uphill, Ivy leading the way.

"Really? Nothing?" I ask. "I thought you were all about Briarcliff's gossip."

"Well, I am. But I've never heard of a student receiving black or white roses. Not even on Valentine's Day."

Drat. I'd hoped Ivy of all people could shed some light on my mysterious admirer ... or enemy. I suppose it would depend on whether I'm talking about the gift of furniture or the rat presents, and I've informed Ivy of the latter. At the moment, I keep the unexpected nicety close to my chest. So far, it's the one unsullied memory I have at this school.

"But you know of the Nobles," I say.

Ivy comes to an abrupt halt, keeping her back to me. "The who?"

"Ivy, come on." I climb to a stand beside her, but she won't face me. "You know what I'm talking about."

"No." Ivy glances at me briefly. "I don't."

She starts walking again, much faster, and I scramble to keep up. "Yes, you do! Remember, in the bathrooms, when I was cleaning up all that damn spaghetti sauce—"

Ivy wheels around and latches onto my arm. She coaxes me to meet her eye before saying, "I didn't say anything, and you didn't hear anything. Okay?"

I'm witnessing fear in her expression. Real trepidation. "Ivy ... you told me that's what they are called. Chase and his friends. Remember?"

"You heard me wrong. I said that their reach was *global*, and for you to be careful. Yeah, they're our age, but their families are rich and powerful. Their influence is never-ending." Ivy squeezes my arm and says, "Do you hear what I'm telling you?"

I shake my head. "That's not—"

The deep, echoing ring of the clocktower reaches our ears, and Ivy releases my arm and shoots forward. "That's our warning—we're gonna be late to class."

"Ivy, wait."

"Can't!" Ivy throws a wave in my direction as she kicks into a run. "We'll talk later!"

"I'm not done with this subject!" I call in a warning, but at this point, I'm yelling at her butt as she sprints up Briarcliff's stairs and runs into the building.

Jeez. That's two people in less than an hour who've pulled a disappearing act on me.

I think of the wilted white rose, crushed at the bottom of my backpack by my books, and I know, with resolute certainty, that I'm not finished with either Ivy *or* Chase.

Ahmar always joked that if my mom was going to pass me down anything, it would be her dogged tenacity. His sobering voice adds inside my head, *Yeah, Calla. The trait that got her killed*.

But I brush that thought away and stride to Briarcliff Academy, my thumbs digging painfully into my backpack's straps.

Nineteen

I'M STARTING to enjoy moonlight more than I appreciate the sun, since the moon's face is the friendliest I see by the time the week is over and a fresh one begins.

Ivy is missing from the dining hall Monday evening—a girls' crew meeting, she said—so I brave the masses alone, without the confidence to join Eden and the scholarship kids when Ivy's not around.

At first, it doesn't seem so bad.

The few students also enjoying an early dinner don't notice me walk in and head to the serving station, grabbing my tray and choosing between steak or chicken cordon bleu. No shoulders bump into mine, nor are there any hisses or jeers behind my back.

I relax, thinking I avoided the worst, since Chase, Piper, and the rest of their posse aren't here yet. The timing was deliberate on my part—I didn't think they'd be so pedestrian as to arrive for 5 o'clock dinner service, crew meeting or not.

Then, a hush falls upon the room, its obviousness exacerbated by the echoing vastness in the uncrowded dining hall, conversations trailing to whispers, then echoes, then ... stares.

Clutching my tray with both hands, I move away from the serving station, a plate of steak with peppercorn sauce and broccoli steaming the underside of my chin.

Piper, Willow, Violet, and Falyn pose at the dining hall's entrance.

I'm starting to differentiate them by hair color, since they stand in order of their ombre hues. Violet is on the left, with her ebony hair. Piper has the darkest brown, then Willow with auburn waves. Falyn, with her hip cocked at the end, is the most (bottle) blonde.

After she finishes scanning the room, Piper's stare knifes into mine.

I pretend not to notice, though my teeth bite down hard as I find a vacant table and sit, grabbing the napkin from the place setting and unrolling it to get to the flatware.

The sound of my fork and knife clanging together when they fall into my palm is the loudest in the room.

Then, the scraping of my knife against the porcelain plate as I cut my steak.

I'm honestly at a loss as to why I've attracted Piper's animosity again. We seemed to have come to a silent truce of sorts during our lunch detentions with Dr. Luke, but I don't think too hard on the reasons why I'm back on her hit list. What I'd like to do is eat my dinner, then escape to the frivolous protection of my bedroom.

Two palms slam down on my table, rattling the place settings within their vicinity, as well as my heart. I startle, my knife and fork dropping from my hands.

Piper stews above me, her cheeks flushed and eyes sparkling with rage. She sneers. "Stay away from him."

I take a moment to finish chewing my mouthful, using it to regain calm and school my expression. I swallow, then buy time by lifting my water glass and sipping. "Who?"

Piper's eyes narrow. "You know who, possum."

"Well." I set my water down, then smooth the napkin resting on my lap, emitting an assuredness my heart isn't mimicking. "Considering you've made it impossible to make a ton of friends, never mind talk to guys, I'm not sure what—or who—you could be talking about."

"You *bitch*."

The insult hurtles around the room before smashing into my face, a hiss of massive proportions. The entire room, already quiet, falls into a thick silence.

I'm confused. "Piper, I've never—"

"Don't lie, rodent, or I'll have the whole school call you a rat instead of a possum," Piper interjects.

"You mean like the rats I found in my locker?" I ask, bolstered by her admission. "A little obvious, isn't it, to threaten me *again* with vermin in public."

"I saw you!" she shouts, and frankly, it sounds unhinged.

I search behind her for her friends. Surely, they want to drag Piper out of here and calm her down. Yet, none do. They watch the show, various expressions of concern, interest, and vindictiveness etched across their faces. Violet is the singular soul that seems reluctant to watch.

I ask Piper slowly, "You saw me what?"

"Showing your slutty tits off. Practically begging him to fuck you when you're alone with him."

I laugh at the absurdity of the situation, but Piper takes it the wrong way.

"*Fuck* you," she hisses, her elbows shooting out like a praying mantis, her face darting close. "You don't get to have him. You can cling to him all you want, plead with him to stick his dick in you, but he won't. He's as disgusted with you as I am."

I admit, the last part hurts, but I avoid the poison arrow to the heart. Piper's accusation flashes me into to the warmth of Chase's arms, the dappled sunlight beaming onto his skin as he smelled of lake water and mint, and his stare, for that one moment becoming a savior's, flickering with warm emotion before he tamped it down.

But that happened a week ago. Why is Piper bringing it up now and not the many times we've been in detention together since?

Because now she has an audience, my suspicious head-voice whispers.

"You're threatening me for nothing," I say. "I promise you, Chase would rather kick me off the dock than screw me."

Piper flinches at the use of his name, and all she can come up with is, "You're *lying.*"

"Oh my God, which is it, Piper? Am I so desperate for him that he can't stand me, or are we screwing behind your back?"

Piper's face goes red.

I roll my eyes, but I'm shaking inside. "He broke my fall into the water. That's it."

"Bullshit. You have an agenda involving your tongue and tits to take him from me."

I sigh in an effort to coax my heart to stop racing. I hate being the center of attention, but Piper's forced my hand. I take comfort in the fact that nobody can see the erratic, untamed beats.

Standing, I mutter, "You're taking this too far. We can talk about it in our room, but—"

"You're no roommate of mine," she snaps. "Tomorrow, I'm going to Headmaster Marron and reporting your ass."

On cue, Piper flutters her lashes, thickened with crocodile tears.

Dread drips into the empty rumblings of my stomach. "Piper, stop. You're being ridiculous."

"This has gone too far, Callie. Your repeated abuses have to stop!" Her desperate shriek reaches the ceiling.

At this point, nobody's eating. My appetite has disappeared, and part of me wishes I'd evaporate, too.

I throw my hands up, matching my voice with hers. "Take what? I haven't done anything to you!"

"Oh, so you think hurling insults at me was nothing? Refusing to do your half of our history essay? Vowing to ruin my GPA and my life? What about vandalizing my bedroom? Smearing my lipstick all over our bathroom mirror? You're fucking nuts, Callie! Fucking *certified!*"

"What the f—?" I temper my voice before it turns into a banshee screech, because I'm not seeing Piper's statements as accusations. I'm seeing them as...

"Piper," I say in an astonished whisper, "Are they doing this stuff to you, too? Are you getting roses?"

For a brief second, Piper's eyes snap to mine, but the movement is invisible to anyone else. A smile replaces any recognition, growing wider with malice the longer she stares. "Like I said, *rat*, you're as dumb as the brain God sized you with. I wasn't going to say anything, since I figure you're acting out because of your mom's murder—"

The entire room gasps, and I feel blood leaving my face.

"—but it's gone too far. Fucking with my room, then trying to steal my boyfriend ... you're messed up, and you need help outside of this school."

"You're not his girlfriend," I blurt, instinctively surrendering to the constant unwelcome loop in my head. *She's not my girlfriend.*

My face rings with a slap, sending me stumbling. Students murmur, but no one stands up to do anything.

I hold a hand to my cheek, as hot and stinging as my eyes. "What's going *on* with you?"

"Which part confuses you?" Piper mocks, but unlike me, appears to the entire dining hall as sleek, collected, and entitled. "My bedroom? My clothes? My boyfriend? Or your mom getting decapitated?"

My mouth works. I'm bent over and clutching my cheek. "All but one," I admit in a sickly whisper.

"Uh-huh. You're so done, Calla *Lily*." Piper bends so she's at my level and whispers so only I can hear, "I warned you. I've tried to tell you to stay away from him, from me, from all of us. This is my last attempt at being kind."

Her baseless threats, coupled with the torrential humiliation in front of the entire school, *again*—and the never-ending rage boiling at the tip of my heart from losing my mother, without choice, without a goodbye...

Yeah, my flip-out is inevitable.

I rear up on a roar, clipping Piper in the face with my elbow and sending her sprawling onto my table. The plate falls to the floor and shatters. Blood bursts from Piper's nose. She screams, and her friends come running.

"You have *no right*!" I scream at her. "To bring up my mother, to threaten me, to think you can control what I—what *all* of us in this room do, like you're some kind of false queen. And why? Because you *think* I'm after Chase? You're desperate to ruin my life based on a pointless rumor! How savage *are* you to do that to a person you don't even know?"

Piper scrambles up on the table's surface, clutching her nose. "It was a mistake to come here, Callie! I will *ruin* you!"

"Hey!" an older male voice calls.

Great. The delayed, biased Professor Dawson is here to save the day.

"Girls! Haven't I told you—"

This time, I'm not waiting around to be framed.

I sprint from the dining hall, Piper's theatric wails and captive audience keeping well behind.

Twenty

"HAVE you thought this all the way through, Calla?"

Ahmar's calming voice flows through my phone and into my ear as I continue tossing clothes onto my bed. I throw a look to my bedroom door, assuring myself that I indeed shut and locked it.

"I don't belong here," I say, getting back to adding to the pile on my bed by rifling through my dresser drawers. "There are things going on that I ... that I have trouble putting into words."

"New schools are like that, kiddo." Ahmar's voice takes on a fatherly tone. "It's hell fitting in, but you don't get education like this anywhere else. Briarcliff is the school your dreams are made of. Your momma always wanted you to go to college, and this is your golden ticket. If you throw it away based on a fight with your room-mate, I promise you, you'll look back and regret it."

"It wasn't just an argument. It was..." I pause and stare at one of my bare walls, my folded T-shirts dropping from my arms. How can I define the clash as just "girls being girls"?

The malice. The vapid hatred. The physical assault, of which I reciprocated ten-fold.

Yeah, Ahmar would be *so* pissed I used force and focus on how I overreacted and possibly broke a girl's nose over a slap and accusation of stealing her boyfriend.

God, just thinking about it that way makes me lose respect for myself, never mind what Ahmar would think.

"Trust me on this, Ahmar. I don't belong. These students are unlike any other humans I've ever encountered."

Ahmar laughs. "You're talking like you're on some sort of safari."

"Maybe I am," I say. *A jungle with nothing but poisonous predators waiting for their chance to bite my head off.*

"Okay, say I indulge you for a moment," Ahmar says. "What are you going to do

84

once you leave? Where will you go? You no longer live downtown. I hate to say it, but you can't go back to your old school. Not after…"

Ahmar lets the rest of his sentence go unsaid, but the missing words ring their wicked truth in my head.

I was close to expulsion once. I can't experience the threat of it again.

"Easy." I add a positive punch to my explanation, though none of it registers in my gut. "I'll go back to Dad and Lynda's. If I show up on their doorstep, they'll have to take me back."

"Kiddo." The pity in Ahmar's voice hardens my jaw. "You're not something they've tossed aside."

"Oh, yeah?" I gear up for an argument, somehow craving it, regardless of how misguided it is. "Where are their phone calls? Or text messages? Or any sort of communication to see how I'm doing? You call me, Ahmar. They don't—they have a family to start, and I'm the dead weight."

The poor joke falls flat on both our ears.

"I didn't mean that," I say. "All I'm saying is … they can't send me here and think I'll be happy. Not with the elitist favoritism that goes on. These kids even have the headmaster in their pockets. I'd rather deal with Dad's cool dismissal."

Ahmar sighs. "It's your choice. Lord knows I can't stop you. But take the night and think about this, okay? This is a big decision you're making—possibly life-changing. And I think you've had enough of those. Maybe, you can see the time away from your stepdad as a good thing. It allows for you and him to start fresh—"

"Dad and Lynda put me here because they didn't want to deal with a problem child." I stop with my one-handed folding, deciding to put Ahmar on speaker instead. Once I press the button, I place the phone on my pillow, so it doesn't get lost in the detritus on my bed. "Hey, Ahmar?"

"Yeah, hun?"

"What would you think of … I mean, if Dad and Lynda are furious I've left Briarcliff and refuse to let me stay with them … um, can I stay with you?"

There's a long pause. Too long and deafening in its answer.

"Calla, I would, honey, but … I'm in a one-bedroom." He laughs in an attempt to lighten the denial. "I can barely fit myself in here. And I'm messy as fuck. This isn't the proper housing for a seventeen-year-old—"

"I get it," I cut in, unfolding a long-sleeved shirt with a sharp flick, then refolding it again for no reason. "You don't have to explain. It was too much to ask."

"No, I don't think you do. I fought for you, honey. But it wasn't in the cards for us. I'm so sorry."

Again, with the pity. I reach for my phone. "I gotta go. Thank you for the talk."

"You sure you don't want to keep chatting? What about this friend of yours, Ivy? What's she think of you leaving?"

"She's—it's complicated," I say, because I haven't told her yet.

"Promise me you'll take the night. Don't be calling a car at midnight and travel with a stranger."

That brings a smile to my face. "I won't. Briarcliff has personal drivers."

"Jesus. And you want to leave that place? I love you, kiddo. Stay safe. And strong."

"Yeah," I say, but trail off.

Ahmar hangs up, and I'm left alone with my thoughts. Piper hasn't come home yet, even though it's been four hours. She's probably bunking with one of her friends, lest Crazy Callie do something vicious to her vulnerable person.

What the hell was that dining hall confrontation about? Earlier this week, we joined forces on the creepy historical project, and I'd believed we'd tolerate each other from there. We had to live together. We could ignore one another just fine once I purchased my own coffee.

Why does Piper hate me so much?

And to accuse me of trying to be with Chase...

She has it so wrong.

I don't know this guy, yet I'm drawn in, despite my current problems always circling back to Chase. My dreams contain him. I remember the feel of his muscles and skin like they're my own. And I've merely touched him once.

But, you've touched him.

Oh, yeah? I sneer to my subconscious. *Now watch me leave him.*

I'm going to escape this place, whether or not Ahmar approves, but I refuse to call it running away.

It's inevitable: Piper will take her fabricated story and real bruises to the headmaster.

Now my packing is spurred by anger. I reach deeper into the mountain of clothes on my bed, and latch onto something sharp. Cursing, I pull my hand back, gripping the object despite the trail of blood traveling down my palm.

It's the inked-dipped rose, the one I'd hidden in my nightstand, but was unearthed when I emptied my drawers. One of its thorns nicked the pad of my thumb.

My lips peel back. I break the stem in half, black petals ripping free with my sharp twist.

In doing so, I curse Chase, Piper, and each of their friends, wishing them all the bad luck a dying, poisoned rose can give.

Twenty-One

THE SUN'S rays stream through the single window in my room, and I sit up blearily, rubbing my face awake.

I must've fallen asleep on the heap of clothing on my bed, which surprises me, since the last thing I remember is deleting all my research on Rose Briar.

Piper can suck it. There's no way I'm gifting her with the information I found before I leave campus. She can start the project from scratch for all I care.

But something seems off. I woke up with an abrupt start, and not with my usual cat-like stretch and slow-blink habit.

Rapid knocking sounds at the front door, and it's sharp and impatient.

I mutter a curse, then peel out of bed. I'm still in my school uniform, with my wrinkled white shirt unbuttoned and plaid skirt askew.

My door unlocks with a sharp click, and I plod into the central room, hazily registering that Piper's room is unoccupied. Her bed's made, and there's no air of perfume from any recent departure, so I suppose she didn't come home.

Good.

Maybe that's why I slept like a baby—there was no one to storm through the apartment and take her unfair intimidation tactics onto domestic territory.

"Callie?" a muffled voice asks through the door. "Are you there? Please say you're there. *Please.*"

"Ivy?" I call, moving faster to the front door. "What's wrong?" Ivy doesn't normally sound so high-pitched and desperate.

I'm hoping it's not to convince me to stay. I sent her a text last night, promising I'd call her today and explain, but that I was done with this school and the snakes it nurtures inside it.

"Oh, thank God," she says, then flies into my apartment and glances around with skittish awareness. "They're not here yet."

"Who?"

"The police."

That gives me pause. "Um. What?"

Ivy spins to face me. Splotches of color rise high in her cheeks, and her eyes are abnormally wide. And wet.

"Ivy, are you crying?"

She sniffs, then pulls out a tissue from her bag and dabs at her eyes. "Have you not heard? Is your phone not blowing up?"

"I mean, it could be." I gesture vaguely to my room. "I've been busy packing, and your knocking woke me up. I haven't checked my phone yet."

"Oh, Callie." Ivy's knees turn to liquid as she glides closer and grasps my arms. "It's bad. It's really, really bad."

I'm so sorry, Calla...

"What's bad? Ivy, you're freaking me out."

Don't see your mom like this. Come with me. Please, kiddo...

Tears pool in Ivy's eyes. She parts her lips, and her despondency unearths a stirring inside my head, a slithering awareness that until now, was slumbering in the trenches of my mind.

Kiddo, Your momma...

I've been here before.

She's...

Ivy's expression is an exact replica of ... Ahmar's.

"Callie," Ivy says. "Piper was killed last night."

Dead.

"W-what?" I stutter. Automatically, I glance past Ivy's shoulder into Piper's room, though I know it's empty. "No. She's not. I just saw her..."

"Last night?" Ivy's grip tightens on my upper arms. "Omigod, Callie, did you talk to her before she fell?"

My eyes flick to hers. "What? No. I saw her at the dining hall." I study Ivy closely. "You didn't hear?"

"No. I do know she missed the crew meeting, though. But listen, there's no time. I came to prepare you."

"Prepare me for what?"

I hate that I keep repeating things back to her, but my brain's in a jumble and my body's going into panic mode.

"They found Piper at the bottom of Lover's Leap."

It can't be. This can't be happening a second time...

I fight through the pulsing muscles of my throat. "Ivy, yesterday at dinner, I—"

"What the *fuck* have you done?"

The deep, masculine tone causes the hairs on the back of my neck to rise.

"Chase," Ivy gasps, releasing my arms. "I-I'm so sorry. I'm so sorry about Piper."

"Get out."

Chase's words are clipped, but lethal. I have no idea if he's talking to Ivy or to me, but either way, he doesn't own this fucking apartment.

I swivel to face him. "You're the one that's unwelcome here."

When I register Chase's expression, I'm shocked I got the words out. Never before have I seen features so flat yet exuding such rage.

"Ivy," he says, without tearing his gaze from mine, "I said get out."

I grab Ivy's arm. "She doesn't have to go anywhere."

He grits out, "Yes. She does."

"Callie, it's fine," Ivy says in a small voice, "I can meet you in the lobby."

"You can wait in my bedroom," I say to her, keeping my stare on Chase's. "Whatever Chase has to say to me, you can be a witness."

Chase arches a cold brow. "You want a second ear for what I'm gonna say? Fine. Where were you last night? What did Piper do that got you so enraged you made her bleed?"

I guffaw. "Are you—is this what I think it is? Are you accusing me of killing her?"

Chase flinches at the word 'kill.' I don't blame him. It's a hard word to swallow when it starts relating to your life. Worse than 'death.' I recognize the pain behind Chase's fury, and the grief. But I doubt my kindred spirit will mean anything to him.

"Who the hell do you think you are?" he says, and for a brief moment, his eyes gleam with unshed tears. "To come to this school and fuck it up the way you have?"

Chase steps closer, his large body overshadowing mine. I don't cower. I hear Ivy back up a step, then two, but she slides my hand off her forearm and into hers. And squeezes.

"I've done *nothing*," I hiss in his face. His anger billows over me with hot breaths. "You're hurting, Chase. You're furious and upset. I can understand that. I'm sorry Piper's gone"—it still sounds so unreal coming from my throat—"but I won't be your punching bag."

"What, you think you know me now?" His eyes transform the tears into glimmering animosity. "Because your mom's been killed and Piper's dead, now we're warm and fuzzy friends?"

I flinch. "I don't give a shit what you think."

Sliding my hand from Ivy's, I storm to the front door, but Chase catches me by the elbow and spins me into his chest, his other hand cupping the back of my neck and pulling at my hair until we're eye-to-eye.

Ivy shouts a warning, but it does nothing to stop him.

This is nothing like it was at the docks. There's no sunlight streaming down, no hint of an angel now.

I'm in the grip of a demon.

"She'd still be alive if you never came here," he snarls.

"You're the one who was supposed to be her boyfriend," I retort. We're both heaving, and a fucked-up, secretive section of my heart wonders if he's pulsing with twisted heat the way I am. "Her protector. What was it you said to me when you splayed yourself across that couch over there like an entitled prick? You *look out for her*. Well, look where she is now."

I've hurt him. I see it in the flash of rage that washes across his overly schooled expression. His hand clenches on my hair where he holds me, and his eyes grow so everlastingly cold.

I may have gone too far, but with such burning confusion inside me, there's no other way to release it. It's all too much, too soon.

The silence between us is thick and nauseating, but neither of us will break.

The weight of Ivy's hand comes down on my shoulder. "Chase, please. Callie, come on. We need to..."

"You have no idea. None." Chase tightens his hold, and an unwilling gasp leaves my throat. "If you thought this is done—if not having Piper around would give you a reprieve—you're wrong. I'm about to get started with you."

I snap out, "You can watch me tremble another time. Now get the *hell* out of my room."

A light knock startles us both, and our heads whip to the sound. A plainclothes detective stands there, with a shield around his neck. Two uniformed officers are behind him.

The detective with the gray hair and rugged face looks between Ivy and me. "Is one of you Calla Lily Ryan?"

"Yes," I say, and disengage from Chase like he's coated with snake venom.

Surprisingly, he lets me go, but he saunters back with a malicious grin maligning one side of his face. What he wants to do to me is obvious in the shape of his lips. He wants to devour me. Destroy me.

"It starts now," he says, then twists to the police. He points at me. "She did it."

My mouth falls into an *O* as the policemen part to let Chase through. The detective doesn't take his attention off me as he steps aside.

"Miss Ryan? We have some questions for you regarding the death of your roommate," he says, and a lump forms in my throat.

A lump the size of a rock at the base of a cliff.

Twenty-Two

DETECTIVE HASKINS WANTS to question me? I tell him he can, so long as I have a guardian present and it's conducted on neutral territory.

That's when he informed me Dad and Lydia were on a babymoon in Tahiti and couldn't be present for any questioning. And Ahmar was too far away of a drive for Haskins to wait.

Faced between dealing with Haskins's stern face alone or having a teacher present in substitution of a legal guardian, I asked for Dr. Luke to sit beside me in the empty classroom they directed me to. He seems the friendliest of the faculty, and the one likely to take my side if things go awry, since I doubt Professor Dawson, who knows me second-best, has bonded with me enough to want to say anything in my defense, should it come to that.

I sit at a school desk and Haskins takes a seat across from me. Dr. Luke stands at my elbow, his arms crossed as he studies Haskins.

I can feel my heartbeat in my fingertips. The silence in the empty classroom doesn't help. It brings back memories of being sat down on my bed and Ahmar bending in front of me, holding on tight to my elbows.

We did all we could. She's gone, kiddo. She's gone.

My breaths patter in my throat like a bird's wings clipped for a cage.

None of this is my fault. I'm not in trouble.

Or so I thought. Yesterday's fight with Piper is glaringly present in my mind's eye, blurring the shining floors beneath me into a transparent movie screen where I elbow Piper in the face and she screams, blood pouring out of her nostrils.

I swallow. I want Ahmar here.

Don't go back in there, Calla. Stay with me. Cry it out. I'll hold on tight.

I scrunch my eyes shut.

A hand comes down on my shoulder and squeezes before retreating. It's Dr. Luke.

"I'll keep this brief, Miss Ryan," Haskins says. He flips through a notebook on the desk, his pen poised as he starts by taking down my basic information. Then, he asks, "When did you last see Piper Harrington?"

"At dinner," I whisper, but force my voice to come forth to admit, "We had a fight."

"That's a start," Haskins says as he scribbles something down. "We know about that from Piper's friends. I'm glad you're being honest."

I nod, aware that being truthful about any friction with the victim is the fastest route to clearing my name and having them move on to someone else.

"Where were you this morning between one and three AM?" Haskins asks.

"In bed," I say. "I fell asleep packing."

Dr. Luke's head tips in my direction. "Packing?"

"I'll be the one to ask the questions, Doctor, thank you," Haskins says. "So, Callie, you were in the apartment you shared with Piper? All night?"

"Yes."

"You didn't go to the party at the cliffs like the rest of 'em?"

I lift my head up. "Huh?"

Dr. Luke's hand squeezes my shoulder again. "Miss Ryan's new to this school, Detective. She might not have been made aware of the mischief these kids get up to once the moon's out. It was a small gathering, anyway, kids Piper Harrington ran around with. I was the professor who found them and broke it up. I'd come from the professors' lodging at around one, and for the record, I didn't see Miss Harrington there. The kids assured me she left the party early because she wanted to go home to be alone."

The longer Dr. Luke's friendly explanation goes on, the more Haskins's features harden. "I'll get to you in due time, Doctor. If you'll let me do the talking?"

Dr. Luke clears his throat. "Apologies. Go ahead."

"Dr. Luke's right," I pipe up. "I'm not cool enough to be invited to those kinds of things."

"Yes, you and Piper rubbed each other the wrong way, didn't you?"

"We didn't become instant friends upon meeting," I admit.

"So, did you see her at all? Did Piper come back to your room after your argument at dinner?"

I shake my head.

"How about after the party?" Haskins glances down at his notes. "Those kids have corroborated Dr. Luke's statement that she left early because she didn't feel well."

Probably because I'd recently bashed her nose in. I flinch at the thought but cover it up in hopes Haskins doesn't read any guilt on my face.

"She refused to be accompanied back, so the rest of the students dispersed around 1 AM," he says.

Again, I shake my head. "I didn't hear her come back. I had my door shut, though." *And locked.* "She could've come in and left and I wouldn't have known."

"Tell me about the altercation between you two. Why was Piper angry and upset?"

At last, the petty reason behind our fight comes into good use. "She accused me of stealing her boyfriend."

My words have their intended effect. Haskins lips lift briefly in what appears as a tired sigh. Dr. Luke frowns.

"And you assaulted her," Haskins says.

I'm talking to the bald spot on his head, since he hasn't lifted his attention from his notepad. "I was defending myself. She threatened me."

"And yet, this is not the first time you've been involved in similar conflict. Your friend from back home—Sylvie Teegarden—you were with her when she overdosed, correct?"

Acidic drops of unease *plink* into my belly. "That has nothing to do with ... Piper and I started off with a misunderstanding. Piper explained it that way when Professor Dawson found us. And again, during detention. Right, Dr. Luke?"

"Miss Ryan's telling the truth." Another shoulder pat, though slower this time, as news of my checkered past sinks in. "Miss Harrington also expressed to me they worked out their differences."

"Mmm. Until new differences came up." Haskins lifts his gaze. "Who's the guy?"

"Chase Stone," I say, without hesitation. *She did it*, that bastard had said.

"The boy who...?"

I give a sharp nod. "The one who was in my dorm room when you arrived and accused me, yep."

"Looks like you have some differences with him, too."

"Of a sort." I pick at invisible lint on my cardigan. My face is too pinched and vindictive to look at Haskins head-on. "Are you questioning him, too? He and Piper were close for a long time."

"I plan on talking with him." Haskins cocks his head. "You can relax, Callie. You're not in trouble. Right now, we're going through all the steps of an investigation, but it's appearing that, well, Piper was the last one at the cliff. Dr. Luke may not have seen her, but all the kids we accounted for insisted she was with them at the beginning. She may have gotten turned around. I hear visibility isn't so good around there at night."

So, she either fell or she jumped, and no one noticed, is left unsaid between us.

I'm practically digging a hole in my sweater, so I drop my hand. "I'm sorry. This whole thing has me ... upside-down. I can't believe it's real."

"I pulled your history," Haskins says, his voice sobering. "I apologize for dragging you through this again, but you understand why it's so important we chat."

Chat. Like we're old friends catching up on death. "I do."

"Any other reasons why Piper might've been upset, or was this just about boyfriend stealing?"

"I've known her for a little over a week, sir. And I wasn't stealing Chase. We're not—we were never together. Piper and I may not have liked each other, but I'd never hurt her."

"Indeed. Well, so far, we have witness statements in your favor, and they line up with what you've told me this morning. Piper threatened you, and assaulted you, on both occasions as well. You were the victim, too. We also have video of you coming into your dorm yesterday evening, and no video of you leaving, so that lines up with your statement of not being at the illegal gathering. But you can see why that may not be sufficient." Haskins crosses his legs. "Briarcliff Academy is known for its hidden passages."

All of this is news to me. My stomach curdles uncomfortably at the realization that Haskins doesn't know I was the last one to throw a punch ... because no one's told him about Piper's accusations about me vandalizing her room or scribbling lipsticked threats on our bathroom mirror. All concocted by Piper's scheming mind, but Haskins wouldn't know that. And it's nothing I can prove as fake, especially when I've done the opposite of endearing myself to the Briarcliff student body.

So, why hasn't anyone told him of the last words she'd said to me?

"Who are the witnesses?" I ask. The dining hall was sparse when I was there. "Piper's friends?"

"Technically, it's confidential, but..." Haskins waves his hand like I'm getting close.

I frown.

Why would Piper's friends ever want to help me?

"Am I under arrest?"

"No, and I'm hoping we've established the type of rapport for your continued honesty."

I nod as if a puppeteer holds my strings, and move to a stand, assuming that was my dismissal.

"We're done here for now." Haskins closes his leatherbound notebook. I stand, the hollowness widening in my chest.

I'm not about to mention the roses, or Piper's continued harassment, because I have the uneasy certainty that it'll be used against me as motive. And I have no idea if Piper's responsible for the secret messages, or if the Cloaks have something to do with it ... should I tell Haskins about the bonfire I witnessed?

I'm questioning the relevancy of it when Dr. Luke chimes in.

"There's an assembly in the large lecture room, Miss Ryan. Headmaster Marron and the guidance counselor will be discussing Piper's tragedy."

It's weird, yet inevitable, that Dr. Luke is using Piper's first name. It makes the finality of her death more apparent, and I'm nauseous at the thought.

"You're all right?" he prompts.

Again, I bob my head, but it's a mechanical motion.

"You and her didn't get along, but the school would understand if this affected you," Dr. Luke says. As he walks over, he lays a light hand on my forearm. "If you need to take the day, I can let the headmaster know, and you can see Mrs. Maisey in private, when you feel comfortable."

"Thank you, but no," I say. "I'll go through the motions today. It ... it doesn't seem real yet."

Haskins clears his throat. "Thank you for your candor, Callie. Here's my card if you think of anything else."

I take it automatically, shoving it in my inside blazer pocket.

Haskins says to my retreating back, "Don't stray too far with that luggage you were packing. I expect you to be available."

With the way he says it, I wonder if Haskins reads more into Piper's and my friction than I initially thought.

"Of course. You have my number," I say, then retreat out the door.

My worries over further questioning from Haskins fade the faster I take the path away from the main building and in the opposite direction to the Assembly Hall.

I'm leaving this place, this school with too many ill intentions weaved between its textbook lines. Piper's tragic death solidifies it, as if the roses, rats, and bullying didn't already. I pick up speed, prepared to bag the rest of my things and drag them out front until an Uber comes to get me.

As I take to the path, I notice lights flashing a quarter-mile away, in rough proximity to Lover's Leap. I've never been there, so I can guess, but chances are there isn't any other reason for police vehicles to be parked nearby.

Oh, Piper, I think, unable to tear my attention away from the blinking lights through the rising fog of the morning. *What happened?*

My feet keep moving despite my distraction, and I'm in front of Thorne House before I register the distance I crossed.

I'm surprised to find Ivy behind the front desk when I enter.

"Callie!" she says, and flies to the front, gripping me in a tight hug. "Omigod, are you okay?"

"Fine," I say, but it comes out shakier than I intended. "It was just basic questioning."

"Thank goodness. I thought you were under arrest, after what Chase said."

My eyelids lower, my vision darkening with held-in frustration. "Unfortunately, it takes more than a flippant comment to solidify me as a suspect. I also think they're ruling it as an accident or suicide."

"Oh. Gosh. That's terrible."

We pull apart, and Ivy walks with me to the elevators. "Hey, while you were out, you got a delivery."

I think of my previous "deliveries," and my steps slow. "Do you know what it is?"

"Some boxes," Ivy says, then hits the UP button. "Return address was from NYC, though."

"Oh." I exhale the remnants of tension. "That doesn't sound too bad."

Ivy laughs as we step into the elevator together. "You poor thing. No wonder you're desperate to leave this place."

We fall into silence once we stride down the hallway to my room. My keycard clicks us in, and I focus on the tower of boxes sitting in the center room, instead of the commotion in Piper's bedroom, cameras clicking and low-voiced mumblings of cops clogging up the atmosphere.

I count three boxes, and notice a note stuck to the top one.

Hey, Callie!

Here's the winter clothing I promised. It's supposed to get cold a lot sooner, so we've sent you proper gear. Did your dad tell you? We're headed to Tahiti for two weeks to celebrate your baby sister. Six months already! Can you believe it? I'll be loaded on virgin pina coladas before you know it.

Anyway, enjoy the clothes. We hope you're having SO MUCH FUN at school and have made a ton of friends, just like we knew you would.

We'll touch base when we get home. Talk soon, hon!

Xoxo, L.

I release the letter from between my fingers, the note fluttering to the ground.

"What did it say?" Ivy asks behind me. "Who's it from?"

"My parents," I say dully. Then, I say it again, with forced pep. "My *parents.*"

"Girls?" A policeman ducks his head out of Piper's room. "You can't be here. Not until we finish processing."

"Yes, sir," Ivy says, then obediently cups my elbow and leads me into the hallway.

My lips spread wide in a vacant grin. "My fucking *parents.*"

Laughter bubbles up, uncontrollable, and soon I have to clutch my stomach, I'm giggling so hard.

"Uh, Callie? Are you all right?"

"My parents!" I screech through my laughter. I lift my head to the ceiling and cackle.

"Callie ... hey." Ivy comes up beside me, peering closer at my face.

"MY PARENTS!" I laugh again, laugh and laugh until tears start streaming down my face.

Ivy starts rubbing my back as I buckle from mirth. "Callie, you're scaring me. Tell me what's going on."

I throw my hand up, signaling for Ivy to give me a sec. Through my gasps and hiccups, I manage to say, my lips salted with tears, "They have no idea."

Ivy asks, "Who? Your parents?"

"Yes!" I cry, my arms splaying out as I straighten. "They have no fucking clue what's going on!"

"I ... I guess that's true." Ivy tries on a tentative smile.

"I'm-I'm bullied, harassed, then my roommate dies, and *they want me to have fun!*"

My knees turn to jelly as I laugh harder than I've laughed before, and soon, Ivy's clutching me, because I can't stand on my own.

The laughs turn to chuckles.

Then, morph into quiet giggles as I turn my face into her shoulder.

Then sobs.

"Callie," she whispers in my ear. "Shh. It's gonna be okay."

"I don't belong," I say in a hitched whisper into her neck. "Anywhere."

"You do," Ivy says. "You're my friend. You belong with me."

I sob into her shoulder. For Piper or for my mom, I can't be sure. Maybe it doesn't have to be one or the other.

Ivy rubs circles on my back. "You're not alone, okay? We'll get through this. We'll get answers."

No, I want to scream. *The answers will never come.*

Twenty-Three

IVY IS an expert at the guilt game. Somehow, she convinces me to stay at Briarcliff, at least until Piper's investigation is completed.

Maybe the "somehow" should be better explained. The boxes of clothes Lynda sent me made my reality a lot clearer. She and Dad are off living their lives, Ahmar doesn't have room for me, as much as he wants to, and the place I have now is ... one I shared with Piper.

There aren't many options, so until I clean up my life a bit more, I'm stuck at Briarcliff.

Since I'm not allowed back into my room yet, I scrub my eyes dry and we head to the assembly. The lecture hall is packed when we arrive, but Ivy finds two vacant seats toward the back. Headmaster Marron is well into his speech about student safety and mental health availability, as well as the dangers of drinking, essentially cementing the idea in all our minds that Piper either committed suicide or became so drunk she fell, before the investigation is officially concluded.

But having heard this all before, I use the time productively and scan students' heads, searching.

I find Piper's girlfriends, seated in the front row, just off center. Willow and Violet hold tissues, their eyes and noses bright red from crying. Falyn is pale—color-less—and stone-faced as she listens to Marron, her hands clenched so hard in her lap, they match the unhealthy white of her face.

Some friends they are. Did they really leave a drunk Piper to walk alone by herself back to the dorms?

Nearby, I see James's strawberry blond mop of hair, Tempest's textured ebony locks, and Riordan's close-cropped one. They sit, stoic and serious, their uniforms buttoned and pressed, the epitome of Briarcliff representation and not the least bit hungover during such a tragedy as they display themselves, front and center, while Marron waxes on about the importance of reaching out for help.

It's who I don't see that grabs my attention the most.

Chase is nowhere to be found, and my mind ponders the reasons why. He was severely incensed in my room, desperate to unleash his fury on the nearest victim. I'd think he'd make himself present, if only to rake his stare across the entire student body, as if someone in this room has reason to know why Piper toppled off Lover's Leap.

"Do you think there are pictures?" someone mutters to their friend in front of me.

"What, like of the crime scene?" the friend asks. "Or is it even a crime scene? She offed herself, right?"

"Yeah, but, like, someone must've taken pictures of the body. How fucked up do you think it is?"

Bile spreads in my throat, and I cough with disgust. Both pairs of eyes glance back, ashamed, until they realize who they're looking at.

"Maybe the possum did it," one sneers.

I sneer right back, surprised at my defense of Piper, a queen whose subjects are ready to turn on her as soon as news hits that she's dead.

Movement in front redirects my focus, and I notice Tempest leaving the lecture hall. I rise to follow him.

"Where are you going?" Ivy whispers loudly.

"I missed an assignment. Need that guy's notes. Don't worry," I say, then duck out the back exit as Ivy whispers furiously, "*What guy?*"

I catch Tempest in the foyer, just as he's about to hit the steps to the Wolf's Den.

"Tempest!" I call, sprinting to catch up to him.

His head turns, his unsettlingly green eyes meeting mine before sliding away in disdain.

"You," he says, once I skid to a halt in front of him. "What do you want?"

Up close, it's easier to spot the hangover. Purple crescents mar his unblemished skin and his hair isn't stylishly messy as usual. More like one side of his face laid flat against a forest floor all night.

Did you watch Piper fall?

The incredulous question rattles my bones, and I gnaw on my lip to cover my thoughts.

I ask instead, "Have you seen Chase?"

Guile replaces the disinterest in his expression. "Why?"

"Because he's a dick," I say, and my frankness makes half of his mouth tilt in a smile, stretching what I thought was a large freckle in the lower corner of his lip. Turns out, it's a hole for a piercing. I add, "And he needs to explain to me why he accused me of murder this morning."

Tempest's eyes flare, but he regains his languid composure. "Nobody knows why Chase does what he does. You might as well ask a fairy godmother for an explanation."

My hand tightens on my bag's strap. "I'd prefer to ask him."

"Well, he's not up there." Tempest's eyes drift upward.

I exhale and bite down on my lip again. "Hey, I'm sorry about Piper."

Tempest's hand freezes on the banister. "She made your life fucking hell, possum. Why are *you* sorry?"

"Because she was a person?" I respond, but I take a closer look at him. He seems so emotionless, so unaffected by the death of someone who—"Wasn't she your friend?"

He shrugs. "An acquaintance, but yeah, it sucks she died."

I set my jaw, but I stay silent, reluctant to agitate Tempest's icy calm.

Tempest must take pity on my inability to properly converse with him, because he adds, "Chase goes one of three places. Here, his room, or the boathouse."

Incentivized, I nod thank you, then turn for the exit.

"Possums are blind during the day," Tempest says.

"Uh, excuse me?"

After an offhand shrug, he replies, "Just a fun piece of trivia for you."

After a pause, I say, "It's their night vision that's limited."

Tempest raises his brows.

"And here I thought someone with *pest* in their name would be more familiar with their species." I add, "See? Creativity has its benefits."

I shoulder through the front doors, having no need to witness Tempest's resultant, vengeful glare.

Twenty-Four

NAVIGATING the trail down to the boathouse is a lot harder when Ivy isn't in front directing my steps, but I manage to make it without breaking an ankle or getting my hair tangled in any branches.

It isn't hard to locate Chase once I hit the clearing, since the broad-shouldered figure seated at the edge of the dock could only be him.

I take the path Ivy showed me and enter the boathouse through the side door. Anger provides the bravery to walk through the clubhouse and equipment room until I'm through a boat bay and onto the docks.

Chase's legs hang over the side of the dock, water lapping at his knees as he lifts something that glints against the light and puts it to his mouth.

Unable to quell the good girl instinct, I glance up at the windows, conscious that a coach or a teacher might be watching. Though, when it comes to Chase, it's anybody's guess how little it takes to turn a blind eye to his blatant disregard of school rules. It doesn't take a genius to notice no one at this forbidden party is being overtly punished. I wonder how much money it took to keep Marron from expelling each and every one of them.

Yeah. Like that would ever happen.

Or maybe, the families and Marron see Piper's death as punishment enough.

I stanch the morality of my thoughts as I approach Chase, my shoes sounding against the wood. His head turns at the noise, showcasing his strong profile with his straight nose and sharp jaw. When he registers who it is, he goes back to gazing straight ahead at the view, lifting the bottle again.

My shoes stop at his back. Chase doesn't react.

"It's not even lunchtime," I say.

"And?" He scans the lake before him.

"You're getting drunk."

"What an astute nose you have, rodent."

The barb doesn't hit its mark. Instead, I volley one of my own. "It's funny, you never lowered yourself to Piper's insults when she was alive."

His back goes rigid.

I involuntarily gulp. I'm poking the beast. But it's too tempting to disturb him like he did to me this morning.

"You're so fucking clueless," he mutters, tipping the beer bottle to his lips.

I drop my bag and sit cross-legged beside him, ensuring no part of me hangs over the edge. "Then why'd you finger me to the cops?"

Laughter bubbles into his throat, and a genuine smile crosses his lips. "Did you actually try to sound like a crime show just now?"

I frown. "No, because that's what you did. You told them I killed her, Chase. Even your overly-entitled ass has to know how screwed up that is."

He allows his head to fall to one shoulder until he's staring at me with his depthless brown eyes, rimmed in thick lashes that he bats adoringly at me. I dismiss the flutter at my core as fast as it comes. "Relax. Nothing's gonna happen to you."

"Oh, so now you *don't* think I killed your girlfriend. How kind of you to be so wishy-washy. It's not like we're talking about a real death here."

Chase winces at my words. He says into his bottle, "I'm aware of the reality of the situation. And it's my fucking fault." He tosses the empty, and it lands in the water with a clunk. Squinting, I notice the few friends floating with it.

"How is it your fault?" I ask.

"I could've walked back to school with her." He shrugs, then reaches into the six-pack beside him for another beer. "Didn't, because we got in a stupid fight over her drinking too much."

"Don't go there. The rabbit hole of despair is a deep one. How could you have known she would turn around? Or get lost on a campus you all know by heart?"

His gaze slides back to mine, but it lands uncertain and unfocused. "I should've taken her back to the dorms. I should've looked for her. Should've searched harder and made sure no one was left behind before I walked away."

Chase's lips clamp shut, and he turns to the lake. I decide to sit with him a while, because he's not telling me to go. A quiet truce settles onto my shoulders as light bird chirps sound from the trees and water laps against the dock.

The reflection of the sun breaks into shards against the soft ripples of the lake, mesmerizing, meditative, and takes my mind off the horror of broken things.

I take advantage of this placid moment to study Chase's features, beautiful in sadness. His arched brows are lowered enough for his lashes to touch, and he's pensive, staring at the water as if the floating leaves can tell him why Piper fell into its depths.

I startle when he throws his arm out toward me. "Want one?"

"Um. No. Thank you."

"If you're here to tell me you've been through it, that you know how I'm feeling, you can kindly fuck off," he says.

"That's not why I found you."

"No?"

"I came here to yell at you."

Chase snorts.

"It's terrible, what Piper must've gone through before she died," I say. "But that doesn't give you the privilege to come into my room this morning, when I'm still registering the news, and yell and threaten to make my life hell."

"Poor Callie, you don't know how it works around here. I did it because I could."

"And now you're lashing out," I say. "Which is, again, unfair."

"Oh, is life unfair to you, sweet girl?" The brown of his eyes resembles sharp chips of wood. "Too fucking bad."

"How did you know my mom was killed?"

He jolts, then glowers upon realizing his tell.

"You said it to me this morning." I hesitate, but barrel on, "Piper said it to me before she ... How did you guys know?"

Chase's shoulders move in an unconcerned shrug, but his hardened features tell a story he intends to keep hidden. "We looked you up once we heard you were coming here." Chase glances at me sidelong. "It helps to be aware of who's stepping onto our turf."

I roll my eyes, but the implications sit heavy on my soul. "You don't owe me anything."

"You're right. I don't."

I glare at him. "While this is clearly a tough time for you, I'd appreciate it if you'd keep the details of my mom to yourself."

"Don't want the school to see you as a murder victim's kid, huh?"

Chase says it so callously, I reach out to smack him in the arm.

It's with cat-like reflexes that he catches my wrist mid-launch, and his resultant glare would freeze this hell I'm in if I let it.

"I'd second guess that decision," he rasps, then pushes my arm back against my chest.

The force makes me wobble, and I slam a hand onto the wood to keep me level. Yet, the rising indignation in my belly won't keep in balance.

"Piper isn't like my mom," I say, hating that my voice is uneven. "But it's still an unfair death. Being angry at something you can't change isn't worth it."

With similar reflexive force, Chase twists and grabs my chin, holding my jaw between his fingers and thumb. "Oh, yeah? So, you're okay with your mom's murder never being solved? You're fine finishing the rest of your life without her? Dead is dead, right? Finding the killer won't change shit."

"You didn't let me finish," I say, wrestling against his tight grip. The pulse at the base of my neck pounds. "I managed to define that anger into seeking justice. I'm determined to meet her killer before I die."

Chase's fingers loosen on my cheeks, but his grim stare keeps its focus.

"It hasn't made it easier," I continue. "My anger just means I have all this love for a person no longer here, with nowhere for that love to go."

Chase lifts his upper lip, but it's not a sneer. It's an indicator of the inner battle he's waging upon himself.

Chase leans in. "Don't take me for a drunken fool. I've recognized my anger, too. I know where it needs to go. What if I told you I don't think Piper's fall was an accident or that she jumped?"

My surprised inhale causes a sharp whistle between my scrunched cheeks. For the briefest of moments, Chase's attention strays to my lips. It stays there, his penetrating gaze seeming to plump my sensitive skin all on its own. His tongue strokes across his lower lip, as if in thought, before he releases me abruptly, twists back to the lake, and tips his beer back until he finishes the whole bottle.

"Neither do I," I whisper.

Chase stills with the rim to his lips.

"I've had a bad feeling ever since I was told she died," I admit.

Chase whips his head around. "Why?"

The question is sharp and accusatory, giving life to the dull-eyed stare he aims my way.

"You have every reason to hate Piper," he continues.

"And what about you?" I dare to ask. My heart leaps into my throat, conscious of prodding the devil with his own pitchfork. "Why would you want her gone?"

Instead of the reddened fury I expect, Chase chuckles as he stares at the water. "Sweet possum, I did *not* hurt one of the few genuine friends I have in this school, I promise you that."

The way he says my deplorable nickname, prefacing it with a sugared compliment, shouldn't have me wanting to savor it, but it does.

I say, adding flint to my voice, "I have a passion for the truth. I'll always search for it."

"That's fucking fairy-tale thinking," he mutters, then lifts his legs and swings them onto the dock.

As he rises, Chase offers me his hand. I hesitate at the unexpected chivalry.

Chase crooks his fingers. "Chill. I'm not about to toss you into the lake."

The sarcasm doesn't ring true, and Chase's expression crumbles for the barest of seconds at his comparison of a body and water so soon after hearing about Piper.

It gives me faith that he's more human than demon, even in his own kingdom.

I fold my hand into his own, and he pulls me up with graceful ease, the strength of his rower's arms obvious with how weightless I become in his one-handed pull.

It's enough strength to fling a girl over a cliff's edge.

I'm appalled at the thought. Two hours ago, Detective Haskins all but concluded Piper jumped or fell. And what, all it takes to flip the switch is Chase's unbacked but passionate theory to make me question it? I'm better than that. I come from cop stock.

But, my subconscious whispers, *no one's explained Piper's reason to want to die.*

Piper isn't someone I got to know well, and her expressions and attitude were merciless and mocking. But the vibrancy with which she directed her malice forces me to admit that above all else, she was alive and determined to leave her mark on whoever crossed her path.

That is not the attitude of a person who wants to die.

Was she drunk enough to fall? Piper's familiar with Lover's Leap. She'd know where the edge was, even while sauced. Wouldn't she? And would she really wait for the party to end to linger near a cliff face?

The answer to my question clicks into place twelve hours too late. I gasp.

"You coming?" Chase asks.

His glowering form has moved closer to the boathouse. During my space-out, he also rolled down the legs of his pants and pulled his shoes on.

"Piper died the same night as Rose Briar. September tenth," I blurt.

Chase goes quiet. He licks his lips. Then, he asks, "And that's supposed to be relevant to me how?"

"Whose idea was it to hang out at Lover's Leap last night?"

His stare narrows. "Piper's. Why?"

I spur forward. "She was was hyper-focused on our history project. Piper fell in love with Rose's story. I just ... the timing doesn't sit well with me."

"We're always at the cliffs, so her idea to go there last night isn't a new one. But, Briarcliff history is a fucked up one, that much is true."

"Why do people keep saying that, but don't give examples? Rose's husband, this Thorne guy, he and his brothers founded the school. That part, at least, seems innocent enough."

Chase says nothing, choosing to regard me in that eerie, unmoving way of his instead.

I notch my chin up. "I'm going to look into it. With or without your support."

Chase's lashes twitch, but he keeps his tone bland when he responds. "Do whatever you want."

Despite all the beers, Chase's gait is steady when he turns. He stalks down the dock, and I follow a few steps behind. When he halts at the base of the path to the academy, I slow my pace.

"Tell me what you find," he says without looking back.

I don't respond, since I doubt it's a question, and when he resumes walking, I do, too. But I stop short of catching up to him. Whatever shaky alliance this is, it's bound to crumble as easily as the soil beneath Chase's shoes.

Twenty-Five

WITH ASSEMBLY OVER, some students go to class while others take the opportunity to skip afternoon subjects in order to "grieve."

Their reasoning is dubious, since the halls I pass through are cluttered with students whispering about taking off to go to the emptiest vacation home. As soon as they catch sight of me, though, hands get tighter around mouths, and lips get closer to another's ear.

I'm antsy at the silent, targeted attention, but try to walk it off and focus on my classes. It kind of makes me sad, the way Piper's death is being used as an excuse to gossip or get drunk, and I think maybe she wasn't as revered by her pupils as I'd initially thought. When I pass by Falyn and Willow with their heads together in discussion, my pity is confirmed. Falyn's vouching that her parents are still in Boston and her lake house is free.

"What are you looking at, *rodent*?" Falyn sniffs.

I jolt, realizing I must've paused in the school hallway to hear what they were saying.

"Nothing interesting," I say, then decide to throw them a bone as I resume walking. "I'm sorry about Piper."

"Sure you are." Willow twirls a curly strand of reddish hair around her finger as I pass.

I slow to a halt at the implication in her tone.

"Judge us all you want," Willow continues. "We're holding a vigil for our best friend at Falyn's lake house."

"That's ... great," I say. "But why do you feel you need to explain yourself to me?"

Falyn laughs, but her eyes are puffed and swollen from crying. "Maybe we're studying your reaction, Callie."

My brows come down. "What?"

"You don't seem upset," Willow says. "Your roommate *died*, Callie, and you're skipping through these halls like it's just a regular day."

"I'm not." I'd love to argue further, but I tamp down the impulse to defend my case. I shouldn't need to convince these witches of anything.

"Did you ever consider that maybe the whole school's talking about you because we think you did it?" Falyn asks, her eyes, so pale they're almost gray, are calculating and cruel.

I cough out a laugh, but even to me, it sounds tight and anxious. "Then why not tell the detective what Piper said to me? About all the 'terrible' things I did to her?"

Falyn's lips twist. Willow sucks in a breath but keeps her cool. Both won't stop glaring at me.

"Maybe," Falyn mumbles, "we weren't given a choice."

"What's that supposed to mean?" I ask.

Willow pipes up. "It means, watch your back. You're protected until you aren't anymore."

I cover up my unease by turning my back on them in an attempt to find the nearest classroom.

Something pulls at my shoulder, and when I'm spun around, Willow's freckled, angry face looms near.

"Piper was fine before you moved in," Willow hisses. "But then you come along, and now she's dead—"

"Stop with the accusations!" I wrest out of her hold. "I never did anything to her. Ever. If you wanted to fuck me over, you should've just told the detective the truth. But you didn't, so don't come after me now."

"Yeah, well, have fun with that while it lasts," Falyn says as she comes up behind Willow. "Because we're all against you. We're positive Piper would be alive if it weren't for you. Whether she did it herself, or *you pushed her!*"

Falyn's yell bounces off the walls. Students slow at her words, and stares that were curious before narrow with conviction.

She did it, I hear someone whisper.

It totally makes sense, another mutters. *Thirsty as fuck.*

Isn't jealousy, like, the number one reason why people kill?

My lips tighten over my teeth, but I peel them back to counter, "Your lies are so much easier to swallow, aren't they? Since the truth is, you left your friend alone to die."

The accusation sits bitter on my tongue and I'm so disappointed in myself for stooping to their level, but it's much too late to take back.

Falyn's face trembles in outrage.

She breathes out enough to hiss, "You bring up *such* a good point, possum. Maybe the police *should* hear all about what you did to her."

"Falyn, don't," Willow says, "We're not supposed to..."

I don't hear their further conversation, because I've widened the space between us and stride down the hallway, their voices nothing but beetles hissing in my ear.

I'm desperate to get as far away from Piper's friends as possible and reach my destination in record time. I enter the classroom, and Dr. Luke lifts his head in surprise.

"Callie," he says. "I didn't expect you here today."

"I, uh, wasn't sure if my detention still stood," I say, and lower myself into a seat.

My attention strays to the seat Piper occupied during our punishment, and a concrete heaviness weighs against my heart. It's not grief, but ... she'll never sit there again.

"I wouldn't have held it against you if you didn't show," Dr. Luke says kindly. "In fact, I'll nullify the rest of your detentions. Consider your punishment stayed because of the circumstances."

Dr. Luke leans back in his seat, arms folded as if he expects me to stand and sprint from the classroom, lightened by a lifted sentence.

"If it's okay with you," I say without moving, "I'd like to stay here."

I pull out my textbooks before Dr. Luke can respond. I'd rather catch up on homework or read ahead for classes than deal with any additional hallway confrontations. The stares and accusations will grow, and the *last* thing I want is to run into Chase in that kind of crowd.

"Well," Dr. Luke says, and when he sees me pull out my history text, his eyes soften around the edges. "You don't have to worry about that project. I can assign you something else or put you in with another group."

"Actually..." I splay my hand across the text. "I'd like to keep writing the paper."

"On Rose Briar? Can you handle her?"

I glance from the pages to him. "I can. I'd like to understand Rose." *And maybe I can also understand Piper* is a statement left unsaid between us, but Dr. Luke isn't so out of touch that he can't decipher my motive.

"Well," Dr. Luke says after a beat, "I never want to tear students away from an assignment they're passionate about, but given the circumstances, if it becomes too much, or you no longer feel comfortable with the subject matter, you let me know, okay? We'll figure something out. I hear Edward Briar is a maniac."

My lips twitch in a smile. "Isn't he the grandfather who lived a full, uncontroversial life before dying of consumption in his seventies?"

Dr. Luke's eyes crinkle. "Yes. Dusty as a chalkboard, that one. But like I said, if you'd prefer to pivot and do a piece on him, you have my permission to go full throttle. Got it?"

Nodding, I open my laptop, and soon, the sounds of my fingers hitting my keyboard are the only noises between us.

I spend the afternoon with my head down, studying hard, and avoiding the catcalls and heckling still going on in my head. What I also hear, though, is my conscience asking why I decided to stay at Briarcliff, when breaking into my Dad and Lynda's empty Manhattan home and living there while they get high on sugar from virgin daiquiris seems like *way* more of an accomplishment.

Because, I reason, I'd be more alone there than I am here.

It's with that crushing thought that I say goodbye to Dr. Luke and plod to Thorne House.

I key into my apartment, staring at the floor as I wander in. A noise sounds out in the direction of Piper's room, and I look up, then drop my bag.

My heart forgets to beat when I see Piper, digging through her drawers.

Twenty-Six

THE COFFEE MUG rack clatters when I stumble into the kitchenette's counter.

"P-Piper?" I stutter.

The girl turns, and as soon as she does, I note the differences. This girl has a pointier chin and angular cheekbones on a thinner face. But she has the same stormy blue eyes and long, brunette hair held away from her face with a fabric headband.

"Jesus." I bowl over while holding a hand to my heart. "You're not Piper."

"No." The girl sniffs and slowly withdraws from Piper's room. "I'm Addisyn. Her sister."

I vaguely recall mention of Piper's younger sister when I moved here. Something to do with the furniture-stealing and the initiation of every wrong thing that's happened to me since. "Oh, yeah. Addy."

"Only my friends call me that," she says, but it's not said with any venom. She seems tired. Sallow and deflated. "My parents will be here soon to help pack up my sister's things. I wanted to be here when they arrive."

"That's fine," I say, but with the way her gaze slides over me, I doubt she would've changed tactics if I'd said no.

Someone pushes in from behind, clipping my shoulder. "Here, babe. I found some chamomile tea downstairs."

The boy Addy accepts tea from isn't in Briarcliff uniform, but ripped jeans and a dirtied white tee instead. He gives me a brief study before laying a kiss on Addy's lips and massaging her shoulder.

"Thanks, Jack, but you'd better go," Addy says as she cups the tea close to her chest. "I don't want my parents catching you here."

"I get it." Jack smooths Addy's hair—though it's as stylishly sleek and flat-ironed as Piper's always was—and kisses it. "But I didn't want to leave you without one final goodbye. Text me when it's over, okay?"

Addy nods and falls into Jack's embrace before he releases her. He doesn't give me any sort of acknowledgment before he leaves the apartment the way he came.

As soon as he shuts the door, I turn to Addisyn. "Is that your boyfriend? He seems ... nice."

Addisyn's response is to cast her red-rimmed eyes over me before heading back into Piper's room.

"I'll be in my room if you and your parents need any help," I say, manners getting the best of me.

Piper's door shuts with a smart *click.*

The idea of sitting nearby while all of Piper's things are boxed up and transported to a place where a person doesn't need them anymore doesn't sit well.

While Addy is shut in Piper's room, I grab the books I need and choose to wait out the packing in the library.

I work in blessed silence among crisp books and the smell of hot-off-the-press paper—strangely fresh for what should be an old, stuffy library—for a few hours before the clocktower rings the dinner bell, but can't summon up the motivation to dig into the history project I asked Dr. Luke to keep working on. The clue is in my finding calculus more interesting than a nineteenth-century soap opera: I'm scared of what I might find between the lines of Rose Briar's death. It's so similar to Piper's in so many ways.

Did heartbreak cause Piper to jump, too? Or was she pushed?

Was Rose *pushed?*

At the bell, I go straight to dinner instead of dropping my bag off at my dorm. The feeling of being unwelcome in my own room is stronger than ever and won't go away until Piper's family finishes what they need to do.

I'm so deep in thought, on Piper, on Rose Briar, that it never occurs to me to avoid the dining hall, too. I push through the doors with my head down and beeline to the serving station, raising my chin enough to notice that today is pasta day.

I choose Alfredo this time, due to my complicated relationship with red sauce.

"*Killer,*" someone hisses behind my back.

I twist to catch the source of the whisper, clenching the serving tongs in my hand. White sauce drops from the metal and onto the floor, splattering like ethereal blood at my feet.

"*Murderer.*"

This time, I hear it to my right and whip my head to the sound.

"*Jealous bitch.*"

On my left.

Despite my hand aching from how hard I'm gripping the tongs, I'm prepared to meet the angry expressions that must follow those words, yet the students around me are benign or relaxed as they fill their trays, almost like I never heard the whispers.

"*You're next.*"

I swear that was muttered by the girl beside me.

"Next for *what*?" I ask loudly. "To fall victim to an accident? To suicide? Be specific if you're going to threaten me about Piper's death over spaghetti."

The girl startles, her eyes wide behind her glasses. "Um ... what?"

"I heard you," I say.

She shakes her head, confused. "I didn't say anything."

"You did," I snarl, then look up at the students watching. "I had nothing to do with Piper!"

Dead silence meets my words as they echo throughout the hall.

"Why don't you all focus on *why* she did what she did?" When no one answers my question, I cry, "What *is* it about this school that turns people into Greek tragedies?"

Someone hooks onto my elbow and starts dragging me through the dining hall.

Automatically, I struggle against the hold, but his hand clamps down harder. I glance up. My insides shrink at the sight.

"Chase, let me go."

Chase's cold gaze stays straight ahead, but he mutters, "Not a chance."

"I said *let me go*." My voice gets louder. "You don't have the authority to control—"

"Do you see who's watching?" he asks through one side of his mouth. "Take a look, then you can tell me whether or not I should drag you out of here by your ass."

I look where he directs, and my lips thin upon seeing Detective Haskins leaning against the wall, arms folded as he witnesses the spectacle.

"Why do you care if Haskins sees my meltdown?" I ask Chase, but he ignores my question and walks us faster.

Chase pushes us through the double doors into the deserted hallway. When they shut behind him, I jerk out of Chase's hold.

"Why are you trying to save me?" I rub my arm where his grip was, a spot that's sore from his touch ... and pulsing hot. "I thought I was nothing but vermin to you."

His stare becomes his surname as he strides past me. "Because you're no good to me in a holding cell. You're going back to your room."

"I'm not one of your loyal subjects. You can't tell me what to do."

He continues eating up the marble floor, pulling me with him.

"Someone in this goddamned school needs to *answer me*!" I scream, then push at his back and drag my feet until he stops.

And turns.

And in the space of a second, closes the gap and claims my comfort zone.

"I'm not saving you, Callie," he says, and it's so low, so threatening that it's seductive in its menace. "I'm keeping you to myself. Because if you have any answers about Piper's death, *I'm* going to know about it. You'll tell *me*, not some podunk detective who thinks true gumshoeing is pulling kids over for a DUI. Isn't that what we agreed to at the boathouse?"

I bark out a laugh, and his spine jerks upright. "Did I just say something *funny* to you?"

"No," I say with a grin, but hold my stomach, nonetheless. "It's just ... you think you have the power of God. That you have the right to information about a suspicious death simply because you demand it. Fuck, maybe you do." I step back from him and rub my eyes. "What universe have I fallen into where a seventeen-year-old can influence my future?"

"Eighteen," he clips out. "And get used to it. Things don't work the way they do in the big city. My family has connections. *I* have power over this school and all the professors here. *My* family gifted the current library. Headmaster Marron? He's golf buddies with my father, a top criminal defense attorney in this *country*. That should make your tits shrivel, considering the school's current opinion of you. And I can use both my father's and my stronghold over Briarcliff to save you, or I can break you. Understand?"

I will ruin you!

Piper's voice rings in my ears.

I gather the courage to say, "Tell me about the roses."

The muscles in Chase's jaw goes tight. "What?"

"Tell me," I repeat. "Because if anyone knows if Piper's death is suspicious, it's the people behind those flowers."

"Those fucking plants have nothing to do with it."

Chase seems so certain, and yet... "So, you admit they exist."

Chase's lips peel back from his teeth. His eyes narrow to a glare. "What part of *go to your room* are you not comprehending?"

"I'm not forced to follow your rules."

"You better follow someone's, because after what you pulled in there, the cops will look at you harder."

"Why would they?" This time, *I* step up to *him*. "It was an accident. Or Piper jumped. Isn't that what you're so confident these hick cops are concluding? Case closed."

One of Chase's eyelids tics. "You said you were willing to get to the bottom of it, anyway."

"Yes, but I'm doing that for *me*, not you. And I'm not listening to the gossip, which you could stop with one use of that flinty glare of yours. Everyone in that dining hall looks to you, their *ruler*. You told me at the boathouse you don't think Piper committed suicide, and now people are calling me a killer, a murderer, unhinged from my mother's death. That all *stinks* of you Nobles coming together and letting the rumors swirl—"

Chase's hands clamp down on my shoulders. He rasps, an inch from my face, "What have I said to you about that word?"

"It has something to do with the roses, doesn't it? This whole thing, it comes down to the cloaks I saw, gold and black..." As I stare into the murky depths of Chase's eyes, the answers become clear. "They weren't pranks, were they? Replacing my furniture, then filling my locker with poisoned rats ... they're warnings."

Abruptly, Chase releases me, his hot breath leaving my lips. "Shut your mouth, Callie, or I swear to God."

My vision turns into two slits. "You want my help? Give me some answers so I look elsewhere. Are you part of it? Of the cloaks and roses? Is that who the Nobles are?"

"I said, shut up!" he roars.

I wince, his echoing shout slamming against my ears. His chest rises and falls with his deep breaths, but he's not moving. He's not tearing his gaze away from mine.

I whisper, "Ask your inner circle about Piper. She and I weren't friends. We were closer to enemies, but I never hated her."

The memory of me tearing up the rose and wishing Piper and Chase bad luck floats to the surface, but I shove it back down. Wishes can't be granted. They're nothing but envy put into words when people don't have control over their own lives.

"Or," I surmise, "Are your friends thinking Piper killed herself, too?"

I don't think Chase will answer me. I'm confident he'll stomp away like he always does, this infuriating boy who sends me all the wrong signals, but my heart argues is so right.

Chase's lips part. "If you're so smart, you'll figure out why you're in the spotlight soon enough."

I laugh dully. "Shocking. Chase Stone giving me a cryptic answer instead of the truth."

"Just be happy you're not in there having a screech-fest in front of the fucking noodle bar," he tosses out.

"You're such an asshole."

"Thank me later," Chase says as his parting shot, then shoves his hands in his pockets and leaves.

Half of me wants to grab him by the shoulder and drag him back here, because I'm not finished. Most of me wants to punch him in the face.

But part of me knows he's doing the decent thing, and I'm better off in my room, behind my computer. Students can't insult me if I'm not there to hear it.

My chief concern is whether Piper Harrington's sudden death will fall on deaf ears, too.

Twenty-Seven

MY STOMACH RUMBLES as I crouch over my desk and force my eyes to keep reading the document on my computer.

I lean back, absently rubbing my belly and wishing I'd gotten in a mouthful of fettuccini before being carted away by His Highness, King Chase.

The dorm room is utterly silent with me as the sole occupant, and I've left my bedroom door wide to get some air, because the longer I sat at my desk and worked on the history essay, the stuffier this room became.

Piper's door is open, too, but it's completely empty, save for her ghost. Her parents and sister stripped her bed, emptied her drawers, and cleaned out the center room and kitchen pantry, leaving nothing behind but empty food packets they'd shoved into our mini trashcan.

If it weren't for the scent of gardenia in the air, it's as if Piper had never set foot here.

My stomach growls again, with wet, bubble-bursting sounds.

At this point, I haven't memorized the campus well enough to search for late night snacks, but perhaps there's a vending machine in Thorne House's lobby. I vaguely recall Ivy mentioning a coffee bar set up there.

Or, if all else fails, I can scour the Wolf's Den for tossed-aside pastries, but that involves traveling Briarcliff's paths at night.

I'm not up for that, cloaks or no cloaks. And there's also Piper's fall into watery depths to consider, and whether someone hides in the shadows to do it to someone else.

Damn you, Chase, for getting into my head.

In more ways than one.

Ignoring my stomach for a little longer, I turn back to my research on Rose Briar, this time containing notes unlike the first round I deleted when I was determined to leave Briarcliff. I'm trying to read between the lines, as if an answer to Piper's demise is linked with Rose's. But with all I've read, the issues surrounding Rose's death are benign, nineteenth century issues. I click onto Briarcliff's library website, attempting to look up texts from that era, but keep getting "NO RESULTS FOUND."

It's freaking strange. Wouldn't Briarcliff Academy's library, of all places, have original founding documents, or copies of it? Didn't Piper say she'd found original papers?

Yet, other than a brief, transcribed obituary, there's nothing much on Rose, never mind any link to Rose and Piper, save for the same cliff, one hundred and seventy years later.

The two couldn't possibly be related. But this was the last assignment Piper was working on. The final subject in her head. Then, she fell off Lover's Leap—*Rose's* leap.

Piper loved the story and fed off Rose's heartbreak, but ... what am I missing here?

Brrrrrrrrrrrruuup.

Ugh. Stupid stomach.

My chair scrapes against the floor as I push it back and wander out of my bedroom, chancing a search through the kitchenette, even though I know what I'll find. Again, I curse my lack of groceries and tell myself I'll carve out some time Friday to grab some snacks, meaning I'll only have to prowl for food one more day.

Like the rat they think I am.

My heart shrivels at the thought. It's infuriating, how I'm giving proof to Piper's moniker of me even after her death.

Sliding on my shoes, I peer into Piper's room, wishing her parents had left some of her binders behind, or that I'd had the forethought to take her notes or emailed them to myself somehow. She never did send me her findings on Rose Briar. And if any clues existed, it would've been in Piper's own interpretation of Rose's history.

Figuring that ship has sailed, I turn for the door and—

Wait.

I squint at the tiniest strip of red peeking from out of Piper's stripped mattress.

Like the brownnoser I am, I glance around on instinct, as if there's someone there to scold me for wanting to step into someone else's room and invade their privacy, but this dorm room is deserted, save for me. Piper's presence was permanently lifted when her family removed all of her things.

Technically, this room could be considered my property now, at least until Marron assigns someone else to it, which he has yet to mention.

Despite my rationalization, I hesitate in my steps. This space shouldn't be invaded so soon. It's as if the air itself contains sacred artifacts from Piper's life that will dissipate as soon as I disturb it.

"Don't be silly," I mutter. I was forced to live in my mom's space for a while after she died, my stepdad not having the funds to move us until he met Lynda. Her artifacts of life were around me constantly, whether they ripped my soul apart or not.

I can enter Piper's room and see what the ribbon is. Now that I'm closer, I confirm it's red satin and attached to something—not a rose, *please*—that's pushed into the mattress.

The ribbon's slipped free from a tear in the cushioning, likely from all the jostling when packing up Piper's life at Briarcliff. But it's a straight cut ... and clean. It's not a hole that happened by accident.

I touch the opening, then after a breath, push my fingers through the padding and hit something hard.

Frowning, I stick the rest of my hand in, grab the object, and pull it out.

It's a hardback book, with a cream background and red roses painted across it. The pages are trimmed at the edges with gold foil, and if I didn't know any better...

I gasp upon flipping the pages to a random section.

Pages and pages of handwritten notes greet my vision. In my brief scan, I see words like *Chase,* and *my heart's broken,* and, *Callie shouldn't be here,* before I close the book with a snap, splaying my hand across the front.

Oh my God.

I haven't just opened Pandora's box by finding this notebook.

I've stepped into a viper's nest.

This is Piper's diary.

Twenty-Eight

NATURALLY, I go straight to the end of Piper's journal and read her final entry.

01.08.05.Ha

Nobody knows that Mr. S and I are back together, and to keep it that way, I'm not going to use his true name, not even during my private thoughts. Plus, he likes that I call him Mr. S when I'm naked. He wants me to moan it before my mouth goes around his dick and I take all of him in. He wants me to plead it when he buries himself inside me and won't let me come until I beg with his nickname on my tongue.

He likes the power. He gets off on it.

And I'm drunk off desire for him, my Mr. S. I missed him so damn much.

I wish he'd let me tell the world about our love. I want us to be real, to go out in public, but he says to wait until we're done with Briarcliff and both of us can leave. But I crave him. I need his arms around me, and the one person that's preventing us from always being together is Callie. My surprise orphan of a roommate is ruining our plans.

Holy. Shit.

My cheeks are hot by the time I finish, my fingers clenched around the notebook.

Mr. S sounds so much like Chase Stone ... but why would he want to keep their hook-ups secret?

My conscience roars its disapproval. Piper's death is likely an accident, so would the police even care if I gave this to them?

Unless there was something in it to indicate she didn't fall or jump. Like ... a secret affair Mr. S didn't want Piper to reveal.

My breaths level out, and I shut Piper's diary. I have to give it to Haskins...

I don't want to be implicated because I gave them Piper's private thoughts. I'm her supposed enemy. They would wonder, why do I have her diary?

"Argh!" I let out a frustrated growl. What would my mom do in this situation?

My inner villainess thinks to plant the diary on Falyn or Willow, but I'm way too clumsy to pull it off and my fear of authority and getting caught trumps that idea pretty fast.

Then, it comes to me.

I'll anonymously mail the diary to the Briarcliff precinct. Being caught with her diary would cause way more of an issue than mailing it. I'm innocent, but ... sending the notebook to them in an unmarked envelope seems like it'll keep me that way.

...There's nothing to stop me from taking pictures on my phone of each page before handing it over, though.

"I'm one of the rare few who believe there's something suspicious to your death," I whisper to her diary. "Me ... and Chase."

I was shaking by the time I finished Piper's final entry, picturing Chase and Piper doing all the things she outlined. And what's most appalling ... I'd wished I were Piper, begging for Chase to undress me.

God, when did I become so twisted with dark desires? He could be Piper's killer.

I reopen the book and turn the pages, snapping photos with my phone as I go along, reading snippets. Piper goes into visceral detail about what they did in private. How Mr. S found her during the day, then whispered hot promises in her ear as he thrust into her at night—until I came along.

My cheeks go hot again. They were doing dirty things in this dorm room, and it's *definitely* why Piper wanted to keep the apartment a single. There's a perverted urge inside me that wants to read more. And picture it.

Most of all, I have to *know*.

I switch to the strange date written at the top of her last entry, the only entry that has this combination of numbers and letters.

It can't be an actual date of the year. In 2005, Piper was 2 years old. Even reversing the numbers doesn't make sense.

I decide to copy it down on a sticky note as well as take a picture of it, thinking I might as well show the string of numbers to Ivy to see if she might know what it means.

"Allow me access this one time," I say, Piper's fragrance lingering in the paper. "I'll find out the truth."

To my surprise, I get midway through her notebook and find a section of torn-out pages. I run my finger along the remnants. Did Piper do this? It could be the simplest reason—she misspelled words, or her handwriting got messy, or the entry was stupid.

Or ... it could be incredibly important.

Where are the missing pages?

I leap out of bed and do a thorough search of her barren room but find nothing. Once back to mine, I finish up the photos, then shove Piper's diary into the night-stand's top drawer, but it doesn't feel safe there. This room has been violated with its gifts of roses and wood. Someone has trespassed with the intent of ownership and a display of power, and if they come back ... if they find this book...

It may never get into the proper hands. I *have* to get rid of it once I get the chance.

But I'm the person to read this. I know it deep in my heart.

Piper's soul needs to be put to rest, because I can't have two ghosts rivaling for my thoughts, demanding justice on their graves.

Twenty-Nine

I SPEND two days wondering how the investigation into Piper's death is going.

On the outside, I'm the perfect student, paying attention in class, avoiding confrontation, and ignoring the sweeping accusations I hope fade as the gap of time between the shock of Piper's fall and campus visits from the police get wider.

There hasn't been a chance to get rid of Piper's diary anonymously, so I use the time to read more. And yet ... I can't find anything suspicious. Piper goes on and on about how she hates her parents' hounding or how annoying her sister is now that she's in school with her. She also thinks Falyn's getting too fat for crew. And Violet has an eating disorder. And Willow's getting too involved with Mr. S—*did they fuck without me knowing? Are they fucking with me? He will be so, so sorry if I find out it's true. He's mine, even when we're not together. Even if our parents refuse our relationship. It'll always be him, my Mr. S. Always.*

It's such drivel that I often have to shake myself awake to finish. So far, the sole intriguing entry is the last one. There are further graphic depictions of Mr. S and Piper's sexcapades. I haven't found much else about Mr. S, other than he could be Chase, and I'm halfway through her journal. I mean, maybe I could make the mental leap and think it's Chase's father because of the "Mister" part, but that would be *crazy*. And Willow sleeping with him, too?

Yeesh, wtf kind of erotic novel am I reading?

My thoughts are yanked away from the journal when Dr. Luke enters the classroom, his expression grim.

"I have some news, class," he says.

The morning chatter falls silent as he leans forward on his desk.

"This morning, the official statement was announced. Barring further evidence, Piper's fall was an accident."

The quiet becomes a pause as we all process Dr. Luke's statement.

Falyn speaks. "But ... how? She's been up there before. I mean—Piper knows the layout of Lover's Leap."

Snickers burst out from students with a tenuous relationship with Piper, but Dr. Luke silences them with a death glare.

"Miss Clemonte, I know you're upset. You have the right to be. We all want answers, but it was especially dark that night with no moon," Dr. Luke says. "There were too many scuff and shoe marks in the dirt. Ultimately, there was just no way for her to tell where the edge of the cliff was."

"But what about her phone? Wouldn't she be using her flashlight?" Falyn persists. Her eyes shine with desperation.

"I don't believe she had her phone," Dr. Luke says, his forehead wrinkling with thought.

"But *why*? She doesn't go anywhere without it. Ever. Why was she up there alone?" Falyn's voice hitches, and Violet moves to comfort her. "Why didn't she go *home*?"

Any empathy I feel toward Falyn disappears when she turns and lasers into me. "In my opinion, the police haven't done an adequate job. There's at least one suspect in our midst."

"Then you have my full support to take it up with Detective Haskins or read the statement yourself," Dr. Luke says tiredly. "Now, this is a terrible subject for all of us, so let's get lost in a little history before real life smacks us in the face again."

Dr. Luke launches into the economic state of Rhode Island when Briarcliff was built, but the buzzing in my ears overtakes his voice.

Piper fell. It was an accident.

But the police don't know about Mr. S.

Chase makes my paranoia worse. His silence on Piper's death propels rumors faster, and I'm having to duck and weave in the hallways in order to avoid the glares and insults cast my way.

Even now, I study the back of his head as we both sit through history class, attempting to decipher through the effortless styling of his hair why his face sports a shiner this morning and his knuckles are cut and clotted over with blood.

"Don't forget, your essays are due Monday morning," Dr. Luke says as he concludes the class. "Just because you're my favorite students ever doesn't mean I'll give any of you extensions."

Doting sarcasm fills his voice, and I offer up a smile along with some other students as we pack up our things.

"Callie."

The tone doesn't match Dr. Luke's and I glance up from my bag. Chase stands in front of me.

His face is flawless, save for the purple-red crescent under his left eye. A cut mars his lower lip, and there are fingerprints on his neck, scarlet marks that frame his jugular.

After a quick hitch of breath, I deploy the most annoyed eye-roll I have.

"Let me guess," I say. "I should see the other guy?"

Chase's brows flatline and his expression follows a similar iced-over state. "It's nothing you need to concern yourself over."

"Oh, don't mistake this for concern." I trace a circle around my face. "Color me shocked that you're talking to me in public."

Chase arches a dark blond brow, a wisp of amusement drifting through his dark cloud. "Only because I have to."

I toss my bag over my shoulder, and it lands against my back with a thump. I'm conscious of what's in it. "And why have you deemed it so important?"

"Did you find out anything?"

His question is direct, biting in its cadence.

I swallow but refuse to shrink under his focus. "About what, Chase? If you're here to accuse me along with the rest of the student body, get a clue. Detective Haskins hasn't spoken to me since, meaning I'm not on his hit list, so why should I be on yours?"

Now, both Chase's brows rise. "Easy. Because I want you to be."

My lips flutter with an exasperated huff.

"I'm watching you, Callie. You keep anything from me, I'll catch it. And I won't take it to the cops. I'll use it for my own weapon."

"You heard the latest. Stop being such a creep," I say, and move to get past him.

His arm blocks my way, pressing into my stomach ... and dangerously close to the underside of my breasts. An astonishing sensation happens around my nipples, and I glance down, horrified, but cover it up fast with a sound of disgust.

"I asked you a question," Chase repeats. "Did you find out anything about Rose Briar?"

A wave of relief passes through me at the mention of Rose. Chase doesn't know about the diary, or my suspicion that Mr. S is *him*. I push on Chase's arm, but it doesn't move. When he speaks to me, his bruised profile comes all too close to my cheek. A simple turn, a quick dip, and he could be kissing me.

No, Chase wouldn't kiss. He'd ravage.

Mr. S uses his tongue like a man, possessive and strong. When he strokes my mouth, I moan...

My molars clench, a painful warning to my brain to stop this bizarre fantasy.

I meet his eyes. A millisecond of movement separates our mouths, but Chase isn't fucking around.

I'm aware of my surroundings and notice the classroom has emptied, including Dr. Luke. Chase has me alone.

I don't back down, and I do not, under any circumstances, let a hint of what I know pass over my features. "If you're asking if I completed my paper, yeah, I did."

"Good for you. I hope you get an A. Now tell me what I want to know."

Under his intense scrutiny, I falter, just a little. "There's a ton of information on Briarcliff's founders. You did Theodore Briar, right? A nod to the odd man out?"

Chase's eyes shrink into slits. "Don't change the subject. It makes me want to pursue this harder."

"Read between the lines, Chase. I could research tons on the men. But Rose? I found zilch," I lie. "Enough to write a basic essay. If Piper knew anything, it'd be in her notes, which are on her laptop, which her family now has." I attempt to push past him again. "So why don't you go intimidate Addisyn?"

This time, Chase backs up a step. And his expression is oddly flat. "That's too bad."

"Too bad?" I echo. "I'm so sorry my research into Briarcliff's catacombs wasn't acceptable for you, Master Scholar."

"Not even close. There's a reason Piper wanted to be at the cliff on the same date Rose Briar disappeared. You're the one who pointed it out to me. But now you find nothing? I guess your usefulness ends there. I'll do the rest of the heavy-lifting."

"Oh, fuck you, Chase! I'm invested in this, but you of all people can't blame me for not knowing who to trust."

He pauses in the doorway, his shoulders leveling. "My, my, Callie, are you saying you don't trust me?" Chase lays a mocking hand on his heart. "I am shooketh."

"The official statement's out. It was an accident to everyone except you and me. So, unless you stayed at Lover's Leap with her that night, or, my bad, Fuckboy's Leap—"

Chase stiffens. When his eyes find mine again, they blaze copper fire. "I'd be careful choosing your next response. Accuse me again, and I'll have you tossed off this campus so fast, you'll lose the granny panties currently cupping your ass."

"Joke's on you," I snipe before thinking. "Because I prefer thongs."

Chase's eyelids flare. Heat snakes into my core, coiling its scales. My response to him is frightening, venomous ... and daring.

I hold a silent breath.

The urge is so sudden and *there*, that I'm desperate to think of something else. To get back to Piper and the mystery behind her fall. To do anything but meander into Chase's clutches.

Chase's focus dips to my skirt, as if he can see the building dampness in my panties. I'm desperate to cross my ankles, but that would accelerate the swelling need, so I clench my hands instead, so hard my nails dig crescents into my skin.

Ire builds in my belly, and wars with this unspeakable craving for Chase. Sheer exhaustion weighs heavy on my expression each time I leave my dorm, because to the rest of the school, theories, rumors, and gossip are easier than checking the facts. Hurled insults contain the satisfaction needed.

Cap all this off with Chase's weird and cold dismissal and his refusal to help despite our private talks, always after *he* seeks me out, it's natural that enraged stupidity spirals its way into my throat.

"I know enough, Mr. S," I say.

Chase's attention comes back to my face. Any passion I ignited disappears with that single flick. "Excuse me?"

"Mr. S," I repeat shakily.

His expression smooths. "Maybe I was wrong about you. Keep your head in your books. You're better at that than any Nancy Drew bullshit you're attempting."

My hands unclench as I watch him leave, my arms trembling with the effort. Chase manages to get under my skin by uttering a simple syllable, and I hate how I can't manage the same effect on him.

Maybe I shouldn't have shown my cards so soon and called him by Piper's secret name. Or perhaps I damn well should've, because I need *something* other than casual coolness from this bastard.

If that flicker of flame in his eyes at the mention of my underwear is anything to go by, perhaps I'm getting there.

Which means, I must identify why it was so crucial to Piper that sex with him had to remain under wraps this time around.

Thirty

THAT EVENING, Ivy comes over to study for our English Lit quarter-term exam.

Yup. Quarter-term grades are a thing here.

We're sprawled at either end of my twin bed, our textbooks and laptops between us as Ivy quizzes me on *Pride and Prejudice,* and I resist the temptation to relate the assignment to its modern twist, *Pride and Prejudice with Zombies.*

"I doubt Professor Parker will appreciate your addition of the apocalypse to a literary classic," Ivy observes as she flips a page.

"Hey, I can't take credit for that kind of originality, but it's unfortunate Parker won't widen his horizons." I stick my pen between my lips as I type out notes on my computer.

"Any other potential questions you can think of? I gotta leave in like..." Ivy checks her watch. "Ten minutes."

"Really?" I pull my computer onto my crossed legs, settling back against the wall. "Where are you off to so late?" I let out a mock gasp. "Are you meeting a paramour, Elizabeth Bennet?"

Ivy laughs, but there's a hesitant pitch to it. "I wish. I promised Eden I'd go over chemistry with her tonight, too."

"Jeez. That's adding some contrast to the night."

"I gotta keep the scholarship alive," she says airily, then runs a hand through her hair. "Unlike many of the privileged douches here, if my GPA drops below a three-point-seven, I'm out on my ass."

Accuse me again, and I'll have you tossed off this campus so fast, you'll lose the granny panties currently cupping your ass...

I wriggle against my mattress, static electricity raising the hair on my arm at the thought of Chase picturing me in the thong I'd told him I preferred.

"Might as well give the privileged douches a name," I say to Ivy, internally begging this extra energy to go to anyone but Chase. "You call them the Nobles."

Ivy's pen stops scratching against her spiral notebook. She doesn't look up.

"Right?" I prompt.

"Not this again," she says.

"You tried to get me to forget about it with that *global* bullshit, but Ivy, you told me about them on the night my entire scholastic future was written on the wall. In garbage."

"Yeah..." Ivy collects her white-blond hair at the nape of her neck, twists it, then lets it fall. "I realize that was a lame cover-up, but is there any way you can pretend I never told you that?"

I angle my head. "You want me to shut up."

Ivy raises her chin, pleading. I hold up my hand. "You're doing a much better job of it than Chase did, basically threatening to have my head if I ever uttered the name again."

Ivy hisses in a breath, and I swear, color leeches from her face in less than a second. "You told *Chase?*"

"It's not like you told me to stay quiet!" I defend. "Not then, anyway."

"Oh my God, *Callie.*" Ivy covers her face with her hands. "Why?"

"Why not?" I push my laptop off my legs and slide closer. "I'm so tired of this game where I toss out an innocuous word and the person I'm talking to flips out. Can someone please be straight with me? As my friend? Explain to me why the Nobles send Chase into a rage and you into a tizzy." I slide a look to the opposite end of the dorm. "And while we're at it, do they have something to do with Piper?"

Ivy doesn't hesitate. "No." She follows my gaze. "Doesn't it freak you out? Living in a place Piper used to make her home? It's so lifeless out there now..."

"It is," I admit. "Which is why, tomorrow morning, I'm going into town and grabbing a few things to make this space my own. Marron says that barring any new students, there won't be anyone filling up her side of the room, so..."

Ivy tucks a strand of hair behind her ear. "It's just you? From now on?"

"I'm not sure how I feel about it, but—hey! Don't change the subject on me!"

Ivy offers a sheepish smile, but color hasn't returned to her cheeks. "A girl had to try."

"Tell me." I lean forward. "Give me something, Ivy, or I'm going to annoy it out of you every minute of every hour, I swear I will."

Ivy sighs, her attention straying to my doorway. "I can trust you, right?"

I grab her hand, and it's cold and clammy in my grip. I squeeze, letting her know that she can.

"Then you can trust me. Don't go to Chase," she says. My hold goes slack. "Drop it, Callie."

I lean back, releasing her hand as a signal that I'll listen to her. For now. Tomorrow morning brings its own stressful complications, so I can leave the subject of the Nobles for later.

"Fine," I mutter. "I won't talk to Chase about it."

"Good. Thanks for the study sesh," she says, and her smile isn't as tight. "I'll see you tomorrow? Maybe I'll join you on this field trip you have in mind."

"I'll text you."

"Sounds great," she calls as she exits my room, color back in her cheeks and a skip to her step.

As soon as my dorm room door shuts with a click, I rifle through my nightstand, pull out Piper's diary, and hold it up.

I glare at it.

"What the hell is the point of a secret diary if you don't write down any of your secrets, Piper!"

Thirty-One

THE FOLLOWING morning dawns with a dreary rolling fog across Briarcliff's picturesque lawn. It's Saturday, which means I should be sleeping in, but I can't get comfortable enough to fall back asleep.

Rereading Piper's diary wasn't the best bedtime storybook before crashing, fully clothed, on my bed. She invaded my dreams, visions of Piper dressed in a nineteenth century ivory nightgown running toward Lover's Leap. Chase ran after her, screaming for Piper to take his hand, until at last, with Piper's long, brunette hair cascading behind her, she takes the leap, without hesitation.

Without looking back.

Trailing behind her, where her footsteps should've been, are black and white roses.

My stomach rumbles when I sit up. Rubbing it, I convince myself it's because of the lack of food in my dorm and not two tragedies intertwining into a sleepless nightmare.

I peel off yesterday's uniform and pad into the bathroom naked, keeping my shower brief, and I decide against eating breakfast in the dining hall. On weekends, seniors are allowed to leave campus, and I can't believe it's taken me close to a month to step away from this cursed school.

A quick blow-dry and make-up application later, I choose basic straight-legged jeans and my mom's college tee. I hug myself once the soft cotton hits my chest, the familiar feel realigning my heart for the time being.

My phone's where I left it—tangled in my bed covers, and I send Ivy a text to let her know I'm headed into town for breakfast, exploration, and groceries, and I'd love a buddy. She responds immediately, and we agree to meet in front of the school in an hour.

I'm early, but it's never relaxing hanging out in my dorm room, so I swing my tote onto my shoulder and step out.

The hall is quiet, girls taking advantage of no classes and sleeping in. The usual "guard" from the local university is at the front desk, glasses perched on her nose and typing on her laptop. She grunts a greeting as I walk by.

Outside, the cool air brushing against my cheeks brings the promise of fall as my feet tread on the path. I'm looking forward to all these trees turning sunburnt orange, bright reds, and chocolate browns—all the colors social media posts promise. Living in Manhattan, I didn't get much fall, New York City basically leveling out into two seasons—winter and construction work. Trees don't change from green to anything. Instead, they turn into skeletons reaching their bare branches toward gray skies. If I ever wanted to immerse myself in autumn, I suppose I could've strolled through Central Park, but it's so overloaded with tourists, cyclists, and joggers, I could never find a moment's peace.

Here, though, at Briarcliff, I could appreciate fall in the quiet.

My head tilts to the left, and I picture my mom walking beside me, as excited about the changing season as me, since her hikes were planned around September and October for this reason.

Picture it, Calla-baby, the colors of painters' dreams. Peek through the fog with me. Go on, look. See, baby.

My throat goes thick, and I pinch the skin of my forearm to drive the sudden pain somewhere else. But my daydream has pointed out how foggy it's become, like the clouds have dropped from the sky to lay their tired forms on Briarcliff's bed of grass.

And ... I'm somewhere unfamiliar.

In my daze, I've gone in the opposite direction of the school, towards the cliffs. My nightmare clung to my subconscious with such tangible firmness that it propelled me in the direction of Lover's Leap.

Alert curiosity propels me farther into the trees, following the sounds of crashing waves until I reach a metal gate with a piece of yellow police tape flapping in the salted breeze.

The jagged end of the large rock is obvious from this distance, even in the fog. It looms majestically, promising a beautiful view but a horrific death, and I can't bring myself to try and get around the fencing.

I step back, the gray mist clinging to the roots at my feet, obscuring the forest floor.

A flash of movement brings my gaze up.

It's a foot, disappearing under a flap of fabric as whatever—whoever—it is, runs back into the forest.

A tightness fills my chest, and the rising nausea tastes a lot like fear.

I'm alone, in the woods, near the cliff where Piper died. Daylight doesn't change that.

"Nope. Not doing this," I mutter, and wheel around to march back to campus.

I power-walk so fast, the tops of Briarcliff's pointed roofs come into view within minutes, but not much else.

A flicker of movement brings me to a stop.

"Hey!" I call into the closest canopy of trees. "I see you!"

Nothing but the faded chirps of birds respond. Gritting my teeth, I dare myself to say, "How about you go back to your boiling cauldron and leave me the hell—"

A figure steps out from behind the thick oaks, clad in a dark cloak, the hood so large, it obscures this person's face.

The fabric falls back from the figure's arm as they lift a finger to their shadowed profile, then whisper, "*Shhh...*"

My brows slam down, but before I can retort, the figure melts back into the fog, and I'm left with the birds.

A low-key buzz emits from my phone in my bag. I dig for it as I continue my trek to the main building. Lifting it, I read:

Unknown Number: WATCH YOUR BACK.
Unknown Number: <calliedidit.gif>

The GIF loads automatically and shows one scene where I'm pushing Piper to the dining hall's floor, in full-on *Carrie* mode with my face and hair soaked with pasta sauce. Then, it switches to a scene of me elbowing Piper in the nose, smiling as blood drips from between her fingers when she clutches her face. Same cafeteria background. Different day.

Importantly, the day she died, and showing evidence that I was angry enough to retaliate.

Three dancing dots appear, then are replaced by a video. The freeze screen shows me enough, but I press play, cringing before Piper's accusations sound out.

"*...so, you think hurling insults at me was nothing? Refusing to do your half of our history essay? Vowing to ruin my GPA and my life? What about vandalizing my bedroom? Smearing my lipstick all over our bathroom mirror? You're fucking nuts, Callie! Fucking certified!*"

I lower the phone, scanning my surroundings for a glimpse of that hooded man, but my mind's severed between the figure and what was sent to my phone.

Someone filmed proof of my possible motive to kill Piper hours before she toppled off Lover's Leap. Enough to reopen the case.

My phone buzzes again.

Unknown Number: STAY QUIET.

Thirty-Two

I'M BEING THREATENED.

Or blackmailed. How do they know what I've found? What I've read in Piper's diary? Is this about the existence of Mr. S?

This video ... it could go to Haskins with a simple 'send,' and whoever gave me this wants me to know they have the power.

I can't walk the rest of the way back to campus alone without fear of the Cloak coming back, despite the relative safety of the school nearby, so I do the next best thing.

I phone Ahmar. He's familiar. Safe.

He picks up after one ring. "Hey, kiddo."

"Hey. Am I interrupting you?"

"Nah ... well, sorta. I'm at a crime scene, but I could take five."

The lightness of his tone lets me know that the scene is more violent than he's letting on. Even in a different state, he tries to protect me from the worst—despite me already *seeing* the worst humanity has to offer.

"What's up?" he asks.

"I kinda ... have news."

"Oh, yeah?"

My pressing need to call Ahmar dissipates. I have to tell him about Piper. It's the type of billionairess death to go national, and Marron already put out a release to the parents and guardians.

Ahmar wouldn't receive that kind of head's-up, and I have no idea if my dad would care to fill him in. I haven't heard from Dad or Lynda since the tragedy happened.

I aim to get it over with in one fell swoop. "So, my roommate died."

"*What?*"

"She—she fell off a cliff. The police are saying it was an accident."

"Jesus Christ, Calla. Are you okay?"

"Fine. I mean, shaken up, but I'm doing all right."

"Should I come visit?"

"No, I'm handling myself. But I can't help but think there's something I'm missing."

Ahmar predicts where I'm going. "Hun..."

"What if there's suspicious evidence being overlooked, Ahmar?"

"Sweetheart, the last time you thought this—"

I dismiss his argument before it starts. "This is completely different. Piper's death doesn't make sense. Kids don't go to this cliff alone in the dark to meditate. They go to hook up, or do drugs, or whatever they can while teachers pretend nothing's going on. There was a party that night. Why did she stay there when everyone else left?"

"If the police are saying it was an accident..."

"Sure, her fall might've been, but what is the reason she *stayed*?" I ask before I chicken out, "Can you look into it? Maybe find out her blood alcohol level and see if she was so drunk that she..."

"Calla," Ahmar asks. "Is this about your roommate or your mother?"

"It's about something fishy in this school," I say, in as calm a manner as I can. "This isn't some sort of crutch about my mom. If you could just call the precinct— his name is Haskins. You're a cop. He's a cop. Maybe he'll be candid with you."

"Hun, it sounds like the case is closed."

"Please?"

Ahmar sighs. "I'll talk to this Haskins guy. I'm not gonna promise anything. He's in a different jurisdiction. He doesn't owe me anything."

"I know," I say. "But I'd like to understand why he called it an accident."

"Okay. But please, Calla, try to focus on your studies and making friends. Getting involved in all this ... it's not healthy for you. Briarcliff was meant to be your escape."

"Now that you're on it, I'll back off, Ahmar. I swear."

Ahmar knows me well enough not to be convinced. But I know that he's at an active crime scene and doesn't have time to lecture me. "I love you, kiddo. I gotta go."

"Thanks, Ahmar," I say, and click off as I'm approaching Briarcliff's buildings.

That last message told me to be quiet. I'll do as they warn, but that doesn't mean I can't coax others to be louder.

And that begins with Piper's diary.

Ivy's sitting on the steps to the main building, absently scrolling through her phone when I arrive.

"Sorry I'm late," I say, breathless as I plop down beside her.

"No worries." Ivy gives me a second look. "Did you run here?"

"Not exactly," I say after a huff of breath. "Did you call a car?"

Ivy pats my shoulder affectionately. "Don't have to. Remember? Briarcliff Academy has a chauffeur service going into town and back."

I raise my brows. "Oh, right."

A town car pulls up the circular driveway, and Ivy and I stand. "See? All I had to do was request it on the app."

"The app," I repeat. "Just when I thought I was an expert on the Briarcliff handbook..."

Ivy laughs as I slide into the backseat. I nod hello to Yael, the driver, when he glances at us in the rearview mirror.

We chat about light topics like course loads and what it was like to rely on a subway in the city and not a car on the way to Briarcliff Village. My phone burns a hole in my pocket, and in the back of my mind I'm desperate to solve the riddle of who could've sent those texts.

Someone who filmed both instances, obviously.

But the second time Piper and I faced off, the dining hall was almost deserted. I didn't notice anyone holding up their phone, but then again, I wasn't too focused on my periphery. A determined filmmaker could've hidden behind the heavy drapery on each of the dining hall's floor-to-ceiling windows, or crouched in a corner, and I would've been none the wiser.

Especially if they donned a cloak.

"Hey, I have a question," I say to Ivy. The car slows with its arrival into the village.

"Shoot," Ivy says. She props her purse on her lap as Yael parallel parks on Main Street.

"How many students know about the Nobles?"

Ivy hisses, then latches onto my wrist once we stop and all but drags me out. I stutter out a thank you to Yael, and he salutes in response, unperturbed by whatever he happens to hear in the backseat.

"I told you not to talk about that!" Ivy says as I stumble to a stand on the sidewalk.

"Correction, you told me not to talk about it to *Chase*."

An annoyed growl comes from Ivy's throat. "Leave it to you to find a loophole."

"I'm sorry, but I need your help," I say, then take a deep breath. "You're the one person I can trust."

"When we talked yesterday, I thought we came to an agreement. Stay away from them—*that's* the warning I needed you to walk away with."

"Ivy, I ... I think they're watching me."

Ivy takes a moment to search my face before she lets out an exasperated puff of air.

"God," Ivy says, massaging the creases in her forehead. "I need espresso for this. Come on."

Ivy latches onto my wrist again and pulls me in the direction of the lobster shack I noticed during my drive through Briarcliff Village ... with Piper.

"I'm known to walk all by myself, you know," I say as I trail behind her.

"And right off a damn cliff," I swear I hear her say, but a passing car's large motor drowns out her words.

Armed with our lattes and lobster omelets, Ivy and I find a secluded seat near the back wall of the shack, which Ivy chose in hopes of nobody eavesdropping.

"Ironically, chatting about this in public is safer than on Briarcliff campus," she says as we sit down. She cups her hands around her mug. "So. Tell me what's been going on."

"Can you start first? And explain how this group works?"

Ivy stares at me, unblinking. I can't shake the unease as she and I silently war to be the winner of this information duel.

But Ivy was my friend and confidant during my first weeks at Briarcliff. It was *her* who brought the name to my attention. She has answers, even if she doesn't think she does. More than I could ever figure out on my own.

So, I give in.

"Okay," I say, and hunch over my coffee so she can hear my low words better. I confess about the roses, the first one black, the second one white. I hold back on my possession of Piper's diary, but I show her the text messages I received this morning.

"Shit," Ivy says as she holds my phone. She drops it face-down on the table. "I'm an idiot, Callie. I'm sorry. This whole time I thought you were stupidly curious about something no normal person should concern themselves over. But now ... jeez, now you're being gag-ordered. For what, though?" Her eyes turn to slits. "What have you been up to that's caused this kind of message?"

"I've been doing some digging on Piper," I admit. "Her death may not have been an accident."

Ivy's expression freezes.

"...And someone thinks they have the clout to frame me for Piper's murder if I don't leave it alone. This video is enough to cast suspicion on me," I say, then lick my lips. "There's one other thing."

Ivy leans back after a long swig of her coffee. "I'm a little afraid of what you're going to say next."

"I'm researching Rose Briar and her jump from Lover's Leap."

Ivy's forehead relaxes. "Okay. That sounds fine."

"It ties into Piper's death. Kind of. Chase and I both think—"

"Wait, *Chase?*"

"Yes," I confess, somewhat chagrined. "Piper's death is too similar to Rose's to be ignored, even if the police want to dismiss it."

"I ... what am I supposed to say to that?"

"We think there's more to it than what the police have concluded. Piper died on the same night Rose did, Ivy. September tenth."

"So now you and Chase are a *we.*"

I'm quick to defend myself. "It's a lonely place, you know, when you're one of two people who think Piper's death is related to a scandal the academy doesn't want revealed."

"Hang on, now you think *Briarcliff's* involved? Like, Headmaster Marron? Come on, Callie."

"I don't have specific proof, but Piper was convinced she had evidence..." I trail off at how this must sound, now that I'm giving voice to it.

"Isn't your uncle a cop? Trust the investigation."

I give a nod, but switch tactics. "Doesn't this school stink of something sinister to you? Like there's something being protected behind the scenes, or hidden under the floorboards, or..."

"Callie." Ivy reaches for my hands. "You've had it tough. Piper zeroed in on you the *day* you arrived here. Then you got Chase's attention. And through them, the rumor mill. Aside from being a drama-magnet, you're going through a lot. For most of us, Briarcliff Academy is just that. An elite school that drives us into the Ivy Leagues, if we're lucky. Have you ever thought that maybe Piper's death is an outlet for you to release all this angst and frustration at being an unfair target?"

I shake my head. "It's not all in my head, Ivy. I got a text telling me to shut up and a Cloak's been haunting me ever since I started looking into Piper's death."

A flutter of confusion crosses Ivy's face. "A Cloak?"

"It's what I call this dude who I keep running into, for lack of being allowed to associate him with the Nobles, lest lightning strike me where I sit."

"Like I said, drama-magnet," Ivy jokes, totally unconcerned over my confession of the obvious stranger-danger on campus.

Now I'm positive she knows more than she's saying. I fold my arms onto the table. "I told you mine, Ivy. Your turn."

Ivy nibbles on her lower lip. "Do you need a refill?"

"Ivy."

"Fine. Okay." Ivy finds a spot on her shirt to pick at. "So, pretty much the whole country wants to send their kids to Briarcliff. You're practically guaranteed a spot at a top university. What's difficult is getting *in*to Briarcliff."

I reach for patience.

"Thousands apply for a scholarship here," she continues. "But if you're a legacy, you basically have instant access to these halls."

"Legacy?"

"You know, if your parents or grandparents are alumni. The academy will give you preference, but you still have to prove your worthiness in grades, or sports, or some extra-curricular."

"Okay..." I say, staring harder at my untouched coffee. "But I've seen no mention of the Nobles anywhere on campus. No clues, either. So, how do you know about them?"

"Well, that's what I'm telling you. The Nobles are the legacies." Ivy smiles, but it seems forced and untrue. "I ... I haven't been upfront with you, but now that you're being singled out ... I can tell you what I know. Which isn't much."

I urge her to continue with a nod.

"It's a kind of preferential treatment that no one talks about. The Nobles are guaranteed a spot in the Ivy Leagues, for example. Through not-so-obvious means, if you get what I'm saying."

I smell bullshit. "Go on."

"No one talks about it because a lot of what they do to get their kids on the elite track is illegal. If it ever came out..."

I think of the journal, and all of Piper's coded secrets. It's all that remains of Piper's working mind, and I'm keeping it from Ivy *and* Chase. I should tell Ivy, but I'm held back by something. Instinct. Caution.

She's lying.

Ahmar's warning sounds in my head. *Getting involved in all this ... it's not healthy for you...*

I ask, "Who's a part of it? Chase?"

Ivy makes a see-saw motion with her hand. Noncommittal.

I let it go, since I'm prepared to find the source and ask Chase straight out.

"Whether he's a part of these Nobles or not, Chase is adamant about keeping it quiet." I pick at my lower lip as I parse through Ivy's explanation. My foremost thought being, *is any of this in the missing pages of Piper's diary?*

"Because the Nobles are to be feared, Callie. Don't let the name fool you. There's nothing noble about them."

My attention drifts to my bag, and the diary that rests in it.

"Anyway." Ivy says in an attempt to move the conversation along. "Why do you keep bringing up Chase? You interested in him or something?"

"Ugh," I say, but even as I make the noise, I'm conscious how overdramatic it is. "He's not my type."

"Chase isn't any girl's type, which is why they all chase after him."

"Not me," I say, and tell myself to *mean* it. "That goes to my point, though. If Piper became exclusive with him again, she'd let the entire student body know he's hers, right? There wouldn't be a dust mite in this building that wouldn't have heard."

Ivy frowns, thinking. "No, Piper wouldn't say anything this time around, because of their parents."

I perk up, sensing a clue. "Oh, yeah?"

"Yup." Ivy huffs out a laugh. "It was the scandal of tenth grade. Chase's dad and Piper's mom met on one of our Family Days. Don't ask. It's the lamest event on the planet, and it involves potato sack races. Anyway—they both left their spouses, and, when was it ... this summer, I think, they announced their engagement. So, to wrap that all up in a neat bow..." Ivy mimes tying a knot, "Chase and Piper were destined to be brother and sister. Their parents forbade them from getting back together, since it would be quite the scandal in Charleston society if they hooked up as step-siblings."

My mind whirs with the implications Ivy's brought forward, but she doesn't recognize any of it as she eats.

I think I've just found out Mr. S's ... *Chase's* ... secret.

Yet, Piper's last words to me won't stop screaming in my head. How she shouted in the dining hall that I was stealing her boyfriend, basically telling everyone within her vicinity that Chase was hers. Was keeping their affair on the down-low becoming too much for her once she sensed my interest in him?

Ivy wouldn't have those answers, so I change the subject. "How can my researching Rose Briar make these Nobles angry enough to send me a blackmail text?" I ask her instead.

"If it was them." Ivy plays with her empty cup by spinning it in a circle. "Piper managed to turn the whole school against you, and even in death, she's still accomplishing it. That text could be from any of her followers who want justice."

"But I didn't kill her! Can't you see how much of an elaborate game this is?" I blurt out, and even to my ears, it's too loud. But hell, I'm shocked and perturbed by *all* of this.

Ivy shushes me, but it's too late. A couple of patrons look our way. One in particular catches my eye.

"Hey," I say to Ivy, unable to move my gaze away. "Isn't that what's-his-name? Addisyn's boyfriend?"

Jack must notice my deeper scrutiny, because he unfreezes and goes back to wiping down a front table, his apron stained with a morning's worth of boiling lobster.

"That's about as far away from elite Briarcliff stock as Addisyn can get," I observe.

"Yeah, I guess. Listen, whatever you're doing to gain attention, I'm better off not figuring it out. And you should put this to rest, too." Ivy rises, and I stand with her, handing over her purse. Before we exit, Ivy presses her hand into my shoulder. "And if you're thinking about Chase offering you any sort of protection while you keep at it—"

Damn her for reading into my thoughts.

"—don't. He's the one with the defenses, Callie. And I have no doubt he'll toss you aside the minute you lose your usefulness. Keep it in your control—ditch him. That's my final advice." She searches my eyes again. "Okay?"

I'm reading between Ivy's lines. She no longer wants to discuss the Nobles, and if I continue to press, if I'm determined to keep trying to decipher Piper's journal ... Ivy won't be any further help, and I can't blame her.

Yet, that inner doggedness of mine rears its ugly snout, and I know with certainty that I won't be able to let this go.

Not until I uncover the truth about Piper, lying within the hidden artifacts of an elite high school.

Thirty-Three

IVY SHOWS me the local marketplace, and I toss some apples, granola, chocolate bars, and potato chips into my basket for midnight snacking. I also buy manila envelopes and stamps. We don't mention the Nobles or Piper for the rest of our morning. I respect Ivy's need for distance, so I keep our topics inconsequential and innocent as we finish up, poke around a furniture store for some basic items, then wait for our chauffeur service on the sidewalk outside the lobster shack. As the cars pass, and I idle beside Ivy, I notice the post office on the corner.

"You know what?" I say, pretending spontaneity. "You go back. I'd like to explore Main Street."

"Really?"

"I like it down here. It feels … real."

Ivy doesn't argue. "I'd stay with you if I didn't have to study for chem. Kinda jealous. It *is* nice in this town."

"Next time." I smile and start walking. "Send me the info on the car app. I'll see you at lunch."

"Okay … um, Callie?"

I turn. "Yeah?"

"You're just exploring, right?"

"You and I made a deal," I say. "I'm not going to involve you."

"My fear is you'll turn to Chase instead."

"All I'm doing is getting some errands done. You don't have to worry."

"What is it about Piper, Callie? I'm trying to understand, but I just *don't*. Can't you leave this to the detectives?"

I deflect the question with a subject I'm coming to learn she's passionate about. "Now you're starting to sound like Chase."

"Well, that proves he has at least one thinking brain cell in his head. But you didn't answer my question."

"Would you mind dropping my food off by my front door?" I deflect. "I'll owe you one."

"Why can't you leave Piper's death alone?"

"Because it's not just my bully's death." I pause for a moment, staring out into the street before I turn back to Ivy. "It's her murder."

"But—"

I'm saved from further discussion when the Briarcliff car pulls up and Ivy gives up. She gets in, but not before sending me an assessing stare above the car's hood.

"Give me your stuff," she mumbles.

"Thank you," I say, and hand over my groceries.

As she pulls the door shut, I wave and promise I'll see her at lunch.

The post office is a block away, and I get to the entrance just as a man is stepping out. He holds the door so I can slip in.

"Thanks," I say, then walk into—

A library?

A row of stacks and the musty smell of well-worn books and much older carpet hits my nostrils. I pause at the turnstile for entry, convinced I walked into the wrong building.

"Can I help you?" a woman asks from the front desk.

She's wearing '50s-style glasses and curled her hair in a vintage bob. She sets down the paperback she was reading—*The Duke's Hidden Duchess*.

"I'm sorry, I thought this was the post office."

"It is," she chirps. "We merged quite some time ago. You'll notice the mailboxes behind me. We're a small town with limited municipal resources."

I nod, then pull out my textbooks until I find the manila envelope I'd stuffed the diary in when Ivy wasn't looking. A quick search on my phone told me the police precinct's location, and I set the envelope on the receptionist's desk and scrawl the address, tilting it so the receptionist can't see. I'm hoping Briarcliff isn't that minis-cule of a town that the librarian/post office clerk will make any connection to me and a newly discovered diary of a dead girl.

I don't have to worry, though, because she's cocking her head at my textbook I tossed out of the way. "Are you searching for something in biographies, hun?"

"Excuse me?"

"Your sticky note there. That's our library's reference code."

She's looking at the note I'd stuck to the front of my Calc text, hoping to ask Ivy about it but never getting the chance. I'd forgotten it was there. "It is?"

I stare at the numbers I wrote down: **01.08.05.Ha**

"Sure, honey." She points to the first number. "Number one means first floor, and eight is the number we give to our biography section. Five is the shelf-level. Then we end with the first two letters of the author's name."

"Well, I'll be," I drawl. I peel off the note and shove it in my pocket before depositing the textbook back in my bag. "So, my mail just goes in there?" I point behind her, fisting the manila envelope.

She chuckles, likely amused by Gen Z kids trying to relate to snail mail. "Yes, dear."

In an attempt to distract, I say, "How old is this library?"

"Oh, ancient in your eyes, dear. Maybe sixty years? Not as old as Briarcliff Academy's, however. Sad, how we lost it."

"I thought Briarcliff's library smelled a little too much like fresh paint," I say. "It's newly built, isn't it?"

"As it happens, it just reopened." The receptionist pushes up her rhinestone glasses and leans forward in her seat. I catch her nameplate: DARLA. "Quite the scandal. The old library burned down."

"It did?" I put extra *oomph* in my gasp, though a lot of it is real. Darla's interest has clearly bypassed what I'm mailing and is on to juicier gossip.

"And the new building was gifted by the victim's family. Can you believe it?"

"Wait..." Didn't Chase say his dad financed the library?

"*Such* a tragedy. If you have the time—" her phone rings, and she glances toward it. "Darn. Anyway, take a look around. Most of the original documents exclusive to this town were destroyed along with it. But this library has the rest."

My heart beats faster. I'm ready to track down the source of Piper's reference code. "Are there papers on the founders here?"

"Another intrepid student, I see. Briarcliff pupils don't think to come to this library for local research. I suppose they don't care, now that the web exists. The last girl here asking for founders documents was ... well, she's a tragedy, too."

The phone keeps ringing.

Piper. She was here and it hits me in a wave, confirming that the jumble of letters and numbers in her last entry point to this place. Piper said she found documents at the library. I assumed she meant Briarcliff's, but she totally meant *this* one.

"You should get that," I say, keeping my voice level. "Um, so, that section you mentioned...?"

Darla lifts the phone, covers the receiver and gestures forward. "Biographies are in aisle eight, dear."

I nod my thanks, then peruse the aisles until I come to 8. I don't run into anyone else as I explore, the library comforting and quiet, save for Darla's murmuring voice. Running my fingers along the dust-covered spines on the fifth shelf, I notice old texts on Briarcliff, most written by someone named Margaret Harris. I spend twenty minutes skimming through a handful and come to the resigned conclusion that I'm not going to find anything but dry material on the school's construction and the town's burgeoning economy. Maybe Piper scribbled the reference code down for no other reason than to come back to this section for additional, drab research.

Or to send me here.

It forces me to think. If Piper's death really is related to what she discovered, wouldn't she try to hide it? I focus harder on Piper and who she was. Vain, self-centered, and uncaring about the lives she ruined.

On a whim, I unfurl from my seated position and keep looking through the "Ha" section. After perusing the row, I find nothing, and I'm about to rationalize that I should be focusing on my *other* running theory, Mr. S, when I backtrack and come across a book by Allan Harrington about his life on the high seas. I have nothing else to go on except for Piper's vanity in choosing an author with her last name, but I pull it out, then let it fall into a random section when I open it.

A sheaf of paper, stuffed between the pages, flutters to the ground.

A surge of adrenaline jolts through me—part of Piper's missing pages?—but after unfolding the single page, it's too aged to be Piper's. But it's a handwritten letter, in feminine cursive.

...he thinks I'm unaware of the Society, but I know. I know, and I demand my part in it.

Much of the writing is illegible with scorch marks. My fingers tighten on the fragile paper as my brain moves fast, making the connection. When I skim to the bottom and find the signature, my beliefs are solidified.

Rose Eloise Briar

YAS!

I glance up, noting Darla's continued distraction on the phone. In a stealthy maneuver worthy of outsmarting any above cameras, I take one of my textbooks from my bag and nestle the letter within it.

Darla's back is to me by the time I get to the front, and without her noticing, scoot out the doors.

My heart leaves lighter, too. I picture the texts and the incriminating video on my phone, but whoever's responsible isn't watching me close enough to know what I've done. How I can curveball the investigation, too.

I've mailed the diary to the police and thus, pointed the finger at Mr. S.

I'm sorry, Chase.

I squelch the unwanted regret. It's a no-brainer that if it came down to him or me, it should *definitely* be him. If the detectives aren't going to focus elsewhere, then it's left to me to redirect the narrative, and if it buys me the time I need to uncover Briarcliff's deepest, most scandalous secrets, then I will.

After being dropped off on campus, I make it through the rest of the day studying for quarter-terms before enjoying the privacy of my room and smoothing down Rose's letter. In the low lamplight at my desk, I read.

They think they have control. They do not. I am the one they should fear, and I must maintain ground by carving my place within. I do not love him. Indeed, I despise him, and he can no longer stand the sight of me. Not after losing his fifth child. Thorne would kill me if he could get away with it. I must act before he does, create a section within this educational system for my protection. My quick thinking will either save me, or doom me to—

· · ·

Indecipherable, charred jumble. Cursing, I move on.

He believes creating a Gentlemen's Society through a boys only school will provide the ample opportunity he requires. It will not. He cannot possibly imagine how far I have come. I must employ my plans now, before it is too late. I aim for balance, and in doing so, summoning a society in secret to operate under the auspices of Briarcliff Boys Academy. An elite group of souls who may protect my name and watch over these children. It is with this letter I deem you to be the wiser, my love. Keep my confession safe, for I am creating the V—

Damn it! Burned edges and holes obscure the rest, but I've been given enough.

A Gentlemen's Society involving Thorne Briar. Rose's discovery of it.

My hand curls into a fist over the page as I ponder Piper's reasoning for hiding this letter. To whom Rose was writing to remains a mystery, but there's a secret written within these pages, one Piper figured out.

For it can only be Piper who's seen these pages, too, and put them in the public library before she died.

After a final read, I switch to my laptop.

There's a way I can communicate my theory, write it out and make sense of it. It's because of them, these Nobles, that I can't think. Can't study like I used to. Can't sleep.

If I'm wrong, then all I'll get is Dr. Luke's brief admiration for delving so deep into Briarcliff lore. He's open to new theories. Piper said he loved out-of-the-box thinking.

And if I'm right, maybe I can flush my cloaked admirer out, and force that person to provide some answers.

After all, *two* girls can't die on campus without garnering a whole bunch of attention.

Right?

While placing my fingers above the keyboard, I tell myself to be brave. I tell myself to write about the *real* founding of Briarcliff Academy.

With Rose's hidden involvement. I open with:

While Thorne Briar and his two brothers, Richard and Theodore Briar, founded the Briarcliff Boys Academy, Thorne's wife, Rose Briar, created a clandestine internal organization as a form of protection against her husband's similar plan within these school halls.

What if, instead of literal skeletons, Briarcliff Academy hides two skulls of secret society members underneath their coveted grounds? One belonging to Thorne, and the other borne in retaliation from Rose.

It begs two questions: Why did these students need hidden protection, and which society was their true protector?

· · ·

Soon, the words start flowing.

Thirty-Four

IT'S BEEN ONE WEEK, and I've heard nothing about Piper's diary.

No news from Detective Haskins, Ahmar, or even my friendly Cloak. I'm walking on needles every day, thinking at any moment, someone will come around the corner and point the finger at me.

Detective Haskins asking, *Why didn't you give me the diary in person, Callie? What are you trying to hide?*

Ahmar, questioning, *I told you to stay away from this, kiddo. You're making it worse for yourself.*

Chase, accusing, *What have you done to me, you bitch?*

Nothing comes, save for quiet murmurings that Piper's case might have new evidence. That tidbit, I heard from Dr. Luke when he was conversing with Professor Dawson outside his classroom. He caught me listening, then went so quiet, I couldn't catch what else he was saying.

Immersing myself with the line of students wandering up the stairs, I don't register bodies getting closer to me until two forms practically step on my head.

The person brushing up against me on my left—James—grabs my elbow.

"What the—?" But I'm cut off by Tempest on my left. His jade green eyes link with mine.

"You're coming with us," he says.

"What are you, the campus police?" I say, attempting to struggle out of James's hold. Students mill around us, heedless of my wrestling.

"No," James says with a tug.

"Worse," Tempest adds, and holds a hand against my lower back, pushing me forward.

Struggling with these two is like trying to kick a tank, and I'm swept up in their grip and through Briarcliff's doors before I can let out an outraged gasp.

Riordan stands at the base of the steps to the Wolf's Den, leaning against the single wall and waiting for us with hooded eyes. When he catches sight of the three of us, he turns on his heel and walks up the stairs.

"This is—you can't get away with this bullshit!" I say, wiry and spry with useless maneuvers. I search around the lobby for any kind of friendly face—or teacher—but see none as these boys manhandle me up the stairs and onto a couch.

"Sit," Tempest says with a firm hand on my shoulder. "Stay."

I glare up at him. "The only dogs I see in this room are you jackasses."

James rounds the couch until he's standing behind me. "So, are we canines or donkeys? You can't have both."

I whip around to give him a piece of my mind, but I'm stopped by a form stepping from the shadows and taking a seat across from me.

Chase splays his legs and rests his elbows on the armchair, his chin dipped low in deep regard.

If it weren't for the Briarcliff crest on his blazer, I would've taken him for a mafia drug lord. His dark blond hair is slicked back from the curves of his face, his aristocratic brows lowered, a thoughtful line forming between. The one spark of light in his gloomy, shadowed form is his eyes, the color of icy scotch. Though, what that stare holds is anyone's guess. His outward purity is a natural disguise for the unmentionable sins harboring within that mind of his.

"Don't make a sound," he says to me. His direct stare communicates the danger I'll put myself in if I refuse his orders.

Perhaps, picturing Chase running an illegal empire isn't too far-fetched.

Up here, the lull of students heading to dinner below is hushed, a low thrum of voices and footsteps dissipating with time.

Chase glances left, toward the balcony overhang, the movement confirming that the lobby's emptied out.

"You can go, boys. Callie, stay here."

Tempest, James, and Riordan—whose position I hadn't clocked until now, near the coffee cart, move toward the stairs.

"Want me to save you some pork marsala?" James asks Chase as he passes.

"I'll take some, too," I pipe up, aware of what his response will be.

"You can have whatever scraps are left," James says before descending. "It's what you're used to, anyway."

I click my tongue, then slide my gaze back to Chase's. "Your friends are so charming."

Chase's expression remains impassive.

"Say, when you order them to harass me like the good little henchmen they are, can you ask them to say *pretty please*? Or, even better, can you have them stay the fuck away from me?"

"I wouldn't want to be you right now."

Oh, how fun. Chase is being cryptic again. I sigh and slouch against the couch. "And why's that?"

"I've just finished being re-interrogated by the police." Chase angles his head, his stare precise. "Did you have something to do with it?"

The diary. Haskins has it. "For the last time—*no*," I hiss at the exact moment my heart turns into an anchor and plummets. "I was as surprised as anyone else when I heard Piper's case might be reopened."

"You don't act like it."

"What's that supposed to mean?"

"You didn't shed a tear when your roommate died. I could easily label you a cold bitch for that. Or ... a cold-blooded murderer."

"What is it you want? For me to buckle to my knees the moment she's mentioned? Sob into my blazer? It's horrible what happened, but I refuse to do what everyone is asking just because I was her roommate for a week."

"You called me Mr. S."

Chase says it mildly, like he's semi-interested by the answer, but I sense the warning.

"Well, your surname *is* Stone," I retort. I cover up my tremors with a snarl.

"Funny, it's the obvious name the police used for me, too," Chase says, and it's so menacing, I wince. "So obvious, in fact, that I'd never use it if I were trying to hide my dastardly deeds."

"Was Piper one of your dirty secrets?" my voice rises with the question, and I let it. "Did you have something to do—"

"Are you a narc?"

Shaking, I reply, "No. Haskins hasn't said a word to me, and I haven't gone to him."

"Do you picture it?" Chase asks. "How Piper must've felt when she went off the cliff? The wind deafening in her ears, the air too fast for her to breathe, her heart beating out of her chest with fear. I do." His eyes glitter with the sharp amber of spite.

"I don't need to," I retort. "Since my nightmares are taken up by my mother sprawled on the floor in a pool of her own blood."

My breath snaps at the end, an audible whiplash that Chase has no right to hear.

Trembling, clenching my hands, I give him my profile, so he doesn't see the sudden tears.

Chase keeps silent, as if basking in the grief.

"My injustice may not come from the same section of my heart as yours," I say. "But we've both experienced the violence of a sudden death. Your girlfriend—"

"Again, with the girlfriend."

"Again, with the denial," I say.

Chase cocks his head, his cold stare tempered with assessment. "Why are you so convinced Piper and I were together? Do you have to sit on my lap to prove we weren't?"

His gaze dips to his spread legs, where I suppose he wants me to look, too. I don't because I can't. I *cannot* keep reacting to him like this.

"Your parents are getting married," I say. "Piper's mom and your dad. You two were about to be brother and sister. That must've horrified you."

Chase's temperament doesn't turn to outraged fire. Nor does he twitch at the mention of his and Piper's future. "Done some digging, have you? Do you find me that interesting?"

"I find Piper's secrets of particular importance, considering she's not breathing anymore."

Chase concedes my point. "That wasn't something we kept under wraps. Only an outsider would find that kind of thing interesting."

"But you would've kept sleeping together a secret."

Chase smiles, but it's not his perfect, half-moon crescent of a weapon, deployed on the female population. "No. We wouldn't have. And I'm sorry to disappoint, sweet possum, but I gave the detective an air-tight alibi. I was with my boys all night. We were at the party together, we left together. Riordan's my roommate, and James crashed on the floor next to my bed. It's been verified, and as such..." He makes an exaggerated sad face. "I'm not their Mr. S. Or yours."

Chase's answer makes me falter with a second's hesitation, but I'm not about to fall for it. James, Riordan, Tempest—they'd all lie for him.

Chase pounces. "If Piper and I were fucking again, we'd do it in front of our parents if we could. I can't stand my father, and Piper despises her mom. Getting back together would've been ideal for both of us, but unfortunately..." Chase trails off into deliberate silence, where only our heartbeats matter. "Save for a few weak moments, my proclivities moved on."

My cheeks warm, but I bite the inside to turn that heat into pain. It's so screwed up of him to be so devilishly hot with me, but Chase excels at it.

Against my better judgment, my gaze drops to his thighs. I kick my attention back up, but Chase catches my perusal with sexual, knowing derision.

I pretend deep interest in our surroundings. "You know, for a place set aside for seniors, you and your Nobles reserve it a lot."

Chase goes rigid. "What have I told you—"

"About the name? Yeah, I get that it's forbidden, but that only makes me want to keep tasting it on my tongue."

I toss a closed mouth smile his way, but my tantalization isn't as effective as his.

"And," I continue, "I think there's some sort of cover-up going on with Piper's fall."

The shadowed skin around his eyes tapers into a glare. "If, after all your digging, that's where you've ended up, you better get a shovel, sweetheart."

"What, you don't think a group of legacy bad boys could be responsible for it?"

Chase snickers, but on him, it's a darting snake bite. "That's what you think they are?"

They. I latch onto the meaning behind his use of the word. *Not we.*

I force a shrug, though my shoulders are heavy with wariness. "If you have a superior theory, let's hear it."

"Nineteenth century bones can't give you answers six feet under. Visit Rose Briar's grave all you like, blame Piper's death on this secret boy band you've concocted, and I'll do the rest." Chase dips his chin. "I figured you for an ally, Callie. I don't like to be wrong."

"The Nobles have something to do with it." I push to my feet. "And the fact that you're so dismissive of my theory proves it. I don't need your gratitude or permission to keep going. When I find the person responsible, you can thank me then."

146

Chase *tsks*. "You're so positive. Yet, your track record doesn't give me a ton of hope."

I freeze. "Don't you dare..."

"What?" Chase rises, then steps, with his shadow looming over me. "While your mom's rotting in the dirt, her killer is—"

He predicts the slap before it meets its mark. My wrist *thrums* under his grip, my pulse spiking to adrenaline levels that would make a racehorse shy away.

Chase waits for my flickering focus to steady on his. "If you're going to be so mean," he says, his gaze tracing the curves of my face, "at least let me get under you first."

It hurts to breathe. Not from pain, but from the amount of space my heart's taking up in my chest, crushing my lungs. Chase has never been so blatant before. Our encounters flirt with sex, but never have they felt so explicit, so *real*.

The animalistic urge to grab him by his school shirt, until my fingers dig into his flesh is insurmountable. The idea of bringing him close, of slamming my lips against his and putting his dark promises to the test kills any remaining rationale.

"Let me go," I grit out. My clenched jaw does nothing to settle the urge for him.

One corner of his mouth lifts, and he steps even closer. "Say please."

His thighs push into mine, but those streamlined muscles of his, refined to cut through the gloss of a lake, are nothing compared to the hard length I'm feeling in the middle.

My panties go damp. My unrefined, sedentary thighs tremble around his confident swell. I'm telling myself not to part my legs for him, even if he comes with the god-like gift of the best orgasm of my life.

"Is something the matter, Callie?" he asks kindly. Too languidly.

A trap.

In one swift arc, I grip his dick through his pants, the shaft encompassing my entire palm.

Chase's eyes flare at the sudden touch, but he doesn't flinch, or waver, or do any of the things I hoped he would when I called his bluff.

Instead, he drops his arms, my free wrist falling listlessly to my side. He lets his arms hang, no longer touching any part of me, but pushes his groin deeper into my grip.

Chase's upper lip curls as he gazes down at me through his lashes. "You ever channeled your anger through sex, sweet possum?" The tip of his tongue darts out when I don't move my hand away. I *can't*. He's too delectable in my grip, but I'll never admit it. Chase is under my control. I'm feeding off it like a succubus.

"Answer me," he says.

My eyes don't leave his, but I have what he wants. My palm rubs against the fabric, against *him*, and he twitches under the friction.

"Mm. Undo my pants."

My self-control is far from reach. The temptation to do as he pleases and act the way he expects is too strong.

But I want him. I've been dreaming of him. Chase Stone, who is under my heel.

I do as he asks. I accept the dare he's put forth and his cunning desire to see how far I'll take this.

"Stick your hand in." Chase smiles, the corners weighted with desire. "I promise I don't bite."

My fingers trace the light trail of hair under his belly button, then spread across the deep V. When I find the hot length of him, I come closer, my nose brushing his, my lips a velvet touch away.

Chase grunts when I tighten my grip, but it's a sexy sound, one that makes me stroke him faster. He growls, his tongue darting for control against my lower lip, but I stay a hairsbreadth back, wanting to witness his every twitch, each minuscule reaction, as I bring Chase Stone to the edge.

Unable to let him have all the pleasure to himself, I use my free hand on myself, lifting my skirt and finding the lining of my underwear.

Chase follows the movement. His hands clench. When he doesn't move to assist me, I realize he's wagering for dominance, too.

I smile, this inner vixen of mine lifting her sexy, deprived head, and she grabs Chase's wrist and trails his fingers across the lace of my underwear.

Chase wets his bottom lip. His fingers curl against my delicate skin. The breath I've been harboring stutters out. I didn't expect to get so wet at his wisp of a touch. I'm not myself. This isn't right. It's dangerous ... and I'm starving for it.

In retaliation, I drop his hand, choosing to finger myself than allow Chase to win any ground.

With both hands working, I bring us up, up, up and under, our eyes locked, our breaths as short and hot as my strokes.

I nuzzle his throat, licking the spot where his pulse patters beneath his skin.

When Chase's lips part, when his chin tips to the roof, I speak.

"Who's in control now?" I whisper near his ear.

"*Fuck—*" he rasps, and I know I have him.

Snick.

We both freeze at the foreign sound.

Chase moves, twisting as my hand goes slack, and I hurriedly smooth down my skirt. But Chase is flying across the floorboards and leaps across the stair's railing before I've registered Riordan's head popping up through the rafters, his phone's lens facing us.

"You motherfucker!" Chase roars, and I back up at the sound, even though he's nowhere near me.

I race to the balcony overhang in time to witness Chase grabbing Riordan by the back of his blazer's lapel and tossing him onto the ground with the ease of throwing a wet noodle at a kitchen wall.

Riordan's head makes a sickening crack against the marble, but he's conscious. "What the fuck, man? We agreed to record—"

Chase bends low, but leers above Riordan with the languidness of a viper assessing its paralyzed prey before swallowing it. Chase says something I don't catch, but I do see him grab the phone from Rio, tap the screen a few times, then toss the phone against Riordan's chest.

As he backs away, Chase looks up to my level. I cover my surprise at being caught under his scope by forming my lips into a tight, grim line.

I expect Chase to say something along the lines of, "Don't worry, sweet possum, it's deleted," but I receive nothing but an enduring glare as he twists on his heel and stalks to the front door, throwing them wide with one push.

Releasing a long, needed exhale, I back away from the railing, and, in need of a cool down, twist my hair at the nape of my neck. The air is a welcome balm, but I can't relax.

The heat in my cheeks … and down there … doesn't fade.

Sitting in the chair Chase vacated, still warm from his body, my palm still tingling from jerking him off, I'm left wondering what the hell I've done.

Thirty-Five

UNSURPRISINGLY, I don't make it to dinner service.

I'm proud of my foresight to buy groceries, so I'm not left hungry when I step into my dorm room.

I'm leaning against the counter and gnawing on a delicious piece of sea salt dark chocolate when it hits me like a sack of potatoes.

I pleasured Chase Stone.

Power has never seemed so wanton before, but I had it in my hand—literally—unexpected and wonderful. The bottomless hole of greed even had me pleasuring Chase by independently pleasuring *myself*, a piece of delicious mastery I refused to give to him for free.

The chocolate melts into cloying sugar on my tongue, and its sweetness burns my throat. I swallow it much like the building orgasm I never got to receive, starting off so sweet and seductive, then ending with the sharp bite of reality.

I am such an idiot.

Never trust Chase. Cornering me in private with his daring grin and come-fuck-me eyes shouldn't have lured me the way it did.

If he's not a Noble, some of his friends are—they have to be—and I just gave them another picture or video to use against me.

Chase's back was to the camera, but I wasn't. I could hope that Chase's actions after turning his friend into a skid mark were meant to delete said video, but why would he?

Fuck. A stubborn piece of chocolate lodges in my throat. I'm dreading tomorrow and what could happen. Will they all see it? Will they all know I almost bent my knees to Chase?

No. I am *not* like that.

Tossing the chocolate wrapper aside, I storm into my room and grab my laptop, prepared to spend the night learning about Briarcliff *and* the Stones. *And* the Harringtons.

The laptop sits on my bed, screen at maximum brightness, and I prop myself cross-legged in front of it while reaching for my phone.

I'm prepared to cross-reference anything I find in Piper's journal with the Harrington and Stone ancestors at Briarcliff, and I'll stay up all night to do it.

I start at the beginning: Rose Briar. It's the one avenue police aren't pursuing, and my one Hail Mary should they start pursuing me.

Planning out a course of action is a million times better than stressing over what Chase could do with Riordan's video. Chase never managed to get to that point before I pulled his dick out and resisted the longing to taste the most intimate, sexual part of him.

To be so intimate and turned on with a guy, without any loving act of kissing....

I'd once told Piper she was dark and twisty, and I'm starting to think that pocket of sin lives in me, too.

My underwear pulls tight against the sudden swell. Dampness coats the fabric as each second with Chase tickertapes across the back of my eyelids, falling through my mind the way explosions of paper rocket into the sky during street parades.

I rub my eyes free from the image and focus on Piper's last words instead, putting Mr. S aside and searching for details of her innermost thoughts, such as any mention, however tiny, of Rose's rival society, starting with a "V," or the Nobles, and whether the Stones or Harringtons were a part of them.

I refuse to give any credence to that gnawing sound in the back of my head, teething its pattern of *denial* all over my brain.

Someone's in my room.

I jerk awake, my sheets tangling with my bare legs when I bring them up to my chest. The wild motion causes my hair to fly into my face, and I scrape it back, keeping my hand on my head as I survey my room, too obscured by night to make out much. The meager moonlight from my single window doesn't help illuminate what I swear is rustling in the corner.

Without saying a word, I fumble for the switch on my nightstand lamp, yanking the chain and flooding both the room and my feeble, sleepy eyesight. Squinting, eyes watering, I scan my room again while maintaining my position in bed, then decide I've made myself too vulnerable and crawl out of it.

Nothing's out of place. No footsteps stain the floorboards, no blood is splattered against the walls—

I gasp, blinking away the interposing nightmare, tugging my nightshirt over my underwear, feeling my clothes and skin, ensuring I'm in reality and not a night terror.

You're not there. Mom's not at your feet. You're okay.

Hefting my binder full of notes in one hand, I fly into the center room, ready to pummel whoever's decided to trespass and terrify me.

I glance left, where Piper's couch and entertainment system used to be. Nothing but the filtered moonlight from the large bay window glides across the hardwood floor.

The kitchenette stands silent, until the mini fridge lets out a gurgle and my skeleton nearly separates from my skin.

The urge to call out is a damn strong one, but I'm no damsel willing to point out where I'm standing for slaughter, despite my room's light illuminating my backside.

Someone was here. I was torn awake by a sound that wasn't supposed to be in my room.

Piper's shut door looms in front of me, proof that I'm not simply shaking off a nightmare. It was ajar before I turned out all the lights and went to sleep.

Same goes with my bathroom.

Gulping, I'm uncertain where to begin. Do I burst through Piper's room, or the bathroom?

And what do I do if I confront a hidden intruder?

I've taken multiple self-defense classes, even excelled in archery that one summer I went to sleep-away camp Upstate, but ... I've seen death. Its bleakness has poisoned me twice in two years, and I lack the confidence in my ability to cheat it the way I did before Mom. Before Piper.

I'm so busy staring down Piper's door that I hear the click before I sense where it came from—the front door.

The bathroom door's open now.

A whimper escapes my lips, and I buckle against my doorframe, the Briarcliff binder clutched tight to my chest.

Whoever it was, is gone, and I have the entrusting notion that the person managed to escape through the shadows because of a black cloak.

Damn my petrified state. Instead of flipping on all the lights like I should've, I gave him plenty of blind corners to escape into before finding the door.

And if you brought him into the light, how do you think that would've gone for you? An inner voice, sounding suspiciously like my mom, whispers.

She's right. The binder slips from my hands, and I race to the bathroom, banging the door against the wall and switching on the light.

The bathroom is as pristine as I left it, meaning there are bottles stacked along the bathtub's rim, and my make-up scattered across the sink's counter with my flat iron's wire tangled inside the sink's rim...

With one thing tucked under it that doesn't belong.

Swallowing, I move closer and lift the foreign object, inspecting it closer to the mirror.

A single white rose petal, softened and bruised from too much handling, is all that remains of my unwelcome visitor, left to rot in my sink.

Thirty-Six

THE SUN IS slow to rise on Sunday morning, unlike me.

Sleep didn't come after my baleful attempt at catching a shadowed figure in my empty dorm room. The rest of the early hours were spent with me sitting cross-legged in bed, holding my lamp as a better weapon, should anyone—even poor Ivy—decide to visit me while the moon was still out. I disregard reporting last night to Headmaster Marron, or even Haskins. What would I say? Someone's harassing me by leaving roses? My room's being broken into, but nothing is taken or moved around?

My breakfast consists of a handful of dry granola and a large thermos of coffee before I pull on a plaid button-up over my white tank and zip up my comfy, ripped jeans—Callie Ryan B.B. (Before Briarcliff).

Having the lonely beats of my heart for company last night, even during someone's scare attempt, I'm eager to surround myself with people, even if they wear Briarcliff gear, and even if they are mostly mean. I decide to do some Sunday study in the library.

It's better than waiting in a room with no security for the Cloak's next move.

I take the stairs instead of the elevator today, choosing the safety of using my feet over becoming easy prey in an enclosed space.

My night wasn't entirely ruined, however. When the lights were on and my brain in peak study mode, I learned a lot about the Stone and Harrington contributions to Briarcliff, and consequently, the small town named after it.

The Stones' donations to Briarcliff were substantial—incredibly so. The very library I'm heading to is even named after Daniel Stone's wife (read: divorcée), Marilee Barclay, called the M.B.S. Library of Studies.

A huge amount of dough is required to donate a building, even from a top defense attorney, and I circled that discrepancy, but never returned to it. Daniel Stone's serious money donations might not have anything to do with Piper, other than him potentially inheriting partial ownership to Moriarty Oil—a company bequeathed to Paul Harrington's *wife*, Sabine Moriarty, when he marries her. Ivy didn't have the whole story—the Harringtons owned the multi-million dollar company, Comfy-At-Home, but she missed the part about them having some serious old family oil money.

All these names twisted in my mind. It's hella difficult to keep rich people's fortunes straight, especially when they intermingle. Yet, arming myself with this information was empowering. I felt less like a goldfish swimming in open waters and more like a baby shark.

In heading to the library, I take the public path. It's a longer trek, but farther away from the forest and in flat plains. If any Cloak wants to introduce himself, he'll have to do it in view of the entire campus.

No one greets me as I enter the pavilion. Students are peppered throughout. It's getting colder, and many are choosing the Briarcliff winter uniform of sweaters and cardigans over their regular clothing today.

The library is behind Briarcliff's primary building, and I detour around the side, still in plain sight, until I reach the modern glass doors of the two-story library.

A light, warm breeze hits me from above as the automatic doors swish open. As I swipe my keycard and step through one of two turnstiles by the librarian's desk, I keep my expression impassive, despite the awe I experience whenever I enter.

It's an open concept, with wide, scarred wooden desks placed in rows in the middle, scores of books rimming all four corners and stacking to the ceiling. A balcony stretches across, midway through the rows upon rows of books, to access the ones shelved higher. Rolling, metal ladders lean against the walls, ready to be used by the librarian upon request. I love the hushed, papered atmosphere of this place, despite the majority of our work being on our computers and online.

I find the closest table, despite most being available. Wanting to be near the exit in case of an emergency—or a wayward bully—is a difficult habit to break.

A low laugh grabs my attention, and I scan the cluster of students who have decided to make their Sunday morning a study session, too.

There. In the far corner, near the stacks with the least amount of sunlight, sit Chase and his posse.

When Chase catches my eye, a half-cocked smirk dancing across his face, I look down, intent on spreading out my textbooks for our English and Calculus quarter-terms coming up this week. My stomach reacts, butterfly wings unfurling at my core.

Echoing whispers and hitches of breath—disguised laughter—emit from Chase's corner of the room.

I curl my hands over a textbook, the words blurring into smudges. Mom's words whisper through my ears.

Falling is a mistake. But staying down? Staying down is a choice, Calla.

My textbook shuts with a smack. I stand, and with hands fisted to my side, stalk over to Chase's table.

Riordan sees me coming and ducks his head, pretending deep interest in his calc text. James catches Riordan's movements, but unlike his buddy, lays his direct gaze against mine, watching me approach as he sticks a pen between his teeth and leans back against his chair. Tempest spins his stylus in a graceful, distracted maneuver, then taps it against his bottom lip as he reads his iPad. The watercolor green of his eyes, however, shine in my direction.

Chase doesn't change his stance, studying his laptop, then writing something down on a spiral-bound notebook.

He's left-handed, I think, which is a ridiculous observation to make when I'm about to ask him if he made a sex tape of us.

James drops his gaze when I reach their table. Nobody speaks.

Hissing, slithering whispers catch my attention at my periphery, and I notice Piper's old friends nearby. Falyn, Willow, and Violet.

My vision turns to slits when I see them, all hunched over their phones.

God, don't let it be what I think it is.

I turn back to the boys, crossing my arms and clearing my throat.

None react.

"What are you going to do with it?" I ask in a low voice, uncaring of who responds. James and Tempest are well aware of what their boys got up to yesterday evening.

James speaks. He feigns confusion and asks, "With what?"

"You know what." I'm hoping my tone cuts through their infuriating ease but know I'm about to be sorely disappointed.

"Chase?" I ask.

One carved, bronze eyebrow rises, but he doesn't stray from his computer.

"Don't you think our attention—no, scratch that—the *school's* focus should be on Piper, not what we—" I catch myself, not even able to say what we did out loud. "I thought Piper was the one deserving the spotlight. Why the hell did you do that to me?"

Chase slow blinks at me. Riordan laughs under his breath, so I shove at his shoulder, turning his laughter into startled chokes.

"And why the hell did you film it, you second-hand creep? Do you get off on seeing your leader's junk?"

Riordan sobers. "Hey, now. That's mean."

"You should've seen my video," James pipes in, smiling with the pen in his teeth. "Hottest Rated for a while there. Maybe yours woulda been, too, had you shown some—"

The table cracks with Chase's fist. The only human who doesn't jump in the whole damned room is Tempest.

A velvet-calm voice floats up to my ears. "You can relax, Callie."

I stare down at Chase. He was speaking to me, but is back to focusing on the screen in front of him.

"See this?" Riordan redirects my attention by pointing to the reddened, swollen skin around his eye. "It's deleted. Believe me on that."

I stop the habit of chewing on my lower lip nervously. "You're sure?"

Riordan lifts his phone. "There's nothing on here. Technically, that show you and Chase put on wasn't supposed to happen, ergo, shouldn't've been filmed…"

"What were you supposed to be filming, little Spielberg?" I ask. "In fact, what else have you filmed? You get off on girl fights, too?"

"Rio," Tempest says, sitting on Chase's left. "Time for you to shut up."

"What's wrong, Tempi?" James asks, letting his head fall to one shoulder. "Is this sort of chit-chat too human-like for you? Should we go back to our lizard forms like yourself?"

"Call me that again." Tempest's stare snaps to James's.

I inwardly flinch at the cool murder in Tempest's expression. It's a miracle I got away with calling him *Pest*.

Chase shuts his laptop. Hard. "All of you, fuck off over to the girls. They look in need of quiet entertainment. James, show them your vintage porn video and get back some of your previous popularity."

"I'm not going anywhere," I say. "Until you explain."

"Not you," Chase clips out. "You can sit."

"Again, with the *be a good girl* talk." But as the boys stand and drift over to Falyn's table, I take Riordan's seat across from Chase. "I don't believe you. You don't put a camera on something like that and just delete it before being able to use it for some gain. I know you at this point, Chase."

"No." Chase laughs. "You don't."

"Then what?" I fold my arms over the table, keeping my voice as low as his. Somehow, the entire exchange with Chase and his boys happened in soft, snappish voices that were overlooked by the librarian. It's undetermined how long this free pass will continue. "What else have you recorded? Piper and me fighting? Did you *send* that crap to me?"

"I wish I knew what you were talking about, sweet possum."

I lean closer. Now that his computer's shut, it's much easier to look into his scotch-brown eyes, as clear and placid as the manmade lake he trains his muscles on. "What you did was an insane violation of my privacy."

"That may be, but with the grave you're digging for yourself, if you go second, I don't want anyone pointing to me as a suspect. Again," he adds drolly.

Ignoring the tarantula-sized creepy crawlies in my gut, I retort, "You were all for my looking into Piper's death. And now you're against it?"

"Not quite. What I don't appreciate is you constantly referencing me as a Noble."

I swallow a scornful laugh. "Are you trying to tell me they have nothing to do with Piper? Because the harder I 'dig,' the faster they tell me to fuck off."

Chase squints at me. "They're communicating with you?"

The dirty white rose petal I found in the bathroom sink takes a spot in my mind's eye. "In a sense. Do they wear cloaks?"

Chase takes his time studying me, the type of survey that leaves invisible goosebumps on my skin. "Callie. At what point are you going to understand they may be warning you away from something and not toward it?"

"Once they start being direct. Like a letter. A *word*, even, instead of skulking around with roses."

"Roses?" Chase sits back and crosses his arms. "You're playing with the devil."

"I am. I even had his dick in my hand, if you recall."

Chase stiffens. But he breaks character with the barest lift to his lips. "How can such a shy, quiet, nerd-girl have such a mouth on her?"

"Who said I was shy?"

Chase stares at me like I should have the answer. Then he answers for me. "You have no friends."

"Correction," I say, despite the sudden lump in my chest. "I have few friends at Briarcliff. That doesn't mean I'm friendless."

Matt and Sylvie come to mind, back in NYC and together, living their new Insta lives without their third wheel wobbling them off track.

"Really?" Chase shuts his laptop, then leans his elbows on the table. His scent drifts into my vicinity, and I pull back on instinct. Now isn't the time to be drawn in by his lure. "Your pathetic month here tells me I'm right."

"Stop changing the subject. The devil isn't a member of the Nobles. It's you, if my earlier opinion didn't point that out. All my problems come from *you* and your salivating followers. So, as long as you can prove there's no video by letting me look through your phone, you can stand down, and I'll leave you alone."

Chase effortlessly tosses his phone, so it lands in front of me. "What if it all comes down to your protection? What if I'm causing you shit in order to distract you and prevent you from taking the path Piper did?"

I hold up his phone for inspection, my grip tight. "Because there's nothing that tells me you have my best interests at heart."

"Oh, no? Was yesterday not enough?"

My cheeks warm. It's one thing to think about it in silence, but when Chase brings it up, in that earthy, dirty voice of his, all the secret, pleasurable areas on my body tingle under his summons.

"If you know something about Piper, you should go to the police, not dangle it in front of me like a rotten carrot," I say.

Chase's phone flashes with a message from James, but I ignore it and swipe to his lock screen. He plucks it from my fingers, types in his code, then drops his phone back into my palm. "I have nothing to say to them. Those Dudley Do-Goods will never get to the bottom of it, and neither will you, sweet possum. Stop while you're still receiving bouquets."

I frown at him, but my focus is on his photo library, scanning the tiles for anything dated yesterday that he could've sent himself from Riordan's phone. No way would Chase leave it as Riordan's sole responsibility. I also look for the day Piper died and any possible fight scenes. But Chase does not record his life in photos. All I see, as I scroll higher, are photos of him training on the water and a few with his arm slung around Piper's shoulder—those caused a tug in my chest— and some random group shots in the dining hall, until my thumb stamps on the screen, stopping at a photo of me. *Me*. In Briarcliff's foyer, staring up.

"That's..." I spin the phone's screen to him. "Is this my first day? Did you take a *picture* of me?"

Chase angles his head, his beatific angles in stark relief. "I took it without thinking."

I study the picture harder. He caught me at a flattering angle, my chin raised, my eyes wide with anxiety and curiosity. Chase had zoomed in, Piper and Headmaster Marron standing somewhere outside the frame.

I appear vulnerable in my mom's old college shirt and jeans. Too innocent for what was to come, despite the shadows of grief harboring in the hollows of my cheeks and the crescents under my eyes. Definitely too war-torn to be filed away as Chase's pixelated prisoner.

I find the Trash icon and send it in.

"I deleted it." I fling his phone, so it lands on his laptop with a tinned thump. "I'm not yours to save."

Chase's brow angles up again. "In more ways than one, I assume."

A commotion splits my attention, and I see Eden picking up textbooks from the floor. Willow's walking away, covering her mouth as she laughs, her auburn ponytail dancing.

I push to my feet with a disgusted scowl, but say to Chase, "We're done here, so long as whatever you caught with your wingman's lens never sees the light of day. If it does, I'll have the NYPD come down on your ass so hard, not even your lengthy appendage will be able to cushion it."

"I'm glad my cock made such an impression on you," he responds, and my cheeks flame. I hate it when I speak before I think. Chase continues, "Take a minute to consider I might not want that video spread around, either. I don't punch my friends in the face on the daily. What happened yesterday ... it wasn't expected. By any of us, I don't think."

Chase waits for my reply, but I turn around instead, ashamed of my traitorous cheeks and the heat at the base of my throat.

No, it wasn't expected.

And, *damn it*, it better not ever be reenacted, regardless of the determined, sexual promise in his hooded eyes as I walk away.

Thirty-Seven

I TELL myself I'm rushing to help Eden and not trying to outrun the angelic devil staring at my back.

"Here," I say once I reach her, bending to lift a textbook. "The filthy rich are clumsy fuckers, aren't they?"

Eden releases a mirthless laugh, but she covers her crestfallen expression by allowing a hank of dark hair to fall against her profile.

"Eden," I say, falling into stride with her and directing her to my table. "You're crying."

"Not about that," Eden says, dropping her books near mine. "That bitch has had it in for me for years."

"Then ... can I help?" I sit beside Eden, in front of my stuff, and spin my legs to face hers. I keep my voice low, since we're closer to the librarian's monitoring scowl.

"No. Not if you're becoming one of them." Eden focuses on positioning her books and laptop.

I jolt. "Who? Like Willow? Hell-to-the-no, Eden."

Eden shakes her head. "With Chase. Nobody will say it to your face, but it hasn't gone unnoticed that you're trying to be Piper two-point-oh."

"I'm *what*?!"

A loud *SHUSH* sounds out, and a quick check shows the librarian zoning in on me, a finger to her lips as her eyes grow small. I nod an apology but get back to Eden.

"Eden, come on. Rumors swirl around here. I'm trying to figure out what happened to Piper, not take her place."

"Yeah, there's that rumor, too. Our own Harriet the Spy."

"I thought I was more of a Lara Croft."

It works. Eden's cheek—the part of it I can see—twitches with a smile.

"Eden." I risk a hand on her shoulder. She doesn't shove me away, and I take that as encouragement. "I will never be like them. I don't enjoy being bullied, but I'd *never* become the bully as a result. I'm not hanging out with the Witches of Briarcliff, and I'm talking to Chase because Piper died, and I'd like to know what happened. If you're wondering why I'm involving myself in a bully's death," I say as Eden stiffens, "It's in my bones. I can't leave her death alone, not when I'm seeing what everyone else doesn't."

Eden doesn't argue or cut in. Her chin tilts ever so slightly in my direction. I continue. "Doesn't this school seem like there's poison in the wood that built it? In the forest? The water? I think Piper's fall was orchestrated, not an accident, and not a crime of passion."

There. I said what I couldn't even form into sentences for Chase. *Briarcliff Academy's responsible.*

Eden tucks her hair behind her ear, exposing her profile. She doesn't look in my direction, maintaining her tunnel vision on her pile of texts.

"Eden, I don't know what it is, but my instinct is to trust you."

"Why?" Eden bites out the question.

"Because everyone here wears a mask, but in the time I've known you, you've never put one on."

Eden's lips part. "Have you told anyone else this theory?"

I shake my head. Eden's warming up to the conversation. If I bring up Ivy, I'm positive it will shut her down. "I'm only realizing it myself."

"Good. Don't." Eden turns, the force of her sage brown eyes as powerful as Mother Nature herself. "This place hides its iniquity, and it starts with your research paper on Rose Briar."

I gasp. "Wait. I'm right about Rose?"

"The alumni, the rich, the privileged, the tenured, nobody gives a damn, so long as they get a diploma or a hefty paycheck."

I bend closer, our heads touching with this conspiracy. "What do you know?"

"You have all the pieces, Callie. Put them together."

"Not when each person I encounter speaks to me in tongues!" I whisper through my teeth.

"There's a reason I notice certain things but stay quiet," Eden says in a hushed voice. "I don't belong here, and neither do you. So, you either become part of the crowd, or you stand out and get banished."

"By who, the Nobles?"

Eden's expression goes blank, but she keeps her eyes on mine. "You've figured out their name."

"The creepy guys who lurk around campus in cloaks? Yeah, you can say I've seen them."

Eden's face falls. "You mean, they've seen you."

"Don't you get all prophetic on me, Eden. Someone needs to give it to me straight, and I'm betting it's you."

"I'm the one who sent you the video."

I stare at her. A ball of saliva lodges in my throat. I cough, and out of pity, she hands me her water thermos. I chug, then, as if my actions weren't obvious, say, "What?"

She repeats, "The video of you and Piper fighting. I sent it."

"Eden—why would you threaten me?"

Eden rolls her eyes. "Please. If I wanted to intimidate you, I'd've tied you up, blindfolded you, and stuck you in one of the hidden tombs under the school."

I choke again, then pretend I didn't.

"I'm protecting you," she says simply.

"By sending me a recording that could get me in big trouble with the police?"

"No, dummy. By sending you something *someone else* has. I'm telling you to be careful."

"I don't understand."

"I stole that video from someone else's phone. I'm quiet, remember. Unnoticed."

"Who?" My face goes numb as all the blood rushes to my chest. "*Ivy?*"

Eden's gaze flits to something over my shoulder, then back to mine. A freakish wave of anger crosses her face. She says in a wet whisper, "You're so fucking clueless."

My back turns rigid. "Hey—"

She adds, much louder, "If you're so positive the ghost of Briarcliff Academy killed Piper, shut your mouth, you crazy slut."

I jerk back. "Eden, what?"

"Take my advice. Stop earning the name Asylum Possum."

I balk. "That's a thing?"

Eden stands, but bends her head close. "Piper wasn't a Noble," she whispers as she puts her elbows into hefting up the books. "She was a Virtue."

"Wh—?"

I'm stopped from finishing the question when I follow Eden's path. Falyn leans over the librarian's desk, so obviously inattentive to what the librarian's saying, it's a wonder the woman keeps talking.

Falyn's assessing stare follows Eden as she exits the library. Eden darts a single look at Falyn, then glances once more at me before walking through the doors, as if communicating the reason for her sudden outburst.

Falyn was watching us.

I pretend to have an itchy cheek, then spin in my seat until I'm facing my computer and my back is to Falyn, but my fingers hover over the keys.

Piper. A Virtue? WTF, Eden?

As if that's not enough, Eden blows my mind further by letting me know she's the one who sent me the incriminating video in the same tone she uses to answer basic questions in class.

Like it's nothing.

But she stole those videos from someone else...

It all starts with your research paper on Rose Briar. And Rose created a society with a V ... the Virtues.

I fall back against the chair.

Everyone else is researching the founders, too. This can't be the first time someone chose Rose. Why did I get stuck with Piper's theories about a secretive woman concocting plans to go against her husband's secret gentlemen's club?

Ugh. My head hurts.

I whip my attention over my shoulder in an effort to mentally will Eden back here but meet Falyn's acute stare instead.

Grimacing and slamming back against my seat, I figure I have another long night of reading between the lines ahead of me.

Thirty-Eight

WHO, in all the hells, am I supposed to trust around here?

It's safe to say that studying at M.B.S. Library of Studies is a no-go, not with Falyn lurking curiously behind my back and Chase hovering dangerously in my horizon.

Before Briarcliff, I was a straight-A, determined student, and I'm not willing to give that up. Briarcliff and all its hidden passages isn't my future. College is.

My cavernous, two-person dorm room with one resident (me) is the best place to get my shit done, but it's also the loneliest. Even Piper's cold, superficial heart was better company than the invisible spirit that's taken her place.

You have no friends.

Chase is wrong. I may be able to count the people at Briarcliff I've endeared myself to on one finger, but she's worth it, because Ivy greets me with a toothy smile the instant I step through Thorne House's doors.

"Hey!" she says, rounding the check-in desk. My worries that she was who Eden got the video from lessen in her presence. She *can't* be the one who filmed it. She was at a crew meeting that evening. "I was looking for you this morning."

"All you missed was my sad attempt to get some studying done at the library," I say.

"M.B.S. Library, also known as the G.P.S. for the latest gossip."

I raise my brows. "And here I thought the single juicy tidbit I had revolved around its name."

"Briarcliff named it after the Stone family, yeah. They're deep in Briarcliff's pockets, tracing back to the founding," Ivy says, propping her hip against the desk as I come to stop in front of her. "In fact, it was through some of their ancestors' trusts they gifted the library, not Chase's parents alone."

"There's my missing piece!" I hold up my index finger. "I was wondering how they got so much money to construct a new library."

Ivy nods, and I'm assaulted with guilt. What did I say to Eden? That she's the one who doesn't wear a mask around here. But Ivy's never been anything but kind to me, welcoming my presence when the majority didn't, not to mention, eagerly providing me with information.

Why then, do I hold my heart back? Is it because of the one moment we've had where she stood back and watched me get attacked by Piper? I gotta admit, that one hurt.

Ivy adds, "Because the old one burned down. It's a crazy story."

I smile wryly, remembering Darla's, the public librarian's, words. "Don't tell me. Briarcliff has another sinister secret to tell?"

Ivy smiles back. "In due time. Where rich people go, scandals follow, and there's many that would make you cringe."

"Now you have me intrigued. Hey..." I hesitate. "Wanna come up and pretend to have a study sesh with me while you tell me all about it?"

Ivy makes a pained sound. "Can't. I have fifteen minutes left on my shift, then some mat work."

"Mat work?"

"Gotta keep this body bangin'," Ivy jokes. "Crew may be off-season, but we still train just as hard in the gym."

I nod in understanding, even though the boathouse resembles a Resort & Spa Lounge, not a high school fitness center. "No problem. I'll see you around."

"Wait." Ivy glances around, as if her boss is about to materialize from a corner at any second. "I can knock off for fifteen. I'll grab one of your snacks and tell you about the burning, then head out."

I snort, but then smile as Ivy pulls out an OUT TO BREAK bronze placard and places it on the desk. "You make it sound like a witch hunt."

"It kinda was." Ivy wrinkles her nose. "Involving the most popular girl in school."

My eyes go wide. "Piper?"

"No, Piper didn't become cool until ninth grade when she started hanging out with Chase. She was invisible before then, but once they started dating, it's like she changed the narrative of the school's social order and crowned them both Prince and Princess of Briarcliff."

"How come we haven't talked about this before?"

Ivy presses the elevator call button. "Why are you interested? Because it could relate to your insane obsession with Piper's fall?"

"Well ... yeah." We step into the elevator.

"I dunno. Maybe because you've been so focused on the days leading up to Piper's death, and not two years before."

I make a noncommittal sound, despite the obvious opening to tell Ivy about Piper's diary. It never seems like the time.

We step out onto my floor, and I'm staring at my shoes as we walk. I wish I could enjoy my time at Briarcliff and stop with the questions and suspicion. I could get to know Ivy better, as well as her friends who sit with us during meals. I could talk to Eden like I want to get to know her, instead of pressing her for information she's reluctant to give. I could be a senior and make senior memories before scoring a diploma at an elite private school, getting into college, and leaving the East Coast *far* behind.

And never solve shit, the meaner part of my mind hisses. *Just like your mom's murder.*

"Earth to Callie, we're at your door. Unless you're thinking of busting through the emergency exit straight ahead." Ivy nudges me lightly.

"Sorry," I say. I dig out my keycard and *blip* us in, our footsteps seeming to echo once we leave the carpeted hallway and enter my furniture-less main room.

"When did they say the couch would be delivered?" Ivy asks, reading my thoughts. "Or the TV?"

"Tomorrow, thankfully," I say, dropping my backpack by the kitchenette counter. "Make yourself comfy on my bed, the only piece of furniture I own at the moment that can fit two people. I'll be in there with some guac and chips in a sec."

"'Kay." Ivy wanders over to my room, which, out of habit, I still keep shut.

She pushes it open, and screams.

Thirty-Nine

THE GLASS BOWL of guac I was keeping fresh in the fridge crashes to the floor, and I slip in the green goop as I hurry into my room.

"Ivy!" I cry. "What? What is it—?"

I slide to a stop in front of her, then hang on to her arm for dear life.

Ivy's gasping beside me, her face bone white. Her free hand goes to her mouth, and her skin is cold beneath mine.

As chilled as the blood that stops coursing through my body when I see what's scattered across my bedding.

Photos. A ton of pictures printed on A4 paper, blanketing my bed to the point where no one would know the color of my lavender sheets.

They're spread across my sheets, taped on my wall above the headboard, and plastered over every flat surface I have.

My desk harbors shot after shot, print after print, stuck and spread and scattered.

"What ... what..." Nothing else can pass Ivy's lips.

My hands might be clinging to her, but my feet want to walk. To bring me closer to the horror.

One word breaks through my throat, one syllable made into a shattered prism of sound. "*Mom...*"

She's not looking at the camera lens in the photo. She can't. I remember how she stared vacantly, blood pooled around her head and her hands curled in a final round of defense. Her irises were milky and clouded with death.

But here, in this putrid reminder vomited all over my room, a large, yellow, smiley emoji takes the place of her face, its inky grin obscuring the violence of her dying expression but made no less obscene.

I fall to my knees, grabbing the closest picture. "Mom," I cry brokenly.

"Oh my God, Callie." Ivy breaks out of her frozen stance and comes up behind me, holding my upper arms and trying to lift me back to a stand. "We need to get out of here. Report this."

Swirls of yellow smiley-faces mock me. No matter where I turn, there's a picture of my murdered mother with an emoji head, the blood obvious around the perfect circle of a grin, until they blur into a nauseating watercolor, because my eyes can't focus, and my stomach promises to produce a similar result.

"You need to get out of here," Ivy mumbles desperately. "Callie, come on!"

"I-I-" My eyes won't close. They'll dry up and blur my vision, but they won't shut.

"This is so *fucked*," Ivy says, then all but drags me out with her athlete's arms.

"You cursed," I say in a daze. "You never swear."

"I'll fucking swear up a fucking goddamned storm after that fucked-up scene, Jesus Christ!" Ivy takes a breath. "Are you okay?"

I stare blankly at the walls, still clutching a picture until Ivy rips it from my hands, tosses it back in my room and slams the door. She pulls out her phone. "I'm calling campus police."

"I..." Gulping, I stand on wobbly knees, and that's when the dam breaks.

Tears pour down my cheeks, my hands start shaking, and my lip trembles on a barely contained scream.

"Callie, sit back down. You're white as—shit, you're gonna pass out. Sit, babe. C'mon..."

I sit, but my gaze drifts to the door. And once I see it...

"*No!*" I cry.

Ivy startles. "What?"

In a burst of energy, I fly to my backpack. The flap is unbuckled, and it wasn't five seconds ago. I dig through it like a groundhog, textbooks flying, laptop sliding across the hardwood, until I hit nothing but fabric at its bottom.

"Fuck," I say. Then scream, "*FUCK!*"

"*What?*" Ivy shouts again, holding the phone away from her ear, color yet to return to her cheeks. "Is there something else in there?"

I tear through my pile of texts, opening Calculus and a flash of relief zaps through me when I find Rose's letter still nestled in the middle.

But as for the rest...

They took my phone! Piper's diary pages are on there!

Someone used Ivy's and my distraction to take it from my bag and sneak out. Or was it while I was in the library talking to Chase?

Piper's bullying, I could handle. She was a basic playground bitch, utilizing tactics better served in a teen rom-com flick, but I managed it.

This, though ... this isn't a simple message of dislike or diversion. This is *hate*, and it's directed at me. Another Cloak warning? He's never been this violently obvious before. Why start now? Why *hurt* me like this?

I lean forward, clutching my temples and moaning. I can't think. I can't *think* with Mom's blood behind my eyes, made fresh by these goddamn pictures somebody printed off like they were nothing but pages for a school report.

Is this related to Piper? Or does it have to do with my continued presence at Briarcliff despite the multiple requests by Piper's friends that I GTFO of this school?

Piper's friends.

They were at the library with me when I got there. But other than Falyn, I lost track of them when I started talking to Chase, every one of my senses attuned to *him* while my background faded to gray.

My nails claw at the hardwood as I form into a leap and fly out the front door.

"Callie!" Ivy cries, but I'm already busting through the emergency exit.

What was it Ivy said?

Mat work.

Boathouse.

My heels tear into the dirt and grass of Briarcliff's perfect landscape before I hit the trail and storm down the hill.

I don't slow until I see the three ponytails ahead of me, bobbing in time as they navigate the terrain in single file, chatting snidely and laughing.

The middle one—Willow—doesn't see me coming. Her ponytail goes flying when I crash into her, the fire in my eyes redder than her hair.

Tackling her to the ground is easy. Pinning her arms on either side of her head as I scream in her face is concerning.

"Omigod!" the quiet one—Violet—cries behind me.

"Get off her, you crazy slut!"

I don't need to tell you who that one is.

"*How could you?*" I scream. Willow twists and writhes underneath me, her starched white Briarcliff fitness shirt dirtied up and wrinkled under my grip. Her maroon sports skort rides up on her thighs when she tries to knee me in the back, but I rear back on a snarl and slap her across the cheek.

She wails. "What the *fuck*?"

Arms grip my shoulders, but I elbow them back. I'm hot all over, my tears cascading lava from the volcano erupting behind my eyes.

I bend close to Willow's face, her head-twists slowing the closer my teeth come to her delicate skin. My throat doesn't emit the sounds I'm used to. They're keening, unhinged wails, its notes hitched with trembling breaths. I manage to speak, broken words that hold the entire meaning of my world.

"*That was my mother!*"

Willow breathes hard, but she gasps out, "What the hell are you talking about?"

"My-my room," I stutter. "What you did."

"I don't—"

"You hate me. You've made that obvious." I glance over my shoulder at Falyn, who's nursing the bicep I elbowed into, and Violet, filming the whole thing on her phone.

These goddamned rich kids and their forest cell service...

I push to my feet and round on her. Violet squeaks and stumbles back into the trees but doesn't lower her phone.

"Stop recording!" I yell. With a trembling hand, Violet keeps the phone on my face. "Why do you all want to catch my weakest moments? Why can't you leave me *alone*? If Piper was a Virtue, who the *fuck* are you guys? *Give me back my phone!*"

At least ... I think that's what I said. Thick tears blur my vision, and it's unclear whose voice I'm using, but it certainly isn't my own. I don't sound like this. I don't talk like this.

I definitely don't want to punch a person tinier than me in the face, but I won't regret it when I smash Violet's—

Strong arms envelop me and shove me to the side, but they won't let go. They're bare, muscular, masculine...

"The fuck?" Chase snarls into my ear, but his warm breath is forced to leave my neck when we stumble over tree roots and rocks, and he uses his balance over mine. "You're spouting off the name Virtue now? Do you have no sense of survival?"

"*Let me go!*" I scream.

"No way in hell, sweet possum," he grits out, then holds me to his torso with a tighter grip. "Not until you tell me what the fuck's going on."

"She attacked me!" Willow screeches, brushing decaying leaves and twigs from her clothes.

"A fucking psycho is what she is," Falyn spits, then flanks her friend.

Violet tiptoes from the foliage, phone still on.

"Turn it off," Chase hisses. "*Now.*"

Violet clicks the phone off and shoves it into her gym bag. My face momentarily goes slack, because of course she listens to Chase's commands the minute his lips move.

"Take it back out and delete that shit, Vi," he says.

I'm somewhat thrown off by the familiar use of her nickname, but it also sends a harsh reminder. These people know each other. They grew up together, always, and have garnered the type of loyalty only decades of familiarity can gift. I can't trust any of them, and most of that distrust has to go to their leader. Their prince.

"I said let me go, Chase." I struggle within his forced embrace, but his elbows don't even tick up with movement.

"Not with your teeth and claws out." His chin digs into my hair. "What the fuck, Callie?"

"They ... they..." I growl in frustration and grief. I can't get the meaning out.

"I told you, Chase," Willow says, her bruised wrists going to her hips. "She attacked me out of nowhere, for no reason. And Violet's going to keep the evidence, because my next stop is Dad's office, and this bitch is gonna be expelled. You hear that, rat-face? You're *done.*"

I spit and snarl with such sudden intensity, Chase has difficulty keeping me in place.

"Not once I show him what you did!" I say. "The pictures, all over my room. That's crossing the line, even for you bitches!"

"Looks like it worked," Falyn says dryly, and that earns her another escape attempt by me.

"Jesus—stay still," Chase says, his voice strained. I'm trying to kick my way out, and my shoes come concerningly close to his groin. "What pictures?"

"My *mother*," I say, my vocal cords tearing as the memory rips through my throat.

"Pictures of her crime scene. Deranged smiley emojis where her face should-should—"

My knees buckle. Chase catches my sudden dead weight and holds me still, his grip becoming less imprisoning as I pull the images forth, pages of my mother's death fanning into my mind's view.

The three of them—Violet, Falyn, and Willow, wobble into my present, but Falyn's catty smile remains clear, and Willow's obvious derision is in the twist of her lips.

Even while messed-up, wrinkled, and pale with shock, they resemble princesses-in-training, looking down at their latest prisoner, asking their knight to ready her for a beheading.

Violet is the disconcerted leftover, pulling her lips in and working her jaw nervously, her reluctance at being a part of this shit-show made clear.

Chase's hold lightens, and he shifts so it's only his body I see. Only him. He lowers his head so his dazzling, angelic face takes their place, and I'm able to blink again. Chase's normally arched brows smooth and his lips turn supple with understanding.

He waits until my eyes are steady on his.

"Leave it to me," he says, then waits a beat to ensure my permission before he turns. "Is what Callie's saying true? Did you three put her mother's murder on blast?"

Chase's voice is so low, it's demonically dark. His cadence slows so the threat is evident in each syllable he utters.

His broad back, covered by his thin unisuit, shades my view, each tensed muscle popping against the maroon and black fabric. I don't need to be a witness to know that the three witches have gone white under their bi-weekly spray tans.

Falyn's voice comes through. "She's a lunatic, Chase, like Piper always said."

"We may not be responsible," Willow adds, "But whoever it was deserves kudos from us. You should be proud, too, Chase, since you and Piper—"

"I never participated in Piper's juvenile cruelty," Chase bites out.

"But you watched it." Willow's voice turns playful. "And you silently loved it as much as Tempest. Laughed like James. Observed with your hand sneaking into your pants, like Rio—"

"Fuck your theories, Willow," Chase snaps. "I'm not a part of your run-down traveling circus as you collect your freaks. Whatever you're hoping to win now that Piper's gone, it ends now."

"And what'll you do about it if we don't?" Falyn trills. "Push us off a—"

Chase rears so fast and hard, his sneakers kick dirt up my shins as he flies in front of Falyn, his fingers twitching with his effort at restraint, but his mouth holding no such reservations.

"Mention her death and my name in a sentence again, you'll see what it's like to bend under my will, and you know better than anybody that I don't use force. I like my games." Chase tilts his head, his face bitingly close to Falyn, who stands her ground, but shakes at the effort. "I love my silent cruelty. I'll inflict every skill I have until you go to sleep screaming. You'll wake up with a voice so raw, you'll have blood instead of a tongue." Chase leans in. "And it will all be from your own doing. My hands'll be clean."

Fuck.

Even I gulp at his words, and I'm the one with a clear view of his perfect ass in tight shorts, the complete opposite of the Satanic lip service Falyn's receiving.

The corners of my mouth tic at the thought. *I'm coming back.* The scarlet vision recedes, and my fingers and toes tingle, like they've been asleep all this time and at last are returning to life.

I breathe.

"Go clean up the shit you've tossed into Callie's room," Chase continues. "I'll explain to Coach you're skipping practice because you didn't want to miss your manicure appointment."

"You know what Coach'll do if she hears we missed training!" Willow sputters, her face blotchy and red.

Chase angles to include Willow. "And you know what *I'll* do if you follow me to the boathouse."

"You're a fucking asshole," Falyn spits, now that his hell-spawned eyes are directed elsewhere.

"There's no need," comes a small voice.

I think it's Violet, but when I look at her, she's clutching her gym bag to her chest and pretending not to exist under Chase's ire.

"Marron's in your room now, Callie," the voice continues, and I recognize its tone.

Ivy steps out from the trees and onto the path. Her eyes are red-rimmed, like she's been rubbing them. Her nails are bleeding from picking at her cuticles too hard.

"He is?" I'm surprised at the rough, off-key tune of my voice, but it sounds more familiar than it did a few minutes ago.

Ivy nods. "The campus police, too. Once they heard what was in there, they, um, they also called ... Haskins is on his way."

Chase asks, "The detective?"

"Yeah," Ivy says, wringing her hands in front of her. "Callie, I think they want you to meet them in Marron's office."

We climb the trail to the school together, Ivy taking my hand at some point and squeezing. Reality continues its shaking camera view as I walk, but I'm happy to leave Chase and Piper's friends in my rearview lens.

They would've had to hack into someone's computer to gain possession of my mom's crime scene photos and used connections they were born with to get it. A password wouldn't be required—all it would take was a simple phone call, an underhanded favor exchanged, or blackmail enforced.

Chase's dad is a criminal defense attorney.

If I looked at that fact on its face, it'd be hard to believe. Chase defended me on the trail to the boathouse. Yet, I can't discount that Daniel Stone had the easiest way to gain access to those photos.

Did Chase do it? Will he defend me one minute, then plow my face into the dirt the next?

He's conniving. I've seen his two faces, one running hot and the other ice cold.

Ivy puts her hand between my shoulders, nudging me into Headmaster Marron's office. Somehow, we'd navigated the Briarcliff lawns and hallways without me noticing.

Haskins sits in one chair across from Marron's desk, where Marron reposes, his elbows propped against the wood and index fingers pressed to his lips. The second visitor's chair is vacant—for me.

Dr. Luke steps out stage left, his arms crossed and mouth grim as he nods his hello, and it's with a quick hug from Ivy that I step into the office and shut the door behind me.

Forty

TWO GRUELING HOURS LATER, I leave Marron's office shakier than when I'd entered.

Stepping into the hallway reminds me that Sunday at Briarcliff continues the exact way it would had I not had my waking nightmares reinvigorated. Students filter through the school, and the Wolf's Den above is loud with footsteps and laughter as seniors drink their caffeine of choice and study, enjoying the time and privilege away from their younger counterparts.

I don't bother to look up as I pass under, but I file away the craving to sleep there tonight, instead of the place where I've been so wholly violated.

Piper, and now my mother, share their final moments with me in that dorm room. I may not have Piper's missing pages, but her feelings stay with me, the fear she must've felt, the betrayal and helpless rage ... the precise feelings I know my mom felt when she'd realized her life was over.

I close my eyes tight once I take the stairs down and hit the pavement outside, intent on keeping the tears in, on forcing my screams silent. The last people who deserve my anguish are those who amble around me, unaware and unconcerned with how their school is run.

My mom's photos being unearthed also meant Haskins's renewed attention on me. I fielded questions from him, with Dr. Luke at my elbow and my stepdad and Lynda on Skype, full of their own questions. Soon, it became Dad and Lynda attempting to understand the situation more than it was any sort of interrogation of me. They didn't know my roommate had died under suspicious circumstances. Had no clue I was being bullied by her, too. Yet, when it came to questioning my motives, Lynda reared up and threatened legal action the minute Haskins's voice bordered on suspicion. She also threatened to pull both me and her family's substantial donation if this line of questioning continued.

I respected her for that.

When she voiced her preference for both Ahmar and her family's lawyer being present if I'm "brought in" again, I appreciated her shrewdness.

Maybe she isn't that bad, after all.

I swipe the dampness from under my eyes, then reach to pull out my phone to call Ahmar, until I remember it's been stolen. During the rare moments Dad spoke, he said he'd overnight me a new one. We've always been strained, he and I, but we're on an entirely different level now that Briarcliff has shown its teeth.

During the questioning in Marron's office, who, in his defense, voiced his deep concern over the "violation" to my person and property and vowed to find the person responsible (yeah, right), I remained silent unless asked a direct question. Even then, I mumbled short answers. My eyes stayed downcast, my hands demure.

What no one caught on to or suspected, is that I. Am. *Pissed.*

Damn if anyone is going to scare me away, cloak or no cloak, Noble or Virtue, past or present.

Somebody doesn't want me to find out the truth about Piper or about this school.

Too bad for them.

I spring from the elevator and into my dorm's hallway with a burst of vengeful energy, but trip on my own feet when I notice who lingers at my door.

Chase unfurls himself from the floor, clad in a pair of Briarcliff sweats and a plain white tee, tight against his pecs. His tawny blond hair is ruffled and askew, like he's been running his fingers through it or just finished an epic work-out, the color to his cheeks mirroring the same energy-sparking habits.

"Can I help you?" I ask, my voice still ragged from my earlier rage session.

Chase licks his lips, something a six-figure, in-demand male model would do once the photographer trained the lens on him. It's endearing and sexy, with the perfect amount of feigned contrition to make a girl want to melt.

"I wanted to see if you were okay," he says.

"How so?" I keep my question innocent. "Because my mom's real, violent murder was plastered all over my walls?"

"Well, yeah."

"Mm." I move deliberately close, and the maneuver is so surprising, Chase steps back, and I'm able to elbow my way to my door. "Sucks for whoever did it, considering I walked in on the real thing. Pictures don't have the same impact, unfortunately."

Chase's heavy breath hits the nape of my neck, and I stiffen at the shiver. I expect a *shit, Callie, I'm so sorry*, at my blunt statement. Instead, I get this:

"Jesus, I wouldn't have wanted to see you then, 'cause today you were a fucking banshee whose tits were just bit off by a werewolf."

I whirl. "What is the *matter* with you? *All* of you? It's like you get turned on by pain! You're all fucking masochists with pretty faces."

Chase's hands cup my face. He ducks low, his brown eyes glittering like he kidnapped the stars to light the way for his inner beast. "Aw, sweet possum, do you think I'm pretty?"

"Stop calling me that."

"You want sympathy? You won't get it from me."

"Then why the hell are you here?" I raise my chin. "To enjoy the aftermath?"

"This may come as a surprise, but I didn't like what I saw today. Blood and murder? Not what I enjoy jerking off to." He bends closer, and I smell the mint on his breath. "Think about it. Piper was your enemy. Stands to reason my motives for finding her killer are a helluva lot stronger than yours. She was my—"

"Girlfriend."

"*Friend.*"

"Sister."

Chase cedes my point, then says, "Not anymore."

"So, what? You want us to work together? You have a fucked-up sense of team spirit, you know that?"

"I'm excellent at leading my crew, sweet possum, and even better at turning their spirit into discipline. Don't think I can't do that to you."

"Ah. So, you're here to threaten me."

Chase chuckles, low and slow. "Not in the way you're expecting."

I force steel into my voice. "What if I told you I'm here to pack up my stuff and leave?"

"You tried that once." He trails a finger down my cheek, and I stifle the sigh that wants to coat my throat like honey.

"This has gone too far," I say.

"I agree. It has." His thumb traces my bottom lip, flanging it out, then letting it snap back into place as he continues to map my features.

"You can't possibly think to seduce me, not after everything."

Chase nails me with a boyish, innocent look through his lashes, as if I can't see the monster as his puppeteer. "Is it working?"

My back is flat against the door. I'm pressing into it so hard, I'm wishing for the superpower to just fall through. But the pieces of me without the bone structure to withstand the pressure surges and piques with need.

I choke out, "Did you use your father to gain access to those pictures?"

Chase doesn't flinch at the change in topic. His hand keeps traveling, keeps *finding*, his fingers playing around my breasts, but not touching them.

Please touch them.

"No," he says. "And to answer your follow-up question, I have no idea who did."

"But you can find out."

"Maybe." Chase's lips take the place of his finger, starting at my ear, the wisps of his breath like curls of smoke, drawing my chin up and my mouth to his jaw, lured by the flickering flames beneath.

My lips brush against his stubble when I ask, "Are you striking a deal with me, Chase?"

"You mean, help me find out about Piper, and I'll help you find your harasser?" Chase nuzzles where my neck meets my jaw, and I suppress a whimper. "What if they're one and the same?"

This is crazy. There are four rooms on this floor. A neighbor could walk through those elevators or the side stairs at any moment—neighbors I've never met, girls who've predominantly ignored my presence.

If they walked in and saw me now, however, I bet my presence would be squealed all over campus.

"What if," I manage to croak out, "they're a Noble? Or a Virtue?"

Chase stills with his lips on my nape, his teeth so close to my jugular.

"You know the meaning of those titles, Chase."

Chase's hands grip my waist, so hard, his fingers create dents in my skin.

"Chase. Tell me—"

My demand loses meaning when Chase rears up and crashes his lips against mine, sealing his secrets with a searing, wrath-fueled kiss.

Forty-One

MY HEART SLAMS its warning against my ribs, my pulse points following their leader's commands, but my hands won't heed.

They rise up, my fingers tangling in his hair, and he tastes like the alcohol I'm too young to crave.

Mint and liquor duel for their time on my tongue as Chase yanks my hair until I'm at an angle he can devour, his mouth as devious and hellbent as his brain.

I'm not supposed to want this, but my body presses against his, the hard length of him spearing against the softness of my belly.

It's twisted and unusual to desire the boy who scares me and wants me to bend to his will any chance he gets, yet here I am, parting my lips so he can possess me deeper, spreading my legs so he can access me longer.

While our lips spar, Chase cups my ass and lifts until my legs wrap around him. He steals the keycard from my fingers and swipes us into my room without the need for sight, and with inhuman, graceful strides, he has us in my room with seconds to spare.

Chase throws me onto the bed, and my eyes pop wide, the mist of seduction waning. I glance around with terrified awareness.

"There's nothing here," Chase assures. "It's all been tossed."

He stands at the end of my bed, devouring me with such intent that my sudden fear must be fueling him.

He's wrong for you. He's too dark, too much a part of the underworld. He'll drag you under—

I stop my inner angel from speaking further.

What if, for once, I want to appeal to my demons?

My lips curl on a hungry snarl, one that takes Chase by surprise, but he doesn't flinch when I rise up to my knees and pull at his sweats, wanting him naked. Vulnerable. Mine.

He catches me by the wrist and pushes me back until my butt bounces against my bed. I push up on my elbows, my expression nothing but a question mark.

"You first, sweet possum."

If I were in a better, less screwed-up mindset, maybe I would've considered Chase's reluctance to come undone before I do, but as he yanks my jeans down, I tug my shirt off, my chest braless and bare, a sight that triggers a rumble in his chest.

Chase climbs on top, pushing me flat, and reaches down to flick the side strap of my G-string. I flinch at the sharp pain and moan.

"Does that turn you on?" Chase whispers against my lips, his hair falling into his eyes the way a turned angel's wings must sag and wither once they descend into wickedness.

He does it again.

Then again.

I cry out, writhing with need, a base desire to have him fill me so instant, I'm choking with want.

Chase hooks the strap, and it snaps apart in his grip, leaving me exposed. His fingers move, dancing across my skin, stroking the soft hairs there, until he finds my folds and spreads them.

Chase rises and sits back on his heels. Once I've sobered and can figure out what he's doing, I move to clench my legs shut, but he keeps them spread with a firm grip on my inner thighs.

The crescents of his lashes are the darkest part of his fair form, and they're all he'll allow me to see when he murmurs, "Just as I thought. Sweet possum."

I *knew* it. When he utters that cursed nickname, sexual promise follows, so much so that he has to be meaning something other than *possum*. And here I am, proving him right.

So, so, bad ... so wickedly against my norm ... I shouldn't ... I can't ... I ... I...

He curls a finger through my folds, and my back arches in the same choreographed movement.

"I'm going to taste that sweetness," he says, then his dark gaze flicks up to mine. "This isn't a request."

"I'm not about to beg," I say hoarsely.

He slow grins in response. I allow my head to fall back into the pillows as his lowers into my personal sin.

Chase thrusts two fingers in before he allows his tongue to play, too. My hips grind with his movements, in no way delicate, and harsher than I've ever experienced.

I'm no sex kitten, having done it one time. Matt was gentle and clumsy, mumbling sorry after every feeble pound, until four seconds later, he was done. My back ached from being crushed against the bodega's cupboards behind the cash register. I'd cranked my hip from him leaning his palm hard into my inner thigh, spreading it unnaturally. My clothes stayed on, with one breast exposed when he pushed my shirt halfway up for a quick grope.

In short, my entire sexual encounter with Matt, Chase could sum up with one finger joint, and he was using a helluva lot more than that.

He's sucking on my clit in a way that makes me throw up my hips and squirm, the ambrosia too much, too sudden and unrelenting. It spurs him on, flicking my clit with his tongue and pushing a third finger in, pounding and thrusting so hard it burns.

But oh, the burn.

It's bliss through fire, a hint of pain with the promise of desire, and I ache for more, *more*.

His fingers aren't enough to fill my craving. His tongue is hot and eager to taste, but not what I want. A mere pittance to what I *need* after the hell his friends have put me through, what *he* might've instigated...

My warnings turn to ashes when my orgasm releases its rays of sunshine, my voice screaming its blinding brightness. I melt in Chase's hands, the thrill so shattering, I can't draw breath as I come down.

Chase lifts his head, his lips dampened by my release, but not his smile.

I glower at him—or hope I do. My muscles are too satiated to care.

"I see my reputation precedes me," he says, then reaches for his sweatpants puddled on the ground and pulls out a condom.

This time, my frown comes easy. "You came here with *that* in your pocket?"

Chase shrugs. "I always like to be prepared."

"I see. So, if a chick crossed your path on your way to my room, you would've fucked her, instead?"

"You have it wrong, sweet possum." Chase stands naked with that reputed cock of his standing at full attention. "I was waiting for you."

My mouth becomes too dry to swallow. "I'm so going to regret this."

"Maybe," he says as he rips the condom packet with his teeth. He does it without his eyes straying from mine, dilated with lust and famine. "But you'll enjoy the fall from grace. I promise."

I never saw you coming, I think, but the scent of sex in the air prevents me from whispering it out loud.

Chase starts to slide the condom on, but I hold his wrist to stop him. He arches a brow, questioning, but I take the condom and slide it on myself, keeping him tight in my grip. He's a Siren's call, and I'm the stupid sailor who can't fight the song, but you know what? Fuck it. I want some release, goddammit, and if it's going to be physical, the person I've wanted to do it with—Chase—is naked and willing in front of me.

I'm not going to look this gift horse in the mouth; I'm going to swallow it whole.

I pump him a few times to keep him rigid and wanting, bemoaning the fact that I've already covered him in bitter latex, because taking him in my mouth would've given me the utmost sense of possession. And to make him come from my choice. My doing...

Chase grips my shoulders and presses me against the bed. He positions his elbows on either side and looks me in the eyes for what seems like a hundred heartbeats before I reach down, wrap my fingers around his base, and line him up to my entrance.

"You scared?" I whisper.

He searches my face, a rare moment of hesitation. "You sure?"

"It's a little late for that, isn't it?"

The skin around Chase's eyes crinkles, yet his pulse is pounding against his neck. "I like to be a gentleman before I fuck you into oblivion."

"Then stop dicking around and *do* it."

Chase takes me for my word. He buries himself in me in one all-consuming motion, then pulls out entirely. He does it again. And again.

I'll be bruised by the time he's done, but I tell him not to stop. His brows crash down with craving.

I use my fingers and find my clit, massaging circles in time to his brutal thrusts, and he looks down in surprise.

"You don't get all of me," I murmur into his hair, and he lifts his head and presses his lips against mine, shutting me up.

My circles become faster, ardent with pressure, the harder he pounds. It becomes so vigorous that my hand starts to ache, and he bares his teeth against my mouth, expelling his roar onto my tongue. The stimulation is so much, and I'm so filled in ways I've never been before, but I push past the ache and meet Chase thrust for thrust, until we're both sweating and gritting our teeth, our rough, animalistic grunts taking over our human forms and bringing us carnal satisfaction.

I hate being the first to come, but I can't hold on. I tangle my free hand into his hair and bring his head down to my neck as I cry out, my thighs clamping around his hips as he furiously grinds, gaining momentum for his own release.

Chase spears up onto his hands, pushing in and out in quick bursts. I'm so tender from the high of my orgasm that it's a wonder I can contain him. The moment he comes, his dick pulses and twitches inside of me, and I take that moment of weakness by curling my legs around him and palming his ass, driving him deeper.

Chase collapses beside me with a heavy exhale, the sheer length of his body far surpassing mine.

I dare rolling over.

I risk curling my arm against his heaving chest.

I chance kissing the salted skin of his shoulder, shocked that I just had sex with the dark prince of Briarcliff.

And liked it.

"What was it like? Finding your mom."

I'd been dozing, but snap awake at Chase's voice.

He's still here?

If Chase had grabbed his things and waltzed out of my room the instant my eyes fluttered shut, I wouldn't have been surprised. Or insulted. It's how these things go, right, when you find yourself in bed with the most popular guy in school?

I am not the girl meant to change his ways. I understood that as soon as his lips crushed mine, slick and demanding. I was in it for the ecstatic release, like him, since the burden of Briarcliff was getting to us both. In different ways, maybe, but the frustrating, unsolvable load is the same.

"Hmm?" I ask, buying time.

I've pulled the sheets around my delicate parts, a lot like Venus rising from the clam, my long hair just as wild and free. But if I were to compare Chase to a stunning piece of art, he was David, full-frontal and confident, spread atop my sheets like the famous sculpture cast in gold.

"Your mom," Chase says again. "You said you walked in and discovered her body."

He says it so coolly, like he's the host of an investigative crime show, but surprisingly, I don't resent him for it. Most people are afraid to broach the subject, and when they do, it's all soft lilts and prying gazes.

Death is everyone's greatest fear. But murder? That's their worst nightmare.

"It was ... like you'd expect," I say, gnawing on my lower lip. "It was a Wednesday. I was late coming home from school because I'd missed my bus. I remember turning my keys in the lock to our door and crashing in—making plenty of noise, because I felt bad. Usually Mom and I went to our favorite Italian place on Wednesdays. I called out her name, but she didn't answer. Not surprising, since she was on call a lot and was probably asked to join an investigation..." I trail off, deciding it's easier to fix the sheets around my body than look at Chase.

He comes up on his elbow, staring down at me. "Go on."

"I don't—I don't like talking about it."

Silky, sand-colored strands obscure his eyes, but not his assessment. I may be covered by bed sheets, but I've never felt so exposed.

I whisper, "She was in her bedroom."

Chase pushes my hair back from my face, tracing my eyebrow, then my cheek.

"On the floor," I continue. "Behind the bed. I didn't see her, but I smelled ... I smelled the tang of blood. Like that sharp, metal smell that you just *know* is coming from an open wound. I climbed over the bed and—and there she was, on her back, one arm flung out like this..."

I find myself in the exact position I found my mom, one hand thrown over my head, the other curled over my stomach. I grimace as she did in her final moments. What she didn't do was clench her fists. What she *couldn't* do was scrunch her eyes shut when her killer pulled the knife out of her chest. And sliced again.

"Is this what you wanted, Chase? To feed off my lows after pushing me to my high? To test my limits?"

"No," he says, and leaves it at that. Or so I think. "My sister used to go here."

Chase's calm tone brings me back to reality. I tilt my head, catching him in my view again. He's eyes are still on me, but the thoughts behind them, they're not soft. Not hard, either.

"Emma Loughery," he adds. "Heard of her?"

I furrow my brows. The name sounds familiar.

"She took our mom's name after the divorce."

"The ... when your parents separated two years ago?"

"No. That was Dad's second escape attempt. His first was with our mother, who he kept around for twelve years, give or take. Dad's a cold fuck, and my twin sister understood that before I did. I idolized our father for a long time. Too long. Emma saw things in him that clouded her happiness, and she thought leaving Dad behind and going with Mom would give her a fresh start."

"I see." I don't see. Chase has a *twin?*

"Ems ran around with Piper's crew when she was here," Chase explains, and I nod, making the connection, except for why Chase is bringing up his sister.

Then, it clicks. "Why isn't she here? Was she...?"

"Killed? No." Chase falls onto his back, causing the sweet, billowing scent of our sex to float into the air before it settles down again. "She was attacked, though. And was trapped in the library's fire, before a fireman pulled her own."

My fingers knot in my sheets. "Here?"

Chase nods in my periphery as we both stare at the ceiling. "In the library. The one before the slab of concrete that was built from my family's pockets."

It's my turn to push onto my elbow and stare down at Chase. His cheek muscles pulse, the curvature of his jaw becoming sharp as a knife. "The old library? The one that burned down?"

He nods. "Who my sister used to be will always be in the soil under the name of his second wife, who lasted what, two-and-a-half years?"

My lips fall open.

Chase slides his gaze to mine. "Told you he was a fucker."

"What happened to your sister? To Emma?"

"She was assaulted in the old library and left for dead. According to the investigative fucktards, no one will ever know who did it. A random event, a stranger break-in, Marron says. No student could've done that kind of atrocity."

I place my hand on Chase's arm. I squeeze, but it's like trying to crush granite between my fingers. "I'm so sorry." I add, "This is why you're so invested in Piper. Why you don't want her forgotten the way your sister was."

Chase blinks slowly but keeps our connection. "We all have our motivations. Emma was fun, happy, and wanted a future. Now, she's one hundred pounds overweight, afraid to leave the house, and refuses to get the help she needs. My father wants to erase her with money. Cast her off to his estate's basement to rot."

I risk laying my head on his chest and listening to his heartbeat. Chase doesn't push me away, but he doesn't wrap his arms around me either. It's simply not what he does.

Ivy had said the fire involved the most popular girl in school. Chase's *sister*.

It's Emma's story that's tied to the burning of the old library, and Chase's father is tethered to it, too.

"Briarcliff has so many sharp edges," I murmur against his skin.

"Both times, with Emma, then Piper, I stood by, because I didn't know." He combs through my hair, lifting and curling it between his fingers. "It's not going to happen again."

I close my eyes at the lull his massage brings and sigh beneath his hand. "Then tell me about the Nobles or why Piper was a Virtue."

His fingers stall in their movements.

"They're a part of this," I push, keeping my eyes closed. It may be because I'm afraid to watch his sated features realign into his iced-over composure. "And now I'm a part of it, too."

"I'm keeping you away from it."

My eyes open. "You don't have a say in what I do."

"Were you not listening to anything I said? I will not let another girl be destroyed."

"That's all well and good, Prince Not-So-Charming, but I can handle my own." I sit up, collecting my hair and clearing it from my shoulders. "You're late to the party, anyway. Someone's been breaking into my room, and I swear it's a Cloak."

Chase's expression smooths. "What did you just call them?"

"I knew it." I point at him, reposed in bed, but his limbs primed to leap. "The Cloaks *are* them. The Nobles." I gather the courage to say what's been nibbling at the back of my mind since I received the initial rose. *No.* Since I saw that mysterious envelope on Piper's desk. "They're a secret society, aren't they?"

Chase snatches my wrist and slams my palm onto his chest. His heart pounds beneath skin, as hard as the bones that cage it. "Feel that? Isn't that what your heart did when you found your mother? Is it a sickening adrenaline you swore never to have to feel again?"

I suck in a breath, because he's much too accurate. That type of pounding, the seasick strain of my heart desperately trying to beat for two ... that memory is a terrible mark on my soul I'd pay Satan to remove.

"Because *I* endure it every damn day I'm stuck in these school walls, which is why I'm here to remind you, *don't get involved.* Your mom's death was a fucked-up twist of fate and not your fault. Seeking out these Cloaks of yours and testing their boundaries? If you do, the smudge her murder left on your heart will be nothing but a cute butterfly tattoo compared to the mutilation they'll inflict."

"And yet they have nothing to do with Piper or Emma," I say dryly.

Chase catches my jaw, holding it as he rises to sit and look me full in the face. "I'll say it for the last time. No."

He releases his grip, and I gasp in a breath, unaware I'd stopped breathing under his hold. Chase stands and pulls on his sweatpants, his back to me.

"Distract me all you want," I say. "I won't stop. I'm not adding a second unsolved crime to my list of life's achievements."

Chase tosses his tee over his shoulder, his bare back rippling with muscle as he prowls to my door without a look back.

"Like you said, Chase, we all have our motivations!" I call.

His answer, predictably, is to slam the front door.

Forty-Two

OVER THE NEXT THREE DAYS, I expected Chase to tell the entire school that I slept with him, ensuring my humiliation by saying he nailed me so hard, I was possum roadkill by now.

It's with that thick, expectant armor that I leave Thorne House and head to the dining hall. But I eat breakfast, then head to calculus without issue. Ivy speaks to me without underlying horror. I make it through the entire day—and the entire day's *meals*—without anyone bothering me, a first since stepping onto Briarcliff soil.

The second day goes similarly, where no one pays much attention, save for the professors when they call my name in class. It is a weirdly lightheaded experience, and it lowers my barriers enough to where I don't have to look over my shoulder every two seconds.

On the third morning, I become suspicious.

Chase is either absent or deliberately obtuse, never seeking me out in the classes we share. His friends, however, do, and within minutes of crossing Riordan's path, I know he knows, and wishes he'd filmed it.

Tempest doesn't have the same eagerness behind his indolent stare, but he watches closely, flicking that spot where a lip ring should be with his tongue as I pass his desk.

The sexual duel between my internal devil and angel has to be put on pause, however, because I have crucial avenues to pursue, like where my phone went, and if the person who stole it is as disappointed as me when they realized all they got for their efforts was Piper's endless drone of unicorn poop. I never possessed the full diary, and now, neither do they.

Which ... they're now looking for, too. When Chase left that night, I'd checked the cloud on my laptop, in hopes my copy would be there, but it was deleted, and suddenly, my midnight intruder made a lot more sense. The only item I have at this point is Rose's letter, hidden between my calculus pages.

I shiver under my Briarcliff cardigan on my way to history, unable to shake the compulsion to do as Chase says—stop getting involved.

Mom wouldn't let this lie. *All victims are the same once they come to me, Callie. They are people who deserve justice, regardless of how they lived their lives. Somebody took that choice away from them.*

Since I'm so distracted and in my own head, history zooms by, and so do the rest of my classes. I cancel dinner with Ivy because I'm so behind on my calculus studies. A certain something happened on Sunday to prevent me from catching up, but I'm not about to confess my turbulent, naked afternoon to my sole friend.

I see Eden a handful of times, but she keeps her gaze away from mine, holding her textbooks tight to her chest, even though she has a rolling backpack she drags around.

I'm desperate to ask her where she stole those incriminating videos of me, and if she had the forethought to delete the original, but she's as evasive as all the other secrets Briarcliff stifles within its walls.

When Falyn kicks the wheels into Eden's path, I stick my foot in front of Falyn while she's busy admiring her handiwork, then smile when she trips over my shoe and mutters an expletive at me.

Eden doesn't thank me. She glowers, then storms in the opposite direction, her damaged, off-kilter wheels bouncing in tune with her steps.

"Miss Ryan," Dr. Luke warns as I pass his classroom door, where he stands and observes the students as we disperse in the hallway.

"Sorry," I say.

"Uh-huh. With more contrition next time, maybe I'll buy it."

I smile with sarcastic contrition, then exit the main building, intent on getting my studies done.

But, as it turns out, Chase has other plans.

For the second time, Chase makes me come.

I'm stripped bare on my bed, lying face-down and ass-up, and what should be a humiliating pose becomes the best oral of my entire, formerly innocent life.

My fingers curl into the sheets, my nails biting into the mattress below as I moan through gritted teeth, wanting to be quiet not for my neighbors, but for my own self-respect.

I push my butt back, my sensitive area too exposed for his tongue to be doing such things. But I can't ... I can't ...

"Shit—Chase! Chase, I ... I..."

He groans into me, the vibrations of his voice snapping the last strands of sanity I have left.

Chase pulls away, and I land on my bed in a heap, pieces of hair fluttering as I blow out meager breaths through my lips.

"You're welcome," Chase says. He stands with a grin, wiping his lips with the back of his hand. He's clothed in Briarcliff gear, while I'm naked and vibrating in front of him.

How did I myself get into this position, you ask?

I'd had every intention to crack open my calculus text when I took the elevator to my floor, my legs too rubbery and sore from my adventures over the weekend to take the three flights of stairs.

The hallway was deserted. It was only when I keyed into my dorm room that I noticed an intruder reclining against a sable-colored, suede piece of furniture.

"Your couch is here," Chase says, head angled as I step in.

"Why is this dorm room such a free-for-all?" I toss my book-heavy bag at him, which he catches.

"The delivery guys were here when I arrived," he explains, letting my bag fall to his feet. "I thought I'd sign for it, then show them where to put the couch."

"How chivalrous of you. I'm so glad my apartment complex has no security measures whatsoever."

Chase tsks. "That's highly insulting to the many college grads who come here and sleep at the reception desk. Or is it Ivy you're pissing all over? She's pretty scrappy security if I do say so."

I cross my arms. "What's your problem, Chase?"

"And your sentiment continues."

"I don't possess the patience for your hot bullshit in addition to your cold shits. Why are you here after ignoring me for days? What do you want?"

"Mm." Chase licks his lips as if deep in thought. My toes curl while watching his tongue run along the pink, sensitive skin. "Solid question. I'm here because I'd rather eat your pussy than whatever the dining hall has to offer for dinner tonight."

"W-what?"

Jesus, I sound like a centuries-old Victorian woman whose consort just threw the word pussy at her. But really, it's that surprising.

"Do you disagree?" he asks. Chase rests an ankle on his opposite knee as he does so, allowing me full view of the strain happening between his pantlegs.

"I can't. I have stuff to do."

Chase rises. He's at a safe distance, but I back up nonetheless. "Are you sure about that?"

"Y-yes."

"Nope. You're not. Take your sweater off, Callie."

Damn it, I love it when he uses my name, how it flows out of his mouth with such familiarity.

"Nope, I will not," I say.

"Mm. You will." Chase slides his blazer off, then tosses it ... somewhere. He loosens his tie, then slips that over his head, too.

My butt hits the wall, and as his body covers me, his delicious scent is the first to seduce.

"I know what you're doing," I manage to gasp when his tongue finds the pulse in my throat. "You're trying to distract me. Prevent me from ... drawing ... drawing— shit, what was I saying? Drawing attention! You don't want me to be involved in Pip—"

"Callie?" he murmurs against my lips. "Shut up."

Thus, here I am, splayed naked in my bed like the feast Chase vowed I'd be.

Watching him round my bed in full uniform, then take a seat on my single chair and cross his ankles on my desk, I have the added incentive to reclaim the unsuspecting part of me that he took.

I roll over on my stomach and prop my head in my hands. "Chase, tell me something."

Chase pulls out a—is that a *joint?*—from his pocket, followed by a lighter. He sticks the joint between his teeth and responds while flicking his lighter against the tip. "Your ass looks great in this light."

I ignore his half-assed attempt at distraction. "Are you supposed to be doing that? I mean—obviously you shouldn't be doing it in my room, asshole, but your sports career. Your rowing."

Half his face crinkles with a smile as he puffs. "Is that what you want me to tell you? Whether or not I'm a good boy to Coach?"

"No. The opposite." I sit up, taking the sheets with me. I've yet to come to terms with being completely naked with a boy in the room when he's not on top of me. "Have you ever been known as Mr. S?"

Chase holds in a waft of smoke, then puffs it out slow. "This again?"

"Is it true? Tell me that much." I hitch the sheets higher. "Did Piper ever call you that?"

"Why is it so important to you? You've never told me where you heard that name."

"It's just something I heard ... around."

"Uh-huh."

"Well, is it a thing?" I grapple for a better stronghold. "Is it the name your girlie fan club calls your dick?"

Chase snorts, flicking ash on my desk, then placing the joint back between his lips. I growl at him.

"You're cute when you try to be rabid."

"It's a simple question."

"Fine." Chase's shoes *clomp* against the floor when he swings his legs down. "No. Piper never called me Mr. S, and my cock sure as hell doesn't have that name. It doesn't have to." He gives me one of his panty-dropping grins. "It speaks for itself."

"Dang," I mumble, then look to the side. Unfortunately, I believe him.

"What's the big deal? Why are you and the cops so revved up about it?" His gaze narrows. "What do you know that I don't?"

"I don't have to tell you." I collect the top sheet, wrapping it around my body and sliding off the bed. "You keep shit to yourself. So can I."

It's tough to discuss a personal item of Piper's that I never deserved access to, sent the original to the police, then lost my copy. Chase would be full of questions and demands. I wouldn't be able to answer them to his satisfaction, earning his wrath. Frankly, these past few days of quiet were like sunbeams on my soul, and I don't want to ruin it when I can't even offer up the missing pages as proof of my efforts.

Chase stubs out the joint and stands, but I catch him when his hand cups my doorknob.

"Chase, um, would you mind staying a bit?"

Chase cocks a brow. "Really?"

He has reason to be confused. The guy truly infuriates me, we whisper veiled threats at each other more than truths, and we don't trust one another. But the thought of being in this room, alone and available for the next unwelcome intruder...

"I need help with calculus. I'm just not getting it," I fib.

Chase's head falls back as he stares at the ceiling in thought. "What if I told you I've been fucking Professor Lacey to get an A in that class and have no idea how to find the derivative?"

"I'd say that's a steaming helping of your hot bullshit."

"Fine. But I can't promise I won't want to fuck you in between."

I go all tingly and wet at the thought. "I—we can come to a deal on that."

"Oh, can we?"

I squeak when I land back on the bed, with him shadowing my body until his hands land on the mattress on either side of me. "I'm calling in that favor, sweet possum."

Forty-Three

CHASE and I come to a ceasefire. Of sorts.

In public, we don't acknowledge each other, except to add any additional information we find about Piper, which so far, isn't much.

I discreetly asked the college receptionists at Thorne House if there was any camera access to the night my mom's pictures were strewn around my room (I left out the part of someone using that distraction to steal my phone), but was told Marron took the footage and handed it over to the police.

That's a positive step. Evidence of my harasser went to the police. Piper's fall was in the hands of the police. The police were in charge of Emma's case, too. I should leave it up to them. Mom would want me to. Ahmar would encourage it. I could lose myself in Chase the way he loses himself in me, carry on at Briarcliff in the relative safety of his protection, then graduate out of these suffocating, deceptive hallways.

Except ... the roses still exist. The Nobles and my hunch they're not a separate danger keeps popping up, despite Chase's lame attempts to convince me otherwise.

The cops are doing shit-all about those doozies. Marron, even worse.

Is Briarcliff just one giant cover-up for a litany of crimes committed under its purview?

It all starts with your paper on Rose Briar.

Eden's voice won't go away. I'll have to scratch that itch after my history and calc quarter-terms today, then sneak away to the public library to see if I can find anything more on Rose. If any old texts exist, it would have to be—

I spear up in bed on a gasp.

"The hell, Callie?" Chase mumbles into the pillow, then searches for my hand and presses it against his groin. Smiling in the waning moonlight, he adds, "Are you waking me up early for a good-luck rub before quarter-terms?"

"What if the library didn't burn down because of Emma?" I say breathlessly. "What if it was the Cloaks trying to hide something?"

"Christ, really?" Chase rolls so he's on his back and peering at me with slitted eyes. "That's reaching, don't you think?"

"I can't find anything on Rose Briar, yet I keep being reminded that in order to solve Piper's death, Rose's mystery has to be looked into, too. The original documents about the Briarcliff founding would've been in the old school library, right?"

Chase rubs his eyes. "I suppose."

"Then that means anything else original to Rose Briar was destroyed."

"Anything *else*?"

Shit. *Shit.* Chase doesn't know about the portion of Rose's letter I found in the public library.

I ignore the slip-up in hopes Chase deems it unworthy enough to ignore, too. "This all dates back to the beginning of Briarcliff, but how?"

"Cal."

"I'm just like the cops. I've got nothing."

"I'm surprised you're not backing the police up. Wasn't your mom a cop?"

"No." I frown at him.

Chase sits up with a grunt. "Seriously? This whole time, I thought she was one. Partnered with your uncle or whatever."

"She was a crime scene photographer," I say distractedly.

"Huh."

"You and Piper's research into me didn't go far, then, if you didn't know what my mom did for a living."

Chase's jaw works, the muscles in his cheeks tensing and releasing, but he says nothing.

I continue. "The library could've been burned down for another reason. We have to cross that possibility off our list."

"No. We don't."

"I see we're back to one syllable demands."

"Just get off that line of thinking, okay? Here. I'll help." He lays my hand back on his junk, rigid and firm under his pants. "I take exams better when my spank bank's empty."

"Gross. And no." I pull my hand back. "This is important, Chase."

"It isn't."

"It *is*. I thought you wanted this. You keep saying you have better reasons than me to solve Piper's death, yet here you are, wanting to have sex instead of talk it through—"

"My sister lit the fire, all right?" Chase's voice crackles in the air. "So, can you please be over it now?"

"She … she did?"

"Yes. Our dad paid people to keep that detail away from the press and prevent Briarcliff from pressing charges. She burned the place to ashes a few weeks after her attack. Became trapped in a fire of her own making. And I can't fucking blame her when nobody would bring her the guy who hurt her. And before you ask, *no*, she did not burn it down to prevent your research of some chick jumping off a cliff almost two hundred years ago."

I can't think of anything to say.

Chase's dark eyes shine in the gloom. "Don't say a word of that to anyone. You understand?"

I nod.

"Good." Chase throws the covers off and leaps out of bed, searching the floor for his pants. "Now that I'm up, I'm leaving."

"Chase, wait."

For the past week, Chase has been sneaking into Thorne House and staying with me, leaving before dawn, but not like this.

"Can't." He scrapes his hair back. "I'll see you in class."

"Chase, I'm—"

"Don't say it. There's nothing to be sorry for. You're doing what I want, and that's asking the type of questions the cops aren't. So, keep at it. Just … leave Emma out of it. She's for me to figure out."

I nod with a noncommittal bob. If Emma and Piper's situations are related, then it's critical I prove that, too, despite the meager access I have to either of them.

Chase pauses at my bedroom door, smacking the frame in thought. "Good luck today."

"Sure," I say, distant. "You, too."

Chase leaves without another word.

I fall back asleep with Cloaks and roses clouding my thoughts, and Chase's confession about his sister ringing in my ears.

A blaring sound wakes me, and I smack my hand across my brand-new phone on the nightstand and drag it toward me to turn the stupid thing off.

It's exam time, and I feel better prepared for them than I do the rest of my problems, which is to say, *not much.*

I shower, dress, then exit the dorms with the rest of the Briarcliff girls, clustered in groups and chatting about possible exam topics. I follow behind, content not to be involved—or noticed—by any of them.

I scan the heads for Ivy or Eden, but I'm disappointed when I don't see them. Maybe they're at the main building or at the library doing last minute preparations. A quick text would let me know, but I've left my phone in my room, as we're all required to do.

History with Dr. Luke is my morning class, and mercifully, it doesn't come in the form of an 8 AM exam. Our papers were our quarter-terms, and Dr. Luke is handing them back today, containing my first grade at Briarcliff Academy.

It's funny, worrying about my GPA when it *should* be my top concern. Instead, bodies fill my head, damaged and dead ones vying for attention.

I'm envious of the girls walking the path ahead of and behind me. They have no idea what Briarcliff truly is, what it hides. Secret societies don't take up their head-space. The founders didn't linger in their minds longer than writing a paper about them. Chase doesn't sneak into their rooms at night, promising ecstasy and escape one minute, then vengeance and truth-telling the next.

Their roommate wasn't here one day, then dead the next.

As if summoned, Chase merges onto the path with the rest of his crew, Tempest and James flanking him, Riordan trailing behind with his nose in a textbook as they prowl.

A group of girls stare at Chase, whispering something to their friends, then glance back at me. None possess the bravery to blurt out what they're thinking loud enough for Chase to catch. He'd rather stare straight ahead and pretend to listen to what James has to say than acknowledge I'm close behind.

We all filter into the school, then spread into various hallways, trudging to class. Dr. Luke is in the classroom when I walk in, sorting through the pile of essays.

"Morning, Miss Ryan," he says without looking up.

"Morning," I reply, and take my seat as the rest of the class funnels through the door. He greets each by name.

"All right, class!" Dr. Luke claps for attention once we're seated. "I have good news and bad news. Good news: three people got an A on these papers. Bad news, the rest of you scraped by with a B minus or lower. To say I'm disappointed is an understatement. These are the people who built the walls you study in and cinched your education for entry into prestigious universities." Dr. Luke strides through the rows, plopping papers onto each desk he passes. "A little more resourcefulness, next time, okay?"

My paper plops in front of me, and Dr. Luke says in a voice meant for me alone, "I expected better from you, Miss Ryan."

Brows furrowed, I glance down at my essay and gasp. **C-minus**. *What?*

"Dr. Luke, I—"

"Anyone who has a problem with their grade," Dr. Luke says as he continues to meander the rows, leaving nothing but his masculine cologne behind, "can speak to me after class."

Students gasp in response. The few who got an A are obvious. Falyn smiles, then shows her paper to Willow sitting behind her with a bright, sharpie-red A. Chase leans back and crosses his arms on a grin, a cock in charge of his roost. Shockingly, James is the third, and he waves his paper like a beauty queen greeting the crowd until Dr. Luke tells him to sit his ass down.

I clear my throat instead of grunting any jealousy, and frantically flip through my paper, scanning Dr. Luke's comments.

My section about the possibility of Rose being part of a secret society is crossed out in red as thick as Falyn's A.

Dr. Luke scrawled in the margins: **While this is intriguing, you have no facts or references to back Rose's involvement in any sort of underground society. This is history class, not creative writing. I need real, historical facts, Miss Ryan.**

So much for appreciating those who think out of the box. I tried to be different and talk about a skeleton that's *actually* interesting, and Dr. Luke crossed it all out.

I sag into my seat, my stomach lurching with failure as Dr. Luke finishes handing out the essays.

"What a fucking douche," the guy behind me mutters. William, I think. "You think with his family inheritance, he'd be more forgiving, you know?"

"No shit," his friend agrees, sitting in the desk beside him. "I thought he took this job for kicks, not because he actually wanted to do it."

"*Mold our futures*," William mocks in a clogged voice. "*Nurture our minds offline, blah-blah-barf.*"

"He's the black sheep of the Stevensons," the friend adds. "His brothers are happily living off their trust funds and parties and tits. Why would you give that up for this?"

I whip around in my seat, startling William. "Did you say Stevenson?"

"Oh, hi, possum," he says.

I ignore his mocking tone. "What do you mean by that name?"

"Uh, it's his last name. Ever heard of Stevenson Banking Co.? I guess he doesn't want to be associated with it since he calls himself lame-ass Doctor Luke, but we all know it, anyway. Except for you, but what else is new."

"Stevenson," I mutter, my eyes downcast. "*Stevenson.*"

"Can you turn around now? You're creeping me out."

I blurt, "Does anyone call him Mr. S?"

"Uh ... do you call him that when you're going down on his dick? Be gone, possum."

I bare my teeth and hiss at him, which causes William to startle again like the little jack-off he is. I twist in my seat, mentally answering his rhetorical question. *I don't. But maybe Piper did.*

My stomach, feeling sick before, creates a tidal wave of nausea.

Dr. Luke stops in the front of the room, turning around with his hands interlocked behind him.

"It's quarter-term day, but do any of you think you deserve the rest of this period free to study?"

Students groan and rustle papers. Dr. Luke's gaze drops to mine, rests there for a few seconds too long, then moves on.

I swallow, an internal fire building in my cheeks.

This can't be the answer. I have to be so, so wrong, just like my essay on Rose Briar. Just like all other avenues of thought I've dead-ended since enrolling at Briarcliff. Piper's death is about the secret society. She *knew* something they didn't want revealed to the public, and Piper would've done that through our paper. The Cloaks didn't begin their stalking of me for no reason. Piper didn't hide Rose's letter for kicks. I have to be right! I HAVE TO.

My essay sags in my hand, answering my affirmations with palpable failure. Piper may have wanted to write an exposé, but Dr. Luke wouldn't have cared. He would've crossed her theories out as easily as he dismissed mine.

Unless he was fucking her as Mr. S, and he's the one who ripped out identifying pages in her diary.

No. *No*, I groan inwardly, lowering my head to my hands. I want it to be the society. It has to be Briarcliff's secrets, not something as obvious and conclusive as a teacher-student affair.

But, it makes a twisted sort of sense. Dr. Luke is the one who broke up the party at the cliff. What made him go there in the first place?

Piper.

She could've texted him. Oh my God—she could've *pretended* to go back to the dorms, when all the while she was hiding in wait for the party to end so she could see Dr. Luke!

"So, who wants to tell me about our guest of honor, Abraham Lincoln? You've all heard of him, yes?"

Dr. Luke uses his usual dry humor to keep the class's attention, his expression serene, kindness and pride in being a teacher exuding out of his pores.

As I raise my head, his wafting scent hits me like the front of a McLaren going at Mach speed, now that it has more context. I'd always associated his masculine, sandalwood scent with comfort, but I was confusing comfort with familiarity. I thought that scent belonged to Chase, but I've tasted the salt of him, and it never washes away no matter how clean he becomes.

No, I've smelled *Dr. Luke* on someone else before. A person I thought was carrying Chase's scent with her when she sat down to tell me about Rose Briar for the first time.

Piper.

Is it just me, or is there a fresh coldness behind Dr. Luke's eyes? So different from Chase's, yet similar in their sharing of ... of what? I can't grasp the word, but I know it's there.

Dr. Luke calls on Falyn, who happily gives him the answer he was looking for: "Abe Lincoln is, like, a president..."

As Dr. Luke gives off every indication of listening intently to Falyn, I slip through his cracks. I study the nuances.

And I catch the word.

Guilt.

Guilt is the darkness lying dormant behind his eyes.

Forty-Four

MY ATTEMPTS to corner Chase after history are thwarted. He leaves Dr. Luke's class with Falyn and Willow skipping behind him like he's the be-all of their existence.

Maybe he is, now that Piper's not there to redirect them.

Eden isn't in this class—heck, I never know where she is on normal occasions—so I can't corner her, and Ivy, as is her habit, has only surface-level Briarcliff gossip to impart.

Not that I don't appreciate it, but as I ask Ivy under my breath before Professor Lacey hands out the calc tests whether she knows anything about Luke Stevenson, she meets me with a blank stare.

"Who?" she asks, her legs angled toward me as we talk across the aisle.

"Dr. Luke," I say. "The history prof."

"*Oh*. The hottest teacher in our school." She mimes hitting her forehead. "Duh. What about him?"

"Does he, I dunno..." I pretend I don't care at all about what I'm about to ask, "flirt with girls in his class at all?"

"Jaysus, I wish." She guffaws. "I can guarantee every girl in the senior class has fantasized about him, but I have no idea whether any of them have done it with Dr. Luke. Why?" She leans forward. "What rumor are you trying to spread, and do you want my help?"

I laugh, but it sounds forced even to my ears. "It's nothing, but—"

"Ladies! Eyes straight ahead, please."

Ivy and I straighten at our desks as Professor Lacey reads the rules before we're allowed to open our exams.

I try my best to stay focused and answer the blur of numbers before me, but instead of equations, I see Piper's handwriting, confessing her encounters with Mr. S and how he insisted the affair be kept quiet. I'd had heavy focus on Chase or his father, but now I believe I didn't spread the net wide enough, too distracted by my gut reaction to Chase and his relationship with Piper.

Could it be true?

Dr. Luke never came off creepy or touchy-feely, and I've been alone with him. He was the teacher I turned to when questioning got rough and fingers pointed to *me* as Piper's killer. Dr. Luke exuded calm and good-naturedness, with an innate motivation to groom and be kind to his students.

I can't put him on blast by reporting my suspicions to the school. Piper's code name, Mr. S, isn't proof.

You know that's not the case. Think back to your fight with Piper.

My mouth falls into an O as I stare at my exam. During that final confrontation, Piper accused me of stealing her boyfriend. I assumed that boyfriend was Chase, but Piper never said it was. At no point did she say his name, and I was so confused at the timeline. My last encounter with Chase happened over a week before Piper screamed at me in the dining hall.

Because it was Dr. Luke. I've been alone with the teacher. I'd fallen into his arms in the hallway when I tripped on a rat. Is *that* what Piper was referring to when she accused me? My accidental trip over a corpse and into Dr. Luke?

It's possible. Piper's diary is lined with more jealousy and hate than goodwill.

I need to talk to Chase. Now.

The clocktower clangs the end of the period, and I blink back into existence, my fingers tightening against my pen when I realized I missed the final ten questions. Professor Lacey's hand comes into my vision, then retracts with my exam before I can do anything about it. I'm left with a blank desk and a cluttered mind.

"Wanna eat lunch together?" Ivy asks behind me. The dull noise of the rest of the class packing up reaches my ears. "It's mac 'n' cheese day."

"I'll meet you there."

"No worries. Come find me."

Ivy trots away, none the wiser to my paranoid convictions. I swear, every day that I dwell on Briarcliff's secrets means losing another chance at true friendship.

I beeline into the halls, taking shortcuts I'm now familiar with, catching Chase as he's about to take the stairs to the Wolf's Den.

"Chase!"

His head turns at my call, and it's with an implacable expression he mutters something to James, who bounds up the stairs ahead of him.

"What have I told you about addressing me in public?" he asks once I come to a stop in front of him.

"Sorry. Your Highness. Your Lordship. Your Majestic Prick."

Chase's eyes narrow into slits. "While I like the last one, I gave you the protection you wanted by getting people off your back during the day, but it has limits. If the girls around here heard I was banging you, the rats in your locker will look like pieces of cotton candy fluff."

"Glad to see your over-inflated ego remains intact, despite lowering yourself to *banging* me." I wave his cutting retort away. "I'll worry about headless Barbie dolls stuffed in my locker tomorrow. What I have to say is important."

I grab him by the elbow until we're under the stairs and out of view to the students headed to lunch.

"What's so important that it couldn't wait until tonight? I had plans for you after crew." The shadows under the staircase assist in shading his eyes with desire.

Ignoring the inevitable pull my nipples seem to feel toward him, I say in a low voice, "I think I've figured out who Mr. S is."

His chest concaves with an exasperated sigh.

"I think it's Dr. Luke."

Chase waits a beat. "And?"

"And?" I give him a smack. He doesn't flinch or move at the contact. "I think he was having an affair with Piper!"

I manage to get a startled eye-blink out of him. "What?"

"Yes! Piper used a codename for the guy she was having an affair with, and it's been driving me crazy because it has to be important, and the police never brought up anything about Piper having a secret boyfriend—"

"Hold. Hold up." Chase raises a hand, and I shut my mouth, but not because he asked me to. Because he never stutters. "I never did ask you where you heard that name. And I thought the police were keeping it under wraps after they questioned me. Motive evidence, they called it. And why ... why am I only hearing about the affair shit now?"

"Because..." I squeeze the back of my neck, needing something to do. "I ... read her diary."

I'm met with silence, but I'm afraid to raise my eyes.

Chase's question is tight with restraint. "What. Diary."

"There was one hidden in her mattress. Nobody saw it, not even her family when they cleaned out her room, and—"

"Show it to me."

"I can't."

A second beat of silence. The school orchestra could be marching by in full practice mode, and I wouldn't hear it, so tunneled are my ears to Chase's every twitch. "Why not?"

"I ... gave it to the police."

Chase's silence contains the pressure to move the tectonic plates beneath our feet. It's deadly, powerful, and I'm at his mercy. He asks, "And you didn't make a copy?"

"I did, on my phone. But it was stolen from me the day ... well, my mom. Whoever it was also broke into my room and deleted it off the cloud on my laptop."

Nothing but breath escapes between us, but I'm hit with an utter need to fill our space. I step into his comfort zone, clutching his hands, though they remain stiff at his side. I search his face for any emotion other than a cruel blankness. Anything.

I say, "I'm sorry I kept it from you, but it can't come as a surprise. You and I, we share what we want to, when it conveniences us. That's how it's been these past weeks, and I promise, I'm growing to trust you. I know you didn't hurt Piper, but..."

Chase's unblinking gaze centers on me. "You don't trust me."

"That's not—"

"I trusted you enough to tell you about my sister."

"Chase, I told you about finding my mother. But this was never a quid pro quo—"

Chase cocks his head and breathes cold fire onto my lips. "Wasn't it? What stopped you from telling me about your friend who OD'd? Or the shit that went down with your dad?"

I stare at him.

"I read all about it, Callie ... how you and this chick went to a party and her coke was laced with Fentanyl and she almost died. Her parents blamed you, but it was a freak miracle that you didn't snort the same shit she did and end up just like her."

I swallow. Excuses won't come, because my mind's too busy flashing back to a lifeless Sylvie who only had me to give her drunken, shrieking CPR until someone thought to call 9-1-1.

"That's not what interested me most about you, though," Chase continues, rounding his sentence in soft tones, but the words are hard. "You accused your stepdad of your mom's murder."

I wince. "You're angry I didn't tell you about Piper's diary. Fine. But don't throw my past at me like it's your weapon to wield."

He ignores me. "You must've been so convincing, with those big, honeyed eyes of yours. The police believed you for a long time, didn't they? You had that detective on your side..."

"Ahmar," I rasp.

"Yes!" Chase snaps his fingers with enunciated conviction. "You raked your dad over some hot fucking coals pretty good. Ruined his rep. Had him arrested for a time, and when he came out, he had to deal with your involvement in an overdose. And all because of what, Callie?"

His tone is mocking, unreal. I'm desperate to cover my ears. "Stop," I whisper again.

"All because of *you*. You almost ruined a man's life over a hunch. You two don't have the same relationship now, do you? It's why you're here and not with him."

"Chase, I mean it."

"You fly after theories you pull from the sky. You drive yourself insane with your unsupported convictions. Didn't your dad put you in a psychiatric hold once he proved his innocence and he untangled you from your friend's near-death? Because you'd lost it?"

Scalding, unshed tears blind my vision. Clog my throat. "That's not..."

"What is it you think you're doing now? Is making Piper's death into a mystery your next psychotic break? Quit while you're ahead, Callie." Chase widens his eyes theatrically. "Stop the madness."

"You're sick," I say through my trembling jaw. "How dare you cut me down like this, after we—"

"Fucked? Yeah. Maybe I've gotten all I wanted out of you."

I ignore the sting. "Is this another diversion tactic of yours? To push me away from the truth?" I search his eyes, praying he sees me. The *real* me. "Who are you protecting, Chase?"

He laughs cruelly. "There you go again."

My fingers clench on his slack ones. "You don't mean that."

"Oh, I do, sweet possum. Thanks for the fucks. It's been real." He pulls away.

"Chase, stop."

"I appreciate you deeming me important enough to hear your latest theory. I'll see what I can do."

I flinch. "Wait."

But he's stalking away, like he always does, and I wish I had the strength to grab him by his infuriating Briarcliff blazer and throw him across the ground like he did with Riordan.

But Chase has already done that. Twice.

Because now he's made a tire mark out of my heart.

Another gloppy, cheesy macaroni noodle falls from my fork.

"Dude, you need to eat that quick," Ivy says around a mouthful of her lunch. "Even fancy, overprivileged mac 'n' cheese goes gummy if left out for too long."

"Not hungry."

"Since when? On the rare occasions you're actually in the dining hall, you turn into a hiker lost in the wilderness for three days when food's in front of you."

I push my plate back, leaning against the chair with a sigh. I can't help but search the dining hall, despite being perfectly aware of what I'll find. Or what I *won't*.

No Chase. Anywhere.

"Then we need to improve upon the source of your energy," Ivy says. "Since biology is next period, and Professor Dawson is no joke."

I'm far away from the importance of exams. It's maddening, considering how hard I used to study, but not as gut-wrenching as facing Chase's accusations, like it's my fault I've kept Piper's diary from him.

It has *nothing* to do with my stepdad.

Nothing to do with Sylvie.

One may have been an accident and the other wrong, but I was right to suspect him. It was a given that I'd put my entire being into avenging my mother.

Chase keeps so much from me. He has secrets that could fill the entire library built by his devious sire, and I'm meant to feel guilty for shoving my possession of Piper's diary in the most private drawer I have? Chase knows everything about me— too much. He's exposed my mind the way he's worshipped my body. He's ... he's felt my heartbeat.

"Callie? You okay?"

"I ... I don't feel well. I'm gonna go lay down before class starts again."

"Don't be late. Dawson won't let you through the door if you're one second past the bell."

"I'll be there. Swear," I say to Ivy, then stumble through the aisles between tables, lightheaded and sore.

Extra energy balls up tight behind my chest. It's desperate to be expelled, but my body is too sluggish to let it. What is this? What's wrong with me?

Heartbreak. It's called heartbreak, sweetie.

I squeeze my temples and scrunch my eyes to rid my mom's voice from my head. It's not real. She's not here, so why must she become my inner voice? I don't want her echoes. I want my *mom*. She'd have the correct answers. She'd hold me as I cried over a boy.

I come close to breaking my nose as I storm around a blind corner. At the last second, I jolt back from the trophy case, leaving smeared fingerprints on the spotless glass.

I almost smashed into the case by Marron's office, and I glance around with an unbalanced waver to my steps, hoping no one witnessed my moment of weakness, or put it on their phone.

The hidden crest, its motto carved in iron, still rests behind a rowing trophy from 1821. The half-wing I can see, spread to the tip of the circle, has those words, the ones so familiar yet impossible to grasp, scored into its feathers.

altum volare in tenebris

My phone's at the dorm, so I can't translate it. Instead, I squint at the writing, hoping I've committed it to memory to decipher it later.

Thump.

Something heavy thuds against the wall behind the trophy case. I jump, but I don't run.

Bang.

A shatter follows from inside the office opposite Marron's, glass breaking.

Human grunts ripple into the air, the last one more laced with pain than the first.

I glance around with wide eyes, then sprint toward the sounds of struggle, and when I stop at the office where the noises come from, I read the nameplate.

"Shit!" I cry, then burst through the door.

Forty-Five

"CHASE! CHASE, *STOP*!"

My yells go unnoticed as two men—Dr. Luke and Chase—grapple for leverage in Dr. Luke's office.

Books have toppled from the shelves. Dr. Luke's desk lamp lies shattered and flickering with exposed electricity on the ground by their feet. Picture frames are crooked on the walls, and one even has blood spray next to it.

A frantic search of both their faces reveals Dr. Luke with a blood-soaked eye. A cut leaks from his eyebrow, and Chase ... Chase is clean-shaven and flawless with his hands around Dr. Luke's neck.

"*Chase*!" I burst forward, gripping one of his arms, but it's like climbing an oak tree out back. Immobile and entrenched.

Dr. Luke's back arches over his desk as Chase bends him at an unnatural angle, teeth bared and saliva dripping, resembling the very wolf Briarcliff touts as its mascot.

"Listen to me. Chase, listen!" I say, my heart pounding in tandem to my words. I attempt to get into his view, but he's channeled his focus into Dr. Luke and is no longer programmed to look anywhere else.

"He can't talk if you strangle him to death!" I say, pulling at Chase's arm despite the uselessness of it. "Chase, look at what you're doing!"

I slip between him and Dr. Luke, between Chase's rigid, jointless arms, and push at his chest. Dr. Luke gurgles behind me, clutching at my shirt, pulling at my hair, begging for help.

"You're killing him!" I scream. "*You're killing him!*"

Chase blinks. His eyes become focused. He glances down at me, the brown of his irises clearing.

He releases Dr. Luke without warning, who sags behind me and nearly takes me down with him. Chase hooks my waist and pulls me into a safer zone, then stands in front of me as a shield.

Not that Dr. Luke appears to be able to do anything but gurgle at the moment.

"You fucked her," Chase spits. Literally. He lobs a loogie onto Dr. Luke's panting chest. "Then you killed her."

Dr. Luke stares at us, sweat and blood dripping from his brows, his button-down shirt torn and sprinkled with blood, both from his nose and forehead. "Mr. Stone, I did not—"

Chase kicks him in the gut. I screech at Chase, pulling him back. "Are you out of your *mind*? What are we supposed to do now, huh? You attacked a *teacher*, Chase. You—"

"What evidence do you have, buddy?" Dr. Luke regains the breath to spit blood, then smile a toothy grin rimmed in red. Chase doesn't respond. He glares at Dr. Luke with such unearthly promise, I have renewed terror over what he's capable of.

"Just as I thought," Dr. Luke rasps. "You have nothing."

"She wrote about you."

Dr. Luke's eyelids flutter. He licks the top row of his teeth, his only reaction to my voice. "Did she now?"

"Explicitly," I continue. "Down to your nightly meet-ups on school grounds. She had a diary."

Dr. Luke stares at me from his place on the ground.

"And I found it."

Chase keeps still beside me.

"You told her to wait for you after the party ended at Lover's Leap, didn't you?" I ask. "For her to act drunk and pretend to go back to the dorms, when really, she found a place to hide until you came along, broke up the party, then met up with her."

"What a silly detective you'd make, Miss Ryan."

Chase's mockery over my dad echoes in the shells of my ears, but I stand with conviction. "You're the cool teacher, the one kids respect the most. If you were the teacher to break up the party, Briarcliff students would listen, because you'd promise you'd keep their secret, so long as they cleaned up and made it look like they were never there in the first place."

"She's right," Chase drawls. "We listened, didn't we, Teach? But you didn't walk back with us."

Dr. Luke's eyes slide over to Chase's. "So, I'm a nice guy. I've been where you are, Mr. Stone. The power of popularity is electric, isn't it? But I got my ass reamed for allowing the gathering to disperse without punishment. You have it entirely wrong. I almost lost my position here, and it's not because I slept with a student. It's because she died while apparently under my off-duty supervision. And you two," Dr. Luke growls, then coughs, "are in so much goddamned trouble for this."

"What makes you think you're not under police watch?" I lie. "What if, the minute I found the diary, I took it to Detective Haskins?"

Which ... I kinda did.

Dr. Luke grunts. "Then you wouldn't've been brought in for questioning over your own involvement, Miss Ryan."

I smile. "You didn't let me finish. What if it was all a ruse? A way to get your guard down, to make you feel safe? Intelligent killers don't just *confess*. You have to give them a reason. Make them comfortable enough to make a mistake."

Dr. Luke glances between me and Chase. "You're full of shit."

I *am*, but he doesn't need to know that.

He points. "Whatever you two are concocting, it's on the wrong side of the law. You assaulted me, Mr. Stone, and you are aiding and abetting, Miss Ryan."

I fake a loud snort. "Who? Me and him?" I thumb over to Chase. "You think we're in cahoots? I hate him, Dr. Luke. You've seen how he's treated me. Like roadkill on his shoe since the day I walked in here. Piper's death didn't change that. Just this morning he made me well aware of the disgust he has toward me."

My voice cracks at the end, and Chase's gaze moves to me, his brief survey unreadable in my periphery, but I see his eyelids flicker, maybe, *maybe* with remorse.

"Plus, our methods are different." I exert all my efforts to stay cold, calculated, and unengaged with the boy I'm falling for. "I didn't want to come in here and beat the shit out of you, Dr. Luke. I just want the truth. I'm a lot like my mother that way."

"Punching him in the face is the quickest way to reach that goal," Chase murmurs, his survey moving to Dr. Luke. He raises his fist. "Shall I continue?"

"I broke up the party and let you assholes go, since any sort of delinquency report is shredded, or forgotten, or deleted," Dr. Luke snarls. "This is what I get for trying to do the right thing when I should've just left you all to drink and smoke yourselves off the damn cliff. I've never, in my entire career, had inappropriate relations with a *student—*"

Chase kicks Dr. Luke in the teeth.

"Chase—" I begin, but Chase throws up his hand to me and takes one step closer to Dr. Luke.

"Callie may be trying for diplomacy here, but you and I both know that's not going to work," he says to Dr. Luke, sputtering on the ground. "Not with men like you. Did you kill Piper Harrington?"

"No—!"

Crunch.

Chase steps down on Dr. Luke's knee, crushing it at such an angle that I make silent gagging noises behind him. Dr. Luke squeals, becoming less and less human to me the further Chase's torture goes.

"I'll ask again ... did you kill Piper Harrington?"

"Christ, boy, how did your parents raise you—"

Pop.

Dr. Luke cries out as his knee's dislocated, and I step forward, unshed tears in my eyes. I'm all for catching Piper's killer, but not like this. Not through someone's physical breaking point...

"Fine! Jesus, fine! I met with her, okay? I saw her that night *to fucking dump her!*"

I freeze with my arm in midair, aiming for Chase's shoulder to pull him back.

Chase lowers his chin. "Continue."

I've never seen Chase this cold and unmoving. Like his sole purpose in life is to hurt and maim to get what he wants, and he's not about to lose any sleep over it.

It unnerves me. Forms a fissure in my heart.

203

"We had an affair, okay? Get off. Get off my leg. *Please*."

Dr. Luke's begging now, his confession turning into sobs as Chase increases the pressure before he releases his foot, Dr. Luke curling into a fetal position on the ground as soon as he does.

In need for balance, comfort ... steadiness, I hold onto Chase's elbow, staring not at Dr. Luke whimpering on the ground, but at Chase.

"Chase," I whisper, unnamed fear curling at the base of my throat. The longer I watch him breathe, the more that fear gains meaning and takes advantage of that meaner, hidden part of me that's grown her fangs these past two years.

"Did you steal my phone?" I ask Dr. Luke, starting off soft.

"Why ... would I take ... a fucking teenager's phone?"

"Because it had sections of Piper's diary in it."

"Oh." Dr. Luke's head moves with a clogged chuckle, then he winces. "Might've. You were looking good for Piper's death, too, Callie."

"Did you record my fight with Piper? Did you plant those pictures of my *mom*?" I put one foot forward, my voice as tumultuous and rough as my step.

"Record...?" Dr. Luke squints up at me with added strain to his expression. "What about your mom? This is about ... Piper, no? And finding her killer? She didn't jump, did she? She was pushed."

Shadows cross his eyes, unrelated to impending unconsciousness. I fixate harder. "Did you do it?"

"Do *what*?"

"Hit him again, Chase." I'm shocked—and terrifyingly satisfied—to say those words.

Chase isn't told twice. He slams Dr. Luke's head into his desk with an open palm, rattling Dr. Luke enough that he spits off obscenities.

"I'll ask again, did you spread pictures of my mother all over my room to stop me from figuring out it was you? Then stole my phone?"

"What? I used Piper for a lay. You got that? She acted all sweet, and cute, and desperate for my attention, and if you'd had the life I've had, you'd understand I couldn't help but fall for a girl like that. Then she tells me she wants to work it out with Mr. Punch-a-Thon over there. Piper wanted to continue fucking me *and* shack up with your psychopath of a boyfriend. What a sad sight you are, Callie. I had higher hopes for you."

I ignore the swipe. "You killed her for dumping your ass."

"I can't say she didn't get what was coming to her," Dr. Luke spits with a copious amount of venom. "She was a *slut*. Am I right, Mr. Stone? A fucking—"

Slam.

Well. I could've predicted that much.

Dr. Luke cowers, covering his jaw against another blow from Chase's heel.

But Dr. Luke won't stop. "How many guys did she fuck, eh buddy? We were two of many. She manipulated, used her beauty, and fed off my dick like a goddamned succubus. Men in this world are better off without a girl like that." Dr. Luke's lips peel back in a gaping, blood-soaked smile. "I was cutting my losses that night."

Chase punches him again.

"Chase, no!" I shout.

"What in God's name is—Luke? *Lucas?*"

Headmaster Marron bursts in, folding his body over Dr. Luke and placing a hand on his shoulder. Once he assesses the situation, he glares up at us.

"If you were aiming for expulsion, Mr. Stone, consider that the tip of the iceberg of penalty that's about to fall upon you. And you, Miss Ryan, I cannot believe the lengths you've gone to prove how much you do not belong here."

Chase doesn't blink. "Tell him, *Lucas*, what you told us."

Dr. Luke nurses his cheek, keeping his eyes closed as he moans.

"Marron's presence will *not* prevent a kick to the balls," Chase growls.

"Mister *Stone!*" Marron cries, aghast.

"I had an affair with her!" Dr. Luke gasps. "Just get that boy away from me. Get them away. Please. Please!"

"Lucas, what...?" Marron rips his attention away from us.

"With Piper Harrington!" Dr. Luke continues, "We had an affair."

"I..." Marron trails off. "Lucas, you're not of sound mind at the moment—"

"I did it! I met with her that night! I didn't 'catch' those kids doing anything. I knew they were there. At the cliff. She called me. Piper hid until everyone was gone, and I waited to see her. But it was to break up. I wanted to end it." Dr. Luke sobs. "But I didn't ... just tell them to stop!"

"Well, howdy, people. How are we all doing?" Detective Haskins says as he gnaws on a toothpick, standing in the doorframe and taking in the scene.

"Detective, I ... this is a formal matter," Marron stutters, attempting to rise.

"Nope, it ain't. I heard it all. Thank you for the tip, Callie."

All eyes, even the bruised ones, turn to me. I nod at Haskins, but I have no idea what he means.

Haskins pulls at the handcuffs clipped to his waist, flicking them open. "*Doctor Lucas Stevenson*, you're under arrest for suspicion of sexual relations with a minor..."

Chase drifts closer to the door, and so do I, but Haskins pauses in his reading of Miranda rights to snap, "You two go nowhere. I have questions once back-up arrives." Haskins's gaze zeroes in on Chase. "A *lot* of goddamn questions."

Haskins's questioning over what occurred in Dr. Luke's office went on for hours. There was the matter of notifying, then getting, my stepdad and Lynda on FaceTime ... again. There was the problem of locating Chase's parents. We each needed a guardian present, and since my former ad hoc guardian was on his way to the hospital in handcuffs, Professor Dawson became my righthand man.

Luckily, the questions weren't as pressing as before, or as suspicious. Haskins, while heading to his meeting with Headmaster Marron, heard the end of the exchange between Dr. Luke and Marron, where Dr. Luke confessed to the affair. He didn't witness how Dr. Luke received so many bruises or a dislocated knee, and I was forced to speak to some of that. I asked if charges were going to be pressed against Chase. Haskins wouldn't expand on an answer.

I told him all I could, what I saw, and what I knew. Feeling terrible at having participated in such violence, I confessed to holding Piper's diary longer than I should have and was prepared for whatever punishment would follow. I couldn't keep the knowledge of Mr. S to myself, not once it led to Chase's impromptu beat-down of a teacher.

"Like an obstruction of justice charge?" Haskins asks, amused as we sit in Professor Dawson's office. My stepdad's silent and fuming face is on the computer monitor, also awaiting my response.

"I had every intention of turning it over to the police," I say lamely. "Which is why I went into town and—"

"Just got it this morning. What a coincidence. It's the reason I was on campus at lunch and meeting Marron."

Haskins's blunt statement brings my head up. "Sorry?"

"You sent the diary to the police station as soon as you found it. That's what your accompanying letter says anyway."

"I ... I see." My brows twist, and I glance to the side, the implications of Haskins's statement pounding against my temples.

"Uh-huh. You also insist you found it as-is and know nothing about the pages that are missing."

I'm caught between a truth and a lie, and I have the sense that the lie is what will save me.

I didn't give them anything this morning. I mailed the diary weeks ago...

I swallow. "Right. Yes."

"Gotta say, I appreciate the apology flowers. Unnecessary, but the letter explained how contrite you were to have found the journal yesterday and read it, but that you made the connection to this ... Mr. S ... right away. As it happens, we already recorded this alleged code name. One of our witnesses mentioned it to us a while ago. But I appreciate your shrewdness."

I try for a humble smile and not one that trembles so hard it'll fall off my face. "You don't have to explain any further, Detective. I know what I wrote."

I didn't write anything when I sealed the diary in the envelope. Someone must've intercepted it before it got to the precinct. Intercepted and ... used this time to doctor up a letter and a lie.

"Yes," Haskins says, his stare never leaving mine. "I'm sure you do."

"If I may ask, what sort of bouquet did the flower shop choose?" I fist a hand into my stomach as I lean forward, popping the acidic bubbles building in my gut. "I requested that it be whatever they thought best for an ... apology."

"Roses."

I keep my voice light. "How nice. What color?"

"White. Beautiful, I must say, in an office of mostly gray cubicles. Our receptionist certainly appreciates it."

"I'm so glad." I fold my hands, hiding the pounding pulse at my wrists. *The Cloaks intercepted my mail.* "I hope they got my request for an ebony ribbon around the vase."

"They did," Haskins says, then snaps his notebook shut. "I appreciate your candor, Miss Ryan, though, next time, just come in with the evidence and be honest.

You're not gonna be arrested for handing it over." Haskins turns to the computer screen. "And you, Mr. Spencer, thanks for jumping on a call without notice."

"Happy to," my stepdad's canned voice responds. He cuts a look over to me. "We'll talk later, Callie."

"Yep," I say, eager to be out of here. It's difficult to look at Dad's expression so soon after Chase brought our unresolved conflict back to the surface.

"Detective?" I ask as Professor Dawson starts leading me to the door.

"Mm?"

"Did Dr. Luke do it? Did he kill Piper?"

"I can't talk to you about the specifics of the investigation, Callie."

"I know, but ... cop instinct. What's your gut telling you?"

Haskins raises his eyes, a knowing twinkle in them. "You know, I never got the chance to say it to you, but I'm sorry about your mother. It's terrible, what you went through as a result."

"Yes," I say, but I don't want to get into Sylvie or my dad. I turn for the door.

"As for your question," Haskins adds, and I pause. "Yeah. I think we nailed him. Sleep easier, will you?"

I respond with a closed-mouth smile, then leave Professor Dawson's office with his droll warning to try and stay out of trouble for at least twenty-four hours.

Forty-Six

"CALLIE! CALLIE, WAIT UP!"

I walk faster on the path outside the main building.

"Hey! Callie!"

My steps quicken, eager to escape the voice.

"*Possum!*"

That brings me to heel. I spin, showing my teeth. "Our fucked-up Bonnie and Clyde moment is over, Chase. Get away from me."

"Not a chance," Chase huffs out as he jogs the rest of the distance between us. His cheeks are pink from the chill in the air, his hair mussed and adorable, and every bit of it infuriates me.

No one should look this perfect after a beat-down *and* a police interrogation. Not even a princely Stone heir.

"You okay?" he asks.

"Dandy. I feel nothing but joy over the stunt you pulled." I stare hard at the clotted cuts on his knuckles, then turn to leave.

He hooks me by the elbow. "Wait."

"For what?" I snap. "For you to decide what to do with me now that we found your girlfriend's killer? After I've given you all that you wanted? That's what this was, wasn't it? I was just a vessel of possible evidence that you fucked to keep happy until I weakened enough to tell you what I knew."

"You're not mad about how I fucked you," he responds. "I've tasted how hard I make you come. You're pissed about what I said about your dad."

That earns him a smack in the gut, which is like fine bones meeting hard concrete.

"I was a goddamn *dare* to you, asshole!" I scream, then sweep my gaze over him. "You don't get to repeat my past like it's an advantage you have over me. You have no idea—*none*—of what it was like to see your mom murdered and think that your stepdad was the—was the—" My voice strains. I hitch in breaths. I have to get away from this.

"Okay. It was bad form." He spins me back around by the shoulder when I twist to stalk off. "Callie, come on."

"No! You know what I hate the most? That you're probably right." I trip over my words. "The Nobles, the Virtues, Rose Briar—it's not my secret to tell. They—*you*—made it clear when you stole Piper's diary from the town mailbox and trussed it up with roses and ribbons. Tell them I got the message."

Chase cocks a brow. "Come again?"

A strangled cry releases from my throat at his utter obtuseness. I push at his chest. "*They* sent it to the police. Your secret society. Not me. To show me who's in control and their power to make or break me. Isn't that how you termed it? You win. I won't meddle in their shit and I'll forget everything I know about them, so leave me alone."

"Callie." Chase's voice softens as mine spikes with hysteria. "I'm sorry."

I'm so outside of my usual self, I don't register the rare apology coming out of him. "What if I was *wrong*, huh? What if Dr. Luke wasn't Mr. S? What if the Nobles decided to protect him and not me? This is what's driving me crazy—I don't know if they're good or bad. They keep doing both. You would've beaten an innocent man—a teacher—and gotten kicked out of Briarcliff. Worse, you could've been arrested. And it would've been because of me. Again."

Chase frowns. "But you weren't. He was the guy."

I recoil. "How could you believe that? Based just on what I said?"

"Because you're you, Callie. You kept Piper's diary from me until you were convinced he hurt her. Killed her. And besides that, I wouldn't have been booted from Briarcliff." He scoffs. "My father simply wouldn't allow it."

"I ... I..." I raise my hand, palm forward. "I can't find the words for this. For *you*. Why won't you mention the Nobles at all? Is it because you won't? Or *can't*?"

Chase sets his jaw. A few seconds pass, silence I'm certain he won't fill, and my heart collapses.

I turn to leave.

"What I said under the stairs ... I've been trying to protect you," Chase says. "Your issues with your dad and your friend, it was wrong of me to throw them in your face. But you have to know, powerful people have access to it."

"Like your father?" I bite out.

Chase's implacable expression doesn't change even when he agrees with me. "He's one of them."

If I hadn't witnessed Chase's unleashing, his pure intent at defending Piper and tangentially, his sister, I'd think this apology was more of his crafted bullshit, wrapped up in a contrite, carefully placed, bow.

Except, I've seen what undulates behind his flawless bronze.

"I'm not *like* you," I say. "I can't beat a man to tears—even an awful one—then leave the scene with a bounce to my step. I can't make another person feel the way—the way you made me *feel*—and use the worst parts of them to satisfy a secret society agenda. I don't feed off people's emotions until they're nothing but husks of themselves." My voice breaks. "You made my position clear once I told you about Piper's diary. I was rat-shit to you after that. You squeezed my heart until it burst in your hands, then left without a second look."

Chase's expression grows dark. "Stop putting words in my mouth."

"Do I have it wrong, then? Were you not walking away from me for good?"

Chase's cheek muscle tics, his single response.

My heart drops to my feet, as useless an organ as it ever was when it comes to choosing the right guy. "That's what I thought."

"I walked away for different reasons," he says, "and if you'll let me talk for half a second, then maybe—"

"You don't deserve half a *milli*second, with the way you've—"

"Callie—"

"You've had your fun at my expense. Our mystery is solved. If you want to tell all your friends what a sorry lay I am, how a former psych patient has been in their midst this entire time, fine. Just take your Noble hounds *off* my scent. Tell them to stop fucking with me, and I'll stay quiet."

"Would you just—"

"Don't worry, I didn't breathe a word to anybody how much you lowered your standards. Your popularity status is intact. We never have to—"

I'm lifted off my feet. His fingers barrel into the soft skin of my upper arms. And he crushes his lips against mine.

"Have you ever thought," he growls after he pulls us apart, "that it isn't *me* who lowered my standards?"

"That's ... that's absurd," I stutter. "I'm not stupid. You used me to avenge Piper. I didn't think about the consequences of how we'd end, how it would affect me—"

His mouth molds with mine, his fire melting my iron with nothing but a match's flame.

That's the kind of hold Chase has over me, and it tilts my world until it's on his axis.

His lips move over my own, his tongue dipping out to taste, then retreating. "Is this cold to you?"

No. You're the danger of blue fire. "It's wrong." I breathe the words into his mouth. "It was stupid to ever let you into my bed."

Chase pulls back again, the merest of inches spaced between us. "Why couldn't you just assume I was pissed over the fact you kept her diary from me for so long and lashed out?" he says, gliding a finger down my cheek. "And that I wasn't doing anyone's bidding and leaving you for trash under the stairs?"

"Because that's not how you operate," I say. "You made that clear when we met. And every other time we slept together."

He smiles, his eyes like chocolate melting through his lashes. "That's a solid amount of times."

I feign an attempt to get out of his hold. Chase is weakening my defenses, and I rein in the yearning to punch him for it. "You're following someone's orders."

Chase grows serious. "There's no one but me and you. Some kind of shift in my reality happened when I met you. And I'm not talking about death and destruction following both of our lives. Or maybe I am. I see the darkness in you, Callie, and maybe I like it. I was beside you when that part of you took over with Dr. Luke.

Perhaps, I enjoy it more than any of the other hollowed-out, happy girls who've skipped into my path, then walked away limping." He tucks a piece of hair behind my ear. "Your past with your dad, I haven't told a soul. There's a strength in you, like you can withstand the rusted and mangled pieces inside me."

"You're dangerous," I whisper, remembering how he looked when he beat up Dr. Luke. How he *felt* in my grip when he did it, cold and unyielding.

He may be content that Piper found her justice, but where will that energy go now? Where will Chase direct the curse of his endless anger that he keeps in a block of ice inside his soul? His sister's unsolved case? Or ... does he want to place it in me, for safekeeping, instead?

Chase responds without hesitation. "You're my compass, Callie. Redirect me."

"I'm no one's morality beacon."

"Didn't say you were. Now." His hands fall to my lower arms, squeezing. "Can we try for a truce? Or if you don't want that," he adds when I open my mouth, "can we fuck the angst out?"

"Chase..."

He brings my hand to his pants, and I feel the length there, the growing hardness that mirrors the throbbing at my core.

"Tell me that finding Piper's killer, that putting it to rest and beating the police to the punch, doesn't turn you on," he says, and my stomach lurches at the truth of it. "I'm so fucking glad he's caught. So *pumped* I got to lay him out, but it wasn't enough. I need to expend this ... this firebolt inside me, Callie. I need *you*."

It will never be enough, I try to say, but can't.

Maybe Chase has a point. I'm as dark as he says I am, and like recognizes like.

"We're in public," is the meager defense I can come up with.

"Then let's make it private."

Chase takes me by the hand and leads me the rest of the way to Thorne House. I won't say we're holding hands, because that's not what this is. His grip is too powerful, his physical intent too direct. We're not showing affection in public. Rather, he's demonstrating to the scattered students outside that I'm his. Those people will tell their friends, who will tell *their* friends, and on it will go, until it reaches the entire school's ears. Not even the scandal of Dr. Luke is sufficient to distract from Chase's claim of ownership.

Don't mess with Callie. She's Chase's now.

She's the Nobles' prize.

But, I can't be hasty. Chase's attention and the Nobles' protection, however surface-level, could provide me with the time to finish out the year.

And discover the truth behind the secret society.

I tell myself that's what I want as we race to my dorm room, our classes long over and dinner a passing afterthought. I focus on the unveiling of secrets instead of the hard certainty of my downfall planting its seed at the base of my skull.

The buzzing of my phone pulls my awareness to the surface, tugging with the type of urgency shaking me awake would.

"What time is it?" I mutter, the cold air of my room hitting my body as I sit up and scrub my eyes.

I'm shivering more than usual and realize I'm naked and just left the comfort of the warm, hard form beside mine.

Chase.

My phone goes silent. I figure it was Ivy blowing up my phone again with her shocked emojis and exclamations once news hit that Dr. Luke was arrested for Piper's murder.

But Chase is here. In my bed. We screwed our brains out and fell asleep. And he ... stayed.

He's never done that before. I don't cover my awe as I memorize the planes of his face, dewy with moonlight, his lashes casting long shadows under his closed eyes.

Chase is softer in slumber. His full lips are supple with dreams, his brows smoothed by the removal of reality.

The buzzing starts up again, and I snatch my phone off the nightstand, reluctant to wake him.

"Hello?" I whisper without checking the ID.

"Calla? Hey, sweetie. Did I wake you?"

"No. It's okay," I say to Ahmar while delicately sliding out of bed. I creep into the main room and shut my door with a soft click.

"I'm sorry to call you so late. There was a gang murder in the Bronx, and I was caught up in that, couldn't get to my messages until later. And, well ... you've had some criminal fun since we last spoke. You good?"

"Fine. Great." I can't help but glance at my closed door with the knowledge of who sleeps on the opposite side. "Piper's killer was caught."

"I know. I heard your voicemail. The fuckin' teacher, huh? What a turd."

"It's shocking." My gaze skirts away from my door, remembering how fury transformed Chase's face when I told him of Piper's affair. That she was having sex with someone else.

Quit it, Callie. It's never like you thought you could have his heart along with the sex.

But it still feels vacant inside my chest.

"Guess you don't need any digging from me, then. I'm sorry I didn't come up with much. It's been nothing but crime sprees over here."

"That's okay. Maybe if you could keep me updated on the process Dr. Luke's gonna go through," I say, perching delicately on my couch. I'm butt naked, after all. I pull a throw blanket over my legs as I talk. The shivering doesn't abate. "So, I can make sure he stays where he should. Did you find anything at all that points to him? There's his confession, but, I dunno, it could be argued it was made under duress..."

Ahmar chuckles. "Always your momma's daughter. Wanting the hard evidence, never the statements."

I'm ecstatic we figured out Piper's killer, but strangely disappointed that Dr. Luke's reasons had nothing to do with secret societies or Briarcliff history. Shouldn't I be relieved that Piper's killer was so obvious, once the connection was made?

But, the stealing of my phone, the interception of Piper's diary, using the distraction of horrendous photos ... it was all them, not Dr. Luke. It has to be, and I'm not crazy for thinking that.

Or is that my desperation coming through?

"I gotta say, Calla, I didn't find much." Ahmar sighs into the phone. "Though I tried, kiddo. Called all the connections I have over in Rhode Island. I did get to reading the coroner's report, though, before it's been made public."

"Oh?"

"It's sensitive information, but I know I can trust you and you got my back. Right?"

"Yeah, of course." Ahmar's like the dad I never had. He can trust me with anything.

"It'll come out once this Luke guy is finished with processing. The victim, your roommate, the girl..."

"Piper," I nudge.

"Yeah. This all goes toward the airtight motive of an affair and spurned love."

"What is it?" I ask.

"Well ... Piper was pregnant. Once DNA comes in on the fetus, that'll be a strong case against your teacher..."

I don't hear anything else Ahmar says, though he rattles off sentences. The roaring dread in my ears won't let me.

I'm frozen, naked, and shivering, and I can't stop staring at my closed door.

Chase is there, sleeping soundly due to an exhilarating round of sex, where he showed me his skills, his prowess, and the utter addiction he's become in my bed.

And Piper was pregnant.

What about Chase?
<u>Sign up</u> to receive exclusive bonus chapters from Chase's point-of-view, only available to Ketley's subscribers.

Virtue

One

THE AFTERNOON SUN shimmers against the landscaped grass behind the academy and a cool, autumnal wind pulls at the loose strands of my kinky brown waves I'd attempted to tame into a ponytail this morning. The maroon ribbon I'd tied around it flaps against the side of my cheek before getting caught in my lip gloss, which I'm pretty sure is a sign I shouldn't be here.

Heck, if the wind so much as shifts, I'm taking that as solid proof that this is a terrible idea, and I'm turning right around and—

"Callie. Hey, you came."

Ivy separates herself from the crowd of students milling in the center of the quad where an elaborate stone fountain spurts water out of a rearing wolf's mouth, the rest of his pack keening beneath the curve of his majestic form.

"I didn't think it'd be right if I avoided it," I say to Ivy once she reaches me. Her pale blue eyes cloud with concern, but she hooks my elbow and drags me into the fray.

"Probably not," she agrees, and to my horror, ushers us to the front.

"Ivy, I'm not sure I—"

"Nonsense. If you're going to be here, you might as well put face-time in."

"Actually, I was hoping for the opposite."

"Why?" She spins to face me, her baby blues turning cold. "You didn't *do* anything. Not to Piper, not to anyone. Why shouldn't you be present for her birthday memorial?"

It's been twelve days since Dr. Luke was put in handcuffs, and the professors agreed that enough time has passed to lessen the trauma of violently losing a student and watching a beloved teacher be arrested for it. They decided the best way to honor Piper's life is to do it on her birthday. Because hers falls on a Saturday this year, the headmaster thought it would be better to hold the service on the Friday before, since on weekends, pupils are less likely to show up.

Oh, and did I not mention that today happens to be *my* birthday?

"Now that Piper's killer has been caught," Ivy continues, "any suspicion over your involvement should be long gone, don't you think? I mean, *you* didn't push her off Lover's Leap. Dr. Luke did."

Ivy's opinion seems to ricochet off the surrounding stone and into each nearby student's ears, and my cheeks burn as heads swivel to the source, then bounce over to the cause.

"Yep. Bad idea," I say as pinpricks of hate-glares pierce my body.

"Ridiculous," Ivy says, then spins us to face the front. "There. Now you don't have to look at them."

"Uh-huh. But now they all can look at me. With my back turned."

"Jeez." Ivy throws an arm over my shoulder and squeezes. "We need to give you some better memories here. After this shindig is over, let's head to my room and celebrate your birthday the classy way: with cake and cherry wine."

Last weekend, Ivy went home to visit her parents in Philadelphia, managing to smuggle her favorite Danish cherry wine in her luggage when her mom was busy baking her *hindbærsnitte,* the most delicious raspberry pastry squares Ivy also had the foresight to bring back with her and shove into my mouth.

Ivy means well, but I doubt the promise of sugar and alcohol will be enough to sweeten the taint left on me when Piper plunged off the nearby cliff just off school property. I was her roommate. I could've stopped it, or at the very least, seen it coming.

Murmurs sweep over the crowd, distracting me from my thoughts. I listen to the shoes scraping against the stone ground until a path forms through the middle of the gathering.

Ivy possesses the gift of being tall, and she sees whatever is making the students part like the Dead Sea before I do.

Her eyes widen, and her lips thin. "Incoming."

I don't look, because I know who I'll see. I'm happy to keep my gaze straight ahead, at the wolf barf fountain, as Chase and his friends saunter down the makeshift aisle.

That is, until I hear one word, whispered by a student behind me, that whips my head around.

Pregnant.

I force myself to look forward again. If caught, my devastation would only fuel Chase's crew. I can't react. I can never let them see.

Not if I want to discover the lies behind their motives and the secrets they've traded in return for their soul.

Two

MY STOMACH CLENCHES as I feel heat start at the back of my neck and prickle down my arm. I glance to the side, catching the source, and I meet the soulless amber depths of Chase Stone's eyes.

We connect for a meager second, but to me, it's ages of time that tether us across the quad, an unblinking connection that shoots ice through my veins yet heats my blood to unbearable levels.

The last time I saw him, those eyes were lit with two candle flames burning their golden incredulity through the bronze. In that moment, he answered the question I posed, the truth that would define us with a simple, "Yes."

Chase's gaze flicks away the moment I flinch at the memory. His attention doesn't return.

His friends stalk behind him—Tempest, James, and Riordan. Piper's former best friends glide around them in beautiful, despondent repose—Falyn, Willow, and Violet. Piper's younger sister and doppelgänger, Addisyn, holds Falyn's hand as they keep close to the guys but force their chins up and eyes forward, while Chase and his buddies glare at the students daring to mumble their opinions nearby.

...pregnant...
Piper's...
...do you think...
Chase's...
Or Dr. Luke's?

Bile forms a waxy ball in my throat, and I swallow the lump as they make their way down a pathway sliced open by simpering student bodies and to the front. Voices ripple into choked whispers as they pass. To my relief, the elite crew takes position on the opposite side where Ivy and I stand. Students who waited early for a front row view scramble back to accommodate their chosen spot.

I'm suddenly desperate to meet Chase's eyes again, maybe find some sort of clue

219

amid the cold bronze and pull out a reality different from what he told me the night I crawled into his arms, shivering from the night's air seeping through my dorm's windows.

"Mm." Chase stirs as I lift his upper arm while crawling back into bed, finding a warm nook under his chin to nestle under. "Who was that?"

I stare at my phone I'd placed on my nightstand, not yet locked and asleep. "Ahmar."

"Oh yeah?" Chase rolls to his back on a grunt, taking me with him until I'm sprawled across the carved muscles of his torso. "What'd he want so fucking late?"

"To tell me something."

Chase idly strokes the top of my head, the movement doing more to lull him into slumber than me. "What did he say?"

My lips part on the answer, but my throbbing heartbeat gets there first. Chase feels my racing pulse against his chest, because he stiffens and says, with careful resonance, "Callie, what's wrong?"

"Piper. She was pregnant. Before she..."

Chase's body, granite-smooth and impenetrable on a good day, turns cold beneath my touch.

I lick my lips, my fingers curling against his stomach. "Is it ... I mean, could it be...?"

"Mine?"

"Quiet, please!"

Headmaster Marron's booming voice, amplified by the surrounding structure of the academy, rips me from the reminiscence. He assumes his position behind the wooden podium centered by the fountain, brought outside for this specific occasion.

His silver eyes scan the crowd as smoothly as his combed back, graying hair.

"We're gathered here today for an important remembrance," he begins, "and what was a tragic ending to one of our brightest, most beloved students, Piper Harrington."

A few students snort their disagreement nearby, but I remain carefully mute.

"Many of you voiced your concern over a professor being responsible for such a heinous act, but while the investigation into Dr. Luke continues, I am here to assure you, and any parents or guardians who contact me, that you are safe on this campus. You are cared for, and your opinion is respected by every faculty member here."

Okay. Now I snort.

Marron cuts a look in my direction, and I cover up my derision with a cough. Ivy smirks beside me.

"We will do everything in our power to ensure your continued trust, including our full cooperation with the police while they valiantly pursue the closing of this matter." Marron clears his throat. "Now, onto the true reason we've assembled on these hallowed grounds. Miss Harrington, please."

Marron gestures to the front where Addisyn stands. She releases Falyn's hand and pulls out her prepared speech from the inside pocket of her blazer as she takes Marron's spot behind the podium.

With a trembling voice, she begins. "Piper was my older sister, my confidant, my best friend, my whole being." She rubs her palm down her nose in an attempt to collect herself, her fingers shaking with the effort. "We grew up as sisters, but we were more like twins. We did everything together, including ... including dreaming about going to the same college. Raising our future children together. Buying a house on the same, the same s-street..."

She breaks down. My heart pulls as I watch, feeling more like an unwelcome spectator to a violent car accident, one who doesn't have the right to be privy to such devastation.

I didn't have a strong connection to Piper, and while a good portion of the school moved on from her death, and the re-shuffling of social stature occurred with the ease of mixing a Vegas card deck, there *were* people affected. Piper's sister is now an only child. Her friends have lost their ride-or-die. Her parents have lost their oldest daughter.

None of it sits right with me. This gathering, Marron's thinly veiled speech to protect the school from liability during what should be a memorial, the fact that it's my eighteenth birthday ... and I'm turning an age that Piper never will.

And whether or not Piper wanted to be a mother, she'll never get to make that choice for herself.

"I need to leave," I murmur to Ivy.

She jolts at the way I grip her arm, much stronger than my voice. "Seriously? We're at the front. We'll make a scene."

"I—I have to," I say. My stomach isn't making any promises to settle. "I can't be here."

Ivy curses under her breath, but scans for a subtle exit-point.

I don't waste time and instead grab her hand and drag her into the space between the podium and the first row of students, bending low so we don't obscure anyone's view of Addisyn's sobs.

Ivy stumbles behind me but matches my speed, until a pair of non-school issued, knee-high boots block my escape.

"Leaving so soon, possum?"

I lift my gaze to Falyn's, her sterling eyes shimmering with well-placed tears.

She waits for my stare to land on hers. "By all means, stay. We haven't even gotten to the part where Addy mentions your homewrecking, skanky ass."

Blood curdles within the broken chambers of my heart.

Ivy pulls on my sleeve. "Don't engage."

I ignore my friend, because it feels so much better to direct my unrest *somewhere*. "Careful, Falyn, your frown lines are showing."

Falyn's bleached blonde eyebrows pull together at my statement. The fact that she's already on a Botox regime is such easy fodder to use, and I'm a little disappointed in myself for not coming up with something better.

I add, "You're right about one thing. I'm not welcome here. So, let me leave."

Marron and the nearby professors lining the front of the makeshift stage eye our scuffle, but don't interrupt Addisyn. Not yet, considering our voices are low, and all they see is Falyn's stricken expression, like we're commiserating on Piper's loss, not testing the strength of our claws.

"No fucking way," Falyn says. "I want you to witness the hell you've caused. Piper's dead because of you."

I stifle the resigned sound wanting to escape from my throat. "And how's that?"

"Let her go."

The deep, leveled words, as dark as the soil beneath stone, causes both our bodies to stiffen. Falyn tenses at the order, and I at the low purr in his tone, a permanent silk that always accompanies his voice.

Chase's gaze is molten against mine, burning into my core with such fierce heat, I can't look away in time.

"Go, Callie," he says.

We haven't spoken in weeks, and he's echoed the very last words I said to him the night he didn't deny that Piper's baby could be his.

My throat's too thick to voice sound, so I give a curt nod, aiming to skirt around Falyn, Ivy frantically pushing against my back. We're drawing too much attention.

Falyn's hand snaps out and wraps around my bicep when I try to pass. She hisses in my ear, "*Listen.*"

"... and while I can't bear to be without my sister, I'll fight for her," Addisyn continues into the microphone. "And bring some justice to her short life. Dr. Luke remains behind bars, but there are others out there who contributed to Piper's misery. A girl who made my sister so heartbroken, she ran into the arms of an older man for solace. A teacher."

Marron stands. "All right, Miss Harrington."

"*You*, Callie Ryan."

"That's enough," Marron says, striding to Addisyn's side and searching for the off switch on the mic.

"If it weren't for you, my sister would be here!" Addisyn screeches, pointing a trembling finger. Murmurs transform into loud voices as they follow Addisyn's direction to witness the center of the spectacle. Me.

I open my mouth. "That's not—"

"Not here," Ivy says, her hands clamping round my shoulders. "Let's go. Before this—"

"Chase was her soulmate!" Addisyn screams. "And you *took* him from her!"

I give in to Ivy's desperate shoves, but I can't tear my gaze away from the girl falling apart on stage. Yet, instead of watching her crumble, all eyes are waiting for me to break.

"Not her fault!" a male voice booms through the crowd.

A sense of relief washes over me at the thought that Chase would stand up for me —but it's not him. It's James, Chase's buddy with the shaggy, reddish-blond hair and hazel eyes sparkling with mirth, but not the happy kind. He gets off at making jokes out of people without giving a shit on where or how he does it, and he's zeroed in on his next target.

James's lips pull wide. "How could Chase resist those tits and that ass?"

I stop listening. The lewd words coming out of such a pretty face should be shocking, but here at the academy, it's not. There's no point in arguing that Chase and I were never together when Piper was alive, if I can even call us a pairing. There's especially no justice in pointing out that despite my "stealing," Chase still managed to possibly get Piper pregnant.

These people have their edicts and the prices they pay to stay at the top of the social chain. Chewing on the fragile bones of us lower mortals is part of their game.

Shoulders slumped more from the emotional weight of this school than Ivy's grip, I walk with her to the edge of the lawn, but not before glancing back, one more time, at James's gleeful maw, still spouting words like "tap that," and "dick her down," with Chase's glacial demeanor beside him.

My steps slow as I study Chase's walled-off features, too rigid and controlled to ever be confused with apathy. His eyes smolder through his visage as he stares straight ahead, a warning sign I notice too late.

Tempest has enough time to shoot his arm out before Chase launches and punches James in the face, toppling all three of them to the ground. Chase lands on James and doesn't stop pummeling his best friend.

"FIGHT!" someone bellows before a mass of prep-school-uniformed bodies jump into the brawl, arms and fists flying.

"*Students!*" Marron roars, and a few other professors join him in attempting to break up the fight. Addisyn hops back and nearly butt-plants into the fountain.

"Holy," Ivy breathes while scuttling me through the new gaps in the crowd. "You'd think it'd be blasphemous to do this at someone's memorial, but you know what? I think Piper's enjoying this, wherever she is."

"No kidding," I respond, my chest tight. "Her ghost must've possessed at least one of them. My bet's on James."

"Please, she had all three of them in her clutches well before her murder."

I squint in Ivy's direction but work to drown any other conflicting emotions threatening to surface. I'm not upset she's so cavalier about Piper's death—Piper wasn't exactly loved by anyone except her followers. I am, however, concerned over Ivy's tidbit that Piper had more influence over the boys than I gave her credit for.

Don't hope that the baby could've been one of theirs, not Chase's.

Ivy has no idea I've slept with Chase, and I'm not eager to confess.

We duck through the outdoor archway connecting the East and West wings, then burst through the doors of the academy, the natural hush of the heavy architecture descending upon us once the doors fold shut.

I take Ivy's hand and we cut through the foyer and to the front. I'm eager to finish this shitty day with some raspberry bars, Netflix, sweet wine, and a good friend.

Yet, Piper's ghost has broken off from the fight, trailing behind me in the cavernous Briarcliff halls, and she's relentless in her wails: *There's so much about this school you can't forget, not even for one night. Don't ignore me, Callie! Don't dismiss my death!*

Ugh. Happy birthday to me.

And happy birthday to you, too, Piper.

Three

THORNE HOUSE IS a modern addition to the otherwise Gothic ski lodge feel of Briarcliff Academy's 170-year-old structures. Automatic sliding doors allow us immediate entry, and the college student manning the front desk lets us through after a careful study of my student ID card. Ivy, she knows on sight.

You'd think I'd have an "in" with knowing one of the front desk staff of the dorms, allowing me ingress and egress well past curfew, but honestly, none of them cared enough to stop any of us.

Not until Piper died.

We take the elevator to the third floor, chatting softly as we hit the carpeted hallway and head to my room.

I swipe my keycard against the hotel-style lock, and when it flashes green, push in. Ivy's so involved in her discussion of how soothing British baking shows on Netflix are that she fails to notice my abrupt stall in the doorway, and *oomphs* into my back.

It's not enough to throw me off balance, but it does the job of jarring the reality of what I'm seeing into my brain.

My mouth falls open. "What the...?"

"Huh?" is all Ivy can come up with. "Is this your stuff?"

"Uh..." I scan the main room as my brows draw in. "No."

A gray leather sectional, so new, the scent of leather cleaner permeates the air, plops its fancy, tightly sewn ass where my pink suede secondhand piece I found on Main Street used to be. At least 45 inches of flat screen TV is bolted to a wall where I'd just installed floating shelves to hold photos of my remaining family, and a monstrosity of an espresso machine gurgles its presence beside us through its sleek nickel finishing, a spot I'd reserved for my Black & Decker drip.

Okay. Maybe I'm not mad at the last one.

But, seriously?

"I think you have a new roommate." Ivy states behind me.

I attempt an eye-roll over my shoulder. "You think?"

My sarcasm is fast overshadowed by a petrified thought when the door to Piper's old room swings open.

Oh God, don't let it be another Piper...

A figure steps through the doorframe. "Hey."

Ivy gasps so audibly that I turn to her with a frown.

"S-sorry," she says while a hand flutters against her mouth. "It's just ... I didn't think..."

The girl smiles with a wry tilt to her thin lips and finishes for Ivy, "...that the ghost of Emma Loughrey would come back to Briarcliff to claim all your souls for the Reaper?"

Well. That's enough of an introduction to leave my jaw hanging. "Holy shit, Emma?"

Deep lines form in Emma's cheeks. "Heard of me, have you?" Her steely bronze gaze, so like Chase's it's unsettling, lands on Ivy. "I see the town crier still has her horn."

I bristle at the connotation. "Ivy's been nothing but awesome, so if you don't have anything nice to say about her, then—"

Emma rolls her eyes. "Let me guess, don't say anything at all? Nice one, whatever-your-name-is."

She turns to her room and shuts the door with a firm click.

"It's Callie!" I call through the thick, mahogany wood. "And thanks for doing what I was *going* to say, which was to fuck off!"

"I don't think that's coming across as intimidating as you hoped it would," Ivy mutters into my ear. "Your voice is kind of high and wobbly—"

Clasping Ivy's hand, I lead us into my bedroom and shut the door. I splay my back against it, while Ivy whirls in the center of my room, her arms spread wide. "Holy moly, do you know who that is?"

I nod, suddenly antsy that some of my first words to Chase's twin sister were *fuck* and *off*.

Not exactly trying to fit into the family's good graces, are we, Callie?

"She wasn't exactly too friendly with her greeting, either," I say in a lame attempt to defend myself.

Ivy isn't listening. She continues a slow pirouette, her voice wandering and stupefied. "I haven't seen her in ... gosh, it has to be over two years. She's changed. Like, *really* changed. I barely recognized her, and oh my God, do you know what *happened* to her before she left?"

After a thick swallow, I nod. In a brief moment of weakness, Chase divulged a little about his sister's assault and the resulting fire while we lay in bed together, our hands intertwined.

A skitter of goosebumps pass over my flesh, at both the tragedy surrounding Emma and the remembrance of Chase's warm, naked body enveloping mine.

"Really?" Ivy asks, her high-pitched question refocusing my thoughts. "How'd you find out?"

"Oh, uh, during my research on the founders in the new library, I think I asked someone why it was called the 'new' library. They told me how the old one burned down and that Emma was trapped inside."

And she's the one who burned it down, but I don't mention that part.

"Yeah." Ivy nods sagely. "I didn't think people still talked about it. Chase put down a terrifying gag order on anyone who dared to mention his sister. Who'd you ask?"

"Can't recall," I say, then clear my throat and move from the door to perch on my bed. "But I was warned she was ... different."

"I knew about the burns," Ivy breathes as she sits next to me. "But I had *no* idea she'd, um, she'd..."

"Gained weight?"

"Yes! She used to be..."

"She's still beautiful," I whisper, recalling those bronze, goddess-colored eyes and streaming natural highlights of elbow-length, blonde hair.

It was greasier than Ivy probably remembered, matted and tangled. Emma's cheeks were dimpled and flushed with natural pink, but they were swollen, her jowls heavy with what I recognized not as weight gain, but a demanding, inner hunger yawning wide, constantly starving because it kept being fed the wrong emotions: anger, hate, resentment.

Only one form of sustenance could stop the clamoring and quell that gnawing ache forever. *Revenge.*

"She also came back mean," Ivy says. "But I can understand the why of it."

And there it is. I take a long study of Ivy, imputing her current expression onto every other student's face who Emma is about to cross paths with. It's an expression of pity. Relief it wasn't them. And while Ivy wasn't wearing it, I knew shock and revulsion would soon follow.

Emma chose to wear defensive armor to protect herself, but I wondered, with the wolves in this arena now led by Falyn Clemonte, how impervious Emma's sarcastic, angry armor will actually be.

More importantly...

"Does Chase know?" I ask.

Ivy shrugs. "You would think so, but, hell, I don't think anybody knew Emma would finish her senior year here. I mean, what kind of therapist would send her back to Briarcliff?" Ivy leans closer, as if divulging a scandalous secret. "She wasn't just trapped in the old library, Callie. She was attacked there, first. Brutally beaten. I think both her eye sockets were fractured, and her back was broken—"

I hold up a hand, the imagery making me sick. "Let's not judge her new self immediately, okay? This is clearly going to be tough for her, and she's my new room-mate. I'd like to maybe not become enemies with this one."

"Okay, sure, Miss *Fuck Off*."

"Yeah," I mumble, sliding my laptop onto my lap. "I'm gonna have to work on that."

Ivy and I finally settle on Netflix's new rom-com and *not* a baking show (Birthday Girl wins), but leaning back against the headboard and sharing a bottle of wine does nothing to calm my racing heart, nor does the sound on my computer obscure the noises coming from the other side of my door.

Emma must have started her move-in process when the entire school congregated in Briarcliff's quad. It makes sense; the campus was practically deserted. There was no one to notice the rental truck's tires bouncing across the academy's cobblestone driveway and to the western edge of the property's surrounding forest, where the Thorne and Rose Houses lie. It certainly escaped Ivy's and my notice when we wandered over here using the student paths.

The speed in which her furniture made it inside is also unsurprising. The rich live as such, with white-gloved positioning, quiet alterations, and seamless decoration. With the gaps of quiet between wood dragging against floors and low-voiced instruction getting longer, I assume Emma is about done with her transition.

One question remains: Where the hell did my stuff go?

Visions of my furniture leaning against the dorm's dumpster causes a shudder, and I shift on my bedding to escape it.

"Meh. That was okay," Ivy says.

Credits roll on the movie I daydreamed through, and I move to close the laptop.

"That part where the monkeys came and devoured everyone's faces was cool, though," Ivy continues.

"Mm." I slide off the bed and place my computer on my desk.

"Dude!" Ivy shouts.

I jump, nearly toppling onto my desk chair. As I right myself, she adds, "You didn't watch a darned thing on the screen, did you?"

"Not really," I admit.

"I get it. You have a lot going on. I mean—more than your usual pile of a lot going on." After a light grunt, Ivy rises from my bed. "Do you want me to stay? I'm not sure how this will go with you and Emma." Ivy grins. "I kind of want to spectate."

"Nope." I give her a firm shove to my door. "I doubt she'll leave her room, anyway."

Ivy says over her shoulder, "She has to go to the bathroom sometime."

"Then I'll be in *my* room. Thanks for the support, but I'll be fine."

"If you say so. But text me for anything, okay? If you need an escape route, I'm pretty sure I can be the Ivy to your ivy."

I raise a curious brow.

"You know, out your window." Ivy gestures behind me. "It's unclear if all that clinging ivy will hold your weight, but I can wait down below to catch you during your grand escape if need be."

I can't help but smile at the image she's conjured. For sure my ass under this skirt would be on full display.

"There we go." Ivy nudges my side. "I was hoping to get a smile from you on your birthday."

My chest warms at her words, but before I can reciprocate, she gets there first and envelopes me in a long hug.

"Love you," she says. "Now you can vote and own a firearm. Happy friggin' eighteenth, my friend."

I laugh into her perfumed shoulder, notes of wildflowers playing against my nostrils. "You're the best."

"Later," she says once she releases me, and when she opens my door, carefully peers around it. "Coast is clear. I'm out."

Shaking my head on a laugh, I pull the door wider as Ivy beelines to the front door, making a U-turn only once when she notices a line of Emma's shoes she's yet to put away. Ivy flutters a longing hand through the air above the Louboutins, Jimmy Choos, and Manolo Blahniks before she shuts the apartment door behind her.

I'm also distracted by the gorgeous array of prestigious color and design, blown away that Emma's brought such expensive footwear to school. One: where will she wear it, and two: what about her self-imposed hermit status?

So what? I chastise myself. *One can be a hermit while donning fabulous heels.*

A shuffling in my periphery draws my eye up. Emma hovers in her doorway, staring at me as warily as I was studying her shoes.

In the fading golden hour of the setting sun through the bay windows, Emma's features are softened, but only skin-deep. One eyelid stretches slightly more crooked than the other. Her hair, as wavy and tousled as a beached mermaid's, is cut short around her face to obscure the pink-tinged scar trailing across her forehead. She's chosen an oversized hoodie to hide her upper body, with a faded Briarcliff crest and two oars crossed behind it, *Briarcliff Crew* written underneath.

I'm so busy wondering if that's Chase's sweatshirt that I almost miss the crooked, re-healed knobs of her fingers pulling at the hem to cover herself better.

My heart swells with the need to explain my staring, but experience has taught me it's no use when a person already sees herself as a target.

Instead, I'm the first of us to experiment with a quiet, "Hey."

She nods, her lips pursed, then scuttles to pick up her shoes lining the wall of our small entryway.

It's a new side of Emma I'm seeing now that Ivy's gone, and I don't think Emma's hesitant, uneven gait is solely due to her injuries.

"I'm not like the rest of them," I try saying. When her metallic stare pings against mine again, so steady compared to the way she moves, I have to force my breaths even. "I mean—I won't bother you. If you don't want me to. You're here for senior year, right? We can always study together, or—"

"Are you as vacant as you look?" Emma spits. My heels knock backward against the floorboards at her vitriol. "If so, let me sum up my newly fucked-up status for you. I've missed two years of classes due to nearly having my skull turned to mush by assholes who probably still attend this school. I'm starting twelfth grade late while finishing up the last of my tenth and eleventh grade papers, because my dad paid the crooked headmaster double a normal student's tuition to allow me back in, and also had the gracious thought to put me in my *murdered* friend's old bedroom, along with the empty-headed roommate that comes with it. Or, maybe you're not such a dumbass. You were a suspect in Piper's death for a hot second, weren't you?"

So was your brother, I want to retort, but bite my tongue.

Emma sneers. "Don't do that. Don't stop yourself from saying what you really think because you're *sad* for me, like the very thought of what I look like—"

I storm forward.

"If you're trying to satisfy your hatred for this school by being cruel to me," I say, "Consider your aim a misfire."

After a beat of hesitation, she lifts a scarred brow. "Putting you down does nothing to lessen how much I despise Briarcliff. Maybe I'm just doing it because I want to."

Ugh. She is *so* like her brother. "I'm not exactly a fan of this place, either, but here we are. Attending anyway, for our own reasons."

"And why would a girl like you hate a school like this?" She laughs dully. "This is the fast-track to the best colleges in the world. The cafeteria menu is designed by a Michelin starred chef. You're practically guaranteed an engagement to the son of some corporate empire if you play your connections right. Or daughter, if that's where your preference lies." She hums in thought. "I don't recognize you from before, and you're not staying on Scholarship Row so ... who did you sleep with to get a spot here? Someone's dad? Headmaster Marron?"

I ignore her goading. "Perhaps I've witnessed the price a soul has to pay for that kind of unlimited access."

Emma narrows her eyes, hopefully stumped by my honesty.

"Can we agree to co-exist?" I ask on a sigh. "Because I have to tell you, living with a person who despises you is exhausting."

A whisper of a smile flirts at one corner of her mouth, but she squelches it with a glower. "I'll get back to you on that." Arms laden with shoes, she turns back to her room, but tosses over her shoulder, "Don't fucking touch my coffee."

Emma heels her door shut.

I let out a singular laugh, shaking my head as I run my hand through my hair.

If there was ever a thought that Emma and I would be bonding over our mutual misfit status at Briarcliff Academy, *holy hell*, was I so utterly misguided.

Four

I'M OUTSIDE.

I rise up on one elbow, squinting at my phone, my tongue thick and fuzzy from breathing through my mouth while I slept. Three dancing dots appear as I'm trying to decipher the meaning behind the text, and the messenger.

Meet me.

At last, my vision clears of sleep, and I sit up, sliding my heavy nest of hair to one shoulder.

"Chase?" I whisper to myself.

He hasn't said a word, sent a text, or exhaled in my direction since our last conversation involving Piper's secret pregnancy. To believe what I'm reading would mean Chase is standing outside the dorms, waiting for me to come out and see him.

This afternoon's events flash into my mind, its dreamlike quality becoming clearer the harder I blink. Chase punched James's lights out because he was saying vile things ... about me.

Chase, the boy who prefers to ignore me when he's not horny, chose to beat up his friend for daring to insult me.

I stare up in thought. Does that deserve a secret, nightly meet-up?

Me: Go away. I was sleeping.

. . .

Blacking out my phone's screen, I move to toss it on my nightstand and nestle into my bedcovers, still warm from when I was snoozing comfortably.

It buzzes while leaving my palm, and on a huff of annoyed, yet curious, breath, I glance at the text's preview.

Chase: If you don't come down, I'm coming up.

Fuck. Chase doesn't bluff. And knowing him, he'd probably be noisy as all hell, waking up his sister and—

Oh, God. His *sister* lives with me now. Does he know that?

Besides that, what time is it? My phone says four in the morning, and I groan. I was hoping to use this Saturday to sleep in and get used to my new dorm environment, or failing that, going into town and studying at the public library, far away from the other students here. Why does Chase have to ruin the tentative peace I've established while trying to finish out this semester?

Chase: 5...
    Chase: 4...

Damn it. I slide out of bed, fumbling for a hoodie to throw over my sleep tank and shorts, then slip into my white sneakers.

Chase: 3...

The bastard is probably already through the sliding doors. I have zero faith in the "heightened" security of this place, especially considering the last month when my nocturnal, cloaked visitor left me rose petals. I *swear* the Cloak is real, even if no one believes me. Even if Chase has made me question whether my convictions are fact or remnants of my previous hysterical break-down...

Chase: TWO

I text two words on a growl, my thumbs slamming against my screen. **COMING ASSHOLE.**

Slipping the hood over my head and tucking my phone into the front pocket, I tip-toe out of the apartment, noting the dim, golden light shining out from under Emma's door with vague curiosity.

My dorm room neighbors the stairwell, and I choose to pad down the steps rather than risk the *ding* of the elevator. Once on the ground floor, I take the second exit out the side of the building so as not to enter the lobby and possibly be spotted by night security.

They were brought in for extra safety, but would I trust their nightly flashlight sweeps with my life? Absolutely not. I have more faith in the kitten a girl on my floor smuggled in under their noses.

I round the corner of the red, brick building, the grass tips wet and speared with a cold dew that brushes against my ankles like tiny skeletal fingers. Once the coast is clear, and I swing around the blind corner, I see Chase leaning against a luxurious, midnight blue BMW, headlights on and engine growling low. It's not the type of BMW I associate with middle-aged businessmen like my stepdad. This is sleeker, lower to the ground, with a lot of black detailing and strange, red, under-wheel lights illuminating the tires.

No security guard comes out to scold him. He probably paid them triple their hourly salary to keep quiet.

"Like what you see?" Chase purrs as I walk toward him.

His voice tightens my chest with tangled nerves, and I hope I cover up the falter in my steps before he notices.

I've always seen Chase in school uniform or athletic gear, never in a T-shirt and jeans. Yet, here he stands, in all his mouth-watering glory, his strong, muscular legs hidden in dark denim that hugs his butt as he leans casually against his car. Chase's shirt is tight against his pecs and tailored to his wide shoulders and narrow hips. The muscles of his crossed forearms ripple with devious intent as I step closer.

"What are you doing here?" I ask, then point at Thorne House. "Oh yeah, and your *sister* is living with me."

He pops off the passenger side, opening the door before he steps back. "I know. Get in."

"You can explain yourself right here, Chase Stone."

Chase rounds the front of the car. He reaches the driver's side and says to me over the hood, "There's coffee in your cupholder."

No five words have ever sounded so sexy.

Chase pounces on my hesitation. "Lots of cream, no sugar. How you like it."

I shuffle my feet, digging my clenched fists into my hoodie's pocket. "Is it from the bakery in town?"

Chase's mouth lifts. "Marta has a soft spot for me."

I bet she does. Not a lot of women would open their doors at three in the morning, unless it holds the promise of Chase Stone on the other end.

But she makes *really* good coffee.

And it would be the freshest pot of them all—the first of the day while the morning employees prepped dough before opening their doors.

"And monkey bread," Chase adds. "First batch."

"Damn it," I mutter, and slide in at the same time he does.

The car's dashboard emits a subtle, blue hue against our silhouettes. Chase's profile takes on a devilish tone, shadows layering with the flowing indigo lights of the interior.

This, right here, is physical proof that demons prefer blue over red.

I study his sharp jawline with unintentional awe before I snap my mouth shut and stare straight ahead.

He's not your personal playground anymore. You're not allowed to keep picturing him naked.

The tug in my belly, tied in his direction, tells me otherwise.

Chase's long fingers grip the wheel as he steers us out of Thorne House and onto Briarcliff's private road.

My gaze flicks back to him, not just for appreciation. I'm searching for signs of the fight, bruises or cuts or fractures. "Are you hurt?"

His lips tilt. "For someone who refused to come talk to me, you sure have a lot of questions."

I busy myself with his promised cup of coffee, lifting it and sipping at the perfection. The scent of cinnamon and caramel tickles my nostrils, and like a hound sensing a fox, my head whips to the backseat.

Chase chuckles. "Had I known all it would take to lure you into my ride was some sugar and caffeine, I would've left a trail of it into the forest long ago."

The relaxed, semi-threat drives my attention away from the white bag spotted with melted butter and to the front. "So, instead of leading me into the woods, you're what, taking me prisoner in your cursed castle?"

"Save the food for when we arrive," is all he says.

"Fine." I settle into my seat, cupping the coffee close. "But I'm not going to leave the question of why you woke me up until we reach our mysterious destination."

"I never thought you would."

The car's wheels turn gracefully under Chase's hands when we exit Briarcliff Academy's gates and merge onto the deserted main road, rimmed with tall, untended trees. For a moment, departing the manmade, landscaped, and carefully chosen flora and fauna of the academy and driving into the natural wildness of the protected forest is jarring, but I stifle the feeling, preferring not to ponder why I'm more comfortable within the school's gates than out.

Especially considering the chauffeur I've chosen.

"Why am I here?" I ask him.

"I thought that'd be obvious. Because I want to talk to you."

Sighing, I rephrase the question to something more specific, since I really should know by now Chase doesn't deal in generalities. "Why didn't you tell me your sister was coming back to school?"

A muscle tenses in Chase's cheek. "You and me, we haven't spoken much."

"A few weeks," I agree. After a beat of silence, I risk adding, "If you want the truth, I knew bringing up Piper's pregnancy would drive a wedge between us, but I never thought you'd—"

"Emma isn't here with my approval," Chase says. We make another turn into the darkness. The speed of his driving sets my teeth on edge. There aren't any streetlights to help us along. I'm relying solely on Chase's fancy headlights to keep me from becoming a crushed soda can against an errant tree.

"I told her it wasn't a good idea," he continues. "But Emma isn't known for listening."

Sounds familiar, I add silently.

"She has this ... strange vendetta," Chase says. "I'm happy she wants to get out of our dad's house, but I was hoping she'd transfer to Dover Shores or hell, some school in California. Anywhere but here."

I nod in full agreement. Briarcliff isn't known to spit out well-heeled, sweet individuals. "So, she refused to listen to you, but what about her therapist? Or doctors?"

"They all had the same opinion as me. It was our father who poisoned Emma against us. He encouraged her reentry into this school. Said it might be healing for her to face her demons."

"But she..." I shake my head while my thoughts realign. "When she moved in, she said that the people responsible for her assault might still be here. She thinks her *attacker* is at this school, be it a teacher or a student or..."

"I know." The whites of Chase's knuckles poke through his grip, notable even in the low lighting. "My dad thinks it's her paranoia talking."

For the barest of seconds, his eyes flick to me.

I tense, but don't add kindling to that fire, since I'm supposedly reformed and no longer victim to the delusion that my stepdad is responsible for my mother's death.

"She could be right," I say softly.

Chase cedes my point by dipping his chin, but says, "Dad's convinced it was a rogue event. A townie breaking into Briarcliff grounds. Marron thinks so, too. And the Briarcliff police force."

"And you?"

"I..." Chase works his jaw but doesn't tear his eyes from the road. Probably because he's afraid of the questions reflecting in my eyes, the ones threatening to unleash the instant he gives me an opening.

"It wasn't your Cloaks," he says.

"Call them what they are," I say. "The Nobles. The Virtues."

"Callie," he warns.

"Hey, I'll even accept Briarcliff Academy's secret society. I *know* they exist, Chase."

"Don't do this."

"You're the one who called *me*. You had your escape hatch all mapped out when you dipped on me that night, and I'd even come to accept you weren't going to talk to me for the rest of the year. I'd made my peace with it." *Not.* "Yet here I am, in your car, on your invitation, because you want something from me. Well, it goes both ways, buddy."

Chase makes an impatient sound in his throat, but his next turn is sharper, and I'm thrown against his side before I can brace. I latch onto the hard length of his arm, so stiff with muscle my fingers don't dimple the skin, as he finishes the turn and we coast up another private road.

I twist my face away from his intoxicating scent, seemingly crafted just for my pheromones, a mix of salted sweat, freshwater, and pine, and focus on where we are.

The forest is heavier here, tree branches and their falling leaves yawning over the roadway, creating a natural, curving archway we drive under. Chase's tinted sunroof is so large, it takes up the entire top of the car, and it's like I'm given wings, taking flight through fantastical woodland under the twinkle of stars.

"Wow," I breathe, the stars' silver specks poking through like sparkling jewels worn by the black, skeletal hands of the branches above.

"You can let go now."

Chase's voice draws my chin down, and I unfurl from his arm. We've slowed to a stop in view of a massive glass structure, a building spanning the size of a New York City block that I'm coming to understand is the length of people's homes around here.

"Come on," he says, exiting the car with slick, effortless grace.

I'm less tranquil, my knees hitting my chest as I swing them to the ground after elbowing open the door. I make sure to swipe the tantalizing bakery bag and balance my coffee before I let myself out.

Chase is already striding down the small walkway, swinging a keyring in his hand. I'm slow to catch up, because I'm too busy clocking the scope of this house, a looming shadow clawing out of its spot in the forest and dominating the sky.

"Is this your place?" I ask his retreating back.

He responds over his shoulder, "It's our lake house."

I swallow the forgotten saliva building in my mouth.

Turns out I was wrong. Chase didn't ferry me to his cursed castle.

The dark prince of Briarcliff Academy took me to his vacation home instead.

Five

I HURRY to catch up with Chase, reluctant to continue hanging out in the darkness. We're still in the middle of the wilderness, and the idea of neighbors other than bears being nearby is laughable.

Wolves, too. The real ones.

"Wait up!" I call, and Chase pauses once he unlocks the large iron doors.

He steps back to let me in first, and I pause for half a second on the door knocker in the vivid shape of a sleeping bat before stepping over the threshold.

"So, your lake house, huh?" I say as Chase steps in behind me. He heads to one side of the foyer, turning on lights. "It's ... quaint."

Chase has illuminated a vast, open area, with a gray brick fireplace built in the *middle* of the room and stacked to the vaulted ceiling, the exposed wooden beams creating a cabin-like feel only the wealthy would consider essential. Thin, white leather couches are placed on one side of the fireplace, and a formal dining table on the other. A throw rug in the shape of a wolf is spread out between the couches, and while I'm hoping it's fake, I'm pretty sure it's not.

The floor-to-ceiling windows on the opposite side probably provide an amazing view of the Stone's private property, but nothing can be seen through the black of the night but our own pale reflections.

Chase laughs under his breath. "Follow me. We'll eat and talk in the kitchen."

"I didn't know you had a place so close to the school," I say, trailing behind Chase down a single step and into the main room until we reach the open, luxury kitchen.

Chase spins to take the bakery bag from my hands, and I settle onto a stool while he opens cupboards.

"Probably because I consider it more of a prison," he says while placing two plates between us. "This is where I'll be riding out next week."

I put my finger to my lips and *pretend contemplation*. "Don't tell me, your decision to club another Neanderthal upside the head for insulting me has resulted in your suspension."

"What'd you expect?" Chase responds, as if *I* was the one who asked him to be such an idiot.

"You shouldn't have hit James."

He slides a plate of still-steaming monkey bread closer, and I stare at it for a minute before giving in.

"He deserved it." Chase licks the drippings of my portion off his thumb while keeping his eyes on mine. An internal shiver wraps its way around my chest. Never have I wanted to be icing sugar more.

Chase bites the pad of his thumb in thought, then says, "James was being an ass."

"He's *always* an ass."

"When it comes to you, my buddies and I have an agreement. You and I may not be currently fucking, but my moratorium on anyone saying anything negative about you or doing anything to you still stands."

I lift another piece of bread to my mouth. The hot caramel and the spicy notes of cinnamon hit my taste buds under pillowy vanilla dough, and I moan.

Chase freezes while plating his piece, his jawline going rigid. Pieces of fine blond hair fall into his eyes, and while I can only see his profile, I sense the solar flare within him, his irises going black with expanded pupils.

My breath hitches as I set the bread down carefully. The raw, tingling pressure against my nipples is almost unbearable. "I don't need your protection."

"No?" His question is soft. Dangerous.

"Piper's killer is behind bars. There's no more risk of a murderer strolling through Briarcliff halls," I say. "And according to you, my discovery of a secret society poses no danger because they don't exist." I add an eye roll as final punctuation.

"There's still Falyn to consider," Chase says as he rests on the stool next to mine. His presence is too close, too warm. "And Addisyn. Without my protection, they'll make it their mission for you to regret ever enrolling at this school."

I grit my teeth. "I can handle a few mean girls." I side-eye Chase. "And mean boys, if it comes to that."

His mouth quirks.

I stare at him for a moment, worrying my lips.

Because, without a doubt, if I stay any longer, I'll jump him.

And I can't let that happen. He ditched me a few weeks ago without a word, and I'm not giving him the satisfaction of coming back for more.

Or perhaps my reluctance stems from him dropping me before *I* could leave him, this high school alpha who will give me his body, but wraps his soul in impenetrable, ancient armor I have no hope of piercing.

Why put my heart through it again?

"Unless you brought me here to appreciate how your virtual learning experience will go this week," I say, picking at my bread, "I'd like to get back to the dorms."

Chase swallows his bite. He stares at the kitchen cabinetry. "I'd like you to do something for me."

I lean back as much as I can in a stool and reach for my coffee, more for comfort than thirst. "What's so important you couldn't text me, or, I don't know, talk to me between classes?"

"This cop connection you have, the guy you talk to in the city," Chase says.

"Ahmar?"

"Yeah, him."

The fact that Chase is bringing up my pseudo-uncle causes my stomach to plummet. I stepped into Chase's car with full knowledge that he needed me for something, but the smallest whisper inside my head wished for it to be unrelated to Piper. For her to be buried to rest so we could all move on.

It's a cold, selfish thought I'd never voice out loud, but that part of me molded to Chase, the piece of me he kept for himself, will always wish to fit against him without the jagged edge of Piper in between.

Chase cups his coffee, his forearms resting against the granite counter, the trail of veins running under his skin matching the threads of gold woven in the marble. "I need you to find out if it was mine."

I inhale, a silent swish of breath that freezes my entire form.

"It's the only way I can know for sure," Chase continues. "The local cops aren't saying a word. More motive evidence they're keeping to themselves, I guess."

"Or they're still waiting on the results," I say, impressed at how steady I sound. Nothing like scientific facts to ease emotional turmoil inside one's head.

Chase shifts his focus, and his copper-toned eyes meet mine. "Is that your honest opinion?"

I shrug as offhandedly as I can. "It can take a while. And think about it. If the results come back to match you, that unravels the entire case against Dr. Luke. If it were yours, they ... they'd pull you in for more questioning."

Chase's head jerks in a nod. "Exactly. I'd like to know before they take me by surprise."

I mull this over. "You're asking me and Ahmar to meddle with an open investigation and interfere with Briarcliff PD's potential plan to interrogate you."

Chase's Adam's apple bobs, the only motion in his perfect form as he stares me down.

This is the moment where I say no. Where I stand up, demand to be taken to back to the dorms, or call myself an Uber.

What I shouldn't be doing is sitting here, contemplating the ins and outs of obtaining such information and the effects that would ripple out because of it.

Worse, I *want* to do it. For him.

"Ahmar may not be successful. It's not his jurisdiction," I say. "He could outright refuse, too."

Chase nods. "I get it. But it's a way to try."

"And if it's yours?" I whisper. "You just punched your airtight alibi in the face. Friends fight. Friends lie for each other."

"I know that, too." His burnished gaze finds the inner heat it needs to flicker with golden flames. "You gotta believe me, Callie. I didn't hurt her. The baby could be Dr. Luke's just as much as it could be mine."

The gears of my mind shift, rubbing together all wrong because of their blatant misuse. I should be planning how to live out the rest of my senior year without Chase and all the problems clinging to the Briarcliff blazers of his entire group. Instead, I'm busy drumming up a solution as to how *I* can benefit.

When the riskiest answer clicks into place, I say, "I'll do it."

Chase's shoulders ease away from his neck. "Thank you."

"On a condition."

Chase stills. Then, once he processes what I've said, his mouth kicks into a saddened grin. "You're learning survival skills pretty quick."

I ignore his statement. "You're suspended for a week, right?"

His brows draw together. "Yeah. Why?"

I sit straighter. "I'll do my best to get the information for you, but in return, you'll let me ask you three questions per day for an entire week, which you have to answer honestly and with the *full* truth."

Chase's nostrils flare. His stare doesn't waver, and I tell myself to be strong against the heat of his microscope. He takes the next few seconds for himself, the mechanics of his mind possessing more expertise on the subject of trickery and traps than mine.

He says, "One."

I shake my head. "Two questions."

"Fine. But the questions have limitations. No asking about your Cloaks. And only one personal question per day."

My heart flutters with disappointment, but I'd factored in that possibility and figured out a few workarounds.

That he's playing into my hands should feel good, but it really, really doesn't. "Deal."

One flawless cheek of his tics with his clenched jaw. "Should we shake on it?"

Dear Lord, if I touch him now, I'll have no hope of leaving this place with my clothes on. I've developed shivers in places that aren't supposed to be sentient, but they're going off on their own anyway, demanding orgasmic release.

"No need." I stand, brushing invisible crumbs off my legs. "Can you take me home?"

After a pause, Chase moves from his eerily still position. "Sure."

Dregs of coffee remain in my cup, but I take it anyway, needing something to do with my hands as Chase guides me out of his lake house and opens the passenger door of his car, an oil-slicked beast waiting silently within the shadows of the forest.

We're silent under the ultraviolet hue of the interior, me taking pretend sips of my coffee. Chase doesn't blast any music on our way back to Briarcliff, and I don't ask him to, preferring the low hum of the vehicle to regulate and calm my thoughts.

At 5 AM, Chase pulls up to Thorne House. I unbuckle my seatbelt, and he leans back from the wheel. I feel his study like the fine pinpricks of sewing needles as I move but pretend I don't.

"Thanks for the..." I pause to think of what this was between us. "Visit."

Chase responds with a closed-mouthed smile, resting one wrist on the top of the steering wheel. "I appreciate what you're doing for me."

After a careful nod, I step out.

"And Callie?"

I bend down to catch his eye.

"Happy birthday," he says.

Chase leans over to pull the passenger door shut, and I stumble back as his vehicle purrs across the driveway before disappearing around a corner.

With my hands on my hips, I watch his departure, a hesitant smile playing at the corners of my lips.

Six

AFTER MY SHOWER the next morning, I send Ahmar a text, asking him to call me when he gets the chance, preferring to get this chapter over with so I can tell Chase I held up my end of the deal.

I scrape my hair into a top knot using the small vanity mirror in my room, some strands still damp at the ends, since I didn't have the patience to blow-dry it all the way.

Before leaving my room, I recheck my bag to make sure I have the supplies I need to go into town.

Emma's bedroom is open and deserted when I slip through the main room, but the smell of fresh coffee is sharp in the air. My stomach gurgles. The few hours' sleep I caught after being dropped off by Chase has reinvigorated my digestion, and I make a mental note to raid the Wolf's Den pastry bar before calling a car.

Outside my apartment, a few of my neighbors mingle, Saturday morning bringing with it a happy need to socialize, make plans, or stay in pajamas all day. A few girls glance in my direction when my door shuts behind me, and with the stares being more curious than feral, I figure news must've hit that I have a new roommate.

Or, for most of these girls, news of the return of an old, traumatized friend.

Relief should settle upon my shoulders at the idea I'm no longer the fresh meat of the week, but Emma's loss of her formal social status doesn't sit well, regardless of her crisp, pissy attitude. Someone experiencing tragedy like that should have friends surround them and be supported by their environment, not smuggled into the cobwebbed corners of a lonely mansion and forgotten about, only to come back to derisive bitches.

I lift my chin in defense of the stares and murmurs, then take a hard left into the stairwell, preferring to chew off my all fingers to the first knuckle than wait for an elevator while these girls mingle over caffeinated mugs of gossip.

A burst of fresh air hits me when I push through the ground floor's side exit, the same one I took to meet Chase. This time, I hop onto the pathway leading to the school rather than hedge around the bushes and soak my sneakers.

I spot Ivy walking with her roommate, Eden, and run to catch up to them.

"Hey," I say once I'm close enough.

Both turn their heads. Ivy smiles. Eden scowls through her curtain of long black hair.

"You guys headed to breakfast?" I ask, sidling up to Ivy.

"Definitely," Ivy says. "I need a load of eggs and bacon to help digest what I just heard."

I frown, hooking my fingers around the backpack's straps at my shoulders while I match their pace, sun dappling their shoulders, and the wind carrying the scent of cut grass and damp wood. "I get why everyone else is whispering, but why are you surprised? You were with me when Emma first moved in."

Eden's brows hitch up. "Emma's back?"

"Is that not what we're talking about?" I ask.

"Nope." Eden snorts, but the delicate skin around her eyes remains tight. "I guess the return of someone beat up and nearly killed in a fire while the school did nothing is yesterday's news."

"I thought the same thing," I say to Eden.

Eden glances my way but doesn't return the sympathy.

"I'm talking about Dr. Luke," Ivy says, her ice-blonde hair bouncing as she strolls. I swear, rumors provide her more energy than espresso. "I spoke to Lisa who knew Carl who heard from Sebastian whose dad is on some sort of state council that Dr. Luke's been released."

I grind to a halt. "*What*?"

Eden stares at the ground and keeps walking, but Ivy whirls to face me. "It's all over school this morning. Apparently, Dr. Luke had an alibi, but she was reluctant to come forward and corroborate because, well, it would ruin her life."

I blink at Ivy, who leans in and lowers her voice to a conspiratorial whisper. "Dr. Luke was having an affair with Sebastian's *mom*. She was with him that night."

"But..." I think back to Piper's diary entries while Dr. Luke's last words to me play in my ear.

I was there to dump her!

"...he saw Piper that night," I finish. "He admitted he was the *last* to see her."

Ivy nods, then shrugs. "He also insisted he left her alive. And if Mrs. Dorian is to be believed, he was with her during Piper's time of death. In her *convertible* on Briar-cliff's private driveway. Ew, right?"

"That can't be true." I shake my head and start walking again, with Ivy prancing beside me. "He all but admitted he killed her."

"Did he, though?"

"*Yes.*" I grab Ivy's arm. "He's the one. Dr. Luke did it. He *has* to be Piper's killer."

"Ow. You're kinda hurting me."

"This is—there has to be a hole in this alibi somewhere. He's lying. She's lying. The police've made a mistake."

"Callie, I don't think so. Mrs. Dorian has a time-stamped video of it."

My grip tightens on Ivy's arm. She yelps, and I shake myself out of it, releasing her. "Sorry."

"What's going on with you?" Ivy asks, rubbing her arm. "Mrs. Dorian filmed them having sex. I guess to masturbate with later? Whatever the reason, it's proof, Callie. Think about it."

"No, I..." I dig a hand into my hair, pulling out strands from my hair-tie. "It can't be. Dr. Luke *did* it. No one ... no one else..."

My vision blurs with the possibilities I'd hidden in the recesses of my mind once I'd heard the *chink* of handcuffs locking around the beloved professor at Briarcliff.

The Cloaks.

The roses.

Rose Briar's secret letter.

The lost pages of Piper's diary.

None of it was supposed to matter anymore. I'd stifled the deep-seated, obsessive need to investigate...

"Listen, I don't know why Mrs. Dorian waited so long." Ivy's voice breaks through the shimmering fog of my mind. "She must've found her morals where she originally stashed them to sleep with her son's professor, deciding *not* to let Dr. Luke rot in prison for the sake of her reputation." Ivy wrinkles her nose. "What a decent thing to do."

In a surge of contorted memory, my stepdad's face replaces Dr. Luke's stricken expression when handcuffs snapped across his wrists.

Dad's shock when his arms were wrenched behind him. The desperate words he uttered when police escorted him past me and out the door.

Cal, what is this? Why do they think it's me?

I'm innocent, Callie!

...Don't do this, please...

Honey, you have to believe me. I loved your mother. I love her.

His pleading didn't stop until Ahmar's arm folded over my shoulder, and he turned me away from the doorway, my cheeks soaked in tears.

"Oh, God..." I moan, then stumble off the pathway and fall to my knees in the grass.

"Callie!" Ivy rushes over, her hands on my back as she bends down.

Why did you do this? You were like a daughter to me...

"It can't be," I say, licking the sudden salt from my lips. I'm crying.

"Here. C'mere." Ivy gently pulls on my shoulders until she envelopes me into a hug, oblivious to the small crowd gathering around us, asking if I'm all right.

"It may not be Dr. Luke," Ivy murmurs into my ear, "but it's someone. And they'll catch him. You're safe. You'll be safe."

"That's not..." My face crumples into the line of her neck and shoulder. "I'm not afraid for my life. I'm..."

Afraid of being wrong again.

More students pause in the walkway, some for concern, most to spectate. Ivy pulls me to a stand and puts a protective arm around my shoulders as she guides me through the collecting crowd and toward the school.

"If you want to go back to your room, I can bring you some breakfast," Ivy says.

While it's tempting to shut out the world and pull covers over my head, I say, "No. I'll be all right. It's a shock, is all."

"No kidding. You and Chase were the ones who got Dr. Luke to say enough to confess, right?"

I wince. *It wasn't exactly a confession.*

Ivy notices and adds, "Not that you're responsible. You're *not*, Callie. Dr. Luke still slept with Piper. And Mrs. Dorian. And God knows who else. He's still a dirty sleezeball who ruined his own life. You know that, right?"

I nod, but don't necessarily believe it. It's one thing to be a jerk-off. Another to be a murderer.

"Piper's parents are still pressing charges, too. Statutory rape..." Ivy continues the morbid pep talk meant to make me feel better, and I appreciate her efforts to reduce my involvement in this clusterfuck, but I never told her how deep I went into Piper's investigation.

How I tend to obsess over these things.

I gnaw on my lower lip, desperate to tell her, but too embarrassed to admit it.

How is one supposed to explain to their only friend their growing habit of implicating the wrong man?

"I'm glad you caught me on the way to the dining hall," Ivy says. "It's all anyone will be talking about over their breakfast. It sure would've been awkward if you puked on their pancakes."

Ivy elbows me after the joke. I smile wanly in response. "I'm not headed there, anyway."

"No?"

"I'm going into town to study at the public library for a while."

"Can't say I blame you. Gossip is so distracting, isn't it?"

This time, my laugh is genuine. "I'll catch you later. You'll text me if you hear anything else, right?"

"One hundred percent. And text me when you're back."

We separate at the academy's front pavilion, Ivy hopping up the steps and into the school with a few other students dressed in their weekend casual.

I pull out my phone and tap on the Briarcliff app to call the personal chauffeur service. After receiving an alert that the wait will be 10 minutes, my thumb hovers over my text list, instinctually tempted to message Chase.

I have to believe he already knows. He has his finger on the pulse of Briarcliff better than most faculty members, and his sources would've told him about Dr. Luke.

So, why didn't he text me? Did he know all this last night?

The realization pisses me off, and I shove my phone back in my bag without bothering to contact him. I'm better off anxiously awaiting a call from Ahmar, not Chase Stone. Ahmar could help me clear up some confusion and possibly shed light on what is now a crucial piece of the puzzle.

The DNA of Piper's secret pregnancy.

Evidence that could mean everything, and not just to Chase.

Seven

BRIARCLIFF'S TOWN car pulls up to the center of the circular driveway, and I greet my favorite driver of the three, Yael, when I slide in.

"Sorry I was late," he says as he completes the half-circle to exit school grounds. "It's a popular morning."

"Really?"

Students tend to avoid the town and the chauffeur service, preferring to use their own cars to get to their nearby vacation homes and mansions on weekends.

Yael chuckles. "You and me both, Miss."

"By all means, Yael, don't ever refer to me as *miss*." I smile at him in the rearview mirror. "Callie's fine."

Yael shows a line of bright white teeth in response. "Sure thing, Callie."

The rest of the drive is quiet, the sun-soaked trees and moss-covered rocks blurring past as I take out my phone but hold it up with an unfocused stare.

The pages of Piper's diary aren't there anymore, but I'd come close to memorizing each and every sheet of paper she scrawled across, full of her thoughts but barren of clues, before the pictures were stolen, then deleted. She never mentioned a surprise pregnancy. But her sexual encounters with Mr. S took up most of the pages, a man I'd convinced myself was Dr. Luke.

It's still him. I know it deep in my soul.

Is he a murderer? Or did Dr. Luke actually dump her, like he insisted he did, which made her so devastated, she didn't think before she plunged into the black sea below Lover's Leap?

Yet, the day she died is the same day Rose Briar is assumed to have jumped off the same cliff, the tortured wife of Briarcliff Academy's founder.

And Cloaks haunt the school at night, a society of students, or faculty, or *both*, whose motives are more sinister than sacrificial.

"*Argh*." I massage my temples with both hands, the phone dropping to my lap.

245

I can't do this again. I can't fall down the rabbit hole with the full confidence I'll climb out.

"Are you all right, Mi—Callie?"

I open my eyes and force a smile. "Project jitters. I'm still getting used to the demands of this school."

Yael murmurs in agreement, pulling on to Main Street and parallel parking by the town's library/post office. "Don't put too much stress on yourself. You have the right idea, coming here instead of using the school library. I hope you find what you're looking for."

"Me too," I say, with a lot more meaning than Yael could understand, and climb from the car.

I fix my backpack on my shoulders, wishing I'd thought to pack my jacket, now that I'm closer to the ocean shore and there's a bitter, salty chill to the air that the academy seems to have walled off. As I'm adjusting the heavy load, I naturally glance down the street, noting how deserted the seaside town is, despite the tourist attractions of a lobster shack, bakery, and candy shop.

It's said the town's income comes mostly from the academy, without much effort going into keeping the small economy going. Almost like the pastel, clapboard shops and fluttering, colorful flags touting the incoming Halloween Festival are window dressing, rather than failing decorations that folks passing through don't bother to look at as they aim for more desirable locations, like Newport or Providence.

My attention lands on the lobster shack, saddened it's not more populated, because they make a mean lobster omelet for brunch, and I pause on the two people out front.

They're about two blocks away on the other side of the street, but it's easy to make out the smooth brown hair and the headband that keeps it out of Addisyn's face. The boy she's gesturing to, Jack, is her boyfriend and works at the restaurant—the gasp-worthy relationship of a prep school darling and a local townie out in the open for anyone to see. And by anyone, I mean ... only me.

I don't judge, or care. What keeps my stare on the couple is the way Addisyn moves, her motions stuttered and sharp. Jack responds with wild gesticulations of his own, both their expressions dark and storm-fueled.

In the middle of a sharp explanation, Jack's head tilts, and he catches my eye. The conversation halts.

Addisyn follows Jack's focus, and when she lands on me, she's not nearly as ominous and glowering.

"The hell are you looking at, possum?" she calls across the street. "Are you so tired of creeping around campus that you've come into town to jerk off instead?"

Aaaaand she's picked up right where her sister left off. How magical.

I shouldn't, but... "If I open a door to a room where you're expecting privacy, *then* you can be mad."

Addisyn hisses, and Jack throws me the finger.

I'm not in the mood to joust, so I turn my back on them and trudge up the library's steps, inwardly eager to get away before Addisyn launches into full attack mode.

Which, she may have a right to, now that Dr. Luke's been released.

Crap. Now I feel bad. Maybe her anger at the world is warranted. Funneling it into me is a sad byproduct, but unavoidable when such a vast amount of torrential hate exists inside you, there's nowhere to unleash it except for on the ones stupid enough to prod and goad at the edges.

I did it, too, and my stepdad was the sorry victim.

"Why, hello! You're back!"

I blink, realizing I've stepped through Briarcliff Library's doors and hover at the reception desk, where Darla sits, her fifties-style glasses perched on her nose while her eyes, enlarged by thick prescription lenses, regard me.

"It's quieter here," I say as a lame explanation. Aren't all libraries naturally quiet?

"I can imagine," Darla agrees, then motions to the middle of the rectangular room, bordered on all sides with stacks of books and topped off with a low, cork-board ceiling. "The place is yours. Well—yours and another young go-getter. Seems your secret's out."

I stiffen at her last sentence, but instinctually search the designated study tables. When I find the person Darla's referring to, my shoulders slump and I mutter, "No wonder Yael was so busy this morning."

First Addisyn, and now Emma.

"What's that, dear?"

"Nothing," I say to Darla.

She smiles, then flicks her fingers. "Go on, now. Studying ain't built in a day."

I shuffle forward, but no matter where I place my butt to do my work, I'll be in Emma's scope. The public library is so small. There are three study tables in total, and all in the center of the room.

As silently as I can, I pad over to the farthest table away from Emma. She's chosen to be nearer to the stacks of books, and mine is closer to Darla.

Emma had the better idea. There's a great risk that Darla will get so bored with her Harlequin paperback, she'll try for idle chit-chat.

My bag thumps on the bleached wooden table. Emma glances up at the sound. When her eyes connect with mine, she sags.

I scrunch up half my face in response. *Sorry. I was hoping to get some space from Briarcliff, too.*

She glares but says nothing as she gets back to her laptop. I exhale in relief, and work on setting up my station.

I toss my phone on top of my spiral notebooks. All signs point to me needing to work on my English Lit paper due in a week. My phone's black screen shouldn't be so distracting, but it is.

Dr. Luke's out.

Someone ripped important pages from Piper's diary that I never saw.

That person could be her killer.

I splay my hands on my closed laptop, mentally prepping for actual schoolwork once I sit, but my eye is continuously drawn to my phone.

Lips curled in frustration, I grab it and open the photos, swiping until the beginnings of Rose Briar's nineteenth century letter scroll across the screen. The original is hidden away in one of my textbooks, but it's so delicate, it's better to reference the copy.

"Damn it," I mutter, and place the screen face down on the table, but it's too late.

I'm not going to get anything done until I explore more of this library and see if it has more gifts to impart.

I ask Darla in a low whisper, "Where is that section on the founders of Briarcliff Academy again?"

"Don't you remember, dear?" Darla responds in a regular voice. Emma's head lifts. "Stack eight is where you'll find information on the Briars."

I briefly glance at Emma in apology for the noise, but instead of facing annoyance, I read a cautious alertness in her expression.

"Thanks," I say to Darla, then slide out from my seat and search for the stack, which, if I recall, is closer to the back of the building.

"That reminds me!" Darla says, *still* in an outside voice. "Briarcliff's mayor has just donated Thorne Briar's original office supplies for our educational pleasure for one whole month. It's on the back wall, honey, in a glass display, along with a few other artifacts from the Briar's time that we like to showcase during holidays. For the tourists, you know."

"Yes. The tourists," I say, my sarcasm at its lowest setting. I doubt the meager out-of-towners who come by want to know the historical progression of a ridiculously pompous preparatory school for the spawn of the nation's 1%, but what do I know?

It doesn't escape me that *I'm* an out-of-towner who is extremely curious about Briarcliff's origins.

"That is," Darla continues, "what remains after the f—"

She stops herself by clamping a hand to her mouth. Her gaze skitters over to Emma with such dismay, my cheeks flush for her.

To Emma's credit, she raises her eyes skyward and shakes her head in disdain.

"Thank you," I say quickly, then beeline through the stacks and to the back, where a map of the Briarcliff township, including the academy's grounds, is drawn to scale and takes up the entire wall.

"Whoa," I murmur, my eyes tracing the detailed forest terrain and hand-drawn buildings interspersed throughout. Gray roads cut through the greenery, dividing into smaller roadways like tentacles brushing against buildings, cliffs and oceanic shores.

An invisible string pulls taut against my vision, halting my scan with anchoring precision. The jagged end of Lover's Leap emerges from the northeast corner, as ominous in acrylic as it is in real life.

"Why are you here?"

The voice smacks between my shoulders and jolts down my spine. I spin, my heart pattering harder than expected.

Emma stands in between two stacks, her hulking form casting her in the light of a fabled hunchback escaping from one of the books lining either side of her.

"Research," I manage to say.

Emma's frown lines grow deeper. "On what?"

"The—the founders." I gesture behind me, where a bench-length glass display showcases the Briar artifacts I haven't gotten a chance to study yet.

"Nobody comes to the public library."

"Exactly." I arch a brow. "I assume that's why you're here, too."

"I have reason to be." Emma takes a step forward, her focus wavering on mine. She ends up losing whatever inner battle she's waging, and stares at the line of Briar-owned items.

"Such crap," she mumbles.

I follow her movements by turning until we're both facing the display. "Why do you say that?"

"They make it seem like he was such a good man. That he did this world a favor by creating this town and building a school for boys."

Emma studies the glass case with dangerous wonder, her upper lip frozen mid-sneer. Standing this close to her, I notice the faint, puckered scar tissue running along the side of her face and cauliflowering around her ear.

Emma's body stills, but her eyes snap to mine with the speed and haunting eeriness of a ventriloquist's doll. "Problem?"

The after-effects of Emma's attack are well-known, but the details kept strictly mute. I never read up on what happened to her, because it was none of my business and—if I'm to be honest—irrelevant to my investigation into Piper's death.

Or so I thought.

I'm disappointed in my reaction, though. This is the type of violence my mother faced as a full-time job when she was alive, and sometimes, she couldn't help but bring it home. I've been exposed to this kind of brutality, in vicious, high definition.

"No," I say, covering my faux pas by focusing on the display. "It takes a lot of hatred to despise not only a school, but the entire town that comes with it."

"It sure does." I feel Emma's stare against my profile burning holes into my pores. "But I've had a lot of time to nurture it."

"Is that why you're back? To get some answers?"

Emma cocks her head in my periphery. "Answers have many different interpretations." She pauses. "Perhaps I'm here to let them know they haven't won."

I turn to her. "Who's 'they'?"

Emma notches up her chin. Something tells me she rarely makes a mistake with what she says ... not anymore.

"You tell me," she says. "Have you discovered anything while doing your *research*?"

"Not much. Just a hidden society within the academy," I deadpan.

Emma sucks in a breath, but her stare remains level, and dare I say, a flicker of respect shines within. "You shouldn't be spouting off about that."

I motion to where we are. "I'm not exactly screaming it from the rooftops."

"But you're certain they exist."

I cling to this brief spurt of bravery. Emma's testing me, and I have the sense that out of everyone, she may be the one to actually speak the truth. "I even have names for them. The Nobles. The V—"

"Don't say it," Emma says in a wet whisper. My side presses harder into the display when her face transforms from assessing to deadly. "Don't you dare repeat that name, not if you don't want them to come for you."

My breath becomes smaller in my chest. Tighter. "Did they attack you? Is that why you set the fire?"

Now, oh, *now*, I wish I'd grown Emma's ability to carefully craft a sentence before giving it the mistake of a voice.

Emma bares her teeth, her eyes like fossilized amber, except hers melts to reveal the creature encased within. "*Who told you that?*"

"N-no one. It was a mistake. I didn't mean for it to come out like that." Fuck, I'm a terrible liar. "I meant did *they* set the fire and trap you?"

Emma steps into my space, so close, her nose nearly brushes mine. Her breath heats my lips to a terrible level, but I can't retreat. Not if I want her to believe me.

"You knew Piper," I say, despite her flaring nostrils. "Do you think she killed herself, or was she attacked by the same person who hurt you?"

"How *dare* you?"

Exactly. How dare I. I'm putting my theories into dangerous existence, threading a needle so deadly, two women have been brutalized from it—one killed.

"If I don't ask the questions," I say, clenching my trembling fingers into fists, "no one else will. Piper deserves justice. You deserve justice."

"Piper was a twat, and you don't know me from shit," Emma says, but she backs off, the stale air of the library reclaiming its place between us. "This is because of my brother, isn't it? Don't tell me, the new girl falls for the perfect, popular guy, but he doesn't return the favor. So, in order to gain his everlasting gratitude, she tries to solve his twin sister's assault and his ex-girlfriend's death. Do I have that right? *God.*" Emma lets out a cruel laugh. "So pathetic."

My lips part on a snarl. "You have it completely twisted. It's this place." I spread my arms. "This school. There's a poison here, and terrible truths are covered up." I point to Thorne Briar's business log, open to some random page of handwritten profits and losses. "I've discovered enough to know that it doesn't start with Chase. It doesn't begin with Piper. Nor did it first strike with *you*. It begins with Rose Briar."

I let out a whoosh of breath, unused to such emotion crossing over my tongue, not since it was capped and bottled in an involuntary psychiatric hold. I vowed never to put myself in a position where dry pills were forced down my throat again.

Yet ... here I've landed.

Double fuck.

Emma stumbles back, her face, stiffened with old scars, spasming with long forgotten muscles. Fear. Apprehension. Denial.

Her skin takes on a ghostly cast, and her hand screeches against the glass display where she drags it, her palms soaked in sweat. "Do you like the way my face looks? Because I'm pretty sure yours will end up this way, too."

"So far," I say quietly, ignoring the spasm of panic in my chest, "not one person has truly acknowledged the possibility that these societies exist. Until you."

Emma regains enough composure to snap, "Both Piper's and my *tragedies*, as you idiots call them, circle around Chase. Why don't you be as unoriginal as everyone else and consider him to be the problem?"

"Is he?"

Emma flinches.

"Because in the rare times he's talked about you, it's been with nothing but love and defense," I say. "And he punishes himself. I hear it whenever he utters your name

—he thinks he's responsible for what happened, not because he wielded the weapon, but because he wasn't there to protect you."

I'm stunned by my statement, and I press my fingers to my lips at the continued passion, draining my spirit faster than I can contain it.

Emma eyes grow small with suspicion. "Chase doesn't talk about me. With anyone."

I swallow, take one last look at the glass case, then come back to Emma. "My mistake, then."

I'm brushing past her before Emma can think up a proper, scathing response, and hurry to collect my things.

But I can never escape. The Briars will follow me, and so will the Harringtons and Stones.

I've introduced myself to their demons, and they will continue their dark suffocation until I unearth the hidden details that can one day set them free.

That is ... if I can do it before they bury me, too.

Eight

THERE'S no wait to take the Briarcliff chauffeur service back home. And thankfully, no forced Briarcliff carpool either.

Addisyn must still be off with her boyfriend, and I left Emma within the shadowed recesses of the library, so I'm safe from them, for now.

My feet hit the asphalt of the school driveway along with a deep urge to see a friendly face and immerse myself in banal activities, like painting my nails or watching garbage TV. Anything to get my mind off the spindly critters circling the back of my brain, spinning their web of names.

Piper. Emma. Rose.

Is their trauma related? *How?*

Leave it alone, a voice whispers from within. *This is not for your wounded heart.*

Nor is sitting on my ass, doing nothing while the person responsible for hurting these girls goes on with their life, merry and free.

They are not your mother.

"Shut up, Voice," I seethe, ignoring the startled looks cast in my direction as I pass them by on the student pathway to the dorms.

I end up bypassing my own, lonely dorm and head to Richardson Place. It's where Ivy and Eden live, and I hope at least one of them is there when I knock on their door.

It pulls wide to reveal Ivy. At the sight of her, I pause with my fist still held up to knock. "What's with the face?"

"Oh, this old thang?" Ivy circles her freshly powdered, foundationed, and glammed-up face with a finger. "It's Saturday, girl. Let's play dress up, and make-up, and drink up, then we're going out. Didn't you get my text?"

I picture my phone, crammed at the bottom of my bag under my books and computer in the hope that it'd stay there. "Nope."

"Chase is holding a huge party at his lake house." Ivy yanks me inside. "We're going."

"A party for what? His near expulsion?"

Ivy laughs. "He's too precious to Marron's bottom line to be expelled. Do you have stuff to get ready or do you just want to borrow some of mine?"

Ivy, here on full scholarship, barely has a chest of drawers to call her own. Her and Eden's room is much smaller than mine, with bolted, standard, grayish-blue furniture and a twin bed that might as well fold-out Murphy-style for each.

Meanwhile, my stepdad's new wife sends me seasonal outfit changes on the regular, my self-conscious rebuffs largely ignored.

"I have a better idea," I say. "Let's go back to my place and you can raid my closet for a dress for me *and* for you."

Ivy's eyes light up brighter than holiday fireworks, and a laugh escapes my throat as she half-pulls, half-drags me out of her room, and we scamper over to mine.

This is precisely what I needed, a friend and a fun time—things I haven't had the beauty of basking in for a while. Chase might be the gatekeeper to my Briarcliff experience, but after the morning I've had, I'm willing to pay his price.

Plus, *everyone* is going, and his lake house is huge. I figure there will be plenty of chances to avoid him until I'm ready.

Emma hasn't returned to the dorms, and after Ivy's tentative questions on how the first night went and what Emma's like, to which I answered noncommittally, we blast music from my computer and sift through the curated outfits Lynda thought would suit me.

When Ivy pulls out a short, black mini dress with a plunging V where boobs should be, I'm positive my stepdad did *not* approve this "seasonal pick" for fall and winter.

Where the frick are my snow pants?

"This says you all over it." Ivy flips the dress back and forth on the hanger, humming and hawing in ways that are newly foreign to me. My ex-friend back in New York, Sylvie and I, often got ready like this, but we added lines of coke to our outfit changes and snorts between eye-liner applications.

The flashback fogs my vision, and for a minute I see Sylvie bending close to my closet mirror, dabbing at the corner of her eyes and sniffling, *"Make a few more lines for us, will you? We'll be so badass at the club tonight."*

"Callie?"

Ivy's face sharpens as she holds up the dress, an unsure smile plastered across her face.

In so many ways, Ivy is the complete opposite of Sylvie. There will be no drugs tonight. No stranger's hard-ons rubbing against the small of my back as I whirl and stumble under strobe lights.

"No freaking way am I wearing that," I say. "That's more Falyn's taste."

"Mm." Ivy's expression is morphing in a way I don't like. She's appearing more as a reality TV fashion judge than my friend, and ... I'm fairly confident I'll be freezing my nipples off tonight. "You're trying it on."

"No, I'm—"

The dress whacks me in the face.

"And this one."

Another whack.

"This, too."

I predict Ivy's next toss and hold my dress-laden hands out to catch it, but Ivy fakes me out and pauses mid-throw. "On the other hand, this purple would totally complement my eyes and hair..."

Laughing, I perch on my bed. "Wear whatever you want."

"And you, my dear, will wear what I tell you to," Ivy says, then spreads her fingers and descends on me.

Ivy won.

A few hours of primping and sipping later, I'm in the risqué black number, my knees knocking together as we wait for a car at the front of the academy. Ivy chose the off-the-shoulder, deep purple dress, its sequins catching the nectarine glow of the setting sun whenever she turns.

Other seniors have taken their own cars to the lake house, and those juniors, sophomores, and freshmen who aren't allowed off-campus on weekends but have figured a way to smuggle themselves out, have long departed.

"Isn't it only cool to attend parties at, like, eleven at night?" I ask Ivy as we wait.

"Usually," she answers through the flat-ironed curtain of her silvery blond hair. Ivy's head is bent as she scrolls through her phone. "But, you and me, we don't have the hook-ups to give us anything more to pregame with at the dorms. Hence..." She lifts her head as she tucks her phone into her clutch. "Why we, and every other invitee, are going to Chase's place early. Free booze."

After the scandal between Piper and Dr. Luke broke, the spine of Briarcliff's student manual cracked open, too. Professors referred to the rules constantly, be it for our curfew or what we could keep in our dorms. Random searches were reinforced, and the first time they were implemented, Thorne and Rose Houses had a *lot* of plumbing issues.

One thing the faculty couldn't revoke was the seniors' privilege to leave campus on weekends. Not if they didn't want a riot on their hands. They did, however, forbid any access to Lover's Leap and put up a new gate with barbed wire curling its metal thorns at the top.

I've only seen the cliff once, soon after Piper died. It starts with a natural clearing in the thicket of trees where students gathered, well away from the dropping off point. For Piper to have stepped so close to the edge, someone would've had to corner her and cause her to back up, her heels scraping against the forest ground until it turned to stone, then ... air.

I shiver at the thought.

"Cold?" Ivy asks.

"I'm good," I say, unfolding my denim jacket from my arm and sliding it on. "Though it's getting frosty."

"Yeah." Ivy glances up at the sky, where burnt orange tendrils are giving way to gray dusk. "It gets bitterly cold here, and soon. October's our last month of pretty."

Yael pulls up, and we both slide in, my dress hiking scarily high when I sit. I mutter a curse, but Ivy laughs, telling me I should showcase my jay-walker legs more often.

"Just because I'm a city girl," I say while elbowing her, "doesn't mean I can't be athletic."

"Oh, yeah? Join crew then."

"No way in hell."

"Figures." Ivy laughs.

Ivy's the only one who knows I can't swim. In a school surrounded by water, where the most popular sport is rowing, vacation homes are lake houses, and cliff faces jutting out into the ocean are the hot hookup spots, my lack of ability to tread water seems like a glaring weakness.

Do you like the way my face looks? a tiny voice whispers. Emma's. *Don't say their name, not if you don't want them to come after you...*

I pull my jacket tighter across my chest.

Ivy's my best friend. She may love to gossip, but when it comes to me, she's reliably mute. She doesn't talk about my mother's murder, despite having an unwanted first-row seat to the crime scene photos, and she's never brought up my inability to swim with anyone.

Relief lightens my chest when Ivy doesn't push the issue.

We arrive at Chase's lake house fifteen minutes later than when I was in his car. Yael slows at the beginning of the thin private drive, the paved roadway clogged with a line of luxury vehicles, most lazily parked without giving much thought to leaving space for other cars to nudge through.

I lean forward to the middle console. "It's okay, Yael. We can walk the rest of the way up."

"You sure?" he asks.

Ivy scoffs. "Speak for yourself."

She lifts a freshly shaved leg shining with moisturizer. A three-inch black heel caps off her outfit.

"It's a short walk," I say as I push the door open. "Come on."

"How do you know how far it is?" she asks but steps out on her side. Our doors slam at the same time.

Shit. I love how I was just thinking what good a friend Ivy is to me, and meanwhile, I'm hiding my meet-up with Chase like he's my dirty little secret.

At least it's a meet-up this time and not pornographic sex that made you blow your load the minute his tongue found your—

"Stupid voice," I mutter again.

"What's that?"

"Nothing." I grab Ivy's hand and we toddle up the drive.

I glance at Ivy, hobbling beside me but maintaining her good spirit as we toddle through cars and people, heading to the front.

My phone rings in my purse as the drive levels out and the lake house comes into view. At dusk, it's easier to appreciate the one-way planes of glass used for walls and the multiple levels of pointed roofs. The home is cabin chic meets million-dollar view, and Ivy unfurls her arm from mine, gaping at the structure.

"Go on in," I say to her, popping open my purse. "I'll find you."

"Don't have to tell me twice. Why did I avoid off-campus parties again?" Ivy asks, then flashes me a bright smile and joins another group heading inside, where music blasts and bottles clink.

AHMAR flashes on my screen when I pull my phone out.

"Hey," I say, tucking the phone between my shoulder and ear while wandering closer to the edge of trees. Someone turns the music up.

"Sounds like you're somewhere you shouldn't be," Ahmar says, but I hear the smile accompanying his words.

"My first weekend party experience. Wish me luck."

"You're the smartest kid I know. You don't need it." Ahmar pauses. "You know never to accept a drink you didn't make yourself, right?"

I huff out a laugh, but I don't miss the hesitation in his voice. He saw me at my worst. He held back my hair when I stumbled to his apartment at 4 AM, because I couldn't go home and face my stepdad, and coughed up vomit for hours. "Yes, Dad. I'm being good. Promise."

The name sounds more heartfelt than I intended, but if Ahmar senses it, he keeps it to himself. "I trust you, Calla. You paid your dues. So, what do you need from me?"

"Well..."

"Uh-oh. I sense hedging."

I pull my lips in, pressing down hard with my teeth, then decide to get it over with as fast as possible. "Could you find out if they've matched the DNA of the baby to anyone?"

Static pops on the other end of the line as I picture Ahmar shifting, wherever he is, clearly uncomfortable. "Calla..."

"I know. *I know.* It's a lot to ask, but it would clear up a lot. Did you hear about Dr. Luke?"

"Yeah, kid, I did, just this morning. I'm sorry. I wanted to call you to see how you're holding up, but—"

"You're on the job. I get it." And I do. "But that means you agree, right? Finding out the DNA of the baby would answer some serious questions."

"Sure, but you have to remember, the paternity of the fetus doesn't necessarily mean it's the perp's. And the vic—sorry, Piper—was only ten weeks along."

I press the phone harder to my ear. "You've been told how far along she was?"

A growl curse into my ear, then nothing.

"Ahmar?"

"Yes," he admits. "Calla, you're like a daughter to me. Even if you hadn't asked me to, I would've kept updated on this case. I've got to make sure you're not in danger by staying at that school."

Warmth encompasses my soul, a comforting blanket I haven't felt since leaving NYC over a month ago. "Thank you for keeping me safe. Now tell me what you know."

Ahmar gives a low, appreciative laugh, but his tone is serious. "The DNA results came back about a week ago."

I breathe in sharp, evergreen air, its pine needles spearing my lungs. I chance a look at the lake house, as if Chase would be standing near one of the massive windows, watching me.

"You ... you know who the father is?"

"It's partially why this teacher guy was let go. Where did you hear the news of his release, anyway?"

"Gossip. Friends. I don't know. Ahmar, *tell me.*"

"Easy, kid. There was a match. It's no one you associate with."

While this should come as a comfort, Ahmar has no idea who I associate with at Briarcliff. He's ignorant to the boys, societies, and mean girls frequenting these grounds, and I'd like to keep it that way. I'd rather he think of me as reformed. An enterprising young student ready to take on the world with a world-class diploma, whose roommate happened to be killed in an accident.

Not as a girl deliberately immersing herself in the elite underworld to solve a murder.

"Can you give me a name?" I ask.

"That's confidential. You know how it works."

"But it's me you're talking to. My roommate was killed. Ahmar..."

He exhales, and I refuse to wince at the pang of guilt that hits when I know I've won.

"I'm already aware of the possibilities," I argue. "Dr. Luke or Chase. And if you're saying it's not Dr. Luke's..."

I realize my mistake too late.

"Chase, huh? Since when are you so familiar with that dude?"

"I ... he's well-known. By everybody. And he's Piper's ex. I'm only repeating what I hear, but maybe if a *reliable* source gave me information, I'd stop listening to gossip."

Ahmar chuckles. "I see what you did there."

"I'm begging you. Is it—"

"This Chase guy? No, it's not."

My chest cracks from the released pressure. I hold a hand to my heart, ensuring it's still beating.

"He's just well-known, huh?"

The dangerous edge to Ahmar's tone makes me grimace. "He's just a guy, Ahmar."

"A guy I gotta meet?"

"No. Definitely not."

"Mm."

It's easy to change the subject. "I don't understand. You said the DNA result was partially why Dr. Luke was released. So, it's not his, either?"

"Nope."

My hand stills in the middle of tucking my hair behind my ear. I frown into the copse of trees, noting the growing, cold shadows creeping onto the asphalt and over my feet.

"The DNA's been tied to a kid in the system. A boy named Joaquín del Pozo. Heard of him?"

My brows pull down, hard and low. "Not even a little bit."

"Exactly. That's the end of that. You don't know the dude. I did you a favor by giving you that name, and in return, do one for me."

Ahmar's talking, but his voice seems so far way, tinned and faint compared to the rush in my ears.

Who the *hell* is Joaquín del Pozo?

"Calla?"

"Yeah." I finish tucking my hair back. "I'm still here."

"This roommate of yours, Piper, it looks like she was involved with a few guys. Her death could be related to this boy, but it might not be. Because of that, I need you to stay back, okay? Let the police do their jobs, and run through their witness and suspect lists, as they've been doing. Are you listening?"

"Yeah," I say, my voice a whispery trace of its usual sound. "There's a process. I know that."

"I'm doing what I can behind the scenes, but I have my ear on this. Leave me in charge. Can you agree to that?"

His question is not a simple request. He remembers, as much as I do, how the weeks after my mother's death went. How I fell apart and screamed for him to arrest my stepdad, then, when that didn't work, turned to artificial mind-altering.

I respond quietly. "This isn't that, Ahmar."

"Not saying it is. But I'll never stop looking out for you."

I smile through the welling thickness in my throat. "I love you."

"I love you, too, kiddo. Now, go try to have some safe, wholesome high school fun. I got this."

We hang up, and I wiggle my phone back into a clutch chosen by Lynda that seems to only fit lip gloss, wrestling it shut.

An adult taking the reins—and a competent one at that—would usually have me feeling buoyant, secure, and hopeful. But ... there's so much Ahmar doesn't know.

I'm not sure how much I can tell him, because my confession would have to begin right here, with the boy I made a deal with. And if I divulge the DNA results to Chase, I have no doubt he'll stage a reaping until Joaquín is found. Then destroyed.

Nine

THE LAKE HOUSE'S front doorway—twice the size of normal entryways—is packed with bodies, shifting, drinking, hooting, hollering, all of it.

I'm amazed at the transformation of the Briarcliff elite, though it shouldn't come as a surprise that as soon as the uniform's stripped off and the weekend's pulled on, revelry ensues.

And ... a lot of belly buttons enjoy their freedom.

I duck under errant elbows and arms, alcohol-tinged droplets escaping from red Solo cups and landing on my shoulders and forehead, but I forge on. The music pushes through my soles and into my chest, a deep, rhythmic bass turning my heart into an 8-count thump.

First, I search for Ivy, but don't see her in the expansive main room. A ring of people surround the fireplace that crackles and spurts, nearby blunts and cigarettes finding the flame.

I look into the kitchen, but can't see Ivy through the throng, and I don't spot Chase, either.

Chase.

Smokey trails of relief float alongside the thought of his name.

The baby isn't his. He won't be pulled in for more questioning ... hopefully. And maybe, his anxiety can be eased over the unexpected loss of something so precious and fleeting in its existence.

Ahmar's warning battles for recognition, his urging to keep the revelation to myself and go on with my schooling like none of this ever happened.

If only, Ahmar, I think dully. *Except, I don't think I've been forged that way.*

An ice-cold rivulet presses into my arm, and I realize that during my musings, I've wandered to the back of the house and against the windows, so black during my first visit, now midnight blue with nightfall.

Branches frame the glass, most barren of leaves, and stretch to some point past my view. A lake glitters beneath a thin, vertical dock, and I picture Chase's silhouette seated at the end, dangling his feet into the fractured blue, his face tipped to the sky.

A *boom* of thunder has me jumping back from the window and staring up, wondering when storm clouds decided they wanted to join the party.

A guttural laugh warns me of an incoming clobbering before the guffawing guy slams into me, and I duck as he stumbles against the glass.

"Fuck, whoops!" he says, the features on his face more diagonal than is probably usual. He thrusts an arm in my direction, his cup sloshing. "Drink?"

"No, thank you."

"Ha! The possum's polite!" the buffoon hollers, then stumbles to his group of friends.

From this vantage point, I can see the packed room in its entirety. People mill, dance, and stumble, the music cranked to its highest level, and there's more spilled liquor than wood showing on the parquet floors.

Is this really Chase's kind of thing?

This doesn't resemble the sleek, deliberate boy I see in the halls of Briarcliff, nor does it describe the naked Adonis curved in my bed, murmuring dark promises in my ear.

Uncomfortable memories float within the drunken haze of my writhing classmates, sharpening the flashback of when I used to be this, free and drug-fueled and forgotten, preferring pills melting on my tongue and powder up my nose to the reality of my murdered mother.

Six months into it, there was an overdose scare involving Sylvie, and I haven't been up to no good since. I wish I could say it was my stepdad being written off as a suspect that made me change my ways and sober up once I realized the power my words could have over someone's life. But, with his innocence came a reckoning of a different sort: I was deemed unhinged. A liar. My voice became an intangible, cloudy mist dissipated with the swipe of a medical practitioner's hand.

Shuddering, I peel away from the windows in search of another room. I could wait out Ivy's fun and collect my thoughts. It'll give me time to sort through the revelation of Piper's third lover.

A darkened hall peeks out from the writhing, dancing bodies, and I carve a forward path, careful to avoid more spill-over. From my dress or people's drinks, I'm not sure, but I keep a forearm pressed to my boobs just in case.

Once I break from the weed-cloud, the empty space of the hallway fills me with oxygen. I breathe, glancing around, and walk farther in, my eyes trailing across professional portraits of Chase and his family.

When I come to a photo of the four of them, Emma seated beside Chase and their parents behind them, I stop.

"My God..." I murmur, my hand going to the picture before I can stop it. My fingers trail across one side of Emma's face—the former one, her cheekbones slim and sharp, exactly like her brother's.

Her eyes seem to shine through the photo and light up the hallway, her hair, a gorgeous cascade of copper-blonde waves, hiding her shoulders but putting her beauty on full display.

All their postures are stiff, the smiles composed and perfected for the photographer behind the lens. Even the navy blue and white of their outfits is deliberate, chosen to match the backdrop of the lake behind them. But Emma's smile lines are deeper than the rest. Her eyes are crinkled with private mirth, and she looks .... the happiest.

My attention moves to Chase, as gorgeous staged in a photo as he is in real life, but a *thump* behind the picture distracts me, my hand falling from the frame.

The music and shouts are quieter here, the party softer around the edges. I've drifted well into the hallway and a descending staircase is near my feet.

Another *thump*.

There's no door I can make out, so after a final glance behind my shoulder, I take the stairs leading down.

They descend deeper than I thought, considering the sprawling, two-story architecture of the lake house, and once I hit the last step, I move to the doorway beside it.

Another hallway forms within darkness—two actually. They're so black with shadow that I shy away from treading deeper, preferring the doorway I can see to the ones I don't.

Besides, I heard the thumps at the top of the staircase. Movement has to be coming from somewhere nearby.

I hesitantly push on the lever.

It briefly occurs to me that I could be interrupting a hook-up, but I can't find Ivy anywhere, or Chase, so I push the lever all the way down.

Hinges in this kind of house don't creak. The door swings open silently, and I step into the haunting blue glow of an office.

Indigo-purple light ripples over a wall of books, shelved all the way to the ceiling and guarded by a heavy, wooden desk. A plush, black leather chair sits empty, but swiveled to the side, as if someone just left it.

Curious, I walk over and press my palm into the seat, the warmth of a recent body seeping into my skin.

Another *thump* draws me straight, but I can't locate the sound. It's coming from in here, but it's ... not.

A large fish tank, nestled against the wall closest to the hallway, draws my attention, and I pass behind the chair and lean forward, instinctually searching for the fish.

I don't see anything but white specks, floating within the water enhanced by blacklight.

"Don't you—"

"But I've tried—"

Thump.

"Try harder!"

My spine goes rigid, and I search the room, positive I hear voices. Both obscured and muffled, but one is easier to hear because of its lighter, feminine tones.

"Are you sure?"

A third voice, a female, joins the conversation.

"...last chance. Otherwise, I'm taking..."

"Tell her."

"No. Lie to her before she discovers the truth."

I force a single blink, long and hard, because I swear these voices are coming from behind the bookshelf, but there was no entry I could tell during my descent that would indicate a room beside this office.

I cock my ear, tucking my hair behind my ears and leaning closer to the books.

"Too close."

"She's uncovering—"

"—we have to go on the defense, not bring in an outsider—"

"She's NOT an outsider!"

"Shh! Look. There's someone..."

I reel back, scanning the ceiling for a vent or something that's allowing me to hear voices that have to be coming from the opposite side.

I splay my fingers across the books, the amateur sleuth inside me determined to find the source. I run my finger along the middle row, then the next, one below, then the ground-level shelving, the tomb raider in me now confident I'm about to uncover a secret room, unlocked by the hidden lever inside a book...

My breath hisses when my finger stalls on a leather-bound spine, creased and crumbling with age. It has no title, no author, but an insignia is stamped at the center in gold.

A perfect circle with raven's wings as its Eastern and Western points.

I pull it out, handling it carefully with both hands. The leather is aged and worn, the gold embossing faded, but I'm able to read the title.

Correction. I can read the name. *Daniel Abraham Stone.*

"You puking down there?"

My knees lock.

I recognize the relaxed cadence, equivalent to a lion licking his fangs before he strikes.

Footsteps round the desk, and I hurry to push the book back in its spot before large, calloused palms move under my arms to lift me.

"Easy, Callie." Chase says near my ear, goosebumps tingling across my neck. "My father vows ruin on anyone who messes up his office."

"I'm—I'm not sick," I say, once my voice fights through the rush of tingles. Man, I wish Chase would stop affecting me like I'm some giddy freshman about to screw the class senior president.

Chase turns me to face him. In the UV blacklight, his skin is lavender-blue and ethereal, like I've been captured by a Faerie Prince.

Ugh. Stop relating him to dark fairy tales. Chase is a guy. A regular dude.

With abs and a pert butt I could bounce a coin off.

Chase searches my face, his stare heating my cheeks. "Then why are you here?"

"Looking for you."

"You found me." His lips close and curve with a smile, but my brows grow tight. I'm certain of the sadness within his grin.

The same expression when he left a few weeks ago, seconds after I told him that Piper was pregnant.

Chase's eyes slide away from mine, and his gaze moves past my shoulder and to the fish tank. "You know what those are?"

"I heard voices," I blurt out instead of answering. "But there's no room they could be coming from."

Chase ignores me, stepping around, but stays close, my nose following the drift of his cologne as he moves. "These are some of the smallest, most venomous jellyfish in the world. Irunkandji, they're called. Their sting is one hundred times worse than a cobra's. They can cause instant brain hemorrhages in humans."

I hedge backwards. "Cool pet."

Chase grunts, his attention on the aquarium. "They're rare, illegal to own, and incredibly fragile, yet my father has them flown in and replaced. Constantly. "

"All that fuss, and they're not even that pretty to look at."

This time, a genuine smile crosses Chase's profile. "So, did you sneak down here so you could learn about the Irunkandji?"

"I told you. I heard thumps and voices, and following them brought me down here." I point to the bookshelf. "Do you have a Chamber of Secrets back there?"

"Is that one of your two questions?"

I jolt, then suck in my lower lip. It's amazing how a little news like Piper having a third secret lover derailed me from my initial goal of pumping Chase for information.

I stare at him hard. I *want* to know where those voices were coming from. "Yes."

He turns away from the tank and angles his head toward the shelving, murmuring, "There's a room. Yes."

My answering expression must amuse him, because he adds, "I promised you the truth. Did you think I'd lie outright?"

"Um. Yep."

He chuckles, leaning a hip against his father's desk, which probably weighs more than an elephant. "I don't make deals for kicks."

"Can you—?"

"Think carefully about how willing you are to waste your next question," he says. "Because, no, I won't show you how to get in, or tell you what kind of room it is."

I grumble, but my mind's already recalibrating. *He won't tell me because it has to do with the Cloaks. And our deal prevents me from getting any information about them.*

I flit my gaze back to Chase and see a reluctant admiration there. He knows where my mind has gone, and that his lack of an explanation equals an answer.

"Fine. Then tell me why a prep school would have a secret society."

Chase sighs and lifts off the desk. "We agreed none of your questions would involve your Cloaks."

"And this one doesn't," I say. "I'm merely asking for your theory on *why* a high school might have a secret society, since most of those cults start in college."

He grunts and crosses his arms. "Cults."

"Prove me wrong." I mirror his posture. "And explain it to me in hypothetical terms."

Chase's eyes glimmer in the shadows.

He exhales, his focus moving to the bookshelves behind me. My concentration becomes a hawk's, anticipating that his attention will go to the leather-bound book with the raven's insignia.

Any tell, however small, will lead me closer to unlocking this mystery. I just *know* it.

"Perhaps," Chase begins, and I snap to attention, shocked he might actually answer me, "the founder of that school created it as a way to both fund and propel certain qualifying students to prestigious colleges, with the intention of placing them into certain careers."

"Like politics, government, top corporations," I say. "Economic influencers."

After a long exhale, Chase casts his gaze to the ceiling. "What a shocking Secret Society rumor you've uncovered. I keep telling you, there's nothing here. Just benign, old-century tradition."

"Yes, but unlike the Illuminati or ... I don't know ... the Knights Templar, Briarcliff didn't start with adults. They wanted their influence to sink into *children*."

Chase vaults off the desk, framing either side of my head with his arms as he presses his palms into the bookshelf behind me.

The backs of my shoulders press into the books, the scent of stale pages wafting over our bodies. I gasp, furious at how loud it is, but I don't cower.

Chase lowers his head, his eyes coming dangerously close to a glittering explosion. "You're in high school. Do you consider yourself young and impressionable?" He angles his head. "How about me?"

Chase presses a thumb to my lips, the hardened, rower's blisters cutting into the soft tissue, but I let him drag my lower lip down. I allow him to watch when his thumb hits my chin and my lower lip bounces back into place.

He shifts, the front of his pants skimming across my stomach, the hard length of him proving how much this stare-down is costing him.

Costing me.

A guttural moan builds in my throat, almost reaching my lips, but I swallow it down.

Sadly, my hips aren't nearly as compliant, and they push against him in a half-circle of lust.

I've missed him.

I've dreamed about the moment when I could have him again, physically and virulently, without thought of recourse.

But these have to be my hormones. The unquenchable sex drive Chase awoke inside me. It's not real life. It definitely doesn't resolve the endless questions, circling in my head like an unkindness of ravens.

I want to get out of here with my heart intact.

"You know who's responsible," I dare to whisper near his lips. "Who's hiding behind these books? What don't they want discovered?"

"I believe," he responds, low and under his breath, "you've exhausted your questions for the day."

Chase doesn't step back. The space between us grows smaller and hotter the longer our eyes duel, and I'm about to crumble, licking my lips at the remembered taste of him, my thighs trembling at the thought of his fingers, then his tongue, inside me.

Chase ducks down, my chin tilts up, and damn me to hell, I'm ready for him to kiss me.

Ten

CHASE'S HANDS move from the shelf to my hips, his face so close to mine, I feel the curl of his lips as he unleashes a hopeless snarl—

"Am I interrupting something?"

The feminine voice might as well be buckshot. Chase and I dive apart, but my muscles are too puddly with untapped passion. I fall back against the bookshelf on a heavy exhale.

Chase spins, slamming his palms on the desk and tipping his head to the person who caused the interruption.

Addisyn.

She stands at the doorway, a languid hand resting on her hip, but the rest of her is stiff with judgment.

"Get out."

Chase's demand is practically a whisper, but it's succinct.

Addisyn's jaw locks at the same time her eyes flash, but she stews for only a moment. "Moving on so fast, Chase?" Her gaze flicks to me. "You can do better than this."

"It's none of your business what I do. I said get out."

Addisyn shifts her weight. "I came down here because everyone's looking for you. There's a party going on without a host."

"Like you give a damn," he mutters.

"I give a lot of damns about appearances." Again, Addisyn cuts her eyes to me. "And you should, too, Chase. My mom just texted. Remember how we were told Piper was pregnant before she died?" Addisyn's eyes shine with tears, pronounced by the purple-blue light encasing this office. "Or have you already forgotten?"

Chase bows his head, the rigidity of his shoulders loosening with grief. "No. I haven't."

"Mom just texted," Addisyn repeats. "The baby wasn't Dr. Luke's."

My vision sharpens on Addisyn. I glance between the two of them, bracing for the knowledge Addisyn's about to impart.

Chase looks back at me, those seconds silently communicating our agreement and what I had promised him.

What I failed to deliver the very moment I saw him.

I frown. Why do I feel bad for him?

As if with a nudge, the book with the raven engraving spears against my calf. I imagine heat emanating from it, steamy tendrils of illicit knowledge circling my ankle.

This is Chase Stone. The guy who hides everything, has everything, and shares his secrets only through deals befitting his needs.

He knows about the Nobles and deliberately cuts me out of it. I'm certain he's aware of the sign of the raven and what it means.

It's how we were first introduced, after all.

Yet, I feel sorry for him when his expression crumbles upon hearing Addisyn's news, before he sets it into his famous Stone scowl. "I didn't get the update."

"Well, there you have it," Addisyn says, her voice growing thick. "It's not his, so it has to be yours."

Chase rubs a hand down his face. "This isn't the place. We can talk about this tomorrow."

"We'd better." Addisyn lowers her chin, shadows creating deeper indents in the purple crescents under her eyes. "Because you have a lot to atone for. You know you do."

"Yes." Chase doesn't hesitate in his agreement.

It's not yours, I want to blurt. I have the impulsive, desperate urge to smooth the bulging tendons in his neck, to take his face in my hands and whisper the truth, lightening his shoulders and his mind.

I peel off the yearning, but its sour onion peels stick to my skin. No matter what I say, Chase will always have darkness inside him. By refusing to tell me about the Cloaks, he protects them, and if Rose Briar's secret letter is anything to go by—a letter Piper was the first to find—these people don't deserve protection.

Addisyn flicks her attention to me, but only long enough to ensure I note how much she despises my presence, then turns on her heel, the sounds of her shoes hitting the stairs fading as she ascends.

I'm so focused on the empty doorway, gnawing my lip at the thought that Ahmar provided me with information the police hadn't even released to the family yet, that I don't sense Chase's whirl until he's inches away, burying his fist in the row of books by my head.

"God*damnit*!" he shouts, then pounds again.

I flinch, but don't retreat.

"Fuck fuck *fuck*!" He beats the shelving again and again, turning to ripping the books from the shelves and scattering them across the floor.

One flies against the fish tank, and I yelp, terrified that those angry things will flow out from shattering glass and search for one last sting before they die.

"Chase." I grab his arm, so hot, hardened, and rough, I have to convince myself I'm clasping skin and not the scales of a dragon. "Chase, stop."

He spins on me with a roar, his teeth bared. "She had my *baby* inside her, Callie."

"You don't—"

"She was at Lover's Leap that night, drinking, smoking, snorting. Did I tell you that? She was at our party and didn't give a fuck if she was pregnant."

"There's still so much unanswered," I say, aiming for calm. "She wasn't that far along. At ten weeks, she might not have known she was pregnant."

Chase lunges for the wall, heaving books, punching wood, and I dance back but can't avoid everything. The corner of one hits my thigh, and I cry out.

Chase's arms drop to his sides. "Shit. Callie." He comes up beside me, leading me to the office chair.

"It's fine," I grit out. "I've never been Charlie-horsed by a law book before, but turns out, those fuckers *hurt*."

He lowers enough for his hands to grip the chair's arms as he watches me massage my thigh. "I wasn't thinking. I'm so s..." He looks down at the floor. "Wait. Ten weeks?"

Shit.

I bite my lip, but don't meet his eyes, instead focusing on rubbing the pain out of my leg.

"Callie."

My name, used as a warning many times before by many different voices, has never sounded so ominous.

"Ahmar got back to you, didn't he?"

"Kind of," I admit, but barely. "I spoke to him maybe an hour ago. They've narrowed down the weeks she was pregnant, yes."

Chase does the math, then bows his head, his silky strands brushing the tip of my nose. "Then it really is mine."

My hand comes up to cup his cheek, the stubble clinging to my palm. "No."

The word is out before I want it to be. I couldn't have stopped it if I tried. He's suffering, and I can't, in good conscience, use the DNA as a weapon for more information about the Cloaks.

It's too cold a maneuver. Too calculating. And the deeper I get into this mess, the more I'm certain that I'm not like these people.

I can expose their games, but I can't play them.

His hand covers mine, squeezing before he lifts his head and meets my eye. "What do you mean, 'no'?"

I swallow. "It belongs to someone named Joaquín del Pozo."

Chase's eyes harden into opaque marbles. He says, with the roughest edge to his voice, "Who. The fuck. Is that."

"I have no idea."

"And why didn't you tell me as soon as you saw me?" His composure cracks, and I don't know whether to embrace him or run. "Callie, do you know what this has *done* to me?"

I nod, lifting from the chair. Chase falls back to give me space, a surprising move on his part. "I'm telling you now, Chase. I've only found out myself. It wasn't like I was hiding it from you—"

"But you wanted to know about your Cloaks, first," he sneers. "Asking me some bullshit about recruitment in high school, and hidden rooms, because they're more important than me knocking up a girl who's now dead, right?"

His tone strikes like a whip, its spiked tail searing my chest. "Don't do that— don't say I'm trying to toy with you, because I gave you the name *knowing* that I can't play your games. I could've held onto the name, tried to see if I could get more information from you—"

"So, you thought about it." Chase's mouth twists. "Using my fear as some kind of weapon to make me do as you please."

"That's precisely what I *didn't* do."

"What would you have done if Addy hadn't come in here? Would you have kept that powerful little nugget to yourself? Become one of my family's many enemies and exploit me?" Chase corners me, backing me up against the emptied-out bookcase, a few missed texts lying flat against the shelves. They tremble when my back slams into the wood.

Chase exhales, brushing his nose against mine, coaxing my chin up. Invisible strings of lust tilt my head, my lips automatically angling to meet his.

Energy, both pissed-off and hot, sparks between us, blanketing my mind from the dangerous consequences and urging me toward satisfaction. Passion blinds me, just as rage blackens him to soot. We can do what we're known for—screw our angst out of our systems and fuck our worries away.

Oh, how I want to.

"You look so fucking hot in that dress."

He dips his hand between my thighs, my legs spreading of their own accord. My breaths turn heavy, his tongue playing along the center of my lower lip, but when I dart to catch him, he jerks away, yet his fingers circle closer.

Chase nudges the tip of my nose, his lips brushing against my skin when he says, "You're right, sweet possum. I'm better than you at getting what I want."

Cold air blasts over my front when Chase retreats on a snarl, and I'm treated to a terrible apathy that crosses his expression as he backs away.

"How does it feel to be played?" he asks me.

I pull my lips in and clamp down hard in an attempt not to cry.

I'm not cut out for this. For him.

Digging my fingers in my hair at the base of my neck, hot and damp from adrenaline and desire, I say, "You're hurt, Chase. And I'm sorry. But can't you, for one second, believe that my digging into the Cloaks is for you and Piper?"

Chase growls and strikes. I dodge to the side, terrified of the cold mask he's slipped on his face, but his movement isn't to charge or trap me. He bends down, pulling the raven engraved book from its spot and tossing it at me.

I fumble to catch it against my chest, blurting out—

"You want more on your fucking Nobles? There," Chase snarls, but he's not done.

He pulls a handful of hardcovers from the middle shelf and throws them over his shoulder, the tombs thumping against the desk and carpeted floor with a heavy, accelerated charge. Delicate spines crack. Hardbound leather dents.

I look from the mess back to Chase in time to see his palm slam against a button that was hidden behind the books, and the wall of shelving sinks in before sliding back.

I gasp, the leather-bound book held in my clutches, as a heavy, metal door is revealed, a security panel at its center.

Chase pushes past me, enters a code, and that door *beeps* and slides open, too.

A single room, cold and sterile, comes into view, a simple couch, a metal kitchenette, and a row of small TVs of cameras lighting up under the automatic floodlights in the ceiling.

"There," Chase spits so close to my ear, I flinch. "A panic room. In case my family is robbed and some of us are inside the home. This is where we're supposed to go." He gestures toward it sharply. "By all means, look around, Callie. Search for ancient textbooks or cloaks in the closet, or hell, fucking underwear Piper left behind. Do all the detective work you want. I'm done."

"But I ... I heard voices," I say.

"This house is brimming with people." Chase scoffs. "You heard nothing but your own paranoia."

The hurt, when it comes, hits my heart with a *splat*. Only Chase is aware of my wrongful accusation and what my misguided convictions did to my stepdad's and my relationship. How I questioned my own sanity afterward.

And it's only Chase who would use it to effectively shut me up.

But pain claws through his composure. It's in the stiffness of his pose and way he curls his fingers at his sides. It builds against the tension in his clenched jaw. Most of all, his eyes shine with barely contained injustice, and he pins it on me before turning away.

I spring forward and try to catch him before he leaves. "Chase, wait."

He pauses at the door, his profile still in shadow. "You can have all the conspiracy theories you want. But this is my *life* being dicked around with. That baby was mine until you told me it wasn't."

I wince.

He adds, with the softness of a snake moving through the grass, "Piper's manipulations beyond the grave are enough of a mess to clean up. I don't need you taking her place."

"Chase—"

But he's gone, and I'm left in the rubble of my own creation.

Eleven

I COLLECT myself enough to exit the office. Music reaches in and pulses inside my skull the higher I ascend, the party more raucous and disjointed than when I left.

Limbs fly in drunken dance interpretations, some choosing smaller crowds along the edges to laugh and chug with. I pass by a keg stand, where someone is being held upside down and told to *drink, drink, drink!* and I wish, so much, to take part in the senior life, to get drunk and do drugs and have sex in an unfamiliar bedroom ... acts the old Callie would've been happy to oblige in.

I'm not her anymore. I'm a broken semblance of myself who seeks out mystery as a healing savior, when all it really does is chip more pieces off, adding to the crumble of ashes on the floor.

A flash of sequined purple draws my attention, and I cross the designated dance floor and find Ivy leaning against the fireplace, laughing as Riordan whispers something in her ear.

"Ivy!" I call over the music. "Hey."

She giggles while she trails her hand up Riordan's bare forearm, and I think: *Well, this is new.*

Ivy catches sight of me when I'm practically on top of her. "Callie! You came!"

"Yeah, I came with you, remember?"

My reasoning is pointless, because Ivy, the sweet girl, is drunk off her ass.

She fixes her eyes on mine for a millisecond before they drift off. "This is so fun, isn't it? Why don't I come to more of these?"

I laugh, shifting the black leathered book to one arm while reaching for her with the other. "Because you can't handle your liquor."

Riordan's expression grows mischievous as he chucks under her chin. "She's handling it just fine."

Riordan is the one friend of Chase's I can't get a proper read on. James is easy. He's the guy with all the jokes, using the comedic relief to probably hide a lonely childhood as the sole kid of two power-hungry parents who are more loyal to their international obligations than what they've left behind in their blood.

Tempest is as his name defines—a gray, brooding storm bearing down on those who dare to show joy around him. He's quiet, assessing, and when he speaks, it's with cruel purpose. And Chase is ... Chase. Mysterious. Hardened. Experienced and, when pushed, brimming with embers of anger he works hard to temper.

I'm guessing Riordan falls somewhere in the middle. Not funny, not sociopathic, but likely the weakest of the four, because I've never seen him participate in the follies of his friends that cement their rule over Briarcliff. Only film them.

Riordan tucks Ivy under his arm, laughing at something she's said and staring at her with a strange sincerity that's missing from the rest of these boys.

Am I confusing weakness with kindness? Is that what I've come to?

I reach for Ivy. "C'mon, let's go home."

Riordan angles himself to block my view as he tightens his arm around Ivy's waist. "I'll watch over her."

"Uh, thanks, but there's something called girl code."

"Callie, it's cool. Rio and I, we're ... hanging out," Ivy says, working hard to blink me into focus.

"That's great, but I don't trust him for shit," I say.

Rather than be insulted, Riordan's dark eyes dart to what I have in my hands. He asks, with a buttery purr and hardened eyes, "What's that?"

I hold the book snug to my chest. "I'm borrowing it from Chase."

His stare narrows. "With his permission?"

Too late, I realize my fingers haven't properly covered the insignia.

"Yes, not that I need yours on top of it," I reply.

Riordan's hand drops from Ivy's waist. She mewls in protest, stroking his chest to retain his attention, but he shakes her off, his attention never straying from the book.

"Hey." I bristle on behalf of my friend. He steps closer. "Back off."

The sharp stones of the fireplace dig into my back, but instead of serving as a warning, it pisses me off. This is the *second* time I've been backed into a corner tonight, and I'm not here for it anymore.

I grit out, as Riordan's shadow passes over my body, "Unless you want a knee to the balls, step *back*."

"Rio, come on." Ivy giggles in an attempt to lighten the growing storm cloud above us. "It's just a stupid old book." She hooks his elbow and pulls, but Riordan doesn't so much as twitch. "What's the big deal?"

Riordan's glare won't stray from mine. "I think you know how important that is, and how much you shouldn't have it."

"Chase gave it to me." I notch my chin up. He may have thrown it at me in a rage after tearing up his dad's office to prove his point that my meddling is fucking up his life, but Chase *did* give it to me. "I'm not lying."

Riordan cocks his head. "Give. It. To. Me."

Why did I ever think this guy was the weakest of the bunch? He's stronger than I am.

Gripping the book, I move to step around him, but Riordan's hand flashes out, tearing the hardback from my grip before I can so much as gasp out, "Hey—!"

He tosses it into the fireplace, red and gold sparks spiraling up the chute as hungry flames eat away the dried, leathery flesh.

"No!" I cry at the same time Ivy yells out something to Riordan.

My answers are in there!

The key to the secret societies that Chase literally lobbed at my head as a finality to our deal is burning to ash.

I'll never know.

I'll never understand.

I'll never discover what the raven means.

In the span of a second, such dreaded certainty shrouds my shoulders that my stomach clenches with the sudden rush of acidic bile.

If I don't do something, any connection to Piper's uncovering of secret Briarcliff writings and her death will turn to unreadable ash.

I'll be labeled unreliable again. A liar. A fool. Chase's last expression before he stormed out of his father's office will forever be etched on his face whenever he looks in my direction.

Don't let it be for nothing.

I leap toward the hissing flames.

In my periphery, I register Ivy grappling with Riordan, her lips peeled back as she tries to get to me first, to stop—

But my hand has already plunged into the fire.

Twelve

A LIGHTNING BOLT sears up my arm, fraying nerves and singeing skin, but I bat the book out of the flames, a crumbling skeleton of its former self skidding across the parquet floor and leaving streaks of black soot in its wake.

Someone cuts the music.

"Are you *fucking insane*?" Riordan roars, but I rush over to the book, holding its delicate pages to my chest and pushing into the crowd rather than respond.

The growing half-circle of witnesses eagerly step aside, unsure what to make of a chick who dives into fire as a party trick.

Falyn separates herself from the crowd. "Was it worth it?" she hisses in my ear as I shove forward.

Willow steps out to block my path, palming my shoulders and sending me stumbling back.

"To look so mentally disturbed in front of the entire school?" Falyn continues. She searches the crowd with overdramatic flair. "Uh-oh. Looks like your knight in shining armor is nowhere around to save you this time. What was so important you had to rake yourself over coals to get to it? I would've happily lit your ass on fire for you."

I twist in a protective maneuver. The movement makes the tightening, blistering skin on my hand burn to an almost unbearable level. "It's not like there was a fire poker lying around." I take a moment to look her up and down. "Chase must've thought to put all safety hazards away before allowing his dumb bitches off the leash."

Falyn's mouth falls open in an *O* of shocked fury.

Well. If I wanted to leave unobstructed, I've pretty much screwed up that goal. But *ugh*, Falyn gets to me in ways Piper never did.

Piper at least had reason to hate me, petty as it was. I took her room and unknowingly prevented her from meeting Dr. Luke without any prying eyes.

273

Falyn inherited Piper's hate, but it's like she's not quite sure where to source it from. Maybe, at first, it was because she thought I killed her best friend. But that's all over now, despite Dr. Luke walking free. I've never been near Lover's Leap, and a part of her knows it.

Not that it matters. All Falyn understands is, she needs to be mean in Piper's place.

"Stop, before you make a bigger fool of yourself," Riordan says as he steps into view, Ivy tottering after him. He hungrily eyes the book's remnants in my arms but pulls out his phone and starts tapping.

"Aw," I say, but my voice shakes with both pain and humiliation. "Are you telling Daddy on me?"

"Someone has to get you under control," he mumbles. "Might as well be your keeper."

My jaw drops in outrage. I'm nobody's *problem*. Indignation stings the back of my eyes.

"How dare you," I seethe. "All I want is to escape you bastards—"

Before I can finish, Willow shoves me again. This time, I spear her with my elbow, clipping her boob. She stumbles away with a cry.

Falyn settles a disdainful glance on her friend, but easily dismisses her, preferring the easier mark that everyone's staring at. She says, with saccharine venom between her teeth, "Oh, honey, it makes sense that you'd want to earn sympathy points by becoming a burn victim, but sadly, that role is already taken in Chase's life. Now you're just a waste of skin that poor Emma could be using."

Shock jolts through me faster than singeing my flesh against flame. Emma was Falyn's friend before the accident. How *could* she?

"Say that one more time."

The whispered warning stalks through the crowd before I breathe a word.

"But louder."

The crowd parts, revealing Chase.

He knifes through, stopping just short of me, but his vision is centered on Falyn. He stares at her with brown eyes so bright, he must be calling upon the forest around him to emit such vicious energy.

"By all means, expand upon my sister's pain." Chase offers a predatory grin, licking the top row of his teeth at the expectant bite. "Then, we'll see how well you'll fare after that."

Falyn blanches under his stare, but unfortunately, doesn't stay quiet. She points at me. "Did you see what the crazy bitch did? If you want to fuck someone over for insulting Emma's name, look to her. She's the one playing in the flames, thinking she won't get burned."

"I thought I told you, what Callie does is none of your business," Chase says.

Riordan joins the conversation, and points. "Did you really give her that?"

"Guys," Ivy says, holding out her hands. She waits a beat while all eyes turn to her, giving a single, slow bat of her eyelids while centering her balance. She lifts her finger at me. "I'm pretty sure my bestie needs a hospital."

So many fingers. Pointing at me. I scan the faces behind them, and the faces behind *them*, all staring, a mixture of awe, mirth, and horror. A few phones pop up above heads, camera light on.

I'm barren. Adrift. Exposed.

"If you're taking such responsibility for her," Falyn sneers, but her voice sounds muffled and far away. "Then explain to your sister why you've decided to fuck a pyro while her burns are still healing—"

"Screw you, Falyn—"

"Fuck, Chase, why have you given Callie access—"

A keening tremble spreads inside my chest until my entire body silently quakes.

"Burn harder, next time, possum..."

"—the bitch dives in after it like she's the fucking Dragon Queen—"

"I'm trying to save you from the biggest mistake of your life—"

"We're elite for a reason. We don't defend pathetic school transfers..."

"You have your orders. Your obligation is over. Let her stake herself in a burning woodpile for all I care..."

Possum. Bitch. Pathetic. Mistake. Obligation.

"Callie, is what they're saying true? Are you sleeping with Chase?"

The last voice, light and sweet, has me blinking out of my fugue, and I lock onto Ivy.

She teeters toward me, yet her expression exudes sobriety after asking the question.

But her perfume's too strong, the colors of her dress suddenly too loud, and burning pain, so hot it's turning my fingers into nubs of blue fire, won't stop pulsing its distress within my skull.

There are so many watching. So few of them care.

Riordan has the time to spit out, "Just fuck her and leave her, the way you were supposed to," before a savage, piercing wail splits through the room.

The small part of my mind that's removed itself from the situation realizes it's coming from me.

My lips are stretched wide on a scream, so loud, so brutal and rough, that I've silenced both the argument and the room.

Hush weaves around me like a blanketing mist, and I glance from face to face, backing up, skittering forward in the meager circle of space they've allowed.

Chase blinks at me, the first show of surprise I've ever seen in him, while the rest gape.

Ivy takes a hesitant step. "Callie..."

"*Let me leave!*" My voice is shredded paper, a nest of hornet stings, eroded rocks rubbed raw from saltwater.

Falyn clutches Willow in stunned horror, and they both dance to the side when I dart toward them. I use those few seconds of their dumbfounded shock to sweep past.

Riordan attempts to say, "Don't let her—"

"Shut the fuck up." Chase's tone is deadly. Final.

I stumble out the door, turning my back on them before the moonlight can illuminate my tear-streaked cheeks.

Thirteen

USING MY GOOD HAND, I call the Briarcliff chauffeur service, enduring the extended wait by crossing my arms around the book—holding my burned hand closest to my chest—and jumping from foot to foot to keep warm. Ivy doesn't come after me. Chase doesn't track me down. I'm left alone to stew or recover. I've yet to decide which one.

My cheeks are sticky with the half-frozen saltwater of my tears, but I've stopped crying, choosing to quell my upset into an inner trembling instead. Sobs will get me nowhere. Breaking down will make me fall. If my goal is to uncover Briarcliff's trove of secrets, I can't keep losing it around Chase, or his friends, or the school.

I swipe a hand across my eyes and find the positive. If anything, my freak-out will serve as a handy distraction while I continue to get to the bottom of things.

After twenty minutes pass, Yael rolls up, and I dive into the back seat without a word.

He takes stock of me through the rearview but remains professionally silent as he drives me to the dorms.

Charred leather scrapes against my fingers as I carefully lay the book on my lap, resisting the urge to begin reading it under pale moonlight and Yael's mixture of scrutiny and concern.

The knowledge between these pages is both the source of my misery and the match lighting my power. I gave up a lot to keep this in my clutches. Trust. Pride. Skin.

Please, mysterious raven book, be worth it.

When Yael pulls up to Thorne House, I murmur a thank you and step out.

"Promise me you'll get that looked at?" Yael asks softly from the front seat.

I glance down at my hand, my fingers curled against my cleavage, the wounded flesh desperate for both the warmth of my chest and the frigid coolness of the October night.

"It's not that bad," I reply.

Yael snorts. "You don't have to put on an act with me. I know how it goes around here. When that wound really starts screaming, at least go to the nurse in the morning, okay? My wife won't forgive me if I don't make sure you're all right. If my daughter left a party all disheveled and hurt, without her parents nearby..."

The heartfelt concern in Yael's tone causes a tortuous lump in my throat. I'm caving at his concern—the first show of in-person, grown-up worry I've received since coming here—and dying at the thought that I *have* no parents at the same time. Any daughter-like relationship with my stepdad, I ruined with two, self-destructing words: *It's him.*

"Thank you, Yael," I manage to croak out before shutting the passenger door. I lean down into his window that he's since rolled open. I manage a shaky smile. "Tell your wife not to worry. I'll see the nurse in the morning."

Yael nods, the lines around his mouth smoothing. "You need to go anywhere tomorrow, you know who to ask."

"I do," I say, and to his shock, reach out to squeeze his hand resting on the steering wheel. "Your concern means a lot."

"Ah, kiddo," he sighs, and my heart *twangs* at his use of Ahmar's affectionate term. "Not everybody gets out of this place unscathed."

He rolls up his window as I retreat, and I give one last wave before entering Thorne House, fumbling one-handed with my clutch for my student ID.

Our shared area is dark when I step into Emma's and my dorm room, not that I expect her to be awake and cracking open beer cans while holding a party on Saturday night.

The question of why she wasn't at the lake house pops into my head, but I dismiss it just as quickly. No way Emma would want to immerse herself in that kind of crowd, with every room at a party-goer's mercy the drunker and hornier they got.

Well. Not *every* room.

I blink from the vision of the Stone panic room, so sure it was a hidden entry into ... what? Secret Society headquarters?

Jesus, I really need to think before I spew my theories into the universe—no, into *Chase's* universe.

I've really fucked it up with him, but I can't linger too long on that thought, either.

Laying the book on the kitchen countertop, I think of how much I've ruined by keeping it in my possession. All those questions I'd bartered for Chase to answer this week? There's no chance in hell he'll be willing to give me information now.

I set that thought aside, too. At this rate, my mind will become such a blank slate, even robots will envy it, and *oh*, how I wish that could be true.

The inner light of the freezer casts its glare directly into my eyes, and I wince as I claw around for a handful of ice to put in a hand towel.

"Do you mind?" Emma snaps behind me. "A starving cat makes less noise at this time of night."

Still halfway into the freezer, I peer over my shoulder. She stands just outside her doorway, her glowering silhouette illuminated by the soft lamplight behind her.

I straighten, moving fast to drop the ice into the towel before my good hand becomes my frostbitten hand.

"Sorry," I say. "This is all I needed. I'll be in my room."

I press the hastily made icepack to the burn starting at the outer edges of my pinky finger and moving down to my wrist. When the cloth contacts my skin, I wince and curse.

Emma hisses in a breath. "What is that?"

Her stare bores into my hand.

"Nothing. Just..." *shoved my hand into an active fireplace to save an unknown text...* "an accident."

She comes closer, her eyes carving a path for her strides, and grasps my wrist.

"Hey—ow!" I whine, but it only makes Emma inspect it closer.

She whispers, "You've burned yourself."

"Yeah, I got too close to the fireplace at the lake house. Don't know what I was thinking, sitting by the hearth."

Emma's gaze flicks up, her familiar, coppery brown eyes searching my hazel ones. She utters two words, and they stick to the base of her throat. "Don't lie."

I stiffen. Against my better judgment, the professional photo I saw of her interposes onto her face, my vision combining the two, the darkness of the kitchen making it easier to pretend to see the old Emma. She still has the same cheekbones, though now they harbor the twisting vines of pinkish scars. She has the same straight, pert nose, the same Cupid's bow lips. Her hair has kept its burnished gold, but it's dulled by lack of care.

For the first time, I wonder if the scars left on her body are but a glimpse of the mutilation she suffered inside her mind.

Without releasing my wrist, she flips the light switch by the door, bathing us in halogen light. I blink at the sudden brightness, but Emma's unaffected. She jerks her chin at the book I've left on the counter. "Do you have a lie for that, too?"

"No, I ... well, I didn't steal it. I can tell you that much."

She spends a few seconds studying the book's jacket—or what's left of it—but I cannot, for the life of me, read her expression. Daniel Stone's name is obscured and melted to ash, but does she know it's her father's? That it was in his study? Is she mad I have it?

Her attention snaps to my wrist with such predatory precision, I have to resist the urge to yank my hand away.

"You shouldn't put ice on a second-degree burn," she says, twisting my hand until I expose my inner wrist. "It could cause tissue damage."

A rush of guilt flows into my stomach. What am I doing, showcasing my minor burn to a girl who was trapped in a fire? "Really, you don't have to—"

"Tap water or cool compresses only," she interrupts. "No sprays, no Vaseline, because that will cause the skin to burn hotter. And don't pop any blisters, either, even though you'll want to. You'll cause an infection."

"Emma..."

"Put your hand under running water." Emma pulls me to the sink and turns on the faucet. She doesn't look at me when she says, "Wait here. I have stuff."

"Thank you."

I don't know what else to say, but Emma doesn't give me an opportunity to expand, anyway. She scurries into her room, and I spin to face the sink, listening to the opening and shutting of drawers as she moves around.

Emma returns, sits me at one of our—new—stools by the counter, and wordlessly cleans and dresses my wound.

We must spend at least fifteen minutes together in silence, but I don't feel the need to cut it with sound. Her movements are soothing, her touches delicate and light, her hands moving with grace and confidence, her full focus on my hand.

I stare at the crown of her head for a while, then watch her wrap my hand with sterile gauze, and I wonder, with a surprising ache, whether the nurses and doctors handled her with the same care that she's showing me.

Don't feel sorry for her, that deep, inner voice of mine reminds. *She set the fire. Chase told you, remember?*

Yes, but she was attacked, first. Her scars aren't solely from burns.

As if sensing my deeper study, Emma sits back, propping my arm at the elbow and raising my hand. "Keep this elevated for an hour or so. It'll help with swelling."

"I ... I don't know how to thank you," I say, my voice sounding strangely weak after not using it for a while. Then I remember—oh yeah, I screamed it to shreds about an hour ago.

"Then don't." Emma stands, cleaning up her first aid kit and washing her hands. She turns as she's drying them, her gaze straying to the book.

I'd known it was sitting there. I felt its proximity like licking flames, though it emits no heat. I'm desperate to dive in, to carefully turn each page and figure out the sign of the raven.

I gather the courage to say, "Emma, about the library earlier—"

"If information on the Nobles is what you're after, you'll find it in that. It's my father's rule book."

My brows jump in surprise.

Amusement glitters in Emma's stare, but it's gone too soon. "Don't tell me you dove into fire for something you knew nothing about?"

I frown at my bandaged hand. "That obvious, am I?"

"Doesn't take a genius to see a burned book—that wasn't barbecued when I last saw it—with a burned hand, and put the two together."

"Yeah." I chew on the inside of my cheek. "Your brother's pretty pissed at me."

"Oh. Of that I have no doubt." Emma tosses the towel she was using to dry her hands on the counter. "But it's not because of what you'll find in there."

I lift my head. "No?"

Emma's lips turn down in an agreeing *no*, and as she passes me on the way to her bedroom, she tosses over her shoulder, "Those answers you're wanting? You're looking at the wrong side of the coin, Callie."

I spin in my stool right as Emma's door shuts.

And if I go and smack my hand on the door, begging for her to elaborate, I know what I'll get in response.

Silence.

If I'm wanting to expose the society and potentially involve them in Piper's murder, it's clear I'm on my own.

Piper.

Her name sears into my brain, and I scramble for my clutch, amazed I've been so distracted, I didn't think to look up her third lover. Her unborn child's *father*.

In my defense, a *lot* happened between Ahmar's admitting of the name and parking my ass on this stool.

But now, under the kitchen lights of a quiet, undisturbed dorm room, I have the time to try and figure him out. Yes, the police are two steps ahead, but perhaps it'll soothe the rush of urgency in my mind if I could put a name to a face.

Is he a student at Briarcliff? Part of the Nobles? The reason Piper fell off a cliff?

Spurred by a new burst of energy, I set the phone on the counter and tap with one finger while my other hand stays raised, starting with the online Briarcliff Student Directory.

Sadly, it's not that easy. No one named Joaquín del Pozo is enrolled at this school.

Deciding on a more generalized approach, I open my internet browser to search his name, narrowing down the geography to Briarcliff and its neighboring towns. If nothing of use comes up, I'll have to figure out a way to cajole Ahmar into either letting me see this guy's rap sheet, since he was in the system already, or at the very least, get Ahmar to admit where this dude comes from.

Now, there's an idea. I switch from the search engine and go to the free criminal background check database and type in Joaquín's full name. If he's a minor, nothing will show, but if, by chance, he's an adult, and considering Piper's proclivity for older men...

BINGO.

Two results pop up, one guy with a DUI rap in Westerly, and I dismiss him at first, moving onto the second result. Both mug shots have yet to load.

My finger hovers over the second name to expand the results, but right before I do, the first picture loads, and...

Oh.

Oh, my God.

I'm staring at Jack.

Jack, Addisyn's boyfriend.

Fourteen

SUNDAY MORNING PASSES by in a frenzied blur.

First off, my hand was *fire*. It literally took on all the components of a flame and turned my delicate hand-bones to dust. I caved and ran to the nurse's office, waiting impatiently with the few students in front with pounding, alcohol and drug induced migraines.

After having it checked out and being administered Tylenol, I gritted my teeth against the continued gnarled heartbeat my wound created and strode to the new library.

I spend my time there not catching up on history, calculus, or English lit like I should be after the disaster that was my quarter-term grades, but instead researched how to safely read old, falling apart, burned books.

When I attempted to lift the flap of Daniel Stone's mysterious "rule book" last night, it nearly disintegrated in my hands. Unwilling to let such important material be destroyed, I set it aside, though it killed me not to absorb the knowledge instantly. But a steadier hand had to prevail.

After reading a few articles off my laptop, I start to hash out ways to use the science room when a *whoosh* of air puffs out beside me.

My spine goes rigid when the accompanying scent tickles my nose.

Citrus. Wood. Crisp weed.

It's similar, but not quite perfect, to Chase's cologne.

"Can I help you?" I ask without glancing over, pretending to be busy typing on my keyboard.

"Not unless you're willing to do a repeat of last night."

Ever so slowly, I pivot to face Tempest.

The green of his eyes pop against the thick rim of his lashes, the same color as his ebony hair. The high cut of his cheekbones, matte rose color of his lips, and lean lines of his body give him a vampiric aura, yet his skin is sun-browned from hours spent on the water as second-in-command in Chase's crew.

He elaborates, without me asking, "Sadly, I only received the video version. Didn't get to see your breakdown live."

"It wasn't a breakdown," I say stiffly.

Tempest angles his head. "Sure looked like one."

"People were crowding in on all sides. No one was moving. So, I figured"—I attempt to keep my voice light—"screaming the walls down would get them to move the hell back. Guess what? It worked."

"Really?" Tempest frowns. "I thought small spaces was Chase's schtick, but maybe you two have more in common than I thought."

My brows pull in, but I work hard not to show Tempest just how interested I am in Chase trivia.

A slow, lupine grin spreads across Tempest's face as he watches me battle for indifference. "The guy never takes elevators. Go ahead, try and make him." Tempest leans toward me, stretching his eyes wide. "I dare you."

A tingle of ... something ... rushes up the center of my back, and I quickly glance away from Tempest and his weird allure.

I face my computer, subtly minimizing the articles I had up. "Is there a reason you've come to chat with Briarcliff's social pariah?" I risk another glance. "Or is that why you've sat down next to me? To let me know exactly how my behavior at the party went over with the school? Spoiler alert: I'm aware."

Tempest doesn't answer. Instead, his fingers drift over my bandaged hand, and my instant, tense reaction causes me to wheeze against the pain of stretching raw skin.

"That must've hurt," he muses, but doesn't draw his hand back. "Was it worth it?"

I lick my lips. "I don't know."

Tempest makes a murmuring sound of agreement, and thankfully, withdraws. My shoulders sag in relief at the distance he puts between us, however small.

Tempest reaches down and sets his bag on the table, languidly searching through, then pulling out his computer and schoolbooks.

I watch all this in horror as the rest of the students using Sunday for studying stare at us and whisper to their friends.

"Um, what are you doing?" I ask.

"What does it look like?"

I resist an annoyed scoff. "You're at the wrong table. Isn't the trust fund seating section over there?"

Tempest runs his tongue along his top teeth. "All my trust fund baby friends have gotten themselves sent into time-out." He bats his lashes at me. "I'm lonely."

"Last I checked, Riordan isn't suspended. Go bother him."

"Rio's otherwise engaged." Tempest's smile is directed at his laptop as he flips it open, but it grates against my nerves nonetheless.

A ripple of guilt follows. I should check up on Ivy. I pull out my phone to do just that, but Tempest covers it with his large hand before I can so much as unlock it.

"Hey!"

"I wouldn't do that, possum. Take a few days before you face the consequences of your actions. Trust me, it's a lot better to judge your foibles at a distance."

I yank the phone—and my hand—from under his. "I don't care what everyone here has to say. I care about my friend."

"And so do I. Which is why I'm sitting here instead of getting my dick sucked off like Rio probably is." He pauses. "Hmm. Now I'm jealous."

"*Ugh.* Stop pretending like you care about me and buzz off."

Tempest's red-carved lips split wide, genuine laughter leaving his throat. "Have I brought out the worst in you by *buzzing* into your proximity?"

"Okay, *fuck* off."

Tempest flicks a brow in response before his expression turns rigid. "Apologies, but I can't."

"Why not? I didn't ask you—"

"Your opinion of my presence means shit-all, but unfortunately—for both of us —the opinion of someone else is written in stone."

I fake gag at his pun, but I stiffen at his insinuation. "Chase told you to sit with me? Why?"

"Haven't you heard? Chase got himself suspended for defending your honor."

I unleash another sigh, this one with a long, drawn out exhale. "Chase wouldn't help me even if I was stuck under the wheels of his car."

"That's where you're wrong, possum." Tempest shifts in his seat to get more comfortable. "He's sacrificed quite a lot for you."

"Oh, come *on.*"

Tempest shrugs. "Believe what you want, but I'm your Siamese twin for the better part of the week. Get used to me."

I groan. "Why? I don't need protection when Chase is here, never mind when his ass is kicked off school grounds for a week."

Tempest responds in a cold, flat tone, "I beg to differ."

My jaw clenches at the ice he's directed my way. Tempest has always been calm and undeterred, but I've never heard him summon so much winter in his voice.

I part my mouth, but Tempest prevents any defense by resting his gaze on my browser displaying the preservation tactics for damaged books, making sure I see him do it, then going back to his work.

Dang. I forgot to close the last tab.

"You're pissed about the rule book, too?" I ask. "Riordan already had me sacrifice skin. What is it you now want?"

Tempest chuckles, but his attention is on his calculus text he's propped on his lap while he leans back, balancing his chair on the two back legs. "What I want doesn't matter. Accept our buddy system and move on. Maybe do some homework instead of becoming Briarcliff's latest Ghostbuster."

I latch on to his unintended meaning. "So, you're saying there was someone before me who tried to figure out the Nobles, too, huh?"

Tempest groans. "You're worse than the paparazzi surrounding my parents' compound."

My eyes cut to his. "Only you would call—"

But I'm cut off by a sudden, shattering scream ricocheting around the room.

Fifteen

THIS TIME, it's not me.

Tempest vaults from his chair, shoving his textbook against my chest, but I shake off the obstruction and sprint after him, toward the sound.

The cry came from the rear, behind the stacks and nearer to the back wall. Tempest streaks into one of the aisles, and I follow suit, both impressed and frustrated at his speed, since he'll get there first.

I swing around the corner in time to see Tempest hunched over a figure puddled on the floor, her bare knees drawn to her chest, and her arms folding around her head as she sobs.

Falyn stands nearby, fingers tapping against her lips, with Willow at her side, murmuring something as she types into her phone. Their third musketeer, Violet, stands behind Falyn, watching the scene unfold with wide, too-bright blue eyes.

Violet notices me first, her shocked gaze holding mine. She mouths what I think is *run*, but I can't be sure.

"Addy," Tempest says, rubbing the hunched girl's back. "What is it? What happened?"

She lifts her head and wails, "The-the police!"

Her face is blotchy and streaked with tears, the pale, robin's egg color of her irises made stark against the bloodshot whites of her eyes.

Chase, I think. Unreasonably. Stupidly. *Something's wrong.*

I step into their aisle, and I know the instant Addisyn notices me, because blood floods her cheeks and she clutches Tempest's arm.

"What's *she* doing here with you?" she shrieks. "She's the reason—"

Tempest shushes her, then raises his chin to her friends. "Anyone want to tell me what the fuck this is, or am I supposed to read the room?"

Falyn shakes her head, her fingers drifting to her neck. "I ... I've got nothing, other than this must be the Harrington way..."

284

"BITCH!" Addisyn snarls, rearing from the ground with her nails drawn, but Tempest pushes her down by the shoulders.

"Jack," I whisper. When I inadvertently get Addisyn's attention, I say, clearer, "Jack is the reason you're upset, isn't he?"

"And just *what* in the good Lord's name is going on back here?"

The librarian, Mrs. Jenkins, comes up behind me, patting my shoulder as she passes by. "Have you lot never heard of the sanctity of a library?"

Tempest rises smoothly out of his crouch. "A simple misunderstanding, ma'am. We'll be quiet."

"I sure hope so. You had me running in heels all the way back here. Everyone okay?"

We all nod, everyone except for Addisyn, her expression hewn with trembling, spasming muscles.

"Any peeps out of either one of you, you're cleaning litter off the grounds for one week. Am I clear?"

We nod like good little soldiers, Falyn adding extra *oomph* in her good-girl facade, and wait for Mrs. Jenkins to depart.

She doesn't.

With the type of glare mastered solely by over-worked and underpaid teachers, she stares down her nose at us, her glasses perched on the end. "If I were you," she says, "I'd scatter."

I spin on my heel, unwilling to garner any more attention *or* detention, and head back to my table. I'm almost through the aisle of books before a hand claws into my elbow and whips me around.

"What the hell do you know about Jack, possum?" Falyn whisper-yells, her usually beautiful, storm gray eyes tightened into beady little balls.

"Lucky guess," I say, trying to pull my arm from her hold. She doesn't give an inch.

Falyn glances down at the bandage around my wrist and palm. In one vicious maneuver, she clasps the gauze, digging her nails in deep.

I choke on my yowl, my knees buckling.

Falyn bends with me, dipping her head close. "Tell me how you know that name, since we, as Addisyn's support system, have only just heard of it."

"Callie has connections," a voice says quietly. I unscrunch one eye enough to see that it's Violet. "She knows a detective. Now let her go."

"I say extend the pain," another voice, Willow, says at my back. She must've gone down a separate aisle, then U-turned into this one to watch the encore to Addisyn's show. "She clearly gets off on it, if last night is any indication. Who knew fire play was a thing? Is Chase into it?" Willow smiles as she enters my view. "Can I ask him? Maybe I'll add hot candle wax to our role play. Aren't those little freckles around his dick just the cutest?"

I flinch at Willow's accuracy, but there's nothing I can do about it, not when Falyn twists me at an unnatural angle and Willow's strangling my heart.

It's not like Chase was a choir boy when I met him. He played, he lured, and I experienced firsthand how well he knew his way around a woman's—

Willow dips forward just enough to whisper in my ear, "He asked for me, just last night. Turns out he was frustrated as all hell and needed to ... vent. God, I'm sore."

She giggles, and Falyn smiles along with her, snide and domineering.

"Stop," Violet says, and puts a hand on Falyn's arm. "Hasn't there been enough violence to last us the year?"

"Not even close." Falyn exposes her teeth. "I'm about done entertaining this bitch's Nancy Drew fetish. Why aren't we allowed to off her already?"

The succinct way Falyn asks about my death should have me worried, but mean girls are at a whole new level in this school. I have no doubt she wants to punt me over the nearest cliff, uncaring of the fact that her supposed best friend recently died from falling off one.

"Jack is Addisyn's boyfriend. He works at the lobster shack in town," I say, pushing against Falyn's hold. We're in a weird sort of arm war, and my burn screams to be released. "And the reason Piper got pregnant. He's been brought in for questioning. Right? That's what has Addisyn so upset. Her boyfriend cheated on her, impregnated her sister, and probably murdered Piper. I'd scream in a library, too, if I heard that news."

Abruptly, Falyn releases her hold, and I clutch my pulsing forearm to my chest, backing away from this half-circle of vultures.

"Maybe Chase was right," Violet whispers to Falyn.

The statement causes Falyn's brows to shadow her eyes as she stares at me. "Unless you decide to use the limited space in that brain of yours for actual study subjects," she says to me, "Your time at this school is ending. Make the right choice, Callie."

Commotion at the end of the aisle draws all our gazes, and Willow steps aside enough to reveal Addisyn and Tempest, Addisyn gripping Tempest's waist like she has trouble even taking one step.

"Have you guys had your fun?" she asks through a quaking lip. "Talking about me? My family? Jack?"

"Ding ding ding." Falyn flips her hair, her lips twisted with disdain. "You're the talk of the school, Addy. Callie should thank you. And what you wanted?" Falyn scoffs. "You're never going to get. Now that your *boyfriend* murdered our best friend."

Addisyn leans out to swipe, but Tempest keeps a hold on her.

My shoulder brushes against a row of books as I attempt to sneak away from the conversation, but no one's looking in my direction, anyway.

I complete a one-eighty by spinning on my heel, and power-walk to my table, collecting my books and laptop as silently as possible.

It's amazing, how not two days ago, Falyn and Addisyn were attached at the hip. I was convinced Addisyn was being groomed as the next Piper, both in looks and poise, Falyn replacing their fallen member as easily as slipping on the Briarcliff uniform.

Now, though ... a rift has cracked open between them, and is it really all because Addisyn failed to tell them about a townie boyfriend?

Secret boyfriend.

Secret lover.

Secret society.

It's all secrets and lies with these people.

Hiking my bag on my shoulders, I mull over Falyn's not-so-subtle warning to fall in line like most students here. Ignore the strangeness and do my time in order to graduate from Briarcliff intact.

But can I do it? Can I let these puzzle pieces I'm collecting scatter and swirl in the salt-tinged air?

Nope. I can't.

And so, I switch my mind on how to best break into the chem lab after hours and not get caught.

Sixteen

EASIER SAID THAN DONE.

For the rest of the week, I'm unable to find any time to bust open Daniel Stone's half-destroyed rule book, Falyn's warning becoming all too real with surprise quizzes, an oral Spanish test, and English Lit paper round-ups.

To add to the fuss, our new History professor, Miss Carroll, isn't nearly as amicable and endearing as Dr. Luke was—err, save for his preference of sex with minors—and she sends all our spines rigid, her voice crackling throughout the classroom, the loose skin around her smoker's throat trembling like a turkey's gullet.

I find myself fascinated by it and can never look away.

Tempest, as he promised, stays close to my side from Monday to Friday, taking Chase's vacant seat if it happens to be closer to mine. And it is, in almost every period.

The electricity dancing across the outlines of my body are missing without Chase nearby, but besides Miss Carroll's unnaturally old appearance, I've developed an advantageous tunnel vision where I'm focused and determined, paying attention in class and finishing my homework a few hours after dinner.

News of my freak-out at Chase's party came as a big wave on Monday but was low tide by Tuesday morning, considering the irresistible ripeness of Jack's arrest, Piper's betrayal against Addisyn, and Emma's sudden appearance in their classrooms were juicy, low-hanging fruit.

Emma and I have two classes together, and each time she came in, whether she was seated there before everyone else or coming in after, the room always stilled, and the students unleashed everlasting stares. She handled it for a few days by glaring and snarling at anyone who got too close, but eventually, I noticed how the attention kept chipping away at her, her snarls becoming sneers, then nothing at all.

Emma isn't around our dorm much. I have no idea where she goes, but when she is around, she doesn't initiate any sort of talk between us. Our schedules are practically opposite—she showers in the mornings while I take one at night, she wakes up at eight, with barely any time to get ready, while I'm up just before dawn.

But our one conversation, held while she bandaged my burn, seems to have made her docile, and my theory turns out to be correct when Emma offers me an espresso before scurrying off to whatever mysterious errands she runs. Despite that one moment, though, she doesn't search me out, and I don't try to find her.

I spend most of my evenings hanging out with Ivy, anyway, catching glimpses of her roommate, but never getting enough alone time with Eden to expand on her knowledge of Piper being a Virtue.

I admit, I'm split between finding out more about the Nobles or the Virtues, and my stagnant week has propelled my unfounded theories to the front of my mind. So much so, it's almost impossible to try to balance a routine of schoolwork while carving out time for detective work.

I stare at my phone, sitting silently beside my laptop as I finish off my calc homework, my legs cramped under the thick wooden desk in my room.

I haven't asked Chase any questions this week. I assumed our deal was off the table as soon as he destroyed, then stormed out of his dad's study. I'm not so brazen as to expect his answers when I've so utterly pushed him beyond patience.

But I miss him. I miss *us*, whatever there was of us. Piper's pregnancy shook him badly, and I have a new understanding on why he cleaved such distance between us after I told him what Ahmar knew. Then, I fucked it up worse by pretending to help him figure out if he was the father, when really, all I wanted was details on Briarcliff's underworld.

I pick up my phone, and after unlocking it, my thumb hovers over the message chain with Chase.

It's Friday evening, and he's expected to be back at school on Monday. It'd be nice to try and smooth things over with him before then, right? It wouldn't be desperate to text and make sure we're on neutral ground.

Besides, he asked Tempest to stay close to me while he couldn't this week.

He punched James in the face for insulting me.

The guy has veins of ice, eyes the color of a frozen forest ground, and the frostiest demeanor, even toward his friends. But he did all that. For me.

I type out a sentence and press SEND before I lose my nerve.

Me: Do my daily questions still apply?

I slam my phone face-down on my desk, then swivel back to calculus. I won't wait for his response. I will not.

A few minutes later, my phone vibrates, and I whip it face-up.

Chase: You don't have much time left.

. . .

Smiling, I pick up the phone. I'll take that as a yes.

Me: Did you

I delete the message, my head falling back on a sigh. *Sack up. You can do this.* Schoolwork and Ivy have made my imagination easier to handle, but it's never truly gone away. Not when all I can picture is Willow's auburn hair mixing with his golden locks, a blend of shimmering metals I could never emulate.

Me: Willow tells me she slept with you at your party.
   Chase: Where's the question.

Does he *have* to be so obtuse? I huff out a breath, daring myself to do as he says and ask, instead of assume.

Me: Did you?

...

Three dots appear, and I watch them with way too much intensity. I'm desperate to see his answer, and I'm not sure how proud I am to feel that way. Nor do I have any idea how he'll react. On Saturday night, he'd said he was done with my investigation, and therefore, with me.

A guy has never made me *this* before. Turned me into a girl who can put all her insecurities, concerns, and the bigger picture aside, just to read his words.

Chase: No. I haven't been with anyone since you.

I fall back against the chair, pressing the phone to my chest. *Okay. He doesn't seem mad.* Maybe I can salvage the wreckage of Saturday night with one simple question, unrelated to Cloaks, or Briarcliff, or Piper's murder.

And entirely centered on us.

Me: Do you miss what we had?

     . . .

I'm nervous.

Holy shit, I'm so beside myself with nerves. I push to my feet, pacing my room while biting down on one corner of the phone.

Nothing.

Oh, Callie. You may have screwed the pooch with this one.

I busy myself with homework and an unnecessary cleaning of my bedroom until an hour passes, my phone annoyingly quiet and black on my nightstand. I check it twice to make sure there's a signal, and still, Chase doesn't respond.

With my stomach settling somewhere near my feet, I go about my nightly routine of a snack, a shower, and then bed, all the while trying to put a positive spin on Chase's no-answer answer.

It's for the best.

You won't be distracted by your crush on a boy anymore and can lessen the pressure of dividing your time.

The hours of hurt can be better utilized by focusing on the Nobles. Use the last gift Chase gave you and read Daniel Stone's rule book.

This weekend, bust into the chem lab, use its tools to open the book, and satisfy your curiosity, once and for all.

Forget. Him.

My eyelids grow heavy. The ceiling I'm staring at grows darker, and soon, I give in to a dreamless sleep.

Well into the night, my phone goes off with a loud, buzzing sound.

I snap awake, rubbing the grit from my eyes, and squint at the screen, swiping open the message.

Chase: Yes. I miss it.

Seventeen

BEFORE DAWN ON SUNDAY MORNING, I decide to do it.

I tossed and turned ever since receiving Chase's answer, both delighted and afraid of our lasting connection. My mind kept firing off instead of spiraling down to sleep, and until I used that time wisely, I wasn't going to get any semblance of rest.

With the sky still indigo with waning moonlight, I slide out of bed and change, choosing warmer clothing for my trek to the academy in the dark. I toss a jean jacket over a crimson sweater and gray leggings, then slip on knee socks and my white sneakers before heading out.

I have my own granola stash these days, so I throw a handful in a snack bag and grab an empty thermos in hopes the kitchen staff has already started the coffee brewing process.

As I'm bending into the cabinet, I hear, "Jesus, I thought you were a raccoon."

I jump up on a yelp, then scowl at Emma as she stands near the kitchen counter, her hair flattened on one side and her nightshirt askew.

"They call me a possum, not a raccoon," I say, stuffing the thermos in my bag. "Or a cat."

"Neither one is very creative," Emma muses, and I harrumph in agreement. "Or amusing."

"Tell me about it."

"In my defense," she says, "I thought an *actual* rodent had made its way up here, but it turns out, it's just you, before sunrise, banging through our kitchen. Again."

After one second of hesitation—because Emma never keeps conversations going, *ever*—I hold up my granola bag as evidence.

Emma grumbles, then gestures to her espresso machine. "Take one for the road, then."

I smile. "Aw. Are you warming up to my sweet, morning charm?"

"No. I'm giving you something productive to do rather than use our cupboards for target practice. Make me one, too."

I keep a straight face, despite the giddiness going on inside me at the thought of a freshly brewed mocha. "Coming right up."

As I'm fiddling with the milk steamer, Emma asks, with a begrudging tone, "What are you doing up so early on a Sunday?"

I doubt she truly cares, so I answer with my back to her, "Getting an early start on the chemistry assignment."

"Okay." Emma doesn't sound convinced. "But we have bio this semester, not chem."

After pouring the espresso into my thermos and sliding her mug over to her side of the counter, I turn. "I'll tell you mine if you tell me yours. Why don't you elaborate on what you're up to during your evening disappearances?"

Emma crosses her arms and glares through her lashes.

"That's what I thought," I say.

I cap the thermos and exit our dorm on a cheery wave.

The soft, golden glow of the school's windows guides me up the hill on the quiet pathway, my footsteps the only sound breaking through the rousing bird chirps and light rustle of wind through the trees.

Not even the enterprising rowing team has left their dorms yet. From what Ivy says, they don't get on the water until about 5:30, and I've beat them outside by an hour.

Usually, being the lone pedestrian on a walkway is a gift, especially coming from New York City, but after being accosted by Cloaks in the forest last month, and Piper's demise, nature hasn't been as calming to me lately.

I pick up the pace, suddenly thankful that Tempest had my back all week while Chase was absent. The mockery I'd expected after Chase's lake house party never manifested, but I still had to manage the usual vermin insults and Falyn's bitter gaze, her expression more than indicating her plans for my removal from this school.

More importantly, no Cloaks have accosted me. Barely a whisper of the Nobles crossed my ears, and since nobody knew or cared what I reached into the fire for (the act itself was enough ammo against me to last an entire semester), there wasn't any reason to. And, by keeping my mouth shut, Tempest didn't ask me about it again. Perhaps he believed I'd grown tired of the hunt.

Not exactly.

I keep my eye on the tree line the entire way to the school, anxious of a Cloak appearing, memories of my previous encounter near Lover's Leap filming over my vision. Clouds of my breath come in shorter bursts, the sounds of my footsteps pound harder and faster, and the bird chirps fade away into silence.

The side-door into the school comes into view, and I scamper the rest of the way, pushing in and leaving the quiet, darkened forest far behind. My cheeks are cold and stiff from both the outside and my concentrated anxiety, but the minute the door thumps shut behind me, my shoulders relax.

The hushed clinking of plates and tinned sounds of pots floats down the hallway, the kitchen staff getting ready for breakfast, but the lights remain dimmed, and won't go on full blast for another hour.

I tip-toe past the dining hall, the low lamplight casting shadows against the stone walls, changing the stained glass motifs into stark, gloomy figures.

Don't look at shadows too long, my old friend Sylvie always said during our childhood sleepovers. *At some point, they're going to start moving.*

Shuddering at the memory, I fly past classroom doors until I find the one I want, thankful it's unlocked when I twist the knob.

I'm conscious of being caught, so I don't turn on the overhead lights as I pick a lab table and toss my pack on the metal counter. I'd carefully placed Daniel Stone's manual in a gallon-sized Ziplock, and after turning on the specialized table lamp and twisting it to illuminate the metal countertop, I pull it from top section of my bag.

A row of beakers and chemistry supplies stand in a row by the personal sink, cleaned and ready for the next class. I slip on disposable gloves and choose a pair of large, lab-grade tweezers, adjust the microscope, and, instead of using my fingers, I painstakingly crack the book open and slip it under the lens.

The pages are charred and brittle, but the magnification helps decipher the writing through the ash. It says, in part:

Those who choose to turn these pages accept thee into thy mind.

Oh, boy.

My conscience flickers to life enough to question why Chase gave me his father's rule book, but my appetite's too whetted to listen to it. I carefully slip the book from under the microscope and turn the page, repositioning it under and adjusting the clarity of the lens:

Upon the second week and the seventh night, meet in the Vault, where your blood will be tested.
   Choose your paper, where your mind will be guided.
   Wear your robe, where your identity will be shielded.
   Wait for the key of your master, so you may be commanded.

What the *what*?

Leaning over so far, I've nearly crawled onto the table, I tweeze my way to the next page. The handwriting's changed, no longer the thick, black ink professional cursive. Thin, blue-inked swipes of hastily written notes take over:

. . .

294

March 16, 1971

I, Howard Mason, class of '74, broke into the Nobles' hidden tomb long enough to steal one illuminating page, and have documented, from memory, what I else I discovered.

The stolen poem above is, in part, the initiate ritual of the Nobles, creating its own chapter, and thus utilizing its own motivations to influence the boys in this school. Its founder, Thorne Briar, as the first headmaster of this academy, thought to enrich the minds of certain promising young men, using his connections to form agreements among hidden collegiate societies to accept these boys, groomed and taught under Briar, upon graduation. Rumor has it, in order to accelerate these individuals, examination topics are given, answers are dispersed, and the boys will earn top grades so their focus can remain on Briar's hidden, and demonic, tutelage.

There is also a symbol, forged in iron, above a hearth of human skulls—believed to be the heads of ancient, English nobleman robbed from the graves where they rested in peace—but that has yet to be verified—of a raven, spreading its wings within a perfect circle. The slogan, altum volare in tenebris, *means 'fly high in the dark.'*

I now have proof. Thorne Briar is manipulating children of the elite so he may form political and economic history to his preference.

I lean back on a deep, pondering breath. The handwriting is faded, the penmanship rushed in parts, but I turn to the next page, and the next, disappointed to see that the writing has become fewer and farther between, fire damage notwithstanding.

I fear I have been caught.

And, among more indecipherable damage, *Thorne Briar's society is nothing but the manifestation of the narcissistic elite, bored with God, turning to the devil instead to manipulate their greed-inspired destiny.*

There is a secret within the Nobles, one they've lost sight of. From what I've witnessed, it is fast getting out of control, and the women they've used—

—they call themselves the Virtues.

—worse than the Nobles, worse than skulls, or keys, or snakes, or wolves. They have motivations so sinful and blasphemous I can hardly put pen to paper and describe—

—find their temple—

. . .

—should reveal their true selves or I'll be forced to inform the Nobles of their transgressions—

—wanton, wasted individuals—

Then, turn after turn, more blank pages.

A good chunk of papery edges has been destroyed, but after about five paragraphs, the rest of the book is empty.

Now, oh *now*, it's becoming clear why Chase gave me free reign on this "hidden" book within his father's personal library.

The book is a decoy. I'm looking at a frickin' ... wooden *duck* trussed up as the sacred Nobles' rule book for members.

The manual's leather-bound jacket was tempting enough, with Daniel Stone's name embossed under a raven insignia—the *Nobles'* symbol. But the inside? It's just a few pages of the investigative ponderings of a former Briarcliff freshman who decided to make it his mission to break into the Nobles' meeting grounds and record his findings for ... a purpose I'm assuming is similar to my own.

Basically, me as a 1970s boy.

I bite down on my index finger. According to Rose's letter that Piper found, Rose created the Virtues to counteract the uncouth motivations of the Nobles. But according to this Howard Mason, it's not the Nobles that are the problem.

It's the Virtues.

Did Piper know this? Had she read the same journals and letters, coming to the same conclusions as me?

Is this why she died?

I shake my head, backing away from the sooty, crumbling ledger, open to its last written page.

Help me.

The thought of looking up Howard Mason and if he survived Briarcliff is a sobering one. I don't know how many more books I can crack open, letters I can read, fucked up warnings I have to endure, before I become so buried in conspiracies, I lose complete sight of myself.

This book, like the other writings before it, provides me with crumbs, and Chase knew that when he thrust it into my hands. As if Daniel Stone would have his super-secret society rulebook hanging out in plain sight for idiots like me to discover.

He doctored this book into *bait* for idiots like me to discover.

The real one is probably stashed somewhere not even his wife would know about.

This was probably a test to see how far I was willing to go to solve the mystery of the Nobles.

And if I was willing to go as far as Howard.

"What happened to you, Howa—?" I start to whisper, but then I notice a shifting near the closed door.

My eyes dart to the top corner of the room, where the blinking red light of the security camera nestled high in a corner goes dark.

And the shadows start to move.

Eighteen

A RUSTLING, hissing sound comes from one corner of the room, but I'm not waiting around for the big reveal.

I hurl my stuff back into my bag, cringing at my handling of Howard Mason's book when I wrap it in the plastic pouch rather than gently tuck it in—

A sharp force hits me in the arm, and I'm sent sprawling before I can secure the book. It goes flying, crunching against the ground, tattered pages drifting out.

My head bounces against the floor, my vision bursting with stars. I push to my hands and try to stand, but a boot to the middle of my back knocks me flat.

Lemony disinfectant fills my nostrils as my face mashes into the floor, but I pry my lips open. "Don't—"

Another shoe kicks me in the mouth, and I cry out, my neck snapping back.

A coppery tang flows across my tongue at the same time a giggle sounds out, girlish and *wrong*.

"Shh!"

"Just get it—"

"—wasting time..."

The whispers swirl, but I don't dare rise again. There's too many of them, whoever they are, and they aren't afraid to get mean.

I keep my eyes stretched wide enough to pick the moving shadows from the stagnant ones, shoes drifting in and out of my periphery, the hem of pale cloaks fluttering around the ankle.

It's them.

My heart scrambles to keep up with the blood rush beneath my skin. "I know who you are!" I cry, and under the influence of such utter realization, I push up, sneering, "*Virtues—*"

Boom.

Another blow across the side of my head, and the sound of glass shattering soon follows.

RUN.

The gut-wrenching, internal warning spears its way to the base of my brain, the spot that's instinctual, ancestral ... reptilian. The part that's telling me to survive and flee.

I scramble onto all fours, then push back on my haunches to sprint past these people—these girls—who were sent to hurt me.

"Hit her harder," comes a whispery growl, but the tone uses the same cadence I heard before. In my classes. In the dining hall.

The certainty that they're here for more than just a prank or a scare burrows to the core of my heart, and I fly forward, my hip banging against a lab desk and my palms smearing across the metal countertops, but I run. I do what I'm supposed to and *flee.*

An amused laugh comes from my left before an arm swings down with another beaker. I deflect it, but not enough. It slices across my cheek before crashing to the floor.

Something else hits me across my stomach, and I curl against the sudden pain before crumpling back to the ground, protecting my bandaged hand as much as I can.

"This is too much," someone whispers. "Stop. Before this gets out of control."

They're all speaking in whispers, as if to disguise their voices, in addition to cloaking their faces, but I know who they are.

The tip of a shoe hits me in the kidney, and I curl on my side with a moan.

"Stop!" the same trembling, hesitant voice says.

"Not until she gets the message." This time, a heavy, rubber-soled foot comes down on my throat. "And since she's so stubborn, I'll make it clear this time."

Sputtering, I grab onto the ankle, as if my sheer panic alone can lift the pressure off my windpipe.

"Piper..." I gasp. "Piper was one of you. I want to know what happened to her. Why are—" I wince at the increase in pressure. "Why are you against that?"

The tallest Cloak leans down, the fabric a shimmering white against the fading moonlight streaking through the windows. "Because you're not doing this for Piper."

"Selfish bitch," another hisses.

"Admit it," the main Cloak—Falyn—says, and though I can't see it through the shadows, I sense her sour smile. "You have some pathetic motivation to study a mystery that doesn't need solving and get into *our* business, read *our* private writings, thinking that by revealing our secrets you'll satisfy your own demons. But that's not how it works, dear possum."

Falyn straightens, waits a few beats, then spits out, "Because *we're* the demons. And regardless of what you discover about us, you won't solve shit. Your mom will still be dead."

I force the tears back, but a few manage to leak out, even as I struggle for breath. Easy, languid footsteps sound out until they stop near the top of my head. Another Cloak looks down, cocking her velvet-lined head, her blue eyes glittering like sapphires.

Addisyn. Somehow, these bitches have decided "virtue" should be part of their names. Despite Rose Briar's best efforts to create a society for good—and deep in my heart, I think her intentions were true—her creation has twisted and curled, tightening around the heart of the Virtues and strangling it until there are no virtuous beats left.

"You've done her no justice," I grind out. "Rose Briar would be ashamed."

Addisyn lets out a tinkling, full-voiced laugh. "You think we care what that ancient, dead bitch has to say? Welcome to our new world, Callie. Now get the fuck out."

She lifts her leg for another blow, but I angle my head at the same time I pivot and twist the ankle pressing against my neck, until its owner screeches and loses her footing, falling alongside me.

"You want in?" Falyn bellows over my head to Addisyn. "Do it, now! Prove you're worthy!"

I bolt upright, scanning the remaining three Cloaks scattered throughout the classroom, one running directly toward me with something metal glinting in her hand. Her hood slips past her hairline, but I have no time for the flutter of truth in my chest when I confirm Addisyn's face. I take stock of the weapon and her manic determination for it to dent my skull. Falyn and I both stand at the same time, and more on instinct than forethought, I turn to Falyn and flip the bottom hem of her cloak well over her head until she's blinded and shove her in Addisyn's path. It's enough for me to gather the distance I need to get to the door.

"*Fuck!*" Addisyn yells, fighting against Falyn's body tripping into her.

It'd be funny, had they not already drawn blood from my face.

A smaller one near the door swipes at my arm as I glide by, but it was a lazy grab, meant to showcase to the others that she tried.

Violet. It has to be her.

I don't want to wait around for Willow's attempt.

Panting, throat swelling, I make it to the door, fling it open, and—

Run into someone whose arms pin mine to my sides.

And they don't let go.

"*Get off me!*" I screech, but it doesn't even sound like me.

I fight against the barricade, but these arms are stronger than mine, the muscles more sculpted, and the torso much broader and flatter.

The perfect canvas to incapacitate a girl against her will.

"*No!*"

My yell is so high-pitched, supernatural and deafening, that I don't hear the voice tumbling out above my head until I stop to gulp in a breath.

"Callie! Hey, Callie! Stop!"

The arms don't loosen their grip, but the less I struggle, the more steadying breaths I can take.

And finally, I process who's speaking.

"Callie, calm *down*."

I swat at the warm hands sliding back to grip my waist, but my fingers get caught on the taut cords of muscle in his forearms, with soft, downy hairs.

My brows scrunch the instant I look up. "Chase?"

"Goddammit, Callie, you scared the shit out of me. What the fuck?" His brown eyes narrow as he lifts a hand to my face. "You're bleeding."

His gaze sweeps over my face and body, taking stock of the stretched collar of my sweatshirt, the burning scratches on my neck, the warm blood on my cheek.

Chase asks, with destructive intent, "Who did this to you?"

I gape at the controlled rage in his expression, his eyes crazed with retribution, as my mind comes back online. "What are *you* doing here? You're suspended."

The wildfire in his gaze tempers slightly. "Suspension ended over the weekend. I have crew this morning and needed to get shit from my locker."

Of course his punishment would coincide with his training schedule. Hell, I'm surprised he was slapped on the wrist at all, considering he assaulted Dr. Luke a few weeks ago and walked away smiling.

Granted, that teacher had an illegal thing for young girls, and we suspected him of murder, but...

"Don't change the subject again," he warns. "Why the fuck are you bleeding?"

I pull out of his hold, and he lets me. I spin to the chem lab, to the door that's conveniently shut, my heart pounding at the same time my brain's assuring me they won't follow me out into the halls, not while Chase is here.

"There was ... I had ... an altercation," I say, still focused on the classroom door.

"At five in the morning? With who?"

There's little point in lying. Especially to him. "The Virtues."

Chase holds his breath, tangible anger exuding off him in heated waves that curl against my back. What is he going to do with that information? Anything? I have the dull sense that he'll keep this news to himself, like he does with all the other mysterious violence that happens to me.

Yet, a cold draft strokes across my cheek as he storms by, headed for the chem lab, his expression so murderous and absurdly angry, it can't be solely because of me.

He throws the door open, and as I come up beside him, we both stare into a messy, deserted classroom.

"They're gone?" My question comes out more confused than factual. How did those girls leave? We've been outside the door the entire time.

I look up at Chase in time to see him bare his teeth, like he wants to chomp this entire lab to shreds, so I round in front, placing shaking hands against his chest to urge him back. "They must've left when they heard you. I think I'm safe now."

"No." His voice is as gravelly as I've ever heard it. "They're showing me you're not."

I stare at him at length before I say, "I was only there because I was reading the book you gave me."

His forehead creases, then he blinks and looks down at me. "You actually read the fuckin' fireball you clawed out of my hearth?"

I raise a brow, though it stings with swelling skin. "I cared enough to pull it out, and it needed special handling. Hence, the chem lab. It was an impulsive decision and no one knew I was here—"

Emma. I told Emma.

Carefully, I school my expression enough that Chase won't sniff anything out, but I can't help thinking, *did she betray me?*

He mirrors my expression. "And did you find the answers you were looking for? Or just draw more trouble to your idiot self?"

"Both." I manage a haughty tone, but inside, I'm trembling.

Chase's shoulders incline on a sigh. His eyes dart to my cheek. "Do you need to get that looked at?"

"It looks worse than it feels." *Lie.* "You gave me Howard Mason's writings knowing exactly what he said in them."

"As a warning. It wasn't meant to be fucking bait for the Virtues." Banked fire breaks through his vision. "Do you think I set you up?"

I ignore the question, because I'm not sure I have the guts to answer it. "And was that your roundabout way of telling me, don't end up like him?"

Instead of answering immediately, Chase gives me a long, silent assessment. The muscles in his jaw go rigid.

I tense under his stare, and though he eyes me like a lion would an elk, I don't have the same flight or fight response I did in the chem lab. My core aches, empty and hollow, under his gaze. It pulses its need for him, despite my internal incantation that he can't be good. He doesn't have my best interests at heart.

He could be my enemy.

"Howard Mason doesn't exist anymore," Chase says over my unseen, shivering undulation. "Is that enough of a warning for you?"

"The more I'm beaten down," I say, with tremulous conviction, "the more I want answers as to why."

Chase scoffs. "You are so reckless, you're bordering on stupid."

"Is this what happened to your sister?"

That shuts him up. His eyes shoot to mine.

"Did they beat her up, too?"

"Don't do this," he warns.

"No, really, I'd like to know. Was she getting too rebellious as a Virtue? Was Piper? Did their discipline start like this, with surprise beat-downs while their supposed friends wore cloaks meant to signify their gentle nature?"

"Callie." My name turns into a whip under his control.

"I'm starting to see the irony in all this." I laugh with hollowed-out breaths. "You Nobles and Virtues are *nothing* like the names you stand for, are you?"

Chase lifts his head and backs away. "Since you insist you're fine, I'm going to be late to practice."

"You told me your sister lit the fire," I persist. "What did she want destroyed?"

Chase freezes in the middle of the hallway, and his answering tone is gritty and rough. "Ask her yourself. Because I'm starting to think I can't protect you anymore."

I watch him pick up the duffel he must have tossed aside once he saw me running toward him. My fists are clenched and shaking at my sides.

But it's when his echoing steps fade and he turns a corner that I experience real, true fear.

I can't linger, alone in a dimly lit hallway, no matter how stubborn my head says I should be.

After one last look at the chem lab's door, I sprint to the closest exit, my lungs spasming with each haggard breath.

Nineteen

EMMA SITS at our kitchenette's high-top counter, her spoon of cereal pausing halfway to her mouth when I burst in.

"Yeesh," she says after a brief once-over. "What happened to you?"

"Nothing you care to know about," I snap, brushing past her.

She slips off her stool and stands. "Hey."

I pause at my bedroom door, throwing my hands up. "What?"

"Need I remind you, I'm the only one with a first aid kit in here, so you might try being nice."

"Nice?" I ask. "*Nice?* You lurk around this apartment pretending you don't give a shit about anything, yet you're so goddamn *nosey*, you know that? Did you tell them I was there? *Did you?*"

Emma jerks back in surprise.

I snarl, "Every *single* person I've come across in this school mopes around with their pissy attitudes and heavy burdens like the whole world revolves around keeping secrets for Briarcliff. But they'll betray good people, *nice* people, for the tiniest entry into a dangerous cult. I'm fucking *sick* of it!"

Emma's brows draw in. "Are we still talking about me here, or have we moved on to my brother?"

I heave out a breath. "The worst part is, the one person who's shown me kindness and that maybe this school won't be so bad if I just enjoy my life and look forward to Winter Formal or Prom—basic, regular, high school yearbook shit—I've ignored. I've shoved Ivy's good intentions aside because I can't control my need to understand you *assholes* better than I understand myself. God, I'm an idiot."

My lips lift in shame, and I whirl into my room, uncaring of Emma's response, if she even has one.

"I didn't tell anyone anything," Emma says through my panting breaths. "You lost the book, didn't you?"

Emma's question causes the air to freeze in my throat.

"If it's any consolation, there wasn't much in there to begin with," she continues.

I slam my palm against my doorframe. "Really? Because my attempt to read it got me attacked."

Emma makes an indecipherable sound in her throat. "That's probably because they didn't know Chase's intentions of giving it to you the way I did."

I stiffen in my doorway.

"It's all about appearances, Callie. You should have figured that out by now."

I hear her dishes clink in the sink, then the door to our apartment opens and closes with Emma's departure. It's only when I lift my head and step all the way into my room that I see the single rose lying across my bed, in pristine, ink-dipped condition.

I unleash a warrior's cry and hurl it against the wall.

On Monday morning at school, I'm told by a student prefect to head directly to the headmaster's office instead of my first class.

Confused but compliant, I step away from my locker and do as I was told.

Paintings of previous alumni leer over my head as I turn into the professors' hall, where all their offices are, trophy and other award cases shining under the lights, recently dusted and polished.

I glare at the hidden raven's crest peeking out from behind a rowing trophy, its deja vu familiarity the sole reason why I started down this secret society's wormhole in the first place.

And how you met Chase.

I flick that thought away when Marron's door comes into view.

There's no time to knock, because the door opens, and I'm greeted with the scowling face of the very person I'm trying *not* to think of.

"What's going on?" I ask, but Chase cups my elbow and drags me in.

I stop the surprise rippling across my face as I take in the other students seated in the office, Marron holding court on the other side of his desk, his frown lines as deep as the crevices on the neighboring cliffs.

Falyn, Willow, Addisyn, Violet, and Tempest are either seated or standing near Marron. Chase takes up position against the far wall, folding his arms so comfortably, I assume that was the pose he took well before I entered into this bear trap.

"Miss Ryan, glad you could join us."

Marron's not glad. He looks about ready to explode.

I scan the room, gauging the temperature, but only Addisyn looks my way, her cheeks wet, eyes red-rimmed, but her expression sly.

"Girls, tell Miss Ryan what you were just finishing telling me," Marron says.

Falyn is only too happy to oblige. "We saw Callie sneaking into school after hours over the weekend, and, concerned for her reasons for being there, we followed."

Falyn peers over her shoulder at me, batting her lashes with innocence, but I note the cut on her temple, probably from when I tripped her up and caused her to fall on shattered glass.

The thought makes me smile.

"Miss Ryan," Marron barks. "This is a serious accusation being leveled your way, so I suggest you meet it with a modicum of sobriety."

I wipe the smugness off my face.

"She's not part of crew," Willow adds, "and since Falyn and I were on our way to training, we thought it prudent that we follow her."

Marron acknowledges Willow's point. Of course he does, since she's his freaking *daughter*. "Very true, dear. This school, when unfamiliar with its layout, can be rather dangerous, especially in the dark." Marron turns a dry look my way. "It's why we keep the doors locked."

"Yes, sir," Falyn simpers. "Didn't you know, Callie, about the hidden entrances and corridors at Briarcliff? The Briar brothers designed this academy with an eccentric millionaire's flair, I'm afraid."

A shiver crawls along my spine. *That's how they got into the chem lab without me noticing.*

"Now, now," Marron chastises. "Let's not speak of unfounded architectural rumors and get to the point, shall we?"

"Callie vandalized the chem lab."

Addisyn blurts it so abruptly, all heads twist to her.

"I did what now?" I ask.

"We were incredibly disappointed to open the school this morning and find the chemistry room so wholly violated," Marron says, his gaze steady on mine. "And these witnesses have kindly come forward to tell me that it was you that destroyed all the supplies, poured chemicals over the countertops, and good Lord, drew entirely inappropriate and obscene diagrams on the whiteboard at the front of the class."

I burst forward, my chest threatening to unleash a boisterous laugh at the absurdity of a single girl—me—doing all that to a classroom, for no reason whatsoever. Luckily, my brain wins out. "Are you kidding? Headmaster Marron, they're lying. I did *not*—"

"Is there a reason we're here?"

The placid calm of Tempest's voice eats through my words like the silent work of termites. He quiets the room yet lifts his hand to check his cuticles as if this is all another day in the life of Tempest Callahan.

"Now that you've brought it up," Marron says stiffly, "Yes. Due to the ... tenuous nature of Miss Ryan's relationship with these girls, Willow has assured me that you two were also witnesses to Miss Ryan's unwarranted outburst. Is this true?"

Absurdity gives way to outrage. I stand in the middle of the room, my face hot and my fists clenched to my sides. Even my uniform skirt trembles with the brewing rage inside my body. But, at Marron's words, I force a ribbon of calm over my skin.

There's no way Chase or Tempest would back up these lies. Tempest wasn't even there, and Chase saw me flinging myself out of that room like the gates of hell were in there.

That's not a girl who draws "obscene diagrams" on whiteboards.

But then, oh then, Chase shatters my world. "Yes."

I whip around to face him, my face going numb with blood loss. "*What*? Chase!" He won't look at me.

"I caught her as she was leaving," he continues. "And she admitted what she did. Tempest heard it, too. Right, T?"

Tempest nods right as a *whoosh* of air leaves my body and shrivels my lungs. I whisper brokenly to Tempest, "You've had my back all week, swearing you were there to protect me, and now you're *lying* for them? Why?" I direct another question to Chase. "Why are you doing this?"

It looks like it pains him, but Chase meets my eye, his jaw grinding. "You need to stop with your delusions, Callie. It's gone too far."

My stomach twists in knots. I feel truly lost, and the words I screamed at Emma last night are the only ones I can find.

...maybe this school won't be so bad if I just enjoy my life and look forward to Winter Formal or Prom—basic, regular, high school yearbook shit...

This academy will always be bad, because of the students they enlist, the broken societies they nurture, and the twisted minds they let rule the school.

I face Marron head-on, and say, in the steadiest voice I can conjure, "I was in the chem lab before school hours because I wanted to go through a damaged book I found. I needed the necessary tools." I throw a long stare in Tempest's direction, since he should know. He read it on my laptop, using it to figure out I'd need supplies, and potentially told these bitches to wait until I skipped along the path, after hours, into their waiting clutches.

And I fell for it. Was drawn to his niceties like the lonely, disenchanted girl he knew I was.

Marron shakes his head. "Regardless of your intentions, you broke into a classroom after hours—"

I cut in, "I'll admit that much. But when I was finishing up and cleaning the *small* mess I made, I was attacked."

Marron's brows shoot up. "Excuse me?"

"Look at my face!" I yell, then point to my cheek. "And look at Falyn's! You think we got those wounds separately? She jumped me, and had her friends help. Addisyn tried to knock me unconscious a whole shitload of times, and Willow—"

The words are out before I can reel them back in, and Marron's expression darkens with rage. "Listen here, Miss Ryan, it is one thing to defend your actions. It is a complete other aggravation to involve my *daughter* in your concocted story—"

Warning laces his tone. And still, I can't stop. "What makes you think I'm the liar? These girls, your daughter, call themselves Virtues, but—"

Chairs scraping against hardwood halt the flow of my words. First, Addisyn rises, then Falyn, then Willow, using their height as a helpful tactic to stare me down.

"Haven't I been through enough?" Addisyn seethes, her fresh tears becoming dew drops in her eyes. "My sister's dead, my boyfriend's in custody, and now you're accusing me of wanting to *hurt* you?" Addisyn gulps in a dramatic breath. "I'm not violent, but I'm forced to think of it every day. I'm trying to heal, but you want me to suffer!"

"Oh, come *on*," I say.

Falyn speaks before Marron can scold me further. "We're trying, as best we can, to take you at face value and not bring up your past, but you're making that super diffi-cult, Callie."

"Last week you humiliated Addisyn in the new library. And now, what, she passed your initiation by trying to kill me with a Bunsen burner?" I back up on instinct, and when I knock into Chase's back, I recoil. He's staring at a spot past Marron's head, his jaw muscles so tense, they're almost bursting through his skin. Yet he still won't look at me. Tempest eyes it all through his lashes, but he won't lift a finger.

"Listen to her, Daddy. She's clearly disturbed." Willow shifts her gaze to me. "First, you steal a book from Daniel Stone's study. An honored alumnus at this school. Then, you burn it. Thankfully, you second-guessed yourself and saved it from the fire—the whole senior class saw *that* insanity—but instead of returning it to its rightful owner, you invade the Stones' privacy *while* breaking into a classroom you have no permission to be in, and now you're saying we beat you for it? Do you take us for barbarians, or are you just confusing us with your stepfather?"

I suck in a breath, my fist reeling back from my waist to punch her in her too-white veneers, but Chase grabs hold of my hand and bends it against my lower back, my muscles aching and trembling beneath his grip.

No one else has witnessed the exchange, and nothing in Chase's expression gives away his battle over my will, but I wish, with all my might, that I had longer nails so I could cut him as deeply as he's cut me.

"Girls, thank you for your input. Gentlemen, you too. I'd like to speak with Miss Ryan alone."

I must imagine the quick squeeze Chase gives before he releases my hand, because he leaves without a glance or a word, Tempest following behind.

I glare at both of them, but I might as well be staring down river rocks.

Addisyn leads the way for Falyn, Willow, and Violet, but she casts an evil, villainess grin my way, mouthing, *fool me once...*

So, the writings of Howard Mason really were a prop. The Virtues thought I had something else more important. More dangerous.

I ignore Falyn's idiotic malice behind Addisyn, instead directing a heavy-lidded glare at Violet. Violet, who never says *anything* and pretends to be good.

"You're just like them," I hiss in her ear as she passes, and she shrinks against my words.

"Miss Ryan, please sit."

I take Addisyn's vacant seat, as instructed, my continued submissiveness to authority becoming more questionable by the second, but I can't help but believe that adults will look into the facts. Marron will discover the truth through his respon-sibility and power, and the proper students will be punished.

That's how a headmaster works, right?

Wrong. Willow is his daughter. He more than likely is aware of what crawls under the baseboards of this school.

Marron steeples his hands under his chin. "I've spoken with your parents."

I respond by keeping straight-backed and tight-lipped in the seat across from him.

After a deep sigh, Marron continues, "I had every intention of suspending you for at least two weeks, but your father has made me aware of your past ... issues."

My teeth clench so hard, they ache, but I don't blink away from him.

"He explained, at length, the troubles you've experienced since losing your mother. The paranoid delusions and obsessive-compulsive disorder that drives you, sometimes unreasonably, and has you taking drastic action against your health and well-being unless proper intervention comes in time."

I can't stay silent anymore. "That's ... that's an incredibly clinical way to apply my mom's murder to the rest of my life."

"Don't you understand, dear? What you do has ripple effects."

"I've apologized to my dad." I wring my hands where Marron can't see. "I was wrong, and maybe a bit unstable after she died, but I'm better now. I swear I am."

Marron lifts a brow. "That is where we differ. But I'm not trying to argue with you. What I'm trying to say is, I'm willing to take your mental struggles into account and will assign you a month's detention, assisting with dining hall and grounds clean-up at the end of your classes every day."

What? I'd rather take a week's suspension like Chase. Throwing parties and basically taking a vacation from this gloriously terrible school.

"Headmaster, I—"

"Consider yourself lucky. Your father should be calling you shortly regarding the ways we can make your stay more comfortable here. For everybody involved."

My brows furrow. "I don't understand."

Marron leans back in his seat. "I have a close relationship with your father's wife, Lynda Meyer. It's due to her conviction that you belong here that I'm amiable to your continued schooling with us. But you are on a short leash, Miss Ryan. I have zero tolerance toward any more acts of aggression coming from you. Keep your head down, pay attention to your studies, and you should get by just fine. Do I make myself clear?"

I stop chewing on my cheek to implore, "No matter how many times I tell you I didn't do it, you're not going to believe me, are you?"

"You're on camera entering school grounds, and I have visuals of you in the chemistry lab, Miss Ryan. Please don't argue with solid evidence."

"But the camera goes black, doesn't it?" I sit straighter in my seat. "All you witness is me doing exactly as I said."

"Reading the book you had no rights to?"

I persist, "Chase lent me—"

"He assures me he did not."

My shoulders slump. *Of course.*

"You don't see me vandalizing anything," I say. "In fact, that camera shows me packing up before it shuts off—"

"Do you recall what I said about ripple effects?" Marron leans forward, folding his arms across his desk. "You're lucky Mr. Stone is not going to his father about the stolen work, though I'm predisposed to do it myself. Continue along this path, Miss Ryan, and I'll be forced to do just that."

"Why are you doing this?" I ask. Pointlessly. Stupidly. "All you have as proof is the bias of a handful of popular kids who are known for their bullying."

Marron goes quiet. As much as I don't want to, I squirm under his study.

"I suggest you leave my office, Miss Ryan, before you say something I cannot dismiss."

More disturbed than I am shaken, I push to my feet, despite the urge to keep arguing, keep *convincing* this man that he's wrong.

But, the defeatist in me has never strangled my voice harder.

"Attend your last period before lunch," Marron says as I walk stiffly to the door. "After it is completed, report directly to our housekeeper, Moira, and she will give you the supplies needed to clean up that godforsaken mess in the chemistry lab before afternoon classes."

"Yes, sir," I say quietly, before stepping out of his office, and into a punishment I swear, by all I believe in, I will prove I do not deserve.

Twenty

MY PHONE BUZZES against the back of my arm as I head to calc, and I realize
I'd forgotten to put it in my locker this morning.

I slide my bag to my front and dig into the side pocket, revealing three missed
calls, two voicemails, and a slew of text messages from both Dad and Lynda.

One eye scrunches before the rest of my face follows with a cringe, questioning
whether I want to deal with this now, or later.

A quick scroll through the messages...

Dad: Call me. Now.

**Dad: Though your actions tell me otherwise, if you have any will to keep
your social life and phone active, you better pick up your phone, Cal.**

Lynda: Honey, this sounds serious. Call us, please. We're so worried.

Dad: WHAT WERE YOU THINKING??????

... tells me I should bite the bullet.

The school's foyer is wonderfully silent when I leave the West Wing and stop
under the chandelier. I glance toward the staircase, and, without another thought,
take them up into the Wolf's Den.

The space is deserted, like I'd hoped, and I perch on one of the stools surrounding the high tops toward the back, the stained-glass Briarcliff crest creating broken patterns of rainbow beams across the wood.

I wriggle in my seat until I'm comfortable, and, after a deep breath, call my stepdad.

"Jesus Christ!" he says after half a ring.

I startle, despite the clues telling me they'd be watching his phone like a couple of cats ready to pounce at the phone's slightest vibration, but exhale enough to tentatively say, "Hi."

"What the hell, Cal?"

"It wasn't me."

Dad blows out a breath that rattles my ear drum. "Not a good lead-in, Cal."

Lynda bursts onto the line. "Honey, are you all right?"

A tentative flutter, like a butterfly landing on the base of my heart, tickles my chest at her caring question. "I'm a little beat up, but I'll be okay."

"Beat up?" she asks. "What—"

"Calla Lily Ryan, explain yourself," Dad interrupts. "And do not do it by appealing to my wife's sweet nature. You tell us the truth, and you do it now, or else I'm seriously going to question the logic in putting you back in school. Maybe you should've stayed at the hospital longer."

I hiss in a breath. "Dad—"

"That's what you've lowered me to, honey," he says, but he honestly sounds upset. "I don't want to do it. You understand? I don't *want* to put you in an institution or send you to the city's answer to wayward girls, but this is the line of thinking you've turned me to. Why did you destroy school property?"

I pop my lower lip from my teeth. "First of all, 'destroy' is a very strong word, and I didn't *do* what they're saying I did."

"Marron tells us there's video footage."

"Well, that part's true," I admit, "But it doesn't catch me vandalizing anything. I was there for personal reasons, reading an old book that'd been damaged—"

"Another lie." Dad sighs. "You stole that book from a prominent figure. Cal, I can't tell you how much of a disappointment you've become."

The barb digs and twists at the very spot a butterfly gave me hope only seconds ago. But how can I recover? I can't tell him about the writings of Howard Mason I discovered in the Stone family's library. I can't admit I've been sniffing out Briarcliff's secret society because I think they're involved in Piper's death, even if they weren't the ones that pushed her. And I absolutely *cannot* confess about my sexual relationship with said prominent figure's spawn and my suspicions that both he and his father are responsible for protecting the secrets of the Nobles & Virtues.

Aw, man. Even in my head, this sounds insane.

"Dad, I'm sorry." The apology comes out more shredded than intended. "But everything I'm being accused of came from good intentions. Can you believe that much?"

Static answers me back. I can picture my dad, holding the phone in a shaking hand, him and Lynda leaning over it as my voice comes from the speaker.

My accusation toward him came with good intentions, too. I wanted to avenge my mother, gain closure, do *something* to stop the demon gnawing on my soul and ripping my heart into its chum.

They'd fought before she died, he and my mom. They were fighting a lot, and during the very last argument, when they thought I wasn't there, I'd heard the slap.

The thump of my mother's back hitting a wall.

The crash of a vase being thrown near her head.

I'm aware of the last part because of her autopsy results. She'd had cuts across her cheekbone from spraying shards matching the pieces of the vase broken at her feet.

I hadn't acted, then. I'd stayed in my room, crumpled into a ball on the other side of my bed, in case Dad decided to unleash his anger on me next.

Because he was mad. So angry, his roars reverberated the walls and shook my lamp on the nightstand.

When I confessed all this to Ahmar on the night she died, his expression darkened, his mouth turned tight and grim, and he arrested my father on sight.

And when my father was released due to insufficient evidence, that demon eating me up inside wore my skin for its own.

"Honey, nothing good comes from retaliation." Lynda's soothing voice comes on the line, brushing against the spindly thorns of those memories. "Whatever happened to make you do this—and Pete, I *know* she didn't do this at random—you report it to a teacher, honey. Or your counselor. Or any responsible adult who can handle the situation appropriately. You understand?"

That's what I did after Mom was murdered, I want to hiss. *And look what happened. I was turned wrong, and my stepdad swore I was too traumatized by loss to see straight. And every single adult responsible for my well-being believed him. Including you.*

"I convinced the headmaster to give you another chance," she continues over the increasing loudness in my head, internal voices that won't shut up, "and I hope you'll take it. We'd also like you to see your guidance counselor weekly, if not every other day. Can you do that for us, honey?"

My mouth opens.

"Do it," Dad says before I can agree. "Or else I'll add behavioral psychiatrist to the list. And I'll make sure they evaluate you for a prescription."

I take a huge breath. Then another. I hope it's enough to stop the quaking of my bones. "Okay. I'll go to the counselor, I'll take the punishment, but I'm not who they say I am."

They're hiding more than I've ever concealed.

I keep that thought to myself, since it will only convince Lynda and Dad of my perceived fragile mental state. Eighteen or not, he can still have me involuntarily committed with this evidence.

"Good," Dad snaps. "You can forget about any parties, too. Halloween is *out*, and the headmaster agrees to keep someone in your dorms to ensure you stay in your room. And if, by Parents' Weekend, you've kept your nose clean, we'll revisit my desire to send you to some serious therapy."

I swallow and attempt to emulate the scolded, contrite, want-to-be-good kid they're determined to hear. "Understood."

"We'll see you in a month, Cal."

"Be safe!" Lynda says before Dad ends the call.

My feet hit the floor with a light thud, and I readjust my backpack with cold, numb fingers. I'm late to calc, and after the talk with Dad and Lynda, it's imperative I wear a squeaky-clean veneer.

I've been exposed to the drugs Dad threatens, and I never want to go back there. Not ever.

I descend the stairs one by one, mentally planning through my growing desperation of how I'm going to keep pursuing the society without setting off more alarm bells.

The Virtues have proven their control and talent for manipulation, but they're so cocky and drunk on the academy's power, they haven't considered who they've come up against. I'm just as skilled as them, if I want to access that buried part of my brain badly enough.

And after this, I do. Oh, I so absolutely *do*.

Twenty-One

THE NEXT COUPLE of weeks inch by with the accompanying snot-trail of a snail.

Halloween night came and went, and I stayed in my room, despite Ivy's How do I know about Riordan's erection? Because after the Halloween dance, Ivy gained access into my dorm, arguing with the college student that she also worked the front desk at Thorne House, and thus, deserved a brothers-in-arms type of trust, and crawled into my bed, delighting me with her summary of hook-ups, fights, and passing outs.

Other than that, the only one other good thing that arose from this time-lapse was the removal of my bandage, revealing a nasty sunburn on my hand rather than an angry, second-degree mottling. The pink-tinged, sensitive skin still needs some doctoring, but as long as I apply ointment and protect it from the sun, I should be all right.

For the remainder of my punishment, I plan to keep my head down (as promised), reporting to my detention and cleaning duties on time and with a closed-lipped smile, despite the injustice inside me demanding I claw at the walls and scream at the top of my lungs.

But I don't, because I've done all that before, and didn't I learn my lesson back then?

Students largely ignore me, and I take enough time to wonder if it's because I remain under Chase's ill-begotten "protection," or if I've just started to smell so bad from picking up garbage, they've all decided I'm not worth the trouble.

The dining hall's become messier than usual, and cleaning up the grounds outside the school is no better. I use the same grasper tool I use in the dining hall, and since it and I have become so close, I've named it Grabby-Hands. We trudge all around campus, sticking everything from fast-food wrappers to used condoms that have somehow been tossed into the hedges.

I don't know why, and I don't want to know.

I've even been designated to empty the trash in the dorms but have been told to only do the girls' rooms.

I suppose Marron has spared me from the truly questionable and haunting items occupying boys' areas.

During class, I sit silently, only answering questions when called upon. It makes me less of a target and much more forgettable, a cloak I'm coming to accept with ease.

Chase goes out of his way to avoid me. On one Wednesday, when I was out near the fountain, clearing off tissues and receipts from Piper's makeshift memorial of flowers and weather-beaten stuffed animals, Chase exited the school, and as he strode down the wheelchair-access ramp and lifted his head, he took one look at me and spun on his heel back inside.

Literally screeched his brakes and did a U-turn.

"Coward!" I'd called after him, but he was no use to me anymore. I didn't give a damn whether he stayed or ran.

At least, my mind didn't care. My heart has other ideas, but I threaten it daily.

Chase lied. He lured me in with a book that turned out to be fairly useless, turned against me without blinking an eye, and sided with the Virtues, basically okaying their attack.

He uses his school powers for evil, and I am so *done* with that bastard.

Instead, my attention turned to Eden, who I've been watching carefully through the veiled lens of boredom as I sit quietly and unobtrusively in the classes we share.

She's the one who told me Piper was a Virtue, meaning she knows more than she's sharing, but I haven't gotten a chance to get her alone.

I plan to change that.

Eden's slippery, though. She's always in some sort of extra-curricular or so intense about her studying, that when I clean up enough to go visit Ivy in the evenings, she actually turns feral if I try so much as to say hello.

But there will come a moment when I corner her. Everyone gets themselves alone at some point during the day, and if I have to back her into a bathroom stall, I will.

Grabby-Hands and I are done for the day, so after swiping sweat-damp hair from my brow, I store him in the janitor's closet and head to the dorms.

Emma might be there, or she might not, but I'm finished pondering over her nightly escapes and where she goes. Ever since Chase showcased his talent for throwing me under the bus, I consider her an untrustworthy accessory.

After keying into our room, I walk into our quiet, deserted central area, peeling off clothes as I go. Emma's door is shut, and I don't bother to call out that I'm home, deciding a hot shower will be a much better greeting than anything I'd receive from Emma.

I spend a lot of time under the spray, enjoying how the water massages my aching shoulders and back, and taking pleasure in washing my hair and scalp. Once I'm confident I smell more like vanilla-orange blossom than day-old pizza, I turn off the faucet and grab the towel.

I'm wiping my face, when my phone dings where I left it by the sink.

The steam I've created in the small bathroom has misted both the mirror and my screen, so I give it a quick wipe before reading the text, continuing to towel off with one hand.

Private Number: You've been accused of something you didn't do.

The towel drops to the floor. I read it again, then reply:

Who is this?

After a few seconds, another message comes through.

It doesn't feel good to be framed, does it? Watch out. They're just warming up. Arresting you for Piper's murder is next.

Goosebumps appear on my forearms, despite the steam.

Me: Whoever you are, you missed the latest. Her sister's boyfriend's been arrested.

Unknown: But did he do it? Or did they?

I worry the inside of my cheek, coaxing my heart into a regular rhythm despite those very words circling my mind every day.

Me: You don't sound too sure either.

Private Number: I have dirt on the Nobles and Virtues, and I'm willing to share it with you.

The phone falls to my side, and I tip my chin up to the ceiling, closing my eyes on a sigh. I'm supposed to be squeaky clean—and not in the literal sense. I shouldn't be dipping into conspiracy tunnels and going off the rails with theories I can't back up. Not now, when my credibility is so shaken. But the temptation is there. No, the *need*.

Maybe I can do this one thing. All I have to do is listen and see what this person has to say. No physical action required, other than being careful.

I go back to my phone.

Me: Meet me in town Saturday morning at the lobster shack.

Private Number: Too exposed. I'll meet you in the public library, at the Briar exhibit in the back.

I suck on my tooth as I stare at the screen. Meeting in the most deserted, low-lit part of a failing library isn't my first choice, but if I scream, Darla will come running. Won't she?

Me: Ok. 9 am sharp.

Private Number: See you then. And keep alert. They're far from done with you.

God. Cryptic as all hell.

I drop my phone in the sink, combing my hair back and studying my face in the mirror. My cheekbones are sharply angled by the new hollows under my cheeks. My eyes, which used to be the same chameleon hazel as my mother's, have dulled to a murky gray. I'm paler than I should be, chewing on multi-vitamins no substitute for food, and my hands resemble blue, veiny claws rather than the soft, long-fingered femininity they once claimed.

A rumbling fear stirs in my belly the more I study my reflection. My inner demon cracks open an eye.

Was that a noise?

I glance at the locked bathroom door, sure I heard the clomp of shoes on the other side.

Emma rarely wears shoes indoors. It's how she creeps up on me so easily.

Another sound, familiar in its clatter, piques my hearing.

Someone's rifling through our fridge.

Visions of my cloaked visitors and the strange roses they leave behind creep alongside my periphery. Nightmares of the Virtues breaking in—Addisyn at the helm—and finishing the job pound against my exposed flesh.

They're far from done with you.

I step back from the door, pick up my towel, and wrap it around my torso. Then, I cautiously unlock and crack open the door.

Twenty-Two

A HUNCHED FIGURE leans into Emma's and my fridge, grunting as he clanks around jars.

I push the door open farther, calmer now that it's clear there's not a hoard of Cloaks ready to descend on my naked, vulnerable form, and pad out into the center of the room.

My gaze narrows.

That butt. I'd recognize that ass anywhere.

"What the hell are you doing with my food?"

My loud question causes him to jump and curse as he nails his head on the top of the fridge.

Chase staggers to his full height and faces me, an open carton clutched in his hands.

He swallows, his glazed stare running over me, then going back to the food. "I'm looking for my sister."

"Well, you're not going to find her inside my pad thai."

Chase grunts, then throws it back in the fridge and slams the door, bottles rattling. "It's bland, anyway."

I lean in for a closer inspection, noticing the red rimming his eyes and how they can't quite focus on a single object. His posture is lopsided, his uniform rumpled, his hair askew.

Yep. He's either drunk or high. Probably both.

My lips go tight. "Haven't you heard the latest? No one's allowed in or out of my dorm room, other than my meandering roommate."

"Mm." Chase pretends to think on the house arrest *he* helped to cause. "My sister's re-acclimating to the academy slowly. I'm allowed in to help her along."

I make a sound of disgust. "You should go back to your dorms, where maybe somebody might be happy to see you."

"Nope. I told you. Looking for Emma."

I glance toward Emma's room but notice her door's ajar and she's nowhere inside.

"Checked there already," Chase says as I turn back to him.

"You won't find her in my room, either. And since I was in the bathroom..." I wait for Chase to finish my sentence. When he doesn't, I sigh. "She's not here, Chase."

"Oh. Damn." Chase leans against the countertop instead of making a move to leave.

When I see where his eyes drift, my grip tightens at the top of my towel.

My nipples, however, have other ideas and demand to be set free, exposed to the air and Chase's sexual survey.

I clear my throat. "Can you leave now?"

Chase angles his head, his attention frozen on my chest. After a moment, he murmurs, "You're gorgeous, you know that?"

Ignoring the traitorous twinge of my heart, I growl, "Fuck off and *go*, Chase."

"I remember what you look like under there." He gives a heavy-lidded blink. "It's singed into my brain, how you curve in all the right places, the way you fit into my hands." His eyes flick up to mine. "Your taste is still on my tongue."

"You don't get to do that," I rasp. "Not after what you've done."

He flinches, and that brief flash of emotion gives me more insight into his thought process than he's ever allowed before.

Chase is ashamed, even though he's made it clear where his loyalty lies. He wants to destroy my time here, or at the very least, ruin it, but I'm starting to think ... is it because he has a personal vendetta, or is there another factor at play?

He doesn't follow up with an excuse, though, and for some reason, that enrages me further.

"Why did you lie to Marron?" I ask him in a stronger voice.

Chase looks up to the ceiling instead of answering, and damn it, I should've expected that. Chase doesn't give answers; he incites more questions.

Yet, he stills as if he's preparing himself for a battering, so I persist. "You *know* I didn't vandalize the chem lab." I suck in a disgusted breath. "If this is some fucked up way of getting back at me for ending what we had, need I remind you, it was *you* who walked out of here after I told you Piper was pregnant. It was *you* who asked me to find out the DNA of the fetus. And it was *you* who gave me Howard Mason's book, pretending like you were trying to protect me when you just wanted to set me up for *them*."

A low rumble sounds from his throat. "There's so much. So much you don't know."

"What have I done to make you want to hurt me?" The question comes out unfiltered, and I wince at the emotional whimper it becomes. "Did you enjoy toying with me? When I fell for your act, when I let you into my bed, were you turned on by the pain you were about to cause?"

In a blink, Chase is centered in my vision, stepping so close that he puts his hands on my waist.

I gasp, losing what little breath was escaping from the thickness of my throat, and look up at him.

This close, I smell the liquor on his breath. The weed.

He's only attracted to me right now because he's lost his sobering armor. That fact is like a bucket of ice water splashing over my head, my shoulders, and my face crumples with the icy realization before I can stop it.

I place my hands against his chest, pushing him back. He doesn't move.

"This isn't you right now," I whisper near his heart. "You can't give me what I want, so I'm not going to give into you."

The barest brush hits the bottom of my chin as he tilts it up. His eyes search mine with bleary melancholy.

At last, he says, "The rules within the academy were written long before you got here. I can't disregard them the way Howard Mason tried and the way you want me to."

"Thorne and Rose Briar created rival societies in this school," I murmur in return. "But what does their twisted past have to do with your relationship with me?"

He strokes a finger down the side of my face, and I turn in to it like the starving, friendless cat that I am. Chase is compromised, yes, but he looks so damn tired, and I wonder if, under his stare, I resemble the same.

"I can't tell you everything but know this..." he says. "I care about you."

I snort, hoping to jar myself back into reality. "But your actions will never show it, will they?"

Chase ensures I meet his eyes, then repeats, "I care about you."

I shove at his pecs. "No, you fucking don't. You *lied* for them. You *helped* them."

He bends close. "Listen to my voice behind my words. I care about you."

My lips slam shut as I search his eyes, the emotion in his tone hitting my ears, but in all the wrong places. It isn't right, what he's communicating. It isn't *fair*.

"So, you lied to protect me? Is that it? You're helping them to protect me?" I push at his shoulders again, but his body doesn't give way to my angry shoves. "My life could be ruined because of your so-called *protection*. I was nearly beaten to a pulp because of it. My dad wants to commit me. Do you know how fucked up that—?"

Chase catches the rest of my question with his lips, the pressure so sizzling, so startling, my body buckles until his grip holds me steady.

We stumble backward, and my head bangs against the wall as his hand cups my cheek and our lips angle to meet each other with a perfect, desperate sear.

My mouth parts to let him in, despite my better judgement's cry to keep him out. I push my chest into his, starving for the friction, aching for him to fill the void he left so wide and echoing when he strode out of here, leaving me in his wake.

Don't think about that, I chide. *Not if you're doing this with him. Take it for what it is. What you want.*

Chase rips the towel from my grip, my naked body molding against his uniform, dampening the school colors with my scent. My hands tangle in his hair when I rise up on my tiptoes, matching his need at the same time he straightens, and I jump so he can catch my thighs around his waist.

He breaks off the kiss. "I care about you," he repeats on a growl. "And it would've been so much worse for you if I hadn't intervened."

I cup his face, my fingers leaving indents in his angular face. "Shut up."

An approving sound comes from his throat as he spins, and it's with the graceful, rower's balance that he carries me into my bedroom and kicks the door shut.

He places me on my bed, but instead of covering me with his body, he takes a long, drawn-out survey, from the top of my head to my toes.

"Chase," I say on a nervous laugh, battling against the need to pull the covers over myself.

"I meant what I said. You're gorgeous."

"You're drunk."

Chase cocks his head. "I'm not so fucked-up that I can't see your beauty."

He unbuttons his collared white shirt, exposing his hairless, carved-in-bronze chest, his six-pack rippling with the movement of his arms.

I try not to gape, because *I'm* not the beautiful one, but I refuse to look away from the visual treat of his muscular, athletic body before he uses its talents.

With a flick of his thumb, his belt's unbuckled and his uniform slacks undone and pooled to the ground. He steps out of his boxers with the same, rapid grace, then puts one knee on the bed as he strokes his straining erection.

And I think, *God, yes. I missed this.*

My core aches for him to fill it, and my starvation must be written all over my face, because he smirks.

With that kind of introduction, I expect him to take me with one thrust, but instead, he moves to settle himself between my legs, but softly strokes my inner thighs. His calloused fingers travel up my stomach, tracing my breasts, leaving shivers along their path, and I'm so lulled by it, so attached to its sweetness, that my heart falls to pieces as his fingers carve their destiny across my naked chest.

Breaths heaving, I internally beg for patience. Noticing my distress, Chase smiles again and dips his fingers down until he's stroking my folds with the same light caress he'd used to trace my body.

I can't meet his quiet seduction with the same amount of grace. It's been so long. Too long. I buck under his hand, twisting and writhing to try to coax his fingers deeper, but he won't comply.

"You're so wet," he rasps out, his focus on his finger, curling it in and out. "So damn ready for me."

"Chase," I moan, so aching and wanton, I have to shut my eyes and whine into the blackness. If I watch him much longer, I'll explode.

His silky voice hits my ears. "Stroke me."

Chase lifts my hand until I curl my fingers around his shaft. During his worship of me, he hadn't touched his dick, nor did he grind it against me. It throbbed and bounced with the same need he was enticing from me, but now I realize, he was doing it to match my desperation, to draw out our need.

Why?

He groans at the tightening of my grip. I stroke, as he asked, then pump, the tender pinkness of my hand and wrist forgotten as I increase the friction, then, needing moisture, rise up enough to draw the tip of him in my mouth.

Chase sucks in air through his teeth at the contact, tipping over the precipice as he watches my lips encircle his cock.

He grits out, "I need to be inside you."

VIRTUE

I release his dick with a *pop*, then ask as I look up at him, "What's stopping you?"

Chase gnashes his teeth, then bends and rifles through my nightstand for a condom. Once he slips it on, he towers over me, pressing my legs apart. But instead of taking me with threatening, animalistic prowess, Chase reins it in, lining himself up with my entrance with trembling, *enraging,* slowness.

"Chase," I beg, but he doesn't acknowledge my pleas.

Inch by tortuous inch, he sinks into my folds, his jaw tight. When his arms come down on either side of me, and I grip his shoulders to bring him closer, I use that momentum to thrust my hips up and wrap my legs around his torso, taking him all the way in.

He buries his face in my neck, groaning, fighting some unseen force. I stroke his hair and whisper in his ear. "You have me. Right now, I'm yours."

Chase lifts his head to kiss me, and it's with such urgent desire, my teeth cut into my lips, but I don't cry out, though it's dizzying and confusing. I press against him harder.

He thrusts, but not with the same possessiveness as before. He's not demanding ownership. It's more like he's asking permission to go slow, to stretch me to my limits with tender strokes.

When the orgasm builds, I bite down on his neck, my cry of release muffled and tinged with blood.

Chase has his own release, his thrusts deep and quick, before he collapses, his chest falling against mine.

I tangle my fingers in his hair, massaging his scalp, and hope he doesn't move. I like the warmth of him, and his weight has a calming effect, like he's squeezing all the angst from my heart so it can maybe find its lost pieces again.

His head moves. "You okay?"

"Mm-hmm," I say, tracing spirals in his hair.

"I don't ... I don't want to hurt you."

My circles stop.

"It's best for both of us if I stay away from you, but I—you're so damn addictive, with your smell and your taste ... and the darkness you try to hide." He lifts his head. "Like me."

We take a long study of each other, but instead of getting lost in the golden flecks of his eyes, I'm the first to break the silence. "It's okay. I know what this is."

He bows his head, blond locks slipping forward. "You don't. And I hope you never will."

My brows furrow, but Chase lifts off me and bends to get dressed.

I want to plead with him to stay the night, but the futileness of the request prevents my tongue from forming the words.

Why should I ask him for comfort, when I swore to hate him the instant he sided with Falyn and her friends? Or how about when he decided protecting Briarcliff's secret society was more important than exploring the budding relationship between us?

With that in mind, I sit up, gathering the sheets around myself, and watch him dress.

323

Though I'm liquid and docile with the orgasm he gave me, I'm reminded that the physical is all he's willing to give.

"Emma's probably in the library," he says.

My brows push together. Why would she go to the very place where her life, as she knew it, went up in flames?

"It's where she goes sometimes," he continues. "You may not believe me, but I really was looking for her when I came in, before you and I..."

I nod but don't say anything else. It's not like he'd answer my confusion over Emma's choices.

"And Callie?"

I watch him carefully. "Hmm?"

"I'm sorry." He shrugs on his collared shirt, leaving it unbuttoned. "For what it's worth."

I set my jaw, folding my arms over my knees and waiting a few more minutes, ensuring he's left, before I reach under my pillow and pull out what I'd managed to dig from his pocket in the midst of our foreplay.

I flip it around in my fingers a few times, watching the light play against the laminate, but I don't feel bad for using his sexual weakness for me. Not after what he's done.

After one last glance through my open doorway, I twist and shove his room card into the crack between my mattress and bed frame, then turn over and try to chase dreams instead.

Twenty-Three

SATURDAY MORNING DAWNS early and bright—for my side of the dorm room, anyway.

Emma came back late, and I assume is still sleeping behind her closed door as I get ready. It's a relief not to face her the night after my impromptu sex with Chase. Not that she and I are known for sharing secrets, but I'm wary she might notice a change in the air, an electric charge to my step, or anything slightly off that I don't think to hide, sending her twin senses tingling.

I couldn't get much rest after Chase left, my mind alive with our sex and his motives and my plans. Too many possibilities flitted behind my eyes. Not only the risks, but the repercussions would be astounding if I get caught.

They've left me no choice. If Chase can't or won't speak about Piper's involvement with the Virtues, I'll have to dig up the evidence myself.

Just the thought sends shivers along my spine, but I refuse to shake the idea that Piper's murder doesn't stop with Jack, just like it wasn't solved with Dr. Luke. Not only is Jack Addisyn's boyfriend, both Addy and Piper have Virtue connections, a secret society created by Rose Briar that, from what I've seen, prefers unscrupulous activities over wholesome ones.

It begs the question: why did Rose create a rival society to the Nobles? And are they still implementing her wishes, or have they gone rogue, beginning with Piper's downfall?

Ugh. I'm so confused.

And determined, goddamnit.

Before I can get to any of that, however, I have an important meeting which I can't be late for.

Ready just shy of eight o'clock, I throw my tote over my shoulder and head out, taking the stairs instead of the elevator.

I have nothing to hide, so I exit out the front this time, lifting my hand in a wave to the campus officer standing beside our usual college girl and her closed laptop. She's looking more alert than usual these days, and not too happy about it, but permission to study in the public library in town couldn't be denied by Marron—especially considering my *relationships* with other girls in this school who are known to use the school's library.

It's better for everyone involved if I stay away.

The automatic double-doors slide open as I approach the exit. When I hit the sidewalk in hopes of seeing Yael (who I requested ten minutes ago), I almost run into Eden.

"Oh. Hey," I say when I come to a halt a few steps away from her back.

Eden stiffens, then raises her head and shoves her phone into her back pocket. She turns, and I'm hopeful the sound coming out of her lips is a reciprocal, "Hey."

But probably not.

"What are you doing here?" I ask.

Eden shrugs. "Are you saying the only place I belong is Scholarship Row?"

"God. No." I step up beside her. "I've just never seen you hanging out around here."

"I have feet," Eden retorts. "I use them sometimes."

I lift my hands. "Okay. I come in peace."

Eden sighs, going back to staring at Rose House across the drive. "Sorry. It's been a rough morning."

"Already?"

An incoming crosswind causes strands of Eden's black hair to tangle around her nose, and she tucks them behind her ear with an aggravated jerk. "Maybe I'm here waiting for you, to give you a message. How's your treasure hunt going? Have they scared you off yet?"

I cross my arms, mirroring her pose. "Pretty sucky, since most people pretend they don't have tongues when I ask questions. Including you."

Eden purses her lips. "Maybe because I've been you. Before. In ninth grade. I got involved in trying to figure them out and they made me pay for it. I wasn't a chosen one." Eden snorts, continuing her stare-down of Rose House. "So, go ahead and construe my silence as trying to keep you from the same fate."

I huff out a breath. "Another protector? Thanks, but no thanks."

"Don't you get it?" Eden turns to me. "You're not allowed to know about them until they invite you to. Give up, Callie."

"Then why tell me Piper was a Virtue?"

"Because I thought it would make you back off out of fear, not blindly pursue it like a moron."

I roll my eyes but decide to change tactics. "I've figured out most of the players. Falyn, Addisyn, you know, the usual witches of Briarcliff. But what I can't quite confirm ... is Emma a Virtue?"

There might as well have been a car backfiring nearby, with the way Eden startles. But she reconstructs her emotionless mask before I can remark on it. "Why, Callie? Seriously. Why keep doing this to yourself?"

"I'm not going to stop," I tell her in a low voice. "These Virtues? They've messed with the wrong girl."

"They're not even *close* to messing with you. Don't you understand?"

"Then make me." My hands go to my hips. "Because if Emma is a Virtue, then that fire she was trapped in had something to do with them. And her attack. It involved the Virtues, too. Didn't it? That's the level of *messing with* that you're warning me about."

Eden thins her lips but won't break eye contact. I take that as my answer.

"So, the Nobles didn't retaliate?" I ask. "What about Chase? Wouldn't he have done everything in his power to protect his sister?"

Eden takes her time answering. "I suppose it depends on Emma's level of betrayal."

As it sinks in, I whisper, "What?"

"It's a rigorous process to even become a prospect of the Virtues. The hazing is even worse. But betraying the society? Even the Nobles' highest member can't protect you from that kind of downfall."

"Highest member? Who, like their father?"

Eden tucks her hands in her pockets, gesturing to the road. "There's your ride."

I glance in that direction, but by the time I look back, Eden's walking away. "Eden, wait! I—"

She waves at Yael, who gives a cheery salute, but Eden might as well be deaf to my voice.

"Damnit," I mutter as I open the car door. "She's escaped me again."

"Hey there, Callie," Yael greets.

I murmur a hello while buckling my seatbelt, unable to bring my mind in the car with me. It's still under Thorne House's awning, interpreting Eden's explanations.

"What were you and my daughter whispering about?" he asks as he turns from the dorms.

And just like that, my attention dives into the passenger seat. "Eden's your kid?"

"So they tell me," he says with a good-natured laugh, but sobers when he meets my eye in the rearview mirror. "She's had a tough time of it, so if you're getting to know her despite her ... prickly nature, I'm grateful to you."

I respond with a thin smile. "I'm sure the more I get to know her, the more open she'll be."

"I was hoping you'd connect with her," Yael says as we slope through the winding roads of Briarcliff Academy. "I wasn't about to push it. Eden would kill me if I did, but I couldn't lose the hunch that you're dealing with something similar involving the privileged kids on campus."

My gaze darts from the window to my hand, and Yael's fatherly concern.

Yael asks quietly. "Are they bullying you, too?"

I lick my lips in thought. "Not quite. Well, not since Piper, you know..."

"Yes. She was the roughest with my Eden as well. Lord, the shit that brat pulled. Excuse my disrespect of the dead, but she was terrible. Eden's been with these kids since fifth grade, for as long as I've been working as a driver. It's part of the deal. My kids get free room, board, and education so long as I'm employed here. My wife and I thought to remove her many times, but Edie insisted we shouldn't. This is where she can get the best education. The best start. Neither me nor her mom ever went to college, and to think of Edie attending an Ivy League? It was one of the most difficult decisions of my life, wondering whether we should keep her here."

I nod in sad understanding. "Eden's stubborn. I doubt she wanted Piper and her crew to win."

"Hit the nail on the head with that one." Yael turns right on to the forested road heading to Main Street. "But it was ... filthy, what they did to her. She tried so hard to fit in with them, but got garbage tossed at her for her efforts. Her uniform ripped to shreds while she was in a swim meet. Rumors spread about her through social media. One time ... they took a picture of her getting changed in the locker room. Circulated it."

Yael's voice has gone hoarse, his dark-skinned hands clenched around the wheel so hard, his skeleton almost bursts from his skin.

Hearing all this makes me yearn to talk to Eden, to assure her I'm not one of them and I could be there for her as a friend if she wanted me, but ... most of me understands these are nothing but futile words until I gain her trust. And that is so much harder to show than pity.

"Did you speak to the headmaster about all this?" I ask Yael.

"Absolutely. But you can come to your own conclusions on what happened."

I grumble in response. Briarcliff's motto shouldn't be *Rise with Might*, it should be *Money Over Child Welfare*.

Yael and I don't speak for the rest of the trip, but I think hard on his confession. The constant brutality Eden faced probably caused her to pinpoint the source of her suffering: the Virtues. Maybe that's why the bullying escalated, because she knew too much and they had to keep her silent. Especially if, according to her, she tried to become one and failed.

My head falls back against the seat. I want so badly for Eden to confide in me, but is it because I want her to heal, or would I rather satisfy my selfish motive to know more about the Virtues?

No wonder she doesn't trust me.

"We're here," Yael says. His eyes crinkle into a kind smile in the rearview. "Thank you for hearing me out. I hope I haven't..."

I give a reassuring shake of my head. "I won't say anything to anyone or make Eden's life harder. You have my word."

"You're a good kid, you know that?"

I laugh self-consciously as I open the door.

"Knew it the second you stepped off that train, all gangly and sweet."

This time, my smile is true, and I wave as he drives off.

Yael's compliment lightens my steps as I climb up the library stairs. No one has seen me in a good light since my mom, and I hadn't known how much of a hole that perception left until Yael reminded me that, yes, I can be destined for good things.

The library's AC is still at full power when I head inside, and I fold my arms around myself as I nod to Darla. She perks right up, her scarlet-red nails glinting under the light and matching her cat-eye glasses. A paperback sits open at her desk, and I have no doubt the Duchess has been at it again.

I don't slow enough to chat, intent on hurrying to the back and meeting my mystery texter.

Sadly, no one's waiting for me when I get there, but I force myself to gather some patience. Maybe they were held up somewhere. Or, they had to get in line for Yael's services. Who knows?

To pass the time, I linger over the glass cases, installed at waist-level and featuring Thorne Briar's personal items, reading the small placards detailing what they are.

There's his watch, the face cracked and fogged, but the gold touches everlasting. I skim over his ledgers, tap the glass over some leather riding gloves, and cock my head at one of the original bricks from the school's building before coming across the original blueprint of the academy, and—

I halt at the proposed design, somewhat shocked that the Wolf's Den was sketched out from the beginning. Even back then, Thorne had it in his mind to call it a senior lounge, the blue cursive faded with age, but legible.

Wolf's Den. Upperclassmen Privilege Only.

My eyes drift up, to the intricate detail of the map of Briarcliff, the roads painted in a bronze type of acrylic. In one corner, just above the glass displays, is a photo of the Briar family, Rose settled in the middle, between Thorne and Theodore Briar, with Richard and the other wives flanking them. With the help of the placard below the picture, I'm able to put names to faces. They're standing outside Briarcliff Academy, and the brief inscription tells me this was opening day. *September 10, 1820.*

I hold my breath. This photo was taken exactly one year *before* Rose plunged to her death.

Rose is dark-haired, her curls a stark ebony in the black-and-white filter. She wears a pale dress with a hint of a smile on her lips while the men and women surrounding her are straight-backed and grim.

She grins just like Emma did in her family photo, I muse. *Except Emma lost her smile, not her life. Barely.*

"Are you finding these items as interesting as my class lectures, or was I the better story-teller?"

I freeze at the voice, then ever so slowly, turn toward the familiar figure.

Releasing my breath, I whisper, "Dr. Luke."

Twenty-Four

DR. LUKE IS MORE haggard than I remember, his natural tan highlighting the aging crevices on his face rather than giving him the healthy California glow I'd admired when I first met him.

His chestnut hair is unwashed and flattened against his scalp, his linen button-up wrinkled as much as his slacks, and his eyes are so bloodshot and purple-lined, I doubt he's slept in days. He offers a reassuring smile, but it's stuttered and incomplete—the opposite of the disarming grin he's used on his students.

I back away in response, almost into the glass case. "Should you be talking to me?"

Dr. Luke releases a forced laugh. "Probably not, no. But you're not in any danger—from me. I like my women young, it's true, but I also like them willing."

My stomach curdles at his perverted candidness. This isn't the teacher I remember—the jovial, good-looking professor who gave boys and girls alike heart emojis for eyes.

Then again, he was never the lovable teacher he purported to be.

"What are you doing here?" I ask, my gaze bouncing around the stacks behind him. I calculate the distance to the front desk.

"Still haven't connected the dots, have you?" Dr. Luke shoves his hands in his pockets. "C'mon, Cal, you're smarter than this."

My gut clenches at my stepdad's term for me, but luckily, my breakfast stays down. "You're the one who texted me."

"That's right."

I cock my head, pretending like I'm not frazzled by his appearance. "Why?"

He sighs and steps closer, but when he sees me skitter back, he halts his steps and moves his hands in a calming gesture, like he's approaching a shy horse.

"I noticed your impressive power of deduction this semester," he says. "You chose Rose Briar for your history paper. Notably, you had a theory that almost two hundred years ago, Briarcliff Academy fathered a secret society who knighted them-selves the Nobles."

"Which you gave me a C for," I mumble, then internally shake my head. My falling grades shouldn't matter.

Dr. Luke raises his brows. "For reasons I'm sure you can understand."

"You made it seem like I failed," I say. "Because I was using my imagination instead of investigative research."

"You didn't cite any materials after your statements that a society was borne under the Briars."

"Because I *couldn't*," I snap.

"Because you were afraid of revealing your source?"

I shake my head, remembering how Chase had managed to fool me with his father's decoy. "It could've been just another way to screw with me. I was afraid to reference something that could've been faked."

"You're lying."

Dr. Luke takes another step forward, but I don't shrink back this time. I'm in public, of a sort. I'm safe.

"You stumbled on a hidden relic. You found writings that were previously thought lost in a fire," Dr. Luke says, his eyes alighting on mine. "Letters written in Rose Briar's own hand."

I give a sharp inhale. "How do you know that?"

Dr. Luke chuckles, but there's no mirth. "I thought you an astute, if misguided, student. Don't fail me now."

I take a moment to think, and a revelation takes hold. I whisper, "Piper."

"Indeed."

I say, "She's the only other person who could've known the letter still existed. Because she found it first, then hid it."

"On my advice." Dr. Luke lowers his voice, before continuing, "She confided in me. I was the only person she trusted. Not even her sister was a reliable confidant."

I refuse to believe him on sight, but I can't fight the curiosity that slithers into the base of my throat. "Did she tell you what was in them?"

Dr. Luke smiles. "Now, there's the Callie Ryan I was expecting. In my time away, you've found out about the other half of the Nobles, didn't you?"

I raise my chin, refusing to give him the name. Just in case he's baiting me.

The crepe-like skin under his eye twitches, amused at my tactics. "The Virtues," he supplies dryly. "Piper was disenchanted with her role among them. She thought there was some disguised malfeasance going on. Isn't that cute? She searched for a forbidden secret within the secret society."

I shake my head, though his statement nudges for attention. "She wouldn't dare tell you something like that. Societies have strict rules. You were an outsider. She'd get in huge trouble if it were ever found out she confided in you."

Dr. Luke angles his head. "She's dead. So, there's that."

I force my voice to keep working, despite my heart pounding in my ears. "The Virtues killed her?" *I knew it.*

"Not quite." Dr. Luke moves closer, until his body towers over mine. I recoil, but it's like I'm caught under a scope of sunlight, unable to escape.

"This is why I asked to see you," he says. "I know who stole those pages in Piper's diary."

I hiss in air, then respond coolly, "Those pages mean nothing now. Jack's in custody."

"That idiot?" Dr. Luke scoffs. "He couldn't kill a kitten if it bit him in the nuts. He's a fall boy, just like I was, and just like you'll become if you don't start listening to me."

He grabs my arm, and I choke on a squeal, fighting against his hold, but he's relentless. He growls, "I know about the chem lab destruction they're blaming on you. The school arrest they've put you under. They're forming the foundation for your instability, Callie. They *know* about your history. The psychiatric care you required after your mother's death. They have people in play who will break your heart *and* your mind if you let them. They're planning your downfall, and if you'll just hold *still* instead of inching away from me, you will have the chance to heed my warning."

Abruptly, he lets go. I stumble at the shift in balance.

"Or not," he snaps. "Your choice."

I rub the spot he gripped, but don't kick into a run and sprint the hell out of here.

Everything he's saying clangs in my head, along with a tolling of names, over and over.

Piper. Emma. Eden.

They all sparred with the Virtues and lost.

Dr. Luke takes my slumped posture as permission to continue. "They've been using you as their pawn to cover up Piper's murder. A Plan C, if you will—if you'll forgive the coincidence of your name starting with the same letter. Or applaud them for their creativity."

Dr. Luke smiles, and for that brief span of time, he resembles the man I trusted to sit beside me when I was interrogated, because my stepdad and Lynda couldn't be there. I wanted him as my guardian when Ahmar was so far away. This bashful, handsome man, whose grin always communicated it was going to be all right.

Dr. Luke speaks, and what he says saves me from the bittersweet spell.

"They led you to me," he says. "They orchestrated your finding of Piper's diary and the name Mr. S., then largely left it up to your clinical obsession to find out who the nickname belonged to. Your convictions may be wrong, but hell if you don't pursue the destruction of your fellow man with all of your unstable heart."

Dr. Luke chortles, and it slithers down my spine.

"And those missing pages in Piper's diary?" he says. "That was their deliberate concealment of another potential suspect—Jack. She wrote all about her affair with him, how she was going behind her sister's back, how much she *enjoyed* fucking the forbidden fruits of her professor and her sister's boyfriend. And yes, Callie, she wrote about the unexpected pregnancy."

I lean against the glass display, hunching over and placing my hands on my thighs. Most of his speech could be construed as crazy conspiracies or a personal vendetta. But Piper's missing entries? What he says they contain could very well be the truth. Why else tear them out?

"How?" I ask through the curtain of my hair. "How could you know what she wrote?"

"Before you moved in, I was in Piper's room all the time," Dr. Luke says above my head. "I snuck in through the stairs after hours and left before dawn. But when she slept, I'd read her diary. Why not? She was an enigma to me, this girl who reigned terror on her classmates but was a mouse in bed. I felt it was my duty to gain insight into her insecure and wretched mind, in case she ever wanted to use our affair against me."

"That only gives you more motive," I grind out, turning my head enough to look at him. "She was cheating on you, and when she got knocked up, that must've pissed you off."

"Oh. I was pissed," Dr Luke responds hoarsely. "But don't take me for a fool. We always used protection."

I straighten, taking deep breaths. I was *not* going to be sick.

"I was going to end things, anyway," Dr. Luke continues. "This only made it easier. She called me from that party, upset and drunk, begging me to help her, and I went there to break it up and break up with *her*. She'd gone too far, calling me when her friends were around. Getting pregnant. She'd become a liability. With the way she was carrying on, there was no way she was keeping that baby, but that didn't matter to me anymore. In that moment, she was stupid and pregnant. And when I left her, she was still stupid and pregnant. Because she was *alive*."

He flings callousness the way Falyn flings insults, but I can't duck in time. I'm so appalled. I can't look away from him.

When Chase found out about the baby and that it was potentially his, he was beside himself. He wanted to be there for Piper and was so furious with himself for not seeing it sooner and saving her.

Oh, Piper, I think. *You chose the wrong guy.*

"The baby's Jack's," I say, eyeing Dr. Luke. I have no idea if he's heard the news or how he'll react to it.

He doesn't flinch. "Yes. And who do you think that pissed off the most?"

Dr. Luke crosses his arms, his heavy silence awaiting my answer. He's studying me as if I should know outright, but it takes me a few seconds. Chase is exactly the type to sneak behind the curtains and orchestrate a scene the way he wants it, but I witnessed the raw devastation in his face when I told him Piper was pregnant, and either he is the best undiscovered actor America will never see, or he didn't know.

Then, there's Piper's friends, who would relish the hypocrisy, not end it by hurting Piper and stealing her secrets. They lived off Piper's rules. Her enemies were their enemies. Her secrets were theirs. It was considered an honor to be part of her group and have her confide in you. Isn't that what Eden said?

The last name I think of, I stumble on. Mostly because it makes too much sense.

I meet Dr. Luke's eyes. "Addisyn."

He nods.

"You're saying Addisyn knew about her boyfriend cheating before Piper died. That she ripped out the pages in Piper's diary."

Dr. Luke straightens, folds his hands behind his back, and levels his shoulders. "No, dear. I'm saying Addisyn killed her sister."

Twenty-Five

ADDISYN KILLED HER SISTER.

The sentence forms a circle in my brain, one end chomping at the other, like a snake eating its own tail, until nothing remains but the husk of Dr. Luke's allegation.

"Think about it, Callie," he says.

The library is suddenly cloying—too hushed, too stale, too warm. My arms itch, and I scrape at them through the denim of my jacket.

"If I didn't work out as a suspect," he continues, "then they had Jack in place as the next one. These people, they *plan*, and human pawns are nothing if not variable. I could've come up with an alibi—which I did. Now, they're directing their efforts at Jack, another innocent man. What if he's next to admit an alibi? Yes, that baby was his, but he didn't kill Piper. I know that, and the society knows that, because I'm positive Addisyn did."

I hold a hand to my head, my fingers digging into my scalp. "How are you so sure?"

"Piper spoke about her sister often, and not on affectionate terms. They hated each other, were always in competition with one another. That need to excel was stoked by their mother, who encouraged their fights and lavished love upon the winner. The loser received the scraps. The chores, the humiliation and disdain, and the worst punishment: complete invisibility. This went on with everything from their academics, to dance, to rowing, to boys."

I level a look at him. "You are not a *boy*."

Dr. Luke concedes my point with what I now know is feigned bashfulness. "All too right. But my point is, Addisyn was always the loser."

"So, what? She killed Piper out of jealousy? Because Piper slept with her boyfriend?"

A shimmer of disappointment runs through me, but I grip it with a firm inner hand. Piper's dead. And if it was her sister, it probably was jealousy. Isn't that the

334

number one reason why people kill? Why should I *ever* be disappointed it's not more complicated than that?

Because you want it to be the society. You want your instincts to be on point. For once.

Dr. Luke clicks his tongue, regaining my attention. "No, Callie. It was jealousy over Piper being a member of the Virtues. Jack's taking her sister as a side-piece merely provided her with an excuse."

I screw my eyes shut, despite my inner devil clawing for attention. *We were right.* "You're wrong. Addisyn's a Virtue. I'm sure of it. She was with the Cloaks who attacked me in the chem lab."

"Uh-huh."

I open my eyes, where Dr. Luke remains straight-backed and focused. On me.

"Continue with that line of thought," he prompts.

"I don't..." I massage the back of my neck, picking up Dr. Luke's facts like bread-crumbs leading me into an oven fire. "Something Falyn said that night. About Addisyn proving herself ... oh, God. Addisyn was *made* a Virtue because she murdered her sister?"

"Ding ding ding! They had to shut her up somehow. Addy was never the bright-est, though she tried. Piper won their family competitions more often than not. And when Piper became a Virtue and Addisyn didn't, well ... to say that caused discord would be an understatement."

"And you know all this because Piper told you. Who would've been sworn to secrecy. "

Dr. Luke nods. "If Addisyn read what I did in Piper's diary, *oof.*" Dr. Luke palms his chest. "What a way to find out the one thing you had over your perfect sister—happiness and a steady boyfriend—was nothing but a cruel joke. *And* Piper received a coveted, rare position in the Virtues, which you bet your ass she lorded over her sister, societal oath or not. I'd be fucking furious."

"Weren't you? When you read it for yourself?"

Dr. Luke makes a dismissive gesture with his hand. "Piper and I fucked. We screwed with each other. We trusted each other with forbidden secrets because *we* were forbidden. But don't mistake what I did with her for love. I've made myself clear in that respect: I met with her that night to end things. I'd moved on."

I push off the display. "That baby, if it were yours, and if she had told someone, could've ruined you."

"She wasn't going to keep it, nor would she sully her perfect scholastic reputation over banging a professor who's not even tenured. Did I not just tell you about these Harringtons and their killer drive for success?"

He's running me around in circles. Using hard-hitting, murderous, circular reasoning to make his facts come at me so hard, I'll have trouble sorting through them.

"Addisyn's a bitch, but I don't see her as a killer," I say, keeping my voice level. "You didn't see her at Piper's memorial. Or when she found out her boyfriend was arrested. She was devastated."

"The Virtues are out to protect themselves, not the Harrington family line. Jack was the next viable option, much better than Addisyn herself, who could blow the whistle on the hidden society while in custody. No, instead they made her a member, allowed her access to all their shiny things, groomed her response to her sister's death, and in return, she had to stay quiet. Even during her boyfriend's subsequent arrest."

"But I—"

"Do you think they want police crawling all over the place? Asking questions? Showing up with a warrant for blueprints to all the hidden corridors and rooms in the academy?"

He has a point, but I don't concede it. I narrow my eyes at him. "What are you getting out of this? Why meet me anonymously when you could just go to the police? I doubt you're allowed to be around—"

"Kids?" Dr. Luke flashes a sardonic smile. "You're eighteen now, Callie. And I'm at least two thousand feet from Briarcliff's campus while I await my hearing. Can't I be seeking you out because of the revenge in my heart? Those bitches ruined my life."

I curl my lip at him. "They didn't force you to have sex with a teenager."

He waves me off. "If you want more convincing evidence, read the missing pages for yourself. They're in Addisyn's room."

Bile spreads across my tongue at the thought of how Dr. Luke could know something like that, unless he was lurking around campus, going into her room ... "Addisyn looks almost identical to Piper. If it weren't for the years between them, they'd be twins. Does that turn you on, Dr. Luke?"

His face turns to stone. "Focus on what's important, Callie."

Dr. Luke turns to leave, but I stop him with one more question. "What is the Nobles' role in all this? Why aren't they doing anything to stop the Virtues?"

He turns his head and smiles at me in profile. "Oh. They're helping you, don't worry."

Dr. Luke retreats into one of the stacks, and I race after him, nowhere near finished, but I can't risk calling out his name and drawing Darla's attention. Instead, I hiss, "Dr. Luke!"

"Don't forget about Plan C," he says over his shoulder, but doesn't slow his steps.

He's gone before I make it to the front desk.

A hard exhale billows from my lips as I stare out the library's large windows to Main Street.

"Trouble, honey?" Darla asks.

I fix my jacket and clear my throat in an effort to calm the raging river of blood through my veins. "I'm fine. Thanks, Darla."

"You spent a while at the exhibit back there. Pretty fascinating stuff, isn't it?"

I glance at her, mustering up a smile. It all seemed like standard artifacts to me. But then, perhaps my perception of history has become a little skewed. "Sure is."

"I'm such a sucker for romance." Darla leans her elbows on her desk, a dreamy look in her eye.

I hate being rude, especially to someone so nice, so I prepare myself for a little small talk, despite the bomb going off in my head. "I noticed. What are you reading?"

"Oh, this?" Darla giggles as she lifts her paperback. "*The Duchess and the Brave Butler*. Good stuff, though Rose Briar's affair is so much juicer."

I go still. "I thought it was her husband who had the affairs."

"Oh, no, dear." Darla pulls herself up in her seat. "Well, he was a womanizer, to be sure, but Rose took up with his *brother*."

Now, my brows hitch up. "Say what?"

Darla leans in close, as if confessing a crucial secret. "She took up with Theodore Briar. Rumor has it, they had an illegitimate child together, one she had to give up in secret."

I point toward the stacks, my cheeks going numb. "*None* of that is over there."

"Well, no, dear. It wouldn't be. This is just some local talk I'm giving you, passed down by the generations. Anything pertaining to Theodore and Rose's affair, if it ever existed, would've been destroyed in the school library's fire, unfortunately. That academy holds on tight to their founders, I must say. It's a miracle we've gotten this much to display."

Huh. I cross my arms, gazing toward the exhibit, though it's blocked by columns of books.

Could the Nobles and Virtues be protecting the more scandalous aspects of their founders? It's not too much of a stretch to believe.

Darla chatters on, but the more I ponder on the limited exhibit items, the more it makes sense. It's plausible that not everything would've been stored in the old library, where any student interested in the history could come across it. Especially when choosing a founder to research is a required American History essay.

If they were smart, the societies would store the greatest scandals and the questionable origins of Briarcliff Academy somewhere safe.

Protected.

Private.

Buried, but not destroyed, because these elite societies have too much pride in their roots to set fire to original documents, no matter how damaging they are.

And it's exactly how Piper would've gotten her hands on Rose Briar's letters regarding creating a rival society.

She was looking into the Virtue's origins, because she suspected a wrongness, a poison running within the veins of the Virtues, or the Nobles, or both.

That gives me pause. Was Piper simply a nasty, spoiled twat, or was she smarter than a lot of people gave her credit for, including me?

Damn it. I guess I'm trusting Dr. Luke's words more than I thought.

"Honey? Have I lost ya?"

I blink. "Sorry. I'm a little stressed out."

Darla titters. "And here I am gabbing your ear off about century-old affairs. Go on back to school now. You're welcome back any time."

I send her a genuine smile. "Thank you for your help."

"Gah." Darla waves me off, but her cheeks blossom with color. "I'm just the town gossip."

"You're one of the nicest people here," I say as I head to the doors, and I mean that sincerely.

Darla doesn't stop beaming until I leave her sight.

Twenty-Six

BREAKING into Addisyn Harrington's dorm room should be easy.

I'll walk right in, because I have access to the girls' dorms through evening trash-emptying on weekdays while everyone is at dinner.

It will be finding the perfect moment that's hard. I'm supervised by the dorm's housekeeper, who keeps an eye on me in the hallway when I enter each room.

Planning isn't my strong suit, but I resolve myself into applying that section of my brain for the rest of the weekend. I'm not responsible for trash clean-up on Saturdays or Sundays. My stepdad and Headmaster Marron both agreed weekends should be reserved for catching up on my studies, not impeding them.

Now that I'm back on school grounds, I feel watchful eyes on the back of my head, tracking me from the windows, guidance counselors and teachers clocking my progress to the dorms.

There's no real reason to believe Marron or even the guidance counselor I'm seeing would be pulling their curtains back and glowering down at the top of my head as I wander by, but with the strict supervision that's been placed on me, I wouldn't be surprised if *someone* was watching me, with their own eyes or through security cameras.

Whether those witnesses are official Briarcliff employees or not remains to be seen.

I can't stop Dr. Luke's revelations from circulating inside my mind. If he's right, if Addy really *is* Piper's killer, and she's being protected, then the purpose of the Virtues is more twisted than I'd originally imagined.

My lips flutter with a sigh, and I dig my thumbs into my backpack's straps as I trek down the hill to Thorne House. Most of the mysteries I've uncovered surround the Virtues, but they weren't created first. There was a reason Rose retaliated—

I halt in the middle of the pathway.

Rose's affair. I can't believe I'm only mulling over Darla's information now. A secret relationship with Thorne's brother? A possible illegitimate child?

Holy jeez, there's a lot to sort through. I've almost become an anchor, detached from its lifeboat and sinking into the depths of the ocean, because of all this.

I screw my eyes shut, giving my head a shake. What did Mom always say? Start fresh with the first point. Simplify it, then attach your theories to facts—not the other way around.

"Okay," I say to the surrounding landscape, the word followed by a hot cloud of air.

It's with my mom's calming voice that I decide to restart with what first grabbed my attention in the first place: The Nobles.

And Chase's key.

With a refreshed bounce, I start walking, turning a small corner around a row of expertly cubed hedges, until Thorne House comes into view.

"Callie! Hey!"

I slow my steps and turn at Ivy's voice.

"I've been trying to catch up to you since I saw you get out of the car," Ivy puffs as she comes up beside me. "You're a speedy devil when you want to be."

I smile an apology. "I have a lot on my mind."

"That must be it," Ivy says. "Because you totally ditched me for lunch."

A little pebble of guilt *plinks* into my belly. "Shit, I'm sorry. I got caught up in the public library, and—"

She waves me off. "It's totally cool. You're here now, but the dining hall's still open. Feel like doing a U-turn and having a late lunch?"

"I want to, I really do," I say with a pained expression, "but ever since I've been tasked with cleaning up the tables during the week, my stomach kind of turns at the thought of hanging out there."

"Right." Ivy mirrors my expression. "Falyn and her witch-bitches have been extra putrid lately, haven't they?"

The vision of cottage cheese poured into coffee, then spilled on tabletops, clots my vision at Ivy's reminder. And gravy mushed into stewed peas. Beef tips mashed into apple juice. The list of gagging textures goes on, especially when I have to mop it up with dishtowels and it slops onto the floor...

How are these girls meant to be so evil, yet so petty?

"Ugh," I say, smacking my lips at the warning saliva bubbling up in my mouth.

"Heck, their hot messes will get anyone's gag-reflex going." Ivy hooks an arm through my elbow, redirecting me back to the school. "Wolf's Den it is. They have some sandwiches up there."

I let her lead me along, since I haven't eaten anything since an early breakfast, and catching up with Ivy would be nice. And normal.

Ivy kicks up a conversation about her crew training, and how intense it is despite it being off-season, and I listen the way a good friend who has no interest in rowing would—with enthused effort—until she mentions a name I've been primed to viscerally react to.

"—until Addy became our stroke."

I swivel my head to look at her. "Addy's a what?"

"She's our stroke," Ivy says on a heavy sigh. "And our new captain. She's a *junior*, and she gets to lead our pace, our team, everything. I'm not one to get upset over these things, but it's really unfair."

"Uh, you can be upset," I say. "You've been wanting to be captain forever."

"I've been working hard for it," Ivy admits. "And no way did I enjoy how the spot opened up—when Piper died—but I thought, this is my chance. I can really show Coach that I have the technique and can lead the rhythm of the boat. I could bring the crew to championships. And now ... well, I'm still the seventh seat."

Ivy has told me boat positions before, and I dig up those memories to better console her. "Seven is still amazing, right? You're still part of the stroke pair. Or stern pair? Whatever it is, you're second in command."

Ivy bobs her head. "Yeah. It's not the same, though, when a girl who's had maybe a semester of training takes your rightful place."

I murmur in agreement but can come up with an answer pretty easily as to why Addisyn got the coveted spot in crew.

The Virtues.

As part of her deal to stay quiet.

I send a guilty look Ivy's way, wishing I could tell her that the whole system is fucked, and no matter how talented she is, that seat will never be hers because of the hidden politics at play. The problem is, would she believe me, or just consider me Callie the Crazy Conspiracist?

I'm afraid of the answer, so instead, I allow part of the truth to come out. "You deserve that spot more than anybody, and it's fucked up Addisyn got it over you. Do you think she's playing a sympathy card?"

"Coach is tough. I'd never think she'd have a bleeding heart under her athletic suit, but anything goes. Addisyn doesn't have the racing stats on the erg to back up her position, but Coach won't hear any arguments about it. She shut us up with a bunch of bull-crap about teams supporting their members."

"Totally screwed up," I agree, squeezing Ivy's arm lightly, but inside, I'm heavy with duty.

Now, more than ever, I have to get into Addisyn's room to see if Dr. Luke was telling the truth. If the Virtues are now guiding Addy's every move.

I open my mouth to impart more genuine sympathy, but a group of guys heading out of Rose House splinters my attention.

Chase.

The hitch in my step is unintentional, but it causes Ivy to pause, too.

"What is it?" she asks, but I'm too distracted by the way the afternoon sun glints across his hair, and how a plain T-shirt hugs his muscles just right as he jingles car keys in his hands and turns to say something to Tempest.

"Uh-oh. Which one?" Ivy murmurs into my ear. "Do you dream of a blond Adonis, or a raven-haired rebel?"

I jerk from my reverie. "What? No. Never."

"My bet's on Chase," Ivy smirks. "You try so hard, girl, but your drool always gives you away."

Ivy pulls me into a casual stroll again, but it's like my chin is attached to string as I continue to follow Chase's moves, how he swings into his BMW and the low purr of the engine vibrates under my shoes the way his voice hummed against my—

Oh, God. Don't go there. He's meant to be the *enemy,* not a relentless sexual fantasy.

That I've made into a reality.

Ivy bursts out with laughter. "Collect yourself, or he's going to notice you."

I blink, then rub my eyes. "I honestly don't know what's wrong with me."

I shouldn't be staring at him like this, desiring him from afar, when I've stolen something from him, and if he ever finds out the way I used him, he'll be...

Unforgiving.

But I can't stop. I don't, until his eyes meet mine, appearing black under the tint of the car's window.

He studies me for an indeterminable length of time, and I him, until Tempest jumps into the passenger seat and says something to Chase.

Does he know what I took?

My stomach coils at the thought. I haven't seen him since last night, and since he's come from his dorm unconcerned and at ease, I'm assuming he found a spare key.

Chase angles his head to his friend, responding, then swings his car out onto the road and roars past us without a second look.

I'm hoping that means he's not the least bit suspicious of me.

Or ... he could be super pissed.

"Dude." Ivy gives my frozen form a playful shove. "Explain."

"I, uh..." am getting *so* bad at keeping my conflicted feelings for Chase in check. Ivy can't know I stole his room key with the intention to search through his personal stuff, so, I go with the most believable. "It's a stupid crush. That's all."

"On the most sought-after guy in school?" Ivy leans into me. "I never thought you to be so basic."

She intends no malice, but I prickle nonetheless. I love her, but Ivy is a gossip whore. I don't know how she'd react if I told her I've been sleeping with him, but even if she didn't intend it, my hook-ups with Chase would be wildfire in this school, and regardless of my cruel intentions, I *like* keeping Chase as mine. It feels good, too good, to share naked, clandestine nights only with him.

"I'll show you mine if you show me Riordan," I say from the corner of my mouth.

Ivy shrieks and shoves at me, as I knew she would, and we both stumble with laughter.

"That was a moment of weakness," she defends. "I'd never get under him, even if I had a ten-foot pole to prop between us..."

"Yeah, right," I say, striding up the hill to the academy with her. "I saw the way you were all googly-eyed at Chase's party, and don't blame Jameson for your bad decisions."

Ivy laughs. "Fine. Maybe whiskey made me weak for *one* night, and I let him touch my boobies."

Now it's my turn to shriek. "You didn't!"

"I did!" she crows.

"Did he record it?"

Ivy snorts. "Maybe he's a little too involved in the goings-on at campus, but can we not at least agree he's a hot voyeur?"

I tip my head and laugh, the heavy load of this morning escaping my body.

In a moment of pure emotion, I throw my arm around her shoulder and pull her close. "You are the absolute best, you know that?"

"Aw." Ivy taps her cheek against mine. "Are you saying we're besties?"

I smile, my lips moving in a way they haven't since fifth grade, when Sylvie pulled me aside, demanding exactly fifty percent of a bestie friendship by offering me a half-heart necklace.

The necklace she was wearing when she OD'd and barely survived.

I don't think on the curse of my friendship when I kiss Ivy's temple, the wind blowing our hair back as we stroll through Briarcliff's pavilion.

All I can think of is my ache for a best friend and the familiar comfort of a kindred soul shining through an open, affectionate face.

Ivy isn't destroyed on the inside like I am. She's sunlight, and I've been starving for it.

So, I look her in the eye with a bright smile, saying, "Fucking right we are."

Twenty-Seven

IVY and I spend the rest of the afternoon, and late evening, hanging out and catching up on subjects I've woefully fallen behind in.

Nothing pointed out how brutally my priorities had shifted than when I received my quarter-term grades. I listen to Ivy as she helps tutor me in my worst subject (ahem, calculus) and she helps me brainstorm with the ones I'm better at—history, biology, and English. We spend most of our time in a corner of the Wolf's Den, other seniors also using the quiet afternoon to get work done, with the added benefit of constantly refreshed snacks.

When we first arrived, the Wolf's Den floor was awash with sunlight streaming through the stained-glass crest above our heads. Students came and went, our breaks were few and far between, and soon, my worries over Addisyn, the societies, Chase, and Piper's death, slumbered for a while as Ivy focused my thoughts and tested my academic knowledge.

We end up being the last ones in the Den, and Ivy's in the middle of showing me a trick to finding the value of the integral, when I notice the floors beneath our feet have gone dark with shadow.

"Huh," I muse, then check the time. "Omigod, Ivy, it's nearly ten."

Ivy lifts her head, her pencil pausing on my notebook. "Yikes, is it? We missed dinner!"

I slide a glance to the pastry cart, a spot we'd been plundering every time a staff member came up to restock it. "I doubt our stomachs will mind."

Ivy straightens in her seat, lifting both hands into the air and turning them. "Look at me, I'm literally throbbing with caffeine."

I snort, then start packing my books and laptop. "That's our cue to leave."

"For sure," Ivy agrees, and we both clean up our table.

The academy remains well lit, despite the time, with electric wall sconces and the large chandelier in the foyer, but I expect someone from the faculty to come up any second and kick us out, since the school closes at about this time.

With the amount of echoing noise we're causing by shutting our textbooks and shoving them into our bags, we're the last ones in the vicinity.

"Thank you," I say to Ivy when I zip my bag shut. "I really needed this."

Ivy pats my shoulder. "You didn't come here to fail, and I don't want to see it happen."

"I can't believe how much I've let this place affect me," I say as we head to the staircase. "I'm usually so good at making schedules and sticking to routines, but I guess, ever since my mom..."

I can't finish the sentence, and Ivy doesn't make me.

"It's easy to get distracted." Ivy clomps down the stairs behind me. "Outrageously beautiful boys, scandalous teachers, suspicious roommate deaths ... you deserve to be a little distracted, ya know?"

I shrug, facing forward. "Not like this. I've been—something like this has happened before, and I swore I wouldn't do it again."

"Like what?" When I don't answer, Ivy turns so I face her at the bottom of the stairs. "Callie, what's going on?"

I hesitate, then scold myself. With everything Ivy's done for me today, she deserves some honesty. "After my mom died, I kind of ... lost it."

"Well ... that's to be expected."

"No, I ... clinically lost it. My stepdad committed me. And when I was released, I went to every party I could find—college, high school, random, it didn't matter—looking to score. My friend Sylvie was down for it, so I never questioned my safety when we both went. But soon, I was going by myself, drinking by myself, then ... snorting powder by myself."

I carefully watch Ivy for her reaction, but the only emotion she's exuding is furrowed brows of concern.

"The drug-use got bad. I, um, I know now it was because I accused my stepdad of murder and .... I kind of fell apart after that."

Ivy says, "Callie, oh my God. You've never—"

"I blamed him," I blurt. "I'm the one who got him arrested."

Whenever I think of it, the lump of coal is still there, burning its embers at the base of my throat. I don't think the guilt of ruining his life will ever go away. It'll just stay buried in the earth until those rare moments when I dig up the black elements, like now.

I look to Ivy for judgment, then jerk back in surprise at her scoff. "I doubt your word alone sent him to jail, Callie. They must've had other evidence to add weight to what you were saying. You know, I've noticed something about you from the minute I met you."

I ask with hesitation, "What's that?"

"You give everyone else such a free pass in life but wrap your own in chains."

I stare at her. "I don't get it."

Ivy folds her arms. "Do you remember when I ran to your room once I heard Piper was dead? And how Chase waltzed in?"

I grumble at the thought of Chase bursting through the door, his brown eyes blazing with the Earth's core as he stared me down. "Yes."

"And when the detectives came, he pointed at you and said you did it."

I suck on my lower lip as it dawns on me where she's going with this.

"Did they arrest you on sight?" Ivy asks. "Put you in handcuffs, send you to jail? No. Because they had other facts in play. A list of other suspects, which, I guess, is growing as we speak. The point *is*, Callie," she says, pushing me by the shoulder when I instinctually hunch over, "is that his word, as strong as it is around this school, still wasn't enough to get you in major trouble." She bops me on the nose, and I wrinkle it in response. "And I'm guessing the same can be said about what happened to your stepdad."

Heart sinking, I shake my head. "I haven't told you everything. There was a fight between him and my mom, which I witnessed, and he slapped her, and I told the police..."

"Yeah. More outside facts proving your word. Like I said."

I frown. "No, I—"

"You're not going to convince me you're a bad person, dude. Not when you're sucking face with Chase in your mind every time he passes by, *despite* what he tried to do to you."

A snort of ashamed laughter escapes my nose.

"Which goes to my point," Ivy says. "Why do you punish yourself so much worse than the people who've wronged *you*?"

Because I was told I was unhinged. Incapable. My opinion drugged and voided.

I peer up at Ivy, who's studying me kindly, and I can't give voice to more truth, not when she's so convinced I'm not that girl.

Maybe she's right, and I don't have to keep recalling the old Callie, the one who wanted to hurt her stepdad, the kid who wanted to punish and maim and destroy the world that had destroyed her mother.

I say, cracking a small smile, "I liked you better when you were teaching me about studies and not real life."

Ivy playfully punches me in the arm. "I only tell it how I see it. C'mon, let's head back."

"You go ahead," I say. "I want to drop some of this stuff in my locker."

"Want me to come?"

"Nah. I know you have an early morning training tomorrow." I point to three custodians who are leaving the maintenance room with cleaning carts. "I'll stick close to these guys."

Conflict crosses Ivy's face, and I'm sure it's her worry over my well-being battling with her need to go to bed and catch a few hours rest before her 4 AM wake-up call.

"What else could they do to me?" I ask. I don't need to say who. "Send me to more clean-up duty? There's a ton of security now because of Piper *and* my latest 'break in.' I'll be safe. Promise."

Ivy chews on the inside of her cheek, but I don't expect her to argue. Not when I've concealed so much from her, including the Virtues attacking me. All she knows is that it was Falyn and her friends who set me up, and I got the cut on my cheek by accidentally breaking a beaker while I fumbled in the dark to read a damaged book.

With her firsthand witnessing of me dousing my hand in flames, how could she question my story?

Considering my track record, I'm deeply reluctant to involve her in my real shit.

And ... I'm *so* afraid to lose her.

After a few more seconds of looking me up and down, Ivy gives in. "All right. You'd better."

"It's five minutes of dropping off my stuff. I'll be fine. See you tomorrow, okay?"

"Yeah," Ivy says, her brows low as she regards me. But she turns on her heel, and I don't look away until I see her duck through a door politely opened by a security guard passing through the foyer, and disappear into the night.

I do feel safer as I trudge down the East Wing to the locker area, as I pass by five other security guards doing their rounds, and even a grumbling Professor Dawson as he locks up his office, telling me to hurry it up before the school closes.

With this much action on a Saturday night, it'd be difficult for even the Virtues to frame me for some other outrageous spoof.

They're forming the foundation for your instability, Callie ... They have people in play who will break your heart and your mind if you let them. They're planning your downfall...

I refuse to let Dr. Luke's words guide me as I turn a corner and find my locker, quickly depositing my things.

All the lights are on. Security and maintenance staff are everywhere. I'm *fine.*

Until I exit the cubicle of lockers, round the corner, and notice that everyone is gone.

Twenty-Eight

THE ELECTRIC SCONCES lining the hallway flicker until they're dim, then turn off.

"Shit," I mutter, but with a lighter bag, I jog down the rest of the hall until the academy's foyer comes into view.

An additional line of sconces goes black, as well as overhead lights, and in a moment of awareness, I skirt to the edges of the wall, unwilling to be caught running smack in the middle of a darkened corridor.

They're here.

It's a visceral realization, felt along all the hairs on my body, but my mind can't believe it—not when I've seen the amount of guards and the cleaning crew scouring the grounds mere minutes ago.

The Virtues couldn't control them, too, could they?

I itch for Ivy's soothing company, but it's for the best that she's not here. I don't want her involved in this fuckery. Whatever happens to me, I cannot take another good friend down with me.

Approaching footsteps draw my head up, and I crouch beside the nearest awards case, most of my body obscured by trophies, as whoever it is passes the East Wing and strides into the foyer.

After waiting a few minutes, I creep out, hunched over and using the lightest steps I can.

As I near the foyer, I notice more than one silhouette, outlines of tall bodies, broad shoulders, and short hair cast in a hazy glow from the dimmed chandelier hanging above.

Men. These are men. Or schoolboys.

One belts out a masculine laugh, cementing my theory, then stifles it when hushed. The guys ... I'm counting about ten bodies ... all form into a single line, until the one in front turns and motions for them to take the stairs.

347

At this point, I should expect nothing less than a mysterious line of men in the foyer of the academy after hours, but honestly, this shit never gets old.

Crouching, I curl my fingers over the edge of the corridor, ensuring that only an eye and maybe a sliver of cheekbone show as I peer into the lobby.

The men silently ascend, and no one's talking now. As I watch, my body trembles like a tuning fork. *They're headed into the Wolf's Den.*

For reasons I want to find out.

When the last foot disappears over the top stair, I scuttle forward, ears perked for any additional sounds coming from above. All I catch is the tiniest *beep*, more shuffling, then silence.

I pause under the indoor balcony, head cocked and braced to run, but I don't hear so much as a squeak of rubber soles against marble.

They can't possibly all be standing in the Wolf's Den saying nothing. Are they watching something on a screen? Meditating? *Sleeping*?

I can't bear the mystery of all those guys going upstairs and then doing ... nothing, so I creep to the base of the stairs and bend slightly over the railing to see the opening above.

I scan everything up there I can see, from the front of the balcony to the top of the stairs, and there are no shadows, creaks, or exhales—anything to indicate there are people up there.

My brows crash down. *Wtf?*

Grasping the handrail, I swing to the front of the staircase and tiptoe up, sticking to the shadows, keeping low and quiet, in case I'm inadvertently crashing one of the extra-curricular club's sleep-ins.

But ... I don't think that's what this is. It's much too quiet.

As each step takes me closer, and I can make out outlines of the Wolf's Den furniture, I don't notice any accompanying people draped over the chairs or clustered in any corners.

I'm so busy studying the interior, I don't register that I've moved to stand in the middle of the darkened room until I'm directly centered with the coffee table.

With not one person nearby.

I murmur my shock and put my hands on my hips, spinning in place. I've never witnessed or been told where Thorne Briar designed secret passageways and hidden rooms, but I'm pretty sure I've just discovered one location.

But the question remains: Where the hell did everyone go?

I make my way to the back wall, since the front is a balcony and the two sides are crowded, one with coffee stands and pastry displays, and the other an elevator door beside the staircase leading up.

I start on the left, faced with a half-wall of books, the other half wood paneling. High-top tables and stools take up the middle section, including the table Ivy and I sat at for hours. Were we really gabbing beside a secret entrance the whole time?

The question brings up Chase's party, and how I acted in his father's office—so convinced of a concealed chamber behind those books. Instead, I was shot down with the existence of a panic room, standard protocol for the uber-rich, and left questioning my convictions.

Here, though, there is no panic room. Ten bodies did not disappear into the back of a senior lounge where no staircase or elevator exists—those are both in the front.

I skim my fingers along the books' spines, but none of them, as I tip and pull at the spines, do anything but puff dust mites in my face.

"Damn it," I curse, tipping my chin up and scanning the top.

What am I missing?

Then, I look down.

The bookshelves take up half the wall. The other half is wood molding, carved in 3D designs often seen in pictures of nineteenth century mansions. Briarcliff decorates with layered rectangles carved vertically, and intricate lace trim in the corners.

I take one step back, studying the wainscoting and trim, but focusing most on the rectangular panels.

Could I ... push one?

Shrugging, I figure I'll have at it, since I haven't come up with any better ideas.

I end up pushing against all ten panels, bending and using all my strength, but none of them move an inch.

I stare up at the ceiling and sigh, thinking, *if only you could see me now, Dad and Headmaster Marron.*

Then I think, perhaps I'm approaching this wrong. Any student could technically push against the panels by freak accident or just plain curiosity.

If I want to know where those guys went, I have to start thinking like a society member, and not simply a student kicking in walls.

So, I start pushing gently on the corners of each panel, starting again from the left. The first four don't budge, but undeterred, I keep trying the others.

It's the ninth one that clicks.

I suck in a sharp breath when the upper right corner presses down, and I'm able to swing open the entire panel.

Omigod omigod omigod.

My heart pounds with the strength of Pegasus wings, and I'm feeling just as high and mythical. *What have I found?*

Fingers shaking now, I pull the panel all the way to the side and peer in, but my nose hits something hard almost immediately.

Cursing, I lean back, and take stock of a small, metal door with an electronic scanner in the center.

"Dang," I mutter, disappointment crashing my new wings down to Earth.

For shits and giggles, I use my room card, but of course, get a low beep and a flashing red light indicating WRONG.

Then ... I remember.

I have Chase's card. I was going to use it to search his room but had put that on the back burner.

His key sits in my bag, hidden in my wallet for safekeeping.

What's the harm in trying it? I've made it this far.

And so, I fish out my wallet from my bag, find Chase's key, and press it against the scanner.

GREEN.

The door unlocks, pushing itself ajar.

"Holy. Shit."

I straighten, glancing around to see if anyone's snuck up on me, but I'm alone, crouched in front of a hidden door that I absolutely *must* explore.

Every fiber making up my brain tells me so.

Fumbling for my phone, I turn on the flashlight and slowly crawl in, my nose instantly assaulted by stale, briny air. The second metal door has opened inward, so I push against it until it hits the wall and I'm all the way inside.

Using the insignificant, white beam of my phone's lens, I spot a small, stone staircase leading *down*, the flattened steps so limited, they're the length of small squares.

Probably a gnome could bounce down just fine, but I'm having issues just picturing sliding, feet and ass first.

Well, I think, *Alice did something similar in Wonderland. Why can't you in Briarcliff?*

With that resolute thought, I slide forward, feet first, until I hit the first step. I stay like that, foot and then butt, for five or so steps before the staircase starts curving, the steps get wider, and the ceiling much, much higher.

Eventually, wall sconces replace my flashlight, which I hastily turn off the closer I get to the bottom ... if there's a ground level.

They're not the electric ones around the academy, though. These are oil-soaked lanterns, lit by a match, and the flames flicker under the light wind of my body as I pass by.

I can't hear much over the pounding of my heart, and my short, adrenaline-fueled breaths, but I put my entire effort into staying silent as I drift down, down, down...

Soon, I hear voices.

And wherever they are, they're no longer being quiet.

Twenty-Nine

"...THEREIN, the second Saturday eve marks our monthly chapter meetings, and I implore all of you to listen intently, study your new members, and remark on your acute abilities that brought you here, as one of us, a Noble member."

I inhale through tight lips and press against the side of the staircase, terrified of being discovered but too vindicated to scamper back up.

They exist. They're here.

And, if it hadn't been for Dr. Luke's revelations today, I would've remembered from Howard Mason's findings that the Nobles meet every second Saturday of the school year.

And *this* is their Vault.

I risk another step, and then another, until a corner wall appears. Instead of peering past it, I turn on my phone's camera, using it as a selfie mirror, and angle it so I can see some of the movement on the other side of the wall.

I'm the shakiest cameraman of all time and will never be hired for any sort of production, but I recognize a few familiar faces lined up in a half-circle around ... three? ... cloaked figures who hold blazing torches. The flames crackle in the silence as the members turn to each other and murmur their motto in Latin, *Fly high in the dark*, as a greeting to their neighbor.

I press a trembling thumb to the camera's button, taking a silent picture.

Behind the cloaked figures is an impressive, massive carving in the stone wall of a raven, spreading its wings and fluttering in motion from the large, hanging chandelier, lit with candles. I gasp silently, in awe of this crypt they've built and the boys standing within it.

James.

Riordan.

Tempest.

Chase.

Of course, Chase.

My camera keeps documenting, and I freeze their faces in time as fast as I can. There are others from lower years, whose faces I recognize, but no other seniors that I can tell. And there are ten boys, in total, the three cloaked figures in the middle making it thirteen.

"Our sisterhood," a Cloak says, his voice gravelly and deep, more middle-aged than youthful, "has had a rough beginning this year, and we must be there for them, always. We've agreed to meet in their Temple for our next ritual, to discuss the loss of their member and who should be the replacement in her stead."

Piper. They must be talking about Piper.

I angle the phone so I can see the speaker better.

"While we don't always agree with their motives, we must keep the Virtues close. And Marquises, you must choose your soulmate on that eve, and be bound to them for life, however you choose to do it."

I suck on the inside of my cheek, eyes riveted to my tiny screen. A soulmate from the Virtues? Does that mean an arranged marriage of some sort?

"Prince Stone, I implore you to think hard on your choice, since your destined soulmate is no longer with us."

I angle the phone to witness Chase's response, but lose my bearing, wasting time trying to find him in the crowd.

"Yes, Father," I hear Chase murmur, and I gasp, this time, not so quietly.

I freeze, my joints cracking from the ice I've injected into my veins to stop myself from moving, but the speaker goes on as if I haven't made a sound.

"To our initiates, I introduce our Marquises, Mr. Callahan, Hughes, Windsor. You three know what to do."

"Yes, sir," they respond in sync, heads bowed.

The speaker removes his hood, as do the other three, and my stare bores into my camera as I clock Daniel Stone, Headmaster Marron, and Professor Dawson as the three caped leaders.

Daniel Stone steps back, Marron and Dawson following suit. He says, his voice booming, "Earls, Viscounts, look upon your higher lords with respect and submission, as they will show you the way. As for our initiates, the Barons, your time has not yet come. This is the last eve you will be seen as applicants, as you have one more ritual to complete. I will leave it to our Marquises to best dispense the choices."

The three Cloaks turn to leave, and I get ready to hightail it out of here, but they don't turn in my direction. They exit stage right, on the other end, at the same time three additional robed figures walk in, this time in thick, velvet, purple robes.

The three purple Cloaks pause at the base of the stone raven, directly under the chandelier, and sweep the robes off their shoulders in synchronized movements.

And ... they're naked.

"Barons," James cries, turning and standing in the middle of these ladies who've bared themselves to freshmen and sophomores. "You have a choice. Take a woman now or save yourself for your soulmate. Whatever you choose, it will be documented in this hour."

Oh my ... oh my *God.*

Are these prostitutes? Escorts? Adults about to sleep with ... minors?

I can't—I can't be here. I'm too chickenshit to witness this—

A face, veiled in shadow, darts into my vision and snaps my phone from my hand. His palm covers my mouth before my surprised cry causes shockwaves into the tomb.

The back of my head cracks against the stone as the body presses against mine, but the scent—*his* scent—tells me who it is before I start to struggle.

My body goes slack in his hold.

Chase bends close, half his profile cast in flickering gold from the sconce above us. His irises are black lacquer. "Go."

He doesn't remove his hand from my mouth until I nod my assent.

Chase's skin scrapes against my lips as he abruptly lifts his palm, and I don't linger. I half-stumble, half-crawl up the steps and don't stop until I fall into the Wolf's Den and hastily close both doors to that forbidden, twisted Noble crypt.

I race home without looking back, my hair cascading in the wind.

The pathway clears of leaves, driven by the same eastern breeze, their decaying, papery skin skittering against the paved walkway as the wind picks them up in handfuls.

I follow the streetlamps until I'm outside Thorne House. I show my ID, then burst up the stairs. I don't stop moving until I'm through my apartment door and my back splays against it.

Emma pauses in the center of our kitchenette, holding her emptied dinner plate above the kitchen sink. She never eats in the dining hall, preferring all her meals alone, and very late at night.

I meet her eye, my chest heaving, then say, "I want in."

Emma arches a brow.

"Whatever you're doing," I continue, exhaling pillows of air between words, "with your late nights in the library—a place you despise—and whispered conversations with your brother, I want to be a part of it."

Emma thins her lips, then goes about washing up her dishes like I'd never asked anything.

"You're trying to take down the Virtues," I say after a gulp. I rest the back of my head against the door, watching her with half-lidded eyes. "Dismantle them. Fuck with them. Whatever you want to call it. I. Want. *In.*"

With her back to me, Emma finishes drying her plate, then perches it on the drying rack. She then pushes off the counter, heading to her room.

"Goodnight," she says over her shoulder, then shuts her door.

I growl, then slap the front door with open palms before pushing off and stomping to my side of the apartment. I only keep the light on long enough to search my furniture for errant roses, be it black or white, but find none.

I rip my comforter off the mattress, then undo my pants and crawl under, burying myself in black as far as the soft cotton will let me.

Dreams blanketed my mind surprisingly quickly, despite what I witnessed this evening, and I clamor through the harmless adventures until sounds on the other side of my door flutter my eyelids, then draw my head up.

My door pushes open, a sliver of yellow light crossing my bed, and then my form, as I sit up and squint against the brightness.

A silhouette comes into the frame. "Emma says you've figured out what she's up to."

Chase. I'd recognize that low, silky sarcasm anywhere.

I skip the preamble. "Yes."

He folds his arms. "You broke into our ritual room today."

I should probably add preamble to this part, but I just swallow. "Yep."

He fishes in his pockets, and something thuds against my bed. I jerk my legs up, in case it slithers.

"Your phone," he barks. Any amusement that was in his tone has long disappeared. "You won't find any photos on it, or video recordings."

I stare down at the black screen, saying nothing.

"What were you going to do with that stuff?" he asks. "Write some piss-poor exposé? Email it to our school newsletter? You forget—we *own* this school. It does what we demand, and if tonight showed you anything, we demand a whole fucking lot."

I raise my eyes to meet his, but Chase's stare is nothing but a glimmer in the darkness. "Who were they? Those women."

He cocks his head. "Exactly what you think they are."

"And that's common? You Nobles bring in escorts for freshmen to sleep with? Do you not understand how *fucked up* that is, *Prince* Stone?"

"I'm more aware than you'll ever be, Callie."

I curl up against my headboard, as if the light he's bringing into my room is poisoned nectar used by royalty to smite their enemies. "I wasn't there to expose you," I say. "I was there to see what the Nobles are. What the point is."

"The point," Chase says, but his echo is filled with venom. "The *point* is exactly what you'd expect. We are an Order that molds boys into men who will end up taking what they want, whether that be in politics, academics, forming corporate empires, influencing the laws, or amassing funds on a global scale. Our rules are the reigning power, and we abide by no other. We influence the president. We provide advice to sheiks. We strategize in wars."

With each statement, I flinch.

"Is this what you wanted?" he bites out. "To finally be a part of an archaic group that still holds as much power as it did in 1820? To watch men use women for sex and gain money for political favors? Are you happy now?"

"N-no," I grind out, his words like razors on my skin. "But my reasons still stand. Piper was involved in this. She was your ... your *soulmate*—"

Chase's hand spears forward. I wince at the violence of his movement, though he's nowhere near me.

"Key," he says.

I shuffle forward on the bed. "Chase, I..."

"*Key,* Callie. Before I really lose my shit."

I bend over the side, picking up my bag where I dropped it. I toss him his keycard. When his fingers close around it, he says, "You're lucky I caught you before you tripped over a goddamn rock and stumbled into our sacred rites. You have no idea, *none,* on how bad that could've been for you."

"Then why'd you let me do it?"

Chase stills.

"You knew I took your key. You were just waiting for me to use it. That's how you knew to keep watch near the stairs for any flicker of movement. It's how you warned me before anyone saw."

Chase shoves the key in his pocket, light and shadow playing across his features with his jerky movements. "You're relentless."

"I'm right."

He growls in frustration. "You left me no choice. I had to gain some control over the situation while giving you what you wanted, hoping you'd stop after seeing what we are."

We. Not they.

At least now, he's telling me the truth. No matter how much it hurts.

I meet his eye again, and he responds with a haggard exhale. "Of course, now you've taken up with my sister on some asinine quest to blow up the Virtues."

"And the Nobles, too, if they're also bastards," I quip.

Chase's features grow darker than shadows, and right when I'm thinking I've over-stepped, Emma comes into view, placing a hand on her brother's shoulder. "Callie's right. Both societies are drunk on power, and people—kids *our* age—are dying. How far back does it go? How many other students had to die to keep their secrets?"

Chase rips from his sister's hold. "It's too dangerous. I told you that before you came here, and I'm repeating it now. And you are *not,* under any circumstances, involving Callie. She's already a target of theirs, and if they ever find out what she's digging up—"

"Um, I'm right here," I say. "No need to discuss me in third person."

Chase doesn't even pretend to look at me. "Haven't you two been through enough? Why be magnets for more bullshit?"

Emma opens her mouth to argue, but I get there first. "Addisyn killed Piper."

It's enough of a verbal boulder that Chase has no choice but to turn to me. Emma, too.

"What?" Emma says, at the same time Chase asks, "How the hell did you come to that conclusion?"

"A source," I begin, and Chase rolls his eyes, muttering how tired he is. My voice is bristly when I continue. "But I planned to back it up by finding the lost pages of Piper's diary. They're in Addisyn's room."

"Let me guess, you took her key, too?" Chase asks.

"No," I snipe, then choose to appeal to Emma, since she and I may have the same goals. "I'm on trash duty on weekdays, and part of that is emptying the bins in every dorm room. I figured I could get a chance then, but it'd be a lot higher if one of you helped."

After a few beats of silence, Emma asks, "What makes you think I care about Piper?"

I shake my head. "You're hearing me wrong. Whatever kind of person Piper was, she was looking into the Virtues, too. But Addisyn killed her before she found out what the society was hiding from their girls. And the Virtues *rewarded* Addisyn for it. They've given her status, improved her grades, gotten her on the rowing team, and she killed one of their own! Come on, guys. You may not be into the whole sororicide angle, but the Virtues assisting in a cover-up of a murder of their member has got to set your teeth on edge."

Emma places her hands on her hips, facing her brother. "She makes a good point."

"Callie makes a lot of points," Chase says on a sigh. "And more often than not, they get her in trouble."

The barb hits exactly where he intended. "That's not fair."

Chase slants his shoulders. "I'm not saying this to hurt you. I want you to stop this, Callie. Finish this year like a normal student, join some clubs, have *fun*. Don't get sucked into our world. It's lethal. Violent. You don't deserve our demons."

"That's where you're wrong," I say, my fingers tangling in my bedspread. "I've been to hell. I know what lurks there, because it was in the bedroom where I found my mom. And I know I broke down—I've paid for that dearly. I accused a man who, while an asshole to my mother, didn't kill her. He just hurt her, then remarried six months later. To a woman he got pregnant."

Emma inhales a pained breath.

"I don't want your pity," I say to her. "Just like you have no time for mine. I made a mistake, and so did he. We're both working to better ourselves because of it. And *this*, exposing a society that recruits children for their own murderous means, *that* is what will heal me. Getting justice. Not playing cheerleader." I look to Chase. "I can't pretend there isn't a hellmouth beneath my feet. The same way Rose Briar couldn't and your sister can't. And you, too." My voice grows softer. "You're here to stop me. Or save me. And I'm sorry giving me access to your society's sexist ritual wasn't enough to get me to scream and run. I've seen things, Chase. I'm not the delicate flower I'm named after. I need you to understand that." I pause. "I need you to help me."

Chase raises his stare from the floor, connecting with mine. As he searches my eyes, I know I've won, but I don't feel our blooming connection this time. Instead, I absorb his tiredness, frustration, and unwillingness to bend entirely to my will.

Emma takes a moment to look between us, her eyes narrowed.

"Not to get in the way of ... whatever this is," she drawls, "but you're thinking by giving the police Addy, you'll be meddling with the Virtues' plans enough to expose them."

"Not to mention, exonerating an innocent man." I flick my glance back at Chase. "Jack's the one who got Piper pregnant, but he didn't kill her."

Chase hardens his jaw under my stare, but grinds out, "You already know who most of the Virtues are. You don't need me."

I hesitate, then ask Emma, "Were you a Virtue?"

Emma doesn't look at me when she gives a curt nod.

Chase says to me, "The Virtues are violent and destructive and barely constrained by us at this point. If pointing the cops to Addy brings them to heel, then I'm all for it—but the rest of the Nobles may not be. By protecting the Virtues, we protect ourselves."

"I can't prove what the Virtues did to me," Emma says, at last meeting my eye, "but if I can show they participated in a murder, then that could be a start."

I want to ask her what she's been planning and how she was about to get her revenge before I offered up Addisyn, but there's no guarantee she'll tell me. We've built no trust, and what's to stop her from resuming her plans if mine fall through and I can't prove Addisyn did anything wrong?

As Chase looks on, watching his sister with protective caution and me with more of a sinister respect, I know he will need more convincing. Those diary pages *have* to be in Addisyn's room, or else this all falls apart and I'll gain nothing.

I stare down at my hands, the open palms as empty as they were when Dr. Luke insisted Piper was killed by her sister out of jealousy.

Am I really believing him? Could I take Emma down this haunted road with me, trusting we won't get lost?

I glance again at Chase, whose features remain inscrutable in the shadows, but the undercurrent of worry is there in his clenched hands and the way his jaw grinds.

"If I can prove Addisyn is involved in Piper's death," I say, both their heads turning to me, "then you'll let me in on your plans for the Virtues. I think it's a fair trade."

Emma's the first to speak. "Show us the goods, and we'll see."

She moves to the door. When she notices Chase doesn't follow, she stops. "You coming?"

"In a minute," he mutters.

Emma sends a long look my way, but her carefully blank features don't tell me what she's thinking. "I'll be in my room."

When Emma steps out, Chase stalks over and shuts my bedroom door. He turns back around, and the face he gives me is ferocious.

"I know I have no excuse," I begin before he can unleash. "But neither do you. You and your sister are planning some kind of coup on your societies while I run around blind. Are you really surprised I stumbled into your lair after being forced to steal your shit? You left me no choice."

Chase stares at me in silence so long, I cross my arms under his scrutiny. But I don't lower my chin.

At last, his voice slips through the air like a black, silk ribbon wrapping itself around my neck.

"If you're going to accuse me, get your facts straight. I'm not out to destroy the Nobles," he says, his features cloaked in darkness. "I want to control them."

Thirty

"YOU ... WHAT?" I sit straighter in bed, my duvet, the only softness in this room, becoming a comforting pillow on my lap.

Chase moves closer until he stands at the foot of the bed. "You saw who guided the ceremony tonight."

That irresistible scent of his, salty, cedar male, drifts its ethereal allure in my direction. To distract myself from his proximity, I bring to mind the three cloaked adults in the ritual room.

"One of them was your father," I say.

Chase nods. "He's the current Noble King, and I'm his legacy."

"Meaning..." I parse through his words. "You're the next leader?"

"Something like that."

"And you want to gain control."

Chase's sharp profile tips to the ceiling. "You just don't see it, do you? How hard I've worked to keep you out of this."

I risk laying a hand on his forearm, the ropes under his skin hard and hot. "You can't keep me away when all I see is secrets and lies." I wait for Chase to lower his head. "If you want me to step back, try telling me the truth so I can understand the danger."

Chase snorts. "You've seen enough to know you're in hot water, Callie. Don't pretend that my telling you more will get you to back off."

I haven't removed my hand, so I give a light squeeze. "Then make me smarter. A part of you knows this can't go on forever. Their power has to bend."

Chase sighs, staring down at my hand. His profile is so dark, he appears in shades of black, the color of doom enveloping his body, as if he's already given himself over to the underworld.

I'm tempted to turn on the light, to highlight his angelic beauty instead of sitting in the dark with his devil, but that would require moving. Disconnecting my touch that keeps him here, with me.

"You're never going to be happy just being normal, are you?"

His question hits hard, and I rub the center of my chest at the phantom pain. "My average life was taken away a year ago. I've never tried to get it back." I squeeze his arm again. "I've seen evil leave its mark, and ... it's hard to explain, but I feel like it's followed me here. And it won't leave me alone until I defeat it."

I'm staring down at my hand on his skin, and jolt at the brush of feeling down my cheek. Raising my eyes, I realize it's him, tracing my profile with a wishful, tentative dance of fingers across my jaw.

"If I tell you what you want to know, will you stop with the sneaking around where you don't belong? The stealing?"

His tone sounds so lost, his touch so forlorn, that I'm desperate for a joke. "Are you saying you didn't enjoy the exchange of sex for a keycard?"

As soon as it's out, I wince at the crassness.

But Chase responds with a lupine smile. "I'll always enjoy sex with you, sweet possum."

I catch my lower lip with my teeth.

"But," he continues, "that was a low fucking blow."

"You ran with it," I retort. "And let me keep your key, so who's using who?"

Chase acknowledges my point, leaning back.

We sit in the quiet, the lateness of the night silencing the rest of the floor. Even Emma doesn't make a sound. I start to think Chase has second-guessed sharing anything else with me, then the shadows shift, skittering back when his voice cuts through the room. "Thorne Briar created the Nobles for competition and manipulation. He didn't understand why grooming for influential positions in government or the global economy started in college. He wanted to mold minds when they were at their most pliable. That way, older members could maintain their dominance and power through the strict regimen they inflicted on young boys, who would have no choice, no aggression, toward their leaders." He pauses. "Not even when that boy turns into a man and is seated in office."

My brows ache with my pensive frown, but my heart feels light with revelation. "Is that why Rose created the Virtues? Because she wanted to protect the kids?"

Chase rubs his jaw. "She wanted to show her husband that children could be guided instead of manipulated, and she chose to prove it by tapping girls who excelled in their classrooms. It was around the time women were granted the right to education beyond homemaking, and she advanced that learning with secret teachings, first at the boathouse, then, once the membership expanded and women came into power, in their own hidden rooms around campus. She died young, but her teachings lived on through the students who loved her and swore to keep the Virtues alive, despite Thorne's multiple attempts to silence them. Some of these women were at the forefront of gaining the right to vote, the Civil Rights movement, LGBTQ rights, key swing votes in the Supreme Court, all because of Rose's determination to thwart her husband's maxim that the only way to win is through terror and destruction."

The implications of what those boys went through—what *Chase* might've gone through—sits heavy between us, and I'm afraid to move and break the spell, conscious of Chase's ability to withhold as much as he tells.

"In the fifties, the Nobles changed under my grandfather's leadership," Chase continues. "He admired what the Virtues accomplished and their quiet dominance in a man-centric world. The Nobles vetted kids in middle school, sure, but the goals were to enlist the clear leaders of the class, in sports, academics, debate, any kid who showed an uncanny talent for domination. But my grandfather ... he wanted to *inspire* them, not corrupt. He wanted our members to go on to do great things for this country, and to use our influence to make a positive difference in the world. He was less about politics and more about mass improvements through power. And with that, came great relationships with the Ivy League Societies, and a brotherhood within the Nobles that hasn't been seen since. Those boys would've given their lives for each other. For my grandfather, too, before he passed on."

"What happened when your grandfather died?" I ask, though the trepidation within me knows the answer.

"My father took over."

Chase punctuates the sentence by sharply cutting off and staring at my closet door across the room.

"And he's rather fond of the Nobles' origins, so he's gone back to the traditional way of tapping initiates."

I swallow, unsure of how far I should take this, so I choose a safer route, away from his personal memories. "And the Virtues?"

"Poisoned." Chase answers without hesitation. "The Nobles use demanding, sometimes vicious, rituals, starting off in middle school but really pushing the boundaries in freshman year, when we're robed. But the Virtues ... they don't bother with the excuse of molding future minds for the good of humanity anymore. They're comfortable with their power, hedonistic, even. They pursue decadence, not control. They feed off popularity, insecurity, beauty, sexual power. So, my dad's done one thing right, I guess. He's tried to gain control of them through the soulmate rite, same as what Thorne tried to do to leash them when he witnessed, firsthand, how women used their accessory status to manipulate the men. And it's what we do now, to ensure the Virtues aren't completely independent, but they keep a lot of their rituals to themselves, as we do to them."

"So, you're allies ... and competitors," I surmise.

"We're a breeding ground for war."

I hug myself, calming the shudders over my heart and the goosebumps over my skin. I'm getting what I wanted, aren't I? Inside access into the Nobles and Virtues, first witness to their brewing destruction.

Chase twists until he faces me on the bed. "If it turns out Addy has nothing to do with Piper's death, I can't help you anymore, do you understand?"

Slowly, I nod. "My credibility will be shot to shit at that point, so yeah, I won't fight you."

Chase takes both my hands, clenching them tight. "I'm not doing this solely to avenge Piper. I'm doing it for you, too. And for me. We're out of control, because now we're killing ourselves and making it look like an accident. As their future king, I can't let this continue."

I pull my hands from his hold, but not to retreat. I cup his face, and he searches my eyes, waiting for my reply. "Thank you," I whisper.

For telling me. For trusting me. For letting me in.

With my entire being, I'm wishing his heart has opened to me, but I don't dare mix up wishes with hopes. Not when the fragile thread that's connecting us could be shredded at any moment.

Chase lingers in his search, his stare grazing across my cheekbones, my eyes, before landing on my lips.

Threading my fingers at the back of his neck, I lean in.

He meets me halfway, and while our lips meet delicately, our tongues are unscrupulous in their demand.

Chase pushes me back until I'm lying down, and he's pressed on top of me, our kiss becoming so deep, we're lighting a fire in ourselves. Our hands scrape against each other faster, our clothes lifted, then ripped off, our underwear cast aside.

We break apart only to remove everything that barricades us from ecstasy, until we're naked and my legs are spread, my folds wet, and he hasn't even touched me.

Chase anchors my waist, then spins until he's on the bottom and I'm on top of him, and I take delicious control, lining him up until his tip is inside me, and I make slow, lazy circles in complete contradiction to the raging inferno at my core that wants all of him, right now, his thickness the perfect size to fill me whole.

Chase groans, his hips begging where his mouth refuses, attempting to thrust, but I keep lifting away.

I smile in the light of the breaking dawn, acquiring more power over a guy than I've *ever* had, and totally taking advantage.

"Callie..." he grunts, his upper lip curling. "Goddamnit. Fuck me."

My next grin shows my teeth. "Ask me nicely."

Air whistles out of his clenched lips. "Don't make me beg, sweet possum, because my answering torture will be so much longer. I'll take my fill, through your mouth, your pussy, and your ass, while you plead for yours."

My smile doesn't falter. "That's big talk for somebody who isn't allowed to come at the moment."

He growls. "Neither can you."

Damn it. Chase has a point. How much longer can I withhold *both* our orgasms? I'm throbbing, hot with desperation, so swollen and ready for his dick that it's making it easier for him to slip farther in, taking more territory.

I grab my breasts, flicking my hard, piqued nipples to try and redirect the pleasure to myself.

Chase notices, but I'm so deep in my own, desperate escape, that I fail to take his widened eyes as a warning sign.

"Fuck this," he snaps, then rears up at the same time he thrusts in, yanking on my hair to pull my head back and keep me at the perfect angle.

I cry out, but he covers my mouth with his other hand, so each time he pounds, my moans are muffled for just the two of us.

He takes, and takes, fucking so hard there will be bruises on my inner thighs, but I meet each pound by burying him to the hilt and clenching around him so tightly, I feel the pulsing of his cock inside me.

Soon, I'm riding him, and he releases his hold so he can lean back on his forearms. I press on his shoulders for balance, bouncing, circling, our thighs damp with sweat and the scent of lust, building until we're at that perfect, painful precipice of release and desire.

"I'm almost there," I breathe out, my voice hitched and tight. "I'm ... almost ... oh God—"

Chase snarls and pulls me against him until we're molded together, our orgasms in tandem, but my release so much louder than his, since he's buried his face in my neck and bitten down.

The sharp indents of his teeth mix with the swirling orgasm that tightens my core and sends my limbs sparkling, and I fall against him, covered in a cloudy haze, the weight of the world lifted far above my shoulders.

Chase trails his fingers up the length of my spine, then cups the back of my neck. He turns his head, murmuring into my ear, "You're going to be the end of me."

I inhale his cologne, and the underlayer of *him* surrounding my naked body like a needed blanket against the chill. My response flows to the back of my lips but won't go any further. I'm afraid, if I say it out loud, it'll be akin to cursing the hearts of our twisted fate.

And so, I mouth it silently into his shoulder, the salted tang of his skin a seal to my terrified vow. *You're my beginning.*

Thirty-One

MONDAY EVENING COMES TOO FAST, despite Emma and Chase's assurances on Sunday that they had a failsafe plan to give me time to search Addisyn's room. I explained to them my thoughts on timing the emptying of Addisyn's floor to the housekeeper's cigarette break, dropping anything I was doing (and any floor I was on) to sprint up to Addisyn's room and do as thorough a search as I can before Emma, guarding the front, or Chase, watching the side of the building, texts me the moment Moira stubs out her cigarette.

With them involved, my chances of success are that much higher, but their presence doesn't lessen the nerves. I've been so good up until this point, receiving texts from Dad and Ahmar, and phone calls from Lynda, that they're so proud of me for focusing on school and keeping out of trouble.

If they caught word of what I was up to while I pretended to be the perfect daughter...

The guilt is worse than the betrayal I'd cause them.

My patchwork family wants nothing but the best for me—even my stepdad, who I *think* I've come to terms with—and who's making an honest, genuine man out of himself, sobering up and taking care of his pregnant wife. They've been so focused on me, and my excuses have been so tunneled to them, my incoming newborn sister has taken a backseat. And yeah, my efforts at proving a twisted sister relationship with Piper and Addisyn aren't exactly helping with that.

When this is done, I'm resolved to repairing my remaining relationships. Forgiving as much as I can. And ... moving forward without a black cloud of grief, if that's even possible.

It occurs to me just how much I'm putting the solving of Piper's murder into solving *me*.

Monday starts off innocuous enough, with classes and lunch with Ivy and her other friends. Ivy's part of crew, but for reasons I've yet to dig into, she never sits with her rowing team at lunch or even acknowledges them much during the day. I've stopped myself from asking her *why* a million times—because I'm turning a new leaf once I prove Addisyn killed Piper and the Virtues' involvement. An unassuming, non-nosy, bright, fresh, green leaf, that will finish her senior year quietly.

If Ivy doesn't want to sit with the mean girls more than she has to, why should I question it?

Because she's on their team.

I shake off the thought as quickly as it comes. This is *exactly* what I'm worried about—paranoia taking over reality, ruining people who care about me.

I say goodbye to Ivy at the top of the hill, me starting the last week of punishment, and her heading to crew practice at the boathouse before the dinner bell.

I'm glad for their insane training schedule, because it means Addisyn, their new captain, will also be down there for the near future and unlikely to trek back through the forest path and to the dorms for a few hours.

My features are tight as I take the walkway to Thorne House, so immersed in the logistics of our plan and where I need to search in her room first (under the mattress. Like sister, like sister, right?) that I don't count the three figures idling by the dorms until I'm practically on top of them.

"Shit—" I blurt, then come to a stop, screwing up my brows. I'm standing with Chase, Emma, and ... Eden?

"Hey," Eden mumbles under her blanket of black hair. She keeps close to Emma while Chase steps forward, hands spread and prepared to argue their case.

I start to ask, "What's she—?"

"She's Moira's daughter," Chase says. "And has been helping Emma and I with our ... research."

My eyes ping between each and every one of them, before settling on Emma. "She knows? About everything?"

"*She* has been working her ass off since Emma's been gone," Eden snaps. "I know a helluva lot more than you, Callie."

It makes sense, especially since Eden's the one who gave me the Virtues' name in the first place, but, "Why tell me this now? Why not yesterday when we were guzzling caffeine and solidifying plans?"

Emma answers. "Because I wasn't sure if Eden would be all for it. This kind of fast-forwards our motives, and Eden's nothing if not cautious."

Eden arches a brow. "That's Emma's polite way of saying I'm a paranoid freak who hates outside involvement."

My eye twitches. "I'm not so sure it's the more the merrier..."

"I could say the same thing," Eden retorts. "I was here first."

"Ladies," Chase says, coming between us. He shadows me until Emma and Eden recede in my vision, until all I see is the glossy, melted chocolate of his eyes. "Trust me. This makes it easier on us, I swear."

Eden pipes up behind him, "I can keep my mom talking while she sneaks a smoke. Be honest, Callie, you're not a subtle one when it comes to unearthing evidence."

I sigh at her words, but don't break my stare with Chase. He lowers his head, as if his sincerity is better seen close up.

But, little does he know, he had me the instant he stepped into view.

I answer softly, "I trust you."

"Okay." Chase smiles, squeezes my shoulders, and drifts to the side, our covert intimacy crackling between us. "Then let's do this."

We confirm our phone numbers through test texts, and the three of them continue to loiter outside while I go in, drop my stuff off in my room, and get ready for clean-up duty.

Chase made it clear yesterday that he doesn't have practice today, unlike the girls' crew. Knowing that, and that his presence will be outside Thorne House the entire time I attempt the downfall of Briarcliff's newest princess, comes as a comfort as I put all I have, all I've *discovered*, on the line, with only Dr. Luke's word as my back-up.

What other choice is there, though? Jack's unfair arrest? Chase's continued suffering? Addisyn living her life of privilege, bolstered by her newfound involvement with the Virtues, and allowing these societies' continued reign and manipulation of Briarcliff students?

I'm no superhero, but if I can get Piper's lost pages, I can get them all. *That's* what's leading me. Not Dr. Luke.

After dressing accordingly in Briarcliff-issued sweatpants and a PE Dept T-shirt, I throw my hair up and meet Moira on the ground floor. She's outfitted in the staff uniform of maroon slacks and a white polo shirt with the school's crest on the left side.

She greets me with a pleasant smile, and now that I'm given context, I see Eden in that mouth—just a smidge, since Eden rarely stretches her lips as wide as this.

I now understand why, though.

"Hi, Moira," I say as she hands me gloves and a broom.

"Ready for your last week of purgatory?" she asks with a lighthearted tone, the lines around her eyes crinkling.

"So ready," I say, matching her smile.

"I gotta say, I'll miss having the extra hands. You've been a big help, honey."

I fall into step beside her as we start at the nearest room. Moira knocks, waits a minute, then swipes her keycard and motions me inside.

Veering into the kitchen, I pick up the small trash bin and dump it into the larger trash bag Moira holds open.

"I didn't know you and Yael shared a daughter," I say.

Moira laughs. "You're an astute one, aren't you? Usually students don't take the time to understand interpersonal relationships of staff members."

"He and I make a lot of conversation when he drives me into town," I say. "Eden came up. I didn't know she was your daughter, too."

Moira cinches the bag shut. Her smile falls. "She is."

She walks ahead of me to the next room, and I rush to sweep up the debris and shut the door.

"I'm sorry," I say after Moira knocks on the second door. "I didn't mean to offend..."

"I'm protective of her." Moira keeps her attention on the closed door. "And get naturally defensive when a student mentions her. Edie doesn't have many friends, and, I'm sorry, honey, you're a lovely girl, but I doubt she's warmed to you."

"Not even a little," I say honestly. "But we've spoken a few times. And have worked on ... projects ... together. I'm not out to get her. I can promise you that."

Moira visibly relaxes. "I'm glad for it. I don't mean any insult. I *wish* Edie would spend time with a girl like you, but she's a woman of her own."

"I think she's strong," I say as I wander inside and find the next bin.

Moira goes quiet behind me.

"I don't participate in gossip, but I do get sucked in when it's mentioned." I turn to Moira's open bag, tipping the bin. "And Yael mentioned a little. What she's been through..."

Moira meets my eye over the crinkling trash bag. "I don't contribute to gossip, either, but I know what you've been through, too. And how hard it's been for you to talk about. So, maybe we should leave it at that."

The warning's obvious, but I can't stop the inquisitiveness from slipping out. "Have you heard of the Virtues?"

Moira's features go flat. "We're falling behind with all this chatter. Come on, now, out you get."

Properly shamed, I exit the room while Moira leans forward and shuts the door.

I don't push the limit any further, but Moira's frank dismissal of the Virtues does add an additional layer of guilt to what I'm about to do to her, and that her daughter's involved in it. Not through my doing, but that's a dumb excuse. I know for a fact that Eden's involvement this evening is 100% due to my actions.

"I'm sorry," I say to Moira's back, though she can't know just how much I'm sorry for.

"It's all right, honey," she says over her shoulder. "Let's finish you up so you can get to your homework."

We work in silence on the first floor, and when we get to the second, my heartbeat kicks up. Addisyn's room is in the middle, which she shares with another sophomore. When Moira's distracted changing out trash bags, I send Emma a quick text.

Me: Second floor.

Emma acknowledges with a thumb's up emoji, and I stuff my phone in my pants' pocket when Moira steps from the maintenance room.

We continue to work in the quiet, but my back is stiffer, my movements jerkier, as adrenaline leaks into my limbs. Moira doesn't seem to notice, but she's not meeting my eye, either.

"The Virtues destroyed my daughter," Moira says, and at first, it doesn't register.

I pause, holding a bin to my chest.

"We didn't know of their existence, not until we started work here when Edie was a baby," Moira continues softly, but she snaps the trash bag open with a loud *pop*. "We mostly tried to ignore the whisperings, because we liked our jobs and loved the benefits and security that came with it. By the time we realized their influence, Edie was already well into researching them. Trying to *be* one, my impulsive child. Back then, she was bright, cheerful, heavily into swimming. But within a month of freshman year, she changed. Became withdrawn, snuck out at night, endured massive bullying at school. They called it hazing, you know." Moira locks eyes with mine. "Testing her limits in a perverted way to see if she was worthy. And that thing is run by *adults*." Moira hisses out a breath. "My daughter's limit was met when her naked body was distributed around school. And instead of my vibrant, dedicated daughter, who loved her swim meets, I have her husk. Don't get me wrong, I will always, *always*, love my girl. But that group of so-called independent, powerful women can burn in hell."

I gulp. "Those pictures, she was a minor. Did you … did you go to the police?"

Moira rustles the bag for me to come closer to dump the contents of the bin in my hands. I do, and when I step closer, notice her shaking grip.

"Oh, honey, we did," Moira says, the underline of her eyes going wet. "But by the time we reported, the pictures were deleted. There were none we could point to, and Edie refused to corroborate."

"Shit," I murmur, my heart sinking. It made sense that the Virtues' influence stretched to the police department, but to think they forced *Eden* to keep her mouth shut … I'm sick at what they could've said, or done to her, to keep her quiet.

Pressure hits my chin, and I realize it's Moira, gently tilting my head up.

"If you're thinking of taking up with them, don't," Moira says, her brown eyes piercing mine. "You are much too sweet and already too tortured to ever endure what they'd have in store."

My swallow hits her fingers, and she releases me, blinking.

"Lord, I need a cigarette after this," she mutters. "Are you okay to do a couple of rooms without me?"

I nod, slightly too eagerly, and work to school my features. "Of course."

"All right, then. I trust you, honey. Hang tight."

After handing me her master keycard, Moira takes the closest staircase exit, and I follow her until she disappears. I'm off-balance and nauseous that I could potentially get her fired. She's had three weeks of trusting me to do my job, and on the last few days, right when she's gotten comfortable with me and even imparted motherly advice, I'm about to betray her.

Then don't. Be done with it before Moira ever gets back.

My phone vibrates in my pocket, and I look away from the exit and reach for it.

Eden: I see her. I'll try for ten minutes. Will text if sooner.

Since we're in a group chat, both Chase and Emma acknowledge the text, and I do too. **Going in now,** I type, then drop my cleaning supplies and jog to Addy's room.

I almost key in immediately before my instincts kick in and tell me to knock first. Stepping back, I do just that, my leg jiggling as I wait for any kind of response.

When there's none after thirty seconds, I key inside.

It takes a minute to figure out which bedroom is Addisyn's. I'm usually only a few steps inside before I empty the trash, then leave. Thankfully, the dorm room is in the same layout as my own, but on a slightly smaller scale.

A few seconds into scoping out the pictures tacked to the wall, I realize I have the wrong room, and sprint to the one across the way.

I'm so bad at this, I think, cringing, but don't take the time to admonish myself completely, because there *is* no time.

I fumble with the bedspread and mattress first, lifting it and finding nothing. I then move to the closet, flicking through clothes, feeling across the top and bottom shelves, opening plastic containers.

Running to Addisyn's desk, I pull out drawers, rifling through but not too hard, finding nothing.

Cursing, I stop long enough to send a text:

Ten minutes isn't long enough. Need more time.

I move to the center of Addisyn's room, taking a moment to *think*. Then, deciding to get creative, I look behind the pictures on her wall and, when that doesn't pan out, move to the backs of the standing photo frames on her nightstand.

Right when I start to believe I'm a genius detective and will find the missing pages behind a photo of Addisyn and her sister, I come up blank.

"Damn it!" I hiss, then return the photo to its proper place.

What would Ahmar do in this situation?

Hands on my hips, I scan the bedroom, cataloguing each shelving unit and drawer that I've searched.

He'd go through it all again.

The answer sets off a lightbulb in my head, and I search the same places one more time, like a true detective would. One sweep isn't enough. One set of crime scene photos won't show everything. Look at all items again, find the spots you missed, thoroughly search the ones you think provide no evidence.

I summon as much of Ahmar and Mom's spirit as I can when I resume my search of Addisyn's closet, stepping in as deep as possible, my face buried in her lavender-scented clothing hanging on the bars.

I burrow deeper, and it gets darker, until I'm all the way in the back, feeling the walls. I'm cross sectioning the area in my head, feeling for ... I don't know, a secret drawer, when my foot hits on a loose floorboard.

"No," I breathe out, stunned as I stare down where my foot rests. Did I just hit the motherload?

Gawking never did anyone any good, so I bend down, using my nails to crack open the floorboard all the way, and reach in before I can second-guess what could be greeting me on the other side. A rat's nest?

A crinkling, papery feel hits the pads of my fingers, and I lift out the sheaf of papers, my eyes feeling bulbous as they bug out of my head.

Is this it?

I rush through the racks of clothes and into the light of Addisyn's room, taking a closer look at the torn, handwritten pages.

. . . .

I'm pretty sure I'm supposed to feel bad for taking Addy's boyfriend away, but all I feel is a win. She thinks she can do better than me, get the hotter guy, make the better grades, be Virtuous, but that will never be, because I won't allow it. There's only one Harrington girl who matters, and that's me.

Then, on another page:

Fuck. Addy's getting a little crazy. It's not like I love Jack. I just love to fuck him. Same as I enjoy Chase's dick and the taste of Mr. S's cum. I don't differentiate in levels of caring, but Addy's acting like I'm stealing her husband and am about to move into a little Cape-town house by the ocean, living in Briarcliff for the rest of my life.
FUCK. NO.
Why would I want to marry a poor boy who thinks he's bad and is working towards a future as a fry-cook at the lobster shack?
I can do way better, and so can she. Can't Addy understand I'm doing her a favor? Always following me around, wanting to be me, and the one time I do something for her, she acts like I should die for showing her what a loser her boyfriend really is.
That's what she said, dude. "I hope you die for this."
Dramatic, much?

With each word, my cringe gets deeper, my muscles sagging with disgust and disbelief.

"Jesus, Piper, you really were a caustic bitch," I murmur, skimming a few more sentences. "Not that you deserved to die, but—"

"I know, right? A total and utter cunt."

My head snaps up at the unexpected voice, meeting Addisyn's cool, murderous gaze in the doorway.

Thirty-Two

THE LOOSE PAPERS crunch in my hands. "Addisyn, I—"

"Don't bother," Addisyn says, wandering farther into her room.

Her tone is calm, her demeanor collected, as she scans her space, pinpointing the sections I hadn't yet cleaned up. The one tell of emotion is the tightness around her eyes, lidding a glare so hard, so lethal, it's only contained by her unbreakable, thick skin.

It's almost as terrifying as if she came storming in, shrieking at me for going through her stuff.

Instead of apologizing for my clear violation, I focus on what I've found—a worse horror. "These pages, they belonged to Piper's diary."

Addisyn's sweeping stare stops on me. "They sure did."

I wait for a more detailed response, but she doesn't move. I add, "And ... you ripped them out."

"Uh-huh."

Okay. Obviously, I'm taking the lead on this, so I go all in. "You killed her, didn't you?"

Addisyn cocks her head, a night owl assessing the mouse skittering below. "What do you think?"

"You were jealous of her," I say, inching toward the door. I have the innate sense that if I reach for my phone or call for help, she'll pounce on me with her talons, turning wild in an instant. If I take small enough steps, maybe she won't notice. "Because Jack slept with her. Because of her easy membership into the Virtues."

She makes a noncommittal sound but won't stop tracking me.

I clear my throat, standing straighter. "I think it's more the latter. The Virtues have a terrible initiation process for those they deem unworthy, don't they?"

Addisyn stiffens. I've ruffled her feathers.

"Compared to those they think deserve the title," I continue. "See, I've been

370

ankle-fucking-deep in this shit—my choice, I know—but with what I've heard and read, these societies *really* prefer the older sibling, don't they? The ... help me find the word..." I snap my finger in thought, feeling more than seeing Addisyn's narrowed gaze. "Legacies. That's it. The eldest kid gets immediate entry, don't they? Piper and Chase are some examples. In fact, they tap them when they're *very* young."

"Fuck you," Addisyn hisses.

"Hit a sore spot. Sorry about that." I'm not sorry, and I doubt I look it, either. "But *you*, you had to go through a ton of bullshit before even being considered, despite sharing blood with your sister. What were they doing to you? Did you have naked photos spread around, too? Or, did they torture you so badly, you had to set fire to a building in retaliation?"

"I'm not Eden, nor am I Emma, so stop using them as fucking examples," Addisyn says.

"Those are the few I've discovered, but I bet I can find out more," I say, ignoring the thickening blood in my veins, urging me to *run*. "If you tell me what they did to you, maybe I won't feel so horrified that you killed your own sister to get in."

"They didn't ask me to do that," Addisyn blurts, but clamps her mouth shut when she sees my smile. "*Bitch*."

"They helped you cover it up, though. Maybe even accelerated your entry into membership because of the dastardly thing you did. Hell, with what I know, it probably impressed them."

"You have no fucking idea," Addisyn says, striding forward.

I almost, *almost,* cower at being run up against her fury, but I hold myself still. "What I can't understand is, why did they reward you for killing one of their own? What was Piper doing that was so wrong in their eyes, she had to die? I doubt it was for fucking your boyfriend, though I'm sure that was enough of an impetus for you."

Instead of snarling like I expect, Addisyn's lips pull up in a sneer. "Oh, yeah? Well, what I understand is, they run this school, not you, and you're about to get your ass handed to you without me lifting a finger."

I raise my brows. "What—?"

"Hey, Ems!" Addisyn calls, without looking away from me. "Eden! Come on in!"

At last, my feet move, but they don't stride forward with confidence. No, they fall back. "What the hell are you doing?"

Addisyn steps aside, revealing the bedroom doorway, and Emma and Eden walking through.

My heart plummets, its descent into cavernous darkness accelerated with the thought of Chase.

Don't let him come next. Please.

"What's going on?" I ask, my eyes bouncing between the two of them.

Emma *tsks*. Eden crosses her arms.

"Maybe next time," Emma says sweetly. "Don't fuck my brother behind my back for favors."

My shins hit the back of Addisyn's bed. "Addisyn confessed. She killed Piper! Why are you here? Eden, where's your mom? Why are you two *smiling* at me like that?"

"You bring up a good point, Callie," Emma says, then gestures to Eden. "Get the pages."

With an agility I did *not* brace for, Eden springs forward and snatches Piper's lost pages from my hand.

"Eden, no!" I cry, but it's too late. She's vaulted back to Emma's side, clutching the writings like treasure.

"And that letter of Rose Briar's you found?" Emma says. "Consider that gone, too. Hiding shit in a textbook? C'mon, Callie, at least encrypt the evidence."

I appeal to Eden. To Emma. Addisyn's off to the side, enjoying the show. "You hate the Virtues. You hate Falyn, Willow, Violet, *Addisyn*—all they represent. Why are you helping them? They hurt you. *Scarred* you. Why would you ever...?"

I can't finish the question, because I'm so bewildered. Here are two girls who've experienced first-hand torture from the Virtues, overheard Addisyn's confession, and yet, they're regarding me like *I'm* the one they need to be rid of.

"You tricked me," I whisper.

"Wasn't all that hard," Emma says. "You're so eager to please Chase, all I had to do was dangle his dick in front of you a few times."

"Ew." Eden giggles. "You're talking about your brother's penis."

I stare on, horrified, my mind rushing to catch up with the *wrongness* of this scene. "Where's Chase?"

"God." Emma moans, her eyes drifting to the ceiling. "You're so predictable."

"You led me to believe you were on my side. Got me here, to Addisyn's room. And I found Piper's missing pages. What was it all for?" I ask.

"First off," Emma says. She looks to Addisyn. "Why didn't you set fire to these pages when you stole them? You're as dumb as she is."

"Probably because I'm not the pyro in this room," Addisyn retorts.

Emma grunts in annoyance, but all the movement highlights are the angry burns down one side of her neck. A scar I thought she got from an attempt to get revenge on the societies after what they did to her.

The fool is me, I guess, because I never asked Emma for the truth. Never took the time to ask her what instigated her attack, to figure out what she did to deserve a beating from the Virtues that unleashed her wrath in the first place.

I just assumed, and that was my downfall.

Maybe all it was, was an initiation gone wrong. And Emma's still trying to get in.

"I can't believe that," I say out loud. "You've suffered so much, Emma. The pain you endured; it can't have brought you to this point."

Emma bares her teeth. "Get whatever halo you have over my head *off*. I'm not a victim. I never was. The only idiot around here is you. And possibly Addy, for leaving crucial evidence in her room. They thank you for tipping us off, by the way."

They. The Virtues.

But I won't give up. "Eden, I've spoken to your mom. Your dad. You're not this person."

"*Ooooh*, you spoke to my parents," Eden sneers. But her eyes drive into mine, asserting another message I can't immediately read. "Unlike yours, mine don't keep me on a leash. The Virtues are everywhere, Callie. They're not about to be stopped by a bitchy sister murdering another bitchy sister."

"Hey," Addisyn says.

"You're protecting Addisyn," I say, so horrifically awed, my voice comes out breathy and unsure.

"You get props for being so determined," Eden continues, then adds with a musical lilt, "but you're done now."

"We're not here to hurt you," Emma adds. "As long as you stop, you can continue at Briarcliff no problem. Focus on school. Find a boyfriend who's *not* my brother. Eat cakes with Ivy and complain about the popular kids."

The mention of Ivy sends shivers rushing down my skin. "If you hurt her—"

Emma laughs. "I'd be more concerned with your own well-being if I were you."

"Can I show her?" Addisyn asks Emma, suddenly gleeful. "Can we add some confetti to our grand exit?"

Emma pauses, then considers the papers in Eden's hands. "I suppose it can't hurt." Emma turns to me. "Happy belated birthday, Callie."

Emma nods at Eden, who shuffles through the diary entries until she finds what she's looking for, then shoves a single piece of paper in my direction.

I automatically grab it, my mouth hanging open as the three of them move to the door.

"Read it. You'll be sorry you ever found Piper's thoughts," Addisyn says to me. "Then get the fuck out of my room."

"Consider this your final warning," Emma says. "And that's coming from the top."

Eden also looks back, an apologetic look crossing her features before they re-harden until she's almost unrecognizable. "You got this far. It's time to turn back."

"And remember," Addisyn adds. "I'm the good sister. You can thank me later."

When they shut the apartment door, and I'm left in the quiet, my knees buckle until I'm seated at the edge of Addisyn's bed, Piper's single diary entry crumpled in my fist.

What the hell just happened? Their wounds bamboozled me. Emma and Eden's emotional stories enraptured and softened until I was nothing but putty to be molded by their hands.

And Chase?

My heart ruptures at the thought.

Slowly, I smooth out Piper's words. The only evidence I have left.

Just got off the phone with Mom. I can't believe it. Can't FUCKING believe it. That bitch's spawn is coming here? To my turf?

Mom thinks it's some kind of play. That the bitch is sending her kid here to get money from us, to show us who's really running the show, but that's not it. I've met Bitch Jr., and she says her mom's dead.

I choke.

. . .

All this time, the bitch hasn't asked for a dime of child support—well, before she stopped breathing. She must've pissed someone else off real good to get that kind of payback. Did she fuck someone else's dad, too? How many dudes did she sleep with? I doubt her husband even knows. I believe Mom when she says the affair has gone on for decades. What I can't believe is that this pathetic, puppy-eyed bitch, who's drooling after Chase like he's some kind of dog bone, is my half-sister.

I already have one idiot bloodline to deal with. And now I have two? No fair. **I'm the only one who deserves to be Virtuous.**

Thirty-Three

I'M NUMB.

Stuck in the cold, even though I'm seated indoors, in a warm room with calming floral smells.

I'm going to be sick.

I launch off Addisyn's bed and reach the toilet just in time, heaving the contents of my lunch. I'm never going to make it to dinner, and at this point, I don't want to.

I want nothing to do with these people. This school.

Coughing, I stand, wiping my mouth with the back of my sleeve and scraping back my hair. I hold the crumpled piece of paper over the toilet before I flush, aiming to mix vomit with vomit, but my fingers can't seem to let go.

On a garbled cry of frustration, I shove it into my pocket and fly out of Addisyn's room.

I run into Moira in the hallway.

"Honey? Goodness, are you all right?"

Moira comes up to me and holds both my arms, peering at my face, but I can't have her touch me. I can't be near such warmth, when she's fostered such coldness and doesn't even know it.

"I can't be here," I mumble, unable to look her in the eye.

"I'm so sorry," Moira says, clucking her tongue at some inner argument with herself. "Yael texted there was an emergency at the house, and I drove over there in a panic, thinking someone was hurt, and no one was there. I called him, and he said he never texted me anything. I called Edie and she said the same thing. I must be going insane, because I have the text right here."

Your daughter stole her dad's phone, probably while he was idling near the school, waiting for a student to ping for a ride.

But I say none of it, because I've seen the heartbreak on this woman's face when talking about her daughter, and I don't want to be the one to add to it.

375

"I don't feel well," I say. "I think I should lie down."

Moira presses the back of her hand against my forehead. "You feel a little piqued, honey. I think that's a good idea. I won't tell the headmaster. As far as he knows, you completed your punishment today."

I nod, undeserving of Moira's kindness, but too cowardly to push it away.

Instead, I escape up the stairwell as quickly as I can, leaving her confused, muttering self behind.

"Shit, there you are."

I halt so abruptly the staircase door hits me in the back when I reach my floor. "Chase."

He comes within inches of me, holding my shoulders. "Where've you been? I've been texting my ass off, trying to locate you three blind mice, but I haven't received fuck all from any of you. I thought you were caught."

I shake my head, but it does nothing to dissipate the bonfire in my soul. "Where were *you*?"

Chase jerks back. "Me? Coach called. Said the girls' Coach needed help with practice today since their stroke was out sick. I texted you about it."

The girls' stroke being Addisyn, who was busy fucking up not only my enrollment at Briarcliff, but my entire *life* as I knew it.

I set my jaw. "Addisyn wasn't sick."

"No shit. I saw her on my way up here."

"Were Emma and Eden walking with her?"

"What? No." Chase's brows slam together in disgust. "That's the last place I'd find them."

"That's what I thought, too."

Chase side-eyes me. "Callie, what's going on?"

"Did you know?"

"Did I know what?"

Bile erodes my throat. "Did you know I was set up? Did you know your sister was playing for the Virtues all this time? Did you *know* Piper and Addisyn could be my half-*sisters*?"

The last sentence comes out as a howl, but that's what I am. Off-kilter, marooned, groundless and without wings.

Genuine confusion crosses his face, but I don't fall for it. I *can't* fall for it. He says, "What the fuck?"

My voice goes raw, even through taut lips. "We're done."

"What? Callie, hold on—"

"*LET GO OF ME!*"

Chase releases his hold on my arm, then raises his hands in surrender. He says, with softness that breaks me, "Please."

"No." The denial rips from my throat, and I push past him before the pleading in his eyes swallows me whole. "I'm not doing this anymore. I hate what they've done to me, but most of all, I hate what *you've* let yourself become under their rule."

The rare, open vulnerability in Chase's face fades with my words, my accusation like a blast of ice in his face, but I can't seem to stop.

"You're the worst one," I hiss. "You're a coward, because you know what they represent, and you do it, anyway."

Chase says, with the sharpened steel of a blade, "The day you truly figure out my motives will be a day you regret, because you are so, *so* wrong."

I glare at him, communicating my hurt, my pain, my poisoned past and dismal future in that single glance.

"You're right," he says, his eyes tracing my face before landing on mine. His expression carefully controlled. "Maybe you are half-Harrington. You certainly have the kind of hate they covet."

My lower lip trembles with hesitation, but Chase turns on his heel before I can respond.

He disappears down the stairs, and when he's a safe distance away, I let myself crumble. I fold into a ball, bury my face in my knees, and let out a keening wail, mourning for the person I thought I was, and the mother I thought I knew.

Thirty-Four

BRIARCLIFF ACADEMY LOVES its cruel irony, because they've labeled the weekend before Thanksgiving, Family Day.

Or, what the students call the Turkey Trot, a weekend of day-drinking between lake houses that happens the very moment the families leave.

And so, while everyone scrambles around, trying on Thanksgiving-themed costumes and discussing the best selfie angle, I sit at my desk, flipping my pen in my fingers and scowling into the air.

"Scary," Ivy muses as she perches on my bed. "You should definitely dress as a scary turkey, or hey, just wear the face you have on now. Freshmen will scatter at the sight of you."

"Funny," I say, giving her the once-over. "Are you going to wear that when your parents come?"

Ivy grabs the front of her costume and flaps it idly. "Probably not, since my dad would lock me in a basement for the rest of my life."

She's dressed as a sexy turkey—since that's a thing—which in her mind, means a sexy fawn Halloween costume with red, brown, and white feathers glued to her suede-clad, minidress ass. A homemade feathered headpiece and white-glitter eyeshadow completes the look. Ivy's dressed so delicious and cute, I'm thinking on her trip back to her dorms, she's hoping Riordan notices her efforts.

Riordan Hughes, who is a confirmed Noble member. I'm watching Ivy's budding relationship carefully but won't say anything. Ivy's the one who gave me the name of the Nobles way back in the beginning—surely, she's cautious around them.

And if she isn't ... well, I wish I had proof to show her, but everything, and I mean *everything*, has been deleted off my phone and my cloud. Piper's diary. Rose's letters. Howard Mason's musings.

Thank you, oh so much, Chase Fucking Stone.

A week has passed since that terrible evening of discoveries, where it feels as though I gained two friends, then lost them that same day. I avoid Chase at all costs, but he doesn't seek me out, either. The thought that he's content to keep his distance doesn't sit well, because the part of me that's still alive and owns a heartbeat wants him to fight, to convince me, of his innocence.

But he does none of those things.

I haven't called Dad to verify Piper's writings, or told Ivy, or confessed to Ahmar. It's like a cancer that sits inside me now, spreading and growing at an alarming rate, but the worst part is, I don't know if talking to any of them will help me shrink this brewing hate.

My mom's dead, and with her went all her secrets. She'd told me she didn't know who my father was—that he was just a one-night-stand who never knew she became pregnant—which was probably a lie.

All my life, I wished for my biological father, but now that I know who he might be, I want to go back to the faceless dad who never knew I existed.

"I should go," Ivy says as she stands, smoothing her mini dress. "And remove this gorgeous atrocity before my parents get here. Are you going to be okay?"

The question comes out tentative, since I've been so distant these past few days, unable to confess, but unable to cover it up well, either. "I'll be fine," I say, pointing at the door with my pen. "Go. I'll see you at the picnic."

"God, I hope my parents don't come in costume," Ivy moans as she leaves my room. "How mortifying would that be?"

"Plan on it," I say helpfully. "Because if I were your mom, that's exactly what I'd do."

Ivy scowls at my answer but breaks into a grin and waves before leaving.

Left to my own devices, I try to work on some schoolwork, but come up empty. I push to my feet and head to the kitchenette instead, scooping some old Halloween chocolate I'd ordered online, but conscious of putting myself out in the open for Emma to see.

My fears are unfounded, because Emma hasn't been around this week. Or if she has, she's done it while I was sleeping, and I do *not* want to think on that possibility too hard. More likely, she's staying at her family's lake house instead of the dorms, an arrangement I'm all too happy to abide by.

I haven't seen much of Eden, either, though I constantly picture them scheming like witches, steepling their hands over a steaming cauldron in the forest as they cackle. Their betrayal is a punch to the gut every time I think about it, but I can't let their stabs to my heart hold true. They were never my friends to begin with. We came together with what I thought was a single goal—to take down Addisyn, then the Virtues—and when that goal failed, I should be glad I walked away unscathed. On the outside, at least.

Instead, I was a tool for their devices. A means to score evidence Addisyn was keeping to herself and didn't tell the Virtues.

I wonder if Addisyn will be punished for hiding pieces of Piper's diary or applauded for it.

It's difficult to know what, or who, to believe.

It shouldn't matter. I'm done.

With the noose of Piper's last words wrapping around my neck, I don't want to think about the Virtues anymore.

A light knock on my door distracts my thoughts, and I pad over to it while dabbing the corners of my mouth with my sleeve.

A light, feminine voice yells, "Surprise!" when I open the door, and my traumatized self almost ducks and covers at the sound.

"Lynda!" I say tremulously, stepping aside to let her and my dad in.

I take note of their matching Thanksgiving shirts under their open winter coats, Lynda's saying, "Momma's Cooking a Turkey" over her bump, and my dad's reading, "I Put the Turkey in the Oven."

"Nice outfits," I say, a smile playing at the corners of my lips while internally mortified.

"We know we were supposed to meet you at the lunch picnic, but Lynda couldn't resist coming up here and surprising you," Dad says.

"It looks exactly the same." Lynda rubs her baby bump in awe as she turns in a slow circle.

"You went here?" I ask.

Lynda turns her head to mine. "Well, sure, honey. How'd you think I snuck you in?"

She smiles and chucks under my chin before wandering around and peeping in first Emma's, then my room. "Where's your roommate?"

"Oh, she's uh, at her family's lake house," I say, at the same time my dad widens his eyes at his wife to shush.

I guess they still think my dead ex-roommate is a sensitive topic. *Oh*, if only they knew.

"How about we go find a good table, huh?" my dad says with forced cheer, trotting after his wife and gently steering her to the front door.

"Great idea," I say, and follow them out.

I'm in Briarcliff sweats and a T-shirt, but I'm not feeling up for dress-up, and Dad and Lynda haven't even noticed. Perhaps they think I'm waiting for tonight to go balls-out and get into turkey spirit now that my punishment's lifted, when really, all I'm going to do is crawl into bed and pray my dreams don't involve my dead mom.

After grabbing my coat, we take our time walking from Thorne House to the academy, mostly because Lynda waddles more than she strides. She thwarted Dad's multiple attempts to bring the car around with a crazed look in her eye—*I will walk, damn it, Pete. This baby's taken enough of my body. Do not take my feet*—so the three of us wander, side-by-side, pointing out pretty pieces of landscaping and gorgeous masonry and stonework around the property.

The small talk is slowly strangling me to death. I can't stand beside my dad without asking the question that's been buzzing in my ears and building its hornet's nest in my throat. "Dad?"

Dad glances down at me. "Hmm?"

"Did Mom ever cheat on you with my biological father?"

Lynda's feet scrape against the concrete. Her hand flutters to her stomach. "Oh, Jesus."

My stepdad pales at the question but launches into action when Lynda looks like she's about to keel over. "Honey? What is it? The baby? Contractions?"

"No." Lynda lifts her hand. "Golly, no. Callie surprised the shit outta me is all."

I raise my brows.

Dad goes to Lynda, anyway, holding a tentative hand against her stomach and wrapping his other arm around Lynda's waist. "It, uh, maybe now's not the time, Cal."

Lynda's lips thin. She doesn't budge when Dad nudges her forward. "Peter. She's asked you a question."

"I..." Dad sighs, digging his fingers into his thinning hair.

"I guess that's answer enough," I say, my stomach turning to stone.

"Cal. Hun. Look at me."

Dad's surprisingly hard tone draws my head up. "It has nothing to do with you. Do you understand me? Your mother loved you. *I* love you."

"But how can you?" My face crumples, and I hate how my vision smears with tears. "After all I've done? After what *Mom* did?"

"Honey." Dad releases Lynda and stumbles up to me, bending until he's in view. His hands clamp around my arms, shaking gentle sense into me. "Meredith didn't deserve to die, and you don't deserve to live a life without a mother and father. She was a flawed human being, and when I found out about the affair, I didn't handle—" He stops, emotion clogging his throat. "I didn't deal with it the way I should've. I lashed out at her, and I terrified you."

"Oh my God." His meaning turns my face numb and cold. "Is that the fight I overheard? You found out about the affair?"

"Callie, baby." Dad holds my cheeks. "Yes. I found out she was seeing this man for years, well before me and well after meeting me. But *you* were right. I'm going to repeat that: You did the right thing. I should've been a suspect, and I should've been held and questioned. And it's because of that arrest that the police found out there was another guy. You did a good thing. Okay?"

"I attacked you," I say, meeting his eye with trembling lips. "When you came home, I tried to hurt you. Badly."

"You weren't yourself, Cal. Your mom's death hit you so, so hard, and I didn't understand it at time. I thought you had no idea. I was floored when you accused me, but I'll never hate you for it."

"But I turned on you." I step out of his hold, and his face falls at the distance. "I became the worst daughter in the world. Partying, drugs, ignoring curfew, screaming at you, cussing at you, wanting you to *die* instead of my mom, and you...?"

"I said I loved you, Callie. That kind of vow means I'll be there for you even at your worst."

"No." I clutch at my temples, unable to mix this version of Pete Spencer with the one that's been in my head the whole time. "You hit my mom."

"I did. And I pay for it every damned day."

Lynda comes up beside him, her cheeks streaming tears, but she takes his hand.

"You put me in the psych ward," I rasp.

"I did. It was either that or lose you, Callie. The court was coming for me, saying I wasn't fit to be a father to you, and I ... you'd lost control. I didn't know how..."

Dad stops, the thickened emotion in his voice making it difficult to continue, but he blinks and forges on, his voice in tatters. "I had no idea how to move us out of our rotten existence. All I knew is that I didn't want to lose you as well as your mother. You had a home with me. I'm sorry—I'm so sorry I didn't say that to you every day, but even when you were in the hospital, you had a home. I wasn't going to give you up, and I promised myself to be a better man, a better *father*, than the one I was turning into."

"Dad..." I say.

"Callie," Lynda whispers, her lower lip shaking. She opens her arms. "Come here. Please. This doesn't change one bit of your position in our family, okay? You're this baby's sister. Her beautiful, admirable *sister*."

She means to draw me closer, but instead, I'm drifting away. My voice takes on a raw edge. "I could be someone else's sister. Was this man, this guy Mom kept seeing, my father?"

Dad shakes his head forlornly. "I don't know that, honey."

"Do you know who he is?"

Again, he shakes his head. "The night you overheard ... she refused to tell me his name. I was hoping, after I admitted it while in police custody, Ahmar could track him down."

My voice cracks into shards. "Ahmar *knew*?"

"Callie."

My name is sent out into the air with such sharp, ragged undertones, that I draw back. But my dad won't let me. He envelopes me into his arms, hugging me so tight I can only take small breaths.

"You're my daughter," he whispers into my ear. "And I'm sorry. I'm sorry. I'm sorry."

His laments repeat into my skin, dampen my hair, and he doesn't let go. He keeps holding on until I wrap my hands around him, until I'm sobbing, too, and for the first time in over a year, I'm hugging the man who stepped into the role as my father nine years ago.

"I didn't show you before," he says. "You were suffering, and I wasn't doing enough to help you. I know that now. And I will fight for you always." I've never heard him cry before, and it's wrenching. "You belong here, with us. I don't want our wretched past to define our relationship. I want this baby to see you as a sister, and Lynda to see you as a daughter, and for you to see us as a family. Could you do that? Can we try?"

His tone comes in broken waves, and with each crest, I'm pummeled, sobbing harder at his words. My fingers claw into his back as I pull him closer, and added, fragrant pressure against my side tells me Lynda's joined the hug, too.

"I can try," I whisper, so low I doubt they'll hear.

I am so, so tired of being alone, and my baser instinct recognizes this as a pivotal turning point—if I deny them, then from now on, I'll be orphaned by choice.

One day, I'll have to forgive my mom for what she did, and although I know it won't come soon or be easy, I'm certain it will happen. Because she was my mother.

If I can't give my stepdad the same consideration, what does that make me?

I'll tell you: it makes me someone who can't keep love.

"Oh, sweetie." Dad kisses my wet temple while Lynda dampens the other side of my head.

They heard me.

Something bumps against my side, and I pull away enough to look down, because all our arms are around our shoulders. "What was that?"

Lynda laughs, then rests a hand on her belly. "That's Blair saying hello. Do you want to feel it again?"

My eyes stretch wide.

Lynda's lips pull into a shimmering smile. "She's not an alien. Well, I'd argue she's more of a parasite, but go on. Put your hand right here."

I hesitantly lift my hand, pressing it right over turkey baby's red cartoon heart.

Another *bop* against the middle of my palm. And another.

"Holy crap," I say.

"Callie, meet your baby sister. She's going to annoy the crap out of you," Lynda says.

I grin up at her, my joy filled with snot and tears, but tangible.

Lynda kisses my cheek, then says to both me and Dad, "Enough blubbering. We're going to miss the turkey roast, and you do *not* want to know me if I don't get my daily meat intake."

We fall back in line and walk close for the rest of the way to the academy.

For the first time since losing Mom, I can't help but think, maybe this cross-stitched family heart doesn't have to feel so knotted anymore.

The picnic area put together around the wolf fountain behind the school is packed with students, parents, guardians, professors, and all kinds of standing heat lamps, and I manage to score us a recently vacated picnic bench while Dad goes and fills our plates.

"Take a seat," I say to Lynda while gathering dirty paper plates and cups. "I'm just gonna toss these."

Lynda doesn't argue, choosing to plop onto the bench with a prolonged groan.

I meander through the crowd, passing the makeshift stage near the wolf-barf fountain where the Music Club has set up their rock band. They're going for the family-friendly vibe and playing soft rock.

The clotted crowds of people choosing to stand rather than sit cause me to zig and zag to the closest trash can, and I let out a squeak of sound when I'm on top of Chase's table before I can safely retreat.

Every single pair of eyes looks up at me. The stone in my stomach gains more cinder-blocks the longer I'm frozen in place.

Chase is the closest, and his face changes when he notices me, an inscrutable pain flashing through his features before he glances away. Emma stares hard with her implacable aim, while Daniel Stone and his estranged first wife, Chase and Emma's mother, look on curiously.

Sadly, they've also decided to sit with the Harringtons.

Those cinder-blocks become body weights sinking me to the bottom of the ocean.

I can't look at Mr. Harrington, at the same time I do, but I cut my gaze away before any emotion flickers across my face. I'm surprised at the lack of feeling when I meet his eye for one meager second. I'm not shocked at the numbness, because it's already been an emotionally draining day, but in that short time, his features were seared into my mind—burnished hair shot with gray, blue-green eyes, tanned skin and the faint lines of a crow's feet smile around his eyes, which I'm sure would crinkle further if he actually moved his lips.

I see him. I note our similarities. Our vast differences.

And I feel ... nothing.

My skirted gaze lands on Addisyn, who gives me a benign smile, fluttering her fingers in a mocking wave, and Mrs. Harrington, soon-to-be Mrs. Stone, a platinum blonde with dark skin, sits regally at the end, squinting as she tries to place me.

Addisyn purrs, "Mom, *Dad*, I'd like you to meet Briarcliff's newest student, Calla Lily Ryan. Mr. Stone, Miss Loughrey, have you met her?"

Chase's dad murmurs something and shakes his head, but doesn't take his eyes off me. And if Ice Queens were real, I would've been petrified into a statue from Mrs. Harrington's gaze alone.

Mr. Harrington—my possible *father*—clears his throat. "I ... I don't believe we have."

"Perhaps ... Calla Lily, is it? ... should be seated with her own family," Mrs. Harrington says, while her eyes politely communicate *fuck the hell off*.

The barest brush tickles my waist, and I glance down to see Chase's hand retreating to his lap, but it couldn't possibly have been him offering reassurance. He's ignored me for days and will probably resume pretending I don't exist once I leave the table.

I'm not sure what kind of warped family arrangement I've stumbled into, but I'm more than happy to prevent this confrontation from happening right on the heels of my healing session with my stepdad.

"It was nice ... to meet you," I force out, refusing to include Mr. Harrington. "I'm just gonna—"

"Addisyn Harrington?"

The rough voice of authority catches my attention, and I blink at the ensuing scene, unsure if it's real.

Detective Haskins leads the way through the mingling picnic-goers, with three cops coming up behind him, the crowd parting with whispers and gasps as he stops at the table.

Annoyance flashes across Addisyn's face before she turns. "Yeah?"

"What's this about?" Mr. Harrington asks.

Mrs. Harrington rises at the same time her ex-husband does, and though she's a head smaller, her very essence fizzles out any authority Mr. Harrington tries to gather.

She can fell a man with her stare, and she directs all that power at Detective Haskins. "State your position immediately, Detective, because I've already called our lawyers."

"Happy to." Haskins positively beams, immune to Mrs. Harrington's intimidation. "Addisyn Harrington, you're under arrest for suspicion of first-degree murder of Piper Harrington..."

Whispers turn to shouts. Gasps turn to screams.

Someone claps.

"*What?*" Addisyn shrieks, but doesn't move. Haskins decides to help her by pulling her hands behind her back.

"Get your *hands* off my daughter, you deplorable man!" Mrs. Harrington bellows, flipping her jacket lapels back as she strides around the table to get to her remaining daughter. Her face is so frozen in fury, it trembles.

Haskins replies, without looking up, "Don't you come near me, ma'am, or else I'll cuff you, too."

Mrs. Harrington turns redder than Ivy's feathered turkey ass. "How *dare* you—"

"Sabine," Mr. Harrington says, grabbing his former wife's arm. "Perhaps you should let the man do his job. We'll call our lawyers, and—"

"You pathetic, miserable turd!" she hisses at her husband. "Your daughter is being arrested, and your other daughter is *dead. DO SOMETHING!*"

Mr. Harrington fumbles in his jacket for his phone, but Daniel Stone beats him to it.

"I'm Addisyn's lawyer. Show me the papers," he bellows, his hand darting out.

Haskins gestures to the officers behind him, who hands Mr. Stone the warrant.

In an attempt to take in more than the central scuffle, I glance first at Chase, who seems just as bemused as me, then at Emma, catching her eye in a way that tells me she's been watching me this entire time.

She smiles.

I clear my throat of the slime that crawls to its base, mouthing, *What the fuck?*

But she shakes her head. Now isn't the time.

I, however, can't close my mouth. Was I just bamboozled by her *again*?

"Callie," Chase says, and I jolt at his sudden presence at my side. "We need to leave. Before this gets out of hand."

"I'm just standing here," I say. "What could possibly happen to me—"

And as if I asked for it, Mrs. Harrington lands her steely gaze on me. "*You.*"

"Now, Sabine..." Mr. Harrington says, throwing a hand between us.

I frown at my supposed, maybe father, at his utter weakness in this situation. Yes, humans are flawed, and yes, his youngest daughter is a kin-killer, but shouldn't he be handling this with a bit more rage right now? Instead he's ... oh, man. The word hits me between the eyes.

He's unsurprised. By any of this.

"We're leaving. *Now*," Chase commands, then drags me back.

We're through the crowd and near the edges before I comprehend my hand in his, our fingers entwined. "Chase..."

He tears from my hold, his warmth retreating as fast as if I doused his flames with lake water. "Go be with your family."

I gape at him. "You can't *possibly* expect me to—Did you know about this? What your sister planned? How did the police know to arrest Addisyn? Why have they made it so public?"

Chase lets out a frustrated sigh but doesn't push me back into the crowd. "I read a piece of the warrant as my dad held it. They have the diary pages, Callie."

I hesitate, but persist. "Are they enough? Is the arrest going to stick? Or is it more of a Dr. Luke situation where she'll be released by fancy lawyers, like your *dad*—"

Chase levels me with a look. "There's a confession tape, too. Now *go*. Before Sabine Harrington loses her shit on you and your secret's out."

My secret. Right. I'm a possible Harrington heir.

Ugh, the thought disgusts me.

Yet, I can't leave. "Confession tape?"

Chase gives me a sidelong glance. "Think about it, sweet possum."

And I do. Addisyn said a lot of culpable shit to me when we were in her room ... and Emma and Eden were standing right outside.

"One of them recorded it," I murmur.

Perhaps, they aren't the savage and heartless lizards I thought they were. But they sure are experts at mind-fuckery.

"Since when was I put on a need-to-know basis?" I demand.

Chase's features go tight, as if he's stopping himself from saying something he'll regret.

I force my thoughts inward rather than argue with him, aware of my penchant for saying and doing things I'm later ashamed to admit.

What Emma and Eden did to me might've been fake, but the words I'd spewed at Chase afterward? Those were real.

"I'm sorry," I whisper, but his only acknowledgment is to put a light hand on my back and gently push me into the gathering crowd.

Thirty-Five

THE REST of the Family Day picnic is a complete wash, Headmaster Marron having to intervene and do a long speech in an attempt to distract from the public scandal involving one of his flourishing, most promising students.

Again.

The gathering parted ways, Lynda murmuring a long, sad goodbye to her untouched turkey platter as we exited the quad and they took me back to my room.

"Let me say, scenes like that did *not* happen when I was in attendance," Lynda says as we amble with the rest of the families down the pathway. Then, her eyes widen with conspiracy. "But what a *rush* that was."

"You must be happy with this, Cal," Dad says to me. "Your roommate's case is finally solved. I know I'm glad to hear it. I was worried about who could be wandering campus, meaning harm."

"Yeah," I say, though I put no conviction behind my statement.

"Do you want to come home, honey?"

Lynda's question hitches my steps, the genuine warmth behind it flipping my stomach.

"You've more than proven yourself," Lynda continues gently. "You've worked hard to show us your willingness to change. But if you're not happy here, you can come with us. Right now. If you want to."

Dad shares an affectionate, admiring look with Lynda, then squeezes my shoulder. "Lynda's right. I may have sent you away ... in haste. Perhaps it'll be easier to mend fences with us all together."

I want to say yes.

It's tempting, so incredibly easy, to leave this fucked-up school with its dangerous societies, fixed grades, and chauvinistic games far behind.

But, coming home would mean facing my mother's treachery. Forgiving my stepdad whole-heartedly. And I genuinely don't know if I'm ready for that.

Besides ... Ivy ... and Chase.

Relationships I'm not ready to release.

"I think I'd like to stay," I say.

"Are you sure?" Dad's caterpillar brows come crashing down. "Because it doesn't seem like you're comfortable here."

I can't deny the observation, so I work on a deal. "I'll stay until Christmas. Come home for Thanksgiving. And we can talk on both of those holidays. I'd like to take my time making such a big decision in my life, you know? I want to make sure I'm doing the right thing, by staying or leaving."

The skin around Lynda's eyes creases with a smile. She notices my prolonged stare, but doesn't take it the way I mean it to come across: *you're beautiful when you smile. I hope my dad deserves you.* "Lord," she says, rubbing one corner of her eye. "I miss my damn Botox."

I snort, and Dad catches me by the shoulder and pulls me to his side. "Deal. We'll reevaluate then, but any time you change your mind, you call us. It's not just you that'll turn over a new leaf at this point. I will, too. And it starts with working on my patience and ... *trying* ... to trust your judgment."

I nod, focusing on his willingness to work with me and not against me, and we part ways outside Thorne House, Lynda squeezing me tight, and the baby kicking me in the gut. Dad's hug is more tentative, but it holds more promise of a fatherly touch than it has in years.

"See ya next weekend, Cal," he says, studying me softly before taking his wife's hand and heading down the drive.

I wait until I can't see them anymore, then enter my dorm with a sort of melancholy cheer. Overjoyed that Addisyn got what was coming to her, happy that my relationship with my stepdad is on the mend, but heavy with Chase's and my argument, the societies' continued rule, and Dr. Luke's strange visit that lead to a crucial clue. Basically—I'm torn over all the unrest Briarcliff protects.

Was choosing to stay the right thing to do?

I step into my room with hunched shoulders, ready to pack it in instead of locate a turkey costume. I'll have to text Ivy, but other than that, I can quietly slip under the covers and...

A folded note on top of my laptop catches my attention.

Curious, I open it, recognizing Chase's handwriting.

Going old school for this, sweet possum, but I feel it's warranted. So, here's a letter instead of a text.

We have a lot to figure out.

Meet me at the boathouse at sunset? I'll be the guy with a fucking turkey painted on his chest.

Oh, and the only dude at the end of the dock.

A wistful smile crosses my lips before I can scold it into a frown. Checking the clock, I calculate about an hour's worth of time to get ready before meeting him.

Because yes, I'm meeting him, and while he has some explaining to do with regards to my phone and all my missing evidence, no, I will not be listening to him in day-old sweats and unwashed hair.

I shower, shave, blow-dry, and make-up until I'm satisfied. There's no time to put together a costume, so I put on leather pants and an artfully destroyed $60 white T-shirt, both "seasonal" and gifted by Lynda, figuring I'll be creative and say I was attacked by a turkey.

The forested pathway to the boathouse is silent as I descend, most students attending off-campus parties or dorm room pre-games, the Turkey Trot in full swing and the drunken recapping of Addisyn's arrest at full tilt. The rare few who would find themselves on this path will probably be here to hook-up, so I clomp as fast and quietly as I can through the trees, hopeful not to see anyone's bared full moon.

I reach the clearing, the golden hour of the sun hitting the placid lake like molten metal, the ripples of the lake glittering with the shards of sunlit diamonds.

I'm early, so I'm not concerned when I don't see any figure waiting for me at the end of the dock.

Moving to the boat house's side door, I creak it open, glad it's unlocked, and head to one of the boat bays opening up into the lake, figuring I'll enjoy the view before Chase and I grow serious, and maybe, have a true discussion for once, with equal give and take.

A girl can hope.

There's no figure, but something—an object—catches my eye at the end of the dock. Tentatively, I make my way over, thinking maybe Chase has left me something in his stead. I cringe as I throw my hands out for balance, the quiet laps of water under the dock more threatening than calming.

Chase is lucky I like him so much. He's the only person who's managed to get me to walk to the end of this floating piece of driftwood more than once.

I stay well in the middle, my boots making clomping, hollow sounds, punctuated only by the lonesome calls of birds not yet asleep in their nests.

Once I'm close enough to make out the object through the fast-setting sun, I notice the white rose laid out at the end, a fluttering note attached to it.

My immediate reaction is to sneer. I hate this form of communication—these damn roses—but if it's here, then someone knew I was coming and wants me to read it before I see Chase.

These secret admirer gifts have never harmed me before, so I walk forward until the end of the stem brushes the tip of my boot.

The same breeze lifts my hair as I bend down to pick up the exquisitely bloomed flower and read the note, attached to the stem with a black ribbon.

Unfolding the expensive, thick paper, I read the simple embossed sentence, then blink and read it again.

You're in.

Huh?

I glance up, staring at the forest on the other side of the lake, like it can provide me with answers.

A howl rises up behind me, but it can't be a wolf. Or a bear, because it sounds too human.

I put a name to the cry, and it rips from my throat. *"Chase!"*

I move—

Until two hands slam into my back and push me into the lake.

Fiend

One

MY DEATH IS SILENT.

On the outside, the quiet is suffocating. My ears are clogged. My limbs hit nothing. My voice is strangled and without breath.

I'm sinking into the black, but my eyes are wide open.

Bubbles of the remaining life I cling to escape my lips, though I can't see them, not even when I tilt my head skyward, my hands curled into claws, desperate to grab *something*.

Water runs through my fingers, thick and viscous, but not tangible enough to lift me to the surface and gasp for air.

I can't swim.

My mind understands this, but my body refuses to concede. It jerks, seizes, *flails*, and yet I'm sinking, down, down...

Inside, I scream. Inside, my heart refuses to die. It pounds against my ribcage, my rebellious pulse transmitting the frantic message to my neck, banging against my eardrums and shrieking into my mind: *Swim! Swim, damn it!*

I try. Oh God, I'm trying, but nothing ripples above. There's no break in the black, the sea claiming me as easily as a stone plinking into its depths.

Chase.

My last thought is of him, the tightening in my chest swelling to unbearable levels. I'm choking because I'm refusing to allow my body to do what it does best: breathe.

There's no oxygen down here. No life.

But I...

My chest seizes. My eyes pop wide. I stop flailing and wrap panicked fingers around my neck, my instincts taking control.

Don't try to suck in air. Don't breathe.

My mouth opens.

393

Lake water fills the one spot it hasn't claimed, rushing into my lungs.

I gag.

Squeeze my throat.

Burn from the inside out.

A strand of hair tickles the side of my cheek as I stare into the horror of dying...

Hands clamp under my arms.

I've curled inward, my eyes rolling back into my head, but a small spot at the base of my brain communicates a crucial fact: *Someone has you.*

Water splices against my body as I'm pulled, up and up, a sliver of moonlight piercing the surface of the lake the closer I'm led to the top.

Those same hands switch to my waist, propping me against their side until my head breaks through the water.

A horrible, grotesque noise I've never heard before escapes through my airways, my nose and throat spluttering. Lake water warmed from my lungs is vomited out.

I scramble for a handhold as I cough with painful heaves, hollowed-out barks escaping my throat as my eyes stay scrunched shut.

They won't open after being stretched to their limits, the underwater prison creating an ironic dry grit that scrapes against my lids every time I try.

"Easy," a voice says behind me. "I got you."

They guide my hand to a piece of wood, curling my hands around its edge. "Hold on tight."

"Wh—wh—..." I'm seized by another coughing spasm.

"Slow breaths," the same person says, rubbing my back as I move to grip the dock with both hands. Water laps at my elbows. I'm exposed to the air from my shoulders up, but too much of me remains buried in the deep.

"Let me—" I gulp. "Get me—get me out. Lift me up."

"I ... I can't, Callie."

That voice, the musical, familiar lilt of it, starts to make sense. I blink, scrunching down hard, then force my eyes open.

At first, all I see is a panel of wood, moist and slippery from mildew and reeking of the same scent. But I twist my neck—*oh*, until the person holding onto the dock beside me, the one who saved me, centers in my view.

"...Ivy?"

Her ice blonde hair is slicked back and flat against her head, wisps of it floating around her shoulders where the lake still claims it. Thick, dampened eyelashes border her wide, worried gaze, droplets of water clinging to her brows, her nose, the crease of her upper lip.

She doesn't say anything, just continues to regard me with that anxious, frightened stare.

"How..." I clear my throat. "What's going on? Who pushed me?"

She licks her lips, a bead of water dissolving on the tip of her tongue. She glances up, over the dock, then back at me.

"You got what you wanted," she whispers.

"I—what?"

"Calla Lily Ryan," another voice says. "My, oh my..."

The careless tone stiffens my shoulders, despite my feet treading uselessly underwater.

Shoes clomp closer, stopping at my fingertips. A heavy, golden cloak flutters around the ankles, and I know, before I continue my upward survey, who owns this unconcerned gait.

"Falyn," I grit out. My hands clamp harder around the dock's edge, readying for her heel to come down on my fingers and send me screaming back into the murky depths.

A full-body shudder overtakes that thought, and I swallow the impending bile.

Ivy's here, I reason. *She won't let that happen to me again.*

But why *is* she here? And why did she allow it to happen the first time? I could blame the grogginess of almost drowning, but in truth, my subconscious has collected more suspicions about Ivy than my present mind ever did.

"Did you find the answers you were looking for down there?" Falyn asks with a smile.

Every molecule in my body wants to *get out*, get dry, get *away*, but Falyn blocks my scuttle to the ladder by laying the tip of her shoe on my fingertips.

She says to Ivy, "Has your time with this water-logged possum softened your heart so much that you couldn't leave her without a swim buddy for two seconds?"

Ivy tips her chin to Falyn, adding a glare. "You shouldn't have pushed her. It's too dangerous. Callie doesn't know the docks like we do. She could've swum up and hit her head. Or been caught in the anchoring ropes. It was a stupid move, Fal."

Ivy and I lock eyes over the rippling water against our jawlines, her expression stiff with a silent, desperate message she tries to send my way. I read the warning through her squinted gaze.

Falyn has no idea I can't swim.

I give Ivy a minuscule nod.

"Everything we do is dangerous," Falyn says. A breeze ruffles her cloak, pushing the hood wider, and I catch the twisted glee written across her features. She looks down at me. "And the beginning of a serious awakening."

My fingers ache with their hard clench. The adrenaline drifts away with the same speed, and I kick my jellied legs in an attempt to raise myself higher. "Not to be a buzzkill, but can we finish your life lessons on land?"

Instead of being insulted, Falyn answers with a low, languid laugh. She glances behind her. I follow her gaze to a line of Cloaks, waiting silently ten feet away. Seven of them stand as straight and stiff as chess pieces, save for the ominous movement of their gold-threaded robes, fluttering in the night breeze.

Falyn turns back to me. "I assume you managed to read the two words in your invitation before you were butt-kicked into the lake."

My mouth turns grim. "Yes. I'm in. Now let me up."

She doesn't step back or lay off my fingers. Instead, Falyn's grin grows wider. "I'm guessing you didn't have time to turn the card over."

"*Stop*, Falyn," Ivy says next to me. "We're freezing. Let's finish this when you give us some towels, at least."

Falyn ignores her. "Let me be the bearer, then."

Falyn picks up the thick card that fluttered from my fingers to the edge of the dock when I was pushed.

"It says." Falyn stops to clear her throat. "'If you choose to accept your first initiation rite, you will land on the path to become one of us.' You're not a Virtue yet, Callie."

Controlling the shivers in my voice, I respond, "I'm still trying to pinpoint when I accepted being pushed into a lake."

"Oops." Falyn's lips curve.

My face doesn't betray my thoughts as I scan behind Falyn toward these girl soldiers who must be awaiting Falyn's orders.

Is Falyn really their leader? I find it difficult, even while flailing around half-submerged from her doing, to see her at the top of a secret society pyramid.

"Do you want the key to our temple?" Falyn asks me, her voice candy-coated and thin.

"*Falyn*," Ivy hisses.

"You didn't go through all this trouble for nothing, did you?" Falyn arches her brows as she regards me below her. "Here's something you can accept: Go fetch."

"What?" I look from Falyn to Ivy in hopes Ivy can explain, but Ivy's face is either too numb from cold, or she's too stunned and horrified to move her muscles.

"This isn't good for me, is it?" I mutter to Ivy.

She blinks. Swallows. Her eyes soften, shimmering with warm tears against the cold drops of water in her lashes. "I'm so sorry, Callie."

"You're one of them, aren't you?" I whisper in return, but my words are so much hotter than hers. She doesn't respond, which is answer enough. "How could you not tell me?"

Ivy answers with a moan. "I thought I was keeping you from the worst."

"Are you done with your pep-talk, Ivy?" Falyn asks from above. "Your bleeding heart can only go so far in this scenario. You know the rules. Callie's on her own. Come up and leave her to it."

Ivy braces her hands on the dock.

"You lied to me?" I whisper hoarsely.

Ivy pauses before she lifts out of the lake, her elbows spearing to the sky. She turns her head and whispers through stiff lips, "Kick off your shoes. Underneath the dock are vertical slats of wood. It's what keeps the platform secure and floating. In between those slats are pockets of air."

I find enough space in my lungs to say, "What?"

"Grip those slats. Hold your breath and pop up for air whenever you can. You can do this."

"What the fuck, Ivy—"

Water sloshes when she lifts herself up in a streamlined move. Once her knees are on the dock, she rises to a stand. Her clothes are stuck to her body and soak my trembling hands when she moves to stand beside Falyn.

"Welcome to your first test of allegiance," Falyn says. "You're a late-term pledge, but that doesn't exempt you from what the rest of us had to endure."

Ivy lays a hand on Falyn's robed arm, and my face spasms with the agony of betrayal, but I do as she says. I toe off my shoes and picture them sinking, down, down, and landing silently on the brackish lake floor.

"Your key to our temple is tied under this dock," Ivy says. "Find it, and you'll succeed in becoming a Baroness."

I go cold on the inside, its spreading icicles leaving frost on my numbed skin. "I..."

"Get it over with, Callie," Ivy cuts in. "I'm not going anywhere."

"Or don't," Falyn is all too happy to add. "Frankly, the queen gave you an easy in. If you can't do this much, then you *definitely* don't belong with us."

Queen?

"Who's your queen?" I ask, my throat shrinking in size. Falyn may not know I can't swim and thinks this task is letting me off the hook, but ... and my stomach sinks as I look to Ivy ... what about the person in charge? Did she require this specific hazing because she's aware of my handicap?

A clawing ominousness clamps around my heart as I quietly answer my own question. Falyn's been put in charge of my initiation—that's evidence enough.

Despite every part of me *pleading* with Ivy, she gives a slight shake of her head. Ivy can't—or won't—do anything besides offer silent support.

"You'll meet our queen when she deems you worthy," Falyn says. "Now hurry up and dunk. We've got parties to get to."

My hands turn into Arctic-level claws. I risk dipping my chin into the water, then choke on a terrified squeal and shrink closer to the dock when it laps over my mouth.

I can't do this. I may be as close as I've ever been to uncovering what Piper might've died for, but I can't face my fear. I refuse to willingly drown for—

"Oh, fuck this," Falyn says, then kicks at my fingers until they rip from the dock.

Two

I DON'T GIVE into the hysteria of freaking out. It didn't do me any good the first time, and I refuse to be rescued a second time ... if any savior would come.

As soon as lake water covers my face, I scramble for the dock, gripping its underside to keep from sinking.

There isn't enough breath in my lungs. Even if I prepared for Falyn's move, there wasn't time for a big gulp of air.

Meaning, I need oxygen. Now.

My heart pounds against my ears, and a blaring panic alarm lances through my system, but I force myself to give into the quiet and think. *THINK.*

In my desperate scrabble, I'm gripping the bottom of the dock. I have no idea where to turn to find the edge, and I can't swim to find it.

I can't swim.

Ivy's words prod the back of my skull. I'd waste precious time questioning them, so I release one hand and let it explore for a neighboring slat, my legs assisting as much as they can with hard, uncoordinated kicks.

The backs of my fingers hit a vertical plank, and I grip it with all my might and do an underwater pull-up until my nose is pressed against the slime and decay of submerged wood.

With my lips pursed and jaw working like a fish's, I search for the kiss of air, however small, to meet my lips.

Water peels back from my face, its waves climbing up my cheeks at each small ripple of movement, but it's enough to suck in the stink of limited oxygen and blink my eyes.

Black. It's so black under here, and my ears are submerged and blocked from sound. But I feel footsteps up above, one pair crashing down harder than the others, and I swear I hear a voice hollering *"Where is she?"* through the clogged clamshells of my ears.

My heart crashes and ricochets along the walls of my entire body, emitting the obvious threat to my life in urgent, pulsing bursts, but my emotions won't get me out of this.

I keep Ivy's advice in mind as I gulp in breaths and tentatively move my grip up and back, testing each hand's strength. Flooded, manmade wood is so different than it is on land. Slimy. Soft. Almost pliable. Certainly not easy to use to keep my head above water.

If I slip ... I'm done for.

As if calling on fate, my arms and hands tremble and ache under the strain.

I can't stay still much longer. If I keep my body this stiff, I'll have no hope of clinging to the surface.

Don't freak out.

Falyn said the key is tied somewhere under this dock. What would it be attached to?

Someone must've swum this path before me to leave the key. Would they be adventurous, or would they want to get the fuck out of here like I do?

Ropes. Ivy mentioned ropes.

With that illustrious amount of information zinging through my mind, I move carefully forward, my fingers slipping with each forced maneuver.

When my left hand catches a sharp piece of wood, I cry out and release it on instinct, water cascading back into my lungs.

Nononono.

I struggle for another hold, kicking and thrashing, and manage to find another thin beam and hold on, angling my head to meet another small pocket of air.

Using my legs this time, I swing out, searching to hit something—hopefully a rope tied from the dock to the lake floor. I keep swinging, keep pressing forward, praying either my leg or my hands hit gold.

At last, I feel a tight, thick rope against my thigh. It's angled, probably from one end of the dock and anchored to the floor, so I use it like a monkey and wrap my socked toes around its width to push my body up and give my hands the tiniest break. I balance on it, my knees bent under me, searching with every sense I can for the feel of a key.

I come up with nothing.

Whimpering, I pry my numbed toes off the rope and find another one.

I beg my hands to keep their strength and help me move a little bit forward, but when my foot slips and all of me falls under, I'm close to failing, instead.

Can I die for this?

My body sings its denial. My brain voices its extreme concern. I'm made up of nothing but bickering parts, my conscience and motivations ceding ground as instinct takes over.

I find another hold on the rope and push up for air, and when I do, my toe catches on a ring of something, hard and unlike the scratchy slime of the rope.

The key?

It's near my foot. Somehow, I have to willingly release my grip on one slat, bury my face in water, and get it.

"*Callie? Callie!*"

The voice is above me, my one exposed ear picking up the hollow clomps of boots.

"*Can you hear me?*" comes a water-clogged follow-up.

"Yes!" I cry, then cough against the sloshing of water around my mouth.

"*Follow my voice. I'll get you out of there.*"

I sense the sound of the voice drifting left, and I instinctively move toward it, my toes curling over the rope as I use it for a guide.

The key.

Gritting my teeth, I try one time. Just once. My legs have bent enough that I have the right balance, and if I keep my left hand on the wooden beam, gulp an inhale, and dunk low enough to...

My free hand closes on nothing but water. But I persevere, my heart hammering its extreme displeasure.

I scrabble forward as much as I can, swiping blindly for what doesn't belong down here, scraping along the rope and searching for the object.

When I hit what feels like a ribbon tied in a bow, I don't question it. I feel for an end, pull to unravel the knot, then grab the ribbon before it floats down, joining my shoes in their watery grave.

Sharp metal hits my palm.

I burst up with my feet, jerking off balance but maintaining it on the rope, and force my lips not to open too wide as I gasp for more briny oxygen.

"*Callie!*"

"I'm here! I'm coming!"

After shoving the key under my shirt and in my bra, I follow the voice all the way, ducking into the water only when I hit the next beam and have to pass under it.

Soon, there are no more beams to grip. My hand smacks against the side of the dock, searching, *hoping* this is the end, and when I feel a warm, calloused palm cover mine, I nearly weep with gratitude.

He pulls, and after a loud gulp of air, I let myself go under with my hand enfolded in his.

My body follows the current of his strength. I give one last push, and this time, when I curve around the dock and my head breaks the surface, I'm surrounded by the wide, empty space of air.

Sputtering, I allow hands to come under my arms and pull me up. I hear Ivy on one side, her voice so panicked that I can't decipher what she's saying.

A towel comes around my shoulders, and when a familiar scent envelops me, I finally open my eyes.

Chase's face eclipses the moon as he stares down at me. He's bare-chested with black feathers painted between his pecs. Some kind of costume for the Turkey trot tonight, a party I was hoping we'd attend together, after I met him here. Before...

I've been propped into a seated position, my legs splayed out, and I'm covered in emergency blankets from the boathouse. He swipes his hands down my cheeks, cupping my jaw, his expression urgent. But his eyes are dark with fury.

I'm certain he doesn't say anything because he's too overcome with rage to speak. His lower lip trembles with the same emotion, his jawline rigid and sharp as a knife. He slides one arm under the backs of my knees and the other around my shoulders—

"No," I choke out, despite the shivering, visceral need to fall into his arms and lay my head on his chest. "I can stand."

"You sure?"

His words are soft but laced with a gathering storm.

I shuffle forward. "I can—"

A mocking, disgusted voice sounds out, "Oh, come *on,* Callie, don't use your epic failure to become a damsel and let Chase carry you off into happily ever after. Have some self-respect."

I glance to the side, unsurprised that Falyn is the first to speak, but Willow stands next to her, and so does Violet, their hoods pulled back and their hair glinting under the dock's singular lamplight.

Yet, they appear frazzled, their expressions twitchy and their eyes darting between Chase and Tempest, who stands nearby, glowering with his arms crossed. The other robed Virtues have scattered closer to the boathouse, risking glances, but otherwise whispering to each other and straying from the scene.

"It's not like that was hard," Willow pipes up, but shrinks under Tempest's answering growl.

"You okay?" Chase murmurs near my ear.

I nod, even though I am far, *far* from okay.

"Too bad," Falyn sneers. "I was *really* looking forward to you becoming a member of our society."

"I'm..." I clear my throat from the lingering panic that spreads across my vocal cords like the jagged pieces of coral. "I'm flattered. Because I have your fucking key."

Falyn's expression goes blank. Chase braces beside me.

She says, "Excuse me?"

Ivy, staying near, smiles at the same time her body sags in relief.

Falyn asks quietly, "You what?"

"Hey, you said this was one of the easier tests, right?" With a trembling hand, I loosen the blanket around my shoulders and pull the key out from my cleavage, its silver curves catching the beam of light as it dangles from my fingers.

I'm awed by its old-fashioned beauty, heavy with solid metal and smooth with its three half-circles at the top. I slide it off the sodden ribbon and into my palm, my fingers curling over the stem.

"I believe this is mine now?" I ask on a rasp.

Falyn's expression goes rigid. She glances at Willow, Ivy, Tempest, Chase—anyone who might have an answer for this unfortunate twist of fate.

When no one offers their opinion, Falyn gathers herself, standing taller. "Fine. Bravo. You've passed the first round."

"Give her more credit than that," Chase says, standing. He crooks out an arm as he rises, so I can take hold and push to my feet with him. My legs ache with the effort. "Since I doubt this was orchestrated by your queen." Chase's jawline cascades with shadow when he pinpoints Willow. "Am I right on that, Will?"

Willow folds her arms into her chest, refusing to meet his eye. Tempest arches a brow at her. "Lies got your tongue, headmaster junior?"

"Like it matters," Falyn snaps out, then points a shaking finger at me. "She would've had to undergo a similar ritual in the temple. I was just the expeditor. Our queen will be—"

"Pissed," Chase supplies. "But sadly, her ire won't come close to the retribution I'm about to seek."

Falyn's lip trembles. She steps back. "You don't have that kind of power over me."

Chase idly checks his cuticles with his free hand. "Don't I?"

"Being the prince of the Nobles doesn't give you the authority to direct me," Falyn says, but her voice isn't as firm.

"You Virtues." Chase clucks his tongue, and while everything about him appears languid and at ease, the arm I grip is taut with barely constrained anger. "Does our mutual rulebook not say that if a Virtuous member attacks a Noble prince's soulmate, the prince may exact any punishment he wishes?"

Willow gasps.

Ivy steps to my other side but stares over my head at Chase. "Are you serious?"

Tempest slides his fingers along his chin, chuckling mirthlessly. "Should've seen that one coming, ladies."

Falyn's mouth works before she says to Chase, "You don't have a soulmate anymore. And our princess can override—"

"You don't have a princess, either," Chase counters. "She's dead."

I add quietly, "I'm—I'm having trouble following this argument."

"Callie Ryan is *not* your soulmate," Falyn says, drawing closer. "Piper was."

Chase withdraws his arm from mine, wrapping it around my shoulders and pulling me closer. "I've chosen a new one. The rules stand."

"*No,*" Falyn whispers, and casts her glare on me.

Her face contorts with fury, hatred, targeted disgust. Her upper lip peels back. "You don't belong with us. You only have access to the societies because it'd be too obvious if we seriously injured you and left you for dead. Admit it. You have no place as a Virtue."

She's right. All I want to do is take them down. For Piper, Emma, Eden … me. And every other girl who's crossed their paths and been veered into their orchestrated trauma.

I'm about to agree—

"Aren't you curious to hear my punishment for forcing Callie to find a key she has every right to?" Chase asks, a soft cadence to his voice. Too lenient.

"You don't choose our members," Falyn hisses at him.

"You're right. The queen does. And she chose Callie." Chase cocks his head. "Get in the water, Falyn."

"*Fuck* you," she retorts.

"Get under the docks."

"I will *not.*"

"And hold your breath for as long as I tell you to."

"*I will not!*" Falyn screams, saliva frothing in the corners of her mouth.

Falyn is so outraged that her entire form shudders, and her eyes, stretched so wide, the gray of her irises leak into the white.

Ivy rests a hand on my shoulder, drawing close.

"Back off, Falyn," Ivy says. "Callie's under our protection."

Falyn slow-blinks, her face twisted in grotesque anger. Then, she guffaws, her stare pin-wheeling between Chase, me in the middle, and Ivy. "Protection?" she asks, then starts cackling. "*Protection?*"

"Either you jump into the goddamned lake," Chase says, "or I'll force your Virtues to do it for you."

"Right, the princely Stone would never touch a girl in such a ruthless manner," Falyn says through her laughter. I'm both horrified and fascinated by the sight. "That's not how you assholes operate. You go behind the scenes, don't you? Orchestrate your enemies' downfall with quiet, sightless maneuvers, but they're just as strong, just as *lethal*, as if you laid your hands on Callie in the first place." Falyn locks me in place with her gaze. "No. They're worse. And you're their latest puppet."

Chase releases his hold on me and storms forward. "If you value your place in the Virtues, you will shut the hell up."

Falyn doesn't back down. "Haven't you told your latest *soulmate* how she's inherited that title in the first place? I'd think that would be some crucial information to impart before you strip her and toss her in your bed."

Dread sloshes against my rib cage. I take one step, laying a hand on Chase's bicep. Trying to turn him, he refuses to cede any ground. "Chase, tell me what she's talking about."

Up until this point, I'd been silent during most of their exchange, drinking in their polarizing arguments for later use, but with the way Falyn's face transforms from distressed rage to snide, *winning* confidence, I'm terrified of this new outcome.

"Oh, honey." Falyn turns to me, widening her eyes with feigned, comical sympathy. "You've already fucked him, haven't you?"

Ivy steps between us, her back to me. "Do as Chase says, Falyn, or go tell the queen what you've done to Callie. Neither choice keeps you on this pontoon."

"I'll get to you." Falyn points dryly at Ivy. "Callie, I'm about to make your trip under the docks feel like *paradise*."

Chase rasps, "If you so much as whisper more lies..."

Ivy's shoulders go rigid. "Falyn, don't. Remember the sisterhood."

"The same sisterhood that's failing to defend me?" Falyn counters. She gestures to the cluster of Virtues hovering at the perimeter, their hoods obscuring their faces. Then at Willow and Violet behind her. "You all want to fall in line behind the prince? Fine. I'll face my punishment, but not before I tell Callie that Ivy was *ordered* to befriend her, and Chase was *told* to fuck her as a distraction."

My knees buckle. I falter in automatic recoil, my heels coming too close to the end of the dock but jerk back just in time.

I may have saved my body from another drowning, but my heart teeters over the edge and splashes back into the black depths. "That's not true."

But it can be. It is.

Haven't I learned by now that the students in Briarcliff are not what they seem? Friends are true enemies, teachers are predators, headmasters are members of secret societies...

Paranoia spreads its spider-legs across my mind, assisting in Falyn's revelation.

Ivy spins to face me. "Don't let her get to you. I can explain."

Chase cups my face. "Falyn's batshit. You hear me? Don't *listen*. I care about you. I do."

The two of them crowd in, and it's with a shredded scream that I push them off. "How could you? *How could you both?*"

"Callie, she's made it out to be—"

"To be what?" Falyn cuts Chase off. "Something other than the truth? If you care about her so much, Stone, then tell her why you singled her out on her first day. How you beckoned her with your looks and your smile and your sex appeal." Falyn slides her gaze to me. "Unfortunately, you're not the first, honey."

I shake my head. "Shut up. All of you, just shut up."

But Falyn's relentless. "Happy with your key now, Callie? Ivy's only friends with you because she has to be. We were curious about you the minute you came on campus, and you certainly didn't disappoint, with everything you've told Ivy you discovered about us."

I blink at Ivy with wide eyes. "You told them everything?"

Ivy's stare gleams with tears. "You have to understand..."

My chest grows tight. There's no water surrounding me this time, but I feel like I've been deprived of all oxygen.

What did I just fight through all this filth for?

"Your life isn't your own anymore," Falyn continues. "It's ours. We tell you who to be friends with. What subjects to excel in. Who you can *fuck*. We're the Virtuous future, and we've just screwed you *senseless*." Falyn beams after her statement. "So, tell me, Callie, as the soulmate who was, and I quote, 'attacked,' you have the option of nullifying Chase's punishment. Still want me to jump in your water? 'Cause I firmly believe I've baptized the shit out of you in this lake—"

I can't listen anymore. Chase tries to catch me, but I push him off, crying with harsh, damaged vocal cords, "*Liar!*"

He backs off, but Ivy comes up beside him, her face pleading with me to stay.

But I don't. I can't.

My world has shifted, and not simply because Falyn has decided to control its axis.

"Let your trials begin!" Falyn calls after me, her laughter echoing across the lake.

Three

I'M NOT sure I can function enough to make it to my dorm room, but I ask for one more favor from my quivering, battered legs to get us to our final destination, where a hot shower and a warm bed await.

Clutching the scratchy boathouse blanket around my shoulders, I wobble as fast as I can up the trail and scurry through Briarcliff's winding pathway until I arrive at Thorne House.

The night security guard raises a brow as I stumble through the sliding doors.

"Rough trot, already?" he asks through his burly mustache.

I shake my head, my teeth chattering too hard to form a proper response, and like he cares whether or not I've taken part in Briarcliff's students Turkey Trot. All *I* care about is warmth.

"I won't ask for your ID, considering I recognize that face of yours," he says when I reach the elevator. "You were in the crowd around that Harrington kid who got arrested for her sister's murder."

I manage a nod, but not much else.

"Looks like you've had a rough enough time of it," he mutters when the elevator door dings open. "Stay safe, kid."

I'm forced to face him when I push the button for the third floor, and whatever he sees in my expression makes his chin jerk back. "And warm," he adds. "Your lips are blue."

The door slides shut on the perturbed crunch of his brows, but I think I've had enough of concerned adults who end up providing zero assistance in this shit-hell of a school.

My keycard is somewhere in my back pocket, and I dig for it with numbed fingers while I wait for the elevator to spit me out on my floor. It takes four tries before I'm successful, my grip on the blanket wrapping around my neck like a vise each time I move.

With my jaw in full-on seizure mode, I stumble down the hall, slap the keycard against my electronic lock, and fall inside, the heavy wood slamming shut behind me.

"Jesus, what—oh my God, Callie."

Emma steps out from her room, annoyance warping into wariness as she strides over.

"S-sh-shower," I say through chattering teeth.

"No shit." Emma takes hold of my elbow, guiding me into the bathroom.

I'm shaking too much to properly peel off my wet clothes, but I try, anyway. Emma turns on the bathtub faucet then helps me undress, her deft fingers taking over where I fail.

"Arms up," she murmurs without meeting my eye.

I nod, but even that much movement causes a searing pain into my brain, and I wince.

"Almost there," Emma says, then unbuttons my jeans and peels them off.

I lose my balance when I try to lift my foot, jarring my hip against the sink and my palms slamming down, but Emma does most of the heavy lifting, pulling my feet through the leg-holes as I wobble above her.

A heavy, metal *clunk* sounds out against the floor's tiles when Emma tosses my pants aside. She picks up the ornate key, turning it around a few times in her hands.

"They had a new opening, huh?" she asks, her voice hollow.

"N-n-not anym-more," is all I can manage to say.

Emma's fingers clench over the Virtues' key before setting it on the counter. She ducks under my arm and helps me into the bathtub.

When my toe hits the water, I wail.

Emma nudges me forward. "It feels like fire because you're getting hypothermic. But the water is barely room temp. I promise. Try to slide in."

I grip her shoulders, whimpering, but do as she asks. This isn't the first time Emma's saved me from my own stupid injuries, and it probably won't be the last.

After a few minutes of coaxing and gentle, *gentle* easing into the bathwater, I'm immersed almost to the shoulders, my shivering limbs and joints turning into soft tremors. I breathe deep, closing my eyes, while Emma lays a warm cloth on my forehead.

"When you start to get cold again," she says, "tell me. I'll add warmer water."

I swallow. "They—they—"

"Don't try to talk. Relax. Deep breaths."

I crack my eyes open instead, my jaw too clenched and my teeth ramming together too hard for my voice to be much use. So, I attempt to communicate my wishes with my stare.

Emma avoids my eye, dipping a washcloth in the water and squeezing out the excess with both hands before draping it on the exposed skin of my chest. I wait it out, because she has to look at me sometime.

When she does, I flare my eyes, pleading with her to give me answers. "A-Addiysn."

After reading my expression, Emma sits back on her haunches and sighs. "I'm sorry for cornering you in her room and making you think we betrayed you. We needed Addisyn to believe we were on her side."

I jut out my chin for her to elaborate, the bathwater rippling with my shudders.

"We had to be believable," Emma says. "Otherwise, the Virtues weren't going to buy it."

"The—the—diary," I rattle out.

"Yeah, you found Piper's missing pages in Addisyn's room. But proving she killed her sister wasn't enough."

"But Addisyn was arrested."

Emma cocks her head. "Were you planning on stopping your snooping into the societies once she was arrested? If so, then great, good job. But I thought you wanted more. I thought you wanted the Virtues."

"I do."

Emma nods. When she moves forward to rearrange the cloth on my chest, the planes of her face are cast in the bathroom's light, the burn down one side of her neck mottled and red. "If the Virtues found out that you knew where Piper's lost pages were and that you were planning on breaking into Addisyn's room and retrieving them, they would've protected Addy first chance they got. Eden and I had to serve as a distraction and make them think we would intervene and bring them the pages instead."

My fingers curl under the cooling water. Emma takes that as a sign to drain the tub a little and add a warmer temperature. When she turns the tap and the stream hits my tingling toes, I sigh in relief.

I say, with my head leaning back, "You've been meeting with the Virtues? Are those what your late nights were all about?"

Emma studies me carefully. "Sort of. They're so up their own asses, it wasn't difficult for them to believe Eden still wanted a chance with them."

My chin comes down. "Eden's been meeting with them?"

Emma nods. "She told them your plans—with my okay. I've been giving her advice behind the scenes and helping her infiltrate the society. She said she would intervene and get the pages from you. Addisyn was in the room when Eden told the queen our plans, and Addisyn demanded to be present when you were steam-rolled."

I frown. "You let me trust you, then you went behind my back."

Same as Chase. Same as Ivy.

The utter recognition that no one I've surrounded myself with has worn their true face has me pushing against the sides of the tub and rising from the water.

Emma catches the movement and stands with me, holding my arm, but I shake her off.

"Callie," she pleads.

"No. Thank you for—for this, but I need to be alone."

"Don't you see it was worth it? We took the pages from you," Emma admits, "but Eden and I, we gave them to the police, not the Virtues."

"No, you blew up your spot with the Virtues by going to the police. Now they'll be pissed. You could've just let *me* do it the way I was supposed to, and your covert operation—or whatever it is you and Eden have going—could've gone on." My voice gets stronger as I reach for a towel, though my thighs are gelatinous and weak.

"Callie," Emma says quietly. She motions up and down my body. "Our plans are still in full effect."

I pause wrapping the towel around my torso.

Emma continues, "You're the newest initiate of the Virtues. Do you believe that was an accident?"

Holding the towel with crooked, thawing fingers, I whisper, "I'm so fucking tired."

"I know you are. But stealth is so important when it comes to them. We've been moving the pieces quietly. We had to get Addisyn out of the way and you into the society, but on our terms, without tipping off the Virtues. If we told you outright what we were trying to do—"

"What *are* you trying to do?"

"They are aware of every step you take. They *knew* you weren't about to stop looking for Piper's killer, or the origins of the Virtues."

"Thanks to Chase," I spit. "And Ivy."

Emma's nose wrinkles in confusion. "Ivy?"

"*Yes,*" I hiss. "All of you, working together without letting me in, watching me stumble around and—"

"Risk your life," Emma counters, her voice more controlled than mine. "*That's* what you were doing. The closer you got to exposing the Virtues, the harder they would retaliate."

"And so, you, what, think you can bribe my silence by making me a member, the way they tried with Addisyn?"

"You have no idea. *None* ... of what they're capable of." Emma points to her face. Not to the burn, but to the scar on her lip. The one eyelid that's lower than the other. "I was beaten because of what they forced me to do. What the queen forces *all* her favorite girls to do in order to graduate as a Virtue."

The exposed skin of my back presses against the cold tiled walls. Wincing, I move away. "Are you threatening me?"

"No." Emma's breath billows out in an exhale.

"You said it. I'm an initiate because you wanted me to be. Am I the next girl to suffer at their hands?"

"Not if we play this right." Emma steps forward. "Listen to me. They won't hurt you so long as you abide by their rules. They think they can control you now. It's why, once Addisyn was arrested, they had to let you in. Eden was never going to be their next member. But you? You've given them so many reasons to get you on their side."

"They could just kill me."

Emma gives a single blink. "Contrary to what you believe, the Virtues don't go around murdering on the reg. They work too hard on their girls to put them in their graves so early."

I ask through stiffened lips, "What will I really be doing, then?"

"Getting what we need."

I rub one eye with the palm of my hand. "I can't be your—"

"It's not just Eden and me working together to expose the Virtues."

My hand drops to my side. My subconscious predicts the name about to leave her lips, but hearing his name out in the open, having *Chase* echo against the bathroom walls, makes it so much more powerful.

And foreboding.
Until she says the name I'm not expecting.
Emma takes a breath. "It was Piper, too."

Four

PIPER.

The girl I lived with for a week, who bullied me relentlessly until the minute she died, still possesses enough of a foothold in this reality to haunt me.

My legs have turned into brittle matchsticks—I barely possess enough energy to balance on my feet, and my eyes are heavy and begging for sleep. But I pop them open to say, "Piper was helping you?"

"Yes."

"Shit." My knees buckle. I plop down on the side of the tub, clutching my towel.

Emma takes pity on me and throws another towel over my shoulders to keep me warm. "She was the only one with access to the temple and the Virtues' documents. When she died, we thought we'd never get back in. None of us had any idea she'd left clues in her diary."

"The library reference code," I murmur.

Emma takes a moment to assess my hunched over form, then scoots to my side. "This is a lot for you to take in. We can reconvene in the morning. You need to sleep."

I don't argue when she lifts under my arm and helps me to a stand. Yet, it's not only lethargy that hangs off my bones. "What happened to you?"

Emma angles her head to glance at me, but instead of answering, speeds us up.

I refuse to be sidelined, so I attempt to ask it in a less personal way. "What do they make all their girls do before graduating?"

"You've had a brutal couple of hours. Can't we leave it for a while?"

"Have you? Left it? After all they've done?"

"Fair enough, but I'm tired, too. I promise. Tomorrow morning, I'll explain more. Until then..." Emma ushers me into my room.

My hand flies to the doorframe. "Wait. My clothes. The key."

"I'll get them."

I let her go, and on my way to my bed, I drag an old t-shirt hanging off my chair back. The towels puddle to the floor as I slip it on, my footsteps heavy, then crawl under my covers, forcing myself to stay awake until Emma returns.

Her shadow flits against my blurred vision. "Here," she says, and something cold presses into my palm. The key to the Virtues' temple. "You earned it."

"Mm." I palm it close to my chest, then bury half my face in my pillow and close my eyes. "What did you have to do? To get yours?"

A few beats pass, then she says, "An abandoned lake house under construction. I had to sleep there overnight and find the key."

"That doesn't sound too bad." I manage to ask, before surrendering to slumber, "Were you afraid of the dark? Is that why they put you there?"

"No." I hear Emma's footsteps pad over to my door. She flicks the light off. "I was afraid of monsters."

Muffled sounds of an argument drift through the black, and I roll over, rubbing my eyes.

"She needs to sleep—Chase. *Chase!*"

I jolt in bed as my door bursts open and scramble up to my forearms, wincing when my sore muscles protest the movement.

"Callie?" he asks as he strides forward.

"I'm—" I clear my throat. "I'd like to be left alone."

He doesn't listen. He sits on the bed, close to my side, light from the doorway illuminating the sharp angles of his cheekbones, the stiff line of his shoulders. Worst of all, it puts a halo around his blond, tousled head.

"I may not be at my best," I say, "but don't think I won't push you off this mattress."

"I came to explain."

"I don't want to hear what you have to say."

"Hate me. Go ahead." His tone turns sharp. "But don't let it be because you listened to Falyn over me."

"I can think for myself." I sit up, wrapping my arms around my legs.

He sets his jaw. "After meeting you..." he sighs. "It's become so *fucking* complicated."

While my heart and my mind war with each other, my hands clench into fists. I'm hurt, hollowed out, and confused, but Chase is here. And he wants to talk.

Falyn's words scythe inside my head, their sharpened blades cutting into my skull with such terrible precision.

Tell your latest soulmate how she's inherited that title...

Chase was ordered to fuck you as a distraction...

Oh, honey. You've already fucked him, haven't you?

I meet his eyes in the gloom with a colorless stare. "So tell me."

"I was told to keep an eye on you. That much is true."

My heart picks up its beats. "By the Nobles?"

His chin jerks down in a single nod. "Piper died, and hell broke loose in our ranks. You were so adamant the society was responsible for her death that my father took me aside and asked me how much you knew."

I frown. "But at that point, I knew nothing."

Chase knuckles his jawline. "You told me you and Piper were working on Rose Briar as your history paper."

"Yeah ... and? The founders are a common topic in senior history."

"You made a connection with the date of Rose's death and Piper's. After that, you started throwing around our society name, then the Virtues'." Chase angles his head to look at me. "Were you expecting them to let you keep tripping over their secrets until you managed to reveal one?"

"I didn't have an inkling of who *they* were until I read Rose's letter that Piper hid in the public library. Then I saw your ritual room and what you do to naked women—"

"If I could explain to you the hundreds of years the society's been given to hone their sexist, masochist ways, I would. But that's not what you want me for. Is it?"

He's right, damn him. I'm not allowing Chase to sit here so I can yell at him about Noble traditions. I'm letting him stay, because... "You were ordered to seduce me."

Chase doesn't bother to deny it. "Yes."

I hug myself tighter. "Then Falyn was right."

"Falyn dilutes the truth to meet her needs, every time."

"Does she? I want to believe that." I'm desperate to cling to his words, to *him*, and forget there was ever a confrontation at the boathouse.

But that would require altering my memories to suit a reality more palatable, more meaningful, for my soul to handle. And I just can't do that to myself.

I force my next sentence to be stronger than the soft edges of my heart. "Then tell me about the first time we slept together."

Chase's back goes rigid.

"Did you sleep with me because you had to? Was that all I was? A task to complete?"

Chase presses his hand against my entwined ones. "It's not that simple."

"Yes or no." My lower lip quivers, but I'm praying for its concealment in the dark.

Chase exhales. "Yes."

I turn my face away so he won't catch the midnight glimmer of my tears. "You can go now."

He doesn't move. He stares at me.

"The *first* time, yes," Chase says. "But the second? Third? Fourth? Fuck, how many times have we slept together? Add them up, because those weren't instructed or ordered. They were mine. I kept coming back to you, because, hell, Callie. Because you shook me loose. You're the first girl who's made me feel like there isn't a collar around my throat, attached to chains against my father's wall."

I hear what he's saying, but he's cloaked in lies. Raised on vehemence and stubborn pride. Chase could form his lips around those sweet nouns for as long as they suit his needs.

"Don't let Falyn come between us. Or allow the Virtues to win." Chase grabs my hands with both of his, holding on tight. "We're *us*, Callie. We don't have to be what they—"

"But do we have trust?"

Chase raises his head. "What?"

"Say I believe you. That we've fallen for each other. That we're attracted and can't resist the need to give in to mutual pleasure. But can you trust me?"

Chase leans back. "I..."

I give a slow, aching nod. "I'm not angry with you for not being able to answer that. I can't answer it, either." I meet his eyes. "And I think that's the problem."

"We can fix it."

"Not right now, we can't. Not with the Virtues and the Nobles trying to direct our every move. We've seen what they can do. *You've* seen more than I ever will. Can you honestly say that whatever information we feed each other, accidental or on purpose, won't reach their ears?"

"That's not fair. It's different now. I'm not their puppet."

"No. You're their prince."

Chase breathes out. "Callie."

"You plan to go against them, remake their values, and that's wonderful. I don't want to be the reason you can't. And they'll use me against you, just like they used you against me."

The shadows caressing Chase's face turn into sharp points on the planes of his cheeks. "I won't let that happen. I'm not under my father's control anymore. I've sided with my sister. I've sided with *you*."

I lift my hand, caressing the dark hollows near his mouth. "You and I, we can't let each other in. Not yet."

And, my heart cries out, maybe we'll never be able to.

Chase takes hold of my wrist, pausing my strokes. "If you can't trust me completely, have faith that I've been doing everything in my power to protect you. Tonight, at the docks..." His billowing breath comes close to a death rattle. "I wrote that letter asking you to come to the boathouse. I wanted to meet you, alone, just you and I, so I could finally be honest with you. If I'd known they were going to use my meeting with you to catch you by surprise ... fuck." He casts his gaze to the ceiling. "Maybe you're right. We're putting each other at risk."

I have no doubts, but I ask anyway, just to hear it in his cadence, a tone he reserves solely for me. "Do you swear you had no idea they were going to push me off the dock?"

"Jesus, Callie—*no*. I wrote that stupid note in my room, then dropped it off on your bed, thinking I'd embrace my fucking dork and you'd find it cute. Thought you might enjoy a handwritten 'hit me up' instead of a text. Then I was sidelined on my way back to the dorms. By James. He had some shit he needed to sort through at the academy and ..." Chase buries his fingers in his hair. "He played me. Kept me occupied."

The urge to reach up and massage the back of his neck, bend his rigid body into mine, is so strong, but I curl my fingers on my lap instead. If Chase can't even trust his friends, how could he ever think we could ask that of each other?

Maybe, because now is the time he needs you most.

I staunch the thought. Too much has been triggered. "I can't swim."

Chase freezes in scraping his hair back. He grimaces. "The fuck?"

"I can't swim," I repeat. "I don't think being pushed into the lake was a coincidence."

"You can't *swim*?" Chase rears off the bed, then whirls to face me. "And you swished around under the docks trying to find a fucking key? It's a vintage prop the Virtues don't even use anymore! Why didn't you refuse? And who the fuck did you tell your weakness to?"

I wince. "I could ask the same of you."

Chase huffs out a breath.

"You could've refused your dad's demands and ignored me. Maybe then, I would've stayed the harmless possum everybody liked to kick around. Instead, after meeting you, I risked everything to find Piper's true killer. I sacrificed a future where I excel in all my classes in a top-tier high school because I couldn't ignore that pained look on your face every time your ex-girlfriend was mentioned. And just when I think this whole thing is finished, that Addisyn is in custody, and you and I can finally get to know each other without Piper's ghost behind us, I've been conned into a secret society by your sister and Eden through some twisted belief that my presence in this group can make up for Piper's absence. I can't do this, Chase. I'm not Piper."

Chase presses his hands to my face, tipping it up. He asks harshly, "Is that what you think? That you're some lame glimmer to Piper's falling star?"

I try to nod, but he holds my head firm.

"Listen to me. I have *never*, nor will I ever, want you to take Piper's place. What you and I have—it's ours. Not theirs. Not hers. And I can't speak for Emma, but when it comes to my sister and her plans to take down the Virtues, she'd only involve someone if she knew they wanted it, too."

I choke on a sob, and my words are lost.

Chase murmurs my name. His thumbs stroke my cheeks, painting curved paths through my tears.

"You're a girl who came into my life at the exact wrong time," he says, bending closer. "And made me question everything I wanted. My future. My choices. I thought I had my tomorrows on lock, but the minute I had you, the second I sank into you, I had no fucking idea what the next day would bring." His fingers knot in my hair. "And I ended up craving that uncertainty. And obsessing over my next fix of you."

His gaze darts to my parted lips. Even doused in darkness, Chase's handsomeness calls to the emptiness inside me, hooks it painfully, and draws it forward for him to satiate. His beauty is incomparable to anyone I've ever met—it makes me greedy and gluttonous. I want to stare at it, touch it, lick it until it's mine.

Chase's eyes lift. They sparkle like tiny stars.

My tongue hits my lip.

His lips break into a smile, and I forget to breathe, yet I don't care. I've lost my breath so many times tonight, but this time, I'll gladly give it away. Our chests rise and fall in tandem. He breathes for me.

Kiss me, he mouths.

My nipples *zing* as I read the silent words. He must sense it, because his grip tightens in my hair, tipping my head back and leaning forward until nothing but a sliver of air exists between us.

Chase tugs me closer, and I shiver as his hand slides from my hair down to the small of my back.

When he finds my bare ass, my body jerks with a small gasp, but I use that momentum to press my lips to his.

His silken tongue glides through my mouth, bringing with it his addictive taste— salted mint mixing with a tang uniquely his. I moan, going pliable in his grip, and he braces his arm at my back to lower us onto the bed, then settles between my legs as he devours me, owns me whole.

"Are you still cold?" he asks against my lips.

It's an effort to open my eyes and come out of paradise. "Freezing."

His pillowy mouth curves into mine, his hands start roaming, and my body curves into his every sway.

Chase traces my folds, slick and ready for him. I raise my hips, and on a groan, he sinks his fingers in.

"I want you to feel me inside you," he says between kisses, "as much as I feel you in me."

Whimpering, I clutch his shoulders, matching his pumps, circling my hips with his. When he pinches my clit between his fingers and twists, he catches my cry in his mouth.

Feeling outmatched, I let my hand wander between us, then under his jeans until I meet his dick, curling the pads of my fingers until I trace the thick vein on the underside of his incredibly long shaft. He groans when I squeeze, when I pace my hand pumps to his finger thrusts.

His knuckle brushes across my clit, once, twice, and I'm so swollen, even my throat can feel the pleasurable, aching pulse begging to release.

Chase's smoky voice curls into my ear. "I'm going to make you come, and right when I have you, when you're screaming my name, I'm going to fuck you."

I tip my neck back, allowing him full access. "Yes."

My legs tremble, but not from cold or fear. Pure ecstasy flits through my veins with the lightness of fairy dust, and as Chase brings me to my peak, when that enjoyable blackness coats my vision, I arch my back and give in.

I'm so lost in the ether I don't notice Chase stand and strip off his pants. I barely register the crinkle of an opening condom. I can't see the way his body covers mine, the sheer width of him blocking out the entirety of my room.

But I spectacularly feel when he thrusts into me mid-orgasm.

The sheer intensity of another building orgasm on the tail of my first one is almost too much, and I bite down on my lower lip to stop the scream.

Chase doesn't let up. He pounds into me, his rhythmic thrusts ignorant to my pathetic attempts to be quiet.

"I've loved fucking you from the first second," Chase rasps, nipping and licking my earlobe. "Love the tightness of your pussy, the feel of you clamping around me when you come. I want you to think about this whenever you're questioning our validity. Remember what it's like to have my cock inside you, to go to class still dripping with my cum and your juices, to have panties soaked with your want for me every time I can't give it to you. Because I would. In public view, in the Wolf's Den, on classroom desks, in Marron's fucking office—I'd have you soaking wet in every damned room at Briarcliff Academy."

My voice hitches. I can't garble out syllables, words, meanings. I'm so close to tipping over another brink, I can't even poise his name on my tongue.

"You like that? Me talking dirty? I fucking love it, too. Come on me, Callie. Come all over me and show me what I do to you."

I can't bear it. I cry out as my body dances under another spotlight of ecstasy.

My nails rake down his back as I instinctively bring him closer, absorbing his heartbeats into my own. Chase keeps drilling into me, cursing once before he thrusts as deep as he can and holds himself there. I wrap my legs around his lean hips to bring him as deep as possible, my body capturing his every orgasmic tremor and twitch.

We hold each other as we come down, Chase burying his face in my neck. Through my hazy, sleepy fog, I hear, "I think I got paint all over your shirt."

Laughing, I let my fingers delicately trace the deep route of his spine, the muscles on either side showcasing it like a ravine on his skin. "It's worth the dry cleaning bill."

Chase chuckles near my ear. "That ratty thing?"

"It was my mom's shirt."

Our movements still. Chase lifts his head. "I'm sorry."

"Oh, that's not—I'm not mad." I push pieces of loose hair from his flushed, angular face. "But I guess I just doused cold water on us, huh?"

The mention of my mom coupled with bringing up the topic of water, are two sore subjects I should've let lie. Instead, I've allowed them to flood their unresolved angst into this room. Into us.

Though it pains me to say it, I murmur, "I'd really like to get some sleep."

"Yeah." Chase's hands come down on either side of me, and he swings himself up and out of bed. "Sure."

He stands, the tendons of his arms and ridges of his biceps flexing. Even in this meager light, the full-frontal force of him is startling.

Chase glances down at me. "I gotta say one last thing."

I nod while slipping under the covers, my body still twanging and vibrating from his sudden, addictive devotion. I don't think it'll ever fade. Chase gives me goosebumps just by looking at me, and hell, I'm in trouble now.

"You got their key, but it doesn't get easier from here." Chase leans forward, his pecs coming awfully close to my mouth, and his evergreen, freshwater scent all-consuming. He grabs the key from where it lays on the cold side of my bed and lifts it for inspection. "All this talk of trust between us ... non-legacy members have to prove they're trustworthy. That you're committed to the society. And that whatever happens, you'll keep the society's agenda, their traditions, a secret you carry to your grave."

"Yes," I whisper into the enlarged space between us.

"They will test you the hardest of all, considering what happened today with Addisyn's arrest. You'll have to do things you will never be proud of. Are you ready for that?"

After a moment, I give another nod and sort through my thoughts enough to say, "I need to become one of them to take them down."

Chase studies me in grim silence. When I don't elaborate, he says, "I'll do everything in my power to help you. So will Emma."

He turns for the door, and I watch him leave under the heavy night shadows.

At the last minute, Chase turns. "Callie. I want to stop you from doing this, but I won't force you to back off. Just know that whatever comes next, I warned you."

Then, he leaves.

The white, predatory glitter in his eyes as he turns is the last image that resurfaces before I fall asleep.

Five

MONDAY ROLLS in with an oceanic storm, and I scramble up the exposed pathway to the academy under my lopsided umbrella, balancing the overflow of textbooks in my arms, as well as my bag, straining at the seams as it bounces against my back.

When the corner of a textbook hits one of my kidneys, I curse, buckling under what both tickles and hurts at the same time.

Other students hurry up the same hill, but they have their shit together as they fly by with extra-large umbrellas and roller bags for backpacks.

And ... is that a golf cart I see buzzing up ahead?

Why couldn't I catch one of those?

Hunched over, huffing, and dripping, I make it to the school's entrance in time to see said golf cart smooth to a stop under the covered section of the pavilion. Chase slides from the driver's seat, brushing his hands down his impeccably dry Briarcliff blazer.

Even in a cold winter storm, his golden brilliance stays intact. His blond hair is sculpted away from his forehead with perfect, tousled texture. He fills out his uniform like a god, straining the fabric in all the right places, without a single raindrop marring his Midas aura.

Chase cuts his eyes to the right, catching me in plain sight as I inadvertently ogle him.

Can't a life and death situation stifle, just a little bit, my foolish attraction toward him? Why does a stupid crush have to feel so unshakeable?

I pick up my pace, horrified to be caught in such a weakened position, especially after this weekend.

"Look, man, she's wet for you," I hear James, golf cart passenger, say. "How many times does it take for you to squeal, possum? Huh?"

I expect James's remarks to be followed up by Chase's fist hitting some part of his friend, but only silence follows.

Daring a peek over my shoulder, I notice that Chase merely sidles up to James with a smirk, Tempest coming up behind them. The fourth musketeer, Riordan, barks out with laughter as James says something else I don't catch.

Chase's attention flicks over to me once more, but then chooses to scan the rest of our surroundings in boredom rather than return to my face.

I whip back around, my cheeks hot with embarrassment and hurt, but I remind myself: Maybe this is how it should be, Chase going back to his rule-the-school roots and me returning to my rodent state. It's safer this way. The Nobles and Virtues are less likely to mess with our heads if they think Chase has grown bored with me and stayed friends with James.

I tell myself that on the way to my locker. That Chase's answering smile to James's insult is an act, and not the real him.

This is what you wanted.

I kicked him out of my room for this very reason. Didn't I?

My locker is—for once—a welcome sight when I come up to it, the dark wood varnish a much better image to focus on rather than Chase's cool dismissal. I spin my combination code and swing the door open, dumping my textbooks with a breathy, happy sigh.

I peel off my blazer, too, considering it's more of a damp overcoat than a fashion choice.

My phone dings in its pocket as I fold the collar over the hook, and I fish inside to pull it out before classes start.

When I see the preview on my lock screen, I frown. It's a text with just a small image, too pixelated to get a good look.

Unlocking the screen, I pull up the message.

And cut off mid-gasp.

I glance around, hoping the nearby students who are also dropping off their things and having lingering morning chats before the first bell haven't clued into my sudden freak-out mode.

But *I* have, and I glance at the picture one more time, to make sure it's real.

It's of Eden, changing in the co-ed bathrooms of Richardson House where she shares a dorm room with Ivy. She's bending down, grabbing a towel off the hook, completely naked. The photo only shows her side, but a picture at any angle, while naked, is still meant to be humiliating if you haven't consented to it.

And Eden is clearly unaware of a lens trained on her body as her damp hair trails down her back, and her tan lines on her shoulders and thighs from a bathing suit are on full display.

It took mere seconds to catalogue the terrible intent of this picture, and my brain screams *delete delete delete* well before my finger hovers over the screen.

But then another message pops up.

Private Number: Create a finsta and share this pic with the entire student body. Caption: FORMER SWIM CAPTAIN EATS PINOCCHIO *AND* THE WHALE.

My mouth falls open. My stomach sinks. I immediately type back: **I'm not doing this.**

It doesn't take long for a response.

Private Number: to learn where our temple is, you'll have this picture making the rounds by noon.

Fuck. *Fuck.*

While still holding my phone, I slam my palm into the side of my locker. Nearby students jolt at the noise, a few lifting their lips with snide disgust as they discover the source of the sound, then go about their day.

I'm not punching wood because I'm at a crossroads and can't figure out the right move—I'm doing it because there is no other current recourse to expel the furious energy running through my veins.

"Callie?"

The tentative use of my name draws my head up. "Not now, Ivy."

"I ... you're mad. That's okay. But I was hoping we could maybe talk at lunch and—?"

New target.

I whirl, punching the air with my phone as I lurch it into Ivy's view. "*I am not doing this.*"

Ivy pulls her books into her chest. "That's—omigod."

"You know who this came from." It's not a question.

She stutters out, "Yes."

"*This* is how the big bad society wants to initiate me?" I point at my screen with my free hand. "By doing ninth grade, social media bullying bullshit? After having me swim for my life under a goddamned *boat dock*?"

"I..." Ivy shakes her head. "It all depends on who's in charge of your initiation."

"Falyn?" My question contains more spit than air. "Why her? Shouldn't it be you? You excelled at duping me this entire semester. You'd think you'd be rewarded by being put in charge of my *worthiness.*"

Every syllable I utter is filled with vitriol—poison I couldn't contain when I was freezing to death, and anger that was stifled by hurt when Chase visited me Saturday night. Now, though, oh, *now*, I am ready to unleash.

And Ivy, a person who I thought was my friend, will be my carnage.

Ivy flinches. "I don't agree with any of this, and you may not believe me, but I was never fake with you. I'm your friend."

"Are you?" I give Ivy the once-over, but all I can see is her swimming beside me, her hair rippling in the water as she allowed Falyn to take control. "What about Eden?

Huh? What will this do to her? It rehashes the exact trauma she had to endure freshman year, and she barely made it out. She lost everything, Ivy. Her passion for swimming, her body, her mind, her *friends*. Everything was taken from her. And I'm expected to do that to her again?"

"She came back to us, asking to be initiated, offering us those missing pages of Piper's diary. But then Addisyn was arrested because of those very pages. Eden betrayed us. If she'd stayed away, she wouldn't be a target. But she wants this, Callie. Eden made it clear in one of our meetings how much she was willing to endure—"

"What kind of fucked up shit are you into?"

Ivy jerks back as if I slapped her. "You put your life on the line to see what crap I'm into. Now suddenly, you can't stomach it? We're not nice, Callie. The Virtues aren't *kind*. They prey on weakness and test our limits to the greatest extent, so we can come out better. Stronger. We're given the ability to leave this school and enter men's playgrounds with the exact weapons required to get what we want."

I stumble back with each breath she takes. "Stop saying those things. This isn't you."

"Isn't me?" Ivy echoes. "Everything you've seen up until this point is who I am. But we've only known each other a few months. I couldn't give you every facet, especially when you started your quest to reveal secret societies on campus. How would you have reacted if I told you I was a member from the beginning?"

"But you're the one who gave me the Nobles' name in the first place." I stare at her, searching for the friend she promised was still in there. "Did you do it on purpose? To test me?"

Ivy's eyes dart to the side, then come back to mine. "The minute your name popped up as a Briarcliff enrollee, you were considered as a possible initiate."

"What? That's not possible. I can't..." Can't believe my best friend introduced herself to me with the intention of planting a seed in my mind to prove my worthiness. Can't comprehend that the instant I stepped on Briarcliff soil, I was societal fair game.

"It can't be true," I manage to say. "How could they be interested in me? I'm nothing. No one. Just a girl from the Lower East Side."

My grip clenches on my phone, and I work to bring our conversation back to Eden. "And I'm still not doing this. Consider me unworthy."

"Come on, Callie." Ivy cocks a hip. "You're willing to give up everything, even after the gaslighting you went through to get to the Virtues' door? Don't be like this. You're so close."

"Shaming another girl isn't something I'll ever take pride in," I say. "I'm really disappointed that you think it's a weapon that will positively shape your future."

I push past her.

"They won't stop, Callie. And whatever task they substitute for this one, it'll be worse. Please. Do as they say."

Ignoring her, I turn into the hallway.

"I'm trying to help you!" she calls. "Please, let me..."

But her voice becomes softer, then fades away entirely, as I put more distance between me and the one person at this school who had my trust.

Six

LUNCH HOUR IS SAFER in my dorm room.

After the last morning bell tolls, I bypass my peers jumping up from their desks and grouping into cliques, ducking from the classroom well before my exit is noticed by Chase or Falyn.

It's not that much of a feat. Their attention was so focused on the professor during class, I could've put a Mentos in a coke bottle, and they wouldn't have turned. When it comes to my presence, Falyn must've decided against threatening me in public, and Chase seems to be intent on keeping up his unconcerned veneer.

That kind of self-control, after the weekend I endured at their orchestration, actually scares the shit out of me.

It shows just how serious they take their positions in Briarcliff's secret societies.

When I arrive at Thorne House, there isn't much activity. Most students take their lunch in the dining hall where they can catch up with their friends, crushes, and latest gossip. My heart pangs at the thought.

Any normalcy I craved when coming to Briarcliff left with Ivy once she jumped into the lake and dragged me out.

Upon entering my apartment, I expect to see Emma at our small kitchen counter, hunched over her food and eating quietly and alone—how she prefers it, and lately, how I'm coming to like it, too.

What I don't expect, once I shed my jacket and dump my bag, is Eden to be eating with her.

"Oh. Hi," I say.

All I can see when I look at Eden is the picture stored in my phone.

Their heads snap up at my voice, and both straighten from their conspiratorial positions on the couch.

Emma speaks first. "Hey." She puts down her chopsticks. "Didn't expect you back so early."

I open the fridge. "I lost my appetite for the dining hall."

Eden says, "I would've brought you some pho, had I known you were coming."

I shrug, preferring to bury my face in the cold icebox of the inner fridge than make eye contact. I'm a terrible liar. If they see my face, they'll know.

"I think there's some jelly back there," Emma says, her voice light as air. "Make yourself a pb and j, then come sit with us."

I do what she suggests. After slathering peanut butter and strawberry jelly between two pieces of bread, I join Emma and Eden on the couch.

Emma finishes her bite of noodles, her attention straying to the sandwich, remaining untouched, on my lap, before snapping back to my face. "I told Eden what you went through over the weekend."

I swallow, my saliva thick and unyielding. "I figured you would."

Eden makes a low sound in her throat. "They think up the most fucked-up things, don't they?"

My traitorous mind flies back to her naked picture on my phone, burning my retinas. I blink against my dry eyes. "I wasn't prepared for that kind of initiation. I wish you would've let me in on your plans after Addisyn was arrested."

Eden shrugs, as if tossing me into a frigid lake was the least of what could've happened. "We weren't sure it was going to work. Yes, betraying you in Addisyn's room was believable, but it wasn't just Addisyn we had to convince. We had to lower the Virtues' guards enough to get them to allow us to be the ones to collect Piper's diary pages from you. That was the easy part, since we had a closer relationship to you than any of them. It was exposing Addisyn and having her arrested before they found out what we really did with the diary pages that was difficult."

"You put yourselves in so much danger," I say.

"Exactly," Emma says simply. "We knew there would be punishment and didn't want to involve you so soon. Not until..."

"I took Addisyn's vacant seat in the Virtues," I finish, then glance between the two of them. "The Virtues are so pissed at the both of you."

"They're biding their time to retaliate." Emma shrugs, but her eyes burn bright. "What's worse than what they've done to us before?"

I lean forward on my elbows. My phone, stuffed in my jacket near the door, blares a Siren's call only I can hear, but not yet. Not yet. "Explain to me what happened to you, Emma. I can't be left in the dark anymore."

Emma sets her bowl of pho on the coffee table while Eden huddles deeper into the couch cushions, bringing her noodle bowl closer to her chest like its warmth can replace what's missing in her chest.

"Don't I deserve to know?" I ask. "After you two colluded—"

"Successfully, I might add," Eden cuts in.

I sigh. "Achievement or not, the three of us are in a whole bunch of shit because of it. I need to know what I'm working with if I'm to take this ruse any further."

And put your entire life back into misery, I silently add, but internally shake myself out of it and push on, saying to Emma, "I can maybe understand why the Virtues believed Eden and that she wanted to prove herself by stealing Piper's diary pages from me the instant I found them, but you? You burned down a library. Why would the Virtues think you would still be on their side?"

Emma's brows jump before her lips turn down. "You may know I set the fire, but you have no idea what's been done to me these last two years."

"Then help me understand."

"My father is the king of the Nobles. My brother, the prince. They've spent their lives working themselves to the bone to keep the Nobles a secret, and because of that, they have to work to keep the Virtues a secret, too."

"And you put all that in jeopardy by drawing national attention to Briarcliff Academy by setting that fire," I surmise.

Emma's chin dips low in agreement.

I set my sandwich down beside her bowl. Emma watches the maneuver.

"My father spent these past two years indoctrinating me back into the Virtuous mindset. He used therapists that were Nobles, trauma counselors that were Virtues, and I spent months being told the societies weren't the problem. I was."

I think of the three days I spent in a psychiatric hold after physically attacking my stepdad, and the pills I swallowed along with the words from doctors and nurses that I was experiencing a break with reality due to the trauma of losing my mother.

If only you'd listen to us and take your medication like a good girl, then you'll be back to normal in no time. Your father isn't a murderer. Cocaine and Oxy and a hard-partying lifestyle are what fuel your paranoid delusions. Your mother isn't coming back.

I was in that suffocating, nauseating fugue for seventy-two hours. Did Emma have to endure it for two years?

"Chase allowed that?" I whisper.

Emma shakes her head. "Not even close. But he was forced to watch it happen."

I wait for her to continue.

"My brother ... I had to make him understand we were playing the long game. Instant retaliation doesn't work. I set the Virtues' temple on fire and look where that got me. The only consequence of my efforts was that they had to build a new one."

I choke on Emma's revelation, wishing I'd grabbed some water. "The Virtues' secret meeting grounds was hidden in the old library?"

Emma responds with a droll look. "Contrary to popular belief, I'm not a pyro who sets revenge fires just because a mysterious masked man who jumped me there was still running free."

"So, it was the Virtues who attacked you."

Emma cants her head in partial agreement. "It was their way of permanently severing me from the Virtues. Fracturing my face..." Her words hit a rough patch, and Emma clears her throat. I take that as a clue that all of us are in need of water, so I hop up and pour three glasses.

"An edict of being Virtuous," Emma says as I return, placing the drinks on the coffee table before reoccupying my seat, "is that you have to be beautiful. If you don't have beauty, you're no use to them."

Eden drops her head, her long, black hair swishing against her cheeks, obscuring her profile. My chest tightens as I glance between them, their minds more battered and disfigured from the existence of the Virtues than their bodies ever will be.

I hate them, I think with ferocious venom. *I hate these societies.*

"So, you tried to destroy the Virtues' property as payback," I say, thinking this through as delicately as I can. "Except, you were somehow trapped inside while doing it."

Eden nudges Emma. "Might as well tell her everything."

Emma watches me for a moment, then parts her lips. "I wasn't trapped. I was locked in."

I stare at her. "What?"

"It wasn't my intention to destroy the whole building," Emma says. "I only wanted the underground temple to burn for what they did. But the queen caught me, and instead of screaming at me to get out, she shut and locked the door in my face."

I hold a hand to my neck, my stomach lurching. "But you managed to escape. You survived."

"Because my brother saved me."

The mention of Chase's name holds the same power it always does, my heart cleaving in two at the thought of him running into flames to save his sister, and the lies he had to weave to ensure both his and his sister's survival at this academy.

And I told him I couldn't trust him.

"Do you see, Callie?" Eden asks, shuffling closer to Emma and putting her arm around her shoulders. "Can you understand why we duped you? We need someone on the inside, to get to the Virtues' written recordings, to collect evidence against them, to expose them for who they really are." Eden waits a beat, both of them watching the information they imparted slip under my skin, erode my bones, and turn my insides to ash. "Are you with us?"

I lick my lips. Take a long, cold gulp of water.

Piper was their inside girl before me. And now she's dead.

So is my mother.

So is the carefree, beguiling, cheerful Callie Ryan that I used to be.

I raise my head, including both Emma and Eden when I say, "Yeah. I'm in."

Seven

"I HAVE A CONFESSION TO MAKE," I say to Emma and Eden, threading my fingers together on my lap. "The Virtues contacted me this morning."

Emma's brows lower. "What did they say?"

I lock my jaw, my gaze sliding over to my bag, slumped innocently beside the door. "It's ... well, let's be real. It's Falyn, and she's teed me up for another screwed up test."

Eden nods. "That's usually how it goes."

"How many?" I ask, mild desperation lacing my tone. "How many will it take before I'm robed?"

Emma answers. "Hard to say. Each girl is different. You're not a legacy, you're a senior, and they're letting you into the society because you've basically strong-armed them."

"*And* Falyn's in charge of your initiation," Eden adds.

"Gee. Anything else?"

"I'm betting on a pretty brutal future for you," Eden says, her eyes as flat as her voice. "But if you can take it, I'll have mad respect for you."

"God." I rub my eyes.

"Sack up," Emma says. "You can do this."

I nod with forced vigor, because I'm not looking forward to what I'm about to say. "Eden, what they're asking me to do is about—"

A hard knock sounds against our door, making all three of us jump. Eden's pho splashes on her white button-up shirt, and she curses.

Ivy's voice floats through the gaps. "Callie? Are you there?"

Emma mumbles something close to an insult then leans back and crosses her arms. She says to me, "Your move. I'm not letting her in."

My attention flits between Emma and Eden—two people on my side, but who've proven their willingness to throw me under the bus if it suits their larger plan—and

Ivy, the girl who saved me from drowning, yet disillusioned our friendship to the point that I'm questioning if it ever existed in the first place.

Are these my choices?

Standing, I sigh. "I'll get it."

Emma frowns. Eden's expression becomes unreadable, but she watches the door.

I stride over and unlock the deadbolt, revealing Ivy, unkempt, windblown, and bringing in the scent of a chilled forest with her. Her shoulders sag at the sight of me. "I wasn't sure you were going to answer."

"I debated it."

She nods, her gaze falling to the floor as she wrings her hands. "Can I come in?"

"No," Eden calls behind me.

"Yes," I say, and step aside. "But if it isn't obvious, I'm not alone."

Ivy tiptoes in, her focus centering on Emma and Eden, both rigid and watchful. Neither have resumed eating.

"Hi, guys," Ivy says to them quietly.

Emma levels her chin. Eden glares.

"I'm glad you're all here," Ivy says. With the way she stands in the center of our room, leaving her coat on and her bag strapped on her shoulders, it's clear she doesn't think she'll be staying long.

My heart aches at the sight. Just a few days ago, Ivy was bursting in here, her jacket, shoes, and books flying everywhere before she splayed on my bed and asked me how I felt about binge-watching baking shows.

"We know about last weekend," Eden supplies. "And what was done to Callie."

The memories get the best of me. I blurt out in defense, "Ivy saved me. When I was in the water, she jumped in and swam me to the docks."

Eden's brows hike up. Emma's lips thin.

Ivy turns to me, her blue eyes lighting up with a familiar smile. "Obviously, Callie. I couldn't leave you to drown."

Eden makes a sound of disgust. "I can't with this drama. The water's like, ten feet deep under the docks. It's not like Callie couldn't—"

"I can't swim," I say.

Eden's mouth falls open.

"Wait a second," Emma says. "You can't swim, and you managed to find the Virtues' key under the docks?"

"Badass," Eden says, her expression turning to one of admiration.

Ivy ignores them both. "Callie, you may think less of me because I hid my membership, but if you keep up your initiation, you'll understand why. The society doesn't play around. I *couldn't* tell you, even though I really wanted to. I tried to leave clues..."

"Like telling me about the Nobles when I first came to Briarcliff," I say. "Then denying you ever said anything."

Ivy slumps. "This world we're in, it's a gift and a curse. With the Virtues, our future is pure gold."

Emma snorts. But Eden's stare becomes almost feverish as she listens to Ivy.

"But the curse..." Ivy continues, "the curse is to sign away your soul."

My eyes narrow at the sudden turn. I study Ivy harder. "We're talking real life here. They can't possibly own your *soul*."

"I didn't come over to convince you to be one of us. I'm here to—I'm here..." Ivy trails off, one hand massaging her throat as she glances at Eden, but lands on Emma. "Eden was humiliated, you were hurt, and Piper died. The Virtues aren't who I thought they were when I pledged in eighth grade. I've seen things, I've—I've *done* things, I—"

"You're the new princess, aren't you?"

Emma asks it so softly; the sound barely travels to my ears. But her head is cocked, her eyes carrying the louder message. Suspicion. Warning.

"Yes," Ivy admits, but she twists and clings to my arms. "Please look at me, Callie."

I do, but the movement's stiff, my muscles slower to catch up than my mind at the word *princess*.

"I don't want this anymore." Her sudden whisper is ferocious, her eyes glistening with tears.

My hands move to cup her elbows, but in my periphery, Emma rises. She comes over to us, and with the gentleness of stroking a caged bird, she lays her hand on Ivy's shoulder.

It's all Ivy needs.

She releases me and folds into Emma, sobbing into her shirt. Emma tilts her chin, not in confusion, but to rest her head against Ivy's, to hold her closer and make the hug more complete. Emma's hand rubs Ivy's back, and I stand there, a sudden stranger to my friend as Emma, the person who's sacrificed the least emotion in this room, opens herself up to provide comfort.

Emma's eyes flick to mine over the pale silk of Ivy's hair. "I was a princess, too, once."

I give a minute shake of my head, figuring I'm comprehending about a quarter of what's really going on. Looking to Eden, I ask, "Are you aware of what a Virtue princess is?"

Eden's expression is the closest to mine. She shakes her head. "I never got that far in their initiation. But if the Nobles have a prince, it makes sense the Virtues would create a princess."

"We don't have to talk about it. Not now." Emma says it to Ivy, continuing to rub Ivy's shuddering back. "That's not why Ivy's here."

"What, suddenly you're on her side?" Eden stands. "She's one of them. She could be setting us up."

"I'm not," Ivy says, gulping air as she lifts her head. The fair skin of her cheeks is splotched in sections, her hair sticking to her tear-slicked face. "I came for some understanding. I've felt so alone since Piper died and thought there was no one. Then Callie and I got close and you came back," Ivy says to Emma. "And Addisyn was arrested for Piper's murder. After that, Callie was tapped for the Virtues. It's too much. This isn't how it was supposed to be. Callie, I didn't want to bring you into this. I wanted you so, so far away, but now it looks like I betrayed you, but I swear ... I swear I only want what's good. I became a member under Rose Briar's teachings, but it's been twisted and broken, and ... and ... when I was asked to step in as princess, I couldn't say no. But it's a pretend power. It wasn't enough to stop them from coming for you, from getting you to that dock, even though I said nothing. I promise you I didn't tell them you couldn't sw—"

It's too much. Watching my friend fall apart is too damned wrenching, and I fly forward and wrap my arms around her.

She doesn't break down in tears again, but Ivy clings so tight, it's like she's asking for my intact soul to become hers, too.

"I had no idea you were so empty inside," I say close to her ear.

"Please forgive me," she whispers into my neck.

My grip tightens around her shoulders. "The Virtues take so much. I don't want them to take our friendship, too."

Ivy nods, sniffling into her sleeve, then slips a tissue out of her pocket.

"Are you saying you're a part of our..." Eden trails off. "What are we? A team? Special ops? Cat burglars?"

"We're the girls the Virtues crossed," Emma says, her expression hewn from stone. "Ivy, if you're to be a part of this, you have to prove you're on our side."

"I am." Ivy nods sharply. "I'll do whatever it takes to help you." She looks between all of us. "What are you doing, exactly?"

Three of us stand in the center of the room. Eden makes it four when she draws nearer, a suspicious gaze cast on Ivy, but somewhat amenable to a new member, nonetheless. She mutters, "All for one, I guess."

Emma takes a breath. "Okay, then. First test. Callie, what were you saying about your next task?"

My stomach sinks. But under Ivy's sympathetic eye, I pick up my bag and pull out my phone. "This," I say, though I keep the screen black.

"We need a little more than the big reveal of your phone," Emma says.

Although I'd prefer to stare at the floor while unveiling the terrible details, I don't. My mother didn't raise me that way. Instead, I stare directly at Eden, and include only her.

"They have pictures of you. New ones. In the locker room. You're changing out of your gym clothes and..."

I can't make myself continue when Eden's eyes die out.

Emma hisses out a curse. "*Fuck* them."

"I agree," I say, leveling my shoulders. "I refused to send it to the entire school like they wanted."

"I'm worried they'll ask for something worse," Ivy says, her voice treading carefully. "I'm fairly convinced they were behind your mom's photos, Callie. The ones of the crime scene."

My focus zeroes in on her, but I blink out of it before my heart can crash to my throat. This isn't about me right now, and I can't say I'm surprised the Virtues were behind that terrible prank.

Ivy says, "They dig into your past, figure out your worst history, then throw it in your face. The things they could do with your most guarded secrets..."

I swallow. "Then I'll grin and bear it, because I'm not putting her"—I point at Eden—"I'm not putting *you* through that again."

Eden, her expression dulled, doesn't even blink in reaction. Emma worries her lips as she squints at her friend, but with the way she keeps involving me in her stare, I can tell her thoughts are whirling toward—

"Do it."

I stiffen, at first convinced the directive came from Emma, but she's just as shocked as I am. Ivy folds her arms in on herself, appearing too gaunt and thin to unleash such a command.

That only leaves one other person.

"Are you serious?" I ask Eden.

She sets her jaw and nods. "This is my punishment for betraying them. I expected it. And if you don't do this, they'll come after you harder, and Emma and Ivy can both attest to the fact that it won't be Falyn behind the next idea. Just do what that bitch wants and be done with it."

"But ... but last time—"

Eden cuts me off. "Last time, I was unprepared. And I—had no friends. None that stuck with me after the photos went out, anyway." She lowers her head, hiding behind her hair.

"Eden," Emma tries.

"Do it, Callie. Before I lose my nerve."

I hold up my phone but shake my head. "I'll take whatever they have coming next. I'm not going to—"

With the grace and speed of cutting through water, Eden darts close and snatches my phone from my grip.

"Eden!" I cry, but I'm the only one who does.

Emma and Ivy both look on, awed and horrified as they watch Eden thumb through my screen. The second she sees her photo, her face spasms before she smooths it into a hardened mask of hatred.

A few minutes later, she tosses the phone back at me. I fumble to catch it, clutching it to my chest.

Eden takes a deep breath. "It's done. I've sent it out through a fake account."

I'm going to be sick. "Eden, you didn't have to do that."

"Forget about it," she says, then swivels to grab her things. "It's nothing they haven't seen before."

My lips tremble. Ivy holds back tears. Emma lifts her hand as Eden walks through our tiny group and toward the door.

"Go home, Eden," Emma says. "*Home* home. By the time Thanksgiving is over, something else will draw their attention."

"That's the thing," Eden says, her hand on the doorknob. She doesn't turn around. "*I* don't forget. But I'll be better, I'll feel whole again, if you bring me their heads. Even if you have to betray Chase, Callie, show me it was worth it, and I'll learn to forgive."

"You have my word," I say softly, but Eden doesn't catch it, because she's already thrown herself into a hallway of laughing, howling wolves.

Eight

I SPEND Thanksgiving in full-on Hates-giving mode.

I don't let it show, to my dad or Lynda. I'm docile, accepting the catered turkey feast and the extravagant holiday party with the smile of a perfect daughter.

To be honest, my relationship with Dad and Lynda moved by leaps and bounds in just one week. I arrive on their doorstep the morning of Thanksgiving, and Dad envelops me in a huge, hard hug. We're both still dealing with our grief over Mom in different ways—he was able to grapple with the consequences of her affair with Paul Harrington for over a year, while I've just found out, and I'm still having trouble with the imperfect image of Mom—but I haven't enjoyed the smell of his cologne this much since I was nine. I haven't let myself look forward to a baby sister this much since I was a kid, wishing for a sibling. And I haven't gotten to know Lynda this much since ... ever.

It's enough to put my anger on simmer instead of boil, but the back of my mind crawls with thoughts of Eden and how she's coping. She didn't show up to any of her classes for the rest of the shortened week. My multiple texts to her go ignored. My calls are declined. Because she won't talk to me directly, I focus on backdoor ways to help her out, like reporting the Instagram posts and sending an anonymous email to Headmaster Marron about the harassment.

It will never be enough.

That slithering thought, with a rattlesnake tail, refuses to uncoil, and I live with it for four days before I can reenter Briarcliff Academy turf and begin my take-down of the Virtues' secret society.

Because that, for Eden, *will* be enough.

After the holidays, the train into Briarcliff arrives on time. I'm saddened to see another driver waiting to chauffer me to campus. I was hoping that my favorite guy, Yael, also Eden's dad, would meet me, so I could poke around regarding Eden's welfare.

Then again, he's probably at home with his wife and Briarcliff custodian, Moira, deciding if this is the instance where they'll override their daughter and send her somewhere else to complete her senior year.

I can't blame them, and I'm sick at being part of their reason, not their cure.

That has to change.

I'm not about to become the Virtues' vessel for getting petty, terrible shit done.

In fact, I'm so consumed by thoughts of Eden, Chase doesn't enter my mind until I'm practically on top of him once I reach the academy's outdoor pavilion.

"H-Hey," I hedge, when he turns around from his group of friends, a hot drink in hand.

Chase doesn't nod. He won't shift. Just stands in my path, his lids lowered, concealing the depth of his eyes.

I lift my chin, despite his attention turning my insides to mush. I'm thankful the weaker parts of me are surrounded by hard, emotionless bone. I ask, with as little care as possible, "How was your Thanksgiving?"

His lips part. "Move along."

"*Possum,*" James adds behind Chase, snickering. "You got some naked pics for us, too?"

I give him a sidelong look, though inside, that slow simmer of mine is hitting a dangerous boiling point. I guess it didn't take Chase long to forgive his buddy for helping to orchestrate my deep-dive into the Briarcliff lake.

Chase steps aside, his movement carrying a cold wind. I chance another look—just one *sign*—that this is an act, and there will come a moment where we can share our true emotions in private, or that James will receive another face-punch, but I receive nothing in return. Not even a ripple of emotion in those river-rock eyes.

He's let James get away with it. Again.

"See you around," I say, keeping strong, staying level, until I'm inside, out of sight, and I can slouch my shoulders without being watched.

I plan to hit my locker and dump the books I'd brought home before walking to the dorms, where I'm hoping Emma will be, and we can have a late dinner together, far from the dining hall.

Maybe Eden will be there, too. Maybe *something* can go right for once, and the three of us can have a quiet evening with noodles instead of rumors coming between us.

As always, unlocking the padlock to my locker causes my spine to stiffen and my feet to brace on the floor. I'm torn between flinging the door open and getting any nasty surprises over with or creaking it ajar with my fingers and peering over the wood.

"Glad I caught you!"

The jarring trill makes me jump, almost into my locker.

"Jesus," I say, heart pounding as I spin around.

"Sorry," Ivy says. "I probably should know by now to approach you with caution."

"I almost used these textbooks on you," I say after catching my breath.

Ivy loops her thumbs in the front pockets of her jeans, sporting a simple white T-shirt on top. "How was your—?"

"Fine," I say, cutting off what will inevitably be the most basic, polite question ever after coming back from Thanksgiving. Our cobbled-together friendship deserves better than that. *And I just used it on Chase.*

I cringe.

Ivy takes my expression another way. "Shoot—sorry, again. I didn't mean to pry. I know you and your dad have problems, and I wasn't—"

"It's fine," I assure. "Better than fine, actually. Dad and I are on the mend."

"Really?" Ivy's raises her brows with pleasure. "Callie, that's awesome."

The genuine warmth in her voice relaxes the tight cords in my chest. "Yours was good, too?"

"Sure." Ivy shrugs. "If you count eating a goose instead of a turkey. Loved seeing Mum and Dad, though."

"I'm glad." Then I cringe again. This is *not* how we usually are with each other.

"Um, so..." Ivy peers over her shoulder. No one else hangs around the lockers. Not surprising, since it's late Sunday night, and students don't normally run straight into the main building after arriving from vacation.

I dump my books in the locker, then bend to grab my duffel and slide it back on my shoulder. "What's up?"

"I mean..." Ivy's cheeks puff out with held-in breath. "We're on such fragile ground, you and I..."

Another cord loses tension inside my chest. "You sense it, too."

Ivy widens her eyes in a *hell yeah* gesture, then digs her thumbs harder into her pockets. "And I'm about to make it worse."

There we go. Knots upon knots behind my ribs. "Don't prolong the torture. Out with it."

"I'm a—ugh." Ivy sighs. "I've been sent as an emissary, and I *hate* that they've chosen me to do this, but Falyn flaunts being in charge of your recruitment so *freaking* much, and I'm seriously about to lose it on her—"

"Ivy. Get back on track."

"Yes. Okay. You need to come with me."

"I'm to what?"

"Right now."

I point to my duffel bag. "I was planning to—"

"Stuff it in your locker."

Ivy's flicked some sort of inner switch, her expression falling as flat as her voice.

"Ivy..."

"Please." For a second, her brows furrow. "Don't make this harder than it has to be."

My hand comes up in surrender. "Okay. Fine. Whatever."

I squish my duffel, and then my winter coat, into my locker, then shut and click the padlock before following Ivy into the hall.

We walk in silence, something we've never done before, and without anything to fidget with, I resort to rubbing the hem of my hoodie between my thumb and index finger.

Once at the back of the building, Ivy pushes the heavy wooden doors open, a counteracting winter wind rushing through the cracks.

I grimace. "I should've brought my coat."

"We won't be long." Ivy points to the adjacent building beyond the howling wolf fountain.

My gaze travels past the roaring snout, and I sigh. "Should've known."

"Come on."

Following her brisk steps, I navigate around the stone fountain (thankfully turned off and thus avoiding a freezing, spraying mist of water) and toward the new library, or, what it's officially called: the M.B.S. Library of Studies, built by Chase's family and constructed over the ashy bones of Emma's revenge gone wrong.

That kind of awareness causes enough heebie-jeebies when stepping through the sleek, chrome-lined sliding doors. Add in the Virtues' hidden temple and ... yeah. I'm not looking forward to my final destination.

They've recruited you because they think they can control you. Don't let them be right.

I reply to my mom's quiet voice: *I won't.*

The lights are dim to non-existent once we step through the turnstiles with Ivy's keycard, and the librarian is nowhere in sight.

Usually, the natural hush of a library is soothing, soft voices and rustling pages some of the only sounds breaking through a quiet solitude. This time, however, my back is up, my eyes alert, and my hands clenched.

We head to the back, single file, until we reach a wall of books. Long, rolling ladders are on either side of us, and what seems like unending stacks of books are behind us. The furniture is magnified, somehow, with just Ivy and me here. The aisles growing smaller in the swallowing darkness, the shelves looming larger over my head.

I shake off the fear, because I've never been afraid of the dark, and I'm not about to start now. I watch as Ivy crouches to the ground and lifts a floorboard, the movement smooth and quiet.

I swear, if an owl hoots outside, I might jump out of my skin.

Crossing my arms, I say, "Is this how you usually enter the temple?"

Ivy looks up. "There's an outside entrance, but it's not used much in winter."

I make a sound of agreement, if only for something to do, as Ivy reveals a small coding panel in the floor and types in a pin. I recall what Chase said to me. "So, I guess the ancient key I snorkeled for is more of a symbol."

"It belonged to the old temple, built when Rose Briar was in charge. With this new construction, we were able to update a lot of things."

Eyeing the wall of books, I step away once the pin pad flashes green. Lately, I've had a lot of back walls move to reveal secret chambers and figure I should keep clear.

Nothing happens.

"Aren't these books supposed to move?"

Ivy rises beside me. She points to the left. "Over there."

When she shifts, I mimic her movement, wary of what will open and how..

A large, person-sized panel in the floor unlocks and lifts with invisible hands. During its slow rise, I glance behind us in automatic caution to ensure we're alone.

When I turn forward again, a rectangular blackness awaits.

"I'll go first," Ivy says with quirked lips, likely understanding that there's no way in hell I'm stepping into a dark hole before she does.

Ivy's covered in complete darkness within two steps, her long legs eating up space faster than mine do, but I keep close to her heels, blinded in both sight and mind. I have no idea where we're going, where to step, or what staircase I'll topple down next.

"Here," she says, and takes my arm, gently guiding me to her side. We inch along a few steps before Ivy does something to cause a ring of sconces to light up around our forms.

My breath hitches as a single room illuminates, the ceiling door we entered through long shut with its silent, ghostly slither.

Gray, flat stone encircles us on all sides, the massive engraving of *altum vultaire in tenebres* carved in classic cursive directly at my eye-line.

"We rise high in the dark," I translate. "You and the Nobles have the same motto."

"Kind of. We interpret it in different ways."

I'm about to ask how the Virtues differentiate such an ominous sentence, but Ivy moves us into the center of the room.

"Holy..." is all I can get out when what I thought was our ceiling lights up with another row of second-floor candelabras, revealing a circular balcony with long, Roman-style columns dividing the circumference into four sections.

Robed figures appear from the shadows, stepping up to the stone balustrade. Their cloaks shimmer gold in the fire-dappled light, but their faces remain darkly obscured beneath their hoods.

Pomp and circumstance.

I think of that pretentious phrase and picture them puffing out their chests as they take their places between the columns, until the eight of them surround us, instead of the sick terror worming its way through my gut.

"Welcome to our temple," a soothing, feminine voice chimes, directly above the carved motto.

It's not a voice I'm familiar with. Not Falyn, or Willow, or even the whispery Violet...

"If you manage to achieve a coveted position in our ranks, this will become your sanctuary."

My throat spasms with a swallow that echoes in the cavernous silence. "I'd hope a sanctuary would contain some comfortable couches. Or maybe some curtains? Except, there are no windows..."

"*Quiet,*" the female voice hisses.

Crap. I'm rambling. I'm not comfortable revealing such a nervous aspect of myself, but with hooded, concealed stares beaming down on my head, remembrances of being stuck in the black, freezing depths of the lake come to the forefront. My near-death becomes real when I think of my face forever contorted with the spasms of lost breaths.

And they watched it happen.

"Calla Lily Ryan," the mysterious voice continues, "you've been summoned here so you may have your curiosity satisfied. What gave you the impression that you could reveal our existence without consequence?"

It's as if she's reading my mind, parting the mists of my thoughts and zoning in on my fear of further reprisal—of something *worse* than drowning happening to me in this place.

"I admit..." I clear my throat when my voice comes out as a warble. "I admit I wasn't careful, or conscious of what I was seeking. My roommate died, and I wasn't satisfied with the simplicity her fall was given. There had to be more truth than she was so drunk, she lost her balance and fell, or—"

"Therein, you found Rose Briar's original writings," the woman cuts in. "And concluded—falsely—that we Virtues had a hand in her murder."

"I didn't ... I wasn't sure what I was uncovering. It was her diary I discovered first. A diary planted by Addisyn. A girl who *was* a current member of yours, until she was arrested a little over a week ago. A girl who murdered her sister, also a member of the Virtues. How could I not conclude you had something to do with it?"

"I assure you, young one..." The woman's tone takes on a dangerous edge. "We are not behind Piper Harrington's death. You would have exposed us for nothing, had we not intervened."

My brows furrow. "Every clue I uncovered led me to your doorstep. Every paper I read, from Rose, to Piper, to Howard Mason breaking into the Nobles' tomb—"

"Planted."

I shake my head. "Not all of it was stashed with bad intentions. Rose Briar's letter was hidden by Piper to protect it, not use it as bait."

"Piper relied on misguided notions rather than coming to us first."

"Piper was killed for her involvement—"

"*Enough.*" The woman's voice crackles against the stone, but the only one who shivers from the electric charge is me. Every other person remains still, serene, and targeted on the girl in the center of the room below them.

"Your grave errors, your rampant mouth, your unfounded theories have brought you to this point, Calla Lily. Remember that, the next time you are given the honor to address the Virtuous Queen."

I glance back at the woman. She lifts her hands, the heavy, golden fabric falling down her forearms and creasing at her elbows as she hooks her hood and pulls it back.

The sconces seem to flicker with exposed power as silky brunette hair cascades down her shoulders, and she dips her poreless face until her features come into the light.

My knees snap together. My nails dig into my palms. My lips fuse into one line as I put a name to that face.

Sabine.

Sabine Harrington is the Virtues' queen.

Nine

"MRS. HARRINGTON," I breathe out.

Piper and Addisyn's mother.

I don't need to see her eyes to recognize the dangerous feel of them crawling across my skin, judging mercilessly..

I reach out to grab Ivy's hand but end up clutching air. She's gone, slipping away during the distracting reveal of the queen.

The back of my throat itches at the thought of being left alone, but my eyes scrape up from the floor, scanning the circular balcony for a ninth Cloak.

I find it to the left of Mrs. Harrington. Ivy may not have asked to be their princess, but she's up there, donning her title and casting a hooded gaze in my direction.

I turn my attention back to Mrs. Harrington. "I'm so sorry for causing you pain. You've lost two daughters, and I never intended to make it worse. And as for my mom and what she did to your family, I—"

"Silence." Mrs. Harrington's voice cracks through the cavernous chamber. "I haven't asked for an apology and don't require one. Talk of my daughters is no longer welcome on your tongue. I've summoned you here not to get to know you—you ruined any chance of a bond due to your unfortunate DNA and your insolent involvement in my daughters' affairs—but due to a development that cannot be ignored."

I shove my hands into my hoodie's front pocket so I can fist them together without anyone noticing. "You don't have to make some grandiose speech to make your disdain clear. I'm partially responsible for your loss of your youngest daughter. The only one you had left. And my mother never took your feelings into account when she—"

"*Enough.*"

Mrs. Harrington's expression is so frozen in time, her frost expands to me, but I grit my teeth and push on. "Why am I here? Why did you choose me to become a Virtue when I so clearly don't belong?"

Mrs. Harrington's eye tics at my questions, but she otherwise maintains her blank, flawless state. "You may have passed our first level of recruitment, but two steps remain before you're invited into our ranks. Are you willing to continue?"

"Do you *want* me to continue?"

Mrs. Harrington's upper lip twitches, the second fracture in her façade. She says, with slow, deathly cadence, "I will ask you this once. Deny us, and you may turn around and leave our temple, so long as you promise never to speak of the Virtues again. However, accept your next two tasks, and the rewards will be everlasting, but once passed, you will *never* be permitted to leave our ranks without severe repercussions. Have I made myself clear?"

"Altum vultaire in tenebres."

The girls' voices combine into a flat lull, but that one note circles the room and prickles against my ears.

Ivy. Where's Ivy? Why won't she let me see her face?

Piper's face swims in my mind's eye instead, transforming into my mother's in a blink. Both expressions are twisted in fear, shriveling my lungs and taking my breath. I lower my head and close my eyes until a vision of Chase takes hold, his lips softened from my kisses, his eyes in vivid, brilliant relief.

I want you to feel me inside you, as much as I feel you inside me...

I search for him now.

Multiple wrongs surround this group and his—wrongs Chase wants to change, suffering I'll expose.

Eden. Emma. Ivy. They've been mutilated by these women, too. What I've experienced is but a quarter of what they've endured.

Their combined hope, directed at me, to infiltrate the Virtues and assist in taking them down, makes my answer come out easy, despite my heart pounding at my mind's door, begging me to say the opposite.

My voice echoes with a strong, sure, "Yes."

A few beats of silence pass, where only the *thump, thump, thump* of my heart is heard in my ears.

"Very well," Mrs. Harrington says, and raises her chin, a power move that ensures she can peer down her regal nose. Her eyes glitter with refractive, ominous light. "Your second task is simple. Confess to us your worst sin, and let it fall on Virtuous ears."

My mouth goes dry. I once again scour the nearest Cloak for Ivy's familiar face but can't find her in all the gold fabric.

"My patience wears thin, Initiate," Mrs. Harrington says.

"Okay, uh..." I search the floor beneath my feet for answers. The memory that floats to the surface makes me squirm. "My best friend. Back in the city. It's because of me she experimented with drugs. At first it was just weed. Then coke. By the end, she ... she took it further. To Molly and LSD, but she wasn't getting it clean. It was laced with other things, like baby powder, and..."

I can't escape the microscopic effect of Mrs. Harrington's stare. She alone regards me without a hood, her expression filled with both judgment and indifference.

"And Fentanyl," I finish. "Sylvie overdosed and almost couldn't be saved. It was my fault. My fault she got into drugs in the first place."

Mrs. Harrington cants her head. The ring of girls surrounding us keep still and silent.

At last, she speaks. "This sounds more like your friend's weakness than yours."

I shudder at the remembrance of my careless peer pressure. "She didn't even want to try a blunt. I had to cajole her, guilt her, into doing one with me. I used my mom's death as a weapon. Sylvie couldn't deny me. I should've kept it at weed. I shouldn't've forced coke on her, too."

"Mm." Sabine gives a slow, bored blink. "I'm unconvinced this overdose is the worst part of yourself. Tell me more about your mother."

My stomach revolts at the word *mother* crossing Mrs. Harrington's scarlet lips. What kind of mother is *she*? Both her girls are—

No. No, I can't fling blame where more than enough resides within my soul. Mrs. Harrington has every right to hate my mother. Meredith Ryan wasn't just a hard worker, superhero mom, and a caring friend. She was a mistress. A homewrecker. A liar.

I squeeze my eyes shut, queasy inside the spiral of my mom's shame. *Human. She was human, and I miss her.*

I exhale. Breathe.

"My mom was brutally murdered," I say, my voice going quiet. "In her bedroom. Her killer has never been found." I look Mrs. Harrington dead in the eyes. "I'm sure we can agree that's punishment enough for her mistakes."

She ignores my goading as easily as a nearby gnat. "But you had a killer in mind, didn't you?"

I flinch. "My stepfather. I blamed him, had him taken into custody, but..."

"You were wrong."

I nod. Forming my costly mistake into words is still too painful to emit.

"Your mother also had an affair."

My gaze snaps up. Will Mrs. Harrington confirm I'm her ex-husband's daughter? Now that she's lost both of hers?

Mrs. Harrington's mouth curves at my expression. "I'm aware, Initiate, as are the rest of my Virtues, of your mother's transgressions, and of whom she had them with. Perhaps another time, we can discuss the sexual relations between her and my ex-husband, but again, her DNA is not the worst part of you, now, is it?"

"Am I his child?"

The question comes out sharp, and I bite my lower lip at the eagerness it exudes, like I'm desperate for the answer.

Mrs. Harrington's eyes grow small, but the power filtering through them doesn't flicker. "You read what my late daughter had to say about it in her diary. What do you think?"

"Piper could've been misled." *I hope she was wrong.* "I don't think I'm related to your daughters. I don't think Paul Harrington is—"

"You don't *want*, is the correction I must make. You're disgusted at the thought of being a Harrington, aren't you?"

I hesitate.

Mrs. Harrington pounces. "What makes you interested in the Virtues, then, if you cannot stand the leaders within it?"

There are no Harringtons left, except for you, I almost bite out. But I'm outnumbered, and while they may all be on a balcony well away from me, I'm not an idiot.

"My mother would've told me." I find more strength as I let the truth flow. "There's no reason she would've kept his name from me all this time. I wouldn't—*she* never—came after you for any kind of support. We were fine. Proudly independent. Best friends." My voice breaks.

Mrs. Harrington pounces on my hesitation. "Maybe she concealed his name in order to protect you. Have you thought of that?"

My breath stalls.

She chuckles. "Enough idle talk, my dear. You're correct. Paul is not your missing father. Your paternity is, yet again, *not* your darkest secret. Your poorly construed accusation against your stepfather is also not among your top transgressions, though you're certainly collecting a stack of them." Mrs. Harrington folds her arms. "I'll give you one last chance. What remains to be confessed to the Virtues?"

My eyes flit around the room, catching upon featureless, obscured faces.

Sylvie overdosing from my drugs was bad. Sending my stepdad to jail was terrible. The possibility of having Mr. Harrington as my real father is a nightmare.

...what's left?

"Tell me, Calla Lily." Mrs. Harrington leans her forearms against the railing, tilting seductively in my direction. "What have you done while at Briarcliff Academy?"

I rack my brain for details. "You mean, other than have a roommate die, accuse a teacher of murder, break into a secret society tomb, and sleep with—"

Oh my God.

Sleep with Chase?

"Dr. Luke," I divert in a scratchy voice. "I accused him, too."

Mrs. Harrington clucks her tongue through a Cheshire smile. "Is that what your new sisters need to hear?"

"What do you want? What are you digging for?"

Mrs. Harrington laughs. "Don't be obtuse, dear. Confess to us who you care for, despite what he did to you. Who you're loyal to, regardless of his cruel intentions. Who you cannot help but follow, despite him not being yours."

Chase.

I step back, but as I'm in the middle of a circle, it brings me to no safer distance. "What's so important about him? He's far from the worst thing I've done."

"Ah." Mrs. Harrington holds up a finger, her nail, painted blood red, visible from my vantage point. "Was I not clear to you before? I asked you to tell me your vilest secret." Mrs. Harrington's red-lined, menacing lips peel into a smile. "I didn't say whose secret it had to belong to."

My brows draw in. I take another step back, toward a nonexistent door. I'm trapped in this corrupt stone temple. "Chase has never made me aware of the secrets he keeps."

"Hasn't he?"

My mind works backward, even as the denial crosses the threshold of my lips. It catalogues and highlights the pieces of knowledge Chase gave me, then comes to an abrupt, alarming halt at his latest confession: *I don't want to end the Nobles. I want to control them.*

Shit shit *shit.*

Chase's dad is the head of the Nobles. Their king. He's engaged to be married to Mrs. Harrington. The last thing this twisted couple wants is Chase toppling them like two chess pieces.

What level of betrayal do I have inside my head?

"He's closed off," I say, keeping my voice level. "We never get that deep with each other."

"Are you saying you only have surface-level fucks with him?"

Such profanity, coming from a Briarcliff parent, is off-putting and creepy. But the girls around her merely sway, their robes fluttering but their shoulders as stiff as the Roman columns framing their forms.

I grit my teeth. "Not that it's any of your business, but yes."

"The truth, Callie," Mrs. Harrington warns, "the *truth* is the only way you will leave this temple one step closer to becoming a Virtue."

"I don't want—"

But you do, my whirring mind slows down to remind. *Think of what Eden is going through this very second. What more will happen to her or to Emma if you don't pretend the Virtues have control?*

Ivy. Where's Ivy?

I pinpoint her when her hood ripples as she turns her head to the side. As a ribbon of light hits her cheekbone and reflects the blue of her eyes.

Her stare is pleading, her lips pulled in. As if she's telling me, *do what Mrs. Harrington wants.*

"Fine," I say. Mrs. Harrington cocks her ear, feigning deafness.

I yell, "*Fine.* I have feelings for him. Does that please you? I care for Chase Stone in a way I've never cared for anyone. I crave him despite the malice he's inflicted and the apathy he gives me, except for when we're in bed. I like him, okay?"

"Like?"

"*Love.*" My voice goes hoarse, gritting with sound. "I'm falling in love with him. *That* is the worst part of myself I can give you. I love a boy who's cruel, who was never mine to begin with, who belonged to your daughter first." I breathe out a few breaths. "And I've destined myself for heartbreak."

"Sweet girl, I can somewhat believe your confession, with your large doe eyes and your thick, pathetic tears splashing over our pristine marble floors. But I can't say the same for Chase Stone. He's slept with you, he's protected you, and he claimed you as his soulmate not two weeks ago."

"That was in retaliation to Falyn's hazing. I would've died from hypothermia had he not put a stop to it."

Mrs. Harrington laughs, and a shiver shoots up my spine at the image of a wolf, with ferocious fangs, chasing a vulnerable girl through a forest.

"Secret societies live and die by their rules, do they not?" I ask. "He invoked the soulmate rite to stop her abuse of power."

A Cloak hisses. Falyn. I flip her the my middle finger, overjoyed that she actually gets to *see* the disgust written all over my face.

"Soulmate protection provides so much more than a shield against your fellow sisters," Mrs. Harrington says. "As you're about to find out. You must admit, after all the hurdles he's defended you from, despite being explicitly told to isolate and humiliate you, that Chase cares for you."

"He might," I say, but my tone is unsure. I have the dizziest feeling that I'm walking into a trap. "You'll have to ask him."

"He does."

My back goes up. "So what? So what if he cares for me despite your stupid threats and orders? If that's all you want, then you have it. Let me leave."

"You've given me exactly what I need, my dear. That is his worst secret you bear." After a slow, satiated smile, Mrs. Harrington pulls her hood over her head and retreats from the railing. "You are that boy's greatest weakness to exploit."

Ten

ONE BY ONE, the golden Cloaks draw back from the balcony and disappear into the ether upstairs.

When I'm alone, the hidden door to the temple opens. I dash up the stairs and burst into the library, my breaths heaving.

The blue hue of sleeping computers guides me through the stacks and to the main doors, and when they hiss open softly, I sprint out, glad to be rid of that place.

Mrs. Harrington didn't have to say it, but I hear her implications echoing in my ears. *Chase is your greatest weakness.*

When did that happen? I'm trying to recall the moment when Chase and I pivoted from enemies, to fuck buddies, to ... whatever we are now.

The foreboding swirl in my gut has me sprinting faster to my dorm, a place where I can find some semblance of peace, of order.

"Callie!"

The familiar call slows my steps, but not my resolve. I don't turn around.

"Callie! Wait up!"

I walk faster.

"Hey." Ivy grips my shoulder, twisting me over my feet. "Couldn't you hear me?"

I regain my balance and wrench out of her hold. "What are you expecting me to say to you right now?"

Ivy's breath puffs next to mine as she trots to keep pace next to me. "It was necessary."

"*Necessary?*" I echo, halting and facing her in the middle of the night-shadowed pathway. "I had to pour my heart out to that witch. With *everyone* watching. Do you know what kind of ammo I gave them? What kind of trigger Falyn's going to pull when classes start tomorrow?"

"She won't. Falyn can't," Ivy assures. "What occurs in the Virtues' temple is sacred. For us alone. Falyn isn't allowed to use any of that against you."

"Like she was forbidden from pushing me off the dock? Or sending me nude photos of Eden? C'mon, Ivy, you can't be so innocent as to—"

"I'm not innocent." Ivy's eyes shine white in the dark.

"Then why allow this to happen?"

"There hasn't been anyone to successfully go against them in years. The Virtues have grown in power, Callie. After Emma, no one was willing to rebel against Sabine. Until..."

I throw my hands up. "Until what?"

"You."

The one syllable strikes my heart like a fist. "Don't put so much faith in me. I'm far from your perfect savior, and Mrs. Harrington proved that tonight. Even my *worst* traits weren't enough for her. She wanted my weaknesses, too. Now she has them. And that *terrifies* me."

"Please." Ivy doesn't have to get on her knees to beg. Her lower lip trembles. "You're not alone."

I catch her eye. Hold it. Even as my heart hurts, it sings. *You are not alone, Calla.*

"Okay." I bite my lower lip. "I'll do the third and final trial. But Ivy?"

"Yeah?"

"If anyone else gets hurt..."

Ivy pulls me into a hug. Her comforting, wildflower fragrance mixes with the bite of winter air, and my shoulders relax in her embrace. "It's not easy, but you're lowering her guard by being honest."

"Uh-huh," I mutter into Ivy's shoulder.

Ivy pulls away. "And hey—that whole Mr. Harrington possibly being your dad was an unexpected twist, huh?"

I give her the side-eye. "Was it?"

"Well." Ivy lets out a laugh, keeping one arm around my shoulders as we resume walking. "Then celebrate that he's not. She wouldn't lie about that."

I turn to look behind us, down the pristine, paved walkway and back toward the library. "I'm not so sure."

"The queen only imparts truth. That's a requirement of leading us."

I scan Ivy's profile, my back tensing under the weight of her arm. She says *queen* like it means something. Talks about her belief in truth like Mrs. Harrington has to abide by it. Really, Sabine Harrington can do whatever the fuck she wants—*that's* one of the requirements of being human.

A flicker of distrust grows its flame in my chest. I sigh, wishing for the Ivy I once knew, not the one who's become the Virtue in my head.

We reach the dorms. Before I go in, I ask, "Are you sure you want to help with the downfall of your sisterhood?"

"I'm wishing for the Virtues of yesteryear. The ones my grandmother spoke of. If that's not possible anymore, then I'm okay if they're disbanded and exposed." She pauses. "Annihilated."

I distance from her when we reach the doors to Thorne House. "You're a legacy?"

"Yeah." Her ice-blond brows lower. "My grandma, and then my dad, were students at Briarcliff."

I wait for Ivy to say more.

"He was kicked out before he could graduate," she says. "And he said it was the Nobles' fault."

"Holy shit, Ivy."

Ivy offers a waning smile. "You and I haven't known each other for long, but you agree we connected right away, right?"

"Sure."

"It's why I stupidly mentioned the Nobles to you so early. The Nobles were told to keep watch on you. They've been interested in you from the very beginning, and I felt so, so bad for how you were treated."

Ivy's not asking a question, but I nod under her scope. I have the distinct feeling that's what she needs right now, even though it's far too late to rewind our choices.

"I'm not just a scholarship kid," Ivy says. "I haven't been the most upfront with you, but you're an initiate now, and I can tell you what my dad did."

I answer hesitantly. "Okay."

"He did some things that got him expelled, and during one of his rants with Mom, I overheard a conversation I wasn't supposed to."

"Go on."

"It's not much, but ... Dad only freaked out once our lives started falling apart. He said it all came back to betraying the Nobles in high school, that he shouldn't have done it, and if he could go back and be a 'good little preparatory prick,' we'd still have our money."

"What did he do?"

"He stole a Stone's girlfriend. Chase's uncle."

I breathe out a gust of air. "Whoa."

"That girlfriend is my mom."

My mouth hangs open.

"Thing is..." Ivy lifts her hands in an empty gesture. "He tried to get back into their good graces by pleading with me to accept the Virtues' invitation to become one of them. That maybe, if I become Virtuous, the perks would stretch to my parents again and he'd no longer be blacklisted from top companies."

It all makes sense. Ivy's hesitation in telling me the truth. Her excuses and lies. "You're trying to save your family."

Ivy wilts. "I'm desperate to. Mom and Dad have scraped by for so long. When I received a scholarship here, my dad became my *dad*. Loving. Attentive and present. I'd never felt anything like it before. He put so much hope in me, in my ability to get our reputation back. I'm sorry you're caught in the middle. I try to do what the Virtues want, but when Piper died, and I took her place beside Sabine—Callie, I—" Ivy's mouth seals shut, her jaw hard but her eyes shining with tears. "There's more to the Virtues than my parents know. My mother was never one of them. I can't be Virtuous anymore. Not after what I—what Sabine made me—"

"Shh," I soothe, drawing Ivy to my side. "It's okay. Let's just go home, get warm."

"I'm sorry for lying to you."

I rest my head against hers. "You don't have to apologize anymore."

Ivy glares in the direction of Thorne House, her forehead creasing. "I'm not finished telling you everything."

I hold Ivy in a light, but secure, hug. "Then we'll sleep on it. To be honest, I need a break from all these big reveals."

Ivy's soft laugh flutters my hair. "Deal. I'll see you tomorrow?"

We separate, and I nod. I back up a few steps, waving goodbye, then swivel to walk through the doors and step into the waiting elevator. When I turn to face the front, Ivy's still standing on the path, her stare unwavering on mine until the elevator door slides shut.

I'm dressed and ready for class well before Emma wakes up, and I pour myself a thermos of coffee before quietly departing our room.

The day dawns bright and frigid, and I huddle into my winter coat as I walk, backpack-free, to the academy. I left most of my things in my locker before my summons last night, and had no urge to run back into the deserted academy afterward to get my things—lest I stumble upon a Nobles' meeting, too.

Only one secret society per night, please.

Gray skies cloud the horizon, and as my breaths puff sharp, white clouds, I wonder when it will snow. In the city, we either received white-out blizzards or blackened sludge piled up on curbs. I've never experienced the true, Christmas effect of blanketing snow on open fields and weighing down thick branches, unmarred and sparkling under the sun's white-washed winter lens.

I'm so distracted by my unexpected Christmas wish that it takes me a moment to connect the dots when I see a cluster of students outside, their neutral-hued winter coats and parkas blending into the cobbled stone of the pavilion and academy.

Heads start popping out of collars and hoods like turtles the closer I get, and the harsh connection of voices and wild gestures slow my steps.

"Fuckin' fight club," a guy murmurs as he passes me by.

He's young, pimply, and thin, likely a freshman, and when I catch his eye, I ask automatically, "What's going on?"

He turns at my question, walking backward, his hands stuffed in his coat pockets. "More elitist bullshit. Looks like there's an opening in their ranks."

I raise a brow. "Huh?"

But he spins around, bypassing the gathering crowd and skipping up the school's steps without a second look.

Me, not so much. I creep to the outskirts of the growing ring of students, too indoctrinated into Briarcliff Academy's clandestine violence to ever turn a blind eye.

I peer above shoulders and through the spaces of arms until I can get a better view. Jeers mixed with encouragement become easier to decipher, and what I hear makes my breath quicken.

"Can you believe this?"

"What'd he do?"

"Who'd he fuck?"

"It's fucking happening, man. Chase Stone. Look what they're doing to him!"

Chase.

His name catches fire in my mind, and I shove through bodies, and ignoring the resulting "hey!" "fuck off, possum," and "rude, much?" I break through the wall of students, finding myself a few feet too exposed in a makeshift circle.

Guttural laughter flows into the spaces around me, as well as its deep, familiar tone. With a sickening *click*, my eyes hit on the spectacle in the center.

Chase stands between his two friends, Riordan and Tempest, with James facing them.

James's lips peel back from his teeth. "It sucks to be on the bottom rung, doesn't it, man?"

My gaze pings over to Chase, searching his face for any clue, any reaction, to tell me what's going on. But he's steadfast, staring James down without the slightest tic or tell of emotion.

Until his eyes wince shut and a grunt sounds out from his tightly shut lips.

Chase's knees buckle, but he keeps his balance.

I step closer, enough to see Tempest draw back his fist to aim another punch at Chase's lower back. His kidneys.

"Wha—" the last letter meant to complete that word doesn't have sound on my tongue.

Chase isn't standing between his two friends. They're *holding* him by his arms.

"Tempest!" I run forward, the primordial part of my brain wanting to catch Riordan by his ear and tear him to bits. But his hand shoots out at the last second, sending me stumbling back with a surprised rush of air exiting my lungs.

Chase reacts to my voice, his eyes flicking up to mine, then darting to Riordan.

But not before I see his flash of warning, the pain at registering my presence.

He roars, fighting against his restraints with sudden vigor, tendons popping out from his neck, his jaw becoming rigid on a scream.

Chase is outnumbered, but he struggles with untapped fury, his once docile, stoic acceptance of being restrained by two buddies bursting into ash.

"Don't you *fucking* touch her again!" Chase roars at Riordan, his voice rough and guttural.

James, who watches the show with thinly veiled pleasure, mutters, "Keep doing it."

"Let him go!" I cry at the same time, but don't risk running up against Riordan again. Not if it will turn Chase feral and reckless.

"Callie, get out of here!" Chase demands between his ragged breaths.

I jump on Tempest instead, clawing at his arms and trying to draw them away from Chase.

But he's Chase's second. They row crew together six out of seven days a week. He's stronger—so much stronger—than me.

His hurricane-green eyes meet mine right when I'm about to use my teeth, and they're direct and bright with warning. "*Leave*," he whispers. "*Before you—*"

I smack Tempest in the bicep, pissed as all hell that I can't do more harm. "What are you doing to him? Let him go!"

Chase cranes his neck to glance at me. "This is none of your concern," he pants between clenched teeth. This close, I register the beads of sweat on his forehead, the tears in his blazer's seams at his shoulders.

How long has this been going on?

"I'm not going anywhere." I clench my hands into fists, and I direct my caustic tone to Riordan and Tempest. "You're supposed to be his friends!"

"I said *do it*!" James roars above us, and, despite Chase's valiant, stronger-than-most, efforts, Riordan lands his foot against the back of Chase's leg, bringing him to his knees.

No! I race to the front, falling to my knees in front of Chase and holding his face. "What's going on?" I whisper furiously. "Make this stop!"

Chase's lids lower to half-mast. Droplets of blood fall from his lower lip onto my thumbs. "This ... this has to finish."

I agree whole-heartedly. "Stand up. I'll help you out of here." I glare up at Tempest and Riordan, who continue to hold Chase's arms back, pushing his torso forward by wrenching his shoulders.

Their faces ... I blink them into focus. They're like soldiers in battle. Blank, determined, and forced into blindness. That way, no color can infiltrate their feelings until the task is done.

"Stop," I plead with them. "You're hurting him."

Pain sears into my shoulders when strong, angry hands clamp down, flinging me aside as if I weigh nothing.

Chase's roar sears my eardrums as I'm thrown, my palms scraping rough asphalt, and my stockinged knees taking the brunt.

James's body blots out the sky as he stands over me, his fair skin blotchy, color riding high in his cheeks. But it's not simply the winter wind that's making his blood swirl. "Quit getting in the way of things, stupid possum, then maybe your boyfriend won't have to pay your dues."

"Chase hasn't done anything," I seethe. When I stand, the torn skin on my palms and knees scream, but my voice doesn't transmit the pain. "And don't you fucking call me vermin. Haven't you heard? I'm an initiate."

James smiles. From a distance, most would see it as his usual goofy, lopsided grin.

But maybe it's because he's facing only me. Maybe this smile shows his canines because his friends can't see, and James is allowing his true self to come out and say hi before he buries it under a joking, *sorry dude, but I gotta beat up your boyfriend* shrug.

As if in confirmation of the creature he hides, James winks at me before twisting around.

"He's my soulmate," I grit out, loud enough for James to hear, but not many others.

James stills.

"Chase announced it at the docks last weekend, and I'm confirming it," I say. Frantically, I scroll through recent flashbacks to find Chase's exact words. "We can invoke protection. Does the mutual rulebook not say that if a Noble member attacks a Noble prince's soulmate, the prince may exact any punishment he wishes?"

James cracks another smile. "That only goes one way, *possum*. You can't invoke shit. And Chase? Chase agreed to these fun times."

The ground drops from beneath my feet. "He wouldn't."

"He refused the Nobles' edict, as confirmed by *your* testimony last night. And he's paying the price." James spits out the last word: "*Willingly*."

I step around James, but fury quickly overrides any logic in my head. "By what? Making him endure a public lashing in the Town Square? Where's your whip, you sick bastard? Why not tear his shirt from his body and lash him until he bleeds? Or wait—I forgot." I throw my hands on my hips and glare. "It's probably because we're no longer in the *seventeenth fucking century*. Let him go, you turd, before I—"

"Before you what?" James's voice takes on a needling tone, and he scrunches his hands under his eyes and fakes a baby crying. "You'll tell the teacher on us?"

I stare at him, my eyes narrowing as his antics draw in giggles and laughter from the crowd. He drops his hands and chuckles, shaking his head in amused disdain. "Go back to your ignorant hole, you rabies infected—"

I spit in his face.

James rears back, color draining from his face until it becomes white with ominous fury.

"Callie!" Chase rasps behind me. I hear a *thump* and Chase's resulting grunt. One of them hit him again. They're beating him up.

With adept slowness, James wipes my saliva from his cheek, his hands shaking with fury and his eyes darkened by it.

I brace for his counterattack, whether it be a hit or a shove—as long as he doesn't direct it at Chase.

What I hear instead is, "Take her. Take her before she does something epically stupid, like put me in a position to knock her the fuck out."

Gentle hands envelop my arm, but my gut reaction is to swing out.

"It's me," Ivy says into my ear. I never heard her come up behind me. "Let's go. Now."

"But—"

"Chase is doing what he has to," she says. "And now so are you."

"Like leave him here to be humiliated? For his friends to use his blood to paint the asphalt?"

Ivy forces up my chin until I meet her eyes. My tumultuous heartbeat must be thrumming into her fingers. "This is the way it is," she murmurs. "You knew it the instant you left our temple last night."

I search her eyes, but I'm not seeing the blue. I'm thinking back. "That I'm his weakness? That's why they're doing this?"

Ivy's eyes soften. "You confirmed Chase refused his orders. The Nobles wanted him to get close to you for their purposes only. To watch you, manipulate you. *Never* to care about you. For that, he has to be punished."

I shake my head, unable to tear my gaze from hers. "We've got to do something. As Virtues, can't we—as his soulmate, can't I—?"

"No. I'm sorry, but we don't meddle with internal problems. This is for the Nobles to figure out."

"But it's my fault."

My heart sinks as Ivy tries to lead me away, but I keep hearing the thumps, the punches, the swallowed, enduring cries of pain.

I tear out of her hold.

Ivy whirls. "Callie—"

Backing away from her, I say, "I won't get in the middle of it. But I'm not going to leave him here, either. I'll watch. I'll watch all of it, to make sure he knows I'm here."

Ivy's mouth falls into an *O*. She re-hinges her jaw enough to say, "That's not how we..."

"I don't care about your traditions. And I'm not going to desert him because of Mrs. Harrington's manipulations. I'm not going to turn my back to preserve more Virtuous and Noble lies."

"You're risking the queen's wrath."

"Our plan to make me a Virtue is still in place," I assure. "She can't do anything if I just stand and watch."

"But will you be able to? They're hurting him pretty bad. Headmaster Marron is a Noble, and he won't intervene."

"I know," I say, then turn away from her, toward the crowd, squeezing through for space until I'm back at the front.

Tempest's frown has grown deeper, Riordan's back stiffer, as they continue to hold Chase down. But James ... James goes in for a kick to Chase's gut, and some students cheer, while most gasp.

A girl with a long braid whispers to her friend beside me, "James is having too much fun. These guys follow Chase Stone's every order. Why isn't Chase fighting back?"

Her friend responds, "I dunno, but whatever Chase did, it's three against one. Even our Briarcliff prince can't fight those odds."

"What'd he do, though?"

"Something terrible," her friend mutters. "Something really, really bad to deserve this kind of treatment."

"Where are the teachers?" Braid Girl asks.

I pull my lower lip in, biting down hard enough to pierce skin, but keep my eyes forward. Chase lowers his chin, covering his wince and grunting at James's kicks, but raising his head after each blow, ensuring James meets his eye between the hits.

Chase's glare could destroy cities.

And James's hesitating blink before he raises his fist tells me all I need to know.

"Grab the back of his head," James snarls to Riordan. "Expose his neck to me."

Riordan stalls.

"I *mean* it!" James bellows.

After a heartbeat, where Riordan and Tempest stare at each other over Chase's slumped form, Riordan grabs a fistful of Chase's hair and pulls until Chase's face is almost tilted to the sky.

James's lips curve. "Not so fun, is it? To be nailed in the face by someone you thought was your buddy. This is for your smackdown at Piper's memorial."

Chase doesn't respond, instead dragging his eyes to the side, where he catches mine.

Stay with me, I mouth, unshed tears building in my eyes.

And with each punch thrown, with each of James's cackles and kicks, we don't look away from one another.

Not until Tempest lays down a final, merciful blow, and Chase is sent into the black.

Eleven

I'VE NEVER MADE myself bleed before.

Yet here I am, pacing back and forth outside Chase's dorm room, chewing my thumb off to the first knuckle.

A metallic, bitter tang coats my tongue, but I swallow it as if it were wine. The bittersweet taste is a telling reminder of where I am, who I've become, and what I'm waiting for.

It's second period, and Rose House is pretty much deserted, everyone heading for class after the violent theatrics were over. It ended when, at last, a sole teacher ran down the academy's steps, ordering James to halt at once.

He did, but not before kissing his knuckles for doing such a good job, and winking at Chase, half-conscious on the ground, and sauntering away.

God. And Chase took it. He submitted to James's cowardly brawl, all but inviting his friend to inflict permanent physical damage. And for what?

My back stiffens when I hear footsteps thudding up the staircase and the low murmur of deep voices.

"Why'd he take it so far?" I hear Riordan ask.

"Deep down, James is a sick fuck," Tempest responds.

"You would know," Riordan says, trying for a joke, but it falls flat. "I mean, I always thought you to be the sociopath, not our fucking comic ginger top."

I wait for the fire exit to open.

Three bodies fill the frame, piling through with Chase's head hanging in the center.

"Fuck," I whisper, my throat growing hot.

I run over, bending to peer into Chase's half-closed eyes. "Shouldn't he be with the nurse?"

"He refuses," Tempest says, grunting as he takes more of his friend's weight.

Riordan digs in his pocket for his keycard and holds it out to me. "Mind?"

I grab it without question and beep us into Riordan and Chase's dorm room, holding the door open for them to drag Chase in.

I've never been in Chase's room before, my mind taking cursory stock of the dark wood and brown leather furnishings, a large flat-screen TV with various gaming consoles, and a lot of black, sleek appliances, before Riordan tells me to take a left into Chase's bedroom.

A calming, grayish-blue interior greets my vision when I step in, surprisingly clean for a boy, though there is a faint, locker room smell emanating from all the sports-gear piled up in the corners.

Riordan is the first to duck under Chase's arm and toss him on the bed in a heap, Tempest being slightly more delicate.

Chase groans at the movement.

"Ice," I mutter to myself. "I'll get some ice."

Riordan stops me with a clear, "Better yet, possum, you should scat."

My eyes narrow. "I'm not going anywhere while he's like this."

Riordan retorts, "It's because of *you* he's here."

"Guys," Tempest warns.

"Oh really?" I put my hands on my hips. "Was I the one holding his arms back so he couldn't defend himself? Was it me who gave James over fifteen minutes with a human punching bag?"

Riordan's face grows dark. He stalks over, pointing his finger. "You have no fucking clue, you stupid cu—"

Tempest attempts to come between us, but Chase's guttural mutter stops all of us cold.

"What'd you say, man?" Tempest asks.

Chase's throat bobs. His eyes stay closed. "She stays."

Riordan curses, spinning away and dragging a hand over his short crop of brown hair. "You're gonna be the end of us."

"I'm not trying to be," I say, and cut around both boys to perch on the side of Chase's bed. "I'll stay with him today."

"It's a bad idea," Riordan says, but not to me. He's talking to Tempest.

Tempest takes a long moment to study me, but I only half see him when I grab Chase's hand and squeeze. "I'm here."

"Might as well give Chase what he wants," Tempest says to Riordan. "We can get to class, make a show of being present and unaffected by what we just did."

I swallow, stroking Chase's pale cheek, but keep my ears open.

"Should we leave *her* here, though?" Riordan asks. "Chase wants it, but our king's made it clear—"

"Who's gonna say something?"

Thick silence blooms.

"It ain't gonna be me," Tempest continues. "We may've been ordered to put Chase on his knees, but nothing was said about the after. We did what was directed."

"Yeah, but..."

Tempest's voice grows ominous. "And now, we leave him be. Whatever occurs after we toss him on his bed is his business. And he says Callie stays."

Riordan sighs. "Fine. *Fine.* But I don't fucking like this."

Tempest says, "You're not going to fucking say anything, either."

I jump when Riordan says, close to my ear, "If we're told to hold him down again, it's on you, Callie. You hear me?"

"I snuck up here without anyone seeing," I say. "I won't be obvious."

"Or do anything stupid," Tempest warns.

I nod.

Riordan stomps out of the room, but I feel more than see Tempest lingering at the door.

In a quiet voice, Tempest says, "You know what would be best for him."

I lower my head. "I do."

"Good. So, take this moment, talk it out, whatever, but then leave. Leave for good."

My answering nod is heavy, my neck unable to hold the weight.

Tempest shuts the door with a soft click.

I stare down at Chase, the black crescents of his eyelashes soft against his alabaster skin, normally so golden and flushed with the rush of endless activity.

Despite my attempt to stay strong, my throat swells, thick and hot, and incoming tears prick the backs of my eyes. I sniff back the threatening sob.

Chase's hand twitches in mine. His pale, rose-colored lips tilt into a smile. "You're not actually crying over my broken body, are you, sweet possum?"

His eyes open, and I'm hit with polished, shining bronze.

"So what if I am?" I mumble, rubbing the heel of my hand over one eye.

Chase's lids lower, softening his intensity. He murmurs, "I'm not brutalized enough to deserve tears."

"No? Because after what I saw..."

"James is a pussy." Chase grunts while pushing himself to lean on the headrest. "He thinks he can wail on me and have me down and out for good, but I'll be fine in a few hours."

My brows spike. "He must've punched you a few too many times in the head, because you were barely hanging on out there."

Chase's lips quirk with a wry smile, but his expression is weighed down and tired. "I know how to take punches. And James doesn't know how to tell I'm softening his blows."

I think back on the way Chase curved his body every time James came after him, his muscles relaxed, his head hanging low.

"It was all an act? The whole unconscious, suffering thing?" I resist the urge to stand and tower over him, but holy *hell*, my heart cracked open when each fist landed on his body.

"I had to keep up pretenses. Make them think they're winning. Not gonna lie, though." Chase grimaces as he pulls his hand from mine and rubs his chest. "He got in a few good ones."

I ask softly, "Why'd you let them do it?"

Chase lifts his gaze. "I had to. If I don't take punishment like the rest of them, what kind of leader will I make?"

"This is all my fault."

He shakes his head, his fingers finding mine. "They would've found out another way."

I flip my hand, so the pads of his fingers trace the sensitive skin of my palm. "Was I..."

"Were you what, sweet possum?" Chase's voice contains a tinge of amusement.

I swallow. "Was I right? Was what I said to Mrs. Harrington ... to Sabine ... true?"

The room becomes so silent, I'm afraid to look up at him. But I force my gaze to meet his. Unwavering. Curious.

He answers with a simple, steady, "Yes."

"I'm your weakness," I whisper.

Chase leans forward to cup my face, cringing momentarily at the movement. "The Virtues have been looking for one for a long time. I've been masking my emotions, pretending I don't have any preferences, for exactly this reason. But I'm human. I was bound to break. And I'm glad I broke with you."

"No." I clasp his wrist, welcoming the warmth against the chilling consequences of his words. "Not like this. We can't care for each other when the Virtues are our enemies. Because that's what they are. The Nobles, too, aren't they?"

Chase sighs. "Piper died. That's widened an already fractured divide. Sabine is the Virtuous Queen, and my father is the Noble King. Engaged to be married. Sabine lost it on my father. Accused him of not doing enough to find Piper's killer, of not inter-rogating the Noble members. It was all of us at the cliff that night. Nobles and Virtues partying. One of us had to be responsible."

"But it was Addisyn. Sabine's other daughter was responsible."

"Yeah. How'd that go?"

I cringe. "Sabine discovered Addisyn was the killer, and she protected her daughter. Made Addisyn a Virtue to keep her quiet and shield her from investigation."

"Sabine blames you. For destroying Addisyn. For almost revealing our societies to the school, the Briarcliff PD, fuck, the NYPD, too, with your relationship with that detective guy."

"Then why did she accept me?"

"Same reason she accepted Addisyn. She keeps her liabilities close, makes her enemies her friends. She'd do anything to keep her position as queen." Chase tucks a strand of hair behind my ear, watching me closely. "You need to be careful. You're not safe."

"Neither are you." I study his wrinkled uniform, the blooming bruises along his collarbone. James was smart enough to keep the most damage away from Chase's face. "This morning proves that."

"I've been dealing with this my whole life. That little show-and-tell they had in the pavilion is nothing. I can handle it."

I frown. "Whose instruction were James, Riordan, and Tempest following? Your father's or Sabine's?"

Chase's touch strokes down my chin to my collarbone. I hide the little tremble under my skin that follows. "Both."

"But ... I thought..."

He traces lower, until the tips of his fingers rest against the open collar of my shirt. I work to control my breaths. "We shouldn't."

Chase gives a sage nod. "We *definitely* shouldn't."

He pops open the button.

"You're coming off a severe punishment because you went against your orders to manipulate me."

Chase pauses at my second button, but the heat of his fingers, the promise of *him*, scores into my skin like a welcome burn. "You watched it. The whole time, you didn't run. Does that mean you forgive me for ignoring you this past week?"

"I have to believe..." I say in a hushed voice, then close my eyes as he flicks open another button and then another, exposing my bra. "I have to believe that our sex was real. That you didn't use it as a weapon."

Chase's hand goes into one side of my bra, cupping my breast and stroking my nipple. I suck in a burst of air. "Our first time, I wanted it to be about my control over you. And it was."

I open my eyes, seeing his face for the first time since he started touching me, his brown sugar gaze, his tightened lips. His short breaths.

"You did that to me," I whisper.

"Not in the way I hoped." His thumb circles my nipple, then he flicks it. I flinch in the best way, tingles traveling from my breasts to my core. "I told myself I fucked you out of Noble duty. Made you come the same way I make tons of other chicks come. But your body fit against mine in a way I didn't expect. Your moans made me hard during a time I wasn't predicting. And those lips..." Chase leans forward and traces his tongue across my lower lip, my nose brushing against his cheek as I tilt toward him for more. "What comes out of your perfect, prissy mouth pissed me off and turned me on. And your pussy?"

Chase uses his other hand to spread my thighs, and when he meets my underwear, I feel his grin on my lips.

I'm already wet for him. Swollen and throbbing with need.

"It tasted sweet, and I kept wanting to suck my fingers to keep tasting you, long after I'd fucked you."

My breaths barely fill my lungs. I'm hot and struggling all over—to be strong, to be timid, to have him despite being warned away from him—but his hands lead the dance. I'm bending and twisting in tandem to his seductive choreography, and I can't stop.

"You don't want to do this," I say against his lips, putting space between us when he tries to win me over with one of his world-tilting kisses. "You're hurt, despite avoiding the worst of it. You're still bruised."

"Then I guess you'll have to be on top."

My core flutters open like butterfly wings as he sneaks past my underwear and dips into my folds, curving his fingers in orgasmic perfection.

"I ... oh." I curse, then push his shoulders, sending him smacking against the headboard.

He growls, "What the—"

But my movements are faster, and he quickly shuts up, choosing interest over yelling as I scramble with opening his belt, then his pants, practically panting over what I'm about to reveal.

"My sweet possum," he purrs.

"Shut up."

It takes both of my hands to cup his entire shaft, and I twist, massage, and play with his balls until he throws back his head and groans.

When a bead of wetness shines on his tip, I bend and lap up the salt.

His chin falls forward. "Fuuuuuck."

I flick his tip with my tongue, my eyes trained on his. "If we're going to do this, this is how I want you."

"Fine. Yes. Anything. Just don't stop. Don't you dare…"

I grin, then shift on the bed until I can better take him in my mouth.

Chase has never allowed this type of closeness—eating me out and fucking me with ease, but never wanting me to see *him* vulnerable and exposed.

But this is my moment. My time to make him mine in the same way he's made me his.

Am I forcing his hand at his weakest point? Maybe. But with the way he supplicates, grinding his hips and fisting my hair … I doubt he'll regret it later.

Especially when I…

"Oh. My. Fucking. Hell." Chase's mouth falls open as I suction my lips around him, then take him deeper, and deeper, and deeper still, until he hits the back of my throat.

His breaths grow harsh, and I rear up before I gag, but I think I got my point across.

"Where in the hell did you learn that trick?" he asks, his voice hoarse with lust.

"I've been waiting to try it out," I say, lining him up to my mouth again. "Only with you."

One side of his mouth tilts. "Do it again."

I do.

When Chase is clinging for control, when sweat dots his forehead, and he clenches his fists with restraint, I grab a condom from his nightstand, slide my underwear off, and, keeping the rest of my clothes on, straddle him while I suit him up.

I don't make us wait. I *can't*, as I'm about to orgasm simply from losing my underwear and hitting air.

He slides inside me easily, perfectly.

Chase's hands grip my waist, and I smile at his attempt at control, but this is my ride. I throw his hands off, and lift my own to tangle in my hair, arching my back so my unbuttoned blouse spreads further. "Watch. Just watch me."

He does.

With every circle and bounce, Chase keeps his hands to himself, though it pains him sincerely. I ride him exactly the way my body demands, clenching around his dick and making sure my clit is rubbed and pleasured with the same satisfying strokes I'm giving to him.

"I'm gonna come," I whisper.

Chase's expression is tight, his jaw locked. "F … I can't … I can't fucking hold on…"

I bend down, pressing my lips onto his. "Don't."

It's here he loses control, gripping my ass, spreading my cheeks, and thrusting so hard and deep, my eyes pop wide.

The orgasm hits me at the perfect angle, and I groan into his mouth, flashes of red and white sparks spreading across the backs of my eyelids and bursting fireworks down to my core. Chase rides the gunpowder fire with me, and we cling to each other's clothes until every firework, every second of our spark, burns down into languid smoke.

Twelve

THE REST of the week goes by with innocuous boredom, which can only mean one thing.

Something sinister waits along the fringes of this pretend normalcy.

But as the days wear on, I manage to ignore the uneasy goosebumps pimpling my flesh, gaining enough distraction from the everyday people in my life, when they're not wearing their cloaks.

Emma and I go about our dorm room business as we usually do, with short bursts of conversation, mostly over our morning cup of coffee, before departing to our various classes.

Not much can be done regarding our infiltration into the Virtues until I pass the trials, and each initiate's tests are tailored to the queen's preferences. Added to that, I'm a senior, and most indoctrinations occur in ninth grade.

A shudder caresses my shoulders at the memory of what I witnessed in the Nobles' hidden ritual room in the Wolf's Den. Grown women and young boys...

I shake my head, dislodging the image. But it serves as a necessary reminder that while the Virtues are more outwardly vicious, the Nobles' quiet acts are just as dangerous.

Chase is the hardest to ignore, even though he avoided the academy for two days, nursing his injuries—or so he told his friends. We left a lot unsaid after I departed his room that night, on what we are, or how far we're willing to bend the rules. But I used the thought of Chase to keep me company while I couldn't see him, the glimmering remembrance of being on top of him, kissing and clinging to him. It's a gravity I'm more than willing to fall into, so different from the sinking, sickly feeling of being sucked into the dark abyss of the Virtues.

And when I finally ran into Chase in real life on Thursday, the hot scrape of his attention over my body and the light, almost invisible graze of his fingers on the back of my hand as we passed each other in the hallway, told me he'd been thinking of me, too.

That happy Thursday ending is why, on Friday morning, when Ivy bursts into my dorm room, I'm convinced my sinister intuition has come to fruition.

"We need to talk," Ivy gasps, out of breath, like she'd sprinted up the three flights of stairs rather than take the elevator.

I freeze with a carton of cream half-tipped over my coffee. "Is there news of my final trial?"

"Not that. I mean—no." She smacks her palms on the counter, and I jump, splashing cream. "Winter Formal."

"I—huh?"

"I know what you're going to say. With all this secret society stuff, what's the point of a school dance?"

"Since you figured out my question, you'll have my answer, too." I finish sloshing cream into my mug, then turn to her.

"Yeah, but this is our *senior year*." Ivy says it like she's whispering a prophecy. "And so far, it's *sucked*."

I cast my gaze to the ceiling and sigh, but I catch Ivy's sunburst smile along the way.

"Think about it," she says. "You and me in some gorgeous dresses, sipping spiked punch and dancing under the lights, forgetting about our problems for just one night. One *night*. That's all I ask."

I lift my mug to my lips to disguise the wavering curve of a smile. "There's no telling what the Virtues have in store for me, Ivy. It might not be smart to flaunt my freedom."

"You should go."

Both Ivy and I swivel at the sound of Emma's voice as she exits her room.

"Are you serious?" I ask. "But it's so public. So exposed. So ... normal."

Emma shrugs. "It's a good way to put face-time in and signal to the Virtues that you're participating in school activities and making an effort to support Briarcliff."

My upper lip curls. "Really? But they're evil. Without morals. Callous and cruel. Why would they ever be interested in a dance?"

"You forget," Emma says, heading to the coffee machine, "The Nobles and Virtues were created from Briarcliff. They may not be recognized extensions of the school and more of an underlying cancer, but they show respect where it's due. All the other Nobles and Virtues will be there."

Chase.

His name hits my tongue one second before I speak it, and I hide behind my mug again.

Chase will be there. We'll keep our feelings private, but our thoughts can be unprovoked. Perhaps I'll catch him across the dance floor, parting the crowd and holding out his hand for a dance...

I cringe at the daydream, my teeth clanking against the ceramic. There's no way we can do any of that. And there's never been a time I've hit any dance floor sober. It was always a sweaty, tangled mess, with rushed highs and pulses of music—my eyes shut and blind to my surroundings.

Setting down my mug, I say, "It's not a good idea. I'm sorry, Ivy."

"Please?" Ivy bounces on the balls of her feet. "It'll be harmless. I swear."

I send a wary look Emma's way. "Uh-huh. And what usually happens after someone makes that kind of promise?"

"Goddammit, Callie, I'm the *princess*."

I jolt at Ivy's rare curse.

"I'll ask the queen's permission. Order the other Virtues to stand down. We deserve this." Ivy's gaze includes Emma. "All of us."

Emma barks out with laughter. "You two have fun."

"If I'm going," I say, crossing my arms, "you are, too."

Emma doesn't bother to answer as she fixes her cup of coffee, turns around, and goes back to her room.

"There's safety in numbers!" I call after her.

She glares at me over the rim of her mug before shutting her door.

"Well. She didn't say no. I think that was positive," Ivy says to me. "Don't you?"

My last class of the day is biology, and I sit through Professor Dawson's lecture with half-glazed vision, science always being my toughest subject. I'd resolved myself to doing better and achieving the grades I used to, but it's becoming remarkably harder when I get so little sleep, my thoughts churning day in and day out.

Unlike me, Dawson is working hard today, calling on students at random, so after a final, firm blink, I straighten in my seat and stare at the whiteboard as he writes about osmosis.

"Miss Ryan?"

Crap. My instincts were spot-on, but I've only skimmed the numbers on the board.

"Um. Yes, Professor?"

Dawson glances over his shoulder, still writing about cell division. "It wasn't me who called on you, Miss Ryan, but proving your utter inattention in my class is always lovely. Look toward the door."

Everyone turns to look at me, including Chase, Falyn, and Emma. Cheeks hot, I pretend not to feel their stares as I glance at the classroom door.

Miss Maisy, the guidance counselor, stands there wringing her hands. "You're needed in the headmaster's office, dear."

Brows pushing low, I stand and walk toward her, but Miss Maisy stops me with a flutter of her fingers. "Bring your stuff as well. You won't be coming back to class."

My stomach pitches, a natural reaction at being called to the principal's office, but the depth of nausea is on a whole other level when that principal is also one of the echelons in a secret society.

Emma goes back to scrawling in her notebook, feigning disinterest, but the redness on the tip of her ear tells me she's piqued. Falyn leans back with folded arms and a smarmy expression.

And Chase ... Chase eyes me the entire time I pack up my things, and unable to help myself, I throw quick glances at him throughout, attempting to decipher any clue as to why I'm being singled out in the middle of class.

It's not for comfort. That's what I tell myself as I keep meeting his eyes, searching for softness in his features. For safety and warmth.

Nothing but burnished bronze meets me at the end of my path.

I throw my backpack on and clutch my biology textbook to my chest as I cross the aisles of desks and follow Miss Maisy out of class.

"Be sure to grab notes from someone, if you feel like passing final exams," Professor Dawson calls before Miss Maisy shuts the door.

"Come, dear," she says, her eyes kind but her expression blank.

"Am I in trouble?" I ask as I follow her down the cavernous hallway.

"I don't know, honey." Her heels hit the parquet tiles at a brisk clip, and I rush to keep up with her.

"Is this related to my meetings with you?" I ask with tentative fear.

I thought I'd been doing so well with her, easing everyone's—including my dad's —minds about my ability to handle the Briarcliff courseload and not fly *off* the handle like so many were worried about.

"Not at all, dear."

We reach the main foyer, where Miss Maisy pauses and sweeps out her hand. "I trust you can get to his office?"

I don't miss the underlying *you've been there a few times before* in her tone.

"Sure," I say, hitching my bag up higher and heading into the west wing.

The hallway of trophies and faculty paintings is silent and yawning as I turn into it, the arched ceilings creating a dome of entrapment I always seem to feel whenever I tread into this side of the school.

Headmaster Marron's heavy wooden door is closed when I come up to it, and after another glance at the hidden iron crest in one of the displays—the forging of a raven, with the Nobles' and Virtues' maxim in curved script underneath—I knock lightly.

"Come in."

I jolt at the tone. That's not Marron's voice. Nor is it male.

My hand hovers over the doorknob, confusion blotting over the foreboding weight in my chest after being called out of class.

It finally hits me—why kids are pulled from their classrooms in the middle of the day. Is this about Dad or Lynda's pregnancy? Is anyone hurt? Is there a policewoman on the other side?

Breaths hitching, I twist the knob, desperate to get to the part where I'm blind-sided, when terrible news is etched into the air, carved down my throat, and pouring blood into my chest, over with before I lose all capability to breathe.

I throw the door open, but my knuckles are white against the frame.

"What is it?" I gasp out. "Is it the baby?"

But I'm met with shadows.

The thick, velvet curtains behind Marron's wide desk are pulled shut, their golden tapestries swinging as if they were recently used. His various knick-knacks and bookshelves are darkly illuminated, a single lamp shining within the gloom.

It's disconcerting, meeting such interior gloom while the winter sun shines bright against the skeletal trees and dying grass outside.

"Take a seat, Initiate."

A shiver barrels down my spine at the voice, recognizable and pristine.

"Sab—I mean, Mrs. Harrington," I breathe out as I round one of the visitor's chairs and sit.

"You may call me your queen."

Her form is carved out in the shadows, lamplight and darkness playing across her features as she reclines in Marron's seat.

The loudest sound is my bag thumping to the floor.

Despite my bones going rigid, I say, "Is there something wrong, my queen?"

The question sits on my teeth like sour candy, too sweet and too cloying to be good for me.

"There might be," Sabine muses. "Considering how you are enduring voicing my title like you would swallowing a rat's tail."

Double crap. I press my palms into my legs, forcing poise into my posture and my voice. "I mean no offense. It takes some getting used to, this..."

"Indeed. Most students exceptional enough to receive our invitation would do anything, say anything, to be in your position. Yet here you are, wondering if my power over you is merely a joke."

"I don't mean to come across that way." Ivy's words come to the forefront. *Your honesty makes her trust you.* I clear my throat. "But I'm confused. I was called out of class and thought something was wrong, with either my enrollment at Briarcliff or my family. I'm surprised to be meeting you in Marron's office."

Sabine pauses for a beat, and a shiver skitters over my skin, as if her view of me is so much clearer than what I see of her. "You'll come to learn, dear girl, that I enjoy throwing my girls off-balance during an interrogation."

I latch onto the word. "Interrogation?"

Sabine cants her head. "Are you honestly surprised, Calla Lily?"

Inclining my head in the other direction, I ask, "I don't think I'm reaching when I say the last time you saw me, I was more open with you than I've been since—" I stop myself, but the maneuver is useless when I see Sabine's teeth flash in the dark.

"Your mother." Sabine leans forward, her elbows poking against the desk's wood. "To be a good mother is a great responsibility. To be a good daughter, even more so. You no longer have yours, and I no longer have mine. We're on similar paths. More kindred than you'll ever come to realize."

I wish for light. For some kind of strobe to land on Sabine, so I can read the grief on her face and see if it matches mine. Because all I hear from her is ... cold.

"It's what I'm asking of you, as my newest initiate. I'm asking you to see me as a mother figure—never to replace yours, mind you, but as someone you can come to and trust. In return, I'd like to treat you like a daughter. Like all my girls."

Bile sloshes deep in my belly. "I'm not sure I need that."

"Maybe 'ask' is too loose of a word," Sabine continues, her voice nothing but languid charm. "If you want the privilege of Virtuous protection, the marker of prestige, you will listen to me."

I force down the growing thorns in my throat. "I've submitted to your trials, done everything you've wanted so far."

"Yes, but have you bent to my will? I do not think so. Chase Stone." Sabine murmurs his name with a serpentine tongue. "You are not to see him. Under any circumstance. Not for academic reasons, or extracurriculars, and certainly not in bed."

My back smacks against the chair. "I haven't spoken to him. Since our meeting in the temple, I haven't—"

"Do not lie to me, dear girl."

Sabine's tone is soft, almost soothing in its allure—if you're not the prey meant for a feline predator.

An exhale whistles through my lips. "He was beaten up and humiliated for going against the Noble rule. I watched it. I'm not about to make him go through that again."

"No?" I feel more than see Sabine arch a sculpted brow. "Then why were you in his room after such an obvious message was delivered to you? Why did you spend hours there? And why, dear, were you moaning and crying out his name?"

I stop breathing. My heart slams against the walls of my chest.

"Here is where you need to listen closely, Initiate. I have eyes where you will never see. Ears where you will always be deaf. Feet and hands where yours have been amputated. I am everywhere in this school."

Then why did your eldest daughter die under your nose? I almost retort, but better judgment catches my tongue. "I understand."

"I hope you do, dear, because this is my last warning. You do not want to put me in a position where I'll punish rather than impart motherly advice. Say it."

I suck in a long breath, my voice carrying more wind than sound when I say what she wants to hear. "I'll break it off with Chase. For good."

Sabine leans back, her forearms gliding down to the desk in soft repose.

"I'd like to ask one thing," I say.

Her shoulders go rigid. "How daring. Go on."

"Why don't you want me to see him anymore?" I bend forward in my chair, inching closer despite every instinct telling me to run far away from this woman. "I thought the linking of a Noble and Virtue was encouraged. Relied upon, even. Isn't it better for the Virtues if the Noble prince were with one of us?"

The room falls into such deep silence, I'm doubting if Sabine will ever answer.

I stand, lifting my bag, and turn to the door.

"You are not one of us yet." Sabine's whisper tickles my ear like the long, furred leg of a tarantula. "And if you ever wish to attain Virtuous status, you will not even lock *eyes* with my daughter's soulmate. Do you understand?"

I rest my hand on the doorknob, my back rigid, my body still. It makes sense, what she's guarding, despite the very real fact that Piper is never coming back. I did it for my mother, and I do it for her still. Yet, the matter remaining unspoken, the one involving Chase and his father, Sabine's fiancé, is what comes to the forefront.

What would Daniel Stone want for his son? Certainly not to be forever linked to a girl in her grave. There is no power play in that, no maneuvers in which he can properly control his son. How long will Daniel let his future wife's wish be fulfilled before his selfish motives become more important?

If I continue to flout their rules, I may be putting Chase in more danger than he's already in.

I look over my shoulder at Sabine, thankful all my questions are masked by her makeshift shadows. "I understand."

"Good." That one syllable is a musical trill throughout the room. "The next time I see you, my dear, will be in better circumstances, I'm sure. I've left a gift for you at the foot of your bed. It's my greatest wish that you enjoy it."

My shoulder blades push into my spine, but I force my body steady. "Oh?"

"You're dismissed," Sabine says airily.

I don't hesitate.

And once I enter the cool expanse of the hallway and shut the headmaster's door behind me, I can finally breathe properly again.

Thirteen

I STARE at the gossamer fabric, its silky, white skirts flashing a rainbow prism of color each time I pace back and forth at the foot of my bed.

Not quite mustering the courage to lift the white rose perched on top, I've been circling the unwelcome dress like one of those cleaning fishes on a shark, staring at it like at any moment, the ivory silk will form into fangs and take a chunk out of me.

But within its gauzy material lies a thick, cream envelope tied to the rose's stem, which, if I stop gaping at it like a dummy, might give me more context.

Tentatively, I untie the black ribbon and slide the envelope out, opening it and reading the simple cream postcard inside.

Dear Initiate,

Wear this beauty with grace, respect its folds with delicacy, and stand within its silk with pride. You are to become a Virtue, and in time, you must prove purity and worth.

Attend the Winter Formal at the princess's behest and the queen's command.

And as a gentle reminder, this invitation is not to be declined. At any cost.

"Damn it, Ivy, I thought the formal was supposed to be *normal*," I mutter, the letter slipping through my fingers and fluttering to the ground. Leaving it there, I grab the long-stemmed rose and dump it in the kitchen trash.

"Another letter from your secret admirers?" Emma asks as she reclines on the couch, her laptop propped on her thighs.

I acknowledge her with a grunt. "I suppose we never should've thought the Winter Formal was optional."

"There's no *we* about it," she responds, before resuming typing.

"Right," I mumble, then stride into my room, figuring I'll be like Emma and try to get schoolwork done in the gaps of time where secret societies and their princes aren't taking up all my mental space.

I grab my stack of textbooks on my desk, and they land on my bed with a *thump*. I climb aboard as well, deliberately avoiding the dress and crossing my legs while dragging my laptop along with me.

Just as I'm opening my computer, my phone I'd stuffed in my hoodie pocket vibrates and lets out a tiny ping of sound.

I try to ignore it, sliding my calc textbook closer and fanning the pages until I find the section we've been assigned.

My phone pings again.

There's the option of silencing it. Or hell, turning it off. But with what I've discovered, been told, and witnessed these last several months, I'm positive I can do neither.

Casting my gaze to the ceiling, I pull it out, then grit my teeth, drop my chin, and read.

Chase: we need to meet.

Breath whistles through my teeth as I contemplate the meaning behind his words. Has he heard of Sabine's visit? Does he know that's why I left class today?

Me: we can't. queen's orders.

Chase: King's orders too, but I enjoy finding loopholes.

He may get off on defying the societies' rules, getting a public beating for it, then learning nothing and returning to his old ways like slipping on a comfy sweater, but I don't have the same liberties.

Me: it's not smart right now. I've been told to stay away from you. And for the good of everyone involved, I should probably do as Sabine asks.

A solid five minutes pass, my text window blank. Thinking I've won, I go back to focusing on math problems.

Until—

466

. . .

Chase: Lover's Leap. Nobody goes there anymore. Meet me at midnight. I'll make sure we're not followed.

Does this boy not understand what it's like to have such a fragile foothold even while treading on solid ground?

Even as my mind whirrs with the potential consequences, my heart is figuring out ways it can be done.

I can see him one more time. Just once. Face to face, I'll lay down the law with firm conviction, and explain to Chase that there's more at stake than our relationship. That I'm working for Emma and Eden ... Ivy, too.

Chase: Don't make me beg, sweet possum. There's something I need to explain to you.

I bring a hand up to massage my temple. My other thumb hovers over the phone's keyboard.

Me: okay. But ten minutes max.

Chase: You're the boss. See you soon.

Instead of texting back, I choke on a frustrated breath. I hope Chase knows what he's doing. And I pray I'm doing it right.

A few hours later, the biology homework is completed, but barely.

My bedside clock tells me it's eleven, so I close my books, rationalizing that I can complete the rest of my homework tomorrow.

I slide off my bed, setting the books in a pile on my desk, then pad into the main room, noting Emma's laptop and notes laid out on the couch and coffee table, but not Emma. I assume she's gone to bed, since her door is shut, and the light is off.

As quietly as I can, I shower off the remnants of the day, allowing the hard, hot spray of water to massage my shoulders and the back of my neck, but keep my hair tied up and dry. After, I slip into the warmest clothing I have, with thermal under-wear under my jeans and a long shirt, hoodie, winter coat, hat, scarf, and gloves.

Briarcliff has yet to experience the full effects of snow, but Jack Frost seems to be

KETLEY ALLISON

giving me the finger wherever I go these days, and if Chase wants to meet me outside at night, I'm going fully prepared for an Arctic trek and not a secret meet-up between the gnarled trees at the base of Lover's Leap fifteen minutes away.

Thinking to warm my insides as much as out, I also craft a decaf latte to stick into a thermos for my walk.

Now that I'm fully loaded and have nothing left to procrastinate over, I creak the front door open and make the softest sounds before clicking it shut behind me.

The dorm's hallway is at its dimmest light setting, but I take a hard left into the neighboring staircase, allowing the red, emergency exit signs to guide me to the main floor.

After that, it's a matter of utilizing the best time to slip out the side exit and avoid the security guard's rounds. I peer around the corner, and as I suspected, the two guards are chatting over their mugs of coffee at the lobby desk before they make their switch.

I slip from the building without anyone noticing, and with one mittened hand clutching my thermos and a knitted scarf covering half my face, I cut through the front of Thorne House and through the backwoods of Rose House, finding the trampled path to the cliffs with the careful use of my phone's flashlight.

It's only when I arrive at the barbed-wire gate blocking students' entry to the edge of the cliff that I take in the forest's stillness, its eerie winter silence sinking into my bones and settling its cold, frost-dampened fingers around my ribcage.

I'd been making so much noise trampling through the brush and kicking aside dead branches and rocks, that once I stopped moving, the frigid December presence made itself known, freezing the air and strangling everything that was once vivid, green, and bright, icing the ground beneath my feet.

Chase isn't here yet, making the nightmare of this forest and the dark creatures lurking within it too imminent to bear. To give myself something to do, I prop my phone, flashlight on, against a blackened, twisted tree root, then uncap my thermos and drink some warmth back into my bones.

I won't retreat. A simple swatch of forest, monitored by a security guard in a golf cart every twenty minutes, isn't going to be the thing that takes me down.

There are far more vicious creatures in my daylight hours.

A low, motoring sound gets my attention, and I inhale icy air into my lungs, shoving the lid on my thermos and shutting off my flashlight before security finds me.

Crouching low, as headlights illuminate my spot, I curse Chase and his assurances that he had the times of security rotation on lock. These guards prowl our campus at all hours these days, December cold or not.

Branches crack and mounds of frozen ground fracture beneath tires, the engine growing closer and the beam of light becoming wider.

Shit. *Shit.* There's still time to escape if I leap up and run *now.* I balance on the balls of my feet and lunge to the side, avoiding the outer edges of the pale, yellow spotlight cutting through stripped-down trees.

"Scampering somewhere, sweet possum?"

Halting with one foot high in the air, I pivot to the golf cart with a sigh. "Should've figured."

"That I'd borrow a cart with heated vents instead of force us to negotiate

468

ourselves into a deep freeze? Bet your ass you should've figured."

"Define *borrow*," I say, but move toward the vehicle, drawn to his words of 'heat' and 'vents.'

As I sidle up to the cart, Chase meets my half-covered face with a closed-lipped grin. "There's nothing money can't buy. Even a slice of time."

"How long do we have?" I ask as I take a seat, leaning close to the hot spurts of air in the console.

"Enough." Chase slides his leather-clad hands from the wheel, puffed-out and comfortable in his black Canada Goose parka.

It's a standard, open concept golf cart, so I'm not holding out much hope for a sauna-like experience.

"Won't these headlights be obvious through the trees?"

"Callie." Chase gently pries the thermos from my hands. "We're fine for as long as we need."

Chase uncaps the lid and tips it to his mouth. "No alcohol," he says. "Disappointing."

"Take this seriously. Please. Sabine pulled me out of class this afternoon for the sole purpose of telling me to stay away from you. Her entire aura *screams* danger, yet here I am." I stare at the dark spots around the twin circles of light coming from Chase's cart. "I've figured it out. I have a death wish."

After a hard exhale, Chase sets down my thermos between us. "I'm taking this seriously. We're meeting here, in the fucking cold, so nobody will see us together."

I slide my gaze back to him. "Do you have any idea why Sabine doesn't want us together? She made it sound like you still belong to Piper, but there's got to be more to it. Your dad, her fiancé, wouldn't want you attached to a—" I almost say *to a ghost*, but catch myself.

Chase stares at me for a long time. I blink uncomfortably under his study, my eyes feeling like cold, hard marbles shoved inside my skull.

Instead of answering, he murmurs, "If you were to have more control over the Virtues, would you take it?"

I press back into the seat. "I've never thought about gaining control over them. I've only ever wanted to dismantle them."

Chase nods, clouds of air billowing out of his nose. "What if I gave you the chance to do either?"

I squint at him, the movement difficult with my fast-freezing cheek muscles. "What are you getting at?"

Chase twists to face me, holding my mittened hands in his. "I'm tired of my father commanding my life and ruining my sister's. I don't want to fucking stand down to his edicts. Not this time."

"Chase." I lean in closer, our clouds of breaths mixing and mingling in a way we can't anymore. "I'm furious with your dad and Sabine, too, expecting us not to be together simply because they forbid us. But we have to be smart about this. You can't thwart his rules with such obvious disregard and be beaten for it again."

Again, Chase searches my face. I pull my hand from his grip and place it on his cheek. "What is it? What are you not telling me?"

He surprises me by diving in for a kiss, my cold lips melting under his, Chase's hot tongue doing more for me than warmed coffee in a thermos ever could.

Instead of fighting him, I grip his shoulders and angle my head to bring the kiss deeper. I thought we couldn't do this anymore. I was prepared to stand back and watch him from afar for the greater good, but the moment he lays his lips on mine, the second his arm comes around my waist and makes me a part of him, my plan to remain calm and collected shatters.

We burst apart, our clouded exhales wider and opaquer.

"I shouldn't have done that," he rasps.

I glance around us, licking my lips, tasting him. "Like you said, we're safe for the moment."

"Ah, sweet possum, we have so much more to do before we can find safe harbor."

"I know," I murmur, looking down at my hands.

"We can meet in secret, in places they'll never find. I'm not about to give you up with a snap of their fingers."

Rather than argue the point, especially when my lips still tingle from his stubble, I say, "We'll figure it out."

Chase catches my chin and tips it toward him. "We'll do more than that. We'll thwart them in the shadows."

I sag underneath his touch but tell myself not to lose my spine. "Not if it means witnessing you get hurt again. I'll endure whatever Sabine has planned for me, but if she uses you again, like she promised she will, I can't prove her right. I can't give her my weakness on a golden platter."

His cold, leather thumb strokes my jaw while his eyes catch the luminescence of our only source of light. "I can't bend to their will. I don't have it in me, and I'd rather James break my arm and Rio kick me in the nuts than forfeit my time with you."

I pull out of his caress, though every ounce of heat remaining in my body begs to draw closer to his flames. Instead, I change the subject from one of pain to tactics. "The Winter Formal. Sabine's ordered me to go."

"It's a mandatory event for us. We dress up, make good face on behalf of Briarcliff Academy, and then attend the real ball underground."

My brows squish together.

Chase smiles indulgently. "The dance continues in the Nobles' ritual room, sweet possum. That's what you're being ordered to attend, and you can't do that until you show your face at the formal."

"And what's the point of it?"

Chase tips his head, his brows furrowing with over-dramatic contemplation. "Elitism? Privilege? Entitlement? All the things the rich and powerful do to separate themselves from the commoners. It's one of the only functions we have together as Nobles and Virtues."

"I wonder why Ivy didn't tell me that when she begged me to go?"

"Probably because her mouth is claimed by the queen, and Ivy bends to Sabine's rules because she's afraid to break them."

Chase says it like it's a bad thing. "She's scared. Ivy doesn't have any sort of fallback like you do if she betrays the societies. Her dad's a disgraced member, her family's broke because you Nobles love your payback."

"Is that what you think?" Chase's tone grows hard. "That I'm only doing this because I have a cushioned life for my ass to land on if things go south? I assure you, if I'm caught, there will be more hell to pay than landing in Hell itself. I'm not doing this for kicks."

"That's not what I meant." I squeeze his bicep. "I'm not trying to lessen your risk. God, Chase, I'm just so scared. I *don't* want you hurt. I don't want Ivy punished."

Chase leans in for another kiss, this one tender and slow. He pulls away once, twice, stroking the escaped hairs from my hat off my face, then pressing his lips to mine again. After one final stroke of his tongue, he draws away, but keeps his hand on the back of my neck. "Trust me."

"I want to."

"Allow me to earn it, then. The Virtues' temple will be deserted during the Winter Formal, and the dance itself will be crowded, all of us, even faculty, wearing masks. If we can time it right and have enough decoys, we can slip into the temple and find the documents relating to Rose Briar that Piper was trying to uncover for my sister."

My heart swings like a pendulum. "Will it work?"

"It has to. This is the only chance we have before school ends for the holidays."

A reminder flickers in the back of my head, remembering my time in the chem lab when I thought it was deserted. "Aren't there cameras? Motion detectors? Something to alert them?"

Chase sets his jaw, staring off over my shoulder.

"Chase. What is it?"

His eyes scrape back to mine. "Tempest. I've given him my father's passwords. He'll log on and put a video of the empty tomb on a loop."

"You brought *Tempest* into this?"

Chase clamps a hand over my mouth. "While I said we were safe here, I didn't mean we were safe if you shouted."

My response comes out muffled, but I make sure the features he can see are carved with a stony glare. "Sorry."

He removes his hand. "How'd you say it last time? Our 'Bonnie and Clyde shit' can't work. We need more people."

"Eden, Emma, and Ivy are more than enough."

"Can any of them mess with a top-notch security system?"

"I didn't know Tempest could."

"How do you think Eden's photos got buried so quickly?"

My skin tingles despite the numbing cold. "I assumed it was Briarcliff's fickle rumor mill. Eden was horribly humiliated by the same tactic years ago. I figured the lack of originality bored most students and they forgot about it."

"Think again." Chase settles back in his seat, interlacing his fingers between his thighs. "We're like vultures. We'll pick at dead meat until it's nothing but old bones. Tempest got in the way of that by intercepting your dummy account, deleting the pictures, and doing other techie stuff I can't even begin to describe to scrub the photos from the internet."

I pause. "He did all that? For Eden?" Then I frown. "Why? He hates people."

"He did it for me. My boy's temperamental, but his loyalty is unmatched."

My voice is soft. "Thank you. For asking him."

"Don't thank me or make assumptions about every member of the societies when you've been part of our fun, secret club for all but a few weeks."

"It's hard not to, with the types of members I've been lucky enough to meet." I turn forward, sucking on my teeth. On the night my dorm room was broken into, the photos of Piper's diary were deleted off my laptop and my cloud without my knowledge.

Was Tempest the Cloak that did it?

Chase speaks before I voice my thoughts. "My beat-down was Tempest putting on the same act I did, assuring the Nobles that his loyalty is intact. But he has his own reasons to bring them to heel and force my father out."

"And Riordan and James? How about them?"

The line of his jaw almost cuts through his skin. "They're loyal to my father. There's no act about it, although Rio less so."

I pull my scarf over my nose and mouth, staring into the dense copse of trees. "My trust is wearing thin."

"Mine, too." He grabs my hand, and though we're both gloved, his grip is firm and stable.

It's nice, a pocket of peace in an otherwise unyielding amount of stress, and while I'm stiffened with cold, I wish I could find more moments like these with him.

As if he can read my thoughts, Chase gives my hand one last squeeze before switching to the steering wheel.

"We'd better go," he says. "I'll drive you closer to the dorms."

Nodding, I cross my arms, reclaiming warmth where it's been lost. Soon, we're rocking and bouncing over the uneven forest path, the golf cart's quiet motor thrumming beneath us.

Chase pulls to a stop near the back exit of Rose House. "It's safe for you to walk from here. Any closer, and we'll be caught."

We spend a long moment staring at each other. I find the courage to say, "We can do this."

Chase cups the back of my head, bringing my forehead to his. "Do whatever they ask. Keep calm. I support you, regardless of how I act during the day. We'll win and take them down. For Piper. For my sister and Eden. For us."

I pull my scarf away from my face and risk another sweet, icy kiss. When I pull away, my lips brushing against his, I say, "That question you asked, about me trusting you."

He nudges my nose with his. "Yeah?"

"I do."

Smiling, Chase kisses me again.

I leave him in the dense thicket of trees, my boots crunching against half-frozen, decayed leaves and branches, peering over my shoulder a few times before I round the corner of Rose House and cross over to Thorne.

At each pivot, he's in the same spot, his eyes brilliant but his lips grim, and I find myself hoping that my white lie will eventually turn into the truth.

That I can trust him with my life.

Fourteen

THE VIRTUES LEAVE me alone for thirteen days.

Whether or not that number will end in an unlucky consequence remains uncertain.

I'm not about to sit around and wonder, instead focusing on my neglected schoolwork as well as our plans to enter the Virtues' temple on the night of Winter Formal. Emma was the first to agree after I outlined my meeting with Chase—out of everyone, she'd be the person to keep my continued association with her brother to herself. Then, we folded Eden into the idea, without mentioning Chase. Once we included Ivy, the only aspect I explained to her was the threat of Sabine, and what she said to me after she pulled me out of class. Sadly, I wasn't sure I could trust my best friend with my secret meet-up with Chase. Ivy has her own bonds to fight against, without enduring mine, too.

With all the piecemeal information I'm feeding to each friend and the different sized holes I'm leaving behind, on the afternoon of day thirteen, I feel more like Swiss cheese than a person. That is why I take the time to sit with Ivy, Eden, and Emma at lunch—Emma, who we coaxed out of our dorm with the assurance that nothing has gone wrong for almost two weeks, and she'd be safe with us.

Famous last words, right?

"Has anybody had time to think of finals?" Ivy asks, pushing her bibimbap rice dish around her bowl with her chopsticks. "Amid all this … stuff?"

"Ugh. Don't remind me." I press my fingers into my temples, not so much feigning a headache as preventing one. "I don't think I've had a worse semester. Ever."

"Isn't it easy to get A's in public school?" Eden asks. I search her face for sarcasm, but surprisingly find none.

"Not always," I say, but I'm distracted by commenting on her sheltered Briarcliff-living when there's motion at the front of the dining hall, Falyn, Willow, and Violet waltzing into lunch late.

The room transforms into a stuffy, cloying environment as they wander through the tables and to the buffet at the back. These girls command the dining hall in a fashion entirely opposite to their male counterparts.

When Chase and his crew walk in, students go quiet, but not out of intimidation. Every move of those boys' is watched by admiring, heart-filled eyes and unrequited hearts. It's hard not to when Chase, Tempest, Riordan, and heck, even James, are carved from beauty, their movie star faces mixing with pro-athlete bodies.

In most schools—including public—there's usually only one guy who claims those kinds of looks. Here? There's at least ten, with Chase Stone being at the top.

Falyn, however ... she and her besties shush the room through fear of reprisal, stealing their throne through opportunity and deceit. Falyn reminds us all of that fact as her gaze sweeps through the room, grazing over heads and landing on nothing, until she reaches me.

"Incoming," Emma mutters. With a few flicks of her fingers, she's holding her chopsticks like weapons. "I knew there was a reason I didn't want to come down here. I thought you said they were independently training?"

Ivy shrugs at the question. "Independent being the buzz word. We don't always have to train at lunch."

Emma curses the closer Falyn looms, and I don't blame her. Here I was, hoping for a predictable, average lunch after almost two weeks of being ignored.

Falyn must've sensed the weakening of my walls. I meet her eye, and her lips slink into a smile.

"So nice to see you all out in public," she simpers when she draws near. "I'd thought you'd have claimed your own misfit island by now."

"It's our school as much as it is yours," Eden retorts.

My eyes flare at her unexpected retort, but I shouldn't be surprised. With the release of her photos and the lack of torture that followed, she regained a small amount of confidence. One side of her hair is even tucked behind her ears, as if she's half-willing to show her face around school again.

I switch my focus to Falyn, watching her carefully, ready to strike if she so much as bats an insult Eden's way.

Falyn laughs at Eden's remark, full and throaty. "My memories at this academy are going to be *so* much sweeter than yours, since I don't have lard coating my fat, pimply ass—"

"Those are big words coming out of a mouth so recently filled with an extra-large, silicone cock."

My gaze pings to Emma. Ivy's breath squeaks with sound.

Emma cants her head. "Wasn't it you in that sex video James circulated last year? Yep. It definitely was. Those lips of yours blowing a fake dick while James stuck his up your ass was verified by Riordan, since he was the one holding the dildo for you."

Falyn sucks on air.

"You're such a wasted bitch," Falyn says, tipping her chin up as she stares at Emma down her nose. "Did you rub one out to the video when your daddy had you locked up in the basement? Was it conversion therapy? Were you so obsessed with Piper, your daddy had to show you amateur videos with dildos and James to make you horny and straight?"

"Enough," I say, rising from my seat. "We were eating our lunch in peace before you came along. It's time for you to leave."

Ivy nods, standing with me. "The public spectacle isn't worth it, Falyn."

I note the attention cast in our direction, some mouths gaping, most whispering, and a *lot* holding up their phones to record. Their interest doesn't capture me the way Ivy's does, though. She's staring at Falyn like she's imparting a silent message, one I'm coming to decipher as *retribution*.

These girls can't do anything without Sabine hearing about it, and either punishing or rewarding them.

With that thought, I wonder how Piper's cornering me in this same dining hall went over with her mother, accusing me of stealing her boyfriend, then ending up dead that night.

It was Addisyn who killed her, I remind myself. *Case closed.*

In a rush of memory, a few of Piper's last words encircle my mind. *I'm doing you a kindness...*

Was Piper warning me away from the Virtues? Or was it really about stealing Dr. Luke from her?

"Did you hear me, possum?"

Ivy elbows me, and I glance up from the section of table I'd been vacantly staring at, lost in thought. I say to Falyn, "No, what?"

"I'm not leaving until you come with me."

I recoil. "Why?"

Falyn smiles but hides her teeth. "You sit with us now."

"But Ivy never has to." I gesture to Ivy, who gives a minuscule shake of her head, like I shouldn't have said that.

"*She* isn't starting at the beginning like you are," Falyn says. "Come join our crew, Callie."

Ivy's whisper touches my ears. "Do it."

"But—"

"Go," Emma says from across the table. "I don't want this table further stunk up with Falyn's presence, anyway. Good luck trying to be popular, possum."

I gape at her, but my brain makes up for my stunned body, assuring me that this is part of Emma's act, that no one can know we've teamed up for anything.

It's better if we look like enemies forced into proximity, nothing more.

"Okay..." I say, and tentatively pick up my tray. My stomach sinks at the obvious answer to my next question. "Is this a permanent thing?"

"More permanent than a tattoo," Falyn says with a succulent, dire undertone.

"Great," I mumble, but after a last, entreating look to my friends, who subtly nod with encouragement, I follow the Wicked Witch of Briarcliff to her lunch table.

Willow and Violet are seated with their food when I arrive. Willow undercuts me with a glance, but Violet pulls out the chair next to her and gestures for me to sit, the cerulean blue of her eyes vulnerable and friendly.

"Welcome," she says.

I perch at the very edge of the chair, ready to bolt if a piece of Falyn's lunch so much as lands on my side of the table.

"Is this really necessary?" I ask the group. "You guys don't like me. I'm not sure why we all have to endure this quality time."

"Coach's orders," Willow says, the hue of her eyes matching the auburn of her tied-back hair. "Like with any new trainee, we have to make them part of the team. Even the ones we think suck."

I lick my lips, parsing through her clues until I reach the conclusion that their rowing team and the title of coach is public code for the Virtues. It has to be, because there is *no* way I'd ever join—

"You guessed it." Falyn's lips stretch wide as her searching gaze centers on my face. "As part of this bullshit charade, you have to join our rowing team."

I blurt out my response without thinking, "No way."

Violet frowns, her small voice somehow coming through the white noise of the crowded dining hall. "It's not that bad. You can join me as the other half of the bow pair."

"Addisyn's absence has to be filled," Falyn barks. "In more ways than one. Stop being so fucking difficult, Callie."

I jolt at her venom but keep my expression calm. I could figure out a way around this. There's no immediate need to be out on a boat, in the middle of bottomless water, without a life jacket or a clue. They're no longer training on water—it's winter, so a lot of their practice is in their weight room or that crazy hydraulic thing they have in the boathouse that simulates a race. I could handle that.

I think. Better to change the subject.

"So, Winter Formal," I segue, stretching my smile until it's sincere. "Are you guys excited?"

Falyn makes a sound of disgust, then picks at her rice bowl. Willow rolls her eyes, but Violet bounces in her seat.

"Absolutely," she says. "Falyn chose the theme this year. Well, it was meant to be Piper, but ... um, you know. We're honoring her with the theme of Snow White."

I push my brows up, but they quickly come down when I recall the ending and the princess encased in a glass coffin, for all the world to see, beckoning her prince with her cold, waiting corpse...

I find my voice again. "That's ... a heck of a way to remember her."

"Relax," Falyn says. "It's not like we can display her. She fell off a damn cliff. We want to remember the *idea* of her, so we'll put a glass case out, fill it with her favorite flowers, and have the rest of the ballroom be winter-themed, including our outfits. Get it?" Falyn waits for my nod. "She'll be the only bright, spring center point in a room full of snow." Falyn settles back in her seat. "I'm a fucking genius for thinking of this."

"You are," Willow assures, but her gaze slides to mine with an eerie, practiced movement. Her red-painted lips curl with a grin. "Everyone will love it, *especially* after the last dance, when Chase opens the case, picks a flower, and makes a speech as the Winter Court King, pledging his everlasting love to Piper."

It's as if my throat picks up the icicles outside and nestles them against my vocal cords. I force out a platitude. "What a beautiful way to honor your friend."

"You won't mind," Falyn says, "since you broke it off with Chase. He's ours now, to do with as we please. Chase will always follow our instructions. Those boys may think they have control over the school, but they haven't for quite some time. Remember that when you're tempted to choose sides."

"Aw." Willow points to my untouched meal. "Lost your appetite, sweetie?"

Violet lays a delicate hand on my shoulder. "Do you need some water?"

"She needs a new life." Falyn snorts. "Because this one's about to get so *brutal* for her."

Fifteen

THE FOREST MUST BE LISTENING, because as a complement to the incoming Winter Formal, Briarcliff is blanketed in snow for the first time this year.

I'm woken by the seeping cold through my window, as if Jack Frost has come through the cracks with his long, gnarled fingers, gripped my shoulder, and whispered in my ear to look outside.

Shivering, I sit up, wrapping my comforter around my shoulders and shuffling to my single window, the sun rising white and pale over the glittering, untouched snow of Thorne House's backyard.

The glass is hard, frigid ice beneath the pads of my fingers as I lean in closer to better see the snowdrops clinging to trees, weighing down the branches and stifling the morning bird calls.

My lips pull wide in a smile.

I've been waiting for this—for my first sight of snow. I whirl from my window, padding around my room with eager feet as I dress in Briarcliff's winter uniform of thermal tights, a plaid skirt, and a long-sleeved, white button-down shirt, throw on my winter coat, and slip on my boots before grabbing a to-go coffee and skipping out into the silent hallway.

I didn't even check the time, but with the beginning sunrise, it must be close to 6:30 AM. No girlish titters can be heard from the other side of the closed, locked doors. I don't run into anyone during my trek down three floors, not even Moira, as I swing through the side exit and trek through virgin snow to the back of Thorne House.

Clouds of my breath and the crunch of my boots lead the way, until I pause next to a first floor window, cup my mittened hands close to my mouth, and sip my coffee while taking in the muted sounds and glaring white of Briarcliff Academy's winter makeover.

With nothing but an acre of thick snow at my horizon, sparkles winking with the rising sun, it's easy to fall into a meditative state, to close my eyes and breathe in the cold, unfiltered air of the nearby forest. I'm immersed in the brief pleasantries of a season that mainly brings blizzards, subzero temperatures, and gray, drab skies, and I'd much rather face the calm of an impending snowstorm than mull over the havoc Winter Formal could bring.

Or the disaster that my time here at Briarcliff has become.

I thought I'd have the upper hand by becoming one of them, but not *really* being one of them, yet the Virtues test me at every turn, hoping I'll fall, ensuring I'll prove my weakness.

Newly-formed icicles on the windowsill beside me crackle against the reflected sunlight, beginning to thaw, and I stare at the uneven spears, my cheeks frozen and my exhales heated, wondering if tonight will finally be the moment I can reduce the Virtues' hold on this beautiful, deadly campus, by finding enough proof in their temple to bring them to their knees.

Is it possible? Would the Virtues store such damning documents? Piper thought it was. She may have died for unrelated reasons, but she was on to something, hiding codes in her diary and planting founders' letters in obscure texts where only someone like her could follow the clues.

I could finally get answers, like why Ivy is looking so broken and sallow since becoming the Virtues' princess, or why Emma won't tell me what she did that warranted so much torture from a group meant to protect her.

If they won't—or can't—tell me, then I'll break into the temple while they're all at the dance.

With the sun glinting above the tallest evergreen trees, I turn my back on the majestic view and plod to the front of the dorms, December's morning bite gifting me with more energy and resolve than a cup of coffee.

The week passes like a frostbitten dream, classes going on as usual, the dining hall—for once—uneventful. On Thursday afternoon, many of the senior girls leave campus at lunch to either drive into Providence for hair and makeup, or have a glam squad come to them in their dorm rooms.

I was so immersed in how to infiltrate the Virtues' temple without being caught that I neglected to plan for any sort of beauty regime, until my phone chirps in my locker. I set aside the textbooks I was switching out for my next class, reading the incoming text with a hesitant twist to my lips.

Lynda: Surprise, sweetie! I've sent NYC's best to glamify you for your first, amazing dance. We're so proud of you. Your dad sends his best and encourages you to skip your afternoon classes (I think he's experiencing a bit of pregnancy brain too, so let's take advantage!). He even says to invite some of your friends if they haven't already booked for hair and makeup. Oh yeah—my glam squad is waiting in your room!

. . .

I lean against the neighboring locker, rereading Lynda's text. I hadn't mentioned a word of the dance to them, and she thought of all this? Immediately, I'm filled with guilt. Guilt over not being a typical high school kid excited for a school dance. Guilt because I haven't asked Lynda about her pregnancy since I was dunked in the Briarcliff Lake, and she's ready to pop any second.

Me: You think of everything! Thank you. I'm leaving right now (but don't mention that to Dad. Hearing that my ditching is actually happening might make him change his mind). How's my baby sister doing?

Lynda responds immediately: **She's enrolled herself in Krav Maga. Can't wait to get her out of the wrestling ring she's built in my stomach. We're still on track for a Christmas due date, so don't you worry yourself tonight. Just have fun and tell me all about it tomorrow.**

Smiling, I pocket my phone and cut through the academy's halls until I'm outside the pavilion and on the pathway to the dorms.

That freshly fallen snow I'd been marveling over this morning has rapidly overstayed its welcome, the plowed walkways turning into black-gray sludge under students' shoes and the wind making the sunny day seem like a lunchtime picnic in the Arctic.

I keep my head down and hood of my jacket up for that very reason, avoiding more icicles on my eyelashes. It's at that exact moment, with the blinders of my hood and the jerky movement of a light jog, that a hand grabs me at the elbow to twist me around.

I squeak, the soles of my shoes scraping over slippery sludge, but ball my free hand into a fist and swing.

"Jesus!"

Chase ducks just in time.

My breath billows out. I scan the walkway, wondering if we'll be noticed. "What are you doing here?"

"What am I—?" Chase collects himself. "You almost clocked me in the jaw."

"I'm jumpy."

"They won't schedule your third trial during the day." Chase shoves his hands in his coat's pockets. On him, the December day looks like he's just broken off from a passionate kiss, his golden skin flushed with rose, and his lips red slashes against the white of our backdrop.

"Tell that to the dead rats in my locker a few months ago," I say. "You shouldn't be talking to me."

Chase dips his chin. "All I'm doing is making sure you're ready for tonight."

"I think so." I sigh. "I hope so."

"Go with what we talked about. What Emma's run you through. We should be fine."

I haven't seen Chase in almost a week, and I'm praying my eagerness to see him, to trace every angle of him with my eyes, isn't obvious. He's been speaking through his sister, as they meet at their lake house most nights to discuss how best to break into the Virtues' tomb without notice. Evidently, Piper told Emma where she found Rose Briar's letter, and how there were many more, as well as other artifacts outlining the secret society's creation.

Piper. Helping Emma. I'm still trying to wrap my head around that.

I raise my brows. "You sure we have the right decoys?"

"Practically every chick will be in some sort of white dress and we'll be in tuxes. We're covered."

I gnaw my lower lip. "And the masks?"

Chase nods in the direction of our dorms. "Emma has them. You can thank Ivy for that."

"I will."

I've unintentionally mirrored his posture by stuffing my hands in my pockets and hunching over, when all I want to do is burrow into his warmth and beg him to take me away to his lake house. Somewhere safe. With him.

My nails dig into my palms as I fight the blooming frustration. "Is that all?"

Chase arches a brow. "You can run along, possum. We're done here."

"That's not..." Chase isn't asking for an apology for my snippiness, but I feel the need to explain. "I'm stressed. Worried. The Virtues keep coming at me with under-lying threats, and I feel like the worst is yet to come."

Chase replies with a low undertone. "It probably is."

"Tonight, at the dance," I say quietly. I force myself to continue, though I've avoided asking him this question almost as much as I've tried not to run into him. "Falyn said you're going to make a speech."

His eyes grow shadows—difficult to do in such a pure, glaring landscape. But in a blink, they're gone.

Chase lifts his hand from his pocket, toward me, but thinks better of it and shoves it back in. He murmurs, "Your feelings are written all over your face."

I cast my gaze to the side. "It's okay if you talk about her. I'm not jealous."

Chase's voice is so soft, I only hear it because it's carried by the wind. "I'm not talking about jealousy."

I blurt out, "Are you making a speech about Piper because the Virtues told you to?"

"They have their reasons, but I have mine. I'm not their mindless toy, Callie, as much as they're trying to make you believe it. Whatever they've said to you, it's only the half-truth."

I search his eyes, amber encased in glass. "You're not doing it under duress? It's your choice?"

His breath comes in small clouds. "Tonight has to run smoothly. This is part of it."

"You're avoiding the question," I whisper. "They're forcing you. What do they have? What is *making* them so powerful around here?"

One side of Chase's lips tics up in a miserable smile. "That's what tonight's about, too. Answers for you and my sister. Let's not screw it up."

Chase spins on his heel, but turnabout is fair play. I grab him at the elbow. "Why do I feel less like a Virtue initiate and more like Howard Mason the longer I put up this charade? He broke into the Nobles' tomb and wrote about what he found. But then it stopped. His last written words were '*help me.*'"

Chase stares me down, rigid and unmoved. "What are you getting at?"

"You're meant to be on my side. I'm doing this stupid thing of staying away from you and being a good little initiate because you've assured me you want them taken down, too. But there's so much left unsaid. If you won't tell me everything, and neither will Emma, how am I supposed to trust that tonight will be okay?"

Chase rests a hand on mine. "Howard Mason is not dead. He's perfectly fine. And you will be, too. Take comfort that this has been going on long before you enrolled. Your presence at Briarcliff accelerated our plans but didn't create them."

I say, firmer, "I swear I'm not checking out."

"You're scared. Understandable. But we have your back." Chase smiles, and for the first time today, it feels like real emotion he's directing toward me. "I hear you have a room full of powders and gels and shit. Go and get ready. Have fun and try not to look so spooked. I'll see you at the dance."

He pries my fingers off gently, and I take a step back, lengthening the distance between us.

"For the record," he says over his shoulder, "I wish you were my date."

Hugging myself, I watch his retreat, his blond hair ruffling with the breeze. He strides unhindered through the flattened, slippery snow on the pathway to the academy. I turn in the opposite direction, holding on to the pretense that everything he's said to me is his honest truth.

Sixteen

I CAN SMELL them before I see them.

A waft of sweetened, chemical fumes hits me when I reach my floor. That sharp, nostril-singeing scent of baby powder and hairspray vapor that seems to have followed me from Meyer House in NYC.

It's not a terrible smell, exactly, but one I associate with Lynda's many summer gatherings when I stayed at her luxurious Upper West Side townhouse with Dad. I'd be holed up in my room, pretending deep interest in a paperback and *not* focusing on the fact that I was imprisoned, while down the hall, Lynda laughed as her stylists regaled her with hilarious stories, a full face, and gorgeous hair.

I unlock my door with blatant wariness.

"*Callie*!" a male voice booms in my direction, making me jump. Today, of all days, is not the one to approach me with a yell.

"H-hi," I stutter out, shutting the door behind me.

I'm immediately engulfed in a superheated room, filled with enough salon tools and foreign products to make an Upper East Side socialite melt.

"You've arrived!" The owner of the loud voice bursts forward, his round body, dressed all in black, bouncing toward me like an Addams's Family beach ball.

I say this affectionately, as whenever I crossed paths with Davide during my rare exits from Lynda's guest room, he'd greet me exactly this way, his small lips pursed between bronzed teddy-bear cheeks. "*Ça va?*"

"I'm doing well," I say, angling my head to accept his air-kisses. "Thank you for coming all this way."

"Anything for Lynda. And at Briarcliff, no less! Lucky girl. This is Suzanne." He points to a twenty-something blonde girl, laying out supplies on a fold-out table they must have brought with them. "She will help."

Davide leans closer, cupping a hand to my ear. "Is your, ah, how do you say, roommate, joining us? We met her, she let us in, but..."

I search Davide's face for signs of horror, or plain shock, upon meeting Emma, but see none. Instead, his dark eyes are alight with eagerness, his expression open and sweet. "I do not know if she wishes for us to touch her."

"I can ask," I say, more out of politeness than in hopes of a positive outcome. Knowing Emma, she'll have locked her bedroom door from the inside.

"Please do. We shall wait. You two can get ready together, yes? Friends love getting ready together."

"Sure." If you can call Emma and I friends.

After heeling off my boots, I head to Emma's side of the dorm, which is ominously quiet when I knock.

To my surprise, she opens her door almost immediately, but only enough to showcase her narrowed, brown eyes. "You have uninvited, very fragrant guests in the kitchen."

"My stepmother sent them over." I say the next part in a rush. "Would you like your hair and make-up done, too?"

Emma's lashes flutter. She purses her lips.

I try not to react to her visible hesitation or show any keenness whatsoever. "Would you like to? Lynda said she was more than happy to cover my friends."

"What about Ivy?"

"Ivy's meeting me here in fifteen minutes. Eden, too. They're happy to do all of us."

I hear Davide squeak behind me, but if I only ask for the basics, they'll totally have time for the others. It's *lunchtime,* for God's sake.

Emma's brows lower. "I don't. I mean..."

"I'd love to do this for you," I say.

It's the wrong thing to say. Glowering, Emma moves to shut her door, but I slam a hand on the wood before she can succeed.

"Alas, my little night-blooming cereus," Davide says to Emma as he comes up behind me, poking his face over my shoulder. "Come join us. You will be missing out on oh-so-much *fête.*"

Emma nails him with a glare, but Davide doesn't so much as shudder. She says, "I'm not going to the stupid dance."

"I did not say that was a requirement, *ma chérie.* Half the fun is getting ready, yes? Drink champagne with your friends—I won't say a thing—make *bonne* memories while you still can. This is your senior year. While you may not dance to-and-fro, you will regret not having my hands upon your face." Davide grows serious. "I am the best in the business. There has never been a woman I haven't made into a goddess, and I shall not back away from this door until you step out of it."

Emma retreats farther into the shadows of her room. "Go away, French man."

"Hmm. A challenge, then." Davide lifts a canister of hairspray from his toolbelt. His eyes grow small. "I can spray you from here, *chérie.*"

Emma looks to me for support, but I shrug. "Talk to the man with the weapon, not me."

Silence stretches between the three of us, until Davide, with an expression of stone, presses the pump in two warning bursts.

Emma winces, but I note the wavering tremor in her lips as she tries to fight off a smile. "Fine. But only because you're threatening me with aerosol poisoning."

Davide breaks into a wide, luminous grin while I step aside so she can come out.

Emma waltzes into the main room, her chin raised regally, but her eyes are hard and flat as marbles as she comes into the light, like she's expecting Davide and Suzanne to comment about her scars or *tsk* that there's not enough product in the world to make her beautiful.

My chest tightens, because the Emma I saw in old pictures, the one before the attack, and the fire, and the Virtues, would've loved to be treated to a makeover before a dance.

Yet, Davide's expression is soft as Emma approaches, before he scampers to the center of the room. "Come. Sit. I have just the things for you."

Emma perches on a stool, and I slide onto one next to her, conscious of how Davide and Suzanne treat her, but soon, he has Emma cracking a smile, and then the both of them are commiserating about their favorite villages in France, and my shoulders relax and submit to Suzanne as she plucks, mumbles, and paints.

Half an hour later, Ivy and Eden join us. We take a quick break to drag the office chairs out of our rooms, but with the speed of stylist professionalism, Suzanne and Davide have us lined up like soldiers as they work on our faces and hair in sections.

While my eyes are closed, I feel Ivy's cold hand clasp mine on my lap. "You ready?"

"Sure." My mouth is so dry, it comes out as a rasp.

"And we are complete!" Davide backs away from Eden, his arms lifted in triumph. "Go, ladies, see how I've transformed you into Snow White beauties."

Eden cautiously tucks her curled hair behind her ears and lifts from her seat. Emma follows. Ivy and I are frozen in our stools as we watch them find the closest mirror in the bathroom and stare at their reflections.

They don't speak.

"Are they okay?" Ivy whispers to me. "I didn't get a good look before they ducked in there."

I shake my head. "Me neither."

Davide waits patiently nearby, steepling his fingers and primed for any movement or sound. Suzanne parts her bright red lips to say something, but Davide shushes her. "Art appreciation cannot be rushed."

Emma's the first to come out.

"Well?" Davide asks.

"It'll do." Emma clears her throat. "It suits our purposes. We'll blend in with everyone else around campus tonight."

Emma's voice may be toneless and unimpressed, but her eyes glitter like diamonds against a flawless application of correcting foundation.

I smile at the sight of her, Emma's brown eyes deeply lined, her cheeks apple-pink, and her lips full and defined. While I've become familiar with her scars, they're almost invisible beneath Davide's expert fingers, only a few indents here and there and a small pucker at her lips.

The same can be said for Eden when she steps out. Her ebony hair shines, and her green eyes pop with the pale, moss-colored eyeshadow Suzanne swept across, and her pock-marks are smoothed and blurred.

"Are you sure you guys don't want to come to the dance?" I ask. "I'm sure there's time to find a dress."

"No." Emma utters the denial with the tone of a girl who has long given up hope for sweet high school memories.

"It's a nice thought," Eden says, "but not for us."

Davide pushes out his lower lip. "I'm sad to hear it, but my talents are never wasted. I see it in your eyes, my little night-blooming cereus, and that is compliment enough."

Emma smiles uncomfortably, and Ivy takes the cue to redirect the conversation by sliding off her seat and pulling at my arm. "Come on. It's gown time!"

I allow myself to be pulled into my room, but gesture for Emma and Eden to follow.

Emma shakes her head. "We have last-minute preparation to do. We'll see you when you guys are done."

It doesn't sit right, leaving them, but then again, nothing has felt okay since becoming a Briarcliff student. Wearing two faces is exhausting—the Callie who enjoys the academy and attends the dances versus the one who has x-rayed through the blackness and sees the broken bones. I wish I could choose one girl to become, and it's with that wish that I allow Ivy to guide me into the gown chosen by the Virtues and don the white-feathered eye-mask gifted by my best friend.

Ivy twists me to face the mirror stuck to the back of my door.

Davide calls his goodbye, and I answer, but it sounds like an echo of my usual tone as I take in my transformation.

My brown, flyaway hair has been tamed into silk tresses drifting to my elbows. My lips are painted a delicate sheen of pink, my usually fair cheeks matching the same color. I lift the feathered, silvery mask to take in my hazel eyes, my lashes thick and black with strategically placed falsies.

Then there's my dress. Lightweight, white silk that reflects a prism of colors as I turn.

A smile creeps across my lips.

If tonight goes as planned, then maybe, just *maybe*, I can permanently slip into this Callie's skin.

"Fabulous," Ivy says. Her long blond hair is sleek-straight to her shoulders, and she wears a silvery cocktail dress.

"I can say the same for you."

She grins, then hooks her arm through mine. "Let's begin the madness."

Eden and Emma are waiting for us on the couch. When she spots us, Emma lifts her phone. "Guess what that tiny, rotund man was calling me? What 'little night-blooming cereus' means?"

Ivy and I shake our heads.

"He was calling me a night-blooming cactus."

A beat of silence follows.

Then, all of us burst into laughter.

Emma pouts, but can't maintain it for long. "Maybe he was *slightly* accurate."

I sweep my gaze over all my friends, caught in such a brief moment of glee, wishing we could feel this free and bright all the time.

Then make it happen, Calla.

"I will," I whisper to my mother, and my friends are still laughing so hard, they don't hear my quiet vow.

Seventeen

THE WINTER FORMAL is held on campus this year, due to Piper's death and the faculty's concern over students leaving the academy's property.

A lot of students found disappointment in the change of venue (apparently, a hotel ballroom in a ritzy part of Providence was rented out well in advance, and now, the thought of holding it in the academy's gym is heinous), but as I walk through the grand doors of Briarcliff's gymnasium—a whole separate *building*—I can't make out the difference between a five-star ballroom and this.

"Holy..." I say, taking in the transparent drifts of white and pale blue fabric and the multitude of fairy lights covering the ceiling.

"Haven't been to a school dance like this before, have you?" Ivy muses as we walk forward.

I think back on the plastic bowls of punch and party store cut-outs of Santas and Reindeer with the scents of rubber, spilled beer, and sweat in the air. "Not even close."

Fake snow lines the dance floor and sparkling glass snowflakes hang down from the ceiling as we wander close to the center, theater spotlights moving back and forth above our heads.

Ivy says something close to my ear that I don't catch. I'm focused on the altar in the center of the room and the clear plexiglass coffin raised on a dais, containing hundreds of stemless pink, red, and white roses laid within its confines.

"Wow," I breathe.

Ivy commiserates, murmuring over the gold detail and the thick folds of white satin holding up the pretend coffin. "I hate to say it, but Falyn and her cohorts embraced the Snow White theme with grace. I thought it was the dumbest idea ever, but this?"

I take in the dance floor circling the altar. "Are we supposed to dance around Piper's spiritual casket?"

"There it is." Ivy snaps her fingers. "I was wondering where Falyn's signature repugnancy was in all this perfection. We're probably meant to be the dwarves dancing around Piper's grave."

"How lovely."

Ivy sidles close. "At least you won't be here for long. Look alive, Callie, and talk to as many people as you can so no one can say they didn't see you. But don't be obvious. Like, still be yourself. It'd probably be suspicious if you started chatting with a ton of students you don't normally talk to. Actually..." Ivy winces. "Have you spoken to anyone outside our circle?"

"Thanks," I say, giving her the side-eye. "I'll be subtle, don't worry."

"Okay. Me too. Oh!" Ivy latches onto my shoulder instead of leaving my side. "And stay away from Chase. Not even hungry eyes across the dance floor. Got it?"

I sigh, then wave a hand at the bed of roses. "It'll be hard to, considering Piper's smack in the middle of it."

Ivy gives me one last squeeze. "It's been hard for you, but Sabine's reasons usually aren't unfounded. I'll find you in a few minutes, see how you're doing."

"Sure." I wave her off, anxious to make nice and do a few meet-and-greets before scuttling out of here and getting the job done.

It's not difficult to toss a few waves and smiles, especially once I take off my mask and let the few people I've spoken to in class put a name to the quick greeting. Like Ivy said, I can't approach a group and just start gabbing. They'd stare at me like fishes shocked onto land, and Sabine is the circling shark sensing the rippling waters.

After making the rounds, I find a corner and fit my mask back on, but my lips have gone chapped with all the nervous licking and my throat dry with the reflexive swallows. I stare across the room at the bar of drinks, then shimmy my way over and ask for a sparkling water.

The bartender acknowledges my order and turns his back to find a glass. The moment he shifts out of view, Sabine appears on the other side, wearing a blood red, strapless dress.

My body stills. Everyone in my immediate vicinity starts moving in slow motion and a white noise rush of blood flows through my ears.

"Miss? Miss."

The bartender's voice sounds hollow, like he's calling out from the curled depths of a conch shell.

I shake myself out of it and accept the glass of water, a thin lime floating forlornly on the top. "Thank you," I think I say, but it's hard to hear my voice.

Sabine smiles thinly and curls her hand in a wave before moving along the edges of the dance floor. Her eyes slide away. I exhale, my shoulders falling from my ears.

It's a wonder she's here as a chaperone. Neither of her girls attend Briarcliff.

Stupid me, I think. She's the queen of the Virtues. Of course, she's present and will always be considered a parent within these walls, whether or not she's the mother of a killer.

She's a queen of a lot worse, hisses that voice inside me. I sip my drink, the water cold and smooth, but the bubbles pop and burn all the way down.

A soft drift of skin brushes my free hand dangling at my side, and I curl my fingers, glancing down when it happens again.

Calloused, long fingers tickle against my own.

"Enjoying yourself?" Chase asks while staring directly ahead.

"I wish I could." *With you.*

Even though he stands a few feet behind me, I sense the heat rippling off him and crashing against my exposed back like white, frothy waves against a cliff. For a moment, I imagine him stepping up to me and lifting his hand, his head cocked in a silent question while his eyes glitter mischievously behind his black, raven-feathered mask. I would slide my hand into his warm palm, and he'd lead me onto the dance floor, gathering me at the waist and pushing me against his hard body, every plane, every inch of him, pressing against my softest parts, ending with our lips...

"You're doing fine," he says, his voice grounding and sure.

It forces me to remember where I am, what I'm doing, and why I can't be with him.

"I'm chomping at the bit to leap out of here. I feel watched in every direction."

As if I asked for it, a tingle skitters up my arm, unrelated to Chase because it has the creepy, measured *ticks* of spider legs climbing my skin.

Falyn stands nearby, flanked by Willow, Violet, and a few other girls I'm coming to recognize as Virtues. With their faces half-hidden by masks, it should be difficult to discern their eyes, but for me, they're all too targeted.

The three of them cast their wicked stares my way, the outer edges of their lips curling with derisive sneers. Violet's is the only one that trembles at the edges, and I file that away, as I've done all her moments of sympathy.

"How am I supposed to escape without notice?" I whisper.

"Leave that to me."

His thumb strokes the side of my pinky finger, and I curl it in hopes of catching him and proving my wishes right—that Chase is here, wanting to touch me as much as I ache to lean into him.

Chase's finger hooks mine. It lasts for a second—not even—but it's enough.

We break apart.

"The crowning of the Winter Formal Court starts soon," he murmurs as he angles away. "Ivy will find you."

"Stay." But he's too far away to hear my whispered plea.

Heart in my throat, I escape the edges of the dance floor and work for farther distance from Falyn and the other Virtues—but then stop.

The Virtues are supposed to be my sisters. As an initiate, I'm expected to socialize.

Setting my shoulders, I backtrack to the group, summoning Eden's eagerness when she spoke of her efforts to become one of them. She did everything she could to belong. Hoped against all barriers that they'd accept her.

I'm my own worst enemy if I don't do the same. And I'd be nothing but a disappointment to Emma and Eden.

"Hey," I say once I reach them.

Violet speaks first. "Hi, Callie."

Willow purses her lips, then finds deep interest in something behind me—or through me, but Falyn says, "Ready for the crowning?"

I paste on a smile. "It's so important that we honor our fallen members, isn't it? Piper would be delighted with what you've done to the school's gymnasium."

Falyn's lips waver between a sarcastic smile and a frown, unsure whether or not I'm complimenting her.

But I'm supposed to be supplicating to these assholes, not low-key insulting them. I force another smile and make sure to include their silvery, off-white gown, exactly like mine, when I say, "Love your dresses. Did the queen purchase yours, too?"

I wince. Even my compliments are turning into sideswipes. I can't seem to help it around these girls.

"It's a privilege to wear our colors," Willow seethes. "If only your pallor could handle it as well as mine."

I suppose I deserved that.

"Attention, students!"

The DJ cuts the music, and we all turn to Headmaster Marron taking the stage.

"The time you've all been anticipating has come," he says, accepting a wireless microphone from the DJ as he passes. "And I'm so proud of each and every one of you for choosing to honor one of our fallen."

I tilt my head to Falyn and smile. She glares at me in response.

"I won't take up too much time," Marron continues. "I'm sure you'd all prefer music to your headmaster's voice this evening, but I'd like to introduce you to your Winter Court King, a boy I couldn't take more pride in, both with his decorum on school grounds and how he's conducted himself after our most heartbreaking tragedy this year. The death of Piper Harrington, a wonderful pupil who you've posthumously crowned Winter Court Queen."

Scattered applause sounds out across the room, but I'm busy trying to find a line of sight on Chase through the glittering headpieces and slicked back hair of all the students.

Falyn has the same idea, but gestures to Violet and Willow to follow her as she carves a demanding path to the center of the room, where a spotlight shines on Piper's altar.

I follow their path, students twisting aside before they're nailed by one of the serrated edges of Falyn's elbows, until...

There.

Chase cuts into their path, acknowledging their presence with an absent nod, his face indiscernible beneath his mask. Yet, I'm taking in more of him than I did when he settled discreetly behind me, like the cut of his tuxedo and the breadth of his shoulders. His hair is windblown, curling into stylized waves at the top and falling into his ears, but there's nothing boyish about him. The raising of his chin commands the room as he takes the few steps needed to assume his position beside the plexiglass coffin and turn, sweeping his stare across the audience.

Marron rests a silver, opulent crown on his head. Chase is so tall, he has to bend to accept the prize.

When Chase straightens, I forget I'm in a school gym. I forget the surrounding students who attend Briarcliff Academy, and that the U.S. has long since shed a monarch rule.

Because we're faced with a king, and despite his face half-hidden in velvet and feathers, the line of Chase's jaw, his confident stance, and his rough voice, takes everyone under his thrall.

I'm staring at the true Noble King, I think, then school my face before anyone nearby can read the awe.

"All of you remember the day we lost Piper," he says. "And every single one of you can recall the days before. She was sharp, she was cutting, and she was mean. I knew her well enough to understand what she disguised: her guardedness, her vulnerabilities, and her easily wounded heart." Chase pauses, allowing the heavy atmosphere of the room to coat his words. "I'm sure you can all name a bully in your life, and many of you would say it was her."

The cavernous gym, while silent to my ears, seems to echo the names whispering into each student's head. A lot would agree on Piper. Many would mention Falyn. And most would be naming Chase, too.

I glance back at the platform when Chase continues.

"I don't think any of you would agree she should have died for her pettiness. I certainly don't. Or maybe you think she got what she deserved, killed by her own flesh and blood."

The gym doesn't breathe.

My attention scatters, pinpointing the furious gaze of Falyn as she twists to Willow and hisses words probably to the effect of, *What the fuck is he doing? He's meant to be mourning Piper, not pissing everyone off!* Then, I scan the sidelines, where a magnetic force draws me to a sleek, form-fitting scarlet dress.

Sabine's expression is so rigid, so frozen, it might fracture with the barest squint. Only the red slash of her lips, the gloss shimmering under the lights from each twitch, each tremor, showcases her carefully controlled fury.

A hand grasps my arm and pulls gently. "Come on," Ivy whispers behind me.

I follow Ivy, carefully disengaging from the crowd and using Chase's primed weapon of distraction to duck out the doors without anyone so much as turning their head—Sabine included.

Eighteen

LIFTING MY SKIRTS, I rush down the gymnasium steps behind Ivy, my dress billowing behind me under the chilled night wind.

"How long can Chase keep up the distraction?" I ask, my voice coming out breathless as cold air shrinks my lungs.

"Long enough to have everybody talking even *after* he finishes his speech," Ivy says, but whirls to grab my hand, forcing my legs to pump faster. In heels.

"Ivy, hold on—*ugh*, I wish I could kick off these things and run in bare feet!"

"No time." Ivy's voice is also breathy, her exhales plumes of smoke near my face. "Chase can buy us about twenty minutes. We have to be long gone by then."

"And Eden? Emma?"

"Already there." Ivy swings left, and my toes scream at the constant impact in such narrow, designer shoes.

Soon, we hit the path to the library, and with the stars as our only witnesses, creep inside the emergency exit that Eden propped open earlier with a stick.

A waft of heat hits me in the face when we shimmy through the door, the exposed skin of my arms thawing under goosebumps and melting snowflakes.

My chest rises and falls with deep, collected breaths as I stand beside Ivy and take in the dark recesses of the M.B.S. Library of Studies.

The stacks stand in the perfect alignment of Underworld soldiers. I instinctively brace for their silent onslaught.

"Let's go," Ivy whispers, though we should be the only ones here.

Everyone else is at the dance, I assure myself. *We're fine.*

Ivy kicks off her shoes then hooks them in her fingers as she sprints to the back, and I follow her lead.

Eden and Emma are waiting at the last column of books. We all nod in greeting, making as little sound as possible, just in case there's an unscheduled security guard belatedly completing his rounds.

Ivy crouches and exposes the keypad, but before she enters the pin and scans her finger, Eden stops her.

She asks, "You sure Tempest can scrub your time of entry?"

Ivy glances at Emma, who says, "He's been texting me. He's in the Nobles' system and found a workaround to the Virtues'. The cameras are off, and as soon as the system triggers Ivy's entry, he'll erase it."

Did I say we weren't *Mission Impossible* agents? Perhaps I stand corrected.

"Okay," Ivy says, then presses her finger on the pad and enters in a code.

The hidden door opens like a silent predator's jaws, but unlike the time before, I'm the first to step through.

A few sconces in the cylindrical room light up at my entrance, but not enough to fully spotlight us. With Eden staying behind as the lookout, the three of us creep along the curved lines of the room.

According to Ivy, there are more than three, maybe five, hidden doors on this floor, one being Sabine's office headquarters.

Ivy stops at an elaborate stone carving directly beneath the spot where Sabine stood on the balcony. Stepping next to her, I study the statue of a sleeping raven, wings tucked in, its talons curved over a twisted branch engraved in the wall.

Ivy wraps her hand around its neck and pushes. As if unable to help herself, she whispers under her breath, "*Altum volare in tenebris.*"

The carving sinks into a perfect square in the wall before it breaks into two pieces and the stone divides horizontally.

I've stopped breathing. My heart thrashes wildly in its cage, and I press a hand to my chest.

We step over the threshold into a large space, stonework turning into brickwork. A fireplace that could engulf me whole is to my right, and a wide desk sits in the center of the room. More carvings decorate the walls, each one a raven in different stages of flight.

Black iron and gray decorate the space, with intricate splashes of red, almost like rivers of blood between bone.

I gulp. "Where do you figure she's stashed her files?"

"Not here," Ivy says.

I'm the only one who jolts in surprise. "But this is her office."

Emma and Ivy share a look I can't decipher, other than it's grim. Then, Emma jerks her chin, as if giving Ivy the okay.

Before I call them out, Ivy moves behind the desk to the back wall displaying a large, vivid painting of Sabine, sitting in the identical, elaborate red chair showcased in reality, but with Piper and Addisyn seated below her in Briarcliff uniform, their legs curled under and their hands demurely resting on their shins.

"This is *so* haunting and creepy," I mutter at the same time Emma tells me to hurry up.

I pry my gaze from the painting in time to see Ivy duck into the fireplace.

Throwing out a hand, I cry, "Wait, what—?"

"It's another passageway," Emma says. "Go with her. I'll stay here and make sure no one comes."

"Shit," I whisper, but the word comes out tight, because I am *so* utterly freaked out right now.

Luckily, when I head into the fireplace, there are no dwarf-sized spiraling stairs into a basement waiting for me on the other side. Ivy's already opened the back wall of the fireplace, and I duck into a beautifully arranged bedroom.

"Sabine sleeps here?" I ask.

A gorgeous four-poster bed with a lace canopy sprawls out in the center, with two intricately carved wooden nightstands on each side.

Unlike Sabine's spine-chilling office space, this one is painted a calming sage green, with century pieces containing a dresser, a wardrobe, and a vanity mirror. The walls are adorned with watercolor paintings, all of white roses.

Ivy pinches her lips, staring pointedly at the paintings and nothing else. "Check the drawers."

I stay where I am. "Ivy, what is this? What am I missing here?"

Ivy's throat bobs, and she won't look at me. "I said you had to see it. So, here it is."

My lips form on *what* ... but can't give the question sound. Ivy's fists are clenched to her sides, her stance rigid and her lips pressed together so tightly, they're bone white.

With my head filled with more questions than answers, I bend to the first nightstand and rifle through the drawers. I sift through sleeping pills, a lavender scented sleep mask, some lace underwear, a box of opened condoms, and something hard and rubbery.

When I pull it out, I screech, then let it loose.

It bounces a few times before landing at Ivy's feet. "Is that a—?"

"Sex toy. Yes."

"But—" Again, I stop myself. Too often, I say things before thinking, and Ivy's stare is so wide and fused onto the watercolor above the bed, it's like she's begging that I come up with the answer myself.

There's a dildo in Sabine's secret bedroom, I think first.

But ... if we were hopping behind a fireplace and exploring Sabine's home-away-from-home, Ivy wouldn't be so stilted. I chance another look at her, wagering my thoughts against her cracking armor, and deciding she's more delicate than stiff. Ivy's so vulnerable that if I stood up and screamed, she'd buckle under the pressure and break.

The more I analyze the situation, the more it makes sense.

Ivy is the Virtues' princess.

I whisper, "Ivy, is this your room?"

Ever so slowly, she nods.

"And..." My empty stomach lurches as I continue, "was this Emma's room, too? Piper's?"

This time, her nod shakes loose a single tear that runs down her cheek.

Bile hurls into my throat, searing the back and making my tongue curl over the bitter, erosive acid. "Do you have other visitors in here?"

Ivy bobs her head, her lower lip spasming as more tears course down her cheeks.

"Visitors..." My voice thickens. My eyes turn hot. "Visitors Sabine chooses?"

"Yes."

"That you're forced to ... host?"

"Uh-huh."

Sleeping pills. Lace underwear. Sex toys. Condoms...

I fill in the horrendous blank, asking, "Men?"

"Y-yes."

"*Ivy*," rips from my throat before I shoot to my feet and envelop my friend in a hug.

Ivy digs her fingers into my arms and buries her head in my neck. I cling to her, absorbing her shakes, inhaling her sobs, my heart fracturing with each erratic beat.

"We can get out of here," I say into her hair.

Her chin digs into my neck. "This is our only chance. In a few weeks, I—I'm meant to return to this room. I don't want to come back here again."

I stroke her hair, exuding calm, though so many questions, so much *horror*, begs to pry open my lips. "Then let's move fast."

Ivy lifts her head and collects herself. "Sabine keeps her confidential papers in here."

After pulling the wardrobe from the wall, Ivy crouches and loosens one of the lower bricks. She stands, a thick, red binder clutched in her hands. "I saw her put this away one night, when she thought I was asleep ... over there." Ivy's gaze skirts to the bed, then away again. "It was my first night here. I was afraid to do anything but lie still ... after. Terrified there were cameras in here. I'm glad you're with me this time. You gave me the courage to show you. Sabine doesn't put anything like this on her computer. Too concerned with unauthorized access."

I take the binder from Ivy's stiff hands, using my side to push the wardrobe back in place. "By whom? Hackers?"

"You can call them that. The society is subject to quarterly reporting, like any other corporation, except it's not through the IRS. It's by the Nobles. Sabine hasn't disclosed the Virtues' true operations for a long, long time."

My grip slides on the leather-bound binder, sweat slicking my fingertips. I cast a furtive glance toward the opening we came through, then open the flap.

"Callie, we don't have time. Someone will notice we're not at the dance soon."

"Just a few seconds."

Time is a gift, a mantra I've learned the hard way. If there is any free moment to glean more information, I'll steal that time away rather than wait for it to be handed to me like a privileged present.

I flip to a random section, using this brief access not to understand Sabine's operations in their entirety, but just a glimpse, a snapshot of worth, so I can be sure our efforts at breaking in haven't been wasted.

A faded, thin page flutters to the floor, and Ivy bends to pick it up.

"What is it?" I ask. "Another letter from Rose?"

Ivy's eyes move back and forth as she reads, holding the paper up to the light until it almost becomes transparent.

It's a newspaper clipping, one with a picture.

The paper trembles in her hand. "Oh no..."

"What? What is it?"

She opens and closes her mouth, continuing to read the fine print.

"Ivy, we have seconds, remember?" I snatch the clipping from her so I can read it myself. She squeaks but doesn't fight me.

Actually, she's very, very silent.

My fingers start to shake as I take in the photo. I realize why Ivy's gone so quiet.

It's a black-and-white photo of my mother, smiling while angling her head, her eyes as lively and her hair just as crazy as if she were standing here today. Even without color, her beauty is startling.

And my heart cracks to pieces.

A vicious killing has rocked Manhattan's Lower East Side. 36-year-old Meredith Ryan, a respected crime scene photographer, primarily employed by the NYPD, was found slaughtered in her bedroom, her throat cut so deeply, she was almost decapitated. Her 15-year-old daughter discovered the horrendous scene mere hours after Ryan was killed. The motive remains a mystery, as does the killer. A spokesperson for the NYPD comments, "This is a tragedy of the worst kind. We don't yet know if this is related to any of the cases she worked on, but we will pull every file and study every page until we either find the perpetrator or rule them out. Meredith was one of our own, and we will work tirelessly to find out why a young mother, a valued crime scene photographer, and a wonderful person, has been taken from us so senselessly."

"Why?" I whisper, the article audibly rustling in my shaking hand. "Why would Sabine have this?"

I stare down at the open binder in my other hand, its weight making my wrist ache, but I stop feeling it as I find more grayish bits of paper poking out, like a goddamned scrapbook.

Flipping furiously, I find more articles about my mom. Journalists who, at first taking a vested interest, peter out as the dates go by and no killer is found. No motive.

Even my dad's arrest is in here. My accusations written for the nation to read. And his ultimate release.

Everything is in here.

"Why would she have these?" I'm screeching, vowels breaking apart in my mouth.

Ivy clutches my hand, then delicately pries the initial article from my grip and places it in the binder. "I'm being honest with you—I have no idea. But we can't stand here and wonder. We have to *leave*."

Her words knock a small amount of sense back into me, and I let her lead us out.

We rush to the fireplace and duck our heads under.

Ivy's gaze is sunken, hollow, as we descend into the shadows. "We'll read everything, and you'll—"

"Dearest Calla Lily, are you so bold as to think you could outsmart me?"

The voice wraps around my ears, tightening with the accuracy of a garrot, before I emerge from the ashy depths of the hearth.

Ivy's ice-cold fingers wrap around my bicep, digging hard. I feel the warm trickle of blood from the crescent-sized wounds she causes more than I do the petrified squeeze.

Reluctantly, I raise my eyes from the floor.

Sabine stands in the middle of the office, with her arms crossed, flanked by Emma, Eden ... and Chase.

Nineteen

"NICE TO SEE you've taken yourself on a personal tour," Sabine says, her storm-blue eyes razoring into me.

I break through the ice of her stare and turn to Eden. Eden, who was supposed to keep watch in the library. I'm filled with swallowed confusion when she won't meet my eye as she stands to the right of Sabine, straight-backed and shaking.

Our backup guard, Emma, is wound so tightly behind Sabine, so pale and stone-still, she won't look at me, either. Her vacant, sightless stare goes past Sabine, through me, and dead ends against the wall.

My arm twitches to help her, but under Sabine's scrutiny, I don't dare react so soon. Not when that's exactly what she wants.

Chase is next to his sister, hands shoved into his pockets, but his gaze on fire. He's targeting Sabine like he wants to kill her.

I do my damnedest to summon a calm exterior and ask the question most likely to throw Sabine off-balance. "Why do you have news articles about my mother?"

Sabine's blood-red lips peel back, but it's not directed at me. "Ivy may have intro-duced you to the Virtuous boudoir too soon. She most certainly spoke out of turn when you were in that room. Ivy—with me."

My gown billows with Ivy's strides as she takes her place next to Chase.

While I'm not surprised at Ivy's compliance, the pull in my belly at watching her resume her position next to Sabine and donning a regal, highborn expression is very, very real.

Chase moves to stare at me with such intensity, such enraged scrutiny, that my feigned, unaffected exterior will crumble once he matches his tone to that expression.

It's not real. It's not real. They're playing a part.

Sabine's voice severs the pulse that happens between Chase and me as we lock eyes—hope, warning, assurance, fear. "You have something that belongs to me."

Sabine lifts her hand, her fingers drooped as if she were already bored with going through the motions of retrieving her binder. "Bring it here."

My fingers tighten on the binder. "You didn't answer my question. Why is my mom in here?"

Her answering smile is kind. Patient. "Why, child, I do a copious amount of research on all the girls who pledge to become a Virtue. All current Virtues are in that binder, and my first impression notes. It's why you can't have it, you see. They are thoughts not to be made public because they can come off as rather upsetting."

I hold my position. Something doesn't feel right. Sabine is much too calm.

"But the dates," I say. "You have articles printed over a year ago, before I ever thought to come to Briarcliff."

"It wasn't meant for your eyes," Sabine continues, but her smile wears thin. "Nor for anyone else's. Bring it here, Calla Lily. *Now.*"

I debate the pros and cons of holding the binder tight to my chest and sprinting out of here. My escape fantasy doesn't last long, however. I said before that Chase and Ivy were playing their parts. As those good soldiers, they would be told to stop me. Restrain me. Rip the binder from my hands.

There's no chance of fleeing this room without doing as Sabine says. I'll have to figure out another way of uncovering the truth behind Sabine's retention of these articles.

And why they matter to her.

Reluctantly, I step forward and push it into her hands.

For the first time, Emma peels her attention from the walls and finds me. Her brown eyes are bloodshot, her lashes trembling. She blinks, but in between those seconds of blindness, her chin quivers.

I take in her hunched stature and what her mind must be forcing her to endure the longer this confrontation plays out. The torture she went through under Sabine's direction. The punishment Sabine could inflict now.

How could I think Emma would be able to withstand this? *Why* didn't I listen to my gut?

"As an initiate." Sabine's voice forces attention back to her. "You have no right, no *business*, looking into such private documents. If it weren't for my dear princess, you may have gotten away with your petty, impulsive investigation, but thanks to her, instead you're about to endure a most painful final trial."

The tiny hairs on the back of my neck rise.

Ivy stares at the floor, her lips clamped between her teeth. Despite my silent prod at her to look up, her focus doesn't stray from the ground.

Sabine chuckles low in her throat. I spare another glance at Chase, but his focus is straight ahead, muscles spasming in his cheeks as his jawline protrudes with a hard, tongue-severing clench.

"You must be wondering, foolish girl, why I'm not exiling you for your disobedience."

At last, I meet her stare. "I'm not your show pony. You got your binder back. So, kick me out, or I'll walk out myself."

Sabine's cheeks tic with amusement. "You've accepted our invitation, meaning, there is no possible way for you to *walk* out. It is up to me whether to banish you, but

I'm inclined to provide you with a choice. Since your acceptance here at Briarcliff, you've been consumed by us. Hungry for our history and societal formation. And now, I hold articles of your mother in my hands." Sabine lifts the binder, dangling the weight easily, despite her waif-like stature. "I doubt you're willing to leave it all behind."

I remain closed-lipped, but Sabine sees past it. She smiles. "Stay and prove this was all a misunderstanding, dear girl. Fall into our ranks and learn our history and all we have to offer. Or, attempt to sever your connection with us and see how far that gets you."

Her veiled threat doesn't hit its mark. *She won't kill me if I leave.*

Piper wasn't killed by the Virtues—it was Addisyn, her sister. Howard Mason is still alive, according to Chase, and after what I've seen in the bedroom behind the fireplace, Sabine likes her Virtues alive, well, and complacent.

Sabine could be calling my bluff.

But as I hold her cool, depthless stare, a tinned, inner voice asks, *Is she, though?*

"You have too many qualities that can't be ignored," Sabine explains. She passes the binder to Ivy, who moves to set it on her desk. "Curiosity, stubbornness, pride, determination, instinctive intelligence—the type of traits that cannot be taught, and which we Virtues covet. It is only your foolishness I must confront, and I can do that easily. So, I either ban you from our society, or I keep you as planned, and thus seal your lips from ever speaking of the Virtues. Or the Nobles, I suppose."

Sabine includes the Nobles with the reluctant tone of including a neglected, middle child.

I jump on the opening. "What is Chase doing here? If the punishment is for me and involves the Virtues, why keep everyone here at all?"

"Oh, child." Sabine gifts me with another serpentine smile. "Breaking you will be so much sweeter than allowing you to cleave yourself from the Virtues."

The image of the adjacent room curdles into my mind, its implications turning those sickening bubbles into pops of acid. Sabine's using some of these girls by offering them out for sex.

I can't leave now. Not after discovering what Ivy is forced to do to keep her place as a Virtuous princess and save her family from poverty.

As if sensing my silent answer, Sabine grins. Gestures me forward. "Come."

Sabine's dress swishes against the stone floor as she spins, her gait over cobble-stones unusually smooth as she leads us to the door to the inner temple.

I step toward Chase, but he stops me with a searing, bone-rattling look, then gives a minuscule shake of his head. *Don't.*

Then, as if he hadn't communicated with me at all, he stalks to his sister's side and grasps her outstretched, shaking hand, murmuring into her ear.

Emma relaxes under her brother's protection, her shudders visibly subsiding.

Sabine pauses at the doorway. "Are you coming, Calla Lily?"

There's pressure at my back, Eden nudging me forward. "Go," she whispers. "We have no choice."

I risk one more glance at Chase before tottering forward, wondering if Sabine's focus on me means the rest of them can get out unscathed.

Foolish girl is right. There's no way Sabine will let bygones be bygones.

The large door guarded by the stone raven slides open, and Sabine disappears into the temple. When I follow her out with my friends at my back, I pause mid-stride and look up at the gold cloaks surrounding the balcony, interspersed with the black velvet of the Nobles.

I gulp, scanning the faceless heads and shapeless cloaks. This can't be good.

They're all here.

Twenty

SABINE COMES to a halt at the center of the temple, sweeping her arms out and raising her head to her audience. "My children, it seems as though we have a minor interlude before we continue our formal winter celebration in the Nobles' tomb. Calla Lily Ryan thinks she can thwart our rules and bring in outsiders to learn our secrets."

The room erupts in chants of *"altum volare in tenebris,"* masculine and feminine voices mixing into an eerie, unisex chant.

I lift my gaze to the rafters, at the mingling of black and gold velvet, for the first time becoming subjected to the Nobles' scrutiny. Up until now, it was always the Virtues who tested my boundaries and stripped my soul. Other than Chase, the Nobles were ignorant of my initiation, or so I thought.

Yet here they are, about to witness my final trial.

Sabine clucks her tongue, disapproval etched into the thin lines of her face as she watches my hesitant and wary study of the room. "Come, dear girl." But her eyes sharpen. "Don't keep us from the night longer than you already have."

Fingers brush against mine, the same touch I beheld at the dance, identical calluses sending a reassuring stroke over my skin.

I feel Chase's knuckles against my palm before stepping forward and pretending nineteen sets of eyes aren't staring at the top of my head, salivating over my potential demise.

Was every member made aware of our plans tonight? Is Tempest up there somewhere? I risk another glance above. Which one of these Cloaks haunted my dorm room at night, taking what they wanted while I slept?

With every step I take, I curse my weakness for authority. My need for companionship. I should be sprinting for the door.

Yet, I walk forward, summoned by the crook of Sabine's finger, pushed by my dread over what will happen to Eden, Emma, Ivy—*Chase*—if I don't bow down and take my spanking like a good, chastised girl.

No wonder my mom and Ahmar always worked alone. Almost nothing could be used against them if an angry criminal decided to take revenge.

Except ... Mom's dead.

As I move closer to Sabine, I'm positive that putting trust in others is vastly becoming my greatest mistake.

A flash of black alerts me to motion at my periphery. I turn. Daniel Stone waltzes out of another hidden entrance, his hood flipped back, his red cloak floating from the breeze of his prowl. When his pale eyes find mine, cold, skeletal fingers wrap themselves around my neck.

Daniel Stone's footsteps echo throughout the temple until he comes to a stop beside Sabine. No sounds emanate from the balcony, no murmurs or shuffles. Complete, utter quiet has stifled all the bodies in this room, every single person, including me, choosing their senses over their motions as events unfold.

Sabine reaches out a hand, which Daniel clasps. "Just in time, Daniel. It seems our Calla Lily needs a lesson in loyalty."

Daniel casts his gaze—briefly—in my direction. "Do as you wish, my love."

An answering growl sounds from behind. It's Chase.

Sabine says, "I'm afraid you're faced with another choice, Initiate."

A litany of possibilities fan through my mind. Back to the boathouse? Falyn's unfettered access to me during school hours? Free reign on my dorm room and locker to plant additional rodent corpses?

I wonder where Marron is, and if he's up there with the others, closed-mouthed and his interest piqued.

I keep my voice level when I ask, "And that is?"

"It's obvious to me, and everyone else in this temple, that consequence to you is —well, of no consequence. It is only if someone else, a person close to you, suffers, that you deign to give obedience any attention at all." Sabine angles her head, adding, "Isn't that right?"

I cover up my wince, but not in time. Sabine's tongue runs along her lower lip at the sight. "The minute Ivy admitted your transgression, I started to wonder, should I punish your father? Your stepmother?" She arches a brow. "Your unborn sister?"

Horrible thumps rattle against my ribcage. I beg my body to stay calm. Don't satisfy her by freaking out.

"Sadly, they're not here." Sabine over-emphasizes a pout. "And I do enjoy a show. Therefore, I am putting your pathetic accomplices up for auction, instead."

A hollow feeling engulfs my center, and I fist my hands in an attempt to keep my hopes from drifting. "Don't do this. We didn't read anything. Discover anything."

"Oh, but I must. Eden, come up to me, please. And dear Emma, come join your former queen. It's been so long since we've been close."

Emma's eyelids fly shut, as if by falling into forced blindness, she can exit this nightmare.

"Don't make me bring out reinforcements," Sabine purrs, but it's the sound of a cat toying with a long-dead mouse.

Gently, Chase pushes at his sister's shoulder, ushering her forward. Yet, the look on his face, fury-born and relentless, leaves me to believe that Sabine thought of everything she could in order to get away with this. Otherwise, Chase would torch this moment and gladly drag his sister from the wreckage he wrought.

"And Chase, handsome prince of the Nobles, you too," Sabine says.

Daniel interjects before Chase can react. "That is not what we agreed."

"I promise you will be very amenable to these new terms, my love," Sabine says, "when you discover that these two have not been keeping apart as ordered."

Silence descends in the room. Daniel's voice comes out as a quiet *whoosh* of steel. "Is this true, son?"

Chase cuts a look in my direction, but I keep my expression blank, my thoughts bland. They can't read it in my face. I will never let them see how I feel for him. Never again.

Chase shakes his head. "I haven't touched her since we got what we wanted, Father."

"Liar!" Sabine shrieks, and for the first time, her face twists to reflect the Medusa she harbors inside, the jealous, reckless, awful recluse of a woman who's lost both her daughters and only has this empty stone temple to show for it.

A lupine, toothless grin stretches across Chase's face. "Prove it. *Mom.*"

Sabine's cheeks blotch to a startling red. She opens her mouth—

"Enough." Daniel comes between them. "If my boy says he's been following orders, then I trust him. He's well aware of the penalty that will follow if he doesn't."

Sabine breathes, in and out, through her nose. "That may be the case, but he's still required to stand among these fools as one of Calla Lily's choices. *Then* we'll see if these two have severed their emotional ties."

Daniel studies his future wife. They share a long look. Then, to my disappointment, he says, "I'll allow it. Come over here, boy."

Chase's focus slides over me as he passes, but soon, I'm left with nothing but the freshwater scent of his wake.

No one's behind me anymore. I'm standing alone.

Sabine preens in the middle of the group, settling her stare on each and every prize, before barreling into mine. "Everyone has their greatest fear, don't you agree?"

I swallow. Nod. I'm so tense, my shoulder blades touch.

"I've yet to fully realize yours, but here are people you've gotten to know. Become friends with, even found a lover in one. With that comes the privilege of sensing their desires, their flaws, and the one thing that will bring them down."

My teeth clench so hard, my jaw shakes with effort, but I force my lips to relax. My stare to remain benign.

Sabine continues, "If you are to prove yourself as a Virtue—that you are worthy of the title—then you have one way to redeem yourself. Choose one of these three to endure your final trial by submitting them to their greatest fear." Sabine smiles, slow, full, and bright. "You are about to prove exactly why I'm keeping you as one of us. Because you've catalogued, with *certainty*, each and every one of their terrors. Emma. Eden. Chase. Haven't you?"

She can't be right.

But ... as if charming a cobra from its basket, my mind betrays me.

I know their fears.

My cheeks go numb. Sabine watches me so closely, her eyes burn when she notes the flicker of realization in my expression.

"Good girl," she murmurs. "Now tell us which one."

Unable to withstand looking at her anymore, I lock eyes with my friends. With Emma, exuding terror through her pores, her face so pale, every burn mark and scar can be mapped. Eden is next to her, head bowed, hair falling forward, but what she's endured is written all over her body—the baggy clothes, the full coverage of her arms, legs ... and face.

Lastly, I come upon Chase.

He meets my study, unwavering and sure. The bronze of his irises darken to a hellish degree and are as intense as black fire licking at my cheeks. His forehead smooths and his lips are one line, closed and silent, but I can read what he wants.

I could understand his wishes even with my eyes closed.

Choose me.

I forget to breathe in those painful seconds of searching my friends.

His nostrils flare as if to say, *I can take it.*

My fingers ache to touch him. *No. You can't.*

Because I'm sure of what will kill him, what will make him suffer the most.

... and I don't think he has any idea of the fear I know lives inside him.

Twenty-One

"MY PATIENCE WEARS THIN, CHILD." Sabine folds her arms, and in the din of the temple, nothing but the cracks and pops of flaming sconces sound out between her words.

I don't want to choose. Eden and Emma have both endured so much, and Chase ... Chase's childhood sounds like an endless SEAL training camp ruled by his father.

How could I subject them to more?

"I choose me," I say.

Sabine chuckles, while Daniel Stone sighs. "My dear," he says, "as much as the books and movies make sacrifice such a bold delight to watch, that is not what we encourage within these societies, especially as a test of loyalty. We battle wills, we push emotions, and we force strength. Those are most encouraged through the sacrifice of *others*—while the one we test watches."

"What my love has failed to mention," Sabine adds, "is that we will choose for you if you do not."

Saliva coats my mouth, thick and bitter as venom. Scanning the faces, I keep thinking *no*. Emma: *no*, Eden: *no*, Chase—

His confidence settles into my center—steady, stable, and sure.

Chase is the one who can take it. Chase emulates the three traits the Nobles embrace: strong will, controlled emotion, incredible strength. But ... can I?

Chase won't back down. Even as my choice scrambles, stretching and fracturing among the three of them, he won't break.

I grasp at one last chance by focusing on Ivy, but her expression doesn't hold support or assistance. It can't.

I go back to Chase, holding his stare as I would the delicate petals of an ink-dipped rose.

"Chase," I say to him, my voice rough and uneven. "I choose Chase."

He nods, offering reassurance where there is none.

"How shocking," Sabine says as she glides forward. "And as our newest Virtuous initiate, tell me, what is his greatest fear?"

Sabine's body blocks my view of him, but I can predict what he's assuming I'll say. *His greatest fear is losing his sister ... or ... he'll lose his leadership of the Nobles ... or ... he's afraid of his father.*

But those are all abstract fears, relating to the future, where time is always variable and risky. Those fears could be conquered through making one single, tailored change.

Deep in my soul, I know that's not what Sabine wants.

No, if I'm to prove myself as a Virtue, then... "Small spaces."

The room seems to sigh, each person's inhale mixing with their neighbors' until it fills the lungs of the entire temple.

Sabine tips her head, her lashes eclipsing over her eyes in careful consideration. Daniel frowns behind her, and Chase—I can't see Chase.

"Are you certain?" Sabine asks.

My lips are dry, seeming to crack open and bleed with each breath. "Yes. He's claustrophic."

Sabine turns her head to Daniel, her neck long and smooth. "Darling?"

The movement brings Chase into view, long enough to witness the surprise in his eyes and the color leeching from his face before he forces his features into such hardened determination, the remaining blood can't escape.

Look at me. I'm so sorry, Chase. I'm so—

But he no longer has eyes for me.

My stomach pitches, and I fist a hand under my ribcage.

"Then I have just the thing," Sabine says. "Don't you agree, Daniel?"

Daniel's lips are bloodless slashes in his angular face. "Yes. But I'll say this, Sabine. It is better for all of us if you exile the girl, not punish my son."

"Strong words coming from a man who dismissed the idea of self-sacrifice as concession stand fodder," Sabine purrs.

"I'm simply—"

"Are you questioning my authority?" Sabine asks him. "In the presence of our young members? Or is your hesitancy to offer up your son merely proving why the Virtues have become more powerful in recent years?"

Daniel sets his jaw. "Do not do this here."

"Do what?" Sabine asks, too innocently.

"Make me bring up your daughters."

In an instant, the air in the temple becomes thick, heavy. Ominous. But I use their bickering to try to catch Chase's eye, but he won't even toss a look in my direction. Or anywhere. He stands behind his father, staring at nothing, while his sister murmurs to him.

In the few seconds it took to state his fear, their roles have shifted, and all I can do is watch Chase's strength ebb, then flow, into Emma.

"I have doubled Briarcliff's grants and donations this year," Sabine growls at her fiancé. "And despite losing two children, my Virtues have blossomed, and the graduates have taken their places to resurrect change in the most powerful of chairs. Do *not* question my authority, my love, and how dare you subvert my claim on Calla Lily

Ryan and all she holds dear. Including. Your. Son. If the situation were reversed, there's no doubt what your actions would be, or can you look me in the eye and protest any differently?"

Low voices circle above us but are shut silent with a raised look from Sabine. She doesn't direct it at any one Cloak, but she doesn't have to.

Daniel glances at his son. Then back to his fiancée. And it is with the blackest of stares and the worst of promises that he finally lands on me.

"As you wish," he says, his lips moving with barely enough space to emit sound.

Sabine spreads her arms, lifting her chin and radiating all the color she's leeched from the temple and into herself. "Then it is to the Nobles' tomb that Chase Stone will endure Calla Lily's punishment for the rest of tonight and long into tomorrow. In twenty-four hours, at midnight, he will be released."

Voices laced with confidence and eagerness float from the rafters and into our ears. The Nobles' code of honor is chanted, over and over: *We fly high in the dark.*

"Celebrations are allowed to ensue," Sabine concludes. "You may all reconvene in the Nobles' ritual room for the true celebration of winter, our strongest and most honored season."

Movement follows, the Cloaks filtering out.

"Calla Lily, you are to come with us," Sabine says, then includes Daniel and Chase. "As for the rest of you, back to your dorms." She stares at Emma. "You must understand by now that you are not welcome here, and if I catch you within these walls again, there will be more than your beauty at stake."

Emma's hand clenches around Chase's, but Chase urges her to the exit with assurances that he'll be all right. Eden stumbles forward and clasps Emma's arm, dragging her away, but Emma refuses to break her stare from her brother's until the stone walls force her to.

In a flash of emotion before she follows Eden and Emma, Ivy sheds her mask, her eyes vivid with sorrow and fury as we connect.

I use that moment to form my own mask, because my night is far from over. Chase will suffer, and it's because of me.

The temple empties within minutes, and Sabine directs me through another door, this one leading down a vast, stone staircase lined with electric sconces.

Daniel leads the way with Chase behind him. Sabine follows next, as if deliberately coming between Chase and I as we walk single file down the winding steps. As much as I wish to be close to Chase, I'm aware of the futility. He won't linger with emotion, nor will he search for my hand.

If Ivy wore her emotionless, blank mask, then Chase has just donned one of iron.

I can't even use this time to mull over where we screwed up, or how Sabine got so ahead of us in such a small amount of time. I'm too afraid of the consequences—if Ivy really did confess our plans to Sabine. Of what Chase will endure and if he can handle it. His *father* wasn't even aware of his phobia.

A loud creak comes from darkness below, and as I hit the last step, I notice Daniel has traversed to the end of a dim corridor and opened a wide, wooden door.

The Briarcliff underground resembles more of the barracks of an ancient castle than a school, and I shudder under the thought of heading into some kind of windowless dungeon.

Chase's strides don't hitch as he follows his father, his gait sturdy and his head held high. I try to exude the same confidence, similar will power, but he's been in this world a lot longer than I.

Once through the door, I take quick stock of the brick walls, and the oil sconces lit by Daniel's hand. Large, dusty gray stone lines the floor, each large tile reminiscent of a honeycomb—if hornets made their nests underground. Chains are attached in the middle of a select few, rising to the ceiling, and stacked high in one corner are broken, splintered pieces of old, rotting wood.

I almost recoil when I follow the chain-link trail to Daniel. He pulls a lever mounted on the wall. Chains clink, and neglected, unoiled pulleys spin, until a cylindrical cage is pulled from the ground through a cloud of dust.

Once the bottom of the cage meets the stone floor, the screaming creaks and clangs stop, but not their horrendous echo.

Daniel stares at the contraption, unblinking. "We haven't used this for over fifty years. It was meant for the foulest of betrayals."

"Then I guess it's time to pop its modern cherry."

Those are the first words I've heard from Chase since this shitstorm began, and my eyes cut to him, noting the sarcasm but studying the trepidation.

The muscles in his neck pop out and strain. His eyes, while focused, count each bar on the cage, wide enough to fit one person.

Him.

"Step in," Sabine says. Out of the three of them, her voice is the loudest. "And dear Calla Lily. Watch."

Chase's Adam's apple bobs, but he takes one step. Then two. After four, he's through the open door of the cage and turns around, facing me.

I mouth his name, because that is the only word that has meaning, and my heart wants to speak.

His brows smooth. He sets his jaw and clasps his hands. But he's shaking. "Do what you've been waiting years for, Sabine. Drop me into a black hole and jerk off to it already."

"*Son*," Daniel snaps.

Chase's gaze slides to Daniel. "Stop pussy-footing around."

My fingers tremble. I take one step forward, then back. I've never been great at family dynamics, but this is another, twisted level. One I should rip Chase away from and run until we've climbed our way out of here, fingers bleeding but hearts intact.

With forced steps, Daniel comes to the cage's gate and swings it shut. He clicks the rusted lock closed. "You brought this on yourself, Chase. I warned you, several times, to keep your relationship with Callie at a superficial level."

Chase stares at his father through slitted eyes. "Then I'll deal with it."

"*Chase.*"

His name bursts from my mouth, filled with too much emotion. It opens a window to vulnerability, but I can't control it.

We lock eyes. He murmurs, "It'll be all right."

But Chase shouldn't be the one assuring me. *I* should be saving him. As Sabine commands Daniel to lower the cage into the ground—into the black—*I* should be protesting. Screaming. Asking them why this needs to happen.

I do none of it.

The Virtue I'm supposed to be takes control, whispering and stroking my conscience until it slumbers under its soothing hand like a purring kitten. Chase can stand a full day in the dark. He'll take it like he endured the beating in the pavilion, the orders of his father, the trauma of his sister. Because he's doing it for the greater good.

I admit, as Chase's feet, then his knees, disappear into the ground by the slow crank of chains and pulleys, it's becoming harder to see the big picture.

"Chase," I try again, his name more rasp than sound.

He doesn't break our stare as he submits to be buried alive, but he can't hide the terror slithering behind the bronze, tarnishing his arrogance.

We are both so composed on the outside as he's lowered into the jaws of his deep-seated fear. But inside, we're destroyed.

The escaped strands of his smoothed-back blond hair go bone white as the sconces spotlight his descent, and I inch forward, my fingers twitching to grab onto the bars and pull him out of there through sheer willpower alone.

He raises his head, and the corners of his lips curve as he attempts a smile. But he doesn't make it all the way. Shadows pass over his face before the gleam in his eyes snuffs out, too.

With a loud *clank*, Chase is sealed in a tomb, the octagonal lines of the roof fitting in seamlessly with the other tiles.

Those borders are the only sign of him in the ground.

Twenty-Two

"YOU ARE to go directly to the underground dance," Sabine says to me, but her attention remains on that middle tile—the one containing Chase. "You are not to mention—not even once—what transpired in this tomb. You are not to return and try to free him, for if you do, my punishment will be ten-fold. Do you understand?"

I blink back unshed tears and nod.

"Lovely." Sabine smiles, her lips remarkably red and unblemished throughout this entire ordeal. "Darling, I believe we're missed at the Societal Ball as well."

Daniel blinks out of his trance, his expression so different from his fiancée's, so silently torn.

"Don't you feel one *ounce* of guilt?" I ask him, my voice ricocheting in the chamber. It's the first time I've truly spoken in this crypt.

Daniel's gaze centers on me, that infamous, Stone cold stare. "My son chose his destiny the moment he decided to abandon his orders and protect you instead of use you."

"And might I add," Sabine says to me, "you are the one who chose to do this to him."

I'm about to scream at her that it wasn't my choice but stop myself. Of course, it was my choice. I said his name. I pointed to him as the recipient of punishment.

"After you, child," Sabine says, motioning to the door.

I can't tear my gaze from the floor. Is Chase screaming by now? Has he lowered to his knees and slammed his forehead to the ground, clutching his head?

The dude hates small spaces, Tempest had said to me in the library one day. *He never takes elevators.*

That seasick swill in my gut splashes into my throat. This is so much worse than an elevator. There's no light. No air.

Can he breathe?

"*Callie*," Daniel bites out, and I jerk to attention, though it physically hurts to leave Chase's prison.

I'll be back, I silently vow. *I won't let them do this to you.*

I stride forward, the soft breeze from the motion chilling me to the bone. My arms are damp with sweat, my chest probably shining with it, and the silk wisps of my dress feel like wilted petals against my legs.

Out in the corridor, Daniel takes the lead.

As I follow Sabine and Daniel through more underground tunnels, ostensibly leading to the Societal Ball, neither of them looks back.

Not even once.

When our footsteps stop echoing off the walls, and instead are replaced by the pounding vibrations of music, we're far enough away to never hear Chase's screams.

Sabine and Daniel take me through a wide archway and into another chasm of space—this one governed over by the large, black wings of a raven crest.

Bodies twist and writhe in the middle, some shedding their cloaks, others pulling down their hoods, and the rest cloak-less and carefree, their gowns and tuxes more stained with sweat and drink than when they started their evening.

Enough light emits from the walls and carefully placed spotlights on the ground. On the opposite side, the staircase I descended one time before blinks in and out of shadow as the moving spotlights crest over and around.

"Callie!" Ivy cries through the music. Once she reaches me, her damp, cold hand clasps mine.

Emitting nothing but joy, Ivy grins at Sabine, lifts my hand to twirl under it, then drags me away.

Ivy spins me in time to witness Sabine's approving nod at her replacement princess, and Ivy doesn't stop until we're well on the other side, and she pushes a glass of champagne into my hands.

"Drink," she says.

Even though my mouth is as dry and barren as the corridors I've wandered through, I say, "I can't."

"You have to." Ivy presses the slim flute to my lips despite my choking protest. "Look like you're having fun."

I ask over the rim, "How am I supposed to do that? Eden and Emma have been taken God knows where, and Chase is fucking *buried*—"

Ivy shushes me, then responds in a low voice. "Eden and Emma are safe in their dorms. Sabine promised only one would be punished. And you're safe now, too."

"You sold us out," I blurt. I've only had one, forced sip, but my cheeks are hot.

The meager light remaining in Ivy's eyes dies out. "I wasn't given a choice. Sabine has Chase *followed*, Callie. She tracked him and his sister to their lake house on multiple occasions, even has pictures of you and Chase secretly meeting up at Lover's Leap. If I wasn't honest with her, what happened a few minutes ago would've been worse. She would've caught you, either way, but with my input, I tried to make the repercussions less lethal."

I hiss, "You could've warned us!"

"You wouldn't have attempted the break-in had I warned you. You would've kept seeing Chase. I would never have gotten the opportunity to show you what she's doing to her princesses—"

"Do you think I wouldn't have believed you if you had just told me?" I ask her, appalled. "Ivy, you didn't have to show me a sick bedroom to prove you were being molested!"

Ivy shushes me, her features rippling with desperation. "You have to act like Sabine to outsmart her, and that's what I did. I'm not ashamed of it. I'm sorry Chase is suffering and you're mad at me, but I'm *glad* I did it, because you're standing here. Livid and *alive.*"

My anger simmers down. "You honestly believe she'd kill me for continuing to see Chase?"

"For transpiring against her." She croaks out her answer, then takes a long sip of her champagne. "She'd kill her own daughters if it came to choosing between them or ruling the Virtues."

"What's that supposed to mean?"

"Nothing. Hate me all you want, but I did this to save you guys. Remember that."

"Instead of being expelled, or beaten, or set on fire, I'm standing here with you drinking fancy champagne in a secret ritual room. Tell me what part of that is supposed to make me feel safe."

Ivy cups her own glass. "Sabine manipulates. You've seen it. Expelling you, beating you, exposing you isn't what would've broken your spirit, like it did Emma and Eden. But putting Chase in a box? You *have* to prove to her that's not your kryptonite, either. Get yourself under control, because if she senses your fractures, she'll go in for the final stab."

"He's in the ground." I breathe, in and out, attempting to regain control. "And I put him there to save my own skin. I can't feel good about that. I can't drink this shit and dance like the rest of you while he suffers."

Ivy scans those around us and pulls me closer, ensuring privacy. "She's keeping you for a reason. We have to figure out why that is."

"The last time we thought of the perfect caper, we ended up as theater for the rest of these assholes."

"Exactly. It's all a show. Outwardly, at least. On the inside, she's poisoning us."

My gaze sweeps around the room, but it isn't calculating like Ivy's. It's furious.

"Listen, I'm all too aware of what it's like to be put on display," Ivy whispers near my ear.

I absorb her words. My shoulders slump. I can't stay mad at her with what she's being forced to endure. Blackmailed and manipulated into Sabine's control. How didn't I see how easily Ivy has to cave to Sabine's wishes when we were planning the break-in? "What you said back there, about being forced into sex..."

She shakes her head. "I don't want to talk about that. Now, it's all about making a happy face and pretending Sabine awarded you the greatest honor by keeping you a member."

"Ivy…"

"Do it." Ivy's expression dims. "It's how I've survived these past few months, and it's how you will, too."

Ivy darts a look over my shoulder then spins me around with deceptively strong arms. There's no time to marvel at her strength—both inside and out—because it's as if the three Furies from Greek Mythology descend on us.

Falyn, Willow, and Violet, their cloaks clasped but hoods down, form a half-circle around our forms.

"Quite a scheme you cocked up, Callie," Falyn says. In this light, her pale-colored eyes take on the yellowish hue of the underground ballroom. "What were you hoping to find, exactly?"

The hidden bedroom comes to mind, and I glance at Ivy. The image must be written all over my face, because in those few seconds of connection, Ivy pales, then jerks her head side-to-side. Falyn doesn't know.

Falyn doesn't know…?

Repeating the question doesn't help. Who are the girls Sabine puts in that bedroom? And how many are there, because so far, I can only count three. Ivy. Piper. Emma.

And only one of them stands in this room.

"I was hoping to discover more information on Piper's death," I answer Falyn.

She snorts.

Willow mutters, "Not this shit again…"

Violet cants her head sadly, like it's hard to believe I'm still on the investigative track.

Falyn says, "When are you going to understand that being a Virtue is a privilege? Acceptance into the Ivies is guaranteed. A job in the Forbes Top 100 is an easy option. Marrying a billionaire is less of a chance and more of a given. What part of that displeases you?"

"What's the price you pay for those riches?" I ask. "Have you ever thought on that?"

Falyn curls her lips. "So far, being me is pretty fabulous. To be you, though … I fully understand why you'd rather fuck up than level up. You're not meant to be successful or admired. You're not one of us." Falyn's gaze rakes me up and down in an assessing, disgusted sweep. "Our queen may want to keep you around in order to contain your screw-ups and prevent them from being made public but understand this: none of us think you belong. Nobody wants you here."

I sigh, having heard this—and predicted it—well before she approached me.

Falyn's eyes grow small. "Then how about this, possum? Chase was once the most sought-after guy in school. Every guy wanted to be him. All girls wanted to do him. And he could choose whatever he wanted in life—who he fucked, where he went after graduation, what top ten company to work for or what billion-dollar start-up he wanted to create. He couldn't afford to show weakness. He ruled this school through intimidation, control, and power. But now? He's in a closed-off room some-where, hyperventilating and looking weak, because of *you*. You ruined the most popular guy in school, merely by existing in his proximity. You're poison, possum. No, you're toxic waste, and it's high time you realized it."

Her invisible knife slips through the spaces between my ribs. My heart doesn't feel the blade at first—but it's so sharp, so expertly cut, that once it does, the blood pours.

Falyn dumps her champagne down my dress.

I gasp, but not at the liquid soaking through the gauze and the fumes going up my nose. I'm gulping for breath because what she says is true.

"Falyn!" Ivy cries.

Falyn shoves her empty flute at Violet, who fumbles to keep it from falling to the ground. "You're next, *Princess*. Better keep an eye on your position and make sure this rodent doesn't nuke it like she did Piper and Chase."

Falyn flounces away, gesturing at her friends to follow.

Willow, not to be excluded, also dumps her drink down my chest, and this time I gasp in surprise.

Giggling, she departs on a wave, but Violet pauses and unties her cloak.

"Here," she says, "to help you dry off."

My response comes out as an accusation. "Why are you being nice to me?"

"Because there was a time when I was you. And I wish I'd had someone to be kind to me in between all the cruelty."

"Then why do you stay?" I ask, while Ivy helps me wipe my chest with Violet's heavy cloak.

Violet's voice goes quiet, almost impossible to hear over the surrounding music and voices. "You heard Falyn. There's nowhere to go but up."

Falyn calls for Violet, a snappish, impatient sound. Violet drifts away, but I watch her departure with a sodden weight against my chest, unrelated to spilled champagne.

"Falyn's jealous she's wasn't chosen as the princess after Piper," Ivy says, swooping in and blocking my view of Violet. "And she's pissed she wasn't chosen as the crew captain after Piper, then Addisyn."

I collect more folds of fabric, wiping at my arms. "That's pretty misdirected rage, if Falyn's taking it all out on me. No—this is something else. She can't stand me and has hated me since the minute I walked into Briarcliff. It's Violet I'm most concerned about. She doesn't belong with them, does she?"

Ivy pauses with her dabbing long enough to peer over her shoulder. "She's too sweet for all this."

"Then why was she chosen?"

"She's beautiful and innocent. A lot of men would pay five figures for a night with a girl like that."

My hands freeze. My blood turns ice cold. "No," I whisper.

"It's not going to happen. She graduates this year and will no longer be an option."

"That's a relief," I breathe out, my heart rate leveling. But I've always questioned the chances of luck. "If that's why she was initiated, why hasn't Sabine used her?"

"Because I took her place."

And just like that, my heart crashes to the ground. I wrap my fingers around Ivy's wrists, stalling her from her busy-work and forcing her gaze back up. "I'm not mad at you. Okay? I'm fucking terrified for you. We have to stop this."

Her answering smile is wane. Empty. "I meet the bill for pretty innocence, too."

I fold her into a hard, *hard* hug. If I could absorb her, I would. If I could steal her away from this room, this world, I'd do it.

My chin digs into her hair, the wildflower wisps of it tickling my nose. Ivy wraps her arms around my waist, accepting the embrace, her chest heaving against mine. But no tears come.

I'm sure she learned her tears were wasted a long time ago.

A tug of warning prickles against my bare shoulders, and I lift my gaze. It doesn't take long to locate the source of my unease.

Sabine stands with Daniel at the front, toasting the room, everyone's masks off and faces on display. But as Daniel's warm tone embraces all the members, Sabine keeps her eyes on mine.

She doesn't blink. She doesn't smile.

All she does is stare as I hold Ivy close.

Ivy and I manage to escape the Societal Ball without too much notice, after pretending to join in on the festivities and fake-drinking as much as the rest of them.

When Cloaks started splitting off and coupling against the walls or passing out in corners, one look from me and Ivy was more than eager to follow me up the stairs and through the hidden door into the Wolf's Den.

Sabine didn't stop us, but that's not a win. She got what she wanted from me tonight, but I've learned it will never be enough.

Ivy and I split up at Thorne House, Ivy assuring me that we'll talk tomorrow after class. With the horrors of tonight under our belts, neither of us feel like more confessions for forgiveness by candlelight.

My dorm room is silent when I close the door behind me, Emma's light off and bedroom door shut. I don't wake her for the same reasons I let Ivy go.

We all need to rest.

After stripping off my ruined dress, I kick it into the corner, hating the sight of it. I'm also happy to shower off the stench of tonight, and I wonder if I'll ever acquire the same taste for champagne ever again.

The pink flannel pajamas Lynda sent me never looked so good, and I slip inside them, hugging the comfort close to my chest. It's with a *pang* of grief that I kiss the picture of my mom on my desk before switching off the lamp and tumbling into bed.

But do I sleep?

My tangled sheets and the pillow tossed across the room would tell you no. All I can think of is Chase. Every moment that passes has me wondering if he's tasted the salt of his tears for the first time in years.

I can't do this. I can't leave him.

I fumble my light back on and shove on my boots and winter coat. A hat and mittens soon follow. I throw my door open, and—

Run straight into Emma.

My resulting scream loosens all the remaining tension from my chest. Emma stumbles away in shock but regains her composure enough to clamp a hand across my mouth.

"Are you asking to bring Mr. Rent-A-Night-Cop to our door?"

I shake my head under her firm grip. She releases me, and I gulp in a breath.

"You scared me," I say tonelessly.

"Good. Stay scared. Because tonight is just the start of it."

I rub my eyes with my mittened hands. "I failed so bad, Emma."

"It wasn't just you." Emma places her hands on her plaid flannel hips. "It was goddamned Ivy and her inability to stay strong under pressure, and my cocky-ass brother who thinks he can take any punishment and survive, and fucking Eden for shrinking to the size of a mouse, instead of warning me, when Sabine burst through the library doors." Emma pauses. "And me. For being a pathetic waste of lard who couldn't bring her dreams of pummeling Sabine into a pulp to fruition as soon as she locked eyes with me. We're all fucking losers."

"I don't believe that." Emma's despondent speech sets my shoulders. "We underestimated her, but we haven't lost, yet."

"That's the problem. She keeps outsmarting me."

"I'm not giving up."

Emma sighs as she takes in my outdoor gear. "You're going to see him, aren't you?"

"I'm not leaving him to—"

"Relax. This is me supporting you. I don't want my brother hyperventilating alone any more than you do. And you're smaller than me, otherwise I'd go to him, too."

My brows crunch down. "What does my size have to do with it?"

"You can't go in the same way you left. Sabine'll kill you. Chase is in the old tombs, right?"

I nod, not bothering to ask her how she knew, since this is Emma, a former Stone and Virtuous princess. She knows things.

"It neighbors their old chapel," she continues. "A piece of the wall swings open just enough to fit you, if you shed your jacket. You can get in and out through there."

"A swinging wall?"

"Chase and his crew sneak in there often to smoke up. James likes to take girls there to terrify them into screwing him."

I work like mad to memorize her instructions to a place I've never been before, shuffling them in with other morbid pieces I've had the bad fortune of collecting today. "Emma, Ivy showed me the bedroom."

Emma's features go flat. "Go. You only have so much time before James sobers up enough to figure out that's a route you might take. He's fast becoming Sabine's preferred righthand man, but nobody will leave the ball for a while yet."

"Thank you," I say, though our conversation is far from over.

"Use the key you swam under the docks for; it still works on a Virtue passageway at the academy. You remember the chemistry room?"

"Yep." My lips pop on the *p*, as I not so happily linger on the memories as to why I'm so familiar with it.

"There's a false door at the back. Find the row of textbooks published in the late

1800s Briarcliff likes to display as a sign of respect to the founders. The third spine has a tiny lock in the center. Slip your key in, turn, go down the stairs, and you should end up at the Nobles' tomb. Push on the third skull from the ground, and that'll lead you to where Chase is held."

"How am I supposed to gain access to the academy? After the chem lab was vandalized, Marron locked up tight."

Emma gives a sly smile. "Your Virtue key works on the side door, too."

She shoos me away, and I leave the dorm as fast and soundless as I possibly can.

It's with the help of my phone's flashlight that I make it to the academy through all the snow, and I use my Virtue key to open the side door at the east wing.

Puffing and shivering from cold, I scurry into the warmth of the silent halls, fly to the chem lab, reach the back where the line of books is, and—

Halt at the many, *many* spines facing out on a shelf above chemistry supplies.

I rip my hat off and toss it on the floor with a curse of frustration, but then think, *fuck it*. What do I have to lose by using my phone's flashlight to find a tiny, tiny keyhole in one of them?

Shockingly, I find it in the first two minutes, right when I'm about to text Emma if she remembers which book.

Probably because Sabine planned for this moment.

I don't care. *I don't care I don't care I don't care.*

Chase is suffering, and he's alone. I am not going to discard him. I *won't*.

When I push the false door open, I grab my hat and run through, wasting no time and following the secret stairs nestled between the school walls until I hit the bottom.

It takes a few missteps and a lot of flashlight to navigate the pitch-black corridors. I don't give up, and on the fourth try, I make it into what most resembles a neglected chapel—if a chapel decided on a skull-lined hearth as its centerpiece.

"So fucked up," I mutter as I peel off my jacket, but count the skulls and settle on the fourth one on the right.

It works. A slim, vertical piece of the wall swings open, and I slip through until it flips shut behind me.

I come to a stop in the honeycomb room I was in hours before, even though it seems like painful decades.

I shed my mittens and sprint first to the pile of broken wood. I choose one, then rest it against the door on an angle. If someone is standing guard, hears me, and tries to come in, the panel will crash to the ground, creating a cloud of dust. I'll be alerted and escape the way I came, ideally before I'm discovered.

After setting the boobytrap, I race over to the lever I saw Daniel use. I twist and pull and use my entire bodyweight to bring the rusted spike down...

And watch as the chains begin to clink. As they start to pull up the middle cage.

As Chase is slowly revealed.

Twenty-Three

AT FIRST, all I see is an empty cage.

The spaces between the bars are clear. There's no sign of Chase.

Did he escape?

That'd be insane. And amazing.

The pulleys keep whirring, but I've stopped searching the cage and debate running out of here, instead. What if this was all a trap? What if Chase was in on this the whole time and never expected to be punished?

That would explain his guileless demeanor as he allowed his father to lock him in. His casual insults to his future stepmother, his *fuck you* attitude to the room, and his sweet, calming assurances that *it'll be all right, Callie.*

A groan snaps my attention back to center. I didn't register the cage coming to a stop or the fading clink of chains.

Something shifts near the bottom, a dark, hunched-over form.

"I'm here." I rush over, falling to my knees and clinging to the bars. "You're not alone. I'm right next to you."

Another muffled sound comes from his collapsed form, a mix between a moan and a sigh. He shifts, his hands, originally wrapped around the back of his neck as he folded down, falling listless by his head.

"Chase, it's me," I whisper. "Can you hear me?"

His head lulls to the side. Half his profile comes into view, blotched, yet blood-less. His eyelashes flutter, as if coming back to consciousness. "C...Callie?"

"Yes." I pull myself flush against the bars, wishing I were boneless and could squeeze through. "I'm right here."

"You ... you shouldn't have come."

"I couldn't leave you."

"T-trouble..."

I glance up at each corner of the room. There are no blinking lights, no eerie

520

black lens staring down. There may be a log of my mindless rush through the maze of corridors, but I doubt it. If the dust and decay is anything to go by, the original, hidden hallways and rooms of the academy haven't been updated in a long time.

I think of Sabine's secret bedroom. It's not just the Virtues who want to keep certain blueprints private.

I reach through the bars as much as I can, stroking his back, tracing the curve of his ear. "Breathe," I say. "Listen to my breaths. Follow them. In ... and out."

Chase's jaw spasms with the effort. "I c-can't open my eyes."

"You can. It's all open space here. Or keep your eyes closed and envision a field, or the peak of a mountain or—or a lake! You're on the water, just you and your scull. Breathe."

Chase's brows crash down. His chest seizes with forced, small inhales.

I rip in two at the sight of him, this unflappable force of will who'll gladly take punches to the jaw and withstand insidious insults by his father. This boy who will risk everything to avenge his sister and face his worst fear to protect ... someone who doesn't deserve it. Me.

I keep my voice calm, my inhales and exhales measured and leveled. Slowly, with great effort, he starts mimicking my breathing.

"Good," I say. "You're doing great."

"You need to ... leave. Before..."

"I'm not here to break you out." I swallow, staring at the thick, metal padlock keeping him in.

Chase follows my attention and gives a weak smile. "You'd sear that off with laser beam eyes if you could."

"Without a thought." I give him a resolute stare, but it crumbles the longer I take him in.

Chase trembles, pieces of hair stuck to his forehead with dried sweat. The snippets of voice I'm hearing from him sound raw and damaged.

"I put you in here." I can't keep the pain from my voice.

"No." Chase's throat moves with a hard swallow as he struggles to sit up. It reminds me, and I crawl over to my discarded jacket and pull out a water bottle.

His eyes spark with life, and he accepts the bottle and puts it to his lips, gulping greedily.

"Gently," I say, but scan his space between the bars. "Although, I'd piss all over this shit hole if I could, too."

Chase's lips curve over the bottle, then he lowers it, wiping his mouth with his tuxedo's sleeve. "This isn't your fault."

I cock my head. "That's sweet, coming from a boy trapped in a cage from the Medieval Times because of my botched plan."

"You think I would've avoided this if it weren't for you?"

I nod.

"Not true, sweet possum. Tempest told you about my claustrophobia because I asked him to."

I stare at him.

"There would come a time when Sabine or my father would force someone into a choice like this, pitting my sister and me against each other, and you against all of us."

"But..." I take in his sallow pallor, the red rimming his eyes, and the hoarseness surrounding his voice. "You *are* afraid of small spaces."

"Yes."

"Then why...?"

"Sabine asked if you knew our fears. Tell me, if you didn't know mine, would you have chosen me? Or would you have gone with Emma, who fears being trapped in a fire, or Eden, who is terrified of exposing herself to the entire school? What do you think Sabine would've made them do?"

"They're not members," I reason. "They wouldn't have—"

"Don't finish that sentence. They'd suffer. Sabine wouldn't tolerate any less."

"That woman," I seethe. "The second you're released, I'll throw my fucking Virtues' key in her *eyeball*."

"Callie." Shadows creep along the terrible hollows in his face, making him appear skeletal. "I will come out of this unscathed."

I catch my lower lip between my teeth. "You're suffering."

"Nothing I haven't been doing since the ripe old age of nine. Now go, sweet possum. Before my father comes and checks on his deplorable son."

My head whips to the door, and the *Home Alone* trap I've made. So far, it's undisturbed. "We have some time yet." Emotion blooms in my chest, then swells in my throat. "I don't want to go."

"I know."

"I can't put you back down there."

"You have to."

"I've weakened you in front of everyone."

Chase squints. "Don't think I won't make a splash when I get out of this fucking thing. I'm okay, sweet possum. *We* are okay." He motions to the bottle. "Thank you for the water. And..." His eyes soften. "Thank you for checking on me. I can't remember the last time someone's done that."

"I'll stay with you. Right here. Whatever happens."

Chase shifts, his hand coming between the iron bars and drifting across my cheek. "You would, wouldn't you? Stay here until someone comes, damn the consequences."

I hold onto his wrist and squeeze. Answer enough.

"That's not the way," he murmurs, brushing the pad of his thumb along my lower lip. "Go pull that switch, then step on the iron lever by the wall you came through and get back to your room. Tell no one you've come here."

"You know how I got in."

"I'm aware of a lot of things, even when I'm put into the black."

"I—"

"Now, Callie." He hands me the empty bottle.

Though every muscle protests the command, I rise to my feet and move to the lever. I glance once more over my shoulder. Chase has risen to a stand, his arms folded. Though he looks in complete control, smudges of dirt mark his tuxedo and his white shirt is missing buttons, like he tore at it in the dark. The whites of his knuckles poke through his skin as he clutches his biceps.

"Do it."

I catalogue every tear, every mark of pain left on his body from having to endure being buried alive. "I won't let this happen to you again."

Chase nods, but his eyes have glazed over with a faraway look, committing to his entrapment by initiating a mental disappearance.

I yank on the lever, a rusted squeal bursting from my hands. The chains begin their rattle, and I'm seized with panic. I can't stay still and watch this. There's no way I can be a bystander for the second time.

I sprint to the cage, grab Chase by his lapels, and pull his lips to mine.

I kiss him, and kiss him deeply, our mouths rubbing together with desperate passion, and I sink along with him, bending my knees, then bowing forward, never breaking that kiss as he's lowered to the ground.

Not until the distance forces us apart.

Twenty-Four

I SLINK FROM THE TOMB, through the chem lab and deserted academy halls, and step outside into the dark, frozen tundra of the Briarcliff landscape, my ribs feeling like icepicks poking against my skin.

Snowflakes catch in my lashes, descending from the ink-black depths of the sky on a silent drift of wind.

My walk to Thorne House is heavier than when I left, my feet filled with leaden angst as I leave Chase in depths without snowflakes, without wind, without … anything. He says it's the right thing to do, but I'm not sure it'll ever feel that way.

When I unlock my door, I'm surprised to find Emma staring into the creamy swirls of her mug. She looks up when I set my bag down beside her on the counter.

"You didn't have your phone," she says as greeting.

Shedding my outerwear, I say, "I had it. That looks good. Mind if I make myself a cup?"

"Why didn't you pick up? I thought something happened to you when you weren't answering."

"And I thought you were asleep."

"How could I sleep after sending you into the Nobles' tombs?"

I pause, lifting a mug from our little tree by the coffee machine. "There's no shortage of blame to go around, Emma. I shouldn't have asked you to be a part of tonight."

"You didn't ask. I demanded. I thought I could follow in Piper's footsteps." She wipes a hand down the unscarred portion of her face. "But I couldn't. I saw Sabine, and I couldn't."

I finish making my coffee, then sit beside her, my spoon clinking as I stir in cream. "If you were testing your willpower, that was a difficult way to do it. You went all-in. Maybe next time, see how you react if you spot her from a distance on campus."

"You made a joke." Emma huffs out a weary laugh. "Impressive, considering our circumstances."

"I'm not sure they'll get any better, so I try for gaps of time when I smile."

Emma slides a saddened gaze my way. "How was my brother?"

I start to lift the rim to my lips, then think better of it. "Surviving. Posturing. Pretending it's all good."

Emma breathes through tightened lips, but her shoulders slump. "He's continually protecting me, but when it comes to needing my help, I'm useless to him."

"I feel the same way. But he seems to think this is all for the greater good." I spin the mug, its hot ceramic searing the pads of my fingers until I lift them for relief, a maneuver I wish I could pull off in real life. "I can't imagine being forced to endure my greatest fear."

But I can, and I did. Drowning in the brackish water of Briarcliff Lake before Ivy saved me. It was the type of explosive, thundering feeling in my chest I never want to experience again.

And Chase has to endure hours and hours of it.

"I'm glad you saw him. I'm glad he was able to speak to you."

I nod. "It was almost too easy. Yes, I used the secret tunnels you suggested, but there was nothing. No one to get in my way."

Emma makes a sound in her throat before sipping her coffee. "I bet Sabine knew you'd go after him."

"And she let me." I lean on my elbows, the mug centered in my hands. "I wish I could get into that woman's head. She's hidden articles—"

I stop myself. The sickly sage color of the bedroom floats into my vision.

"What?" Emma asks, but her expression holds warning. *I'm not ready to talk about it.*

I say, quieter, "I found newspaper clippings and articles about my mother's death in a binder Sabine was hiding."

"She was researching your past."

"Well before I enrolled here. The dates are from more than a year ago."

"It makes a sick kind of sense. Your mom was having an affair with her ex-husband, right?"

"Yes, but remember when I confronted her tonight? Sabine explained the binder was for Virtuous prospects. Why would she ever consider me as a Virtue, after what my mother and her husband did? I was his illegitimate child for a hot minute there."

Emma shrugs. "With that theory, why has she let you in now?"

"Because she assured me I'm *not* Mr. Harrington's bastard daughter. And hell, she could be enlisting me as a Virtue now as a sick sort of revenge on my dead mom's ghost, by making her daughter a kind of Virtue not even the Nobles know about—"

Again, I stop, inwardly cursing.

Emma visibly stiffens beside me, her fingers flattening against her mug.

She asks, her breaths shallow, "Where did you say you found those articles?"

My hair falls on either side of my face, and I find more solace in the dregs of my coffee than I do by looking up. "I didn't."

"Tell me, Callie."

I sigh. Tuck my hair back. "I mentioned it before I left to see Chase. It was in a kind of ... bedroom."

Emma's brows lower. "Is it the kind of bedroom that can only be accessed through the back of a fireplace?"

I lift my gaze in answer.

"So, it's official. Ivy showed you the irony of becoming a Virtuous princess. Did she tell you all of it?"

"Most. The rest I could glean for myself."

Emma moves to stare vacantly across the room.

"You don't have to talk about it." I lift my hand to offer comfort, to rub her back or squeeze her shoulder, but instead of doing any of that, my arm comes back down. She's not the kind of person to seek comfort, only strength.

Her attention shifts, her eyes sharpening as they land on me. "Maybe it's time I did."

I'm wary of spooking her, so I say nothing.

"In ninth grade, Sabine awarded me the title of princess. I thought it was an honor. Took it as entitlement. For as long as I can remember, my family has drilled into my ears the importance of becoming royalty in the Nobles and Virtues. And it was about time, too. Chase had become prince two years prior."

I push my brows together. "In seventh grade?"

Emma shrugs. "The Nobles don't have the—responsibilities—that we do. To be prince means to be groomed for leadership and granted privileges unavailable even to other society members. Like the best dorm room, a rigged top of the class ranking, make-up exams when you don't feel like taking them at the time, first seat in Briarcliff's nationally renowned rowing team. All orchestrated by the headmaster. *All* so it looks terrific on an Ivy League application."

I drum my fingers against the laminate counter. "He doesn't act like any of his positions were bought and paid for."

Emma offers a jaded smile. "Because they weren't. Chase gave the best boys' room to Tempest. He's at the top of the class because he earned it and is both captain and stroke of crew because he has the racing stats to prove it."

I smile. That sounds exactly like the Chase I've come to care for. "And what about the Virtues? How is the princess awarded?"

Emma's chest concaves. Despite the thorns she rims around her body and the steel she wraps around her heart, she seems so fragile right now. So brittle and broken as she hunches over her cold coffee. "It used to be that way, too. When my grandmother guided the Virtues, we had all those privileges, but ... it's a man's world. We were never awarded the status of a Noble Prince. The princess was ranked second in the class, given stroke and captain of crew, but the girls' rowing team isn't as widely recognized as the boys'. And exams..." A mirthless laugh escapes her lips. "Most of the time, the princess did better than the prince. But who got the top marks?"

I nod. "My mom, she worked in a male-dominated industry and was made to feel like a bitch when she wanted to be seen as an equal, and a single mother when she needed to take time off when I was sick, like it was some kind of handicap to gaining respect. I'm pretty sure I was aware of gender norms when I was five."

Emma snorts in agreement. "Yeah, but what did your mom do to combat it?"

"She stayed the course, got together with the other two women at the precinct, demanded equal pay, and worked hard to change perceptions, even to the smallest degree."

"Yep. The hard way. And I'm sorry you're mom's dead, but she didn't make much headway, did she?"

I'm forced to agree.

"Sabine Harrington, or Sabine Moriarty, back then, when she took my grandmother's place, didn't want to work that hard for recognition. She wanted it now. She made deals behind the Nobles' backs—starting with Nobles who'd automatically graduate into top positions in the country. She married one. You'd think they'd stay loyal to their own society, and most did, but there were some willing to bend the rules, including Paul Harrington."

I force a deep breath, waiting for what will come next.

Emma whispers, "Sabine used the most ancient power a woman has over a man. Sex."

I wrap one hand around the back of my neck, massaging out the goosebumps. "She negotiated the bodies of the girls in the society to gain favors from these men?"

"Only some girls. The most innocent, the sweetest. The ones less likely to talk." Emma shakes her head, a hollow swing, side-to-side. "I wasn't like my brother. Not boisterous, or sociable, or aggressive. I preferred *Harry Potter* in bed to societal events, Comic-Cons over sports, Reddit forums to talking to friends in real life. That's why, when Sabine picked me, *me*, I was shocked and over-the-moon. Yes, I was a Stone, but for the most part, I went unnoticed as a Loughrey. I chose my mother's last name instead of becoming a Stone. I was a legacy in the Virtues, because I had to be, not because I earned it. And my dad, he was so proud I'd taken the Stone status. My mom, too. I'd never experienced so much warm attention, not to mention, the open respect it caused. And it's because of that I was willing to do anything to keep Sabine happy. Anything."

"Emma, I'm so sorry." Though it's never enough. The platitude, even genuine, will never bring back what was lost.

"It was Piper who figured out what was going on, first. Why I always disappeared the first Tuesday of the month and came back quieter, lesser. And she wouldn't stop asking questions." Emma rubs her eyes, but a smile creeps along the edges of her mouth. "God, she was so fucking annoying. But I thought, being Sabine's daughter, she was on her mom's side. I thought she *supported* what Sabine was doing. Turns out I was wrong."

I bite my lip in thought. "Was Sabine keeping her daughters blind because she wanted to protect them?"

"Maybe. But remember the qualifications were innocent, quiet, sweet. Piper was none of those. She couldn't fake innocence if she tried. Same with Addisyn."

Remembering the Piper I met, I murmur, "Good point."

"I'll never understand it, not in a million years, but one night, I decided to tell Piper the truth. Scream it at her until it tore her open. I didn't care if she told the entire school. Didn't give a fuck if she called me a slut. I wanted it out." Emma clutches her chest, as if she can feel a bullet wound. "I wanted the *poison* out."

I ask, with bated breath, "What did she say?"

"Piper did the last thing I expected. She offered to help me."

The dorm is silent, but Emma's words trickle into my head with the steady drips of a faucet, pooling into a watery puddle of answers, growing hotter the longer I study Emma's face.

Her wounds.

Her scars.

"Back then, we only knew of one way to get out of Sabine's control, and that was to make me no longer desirable for her needs."

I cover my mouth. "Oh Jesus, Emma..."

But Emma forges on. "We agreed to meet at the library—the old one. The Virtues original temple was underground, built almost as a mirror to the Nobles. We figured the best way to really piss off Sabine was to do this on her turf. Piper brought along a baseball bat."

"*She's* the one who attacked you?"

Emma raises her head. "With my permission. I didn't want to be me anymore. Didn't *want* to be desirable, or special, or Sabine's princess. The men, they were old, stinking, *vile*, and I couldn't take it. I needed it to stop. How else was I supposed to do it? Go to the school? Marron wouldn't believe me. My own *father* didn't. The one time I tried, he asked why I was back into reading fantasy again and that Sabine would never do such a thing to the future accessories to our country. That's what he called the Virtues. *Accessories* to the Nobles. Like we're the arm candy to the true leaders. And my brother ... Chase was too busy being Mr. Popular and proving to our father he deserved to be a prince on his own merits."

I scrape my hair back from my face. "Holy fuck. This is—I can't even."

Emma nods sagely. "I asked Piper to hit me as hard as she could. Multiple times. In the head, in the ribs ... if she killed me, I didn't care."

I reach for Emma, but she recoils, and I'm forced to sit there, arms hanging limp, as Emma's trauma unfolds in my head.

"She was scared at first, but it's like ... a switch went off in her once she really got going. I don't know what was going on in the Harrington home, and I still don't, but that night told me Piper had hidden rage in her, too." Emma takes a breath. I use that time to grab her mug and push it under the coffee machine. If she won't accept my comfort, then I'll give her another form of warmth.

"I blacked out and didn't come to until I was in the hospital, with Sabine leaning over me."

Tears pool in Emma's eyes, and I rush to set the fresh coffee down and rub between her shoulders. If she shrugs me off, so be it, but she doesn't.

"Guess what that bitch said? None of my injuries would cause too much scarring. And any that formed, she'd personally pay for a plastic surgeon to fix. I'd be back to beautiful in three months and could resume my princess duties after that time."

The coffee I'd gulped down rolls in my stomach. "I can't believe..."

"That's when I knew there was no escape. And that's when I decided to start the fire and burn the whole fucking place down."

I risk prodding, "You said you were trapped inside, against your will."

Emma looks down at her untouched coffee, but her hands wrap around the ceramic. "Sabine caught me before I lit the match, and the look on her face when she did... it was like she was some kind of demon. I saw her true self that night, just like I was showing her mine. She pulled out a lighter in her purse, sent the bookshelf next to her up in flames, then turned around and locked me in."

Black stars come across my vision. I need to lie down but can't. Won't. Not until Emma finishes.

"Piper followed me that night. She'd hidden behind a tree when her mother stormed out, saw the smoke, and ran to get Chase. I was cornered by fire and smoke. I couldn't see or move. They unlocked the door, dragged me upstairs, broke a window and escaped, and the next thing I know ... I'm scarred. Burned. The fire is labeled arson and connected to the same perp who attacked me a few weeks previously. It remained unsolved and then ... forgotten."

I stare unseeingly at the fridge, the conjured scenes of Emma's confession playing out in my head as if I were there. "This is terrible. Worse than I could ever have imagined."

"Which part?" Emma tries for a smile, the scarred ridge of her face moving with rediscovered mirth. "That Sabine is, at the very least, an attempted murderer and pimp, or that Piper was nice and saved my life?"

I answer honestly. "Both."

"Piper changed after that. She took the role of the princess, which Sabine accepted, since my situation was so costly to the Virtue reputation she'd garnered. While Piper was princess, there were no 'meetings' with men. I guess Sabine had a line—her own flesh and blood couldn't be trafficked. I could've spoken my truth. Piper would've backed me up, adding heavy credibility as the queen's daughter. But we both decided to stay quiet and bide our time, because we only had my word as evidence. Piper was working to find more. She went all the way back to the origins and Rose Briar, started collecting secret messages Rose had written to Theodore and even unearthed a Briar's birth certificate she wanted to talk to me about, but then she..." Emma changes tactics. "She'd be the expected bitch by day and the Virtuous princess by night. But in between, Piper was my savior. And she was working to save all of us before she died. Then she was pushed off Lover's Leap, and ... it's like a reset button was hit. Sabine could begin again."

This time, I really am going to be sick. "And she started with Ivy."

Emma spins to watch me as I fly into our bathroom and dry heave into the toilet. When nothing comes up and my stomach proves its dire emptiness, I rise, wiping my mouth with a hand-towel.

"Now you're aware of Sabine's motives and how she can so easily manipulate. Even the Noble King isn't aware of the influence Sabine wreaks inside this school and out. My only question is this." Emma comes up to the bathroom, folding her arms, but looking upon me with desolate wisdom. "What is she planning to do with you?"

Twenty-Five

I GREET the next morning with a massive headache and roll over to check the time with a wince.

The over-extension of my body, my mind, my *emotions* last night shouldn't come as a surprise, but I'd argue that I shouldn't feel like a 90-year-old woman creaking out of bed at the crack of dawn.

Then it hits me.

Chase.

He doesn't have a morning to greet. His time consists of preventing his black environment from seeping into his soul.

Picturing how the rest of this day is going to go, I don't think I'll be able to take my mind off his suffering in order to properly listen to Professor Dawson in biology.

"Morning," Emma says as I pull my door open. She lifts a mug.

I garble a sound close to *yes, please*, and yank the hot coffee from her hand.

"You gonna be okay today?" she asks.

"I'd rather ask you the same thing. Are you okay after what we talked about last night?"

Emma purses her lips. "I doubt you or I will be able to focus on our studies while my brother is buried in a basement."

I nod, and my shoulders *finally* relax. Out of everyone, Emma gets me the most. "Let's not go through this day alone."

"You mean..." Emma arches a brow. "We'll have each other's backs?"

"Maybe." I flap my hand. "Let's not get ahead of ourselves."

"Thank you."

The room goes quiet. I stare at her.

"For last night. For everything." Emma continues, "I thought I knew what to expect when I returned to Briarcliff, and I gotta say, you weren't it."

I give her a half-smile.

"But it's been easier with you—if you can call what we're going through easy. I don't have a lot of friends, and I'm not saying you're, like, my bestie or anything, but it felt good to tell you my story last night and not have you judge me. There hasn't been anyone like that in my life, not since Piper, and—"

"Emma." I lay a hand on her shoulder. "I like you, too."

Emma fights off a smile. "Yeah, yeah."

She pushes my hand away and absconds into her room.

I snort, buoyed by this small moment of normalcy, but Briarcliff doesn't award an average day without a price.

A knock sounds at our door.

"Hey," I greet Ivy, but she brushes past me, her cheeks flushed, and her hair tangled. "What's ... up?"

"I was hoping you wouldn't be at school yet." Ivy tears off her winter coat and tosses it on the couch. "Is Emma here?"

Emma pops her head out of her bedroom. She takes one look at Ivy and says, "What's wrong?"

Ivy turns to me instead. "Have you ever looked at past Briarcliff yearbooks?"

"That's random." I arch an eyebrow, but answer. "I was thinking of looking up Howard Mason at some point but haven't gotten the chance." I lean forward, resting my forearms on the counter. "Why?"

"Well, after you found those news articles Sabine saved about your mom, it got me thinking."

Emma comes out of her room and stands beside me. If I didn't know any better, I'd say she was taking a protective stance, her suspicions of Ivy coming to a head after last night. Emma says, "I figured the mystery stopped at Callie's mom having an affair with Sabine's husband."

"Me too, or so I thought," Ivy says. She thumps her backpack on the counter and unzips it. "But Sabine is rarely that surface-level. You assume she wants one thing, until she turns it around on you at the very last second and slits your throat, amirite?"

Emma makes a sound of agreement. "Couldn't have put it better myself."

"I went to the library as soon as it opened." Ivy pulls out a yearbook, the silver foil flashing 2002. "To look up Sabine's class."

Ivy cracks open the yearbook, both Emma and me hovering behind her shoulders. She flips it until she finds the graduating class. Her finger lands on one photo in particular. "Look."

I squint. Then, I hiss in a breath. "That's Lynda."

"Yep. And there's more." Ivy flips to another page, points to another teen.

Emma says, "And Mr. Harrington."

"Makes sense," I murmur, "Since Sabine would've been pregnant with Piper around this time."

Picturing Sabine as a teen mom is an entirely different image than the one I have of my own. Mom had me at nineteen, but she didn't have a rich boy to fall on or a billion-dollar furniture company to inherit by forcing his hand.

Except ... wasn't Sabine part of an oil family? *Moriarty Oil*, that's right. So, why would she—

The answer comes to me in a harsh wave. *She made deals behind the Nobles' backs,*

Emma had said. *Starting with Nobles who'd automatically graduate to top positions in the country. She married one.*

Sabine started her control of the Nobles early, using Piper as her first weapon.

I blink out of my fugue when Ivy finds another face, to which I say, "Daniel Stone."

Then, with the slow, careful push like the triangular pointer on a Ouija board, Ivy lands on one last photo.

I stumble back as if scalded. "That's—that's not possible."

"Holy shit," Emma says, her eyes as wide as the mugs we've forgotten to drink out of. "Callie, your mom went to Briarcliff?"

"No way." I shrink away, like the yearbook is about to rear up and bite me with traitorous fangs. "That's someone else named Meredith Ryan. It has to be."

"But her face," Ivy supplies, lifting the book so I can see. "She looks just like you."

The denial shrivels inside my throat the longer Mom smiles back at me. "She never told me ... she never ... how could she not have said anything about attending an elite private school?"

"Callie," Emma says. "Your mother kept a decades-long affair from you. She was murdered in a way that seems personal, and her killer has never been caught. And now she attended an exclusive school she never mentioned. Looks like your mom didn't tell you a lot of things."

"But why?" My voice cracks. "We lived in a one bedroom and shared instant ramen for *years*. We told each other everything. She was my best friend—my *only* friend for so, so long. I trusted her. I—I *loved* her. How could she have...?"

I trail off, the rest too difficult to comprehend.

"Callie." Ivy grabs my attention by gripping me by the shoulders. "That's not all."

"What?" I ask, pressing my hands to my cheeks. The ground tilts, Chase is below dirt level, and my mother, the only person I trusted in the *world*, is a certified liar. "What could be worse than that?"

Though it clearly pains her, Ivy turns back to the yearbook. "There are so many players in this class, I had to look at the underclassmen, too. Just to be sure I'm not missing anyone. And here. In the tenth grade. Do you recognize this guy?"

Ivy lifts the yearbook again, and I force the papery lump in my throat to dissolve. I look.

When I do, the lump comes back twice its size.

Emma leans over me and asks, "Who's that?"

I lick my lips, but they're so cracked and dry, I only cause a sting of pain. "That's my stepdad. Peter Spencer."

Twenty-Six

I FLEX my hand above my notebook, the pen bouncing across the page. The new history professor drones on, and up until now, I'd been furiously taking notes. Who knew such desperation would provide copious amounts of energy to focus, my ears tunneling to the professor's voice and my handwriting following suit?

It was easier to avoid Chase's empty chair that way.

The vicious noise between my ears quieted down, and the images of my mother's Briarcliff Academy yearbook photo became a backyard blur in my head.

That is, until the bell rang.

I jolt, glance around, blink. Then pack my things like everyone else.

A heavy hand hits my shoulder the instant I stand. Tempest leans forward, his breath hot. "Are you done fucking around in our lives? Chase asks me to do him a solid, and I do, only to find out hacking security systems are pointless when the head honcho is already aware of the hamburglars. You not only put my boy at risk, but me, too. I don't like being duped by pretty faces."

I stare straight ahead, but his breath wafts strands of my hair near my cheeks. My voice comes out steady through the intimidating shivers. "I'll be done when you people stop fucking around with *my* life."

Tempest backs off, and I regain my own oxygen. "That supposed to mean something, possum?" he asks.

Shoving the textbook in my bag, I say, "Not to you," and storm away from him.

Tempest doesn't follow, but I'm forced to pass James, then Riordan, both with flat, predatory stares.

"Chase should've laid you to waste the minute he got the chance," Riordan mutters.

"She must have a lollipop pussy," James replies, "for him to take a day off for her."

I slam my hand on the doorframe. "If you idiots had the decency to really learn about your stupid club, if you're so protective and proud of being members, then you should recognize the stink. It's not Chase's fault, but it's not mine, either." I hiss, "Figure out your *shit*," before exiting the room.

I storm down the hallway, furious and already wishing for hindsight. I should've told them what Sabine is doing to the Virtues. Should've told them what Ivy will go through—*again*—on the first Tuesday of the coming year.

Except, when I snuck into the Nobles' ritual room, there were those women in purple robes. I recall the look on James's face as he presented those women to the new initiates.

James won't care and is probably well aware of Sabine's embellishments to the Virtues, and while Tempest and Riordan were hooded and ambivalent when the women shed their cloaks, I doubt they'd give a shit, either.

It's up to us girls to put a stop to this. And it's up to me to figure out why my mother cloaked her past in the same secrets that are shrouding me now.

I spin the lock and open my locker, transferring my texts for the next class, but I pause when my phone lights up on my shelf.

Lynda.

Snatching it, I press the green button before I think too hard on it. "Lynda, I need you to—"

"Hey, girl!" Lynda trills on the other line. "I'm in labor!"

"I—huh?"

"Blair's coming a week early! Your dad's driving me to the hospital now."

"Shit," I breathe out, and Lynda laughs.

"Don't worry, sweetheart, this pain is easy-peasy considering the bulldozer I've been carting around in my belly for 38 weeks. I'll take a few hours of screeching cramps over one more week of this waddle I've got going on—*oh*. Oh, here comes another one!"

"I—should I come?" All thoughts of the past dissolve as I picture my future—my *sister*. "I can get on a train and be there by tonight—"

"Cal, we're fine!" my dad calls out. "Finish your exams. I don't want you missing out on this semester!"

My exams? "Oh *shit*, exams are next week."

I envision my father's deep, drawn-out sigh. Lynda says, "Exactly, hun—*ooooh. Faaaaaaaack*. Okay. I'm good. Come when exams are finished. Once Blair's out, she's out, but she's not going anywhere. And I'll be able to introduce you two in much better conditions than *aaaaaaaaaaaaaagh*!"

I grimace and hold the phone tighter against my ear, as if that could help. "Okay. As long as you're sure."

"I didn't get you into Briarcliff to coast by, Callie," Lynda says, panting. "You get those A's, then come meet a B. God*dammit*, she's a bitch!"

"I can't wait," I say, "though I figure I also got into Briarcliff because I'm my mom's legacy."

Lynda breathes heavily into the phone. "Um, what, hun?"

I respond with a grim smile. Her words are too carefully placed between her gasps.

She knows.

"Can you put Dad on the phone?"

"Sure. I need to recline and scream now. Bye, love."

"You got this, Lynda."

"All good, Cal?" my father asks when he comes on the line.

"I should ask you the same thing. You ready to be a baby-daddy?"

He gives a shy laugh. Pete came into my life when I was nine, and I doubt he's been around a kid, since. "I hear the whole afraid-to-hurt-the-baby is natural and will go away after the first fifty diaper changes in a day."

I can't help but smile at the true terror in his tone. "You'll do great. And you'll be there for Lynda the entire time. That's something my mom didn't have."

"Ah, Cal." Dad's voice goes thick. "If I could've been there for her, too, I would've."

"But you didn't know each other back then, so I get it."

"That's right, honey."

"Well, good luck, Dad. Facetime me once everything goes well."

"Will do. Love you."

"You, too," I say through a forced smile, ensuring the feigned brightness transmits through my voice.

Then I hang up and toss the phone into the locker with a *thunk* and slam my locker shut.

I clued Lynda into the unraveling of their lie, and I caught Dad in the same, sticky web.

Lynda may be screaming her face off at the moment, but once things calm down, let them figure out how much they fucked up in that one, simple conversation.

Twenty–Seven

THE SHEER INTENSITY of the stars in the black sky tells me that it must be close to midnight, but sleep was never an option.

I chew my lip, watching the night grow darker and darker, lights on the student paths flickering out one by one, and the night security's flashlights bouncing against the white snowdrifts less and less.

He has to be out by now.

Chase, not my sister, but yes, I do see the parallels in both scenarios. If I really wanted to think about it, I could postulate about a newborn being dragged from the black into a new life, and Chase being pulled from the pit because of old traditions, but I'm not interested in getting philosophical.

I just want him.

Unable to hurry-up-and-wait any longer, I shoot from my chair and don my winter gear, prepared to wait outside Rose House all night.

I grab the thickest scarf I own and wrap it around my face while clomping into the main room, until I come to an abrupt halt, and not by my own volition.

I look down at Emma's hand, firmly encased around my puffy jacket as she slams it against my chest.

"What the hell?" I ask.

"Where are you going?" Emma retorts.

"To—" *see Chase*, but from the look in her eyes, I've been caught doing something stupid. "I don't want him recovering alone," I finish lamely.

"He won't. He has his friends, probably even my dad. You won't be welcome there."

She's right, but it doesn't lessen the pain of hearing it.

At my expression, Emma moderates her tone. "You care about him. And I'm sure he wants to see you, too. But you guys can't do this anymore. Not until we understand why Sabine and Daniel want you two apart."

The ends of my scarf flop over my hands. "Because he's Piper's, and I can't compete with a secret society's soulmate, in life or in death."

"It's true no one can escape the society, but that reasoning is off," Emma muses. "My dad following Sabine's every whim is off. He's a horrible man, but he has excellent business sense. He'd never approve of what she's doing with the Virtues. He'd see it as devaluing currency. Diluting assets. And because of that, I don't think he has any idea what she's up to."

My hands drop to my sides. "Does that mean your dad has no idea what Sabine did to you?" *You never told him?* Is my next question, but I wisely keep it to myself.

"No. He and Chase have no clue. I've made certain."

"But, why?"

"Because, despite what Sabine's done to the Virtues, they'd try to keep the society. Restore it, make it beautiful again—whatever. I don't want that." Emma's eyes go hard. "I've worked my ass off to regain their trust and get back at Briarcliff to destroy, not repair. Those two noblemen would only get in my way."

I see her point but my heart sinks for Chase. He'd want to know. Perhaps if he did, his whole perspective would change and he'd see the truth of these societies. The deadly, irrevocable poison seeping into us.

I ask, "Does that mean you don't think he truly understands why Chase and I can't be together?"

"Not a damn clue," Emma intones. "Strip yourself out of this marshmallow you've encased yourself in. You have no time to pine over my brother. We have work to do."

"Like go back to the yearbook."

Emma's hand smacks down on the silver crest of the Briarcliff yearbook on our coffee table. "Yep. And since Sabine and your mom probably knew each other..."

I pull my lips in, stare hard at the seemingly innocent maroon and silver hardcover and toss my jacket. "Let's search the internet for anything we can find."

Emma smiles, slow and cat-like. "I'll make the coffee."

Two hours and a thorough delve into the dusty pages of a three-decades-old yearbook later, we have as much to go on as we did when we started. Mom isn't in any additional pictures—no clubs, sports, or written honors. It's like she was a ghost haunting these halls, taking her classes, then quietly blending into the stone—unremembered, intangible.

That sounds nothing like my mother. I flipped through the yearbook and did over a thousand internet searches to prove the theory wrong, but it's like she popped into existence when she became a crime scene photographer. Everything before is an empty data mystery.

It's hard to believe I missed such an important gap in her life while she was alive.

I've been staring at the 74 faces surrounding her, wondering if my dad is also in here somewhere.

Fuck. That's a barrel I do *not* want tumbling down the waterfall of emotions I have right now.

"You're sure your mom never mentioned Briarcliff?"

Emma sits with one hand squished against her cheek as she rests her elbow on the counter, half falling off her stool.

"Positive," I reply. "As far back as my memories go, at least. I can call Ahmar in the morning. He knew her best—as far as I can tell."

I slump in my seat. *As far as* is becoming the new preface whenever I talk about my mother. *As far as I knew, as far as I can tell, as far as I understand...*

It feels thick in my mouth. It weakens our relationship. But I must utter those words and prove to the world that I didn't know my mother as well as she knew me.

My fingers drift over her smiling face in her class photo. Her long, kinky, reddish brown hair. The pert nose I never inherited, and the large, close-set eyes that reflect my own.

I stroke her cheek.

And I pretend not to hurt at the idea that I'm the same age she's frozen in, her uncertain future encased in a grin.

"I'm sorry she died."

Emma's quiet words bring my eyes up.

"I don't think I ever said that. I'm sorry you're entrenched in Briarcliff as much as I am and that it's caused you the exact amount of pain needed to keep you here."

Her sincerity circles in my head, less like vultures and more like seagulls searching for an offering. "My sister's being born today."

Emma blinks. "What?"

"Yeah. My dad's at the hospital with Lynda right now. Last they texted, she's still in labor, but all signs point to Blair coming today."

Emma hums in thought. "So, she's not blood-related to you."

Emma's bluntness doesn't grind against me like it used to. "We may not share DNA, but this one beats the imaginary one, named Dragoon, I concocted as a kid."

Emma's lips even out in a smile—a symmetry of muscles Emma rarely deploys. Usually, she holds the scarred side of her face frozen, unmoving.

"My mom was seriously concerned when I started blaming Dragoon for all the dead cockroaches around the house."

A beat of silence passes, then Emma laughs. "You were one creepy kid. But that comes with sibling territory as well as imaginary. Chase *constantly* pinned shit on me that I didn't do."

I almost grin, but the mention of Chase sobers us both.

"Running isn't the way to solve this," I murmur, stroking my mom's picture. "And I think that's what my mom tried to do."

Emma sighs. "You might be right. And since she's not here to explain, we'll have to figure out the rest of her story ourselves."

I manage a small smile. "Thank you."

"For what?"

"For not judging. For having my mom's back when you never met her. For trusting me when I say she was a good person."

Emma's lips press shut, trapping whatever she almost said next. Instead, she says, "Maybe we should sleep."

I gaze out the bay windows, wondering if Chase is in his bed, thrashing, sweating, his mouth stretched wide with silent screams. "I don't think I can."

"You've barely slept since the formal." Emma slides off her stool, then all but wrestles me out of mine. "If we're meant to take down the biggest, most dangerous bully Briarcliff has to offer, I can't have your bleary, googly-eyes beside me when we do."

"Fair point," I say.

I do as she asks and head to my room, going through the motions, changing into my pajamas, and turning off my bedside lamp, revealing the grayish, dusky sky leaking through my windows.

I lay in my bed, convinced I won't be able to find solace in sleep.

Three hours later, my eyes are still wide open, staring into the creeping dawn.

Twenty-Eight

A LOCKER SLAMS shut beside me, and I jump. The girl responsible sneers at me with her tongue on her upper lip, then saunters away.

Rubbing the sleepless grit from my eyes, I mutter to her back, "You must be friends with Falyn," then resume collecting my notes and books for my next class.

I've coasted through the day in a hazy, here-but-floating state. Emma, my wise night owl, is right, and if I don't find time to sleep soon, I might timber over in the middle of a confrontation with Sabine.

My mind doesn't seem to care about my body's needs. It wants justice, it demands to *think*. About my mother, the Virtues, the Nobles, and Chase.

I haven't seen Chase all day. He didn't show up to the classes we share, and I can't ask his friends about him without raising suspicion. All there is to go on is Tempest's expression, and it's like he's been raised by a gargoyle, with his flat, one-note expressions and stone-heavy eyes.

Sighing, I heft my bag from the floor and head to English Lit.

"Hey there, sweet possum."

Tingles prickle along the back of my neck as I spin around. Every piece of me itches to jump into Chase's arms, but we're in the middle of a crowded hallway. I settle for a breathy, "Hey," but know my eyes shine with relief.

He tucks his hands in his pockets, his blazer flaring out behind his wrists. "I'm okay."

I take in all his parts, starting with his face—fatigued, pale, flawless—and his slightly stooped but otherwise strong and confident posture. After a quick check to see who's around us, I risk one step closer.

Chase's eyes run over me as I move. "As for you, I'm now wondering if you're worse for wear."

"I'm fine." The tremble in my voice indicates just how much I'm *not*.

A strand of hair falls into his eyes when he tilts his head. "I've been gone twenty-four hours, sweet possum, not deployed to Afghanistan. What have I missed? Don't lie," he adds, as I open my mouth to do just that.

"Now's not the time," I say instead.

"It's never the time." Chase clamps onto my elbow and drags me into a blind corner, hidden from view of the hallway. "Tell me, anyway."

I release a breath, staring past his shoulder as I force my heart to stop its pounding, traitorous beats.

Chase tips my chin, forcing my eyes to his. "Tell me, Callie."

Leaning into his fingers, I close my eyes. His warmth, his presence, he's *here*. And he's in one piece.

My brows come down over my deliberate blindness. Maybe it's the sadness inside me that makes my heart want to speak, because I blurt, "All I want is to wrap my arms around you."

Chase growls, low in his throat. "We can't."

"It's stupid, and I wish I—"

Strong arms envelop my body, and my eyes flutter open when my cheek hits his clothed chest. Chase's freshwater fragrance hits my nose, and I burrow into him, just like I said I wouldn't. His chin comes down on my head. He strokes my hair. Chase holds me so tight I can't breathe, and my own grip on his waist will leave bruises.

"I'm so glad you made it through." My voice breaks on the last word.

He kisses the top of my head. "I've been around worse." Chase traces a final trail down my cheek, then releases me.

Cold air replaces the heat of his body, and I shiver with sudden emptiness. Instead of buckling, I siphon Chase's burst of emotion until I mimic it.

Lifting my head, I tell him about the news articles Sabine's hoarding.

Throughout the exchange, Chase's lips turn down, harder, deeper. By the end, he's forced his mouth down so hard, he's revealed a small dimple I never knew he had.

"It could be related to your sniffing around the Virtues when they didn't want you to," Chase says.

"I initially thought that, too, but she has clippings and print-outs from well before I enrolled at Briarcliff." Then I tell him about his father, my stepdad, and Lynda all attending Briarcliff at the same time. "Chase—my mother was a student here, too."

I expect a widening of eyes, at least, but all I get from my big reveal is a slight tic of an eyebrow.

"Don't you think that's a little suspect?" I prod. "What if they're all part of the secret societies? What if my *mother* was a Virtue?"

"That's taking it a little far, don't you think?"

"Sabine's remodel of the Virtues is taking it too far. Putting you in a glorified coffin. Dumping me in the Briarcliff Lake in winter. Assuming our parents all knew each other? That's a drop in the fucking bucket." I take a closer look at him. "Why aren't you as surprised as your sister was?"

"Surprise looks different on me. And I'm wondering..." Chase trails off, deep in thought. "My father's study. He has files there relating to the societies related to our quarterly reporting. Financials, official documents, and records of membership dating back to the beginning."

My heart leaps. "Could I see them?"

Chase licks his lips. "My father's doing business in New York for the next few days. I believe Sabine's going with him." His eyes flash with freshly forged bronze. "I'll take a look tonight."

"I'm going with you."

"Hell no, sweet possum."

"Hell to the *yes*. This is my mother." My shoulders heave with my determined breaths. "And she's not here anymore. Anything that's found out about her, I want to be there. Read it *first*. I deserve that."

Chase shakes his head, releasing a heavy sigh. "It's not a good idea. We're being watched. And this conversation has to end."

"Then be mean to me," I blurt out.

Chase narrows his eyes.

"All day. All week. Do your worst. Enlist James and Rio, even Tempest. Be assholes, and get Falyn off my scent. I'll even cry."

Chase rumbles his disagreement, but I continue.

"I'll convince Ivy, Eden, your sister, that I'm devastated. Then I'll sneak out with you tonight."

"It's not a good idea."

"None of this is good or right."

Chase takes a longer assessment of me. "Are you sure? I won't be easy on you. Or humane. I'll have to make your day brutal, and sweet possum, after the past twenty-four hours, I'm fucking hellbent on letting loose right about now."

I set my shoulders. "I can handle it."

Chase grunts. "And if we get caught?"

I smile when I have him. "Sabine and Daniel aren't here. Who would dole out our immediate punishment? Falyn? Marron?"

"They'd wait."

"Then I'll gladly take the repercussions, because I would've read everything your father had on the secret societies."

Chase rubs a hand down his face, and a twinge of guilt follows the movement. He's gone through so much and has only recently been taken out of a hole of his nightmares. How much more can I ask of him?

But this is about my mother. Not him. Not us.

"Fine," he says, then glances to the side at a noise echoing from down the hall. "We need to get to class."

I give a resolute nod, but my voice isn't nearly as strong. "Thank you."

"Don't thank me yet." The forged bronze dies out the longer he looks at me. "You may not like what you find."

"So be it if it's the truth. Because so far, everything I have has been built on other people's lies."

Chase starts off mild.

I endure a few muttered vermin insults during class, but having heard it all before, I don't grow concerned over the increased participation he's gathering—first from his boys, then Falyn and her girls, then the rest of the class.

Professor Lacey turns to write something on the board. The slogan "slut muncher" is uttered nearby, but I steel my shoulders and feign detachment, writing down every single letter the professor scribbles on the board.

Then something wet hits my temple. I raise my chin but keep my expression blank, despite all the gasps. And I wipe it away, assuming it's a spitball.

The girl next to me screeches, scooting herself and her entire desk away. Hoots and laughter follow.

My stomach pitches, and a hot, scorching blush creeps into my cheeks before I even figure out what the cause is.

"Gross, possum!" a male student cries.

"Wipe your fucking face!"

My gaze skirts to Ivy. She flips around in her chair and stares at me, her face white. Oh God, I don't want to look.

...but I do.

A used tampon lays near my feet. I scrape my chair away, vomit surging in my throat, but all of this is too late. It's already hit my skin. *I have someone's period blood on my face!*

A strained whimper escapes my lips at the same time someone else says, "Period possum!" and starts applauding.

The rest of the class makes gagging and retching noises, but I can't bear to scan the room to see which voice belongs to who.

Professor Lacey spins around. "Class, what the heck's going on—oh. Oh, Christ. Miss Ryan, what...?"

She scrutinizes the mess in the aisle, and when I follow her gaze, I realize someone has dared to kick the tampon under my seat, leaving a bloody streak on the white marble.

"Dig into your vagina in the bathroom like a normal chick," James cries, then stands, plugging his nose while he stands. "Should we call her bloody possum twat or rat vagina now? I can't decide."

"*Mr. Windsor!*" Professor Lacey cries, her voice so high, it screeches. "Headmaster Marron's office, *now.*"

James grins. He slams his palms on his desk, then high-fives Riordan on the way out. "Worth it."

As his final encore, he winks at Chase then gives the thumbs up.

I swallow thickly.

Chase leans back in his seat, his gaze cold and inscrutable, but directed at me. With a face that blank, eyes that dead, Chase's stare can only mean one thing: *I warned you.*

You did, I silently respond. Tears betray my vision, but I wipe them away and turn in my seat, facing forward. "Professor, can I go to the—?"

"Yes. Absolutely. Go, go." Professor Lacey eyes the mess on the floor with appalled trepidation. "In fact, class is dismissed. A custodian must get in here immediately."

I scurry out of my seat as the class whistles and claps at the dismissal, but most choose to keep commenting on the mess.

Ivy tries to grab my hand as I pass, but I sprint out of class, find the nearest bathroom, and scrub my cheek until it's raw.

Twenty-Nine

A KNOCK SOUNDS at my bedroom door.

Ivy's hesitant voice calls through the wood, "Callie? You in there?"

I burrow deeper under my covers, the sheets scratching against my tender cheeks and wicking away the lingering tears.

I'm supposed to be devastated, but to be honest, it's not difficult to play sad this evening.

"Can I come in?" she asks.

I sniff and rise out of my hovel, brushing away pieces of hair stuck to my face. "Sure."

"Oh, Callie." Ivy rushes over, the mattress dipping when she sits, and she wraps her arm around me. "I wanted to comfort you sooner, but you ran away so fast."

I nod, sniffling into her shoulder. "It was easier to escape."

She rests her head against mine. "Want me to bring some chocolate and vodka so we can really commit?"

I chuckle, pulling away and wiping my eyes. "I just needed a few minutes to cry. I'll be okay."

"That was brutal. And *ugh*." Ivy makes a face. "Whose tampon was that? Did she just—" Ivy mimes pulling a string from between her legs "—and *plop*? Like what? How is *she* not ridiculed for that?"

Ivy is so appalled with herself for even mimicking the maneuver that she gags. I laugh, and that laughter travels to my belly. "Can you picture Falyn resorting to that level?"

Ivy topples over in a fit of laughter. "My goodness, imagine the horror of anyone who *saw* it happening."

I fall next to her, joining her in laidback repose. "Right when I thought the Witches of Briarcliff had given me all they had."

"No way, this was part warlock." Ivy props herself up on her elbow. "This isn't something Falyn or her cohorts would think up on their own. This, my friend, is dead rat territory."

I recall the mass of rat corpses slopping out of my locker mere days after coming to Briarcliff Academy. "What girl would willingly do that in public? And smack me in the face with it?"

"A girl who was blackmailed." Ivy grows serious. "Callie, Chase has picked his side. Only someone like him could make a girl be so grotesque. He either promised her a world of sex, or..." Ivy purses her lips, "used her worst nightmare against her, same as what happened to him."

I roll and stare at the ceiling, folding my hands over my stomach. I'm worried if I look at Ivy, the smallest tic of inner knowledge will show on my face.

It doesn't feel great to dupe my friend, but Chase's and my deal is working. Ivy believes he's turned.

"He's angry," Ivy continues. "After what happened to him, I was worried he'd take his anger out on you, and it looks like I'm right. I think you should be sick for the rest of the week. Catch up on some sleep. Stay away from him and wait for his rage hurricane to end."

"I would," I murmur, "but I'm failing my classes and finals are in a few days. I can't miss them."

Ivy grabs my hand and squeezes. "Then I will do everything I can to help you stay out of his way."

My mother, I think as a wave of guilt crashes inside me. *Think about getting answers. Not about hurting Ivy.*

I turn to her and envelop her in a side-hug. "Thank you. I love you ... you know that?"

"*Ack.*" Ivy laughs tightly. "You sure you don't want to row? You're squeezing me like you *want* me to be an oar."

"Maybe next year," I say as I release her.

Ivy frowns. "But we graduate this spring."

"Exactly."

Ivy smacks me on the arm as I roll and pull the covers over my head. "I'm glad to see you sassy, at least. Get some sleep. I'll come by tomorrow morning and walk with you to class. As the Virtuous princess, I can order Falyn to stand down. But Chase and the Nobles..."

"You have your own shit to worry about, too. I can handle stupid school pranks."

"That's just it," Ivy says, her pensive face growing smaller as my lids get heavier. "We've moved way beyond hazing."

"Mm?" I mumble sleepily.

"I'm worried about you, Callie. The Virtues and Nobles are out of control."

"Callie? Possum. *Possum.* Hey. Baby."

My shoulder's jostled a few more times, the last few shoves so hard, I'm positive I'm no longer running toward a cliff with ravens nipping at my back.

"Wha...?" I crack open an eye, but I shouldn't have bothered, since my room is as dark as my dreams.

"There you are." A vague outline of Chase's large body takes shape. "You were so KO'd, I was about to leave you to the Sandman."

I sit up, scrubbing my eyes, then scraping my hair back. "I'm ready. Just give me..."

"Callie." His hand falls on my shoulder, a leveler on most occasions, but it feels like an unwanted anchor tonight. "You should stay here. It's obvious you need the sleep."

I throw the covers off and my feet hit the floor. "I want answers more than a few more hours of rest. I'll get dressed, and we can go."

"If you say so."

Chase backs off, but his residual grumble makes it clear he's not happy about it.

I pad around my bedroom, finding my sweats and socks and pretending I don't see the cool, unbothered Chase reclined in class today instead of his current shadow waiting along the edges of my room.

His lack of features in the night makes that impossible, and my movements are stilted and clumsy, reflecting the emotions toiling away in my chest.

"You good?" he asks after my third curse when I bang my toe against my bedside table.

"Fine." I fumble for my hair-tie and call myself ready. "Let's go."

"You can change your mind."

"Nope."

I lead the way from my bedroom into the low-lit gloom of our kitchen appliances. Emma's light is off, and while she spent time eating with me at our counter tonight, I was so shell-shocked and desolate, she wisely left me alone with my feelings for the rest of the evening.

"Emma doesn't know?" I whisper over my shoulder, verifying that she's sleeping on the other side of her door.

Chase's voice, rough even when controlled, responds, "Not a clue. And I'd like to keep it that way."

These twins keep too much from each other, I think sadly. But right now, my mother is the priority.

Chase cuts past me at the apartment door while I'm putting on my coat and pushes the stair's door open to slide through. We silently descend the three flights, and when we burst into the frigid, winter air, I let myself squeal into the collar of my coat as I follow him to his car.

We take a hidden path through the forest to a back road, probably for vendors and staff to travel unnoticed around the edges of the academy. Chase's car lurks quietly on the plowed drive, shining iridescent black against the opaque darkness of the trees and sky.

He opens the passenger door, and I'm thrown into the memory of the last time I rode in his car, with the smell of caramel, fresh-baked bread, and *him* permeating the interior, stimulating both my stomach and pheromones.

Just the thought has saliva building in my mouth and clenches my core. I'm desperate to tighten myself around him again. Rules be damned—I want him to take me in his car, surrounded by forest, and out of sight from our enemies.

Chase gets in on the other side, his eyes dark but shining when they land on mine. Every line of his shadowed expression communicates his same need.

"Chase, I—"

He growls, then clamps his hand on the back of my neck and pulls me in for a hard kiss. Chase's tongue plunges, explores, and I part for him easily. A needy mewl sounds from my throat, and I guide his free hand between my legs, aching for him to fill me and for my walls to clench around something other than emptiness, but he rips away with a curse.

"I knew this was a bad idea." Chase swipes the back of his hand over his mouth, staring straight ahead.

"I told you, I have to be the one to discover anything about my mother. She's mine, Chase. She was everything to me."

"That's not what I'm referring to." His gaze slides over me but flicks away the minute heat builds between us. "If I'm to follow orders to keep my hands off you, we can't keep finding ourselves alone." His tone falls into velvet when he continues, "Because I will take every advantage. I'll have you naked before the end of the night. I won't be able to bring you home until I've tasted you again. Fuck, I miss your taste."

I lick my lips, but they're not the flavor he's looking for.

A tingling hollowness builds low in my belly. I squirm in my seat.

"Drive," I manage to garble out. "Before I climb on top of you and end this charade."

The engine rumbles to life, and my head falls back on a sigh when the vibrations hit my seat.

It's not enough, it will never be Chase, but it takes off the keening edge building at my middle.

We don't talk as he navigates the private road and onto the main passage of Briarcliff Academy, and I'm grateful, because that time of quiet allows me to regain rationale and logic. And memories of today.

"You're quiet," Chase muses as he turns out of the academy gates. "But I can hear you thinking."

I stare out my window. "It's nothing."

He turns left, the wheel gliding between his skilled fingers. "You come better than you lie."

My cheeks grow hot.

"Fine. I don't need your words to be confident in your hatred for me at the same time you want to jump my bones."

"Don't simplify it like that."

"Why not? It's exactly how you're feeling."

"I had a used *tampon* thrown at my face."

Chase arches a brow. "I told you I wouldn't be kind."

I rear away from my seat, so incensed, it's difficult to form a sentence. "What the hell is the matter with you? I expected name-calling. I practically guaranteed Falyn's bitchy involvement in some way. Hell, I wouldn't have been surprised if James joined in and my locker was fucked with again. But you convinced a girl to yank on a string between her legs in the middle of class and *toss* it, then you sat back and enjoyed the show. That's fucking gross, Chase. It's despicable. And you orchestrated it."

Chase's hands relax on the wheel, and I note the small smile playing against his profile. I'm about to punch it off his face.

"Did we not agree to convince the Nobles and Virtues that I've taken their side? Bowed to their rules after a night in a cage? I couldn't play by the normal bullying rules. It was the only way, and the reason you're in my car right now. Sabine's cronies won't be tailing us after that display—and even if they are, I went through a lot of bullshit and dollar bills to make it look like I've locked myself in my room with a random sophomore tonight."

The thought of Chase with someone else—even pretend—makes me sick. But I can't argue the point, so I fold my arms and counter, "Don't be surprised if I pee in your sports bottle before your next rowing practice."

"Now, Callie," Chase says as he pulls into the driveway of his lake house. "That's just gross."

Thirty

THE LAKE HOUSE is quiet and undisturbed, the small porch light offering mild illumination of the front steps, and I follow Chase through the front door.

We don't stop in the kitchen and talk over coffee like last time. I try not to reminisce on how close he was when we sat next to each other and how the heat of his skin acted like a magnet to the little hairs on my arms, drawing me closer, my lips softer, my body on fire.

Chase tosses his jacket on the couch and descends the stairs two at a time. I scamper to keep up with his long legs and sure footing. He turns on the study's light before I arrive at the bottom, and I swing into the office right as he's rounded the desk and started typing on the keyboard.

I come up beside him, admiring the toned bulges of his muscles through his shirt as he bends, but getting to the task at hand. "I thought you said your dad used hardcopies."

"He does, but he keeps a catalogued system on his computer. Rather than search through all his file cabinets, I'm going to locate the ones we need in his spreadsheet."

"And he's given you his password?"

"He gave Sabine his password. Piper watched her type it in one night, then she told me."

Piper's name causes a squeamishness in my gut, more because of my inability to see just how good she was at working the room while being a completely different person behind the scenes.

"I underestimated her," I say, folding my arms.

"If you're wishing you had the time to get to know the real Piper Harrington," Chase says, while a spreadsheet pops onto the screen, "I tend to agree with you."

My lips pull into a sad smile. "I'm hoping I can properly avenge her instead by picking up where she was forced to stop."

Chase turns to me. "I love you for it."

I shift on my feet, unsure of his proclamation and where it should land. Chase has never said anything *near* that level before.

And, because I'm a coward, I pretend I didn't hear it and ramble, "What's your opinion on Addisyn being the killer? Now that I'm an initiate, I'm seeing all these holes…"

"Nah. Piper may have been a double agent, but she wasn't killed by her mother. Addisyn did it. To be sure, I visited Addy in holding. Ah. Here we go."

Chase taps the screen and straightens.

"Wait, you visited Addisyn?"

He nods, his posture loose, like he just told me he had a burger for lunch. "I had the same misgivings you did and needed to hear it from Addisyn's lips. Why she killed Piper. *Why* she worked so hard to eliminate her sister."

I raise my brows. "And?"

"It was jealousy, through and through. Over Piper being a Virtue before her, then becoming the princess. Then, Piper sleeping with Addisyn's boyfriend and getting pregnant. Those two … Addy and Piper … they didn't have the best upbringing."

I think back to Sabine's graduation photo, and the realization of what Piper was to her. Addisyn might've been the same thing. A weapon. A leg-up. A *power* play. It must have affected those girls. So much so that it ended it murder. Both their lives, over.

I say, "It's just so hard to believe, especially after hearing about what Sabine is doing to the Virtue name and to her princesses…

I stare at Chase, watching for his reaction. It's hard to believe that he'd be aware of the trafficking and not become an apocalyptic incendiary device. Emma's keeping the worst from him to protect her cause. Can I take away her right to confess when she's ready?

In this office, surrounded by the Stones' trinkets and deadly creatures, I dare to add, "Chase, do you know the full story of Emma's—?"

He spins to the wall of books behind us. "The files we need are in the panic room."

I allow the change in topic, since I haven't even collected more information on Mom yet. "Oh, so it's not just for robberies, huh?"

Chase sends me an unamused look before typing in the code. "That was before you stuck your nose in this shit and got yourself initiated into a dangerous secret society."

I stand back as the wall pushes out, then slides apart to reveal an industrial gray door.

Chase motions to follow him through the door. "In here."

Despite my resolve, guilt remains heavy in my gut. I can't *know* these things about Emma and not lay down clues for him. "Addisyn was made a Virtue after killing Piper. Don't you find that suspect? Wouldn't you think Sabine was complicit in the murder by protecting Addisyn?"

"Both are her daughters, and both had deep-seated issues with their family. I believe Sabine was shielding the one legacy she had left, regardless of whether she saw Addisyn as her second favorite. Her favorite was gone. And as a mom…" Chase shrugs but continues striding to the back of the panic room where a set of file cabinets are built into the wall. "I'll never say what she did is forgivable. I miss my friend a whole fucking lot. But when it comes to family, to my sister, I would do anything to protect her."

"That's different. You did that out of love. I don't think Sabine's capable of that. Every action she makes comes with a plan."

Chase pauses near the gray cabinets. "You're right. But I thought we were here about your mother, not Addisyn or Sabine."

"Pretty sure it's all relative," I mutter as I sidle up to him, but he's so focused on locating the correct cabinet, he doesn't hear me.

"Got it." He pulls one open on a squeal of metal wheels. "These are the members from the 1980s and before. After that, we were put into a computerized system, but after Y2K, my father preferred to keep the originals, too."

"Thank God for that," I say, and lift my hands to dive in. I'd heard about that strange year in 2000 when everyone was terrified computers would either crash forever or take over the world.

Chase blocks me with half his body as he sifts through the files with sure fingers. "Your mom was in the same class as my dad. If she was a Virtue, it'll be in here."

My heart leaps, but it leaves a nauseous wake. "And my stepdad. Peter Spencer. And stepmom, Lynda Meyer."

Chase nods, pieces of hair falling into his eyes as he focuses on the files. "I'll find them."

I swivel to the opposite side of the open drawer. He tracks me with his eyes. "Let me do this. I'm familiar with my dad's system."

"Sure. But I want a front row seat."

Chase stares at me, setting his jaw as if preparing for an argument, but must second-guess himself, because he returns to his search.

After a few seconds of rifling paper and the low hum of air vents, Chase speaks. "I found her."

"Oh my God," bursts out of me, and I reach for the file before he's pulled it all the way out. "Let me see."

"Hang on." He lifts it out of my reach.

"*Chase*," I warn. My muscles are primed to leap. "I will tear that thing out of your hands with my teeth. Give it."

Chase levels me with a look. "Despite you being here, the Nobles require plenty of confidentiality. I need to make sure there's nothing in here you're not meant to see."

"Like what? My mother would've been a Virtue, not a Noble, and that negates any confidentiality you may have, because I'm a—"

"You're not a Virtue yet. And at the rate you're going..." Chase gives me a droll look.

"I don't give a shit, so long as I understand why my mother *died*."

Chase freezes with the file dangling high above my head. "What did you just say?"

I clamp my mouth shut, but my chest heaves. "I didn't mean to say that. You have to understand. With Piper's death, and all these secrets surrounding my mom and Briarcliff, can you blame me for thinking her death might be related? Her killer's never been found."

"The societies don't murder."

I scoff, shaking my head. "Even now, after all they've done to you, you're still loyal to the Nobles."

"I've told you before, sweet possum. I will lead them. In a different way than my father, sure, but I'll never leave them." His voice goes quiet. "I don't bow to them. They submit to *me*."

"I ... just give me the file, Chase. Let me see what the Nobles have on my mother."

Chase lowers the file, but with the open cabinet still between us, he's able to fan it open and read it before I can get to him.

"She was a Virtue," he says, right as I'm about to snatch the papers away. "Says it right here."

He points to a list of the graduating class of 2002. After their full names, the students are ranked by status.

And there, right in the middle, is my mother in typed font. **Meredith Ryan.** "She was a marquess?"

"Meaning she was initiated into the Virtues, but not as a legacy. Instead, she was a promising achiever."

I run my finger along my mother's name. She was never one to talk of academics or brain power. I remembered her with an insane work ethic and an encouraging smile whenever she caught me struggling over homework. She always assisted me with the harder problems and the heftier math equations, but I never, for one moment, assumed she was a genius achiever great enough to be noticed by a coveted secret society.

I suppose all kids just think of their parents as starting their lives once their kids are born. Anything previous to that is an unnecessary blur, because they now exist to care about and protect you, their own goals and dreams dull in comparison.

But this goes beyond thinking your mother is just your mother. She lived a completely different life than what she set up in my brain.

I close my eyes, lingering in the dark for a moment. After a breath, I open them. "And my stepdad? He was two years below her."

Chase flips the 2002 file shut, but I grab it from him and press it close to my chest. "I just want to hold onto it for a minute. Before you put it away."

Chase's lips twitch in what might be understanding. He nods. "2004 should be..."

"Wait." I put a hand to his wrist to stop him before he keeps shuffling the files. "What's that?"

He surveys the cabinet. "What? I don't see anything."

"That. Right there." I push his hand away and pull out what caught my eye. "Is this a birth certificate? And ... holy shit, it's old. Emma said Piper wanted to talk to her about a Briar birth certificate..."

The single piece of paper is laminated. I'm not worried I'll crumble it with the oils of my fingers, but it's yellowed with age, and covered in ash.

"It probably has to do with the origins of the societies." Chase moves to pluck it from my fingers. "Which we already know."

"No, it's..." I squint at the same time I spin to keep it away from Chase's sticky fingers. "Rose Briar is listed as the *mother*. Oh my God—I remember. The librarian in town said there was some kind of illegitimate child born between Rose and Theodore Briar."

"Callie, this has nothing to do with your mom."

"Yeah, but it's near her file and ... I thought this child was adopted out and made to not exist. Thorne Briar exiled it, right? I shouldn't say 'it.'" I correct myself. "Says here it's a girl. A Daphne Wilmington. Maybe that's Rose's maiden name, since a father isn't listed ... wait. Why does your dad have this? Isn't this Virtue property, since it's related to Rose Briar?"

"Callie, we need to go."

"Does Sabine have any idea this exists? I mean, yeah, she has the password to the location of these files, but was this listed as an item on your dad's spreadsheet?"

Chase sighs. "Not that I saw."

"Let me just get a picture of this."

"Do you really think that's necessary?"

I nail him with a look. "If you know what I know about the Virtues, *everything* is necessary."

That stops him. "Fine. But be quick about it."

I pull out my phone and take a photo. I also take a snapshot of my mom's listing. Chase doesn't find anything with regard to my stepdad, but he does find Lynda's name, and I take a snapshot of that, too.

"Let's go," he says, stuffing the file back in. "I had the motion detectors turned off in the room, but Tempest can only keep them black for so long."

"Way to tell me that now."

"You'd've been skittish and set them off with all your twitching had I told you earlier."

Frowning, I turn with him to the door, but the faded edges of the birth certificate linger in my mind.

Where did the baby girl go after leaving Briarcliff?

And ... why is it considered so important that Daniel Stone has it safely stored *away* from Sabine?

Thirty-One

CHASE DROPS me off in the woods near campus. He offers to walk me through the forested pathway to the back of Thorne House, but I decline, my head too filled with my mother's cloaked past and my body too attuned to him to withstand more of his presence with no pay-off.

Yet, his headlights carve my way back to the dorms and don't wink out until I'm safely in Thorne House's backyard.

Once I'm sure no security guards are idling outside, I sneak in through the side-door I propped open with a rock, then creep up the stairs into my dorm room.

It's close to 4 AM, a time when Emma begins to stir. I tip-toe into my bedroom and shut my door with a soft click.

Then turn on my laptop.

Sleep is not a priority. I pull out my phone and flip to the photo proving my mother's involvement in the Virtues.

It doesn't stop there. Lynda is a Virtue. And my stepdad may not be a Noble, but he went to school here, too. Two years below them.

Why didn't my mom tell me she met my stepdad in high school? And why did Lynda and Dad send me here without cluing me in that Dad was an alumnus, too? Is my dad's second marriage to another Briarcliff alum a coincidence, or a secret society set-up?

I'm staring at a blank search screen, but so many questions flit through my head. I don't know where to begin, other than to call the responsible parties, but it's too early for that.

I straighten from my computer. *Or is it?*

Swiping through my contacts, I find the number I'm looking for and call.

"Calla? Everything okay?"

Unanswered questions may be swirling through my mind with suspicions cast over my every move, and suspects are more involved in my life than friends, but Ahmar? He will always be my heartening escape.

"Everything's fine—well, sort of. I can't sleep."

"What's wrong?"

Ahmar's voice sounds tight. Clipped. "Are you busy right now? At a crime scene? I can call back."

"No, no, you're good, kid. I just got home after a rough one, is all. But I have the morning off, so I'll sleep in a bit. Which means I have the time to hear you out on why you're calling me before dawn."

I cut to the thick of it. "It's about Mom."

Ahmar goes quiet. "Shoulda figured. How can I help?"

"I've just found out she was a student here at Briarcliff." I decide to leave out the Virtue part, since Ahmar has no idea about the societies. I'm starting to wonder how much longer I should keep it from him. "And so were Dad and Lynda."

"Really."

I shuffle into a cross-legged position on my bed. "That wasn't the exclamation of surprise I was expecting."

"No, kid, it's not." Ahmar sighs.

My thigh muscles clench. "You *knew*?"

"About your mom? Yeah, honey. Don't freak out on me. I plan on explaining that. As for your dad and Lynda, I knew about them, too, but it's high school, honey, that they went to decades ago. Nothing at Meredith's crime scene pointed to Briarcliff Academy."

I rub my forehead, the friction causing a small, needed amount of pain. "Why didn't you tell me? Why didn't Mom open up to me? What the hell is going on behind the scenes of my *life*?"

"Calla, honey, calm down. I'll tell you what I know. And I'm sorry, I'm so sorry, you're hearing this from me and not from your momma."

"I feel like she's a stranger." My throat constricts. "Like I never knew her. Like she's this girl who became this woman who had a child, then decided to erase her past life. Is the person I grew up with the woman she always was? Or was it all an act for my benefit? Who *is* she, Ahmar?"

"She was happy with you. Don't you ever think she lost herself when she had you. There were times when I was over, and you were playing at our feet, that I'd catch your mom—in the middle of one of our serious conversations—staring at you, and she'd smile with this special curve to her lips. It lit up her whole face, that grin. The *pride* she took in you, baby girl, was unlike any kind of love I'd seen before.

"Looking back, it's the reason why I let her get away with her secrets, because she worked so hard to be good at the mother thing and the single parent rap she got served with. Part of me also knew there'd come a day when you'd find out, especially once I heard you were being sent to Briarcliff Academy."

"Did you ask Dad about why he chose Briarcliff?"

"It never occurred to me to ask them about it. Briarcliff is a top tier school, and parents across the city try their damnedest to get their kids enrolled. As alumni, they had an easy in. I figured it was his effort to give you something more, especially after the friction between you two and how much you were suffering in the city. It seemed like a good idea."

"But you're a detective. You don't believe in coincidences." My hand squeezes the phone against my ear. "What about my mom? What did she tell you about this school?"

"She mentioned it one night, I think. You were, I dunno, two? She'd just put you to bed, and we'd had a rough day on a scene. It was a teenaged girl ... she was brutally murdered, and the entire time your mom took photos, there was this glazed look in her eye. Like she'd checked out. So, when we got home and she relieved the babysitter, I poured us a stiff drink and asked her, point blank, what the fuck was going on with her that day. We'd had bad scenes before, with younger victims.

"She told me it had to do with her past, and while she wanted to get it off her chest, she swore me to secrecy. I swear, kid, it's like she knew her future, 'cause she stared at your bedroom door the entire time."

I fold my hand over my eyes, bowing forward. "She wouldn't have wanted me to attend Briarcliff Academy. But you encouraged me to go."

"No." Ahmar's hard exhale causes static against my ear. "But Pete had a different experience at Briarcliff. He loved it. That kind of diploma is prestigious, an honor, all that bullshit. And frankly, I thought your mom was taking it a bit too far, closeting her high school like this. It's a building, for chrissake. Not a haunted house."

If only you knew...

"On that same night, your mom told me she had some bad blood with kids she went to school with. She was involved in some kind of extracurricular, she called it, that didn't go well for her. Somehow, she got on the wrong side of some popular chick. Meredith was ostracized, bullied, her senior year made into a living hell. Your basic high school bullshit."

"It's not basic at all."

"Ah, kid, I didn't mean to simplify it like that, especially while you're going through something similar—but that's what I mean. It's like a rite of passage at that snob school, am I right? Girls who don't come from much are the first to be kicked down. And shoved, and belittled, until they start fighting back.

"That's what your momma did. She told me she had grown fed up and enlisted the help of some guy. It only pissed this popular chick off more. Your mom's grades dropped, she barely graduated, and the way she told it, this girl made her suffer long after she left Briarcliff, until she was forced to become incognito and live—in her words—an unaccomplished, boring life where she no longer made any waves. When that happened, this chick got bored and moved on. In my mind, at least. Mer made it clear to me that this chick didn't know you existed and wanted to keep it that way."

"Why didn't she want anyone in her high school to know about me?"

"Unfortunately, the answer to that lived in your mom. She made me promise, if anyone from her past ever reached out to me, never to mention your name. But you see, no one did, Calla. And everyone she was involved with graduated. You went to Briarcliff on a clean slate. Your mom and you, you guys had a great life, but that night, she acted this school had fingers that could grab you in your sleep. It was ... unsettling."

"Paranoia," I finish. "Just like when I went after Dad for her murder and was dead wrong. So, you decided it was easier to go with Dad and Lynda's perspective of Briarcliff, huh?"

"Baby girl, I ain't saying what you think I am. You are all the best parts of your momma, don't you ever forget that. And I loved her. She was my sister, my best friend. And you're like a daughter to me. I promised to protect you, but I couldn't keep you away from a school that showed no evidence of being a danger to you. Meredith's experience there was decades ago. *Decades*, Calla."

I cast my eyes to the ceiling, the popcorn pattern becoming a watery blur. "Tell me you looked into Briarcliff before sending me, anyway."

"What do you take me for? Of course I did. That request she made, that I never tell any of her past classmates about you? Strange as fuck, considering she married Pete, who while not her classmate, was a graduate of Briarcliff. I was on this school like spunk—I mean, like glue—the minute your momma was murdered. I made the calls, even visited the campus. I conducted interviews with her former classmates, though she wasn't friends with many. At that time, Lynda Meyer came up in the investigation but was ultimately dismissed as a suspect. She hadn't reunited with Pete at that banquet yet, and she and Meredith didn't run in the same circles at school. And, when she and Pete *did* start dating, I looked into her again, since she was gonna be around you, but she has no criminal background. Lynda was a straight A student and didn't participate in any drama at Briarcliff. She barely knew your momma. The rest of the people I interviewed from your mom's class couldn't say much about Meredith. She wasn't outspoken or extroverted. Nice and polite but didn't seek attention. I will say, though, she was Winter Court Queen in her junior year."

"Why didn't you tell me any of this?"

"Because I wanted you to be a kid, kid. You went to Briarcliff to start a new life and heal. If I told you your momma walked the same halls, went through some shit, and graduated by the skin of her teeth, what would you have done?"

"That should've been my choice to make. I should've been able to make the decision to go here based on my mom's experience."

"I did what was best for you, Calla. You were in a rough place. I wasn't about to add to your pain. I ain't standing down from that."

My phone grows hot in my hands. I don't want to argue with him. "What about Sabine Harrington? She would've been called Sabine Moriarty back then."

"Funny you should mention her. She was the chick who went after your mom in school."

"And the mother of my dead roommate." I go quiet, allowing the dominos to settle in place in Ahmar's mind. Although, knowing him, they probably already had.

"Remember, kid, Rhode Island isn't my jurisdiction. Your roommate's death wasn't something I could investigate officially. I did compare it to my notes on your mom, back in the beginning stages when I'd interviewed Sabine—who, while a bitch in high school and a real doozy now, had no contact with your mother since and has an airtight alibi on the night Meredith was killed."

I rub my eyes with my free hand. "Did my real father go here, too?"

Dead silence. Then: "I wish I could tell you the answer to that."

"She was nineteen when she had me. Eighteen when she got pregnant. Ahmar, my dad..."

Ahmar's response is gentle, yet firm. "None of my interviews raised red flags. Your momma was a loner, honey. There were no guys she was noticeably close with that I could find. She never told me who your father was."

"What about the Winter Court King?"

"Some senior. I'll look him up, but that shit is based on votes, and she wasn't in a relationship with the dude."

"I should've been told this. All of it, while you were investigating."

"Kiddo, because you're like a daughter to me, I treated you like one and protected you from unnecessary stress." Ahmar no longer sounds like he's satisfied with his answer, and the aching hole in my heart is glad for it. Then he ruins it all by saying, "I hear your relationship with Pete is better now since enrolling at Briarcliff. Am I wrong?"

I don't enjoy proving Ahmar right, so I follow up with, "It could've improved faster if I were kept in school in the city."

"Calla."

My shoulders fall. "Fine. Dad and I are back on track. But there's more to this story ... more than what anyone involved is telling you."

"Kid, me and my team squeezed that school dry. I hate to tell you, it's a dead end."

I take a deep breath. "What I've found out won't be on any records. It's not spoken about publicly. And anyone involved will deny it well after their death."

"I think you need to get some sleep. You're making me a little worried, kid."

My stomach flips, my throat so thick with fear, but I forge on. "That extracurricular my mom was talking about? It's more of a cult. And I think she tried to back out of it, which is why Sabine took her as such a threat."

"Let's not get ahead of ourselves. We're talking high school shenanigans. After time passed, your momma lived a good life—"

"Until someone took it away. Someone took her from *me.* I'm going to send you some documents, Ahmar. And before I'm labeled as a psychiatric threat again, I want you to not just read them, but research them. This is so much more than a school club. It's a rigged college acceptance scheme, interference with the economy and political agendas, and a sex ring. *That's* what my mom was running from, and what Sabine is in charge of now."

My breath *whooshes* out. My heart slams, pounds, ricochets off my chest and races all the way down to my fingers and toes. But I said it. I put it out there.

And I pray I haven't just handed Ahmar a bomb that could put him in serious trouble.

At first, I think the line's gone dead. I hear nothing from Ahmar's side.

Then: "Those are some heavy accusations, kid."

"Please believe me. Or, if you don't, look into it and prove me wrong. *Please,* Ahmar. I'm in over my head. I need help."

I squeeze my eyes shut, remembering the last time I begged for his help, and he cuffed my dad and arrested the wrong man. Ruining my dad's reputation, and destroying his trust in me.

"This is different," I add. "I have proof. Evidence."

He doesn't answer. Too much silence has passed since I last spoke. "Ahmar?"

Ahmar breathes audibly. Soon, careful words follow. "Kid, I didn't need to promise your momma I'd be there for you forever. I'd do it anyway. Yes, I will look into it. Send me what you have, but I can't promise you there will be a change."

This time, when I close my eyes, it's with a sigh of relief. "I appreciate it."

"Do something for me. Get some sleep before school."

"I will," I lie. But my next words hold nothing but the truth. "I love you."

"Love you, too, kiddo. Too much, sometimes. Talk soon."

When we hang up, the first thing I do is send him the Virtue Member List containing Mom and Lynda's names, proving Lynda could know more than she said. Then Dad's class photo. And, as a mysterious cherry on top that I'd love to know the flavor of, the birth certificate of Rose Briar's illegitimate baby girl. Maybe Ahmar could trace the lineage. His knowledge of Rose Briar's family could perhaps lead him to physical proof of the existence of the Nobles and Virtues.

Balling my hands into fists, I curse losing my copies of Piper's diary. I mourn the brief existence of Howard Mason's writings hidden in my calc textbook before it was stolen and given back to the societies.

I'm relying on my gut to lead me in the right direction, at the same time it churns with uncertainty.

And for the second time, I've used that instinct to involve Ahmar.

Thirty-Two

I BOUNCE on the balls of my feet, waiting for Ivy to notice me. When she finally turns into the hallway, she yelps and trips to a stop seconds before bumping into me.

"Lord, Callie! Save the creeping around in the shadows for our nighttime adventures, would you?"

I offer up lamely, "I wanted to catch you before our next class."

Ivy shifts the pile of books in her arms. "For what?"

"I'm wondering when I get the rulebook."

Ivy clutches her texts to her chest, then elbows me into the empty classroom. "Are you out of your mind? Don't ask for things like that in public!"

Expecting that answer, I interlace my fingers, and ask, with innocent charm, "I take that as a *not any time soon*?"

"Your third trial's complete. Sabine will schedule a date for the ceremony where you'll pledge your loyalty, accept your robe, and become an official Virtue."

"I assume Sabine's scheduling is at her leisure."

Ivy responds with a pained look. "Sorry."

"There's no time to wait for her. I might have a lead on something. Can I borrow yours?"

Ivy squints at me. "This was a setup, wasn't it?"

I give an offhand shrug. "Do you have it handy?"

"It's in my room, in the locked drawer of my bedside table. Here." Ivy digs in her blazer pocket and pulls out a silver key. "Go and satisfy your curiosity, but don't tell anyone I gave you access."

"Never. We're on the same side, Ivy."

Ivy's fingers tighten around the key before releasing it into my hand. "I hope you're right."

When the key drops into my palm, I hold her hand and squeeze. She looks up at me in surprise.

"I will not let Sabine schedule another Tuesday, do you understand?"

Ivy blinks. Swallows.

"However I can stop this, I will. You are no longer Sabine's slave."

Ivy holds my stare and whispers, "How can you be so sure?"

"My mother was a Virtue. She and Sabine had beef long before you and I were born. And like us, my mother tried to leave them. They punished her, made her suffer the rest of her year here, but ... she went into hiding and was able to live a life without them. Up until my enrollment, she kept me from becoming a legacy."

Ivy shakes her head. "That's not possible. Once you become a Virtue and accept their privileges, you're indebted to their cause for life."

"Which is why I need that rulebook. I don't think my mom became invisible like she thought she did. The societies must have kept track of her somehow. She married my stepdad, who went here. And now he's married to her classmate. And after her death, I became a senior at the very school she ran away from. It took me a while to figure out, but ... it isn't just about Sabine bringing me under the society's control to stop me from exposing the Virtues. This is about my mother. Whatever's in those pages might tell me what *she* found to get them to let her go."

My confession to Ivy leaves me out of breath but determined to trek through the bitter cold to Richardson Place. The afternoon air is so frigid, it's like walking through a block of ice, and I pull my faux fur-lined hood closer around my face as I clomp down a paved walkway that's begging for another snowplow to come around again.

It's supposed to blizzard tonight. I forgot that nugget of relevancy when I shot up in bed this morning. My dreams were so relaxed (for once) that my mind was able to toil away behind the scenes, picking up jagged pieces of collected information and fitting them just right before the answer slapped me awake.

And when I stared blindly at the wall across from my bed, my eyes stretched wide, I thought, *There it is. The missing clue.*

There is a deeper connection to this school and my mother than I was initially willing to consider. A festering one. Why else would Meredith Ryan, the strongest, most independent, and fiercely loyal woman I knew, capitulate to a mean girl like Sabine?

Mom worked herself ragged when I was young. Her hands were nothing but reddened, knobby stubs from all the detergent she was forced to work with while she cleaned office buildings at night. It wasn't until she began cleaning the precinct, that she noticed someone left a folded newspaper by their computer with a half-completed crossword. During one break, she finished that crossword and left it on the desk. The following night, that day's newspaper was left open again, this time a quarter completed. She filled in the words once more. It became a nightly ritual that eventually had her meeting Ahmar, working late, and he used her innate strategic abilities to help convince her to be more.

Looking back, I see that my mom was a broken version of herself. Somebody swung down a power stick, and it shattered across my mother's back. And a woman like my mother—boisterous, pragmatic, sincere, smart, and an expert at spotting the smallest details—would never have been put in that position unless she was given no choice.

She may not be alive anymore, but I'd like to gift her that freedom back.

When she died, and after the initial investigation was over, Dad packed up her things and put them in storage to go through later, when I felt ready. More clues might lie in the items she left behind, and I make a mental note to call Dad and ask him to send a few boxes over—once I've prepared myself enough to talk to him.

He and Lynda are on my list, but I must see this theory through, first. Ahmar may have thought it a coincidence, but I never inherited my mother's pragmatism, nor did his wash off on me.

The last time I confronted my dad, it ended horribly and with me on a mental hold. This time, I'll be holding evidence of Briarcliff Academy's duplicity in my hands before I accuse him of helping the Nobles and possibly *marrying* my mother to ensure her continued docility.

The thought makes me unsteady, and I walk faster through the falling snow, eager to breathe air that isn't filled with microscopic icicles taking up space in my lungs.

I key open Ivy's door, but since my departure from the academy, the wind kicked up, and a boatload of snow follows me in.

"Damn it, Callie!" Eden pops up from her desk chair, runs past me, and slams the door shut. "I *just* got the room to a decent heat level!"

"I didn't think anyone would be here."

"It's independent study this afternoon. Remember? Exams start tomorrow."

"Oh." I blow a lank, half-frozen strand of hair from my face while I pull my hood back. "Right."

"What are you doing here?"

I hold up Ivy's key with numbed fingers. "Her copy of the Virtues' rulebook is by her bed. I'm here to read it."

Eden blinks. "Points for blunt honesty. Fine, go ahead."

While Eden goes back to studying at her desk, I slip off my coat and make sure to hang it on the coatrack under Eden's hairy eyeball. My socked feet make no sound as I head over to Ivy's side, sit on her bed, and unlock her bedside table.

The rulebook is where she said it would be, and I pull it out, sliding a palm down the buttery leather and gold foil lettering of her full name: *Ivara Alling*.

How must it have felt to receive this kind of belonging? I trace the edges of her name. How must it have felt to have that belonging ripped away from you and replaced with fear?

I carefully open the book, my head bowed over the pages.

My hovering doesn't stop the watchful prickles from heating my neck, however.

"Eden, are you interested in reading this, too?" I ask without moving.

After a creak and a shuffle, the bed dips under me when Eden takes a seat. "What are you looking for?"

"Anything relating to my mother," I say, turning the page.

"Your mom?"

"Oh yeah, she's a Virtue." I read the next page, containing the rules and decorum of a Virtuous member.

"Jeez, I miss one day with you guys and already I'm way behind on the revelations. She went to Briarcliff?"

"That's the theory." I flip to another page, my brows growing tauter the more I find block paragraphs of etiquette and appropriate dress codes. "When was this written?"

Eden slams her hand on the open pages, smacking it into my lap. "The 1820s. And your confused face is correct. The moral code is way out-of-date from current Virtue practices. Mrs. Harrington thinks these books are wasted materials modern women don't need. Ivy didn't tell you that?"

"She didn't have to," I say on a sigh. "I told her I wanted the rules, and I guess I have them. But I thought it would give me more clues. This is so *frustrating*." I push the heels of my hands against my temples. "I feel like all I do is sift through papers written in a secret code I can't read."

"You haven't tried asking me." Eden stares at me attentively. "I've broken into Ivy's drawer and read that thing a thousand times. Whatever you're looking for, I might be able to save you a ton of wasted reading time."

"You go through Ivy's things?"

"You went through Piper's. Now ask me your question."

Touché. "I've just found out my mother went to school here with Sabine and Daniel."

"The two current leaders of the secret societies," Eden muses. "Interesting."

"It's why I'm scouring the Virtues' rulebook, because I think my mom was also a member of the Virtues." I lift my head and stare at the ceiling, allowing my thoughts to take over. "When I first came here, I found the societies' crest, hidden in the trophy case by Marron's office."

Eden nods. "I've seen it."

"It had a familiarity to it ... one I couldn't put my finger on. It might be because I recognize it from somewhere in my past. I plan to go through Mom's boxes when I'm home for Christmas. See if I can find ... something."

"Well." Eden lifts the rulebook from my hands. "A lot of this is moot because of Sabine's overhaul of the Virtues' record-keeping. Back when your mom was attending, it wasn't. So, hmm..." Eden fans through the book, running her finger down the pages as she skims. "Here it is."

I lean over her shoulder.

"The Virtues have differing opinions from the Nobles, even back then. When these societies were first created, Rose Briar adopted the same rules and initiation rites as the Nobles."

"Like what?"

"Tradition over change. The men handled all the money, like alumni donations, robe purchases, site maintenance. If the Virtues had a leaky pipe in their toilets, they had to go to the Nobles for approval to obtain funding to fix it. That sort of thing."

I wrinkle my nose.

"Exactly," Eden says. "The women members wanted to carve their own paths and obtain independent power over the men. So, while they used *this* in obvious sight of the Nobles, secretly, they created rules to reflect their views, *not* the Nobles'. The queen who replaced Rose figured out a way to siphon money from the main bank account into a secret one, only for the Virtues." Eden brightens. "Which, I think, is the first documented case of embezzlement in Briarcliff history."

I laugh under my breath. "Good for her."

"Back then it was good. *They* were good, decent, and damn smart. That's what you get for harboring the best and brightest women under your wings but become blind to what goes on in between the thick feathers. These women toiled, conspired, and fought for their independent rights. They married CEOs but handled the bank accounts. Started dating future presidents while advising them under her breath in their ear. Founded their own companies, spearheaded some of the most successful non-profits in the world ... all under the Nobles' unassuming eye."

"That's wonderful." And I mean it. "I always thought Rose had good intentions creating the Virtues."

Eden side-eyes me but doesn't expand on the topic. I wonder if she knows, whether by going through Ivy's stuff, or because she keeps an ear to the ground, what Sabine asks of her top girls in order to keep those accessory positions these days.

"Getting to my point," Eden says, then taps a section of the rulebook. I peer closer. "Most of these rules are inapplicable except for this one."

I squint, then reread the bold title. "The rules of succession?"

Eden reads the paragraph out loud. "'A direct descendent of the blood of a Briar will forever maintain leadership and accord over the prestigious Virtuous members.' And look here." Eden skims over the requirements of being considered a Briar blood-relation to subsection (c). "'If a member of the Briar lost lineage is subsequently revealed, herein after referred to as a 'Hidden Briar,' that Hidden Briar has the automatic right to overthrow a Queen in power over the Virtues, provided the Hidden Briar possesses a relation stronger than the current Queen.'"

I straighten. "This is to be expected. From what I've gleaned of the Briars, they were egotistical, power-hungry males, willing to leave anyone considered below them behind."

Eden looks up from the book, her cheeks blooming in a flush of excitement the longer she studies me. "Uh-huh. Keep going."

I give an uncertain smile, unused to friendly encouragement from her. "Okay. Well, does the blood-relation requirement include illegitimate children?"

Eden's smile stretches wide. "Yes! It's like you said—the Nobles were assholes with a hero complex, and they gave rights to their illegitimate heirs. Granted, the rightful heir had a stronger hold on the throne, but an illegitimate son, born to Thorne Briar for example, had more of a claim to leading the Nobles than, say, a distant cousin."

I lose my breath for a moment when I latch on to Eden's explanation. "And the Virtues copied the text directly from the Nobles' rulebook."

Eden's answering smile shows a row of bright, white teeth. "And never changed it."

My heart pounds in my ears. "Rose Briar had an illegitimate daughter with Theodore Briar, Thorne's brother. I found the birth certificate hidden in Daniel Stone's personal files."

"Looks like you've found yourself a Hidden Briar. Buried into nonexistence. You discovered it in Daniel Stone's study, but where was it before? Why have the Nobles been keeping it a secret?"

I whisper, finishing, "Instead of destroying it?"

Eden snaps the book shut. "It's the Nobles' leverage over the queen. I guarantee it. Because I will bet you more naked pictures of me that Mrs. Harrington is not a descendent of the Briars. In fact, ever since Rose died, there hasn't *been* a direct descendent in power for almost two-hundred years. The Briar brothers all had sons."

"Holy shit." I stand, move, my footsteps matching the pace of this revelation pounding into my brain. "So that means we have—"

"A traceable way of finding the true Virtue queen." Eden spears up from the bed, throwing her arms wide. "And kicking Sabine to the curb. Holy fuck, Callie. Holy, fucking, FUCK."

"Wait." I raise my hand, though my heart is slamming into my throat. "This is big. We have to think this through. If we have a weapon to overthrow Sabine, we need to protect it. I *have* to tell Chase how important that birth certificate is before he accidentaly reveals it to Tempest or someone else."

Eden cocks her head. "Wait, you think the birth certificate is the weapon?"

"Well, yeah."

"Oh, dear." Eden comes up and puts her hands on my shoulders, searching my face. "You haven't thought this through as much as I hoped."

I search her eyes just as thoroughly. "I've had two minutes since reading the succession rules."

A harsh laugh leaves Eden's throat, but she doesn't let go. "I've grown to like you, so I'll say this quick. Think about every minute of your stay here at Briarcliff and who glued themselves to you. Your stepdad went here. So did your stepmom. Your best friend is the Virtue princess. Your not-so-secret crush is the Noble prince. It's all been orchestrated. Ivy *knows*, Callie. Chase does, too. Daniel Stone has probably long ago traced the lineage of Baby Girl Briar."

I lick my lips, but realize my tongue is numb. The weight I thought was coming from Eden's hands has moved into my belly, dragging me down, sinking me through the ground.

The longer Eden stares, the more the weight claims a name. Dread. Sick, inhuman, soul-eating dread.

I try to get the answer out, my lips are stiff, uncooperative. "Y-you think..."

"That your mom was Rose Briar's descendent? At this point and with the people we're dealing with, I'd be surprised if she wasn't. Or ... *dude*."

"What?" I practically shriek.

"This dad you don't know about. What if *he's* the tie to the Briar line? Either way..."

"That would mean..."

"That you are, too." Eden's smile turns grim. "Your coming to Briarcliff was not a coincidence, Callie. Someone wanted to keep tabs on you and keep their enemies close."

"No." But it comes out soundless, and I spin out of Eden's grip. My features contort as I twist back to my friend. "*No*, Eden. That can't be right. Because that also means—that means—"

"Your mom's murder may not have been so random," Eden says. "Especially if, through Daniel Stone, Sabine discovered who Meredith Ryan could be the mother of."

Hot, sticky tears well in my eyes. I don't wipe them away when they fall. I stand my ground. Stare soullessly at Eden. Then I give voice to the demon blackening my bones.

"If I'm a descendent of Rose Briar, and Sabine found out … she killed her. Sabine killed my mom to force me to go to Briarcliff."

Thirty-Three

BETRAYAL ISN'T SUPPOSED to make me blind.

Yet, I can't see anything as I shoot out of Eden and Ivy's dorm and into the frigid evening air, the stars so dim, they vaguely light my way home.

Snow crunches beneath my boots as I finish zipping my jacket and stumble up the jagged walkway to Thorne House. My fingers shake as I pull out my phone and try to send a text, but the screen is too bright, and I can't read the message chain even when I squint.

Eden doesn't cry out for me to come back. If I turn and take one last look at Richardson Place, I doubt I'll see her in the doorway I left open when I flew out of there. She dropped her nuggets of wisdom, then sat back to see what I would do.

It's not her mother whose past has been broken open. Eden had never heard of Meredith Ryan before she was brutally murdered in her own bedroom.

By the Virtues.

"No," I whisper, shaking my head. "It's not true. It's not real."

My paranoia's taking over. My unfounded convictions are building in my throat, desperate to be torn out with one long, never-ending scream.

I blink, and I'm in the psych ward, restrained and flailing in my hospital bed.

I open my eyes, and my stepdad faces me, until he's marched out of our home, his hands cuffed behind his back.

I trip, my hands plowing into a mound of snow, and I'm blinded by the white noise of my actions, the wrongness of them swirling around my head and telling me to *stay down.*

"I-I can't," I tremble out while resting on my haunches. My bare hands have immediately gone red and ache with cold. "I can't be silenced this time."

I can't be wrong.

My phone bounced into a snowdrift nearby when I stumbled, and on a hitched sob, I reach back into the cold and grab it. I say into its speaker, "C-call Dad."

Lifting the phone to my ear, I wait for him to answer.

And when a bubbly, audibly exhausted new father answers, the stone in my gut sinks deeper. "Cal, hey!"

"H-hi."

His tone immediately changes. "Honey? You okay? You sound a little distant."

"I'm..." I breathe out, my exhale turning white against the darkness before dissipating. "I'm outside, walking back to the dorms. That's all."

"Ah. Okay, good. Say, why don't we FaceTime? I have someone who'd love to meet you."

I squeeze my eyes against the ache at the same time I say, "Dad, did you go to Briarcliff?"

A few seconds pass. Something squeaks in the background, and though I've never heard a newborn before, my baser instincts tell me its Blair. "What's that, hon?"

I stumble out of the snowdrift. "You're a graduate of Briarcliff Academy. Class of '04."

"That's—"

"And so is Lynda. 2002, the same year as *Mom*." My voice becomes pitchy, my steps uneven. "The three of you went to this school, and neither you nor Lynda told me you did before sending me here. Why?"

"I didn't want to skew your view of the academy by admitting your mother went there. You were hit so hard by her death, honey. We all were. But when Lynda said she could get you in—through no urging of mine—I couldn't pass it up. It could open so many doors for you. It provided so many possibilities you weren't getting—"

"Like it did for Mom? We were *hermits*, Dad." I bare my teeth despite the flickers of snowflakes coming at my face. "Before we met you, Mom was barely getting by. She had me dumpster diving for our dinner so she could work two jobs. I'd wait up for her every night until she came home because I wasn't sure how safe she was. We had nobody, *no one*, to call a friend. Not until Ahmar. And then ... you."

I hear Dad's sharp inhale at the insinuation. "What are you getting at?"

"Were you told to meet my mom? To seduce her and marry her?"

"Oh, Jesus. Honey, don't do this. Not again."

There's true terror in his voice, but I can't contain myself. Not after I held in my hands the very reason my mother could've been killed. My voice crackles in the air, splits and divides into scattered explosions, and I don't relent. "Did the Virtues tell you to find her, to make us feel safe, then for you to step aside while they *killed* her?"

"Callie—"

"And then assured you Lynda would be waiting for you on the other side, with her wealth and privilege and safe haven, so you could forget about the murder you helped commit—"

"Calm down. Calm down this *instant*, Calla Lily!" Dad roars.

"*She's dead because of them!*" I shriek. *Because of me.* "The Virtues! The Nobles! They killed her because of some *rulebook!*"

"CALLA LILY RYAN!"

I yank the phone from my ear, grimacing, crying, howling with the building wind.

"That's it," his small voice says from the phone's earpiece. "I'm coming over there and we're packing you up early. You're coming home, young lady. Briarcliff was a mistake."

"It was," I sob, then crumble to the ground, my knees sinking into the snow. "It's shown me too much. I didn't want to know my mom went here. I want the mom I knew. I want my mom..."

My sentences fade away, taken by the winter air, and my head bows, tears trickling down the tip of my nose and splashing into the snow.

"Give me the phone, Pete."

An argument sounds out on the other end, Lynda jumping in with indecipherable sentences, until the phone shuffles between them and she becomes clearer.

"Pete may be afraid, but I'm not anymore, honey."

My head lifts. "W-what?"

"You are not crazy, okay? I don't think you're having a break down. I don't believe you need any medical intervention." Her voice is soft, soothing.

Until Dad argues something I can't catch.

"*Enough* of this, Pete. I'm tired. You're exhausted. We have a new baby. I'm not playing this game anymore. Are you still with us, Callie?"

I wipe my sleeve across my nose, my breathing coming out in faster puffs. "I'm here."

"You mentioned the Virtues. You know they exist."

I swallow through the swollen, aching emotion in my throat. "Yes."

"Then I'll tell you what you don't know." Lynda's tone, so matter-of-fact, sets me on a bated edge. "A few weeks ago, Pete lost his job when he did nothing wrong. There was no warning, no list of circumstances offered as to why he was being let go. All he understood was the subtle crest of the raven imprinted on one of his boss's office photos."

I think back to when Chase was punished for my breaking into the temple. I thought it ended there. What a fool I was. "The Nobles fired him?"

"I'm convinced it was under the Virtues' direction. Honey, I'm a Virtue, too. And I never spoke to her much, but I ... I knew your mom."

Though I'm not surprised, my face still falls. "You never said a word."

"For your protection. I figured out, pretty early, Sabine's hatred for Meredith—your mom. At that time, I couldn't do much about it. We were just freshmen. Powerless. And Sabine, while a freshman, had the ear of the queen of the Virtues. Her grandmother. For reasons I don't quite gather, Sabine was able to convince her grandmother to make Meredith's initiation difficult, almost impossible, to pass. Meredith and I weren't close, and I was never a witness to her initiation rituals, but I ... I saw her fading away. Bit by bit, as the days passed, and the hazing didn't stop. It's hard to explain, but I saw Sabine grow healthier, glowing, enjoying every moment of your mom's torture."

My lips tremble, and it takes everything I have left to hold them closed. I imagine my mother, forcing herself to continue the ritual because of the promise of being a Virtue. The possibilities. The prospects.

The forced sexual favors.

"Did she ... was part of her initiation being involved in a sex ring?"

For a moment, all Lynda does is breathe. "Honey, I wish I could explain what really happened between her and Sabine, but your mom didn't tell a soul. When she passed the trials and became a Virtue, she never spoke about her initiation. But she— it's so hard to be an outsider for this, and I'm so *sorry* I didn't do more at the time. Meredith left abruptly during our senior year and finished her schooling through distance learning. I was never sure why. Not until I received a phone call, a few months ago, to transfer you into Briarcliff Academy."

I scrub my eyes. I still can't *see* straight. "Why didn't you go to the police? If the Virtues threatened your family, why didn't you tell Ahmar? Or me? Or *someone*, that this was going on?"

"You and I both know that I couldn't."

Blair cries out. Dad's quiet shushing follows.

I say what Lynda doesn't. "You didn't want to say anything because you were making a family. They threatened you when you were pregnant."

"*You* are part of this family, Callie. We did this to keep you safe. Please believe me. If I didn't do as they said, if I ignored their orders..."

"They would've gotten me here another way." I stare off into the white-washed forest, a strange dullness taking over my body. They'd already moved my mother, the one force blocking my entry into Briarcliff, out of the picture.

"Not all of them, honey," Lynda says quietly. "You have allies."

None of her assurances hit where they're supposed to. "Was Sabine responsible for this? For getting me here, watching me, and making sure I didn't solve my mom's murder?"

"I assume your presence there is related to your mother, but I can't tell you if Sabine is responsible for your mother's death."

Though I'm so stiff with cold, I push to a stand. "So, what *do* you know? What were you and Dad planning behind my back?"

"Oh, honey." Lynda sighs, the saddened vibration tickling my ears. "We were at a loss on what to do. Pete was terrified. When it came to the Briarcliff societies, we couldn't escape. And a part of him—a part of *me*—hoped you were just as much protected as you were monitored at that school. Not all Virtues are cruel. Not all Nobles allow the rules to bend until they're non-existent. I know, because I'm one of those members."

I hold my breath, then blow it out, the sifting cloud of my exhale dissipating in the frosty air. "What about Dad?"

"Pete's not one of them, honey. I had to explain the existence of Briarcliff secret societies when we received that phone call over the summer."

I close my eyes and massage my forehead, but it feels like being soothed by frozen ice-pops on my skin.

"Meredith died eighteen years after high school, honey. I had no contact with her after she left Briarcliff. And your father and I, we recognized each other at the banquet as alumnus from Briarcliff. It's how we struck up a conversation. Pete and I getting together had nothing to do with my or your mother's involvement with the Virtues."

My boots crunch into the packed snow as I resume a shaking, unsteady walk. I believe Lynda when she says she had no ulterior motives when meeting my stepdad.

She's sweet, open, kind. And so far, she's the sole Virtue, who, when pressed, has told me everything she could.

I can't disregard that.

I also can't ignore the niggling in the back of my mind. "That banquet you and Dad attended at the Met. Was Sabine there, too?"

I sense more than hear Lynda's hesitation. Blair whimpers in the background. "Yes. Yes, she was."

My eyes fall shut. "How sure are you that your reunion with Dad was a coincidence?"

"I ... oh." Lynda trails off, her voice trembling.

"It's okay." I look up at the lights of Thorne House, growing closer with each step. "Go back to Blair and Dad."

"Honey—"

"It's almost the holidays. I'll see you then. I love you."

"Are you safe? Why don't you come home?"

"Not yet." My breathing grows steadier, my strides longer, as I hit the entryway to Thorne House.

I don't leave room for more argument, or for my dad to come on the line and order I come home. They put me here.

And now it's up to me to figure out how to best utilize the remainder of my time at Briarcliff Academy.

Thirty-Four

WHAT FEELS like a thousand texts to Chase go unanswered.

He won't pick up his phone, either. I chew on my thumbnail, staring at my screen, waiting for the elevator to open onto my floor.

I wish he were here. I ache for his reassuring weight against my side, or the way he tucks my head under his chin, squeezing me close.

I'm empty without him. There's no one to receive my worries or help figure out just how the Virtues got to my mother.

As if called upon, logic sifts through my frantic thoughts, asking, *Whose side would he take?*

Chase has never once proclaimed his separation from the Nobles. He wants to stay a member and become their leader. He's sure of his ability to turn them around.

Would my belief that the Virtues killed her ruin his plans to preserve the Nobles? *Yes.*

That singular conclusion leaves me standing in an elevator, bleak and alone.

Providing exam answers and manipulating college acceptances is one thing. But murder? If proven right, I could never keep that from Ahmar. I'd happily expose the secret societies in order to avenge my mother.

I stare down at my phone.

Chase must've figured that out, which is why he isn't answering.

I unlock my door and scan for Emma. If Chase can't take my side, maybe she can. "Emma?"

No answer.

I hang up my damp winter coat, melted snowflakes landing silently on the floorboards.

Scraping back my hair, I finish my brief search of the central area and her room, both empty. Phone still in my hand, I walk to my side of the apartment and text:

. . .

Emma, where are you? I need to

When I glance up to enter my bedroom, I stop mid-sentence.

There, on my bedspread, sits a perfect white rose with a note attached.

I don't want to know is my first thought, but I quench it as quickly as I drop my phone beside the flower. After the revelation of my mother, I must keep up the pretense and play to Sabine in hopes I'll find something more concrete to hand over to Ahmar or Detective Haskins.

Your death won't go unnoticed anymore, Mom. I swear it.

Grimly, I pick up the letter and unfold it at the single crease.

You are hereby summoned to the temple post haste.

My cheeks puff out with an exhale, and I throw the note back on the bed. Sabine wants me on her turf? Fine.

I spin to my closet.

This time, I refuse to face her unprepared.

After pressing my finger on the hidden panel, the back wall of the library opens to the Virtue's Temple.

It's incredibly well-lit compared to the darkness of the closed library, and I squint at the unexpected brightness, costing me precious seconds.

I step through, my gaze adjusting and landing on three figures in the center, one taller than the rest.

I tread faster, the figures snapping into focus—

"That's far enough, my dear."

Sabine's liquid voice soaks into the air, and my feet follow the order before my mind has a chance to catch up to the scene. When it does...

I shake my head as if to dislodge a hazy dream clinging to me as I wake. Yet, ice water shock floods my system, proving my wishes wrong.

Sabine smiles coyly as she lays her hands on the heads of Chase and Ivy. Both on their knees. Both with their arms tied behind them.

I meet Chase's eyes first, so intense, so level, and filled with the promise of impending fury. His rebellious will soaks into my bones the longer I hold the connection, and I pull on that strength and hold it close. It hurts to drag my gaze away from him, but I have to see if Ivy's okay.

She is, but her stance isn't nearly as defiant. Her entire body shakes, and her eyes turn wet at the sight of me.

Both Ivy and Chase's mouths are unbound, yet neither say a word.

I meet Sabine's stare last. "What is this?"

"My sweet Virtues tell me you've learned a secret."

I don't let the surprise show on my face, but my thoughts tick back in time frantically, wondering where, how, Sabine could have heard.

Eden? Would *Eden* have said something?

"Where's my sister?" Chase growls.

Sabine takes her time looking down at him, but her warning is imprinted in every subtle, cruel line on her face. "One more word, little prince, and I'll show her to you."

That isn't a reassurance. Chase's expression grows dark, black caverns forming under his eyes, but he tears his attention from Sabine and turns to me. "Let her do whatever she wants to me, Callie. Just save my sister."

I nod, my face numbed with terror, but I force my voice strong when I say to Sabine, "What's to stop me from calling the Nobles? You can't treat their prince this way. Not without consequence. And your own princess? What are you doing, Sabine?"

"Ah yes," Sabine says, her voice tranquil and light. "We societies do have our rules, don't we? We follow them rigorously. To the letter. At least, my counterparts do. As for me? I prefer to do whatever it takes to stay in power. Look around, Calla Lily."

I do, noticing the empty balcony above. The closed temple door behind me.

"This is not for my society to witness, nor is it for the Nobles to take part in. The Virtues have claimed independence with my rule, and what can the Nobles do about it? *We* have the highest positions in the country. *We* have the longest reaching influence. And if the Nobles want to continue, they'll curtsy to my commands."

"*You* have committed murder!" My voice ricochets off the walls, echoing my vitriol.

"My, my, you've been busy."

"You killed my mother." I'm not as steady now, but I call upon Chase's fury and absorb it into mine.

Ivy gasps, but one look from Sabine, and she droops, hiding her face in her hair. She's so afraid, so desperate to save her family, she'll fall to her knees and allow her queen to tie her up despite everything Sabine's done to her. *Oh, Ivy...*

"You put your girls up as prostitutes," I continue, fueled and hungry for hate. "Emma had to disfigure herself to get away from you."

Chase goes white, a marble statue carved in rage. *He really didn't know* hits me between the eyes, but I barrel forward.

"Your own daughter turned against you and helped Emma. Then you locked Emma in a fire in case she talked, but you failed, because she survived. Your *other* daughter will rot in prison for the rest of her life. What kind of leader does that make you? No wonder my mother wanted nothing to do with you. No *wonder* she was willing to give up her natural-born right to the Virtues and escape the filth your family created—"

"*How dare you*," Sabine hisses, her venom permeating the air. "You think reading some old papers gives you the right to question my leadership? My abilities to turn these girls into strong, hardened women who bow to no man? It is because of me they thrive outside of this school. It's because of the Virtues' continued reach that we possess power, prestige, *riches*, for lifetimes after."

"My mom wouldn't know about that. Ivy sure doesn't." I angle my head. "And neither do your daughters."

Sabine's cheeks splotch with rage, a sound like a death rattle emitting from her throat. "You mistake the reason for your presence here, dear girl. You will never smite me. You *will* bow to my will, just like every other girl who's attempted to thwart me, and dares question my reign."

I level my shoulders, notch my chin, but I look to Ivy, and then Chase. "You didn't kill all the Ryans. The societal crown belongs to me."

Chase doesn't blink. His granite eyes are hard and his jaw tauter than a predator's on its prey. And as I speak, his expression holds.

Eden was right.

He knows.

My frantic blinks can't be helped, my heart hammering for my body to respond to the shock. I move to Ivy, my sweet, loyal friend ... and her forehead creases. Her eyes slant with sadness. But her mouth doesn't go slack.

This entire time, they knew about my heritage.

"Child." Sabine laughs, but it is brittle and empty in such a vast room. "You truly believe I killed Meredith?"

I stand my ground, fuming silently.

"I take that as a yes. Well, dear, I have more important tasks than hunting down a former housekeeper turned smut photographer."

Outrage spirals into my throat. "You don't have the right to lead the Virtues, and you haven't for a long time. You hid the truth, Sabine. And you indoctrinated those who'd continue hiding it for you." I take a long look at Ivy, at Chase. "Not anymore."

"And what will you do about it, little lamb? I have years of experience over you. Decades of duplicity. You. Are. Mine."

"I'll never be yours to control."

"Nor will you ever reach your full potential then, I'm afraid. Already you've shown your crutch." Sabine's expression grows sly. "You came here thinking both you and your mother were meant to be killed. I'll provide you a counterargument. Your mother proved her unwillingness to surrender to the new Virtue rule when she ran and left Briarcliff far behind, thus becoming expendable. But you, my dear, you are young. Impressionable. Moldable. And if Rose's child's birth certificate ever surfaced, it was best to manipulate you onto the right side. Isn't that right, Chase?"

My heartbeat thrashes so hard, it pulses in my fingertips and booms in my soul. I can't move, because I'm quaking.

Chase seethes, but as he replies to Sabine, he only has eyes for me. "We had that birth certificate under Noble protection for a reason. It was meant to keep the Virtues under our thumb."

"So, dear, did you seduce Calla Lily for the Nobles, or the Virtues?" Sabine smiles. "That's a lovely thought, that the boy you love has manipulated you either way."

I feel sick, yet I'm starving. Aching for the truth, I ask Chase, "Did you know? What she was doing to her top girls? To Ivy, to *Emma*?"

"No." Chase's answer is almost a howl, grinding against his teeth.

"Did your father?"

Chase opens his mouth to respond but can't.

"Daniel understands the importance of power as much as I do," Sabine supplies. "He and I agreed, so long as I was successful, there was no need to reveal Rose Briar's secret line."

"Until your daughter found out." I dare to step forward. "First Piper discovered what you'd done to Emma and the men you expected her to have sex with. Then she found out about Rose's baby. Didn't she?"

"Callie," Ivy pleads. "Stop. You're saying too much. Please."

"Why?" I ask my friend. "The secret's out. I'm not the only one who plans to stop her." I raise my eyes to Sabine. "Do what you want to me, but it's too late. People outside this room are coming for you."

Instead of backing into my trap, Sabine's stare glitters with malice. "Dear girl. When will you finally concede that I will always be one step ahead?"

Suddenly, I tune into the sounds of my breaths, loud and extraordinary in a room that houses at least four people.

Then, realization hits.

Because Chase has stopped breathing. And Ivy looks on with a sickly, silent, dreadful cast.

I anxiously search their faces for answers. *What am I missing?*

Too soon, Sabine provides the missing link. "Shutting you up is much too easy. I can't kill you, but I do want to hurt you, and I don't have to pierce your body to know I've torn out your heart."

My mouth forms on a *W.* But I don't give my question voice. My shock doesn't have sound. Sabine draws a knife from her bodice, and it glints in the sconce's light. Lances down. My scream unleashes with the steel.

"*No!*"

I fly forward, rushing for them both, desperate to save them *both*, but instinct tells me who Sabine is after before my feet hit the air.

I hit Chase, and he braces for me. I topple him, sending us to the floor and digging my chin into his neck, prepared for the blade to sink into my back...

But nothing comes.

Thirty-Five

A WET GASP sounds out to my left.

I raise my head, hair falling into my face. Through the tangled strands, I meet widened, glistening, terrified blue eyes.

"*Ivy*," I whisper, but her name is so raw with emotion, it comes out as a desolate moan.

"M ... my..." Ivy's hands skate to her neck, where a thin, intricately carved silver handle sticks out of her flawless, white flesh.

Sabine backs away with a cruel twist to her lips, her eyes alight with a vulturine thrill as she watches Ivy flail. I launch to Ivy's side, heedless of any impending danger, and bring my fingers up to Ivy's neck as hers dance around the wound.

"P-pressure," I stutter out. Somehow, my voice can be heard through the desperate swelling in my throat. "We need to put pressure on it. Ivy, stay with me. Look at me. Don't ... no, Ivy, don't close your eyes..."

But Ivy's lids flutter closed, and she collapses to her side as she gasps for breath. A keening wail escapes my mouth as I follow her to the ground, tearing off my coat and holding the fabric close to her throat.

"She's choking on her blood. Call 911!" I scream at Chase. I glance over my shoulder and see him standing, but his expression is so sad, his demeanor so dismally accepting, that I screech, "*Call an ambulance!*"

He comes to his knees beside me. "Callie. It's too late."

"It's not! Look at her! She's—she's—Ivy, no. Why isn't she breathing? Wake up. *Wake her up.*" My face crumples. I lean over her, stroking her temple, brushing her hair off her forehead, tracing her cheeks. I croak out, "Please, Ivy, open your eyes."

"Understand this, dear child." Sabine's voice comes from the depths of the temple, despite every section of the circular room being illuminated. Her voice alone brings the darkness, shrouding my hold over Ivy, skittering along the tenuous grip I have on my mind.

She continues, "I have the control over the Virtues, Briarcliff, the Noble prince, *you*. Anyone you attempt to turn against me, I will ruin. I don't have any ties. No reasons to withstand the Nobles or any uprising within my own society. My daughters are gone. You are the daughter to no one. It is essential you understand that, if you wish for any kind of future."

Chase grips my shoulders, but I wrench out of his hold. "Don't you dare drag me away. I'm not leaving. *I'm not leaving!*"

"We have to go." Chase's command is so unsettling, offering a gravity I have no desire to sink into.

"You're *hers*," I hiss. "I refuse to go anywhere with y—"

Chase swallows the space between us, bringing us almost nose-to-nose. "I will *never* follow Sabine's rules." His guttural whisper coats my lips. "But if we don't get out of here, we'll have to follow Briarcliff PD's. Sabine's probably called the police."

I tear my attention from his face, scanning our surroundings, my hand tightening on Ivy's lifeless, slackened fingers. "She's not gone."

Chase grasps my arm. "Get up, Callie. *Now.*"

"I don't care!" I sob, folding over Ivy, my forehead pressing into her still chest. "She's not dead. *She's not dead!*"

"Swallow the emotion. I know it hurts. Keep the grief inside for just a few minutes. Can you do that for me? We need to get out of here. Get. *Up.*"

My fingers knot in the fabric of Ivy's school uniform. "I can't—I can't leave her. She'd never leave me. I left my mom. It's so cold in here. I have to—"

Strong hands hook under my arms. Chase lifts, but I fight off his grip.

"If I have to drag you out by your fucking hair," he bellows, "*I fucking will!*"

"Ivy!" I sob, scream, howl, my hands clutching at air as Chase encircles my waist and pulls me from the temple.

By the time we burst through the library doors, sirens wail in the distance and red takes over the night sky.

Reign

Callie

CHASE and I sprint down the pathway, keeping to the pedestrian trails so our footsteps can't be tracked. Somehow, Chase managed to snag my coat as he struggled to get me out of the building and throws it over my shoulders as we escape.

A sodden piece of the coat hits my cheek.

Ivy's spilled blood is still warm.

My tears are frozen, turning into salted ice that stiffens my cheeks as we fight through the winter chill, but Chase doesn't leave my side. I feel his hot breath on my neck with each exhale, his steady hand landing between my shoulders and coaxing me forward every time a fresh image of a dying Ivy hits the backs of my eyes, and I buckle between sprints.

"Almost there," he says, his breaths heavy. "Keep going."

My exhale hitches on a sob.

"Don't fall apart yet. I promise, baby, as soon as we get to your room, you can fall apart in my arms. I'm right here. I'm not leaving."

I grip his arm as we run, the hard sinew of muscle bulging against my fingers as he uses every ounce of energy he possesses to get us out of here.

There's a tickle of realization as I hold onto him. Chase doesn't have a jacket. The thin material of his white Briarcliff button-up is all that separates him from the December winter moon.

He must be freezing.

I think this fact, but it doesn't register past the surface of my brain. The only worry I can come up with has to do with Ivy. The only anxiety I'm concerned about has to do with my friend.

My former friend.

My dead friend.

"Oh, God," I moan, and Chase takes my weight for his own.

He half-carries me the last few feet to Thorne House and hauls me against his side as we sneak through the back. Chase props me up just inside the door, then exits briefly to use a fallen tree branch to obscure our footsteps in the snow.

He brings the cold with him when he shuts the door and carries me up three flights. I grip his neck like a lifeline, breathing in his familiar scent laced with snowflakes, and work to calm my broken heart.

"Almost there," he says into my ear.

I bury my face into his neck but hear when the lock turns at my apartment door and register the blanket of warmth as soon as he steps out of the hallway.

"What happened?"

Emma's soft voice floats in my periphery, but I've yet to lift my hanging head.

In fact, I've yet to register Chase depositing me on a kitchen stool as he goes to talk to his sister.

"Thank fuck you're here," Chase says, and my eyes lift from the floorboards enough to see him embrace his sister in a hard, emotional hug. "Are you all right?"

"It was the strangest thing," Emma says once they pull apart. "I got a text from Ivy to meet her at the lobster shack in town, but when I went, it was Falyn and Willow waiting for me."

"Goddammit." Chase scrapes a hand down his face. "We thought she had you. That Sabine had taken you."

"Hell no. Just a couple of bitches thinking they could dangle my re-entry into the Virtues like it'd be something I'd desire. Why? What's going on?"

It's here I see the cracks in Chase's glacial demeanor, the stricken lines around his eyes and mouth as he speaks close to Emma's ear.

Emma gasps and rips from his hold. She's immediately at my side, pushing my hair back and eclipsing my vision.

"Callie? Callie, can you hear me?"

I say nothing. Do nothing. Do I blink?

Emma pulls her lips in. "She's in shock."

Chase's presence, as soon as it's close again, fills my soul, and my arms ache to tangle around his neck. Yet no part of me moves.

His voice carries above my head. "What were you thinking, Callie?" His tone dips and dives with emotion. "I should've taken the blade. Not Ivy. Not *you*. Why did you get in Sabine's path? *Why* did you protect me?"

My only answer is motionless lips, soaked in tears.

"It should've been me," he whispers. "It should've fucking been me on that floor. I should've protected you both."

Emma cuts in, "Chase. Please. Look at her."

Chase stills. Gives me the once-over. Something at my middle catches his eye. I curl my fingers, but they're stiffer than normal, like a new layer of skin has caked over them.

Not skin. Blood. Dried blood. Ivy's.

I'm lifted in a *whoosh* of strength and carried into the bathroom where Chase resolutely shuts the door in his sister's face.

I want to tell him Emma's seen me in this state before. Naked, shivering, scared. But I can't.

584

Chase sets me on my feet, running his hands up my arms as he straightens, so gentle, so barely there. He searches my eyes for a moment.

His stare hardens, coming to a decision. Delicately, he unbuttons my blouse and strips it off my form. My skirt is next, my bra, my underwear.

When I'm naked in front of him, his expression doesn't waver or flush with need. He doesn't grit his jaw or indent my skin with his hard grip before he can't contain himself anymore, covering me with his body.

He does none of that, and I wish he would. I wish for normalcy, for a regular day, for a rewind.

Chase turns on the shower, then strips off his shirt and pants.

Bared, beautiful, he steps up to me, trailing a finger down my cheek. "We'll get through this."

I'm lifted into the shower the same way he swept me off my feet in the main room, the warm spray covering my shoulders and splashing his chest as he steps in.

In silence, Chase lathers my body, his sweeping strokes as effective as sweet, whispered *shushes* against my ear. He soothes as well as he commands, and I wonder if he knows that.

He washes my hair, rubs the blood from my fingernails, and massages the tender spots of my body with athletic expertise. He doesn't stop until he hears a relieved, long sigh leave my lips.

When he's toweling me off, he asks, "Can I carry you to bed?"

It takes effort, will, my every fiber, but I meet his eyes and give him the barest of nods.

His chin lowers. "Okay."

Chase settles me against his chest, his heart beating into my ear.

It's fast, hard, relentless in its pulse, but it's soothing compared to my erratic rhythm.

I'm laid on top of my covers, my pajama shirt and shorts slipped on with the same ease as when he'd peeled off my clothes.

"I'm staying with her," Chase says above me.

"I wasn't about to question it," Emma responds. Somewhere during our trip from the bathroom to my room, she reappeared. "Sleep, if you can. We'll talk more in the morning. Is there any chance the police will knock on our door tonight?"

Chase sighs. "Likely. Callie was Ivy's best friend."

"I still can't believe it. Sabine's out of control." Emma pauses. Then she asks, in a much softer tone, "Did you leave her body there?"

"Yes, but I doubt Sabine wants Ivy discovered in temple. She could've used some Virtues to move Ivy into the library when we left. These girls ... Jesus Christ, Ems. These girls do anything for her."

"This is what our father has missed for *years*. Even with his own daughter. Sabine grooms us like a predator. She has complete manipulation and control. But..." Emma pauses. "I've always thought, maybe Father knows and encourages it. He certainly encouraged me, in no uncertain terms, to return to the Virtues' fold when I re-enrolled at Briarcliff."

"I had no idea. No fucking clue you were being used like this. And what you did to yourself? What Piper helped do to you? She beat you with your permission.

Emma." Chase's tone breaks off at the end, the first, and only, clue of grief he has allowed to permeate the air. "Why didn't you tell me? I could've done something. Exposed the Virtues to the rest of the Nobles. I can guarantee not every one of us would be so accepting of our sisters used as fucking *sex* slaves."

"Some of those very Nobles you speak of stepped up to the side of my bed."

Chase's breaths heave in response, a bull readying his horns for a disemboweling.

Emma continues, "Would it have stopped Sabine from using you to seduce Callie for her own means? From Piper falling off a cliff? From the Virtues threatening, blackmailing, then killing Ivy? I don't know, Chase. This is what I think about every day. But you've been following Father's rules for so long. I couldn't be sure you'd be on my side."

"How could you think that? I *pulled* you from that goddamned fire!"

"And there, right there, is your damn hero complex bursting out of the gates without any reins. You always have to save the girl, don't you? You ran into those flames without giving a damn about yourself, when really, you should've given thought to the fact that I didn't want to be pulled out."

Chase sucks in air. "Emma. You don't mean that."

But she's relentless. "You even have the gall to blame yourself for Piper's death. *You* didn't push her off the cliff. *You* didn't get her pregnant. It was Piper's choice to dig into the Virtues. *Her* decision to become the Virtuous princess instead of me. But because you just can't stop yourself, now you go after Callie for daring to try and sacrifice herself for you. Maybe she wanted to. *Maybe* it's not all about you, Chase. We need to make our own decisions. I needed to save other girls from becoming Sabine's puppets. Piper needed to save me. Callie needed to save her friend and *you.* For once in your fucking life, allow us to be the noble ones."

"I'm not going to apologize for wanting to protect the women I care about."

"You guys are fighting about who has the right to die first," I whisper, "when Ivy's already dead."

Both go silent.

Emma's the first to speak. She covers her face with her hands. "I'm sorry. My brain is everywhere. I'm so sorry about Ivy. And I'm terrified for my brother, for you, and I'm taking it out on anything that moves."

"It's okay," I murmur, but the tears well anyway.

Emma lays a hand on my shoulder. "You'll tell me tomorrow. Try to rest." She then lays a hand on Chase's cheek, staring long and hard into his eyes. "You, too."

"Yeah, sis." Chase squeezes her wrist.

Emma steps out of the room and the bed dips as Chase settles beside me. His body molds to mine, and he says, close to my ear, "Can I stay?"

I turn into him, my damp lashes cool against my tender skin as I close my eyes. "Don't leave."

He brings an arm around me, tugging me close. "I'm so—I should've—"

I nuzzle his neck. "Your sister's right. You take on too much. Let us have our faults. I could've saved Ivy, too."

"I wish you had."

I squeeze my eyes shut, asking, for just this moment, that my crying stops.

"Sabine was aiming for you. I know it in my bones. And I couldn't stop myself from protecting you if I tried."

"Callie." My name sounds so pained on his tongue. He kisses the hair at my temple. "I hear the guilt in your voice. There's no way you could've saved us both. One of us was dying tonight. There was no way out."

"There's always a way."

I'm surprised at the grit in my tone, the instant anger. Yet, the more I stew on the words, the more certain I become.

"Tomorrow will be rough." Chase fits me against him when he moves to his back. "Rest. Sabine's not touching a hair on your fucking head."

I lick my lips, truly wondering if Chase can claim such invincibility when tonight has shown us there's no such thing.

My best friend is dead. That caring, smiling, bursting-with-joy person is dead. Because she wanted to save her family. Because of Sabine.

Those thoughts grow vulture's feathers until they form into jagged, black wings, and they silently circle my mind, flying lower and lower, ready to eat into the carrion I've become.

But with Chase's arms around me, I manage to slip away and avoid their gnarled beaks, falling into a fitful sleep.

Callie

I CRACK MY EYES OPEN, and for a moment, think they're still closed. Darkness blooms out of every crevice in my bedroom, so blinding I can't possibly be awake.

Then it hits me.

This blackness has exploded out of my soul and blanketed the room. Ivy's dead.

"Are you up?"

Chase's soft whisper tickles the hair around my ears. On my exhale, my body molds into his. "Yes."

He squeezes me closer. "You were having a nightmare."

"It's not a nightmare if it actually happened."

"Baby." Chase lifts to his forearm, stroking hair from my forehead and kissing me gently. "Don't take this poison in. It's for me and my sister. We're the ones who brought you closer to the societies. Maybe..." Chase's dark eyes are the only glimmer in the room as he looks down at me. "I wouldn't blame you if you wanted to leave. If you want to run out of these doors this morning and never look back."

The thought occurred to me, but I don't allow any flicker of it in my expression. "I'm not leaving Ivy. She deserves—"

Justice.

They all do.

Piper. Ivy. My mother.

Chase sighs. "I understand. I want to avenge her, too. Fuck, I want to rip the Nobles to their bones and have them grow new, untarnished skin after this. We have to take responsibility for her. Sabine and all her Virtues."

Chase comes to a sit, staring out at the gray dawn coming from my window. "I'll start today. Call a meeting and tell them about what Sabine's done."

"No." I sit up with him, my joints feeling like a middle-aged woman's instead of an eighteen-year-old's. "If I've learned anything about Sabine, it's that she excels at grooming her charges. She's prepared for this moment, Chase. She *wants* you to stand in front of your Nobles and accuse her of murder. I bet you she has a plan to discredit you, to make you the enemy and strip your Noble title." I bring my knees up to my chest, digging my chin into the cartilage. "She wants both societies for her own. And while she started with me, she's ending with you."

Chase shakes his head. "I won't allow it."

I approach my next question delicately. "How did she get you to the temple?"

"Ask it like it is. You mean, how did you find me on my knees in front of her?"

"I didn't mean it like that."

"I wouldn't blame you if you did. A fucking pillowcase was tossed over my head when I was at my desk in my room, and I was dragged to the temple to face her. She knows my weakness, that bitch. Sabine used you and my sister against me, said she had both of you locked up in the crypt's cages, and I lost it. Didn't think..."

"You were taken against your will?" I stare ahead, wondering how many Virtues it would've taken to bring down Chase Stone. "They must've caught you by surprise."

"It wasn't the Virtues. These arms were stronger. Broader."

"They were guys," I conclude with him. "You think Sabine's turned some of the Nobles."

"She's not a damn super villain. I *will* take her ass down."

"Did you know about my lineage?"

The sensitive change in topic shuts him up. He swivels to look at me.

"Don't lie," I say before he can open his mouth to do just that. "If you respect me at all, if Ivy's death truly means something to you, don't keep hiding the truth."

His tongue darts out, sliding across his lower lip. In the hue of dawn, his blond hair has become a glimmering sterling, his skin in an alabaster cast, as if his soul is floating just outside the edges of his body. "I didn't know the whole time. I found out a few weeks ago."

My shoulders curve over my knees. "How could you keep something like that from me?"

"Because I had a deep desire to keep you from getting hurt. Or worse."

I ignore his gruff tone. "I deserved to know."

"Callie, your lineage is a *weapon*. One that's been hidden for almost two hundred years. The Nobles hid the survival of Rose's baby for their advantage—so *they* could choose the new queen of the Virtues and regain control, and they did." Chase casts his gaze to the ceiling, his fingers tangling in his hair. "It's been nothing but push and pull with these societies. Who's the strongest. Who's the smartest. Who has the most influence. Theodore Briar convinced his brother—the first Noble King, Thorne Briar, to choose a Harrington woman to become the new Virtue queen after Rose died and squirreled away his own daughter. Why do you think that is?"

"Theodore didn't want his daughter, his secret baby with Rose, to inherit the Virtues."

"Exactly. The Virtues were already poisoned at that point, even at their origin. Without Rose to guide them, competition with the Nobles flourished. In protecting his daughter, Theodore didn't anticipate that once the Harringtons took control, it turned into a covert war of who could become more powerful and gain more allies as they grew in size and influence."

"Did the Harringtons have Rose killed so they could take her spot?"

"I don't know. Her death was ruled a suicide."

"Yes, the story is that she killed herself because she was desperate for a child and she couldn't have one. But she *did* have one. After what Sabine's—after how she—" I swallow. Collect myself. "I wouldn't put it past the Harringtons, even the two-hundred-year-old ones, to commit murder."

"You could be right. Hell, everything I've studied and memorized in the Nobles' rulebook could be nothing but lies. The Nobles overlooked the Virtues, convinced that women would never come into the kind of power they possessed. They didn't consider the Virtues' drive for success and the motivation that can provide—needing to claw themselves to the top. The Nobles didn't have that type of drive. We were men of privilege, of high-class riches, meaning we never had to consider what it was like to prove ourselves over and over again. I'm coming to understand that in an effort to manage that kind of desperation, the Noble successors never told the Virtue Queen about Rose's surviving lineage. If they did..."

It takes a moment to sort through everything Chase explains. "In hiding Rose's surviving bloodline, the Nobles maintained the power to choose the queens, instead of leaving it up to the Virtues. What I don't get is, why continue to hide it? The Virtues were under a new rule. Since these societies are following the rules of the monarch, a hundred years later, it's not like the power of Rose's bloodline could derail that kind of history."

"Actually, it can. Secret societies are sworn to their rules and oaths. Especially the original law. Think about the US Constitution. It's like that. We strictly follow the will of the founders. *Including* Rose's will, which was to have her heirs be the first in line to rule the Virtues."

I mull this over. "By that reasoning, if baby Delilah Briar ever realized her history, she could replace the queen immediately."

"Worse." Chase searches my eyes. "Think about that baby's blood, Callie. *Really* think about it."

I pinpoint the sparks, the brightness of comprehension he wills in my direction.

It hits me. I gasp. "That baby had *both* Noble and Virtue blood. Theodore and Rose. She came from two of the founders." I rub my fingers against my lips, tearing at the chapped skin. "What does the rulebook say about a member who descends from both a Noble and a Virtue?"

A faint, proud smile pulls at Chase's lips, but he tamps it down. "Congrats. You discovered our problem. If you recall, Thorne never had children with Rose. They were all stillborn or miscarriages. He had kids with his next wives, but that bloodline is diluted. Thorne never thought past his own lineage, so he never wrote anything in our rulebooks about founder blood on both sides—meaning, if the original Noble King and the first Virtue Queen had a child. He had no idea his brother, the next king in line, was having an affair with Rose, or of the baby who came from said affair. So, nothing was ever written about it. When Thorne died, he believed his inheritance died with him. Theodore became king for a time—solidifying this baby's inheritance of the societies."

"Why would he do that? He didn't want his daughter to ever know about the Nobles and Virtues."

Chase cedes my point. "After Rose died, Theodore passed Delilah's real birth certificate on to the second-highest official of the Nobles, a friend and confidant. Theodore knew if Thorne ever found out, the baby would be killed. For her safety, the baby was smuggled out and given to a middle-class family with a forged birth certificate. From then on, the original birth certificate was passed down to only one living Noble at a time—no more. My grandfather was the last one to legitimately receive the information. Then, my father found out. And instead of keeping it safe, he decided to use it to his advantage. He wasn't about to let a Rose Briar descendent languish until someone smarter and more cutthroat got the same idea he did. So, he told Sabine. They traced Delilah's heirs. And they brought you here, Callie, under the guise of recruiting you."

"I can't—I need a minute." I shuffle to the foot of my bed, my feet hitting the floor as I fold my arms around myself. "If what you're saying is ... Chase, was my mother killed so I could come here?"

The sparks in Chase's eyes die out. "Would your mother have allowed you to come here otherwise?"

"*No*." Even as the denial leaves my lips, the truth wraps around my neck with a stranglehold. "It's not true! My mom wasn't killed over some fake laws concocted by a small-town secret society!"

"Callie," Chase says, his lips barely moving with my name. "Come back. Sit with me."

I stand and whirl to face him instead. "My world—my *everything*—was taken away because of some godforsaken rule Sabine decided to break? Why? Mom escaped. She didn't *want* to be a fucking Virtue Queen!" My palm slams into my chest. "*I* don't want to be queen! She could've left us alone. We would've lived our lives in New York, and I'd've never figured out their existence!"

Or yours, the dark trenches of my mind whisper. *I never would've met you.*

"Sabine and my father couldn't take that chance. Your mom knew of her inheritance somehow. Sabine couldn't let that kind of fatal flaw lingering in the air around her."

"She took everything from me," I hiss through clenched teeth. "And because that wasn't enough, she took Ivy, too."

"Good. Get mad, Callie, because that's the only way we can move forward and leave this fucking bedroom. My father and Sabine wanted to watch you, on their turf, to see if you were malleable enough for them to admit your heritage and rule through you. If they had you on their side, what did it matter that you had the ability to be the ultimate ruler of both the Nobles and Virtues?"

"This is so crazy," I whisper, digging my fingers into my hair. "We're talking of kingdoms and thrones and who has the right to rule, but we're in the twenty-first century! At a high school! And *I'm* the one who's told she has a screw loose for thinking my stepdad killed my mom?"

"It sounds ridiculous, but this stuff has been ingrained in us for centuries. I've been groomed as a secret society member since I could crawl. My sister, too. And my father, grandfather, great-grandfather before that." A shadow ripples over his expression. "You've seen what they're capable of. Don't discount their power simply because they covet pretend royal titles."

KETLEY ALLISON

Ivy's fading gaze forms into the air around me. Her eyes locked on mine, wet with silent pleas as she took her last breaths.

I was so useless in that moment. So benign in my ability to assume my rightful position and kick Sabine off this so-called throne *before* Ivy had to die.

I think about what that does to a person, when someone they care about dies unexpectedly and violently. It derails the heart, imprinting a permanent mark that trails behind them like an oily shadow...

Even Sabine isn't immune to grief.

My chin jerks up. "Piper died. That wasn't in Sabine's plans when she brought me here, was it?"

Chase takes a moment before he answers. "No."

"It makes perfect sense now. Piper's death really wasn't because of the societies. Sabine and your father didn't know Piper was digging up dirt on Rose. They had no idea she was helping Emma escape their underworld. Addisyn's jealousy was a variable they didn't consider."

"You started looking into the existence of the Nobles and Virtues before they were ready. My father had to pivot hard and fast. That's when they tapped me to do their dirty work." Unreadable lines deepen his frown. "I was already in position."

"They wanted you to gain my trust. Weaken my will." My statement burns my throat, clotting my voice.

"Father admitted why it was so important I keep you close. He told me about your relation to Rose."

"And to Theodore." I massage my neck in thought. "My ancestry gives me control of both societies. Why not kill me, too, and end the bloodline for good?"

"Our pairing meant I naturally maintained more power over you, as a future Noble King. Especially if you never figured out your heritage. But I started caring. And they weren't so sure I was willing to hide the truth of your blood for much longer." Deep crevices form around Chase's full lips. "If they ever figure out just how much I've fallen for you..."

I give him a level stare. "Their plans would change again. They'd want me dead and lose the bloodline forever. Even if the rest of the Virtues and Nobles find out about their duplicity, they won't mind, because I'm already gone."

"Sabine might've killed your mom. She *definitely* killed your best friend. She's not going to stop. I have to protect you."

I peel off my pajamas and start pulling on clothes strewn about the floor.

Chase's back goes rigid. "What are you doing?"

Once I pull the Briarcliff sweater over my head, I turn. "Sabine and your dad are so ego-driven, they never gave thought to the fact that I don't *want* to rule the societies or keep their secrets. I'd rather blast them open and expose them to the world, with Ivy and Piper's ghosts cheering me on. The Nobles and Virtues may not believe you, but perhaps they'll believe me."

The word is strange on my tongue: *believe*. A definition that's been twisted, maligned, and meaningless when it comes to my life.

But this time?

"This time," I say, "I'm not going quietly. I'm showing everybody, the entire *school*, everything I've found out. Piper's diary. Rose's letters. Howard Mason's discoveries. All of Briarcliff will learn about the academy's dirty secrets, and then it's up to them to do what they want with the information."

Chase sighs, readying for an argument.

"It's not up to you anymore," I say. "My only friend in the world is dead. I'm not going to sit down or be quiet or *hide* like Sabine wants. She thinks this will shut me up or bring me to her side. But I'm going to do what she least expects. I'm publicly outing her, Chase. And the Nobles. I'm done with this charade." My voice cracks. "*Done* being told what to do. I'm taking it back." I swipe under my nose. "I'm getting Ivy justice. Avenging my mom. Representing Piper. And keeping you. The last person I have left."

Chase's shoulders slope, but he lingers on my face. His lithe body slips from the bed like silk, and he prowls closer.

Cups both sides of my face.

And says, "My sweet, sweet possum. My reluctant princess. My vengeful queen. *My* girl. I am on your side. And I will stay there, whatever you decide to do."

I write long into the night.

The police presence we predicted never comes, but just as quickly as that concern sparks, I squash it and focus on finishing the most important paper of my life.

"Got it," Chase says behind me.

I tilt my head enough to the side without tearing my attention from my laptop. "Dr. Luke got back to you that fast?"

"He's willing to give us his copy of the Briarcliff email list."

I make a sound of approval, then ask offhand, "He's a Noble, isn't he?"

"He was, before the scandal."

When I don't fill the silence, he continues, "We Nobles are fine with affairs, crimes, acts of idiocy, so long as they're done discreetly. Dr. Luke's blowback carried too far for the Nobles to protect him any longer."

It's comforting that Chase doesn't bother to hide the obvious from me anymore. "Send it to me."

If Chase is concerned over the flatness of my tone, he doesn't say anything. My email *dings* with his message, and I toggle to my inbox and copy it. "Thanks."

Chase comes up behind me, laying his hands on my shoulders and bringing his mouth to my ear. After a light kiss, he says, "I'm only going to ask this because I feel it's warranted. Are you sure you want to do this?"

I spin to capture his lips with mine. When I pull away from him, I stare dead-on into his eyes.

And in answer, I click *send*.

Chase blows air out of his mouth. "Fuck. Lady Luck be with us."

"We don't need luck," I say when I stand. "All we need is desire. And I have the crushing need to fuck that woman over in spades."

Chase

I LEAVE Callie drifting between her sheets, but not before smoothing the lines of grief on her forehead until she at last fell asleep.

Dawn floated away with her, the glaring blue of the sky taking its place as I sneak out of Thorne House and prowl into mine, taking the side stairs where security thoughtfully (and with enough bribery) turns their back until I reach my door and stalk in.

I prod a sleeping Rio with my boot, right in the ass. "Up."

Rio twists in his bed, mumbling something close to "No, motherfucker," before throwing his arm over his face.

As a Plan B, I rub the gray sludge of former snow from my soles onto his exposed abdomen.

He screeches, bolting upright. "The fuck, man?"

"I said up."

"Fine. I'm up. What do you want?"

"Out."

"Multiple syllables not your forté today, huh?"

"Last warning."

"It's my room!"

"And mine. Which I'm commandeering. As your prince."

Rio stares at me a moment, the brown of his eyes resembling murky, hazy sludge, likely remnants from smoking last night. "Pulling the Noble card on me at the ass-crack of dawn. Thanks a bunch, *Prince*."

I eye him as he slides out of bed, his footsteps as heavy as the headache I'm sure he's nursing. When he scratches the top of his head, his dark hair tangled and unkempt between his fingers, I wonder if he knows.

If he participated.

"You seeing Ivy before exams?" I ask casually.

594

"Nah." Rio steps into his pants, then goes for his belt. "Meeting her after, though."

I make a sound, though if you ask me, I'm not sure what it's supposed to communicate. All I can see is Ivy's diluted blood circling down the shower drain beneath Callie's bare feet.

After buttoning his shirt and throwing his blazer over his shoulder, Rio says, "Whatever you have planned this morning, she better be worth it. You haven't even shaved. Do you think she has?" He winks.

Hell. He thinks I'm kicking him out to receive some pre-exam fuck from some faceless co-ed, like we used to do before senior year reared up and sank its fangs into my neck.

Or ... before Callie showed her face at Briarcliff.

Her eyes, rimmed in gold and filled with shattered jade, cloud my vision until I blink them back, but the beauty of her refuses to be dimmed.

Growling, I follow Rio out of the bedroom, my glare so tangible, it should leave marks on his back.

Rio opens the door, where Tempest is not so surprisingly leaning against the frame. He tips an imaginary top-hat the moment Rio notices him and jumps back in surprise. "Howdy."

"You assholes keep ruining my morning. This is your booty call?" Rio turns to me. "I'm disappointed, man. I was hoping you were back to your old ways. Then, at least, we could all get back to ours."

"Go find Ivy." I spit out the words before my better judgment can properly contain them, but Rio, senseless, ignorant jackass that he is, doesn't blink at the undertone.

"Great idea. *She* follows our rules. I can fuck her and not have Mommy and Daddy be angry at me," Rio says, then dips around Tempest before I can think of a proper retort. Or better yet, before I can grab him by the back of his collar so I can drag him back in here and invert his goddamned nose.

"I see he's his usual maggot self," Tempest muses as he strolls in, shutting the door behind him.

I dart a final look at the door. "He's not our problem."

Tempest grows serious. "Talk to me."

I gesture to our kitchenette, where we start to sit on the two stools, but I pop off, unable to contain the tight wiring of my body for one meager second. "What do you know about last night?"

"Last night?" Tempest cocks a brow. "I studied, drank a tumbler of smuggled whiskey, then curled up in my bed and slept like a milked kitten. But I assume my bedtime routine isn't why you texted me so early."

I get to the meat of it. "Sabine killed Ivy last night."

Other than his body going still, Tempest doesn't react.

"I was there. So was Callie. I'm convinced the bitch was aiming for me, but..." *Callie stood in front of the blade* "...she changed her mind last minute and stabbed her current princess instead."

"Why in the fuck would she do that?"

I shrug, but it doesn't convey nearly enough meaning, so I scrape a hand down my face instead. Fathoming the unexpected death of Ivy rubs me raw, but adding Callie on top of it—a girl who dove in front of me, whose vanilla-scented hair cascaded over my face with the force of her jump, and the heat of her haggard breath dampened my neck as she clutched me—is another thing entirely. I don't feel things for girls. I *never* feel the need to claw them off my body and throw them behind me, teeth bared for battle.

Yet I wanted to do all that and more for her. To end her heartbreak. To rewind those moments until I'm holding the knife and cutting out Sabine's heart instead.

"I'm not so dense as to believe murder doesn't happen in our ranks, but to do it so outrageously? Sabine believes she's invincible, Temp. She doesn't think anything will come of this."

Tempest stares at the dark marbling of the countertop, his gaze hooded and unreadable. "Who else knows?"

"No one other than Callie."

He sets his jaw. Looks up. "Good. We're gonna keep it that way."

"No," I correct, "we're going to kick down Sabine's doors and drag her out in front of all our members and behead her."

"That's a quaint image, but you and I both know if you take her actions to the king, nothing will come of it."

"I'm so sick and *fucking* tired of nothing coming of shit! First, my sister's mutilated and nearly killed. Then Piper dies. Now Ivy. We swore to lay low until the right time, and I was with you on that oath—but this? This makes three. I can't let this go on any longer."

"Here's how I see it." Tempest rises and tucks his hands in his pockets. "Sabine went into last night with the sole motivation of ending your life. Likely she had a plan for when you were a corpse at her feet. I'm thinking, Callie's psychiatric history got the better of her, and she stabbed the shit out of you, and Ivy, poor dear, tried to intervene but was gutted for her efforts, too."

"That's cold, T."

"Forgive me for the brief summary, but even you have to admit that Callie's mental history is like catnip. Using it isn't even diabolical. It's such pluckable, low-hanging fruit."

I do my best to control an unwanted eye twitch.

Tempest sweeps out a hand, continuing his one-man, fucked-up Shakespearean theater. "But alas, circumstances occurred, and variables came into play that Sabine didn't quite plan for, like your girl throwing herself in front of you. Death by literal backstabbing can't work if Callie's supposed to be the villain wielding the knife. So, Sabine used quick-thinking and switched gears, deciding to sacrifice her top girl because sending you a message was more important. Think on that, Stone. The consequence of killing someone close to her was less important than screwing you over. There is no way you and Callie can stay together after this."

"Stand down." I curl my lip at him. "This isn't some Romeo and Juliet moment where I take a vial of poison and sacrifice myself for a love story. Our society is under threat. Our ranks put into question. My *princedom* at stake."

Tempest grips my arms, not to shake sense into me, but to assist in having me sink to his level. "I certainly hope you see it that way," he says, his lips barely riding over the words. "Because from an outsider's point of view, you're doing a helluva lot to fuck up your takeover of the Nobles for a girl."

"You know who she is." I shove out of his hold. "You're the *only* other person who understands the dangers of Callie's legacy and why I kept up the charade of seducing her to keep my father happy, and why I'm still keeping her close. We need her on our side, T. And after last night? She's gone rogue. And that's not a benefit to any of us."

I tell him about Callie's mass email that's likely hit everyone's inbox by now—including his. Tempest's expression grows shadows, but he stays quiet.

"Why'd you let her do it?" Tempest asks after I finish.

"Because I need her to trust me. Her best friend was violently murdered in front of her. How would it have looked if I tried to convince her to do nothing?" I start pacing the room, my veins throbbing, my arteries pumping. "She was silenced when her mother died. Labeled unhinged and kept separate from any information regarding Meredith Ryan's murder. Who was a former Virtue, by the way."

Tempest doesn't flinch at my fact-drop. He wouldn't, since unearthing long-forgotten, scandalous secret society mysteries is part of his deal as my second-in-command. Tempest is the sole recipient of my wants, theories, and terrible truths. He alone understands the desperation behind my goal to steal the Noble reins from my father.

"I had to give Callie some control," I say through his silence. "Some ability to seek revenge. Otherwise, she'd be kicked down, locked up, voiceless, and betrayed. She may not have gotten back up this time."

Tempest studies me. "Are you sure your concerns for her are surface level?"

"I'm protecting her as I've always done." Then, to cover any missteps I may have made, I add, "Causing her to become strangled and unsure again does neither of us any good. We need Callie at the top of her game, ready to do anything we ask. Curled up in a ball and wailing at the walls isn't her ideal state."

"There will be a lot of blowback because of that email."

"How about another girl's murder? You think there'll be issues with that?"

Tempest ignores my sarcasm. "I'd bet my parents' next blockbuster movie that Sabine has prepared for this moment. And that's fine, because you're coming out with your own story."

Tempest stops any retort by lifting his hand, silently asking me to hear him out before I lose it.

"As your only ally, my duty is to keep *you* safe. Not her, not Ivy, not even our boys. You first. Listen to me, and listen well. This is how we'll play it—you're going to resume making Calla Lily Ryan's life hell."

I lift my brows, sucking in breath for a sweeping denial, but my throat constricts before I voice sound.

Tempest senses the opening. "If you want to keep her safe, this is how you'll do it. Callie's figured out her heritage. Great. Sabine saw her as a threat before, but now it's an impending avalanche. And there's also you to contend with. You care too much about the new girl, and she's developed feelings for you, too—which, thank you both, was showcased in front of our evil queen last night. With that kind of proof, Sabine's on the warpath. She's so keen on ending you, she was willing to sacrifice Ivy to prove her suspicions that you've continued ignoring your father's instructions, despite the public lashing."

The sound of the dagger sinking into Ivy's skin, then Callie's piercing scream, stirs the air around me. For a minute, I think I'm holding Callie's weight again, bracing her against my chest as her tears drip from her chin, cold by the time they hit my collarbone.

I blink, and Tempest comes back into focus.

"We can't take their perception of your treachery at face value," he continues. "In order to get Sabine to back off, you need to shut up about Ivy and distance yourself from Callie. No—that's not enough. You have to make Callie hate you, Chase. Like *fucking* despise you. If Sabine can kill her princess without a thought, she'll kill you and Callie with just as much ease and take the Nobles and Virtues for herself."

I rub my fingers against my lips, air heaving from my nose, but I can't argue his points. "Sabine has my father. She's taken the Virtues and made them into her playthings. She has powerful men at her disposal by placing key girls in positions to annihilate them. Why isn't that enough for this cunt?"

Tempest's pale eyes pin mine. "After Piper's death, this runs deeper for her now. I don't think she'll rest until she has you by the balls. Your sister was first, but I'm confident Sabine's ultimate goal is your destruction. Do me a favor, don't help her along."

I grit my teeth, my jaw aching with the force. "I won't rest until I avenge my sister and keep Callie from the same fate. That clear?"

"Crystal. And we can do all that. Intelligently and without this whole cocked-and-loaded thing you have going on right now."

"I have to warn her."

Tempest's eyelids lower to half-mast. "Do what you must, but don't draw any more attention to yourselves. You two are done. Do *you* understand?"

"Yeah." I massage the back of my neck, staring at nothing but seeing everything. "I have to ruin her at the same time I'm falling in love with her."

Callie

BY THE TIME the sun crests over the polished stone landscape of Briarcliff Academy, I'm dressed and on my third cup of coffee.

My hand shakes as I set my mug on the counter for the final time, my stomach growling for more sustenance. I tried to satiate it—with cereal, a string cheese, a banana, even a damn cookie—but I vomited every time.

Ivy's not alive.

She's dead because of what I represent. Some fake queen meant to rule a concealed class of pompous, psychopathic assholes.

And my mom died for it, too.

No wonder I can't keep anything down. How am I supposed to reconcile that kind of mindfuck with a complete breakfast?

Emma's door creaks open, and I break out of my vortex stare into our granite countertop.

"The craziest thing just happened," Emma says in greeting. "I got the most hilarious email this morning."

I give a curt nod, then push away from the counter and toss my backpack over my shoulder.

"Holy shit, Callie. What have you done?"

"Told the truth."

"You've outlined *everything*." Emma holds up her phone. "Rose Briar's letter. Howard Mason's journal. *Piper's* diary. Jesus—Ivy's murder last night."

"It's the only way I know how to fight back and protect us at the same time."

Emma gapes. "How the *fuck* is this meant to be a defense? Who did you send this to? Everyone? The entire school? The national news stations? *Callie.*"

I don't react to her heightening panic. "Did I ever tell you that Ahmar and my mom used to catch up over coffee some nights?"

"I can't wait to see where this is going. Did my brother agree to this?"

I ignore her question. "Most times, I slept through their meetups, since it was largely them decompressing, shooting the shit, that kind of thing. But one time, I couldn't sleep. I went into the kitchen to ask for a glass of warm milk, but right when I reached the threshold, I heard Ahmar say, 'Seriously, Mer, you can take all the photos you want, provide all the evidence, but sometimes, the cops just can't act. Funds are too thin. Man-power too spread out. So, you know what I gotta do sometimes? Take it public. *Nothing* makes a commissioner act faster than throwing scandal at the press.'" I shrug. "So that's what I did."

"There are no facts. Everything you collected was stolen from you. How is anyone supposed to believe this?"

"I don't need truth. I need panic. Interest. Rumors. The Virtues can't touch us while the gossip swirls."

Emma's phone dangles at her hip. She takes one step back. "I don't know whether to admire you or fear you. You don't ... sound right."

I respond colorlessly. "I don't know how I'm supposed to act. Sabine wants to take everything from me until I can't rely on anyone but her or the Virtues. I'd rather face public ridicule than become her next princess. And with these kinds of accusations sent to parents, faculty, and the Briarcliff Academy staff and Board of Directors? I'm dragging her out of her protective cave and feeding her to their stockholders. She can figure out how to explain Ivy's blood on her hands. Because, after this semester, I'm out." I breathe in deep, then level my shoulders. "I'm going home."

"I don't blame you," Emma says quietly. "Though I don't think it'll remove you from danger."

"My mother knew she didn't belong here. If she were alive today, she'd never have let me step on this soil to even glimpse the academy."

"What about my brother? Does he know you're leaving?"

Chase. *My* Chase. He left soon after I fell asleep, deciding that if the police came, he probably shouldn't be here. Haskins never knocked on my door last night, but that doesn't mean he won't find me this morning.

But Chase is different. I can't let him find me, because if I do, I'll break. I'll fall into his arms. I'll stay.

"He'll understand," is all I can say.

"He might say he does, but he's lying. You're the one person he doesn't have to play games with or be one step ahead of. You're real—you're showing him what an *actual* person is like outside these walls and away from Briarcliff's chains. If you leave, I might lose the remaining piece of him that's been able to withstand our father's tampering."

My lips twitch in hesitation, but I don't think Emma notices. "Chase will be fine. He's strong."

I turn for the door.

"Hey, Callie?"

"Yeah?"

Emma sucks on her cheek in thought. "This may come out strange, even though we *are* here for a high school diploma. But I feel like I should remind you: exams are today. Assuming your mass email doesn't screw over the curve to epic proportions, that is."

With any other person, I'd be concerned over Emma's mention of exams the day after I watched Ivy die. But Emma isn't any person. She has her own tragedies inside her and her own ways of dealing. Sarcasm and compartmentalizing are the top tools in her box.

But the calculus final? Neither of us has the mental bandwidth to handle that this morning.

I say to Emma on a sigh, "Fuck."

Ahmar calls me on my walk to the academy's main building.

"How's it going, kiddo?"

I choose my words carefully, while clomping along in the snow. "Have you found out more about the Nobles and Virtues?"

Ahmar reacts to my cheerlessness with a short, "Calla."

"It's bad here, Ahmar. Really bad. Ivy"—It *hurts* to say her name—"Ivy was killed last night."

Silence.

My story comes out in a rush. The knife. How it cut Ivy's throat. How she bled to death in my arms. And just ... how.

"Ahmar?" I ask, once the sickness surrounding my words subsides. "Are you still there?"

"Kiddo, I'm working on processing all you've said."

"It's a lot, but it's true. I was *there*, and so was Chase, and Ivy ... Ivy..." I end on a sob.

"Baby girl." Ahmar's sigh is filled with love. "I think I gotta come over there."

Nodding vigorously, I blurt into my phone, "That's a great idea. I don't know if Haskins is in the societies' pockets, but a lot of the Briarcliff PD sure are, and I'm positive they're working on covering up Ivy's death. She was *murdered*, Ahmar. Just like my mom." I halt in the middle of the walkway, the overnight snow clumped and packed to the sides. "Oh my God, Ahmar, I haven't told you who did it—*Sabine* had Mom killed—"

"Callie. Honey. Take a breath."

"I can't, Ahmar! Don't you see? It all comes back to the Virtues. I have the blood they've been looking for! They don't want me to—"

"Jesus Christ, honey." Ahmar's voice grows thick before it cracks. "Please stop."

"No! They can't kill any more people I love, okay? I won't let them. I can't let them take Chase!"

"*ENOUGH!*"

Ahmar's yell has me careening, but I right myself before tripping over a mound of plowed snow.

"Sweetheart, think about what you're saying. *Think* about how crazy this sounds!"

"But it's the truth!" My voice shreds into the air.

"You can't go down this road again. I won't let you. I'm coming over there, and I'm taking you home."

"What?" I blink, staring into the blinding white until tree-tops blur into the horizon.

"You're scaring me," Ahmar whispers. I've never heard him whisper before. "All this crazy-talk ... I thought I was helping you by listening to your theories and letting you work them out until you came to the solid conclusion. The *right* answer. But you're not. You've spiraled, and I'm taking the blame for that."

"*Spiraled*?" My shock echoes through the landscape. "Ahmar, please. This isn't like last time. This is *real*. I watched my friend die last night. I-I felt her die. I'm not making this up or chasing wild theories or seeing things—don't come." My lower lip, dampened and chilled with sudden tears, wobbles. "Don't come to try and put me away again."

"Anything I do, *anything*, is because I love you. I even looked into these societies you keep mentioning, and yes, they do exist."

"See! I told you!"

"They're as legitimate as skulls and bones or locks and keys or whatever those Ivy Leagues call their secret clubs. Calla, what I'm saying is, they are the high school equivalent of massive donations from their alumni and ego-stroking meetings and dumb rituals well after graduation. These exclusive clubs are nothing but a way to reward over-inflated, privileged egos for being rich and contributing to the success of capitalism."

My heart sinks. "Ahmar, don't say this. The Virtues are so much worse than that. There are sex rings involved, and pay-offs, and blackmail."

"That may be, but it's impossible to prove."

"*I've* just proved it! I saw everything!"

I hear Ahmar's slow inhale and exhale. "Sweetheart, I love you with all my heart, but you are not a credible witness."

"Then find somebody who is! Dr. Luke. He was a Noble but was kicked out for getting involved with Piper. If you talk to him, I bet he's pissed enough to—"

"Baby girl, I'm gonna stop you right there."

My face crumbles, the collapse made all the easier by the crippling cold. "You've always been in my corner. Believed me when no one else did. So, *believe* me when I say my mother was killed by the Virtues for her automatic inheritance of the society. Ivy was killed to teach me a lesson. And Sabine only wants me alive to become her puppet. I'm in danger, Ahmar, and you're the only adult who will help me."

"God. *Damn it.*" I can picture Ahmar's internal arguments with himself and the way he'd be running his hand down his face. Balling a fist in his hair. Punching a nearby wall. He did all those things directly after we found my mother. "I wish you would hear me, kiddo, loud and clear. I want to help you. I do, and that's why I'm offering to come get you before I call your Dad and let him know you're falling apart."

"Do it!" I dare him. "He and Lynda will *both* admit the danger of the Virtues."

But ... will they?

Blair's in the picture now. A baby girl they have to protect better than they did me.

"Calla, I've been threatened with losing my job if I pursue this any further."

That has me whirling. "What?"

"I'm not supposed to be messing with other jurisdictions. You and I both know this. But now my lieutenant is involved, and he's telling me if I keep looking into Briarcliff crimes, I'm out on my ass. We're overloaded as it is. He can't afford to have me split my efforts."

"But ... you're doing it during your down time. He can't relegate the hours you're not working."

"It's come from the top. The commissioner has told me, point blank, to end my research on Briarcliff."

"I don't..."

"Baby. You do. You do understand. This is out of my hands. You have to let Briarcliff PD do their jobs, and you have to come home."

It's amazing. Not ten minutes ago, I'd told Emma I was going home. Leaving. Escaping. Into another cage, all the same. "I can't. I won't. Ivy's body is barely cold, and my mother's has been cold too long."

"Ah, sweetie." Ahmar sniffs, and I swear to God, I think I'm making him cry. "You're breaking my heart. You scare me so much. More than I've ever felt fear in my life. I need you to come back. You can't be there anymore."

"If you can't see what's in front of your eyes..." I take a deep breath. "There's no reason a commissioner and lieutenant would be so concerned with your off-hours, especially if it's not affecting your work, and I know you. It's not. They're probably former Nobles. And you know what? One is likely been back to the Virtue temple and used that bedroom with underaged girls—"

"Do *not* keep going with that line of thought, Calla Lily."

Ahmar's use of my full name brings me up short. He's never, in all my years of knowing him, released my birth name like fire escaping his mouth.

"Mom *went* here, Ahmar!"

"That doesn't mean she was killed because of it. Your momma photographed a lot of crime scenes, mainly gang-related. We've looked into Briarcliff, and to put it simply, the evidence just isn't as strong as possible gang retaliation."

"What about my roommate being pushed off a cliff? Are you going to disregard that, too?"

"I'm not dismissing you, honey. I'm laying out the facts—"

"People are dying all around me!"

My yell causes the few Briarcliff students heading to exams this early to falter and look back at me.

"Everywhere I turn," I continue, aiming for calm, "somebody I care about dies. You can't pretend not to see that."

"You are not the reason, honey."

Instead of a comfort, the sweetness in his tone only angers me further. "Stop saying that like it's true. I *am* the cause. It's my bloodline that's done this."

"We are not in the stone ages. You can't expect me to buy this descendent business like it's a bona fide recipe for murder. Your momma was in a high-risk career. Your roommate was involved in multiple affairs and was knocked up by her sister's boyfriend, thus becoming a victim to her sister's rage and jealousy."

"And Ivy?" My question is nothing but a tremble of sound. "What about her?"

"That, I don't know. I haven't heard anything. Baby, I'm sorry."

He doesn't believe me.

My voice comes out softer. Flatter. The Briarcliff forest dulls in my vision. "I understand. I'm on my own. If you won't believe me now, then I have to gather more evidence. I'll do just that."

"Calla, don't you dare hang up on m—"

The phone drops to my side.

I trudge the rest of the way to school with the same misery I carried when I found my mother, massacred on the floor.

Callie

I SHOULD BE on a first-name basis with the Briarcliff prefects at this point, but to be honest, when I'm summoned by yet another one as soon as I enter the academy, her face doesn't even look familiar.

Her expression, however, does.

Callie the troublemaker, drawing the attention of the headmaster. Again.

Shoulders hunched, I make a left into the faculty wing, not bothering to toss my things into my locker.

With each step, a viscous film grows around my heart, becoming thicker and slimier the more time that passes between Ivy's last breaths and bringing her murderer to justice.

Like today, for example. Why is everyone still in school? Shouldn't we be holding a memorial or an assembly for another tragic victim at Briarcliff?

I hate to think on the reason for the silence, but it's obvious in the roots of this academy. Unexplainable events, secrets, lies, mysterious deaths ... all of it grows in Briarcliff soil, yet everyone just steps over the weeds.

Marron's door is open, leaving me exposed in his doorframe before I'm ready.

"Ah. Miss Ryan. Come on in."

I jolt at my name. A quick scan of his office leads to further confusion.

Haskins isn't here. And now that I think about it, I didn't pass one patrol car on my trek to the academy.

"You're looking rather pale," Marron says as he rustles papers on his desk, flicking a glance in my direction. "Do sit down."

With stiff legs, I do as he asks, dropping my bag at my feet before taking a visitor's chair.

"Now." Marron stacks the same pile of papers. "I assume you're curious as to why I've called you in this morning right before your first exam."

"Actually, I know exactly why I'm here."

At last, Marron's gaze steadies on mine. He arches a brow. "Am I correct in assuming you will take responsibility for the dissemination of complete misinforma- tion *and* the unauthorized use of parent and faculty email addresses last night?"

"I'd think you'd be more upset that your secret societies are outed," I observe, neither confirming nor denying. "But in this place, I guess it takes a lot more than attributing a second girl's murder to the Virtues to deepen your frown."

"Excuse me?"

"Ivara Alling." My voice shakes, and I fight for control. "Ivy. She was killed last night by Sabine Harrington."

Marron leans back in his seat. His stare doesn't leave my face.

I continue, "You know who Sabine Harrington really is. The queen of the Virtues, a secret society created by Rose Briar, and after her death, continued on by women anxious to claim power in a man-driven world. Namely, the Harringtons, which Sabine married into."

"Good gracious, you have quite the imagination. I'm not surprised that it's largely in line with the anonymous email sent out."

I squint at him. "The Virtues weren't the first. Thorne Briar created the Nobles, an elite secret society meant to groom and prepare boys for the ultimate status within college, then the workforce, and ultimately, key positions of political power."

Marron sighs. "Miss Ryan, as much as I enjoy a good story-telling—"

"You're one of them."

A muscle under Marron's eye twitches.

"A Noble Viscount. I saw you in your red robe, telling what I can only assume are high-class escorts to strip for the freshmen initiation this year. I also heard your talk of soulmates—a lame attempt at controlling the Virtues, if I've ever heard one, but I'm guessing you Nobles haven't mentally surpassed the whole 'let's marry the woman and that'll keep her out of trouble' trope."

I wait for my theoretical mike to drop—I'm so angry, so helplessly enraged, that all I want to do is affect someone, hurt someone, *wake them the fuck up.*

"Why, yes." Marron lays his forearms on his desk. "I read all this in the elaborate, paranoid rambling you sent to all faculty and parents last night."

"There's nothing delusional about an anonymous email I happen to agree with," I hedge.

"You are treading such dangerous waters." Marron clucks his tongue. "And I sincerely don't think you care." He lifts a sheaf of stapled papers, turning them so I can read the first page. "Indeed, your psychiatric transcripts assure me of your inability to discern fact from fiction when you're in such a dissociated state." He holds up a hand to prevent argument. "Allow me to elaborate."

Marron licks his finger, turns the page, and reads, "'The patient suffers from para- noid personality disorder. On a recent occasion, extreme paranoia occurred in the form of the patient's insistence that her stepfather killed her mother. PPD can also include an unrelenting mistrust and suspicion of others, even when there is no reason for those suspicions to be cast, of which the patient also displays.'" Marron looks up at me over the top of the paper. "Does any of that ring a bell?"

"You bastard," I hiss under my breath. Marron doesn't react. "Ivy was stabbed in the neck by Sabine because that woman is so starved for power that she'd rather traffic, maim, and kill the girls she enlists, while you just sit there and preside over your over-priced, over-privileged, garbage dump of a school, uncaring of the senseless deaths of your own students."

"Although you have yet to admit it, you've caused quite a stir with our parents. I assure you, I have easily quelled the hurricane you've attempted to create with one, simple attachment to your diatribe." He lifts my hospital transcripts again. "This."

"Throw my past at me all you want," I seethe. "That doesn't change what I saw last night. I had Ivy's blood under my fingernails—"

"Ah." Marron sits back, giving me the once-over. "You're looking rather clean from my perspective. Did you shower?" His expression grows coy. "Did Mr. Stone help with the cleanse? Indeed, did he convince you to write this email that can so easily be discredited with your fragile mental state?"

My heartbeat kicks up, pounds, slams in my throat, but I keep my voice level. Pray for it. "My friend's *body* is in your library. I saw the police lights last night. Soon, you'll have to answer for another death on your watch."

"Hmm." Marron puts his index fingers to his lips and turns his attention to his desk. "I don't normally break confidentiality, but I believe I have something you should listen to."

I balk. "Why isn't anybody *hearing* me? There's no time for more stupid games! Your Virtue Queen is out of her—"

Ivy's voice fills the room.

"Hi Headmaster, um, I'm sorry to call so late, especially before finals, but my mom's sick. Like, really not doing well. She's been diagnosed with ... with ... ovarian cancer, and I'd really like to be with her. I hope you can understand. I'll defer this semester in hopes you will allow me to repeat my senior year. You understand, family comes first. I need to be with my mom. Please send anything my parents need to sign through email. Thank you."

Once the grief at hearing her one last time runs through my veins, once shock filters through my head—"No. *No!* Can't you hear the fear in her voice? Ivy's terrified! Sabine must've made her say this before she put Ivy on her knees. Sabine plunged a knife into her while Ivy had her back turned! And she *trusted* her! All Ivy wanted to do was save her family!" I stand so abruptly, my chair falls backward, knocking into a side table and scattering picture frames across the floor. "How could you defend such a woman? How can you encourage such hate against children?"

Marron watches my tirade in such a bland and non-reactive state, I'm actually terrified.

"Headmaster..." It comes out as a whimper. "Please."

Marron purses his lips. "I'm sure you won't be surprised when I say, as soon as I can prove you were the one who sent that baseless stream of consciousness to Briarcliff's parents, you will be expelled from these grounds."

"Don't fall in line. Just once, do the right thing. Sabine can't get away with this."

"I'm afraid, Miss Ryan, that your disorder has clouded your better judgment. You're an adult now, so there's no possibility of forcing you to get the help you need, but I implore you, seek that rehabilitation. Not only am I genuinely concerned for the students around you, I'm also concerned for your well-being."

"Fuck you," I spit.

Marron *tsks*, then sighs. "Do I need security to escort you out?"

I turn my back to him in answer.

"Good girl," he murmurs, but his voice no longer registers. "And I wish you the very best of luck with your exams today."

I have to step over the scattered pictures, quelling the urge to kick and stomp on them until they're as destroyed as my insides feel, but one overturned frame distracts me enough to pause. There's a strip of masking tape on the back, and the name MR. MARRON, AKA HOWARD MASON, circa 2001, scrawled over it with black marker.

I'm bending and picking it up before my mind accompanies the movement. When I turn it to see the picture, my mouth drops open in awe.

"Who is this?" I whisper. Most of me doesn't care if Marron heard me or not.

Yet, he stops his mindless shuffling of papers as soon as he registers what I'm holding.

"My old faculty photo," he snipes. "I was a teacher here before I became headmaster. Do put it down before you ruin it further."

"You ... you're Howard Mason?"

Marron licks his upper teeth. "I haven't been called that since my attendance here."

I ask through the massive lump in my throat, "Why did you change your name?"

Marron's expression hardens. "Miss Ryan, you've vastly overstayed your welcome. Leave my office before I'm forced to initiate a school lockdown and have you dragged out by police."

His overdramatic warning doesn't affect me. "You were against them. When you went to school here, you made it your mission to expose the Nobles, but now you're one of them. Why? How?"

"Miss Taskin!" Marron hollers. "Allow security to escort Miss Ryan to her first exam, of which I have no doubt she will excel."

But I'm not finished. "2001 ... that's when my mother went here. Did you know her? Were you her teacher?" My face goes numb. "Were you involved in her—?"

"Miss Ryan, you're to come with me."

I look over my shoulder to where a beefy school security guy in a dark suit stands nearby. And he looks ready to drag me out by my hair.

"You're not getting away with this." I whirl on Marron, even as security moves to stand between the headmaster and me. "You're just as culpable as Sabine. You covered up a murder last night, and the fact that you can just sit there and pretend an innocent girl isn't dead *sickens* me. You're pathetic. Disgusting. And when justice finally comes for you and you cry out your last words, I hope they're the same ones you wrote in your journal—"

Marron's eyes flicker.

"*—Help me.* This time, no one will. Nobody will come to your rescue. I'll make sure of it."

Security's broad body wrestles me out simply by shadowing my smaller form, but I make sure my eyes are bright, that they're made of starlit fire, for every second Marron holds my stare, until security pulls the door shut.

Callie

I JOIN the swell of students heading to class, having no choice but to merge into the mass and become as inconspicuous as possible.

Anonymity turns out to be insanely difficult when all I hear is talk of the email last night and the big reveal of secret societies on campus.

This psycho says Ivy's dead, someone whispers.

If dead is going home and avoiding finals, then I guess she's gone to fucking heaven, another says and laughs.

Do you think it's true?

Nobles and Virtues? What the hell? Why wasn't I chosen?

Piper and Addy's mom? Are you serious? The asshole who wrote this ruined my MILF moment. I don't want to have my cock slit while I bang her.

Fake news. Total bullshit.

No proof.

Gossip Girl wannabe.

Russian hacker for sure.

As we progress down the hallway and my exposé turns to fodder, my heart sinks to the deepest chamber in my chest. I was so convinced that all Briarcliff Academy needed was a rumor. It's fueled so much before—Piper's death, Addisyn's arrest, Rose Briar's mysterious disappearance...

Why *shouldn't* more uncertainty taint student thoughts and cause faculty to second-guess their career choice?

They should be rewinding their memories, where sudden inconsistencies become obvious, now that I've given them context. Like the academy's hidden rooms and hallways and the random disappearances of their roommate at night. The sudden propulsion of their average-grade friend being awarded all A's in every single exam. The pairing of two people who are complete opposites, yet now call themselves soulmates.

Something.

... yet, nothing comes out of these mouths except ridicule.

Don't they know what they're treading over every day at this school? Can't they feel the ghosts they pass or notice the dried blood under their feet when they go to the library to study?

I clamp down on the banshee that wants to wail its way out of my throat and into these ignorant, stupidly neglectful ears.

If clear words and accusations will never convince these people ... I need the blood on my hands.

My tongue feels like a swollen lump in my mouth, a useless muscle mass that's done nothing to help. I'm at a loss on what to do, other than retrace last night's steps, so I can personally witness what they've done to clean up the library and temple.

My best friend. My *lost* friend.

Tears well, but I sniff hard and order my eyes to stop getting so hot. As soon as I'm able, I'll find Chase. As soon as I can talk to someone who saw what I did, things will be better.

I step into calculus in an anonymous wave of movement, silently taking my seat, yet staring hard at the vacant chair across from mine. My eyes don't leave Ivy's permanently empty spot until that special part of me that seems to conjure him when I need him the most flickers to life.

On a hitch of breath, I look up.

Chase meets my eyes and holds on, giving a single, imperceptible nod before he takes his seat.

Professor Dawson passes out the exams and calls for us to begin, but all I can focus on are Ivy's last words. All I hear are her wet gasps for breath as blood fills her lungs.

And the only picture on the backs of my eyelids is of my mother, interposed over Ivy in the same helpless, dying state.

"Time!" Dawson announces. "Pencils down."

The hour went by with nothing but one breath filling my lungs. Blinking, I study the stapled exam, apparently sifted through by my fingers since the pages are dog-eared and fanned through. My hand aches from my prolonged grip on my pencil, and for the first time, I notice the lead is worn down to the nub.

Curious, I go back to my exam, staring at the answers for each equation.

For every single question, I wrote the same answer: **2.**

For a pair of unanswered deaths. Ivy and my mother.

Over and over, scrawled on each page and on the backs, in cursive, then block numbers, until there's nothing left but faded scribbles as my pencil wore down.

As Dawson comes by to pick up my exam, he frowns, yet says nothing as he tucks it in with the others.

I stare at his back as he continues to gather exams.

Has Headmaster Marron already warned the professors of my disintegrating mental state and imminent departure? Is that why Dawson's so unaffected?

He's a Noble, too.

Once finals are collected, the classroom bursts with noise. Voices pile on top of one another, discussion of the strange midnight email quickly overtaking any comparisons over the toughest equations.

Chase finds me through the crowd. "With me."

We don't create the stir we normally do when Chase hooks my arm and escorts me out. Too much attention remains on the anonymous email.

"Where should we go?" I ask him under my breath as we filter through the students in the hallway.

"Our Vault."

I almost trip over my feet. "You mean, back to the—?"

"Yeah. I do."

We veer around a corner and stop in front of a custodian's closet. After a brief scan of the area, Chase uses his keycard, and the lock beeps green.

"What about the rest of your finals?" I ask, genuinely concerned. My grades, I've all but given up on and passed over to Marron for the final F, but Chase? He has roots here. Priorities. Loyalties. *Rules.*

All I get from him is a steady, "It's fine," before he shuts us into the black.

I don't bother to ask more questions, relying on my sense of touch instead. I keep my hold on Chase's arm as he navigates seamlessly around shelves of cleaning items until we reach a wall.

Another small light flashes green, followed by a low whine of hinges.

"Of all the places," I whisper as he pulls me deeper. "I wouldn't have thought to search the janitor's storage space for hidden access to a Noble room."

"This didn't used to be a supply closet. It was Thorne Briar's office before the faculty wing was created, moving the headmaster's office."

The mention of the word *headmaster* has goosebumps skittering under my skin. "Chase, Headmaster Marron's not who—"

"Shh. We're in the walls right now. If we talk loud enough, people can hear us in the hallways."

Good to know. I hunch forward and keep my hands on his shoulders as we traipse through the darkness.

"Steps ahead."

I feel around with the tip of my shoe before descending the first step, Chase's tight, reassuring grip on my hand leading me the rest of the way down.

After what feels like fifty steps, Chase finally begins lighting sconces with his pocket lighter, the dampened stonework of the walls gleaming into focus.

It doesn't escape me that the Nobles have largely stuck to old traditions and their original rooms, unlike the Virtues. Granted, the Virtues' original temple was destroyed in a fire, but Sabine allowed it to happen. She shut Emma in and never called 911. She was probably glad to sacrifice the rotting, mildewy nineteenth-century architecture in favor of more modern amenities.

And be gifted a circular room where she could be the center of attention by her future husband.

The thought gives me pause. I wonder if the name of the new library ever gives Sabine hives.

I certainly hope so.

"We're here," Chase says as we step into a low-ceilinged, stone-lined room with rows of wooden pews laid out in front of a large, skull-framed hearth.

"Holy shit," I murmur, breaking away from Chase to wander closer to a fireplace taller than me. Above it is a life-size, iron insignia of the societies' raven. "I've been here before. Snuck through there to get to you when you were—" I glance at him.

"In the cage. I remember." Chase throws his lighter into the fireplace, the dried, corroded wood igniting with a *whoosh* of heat.

I watch the fire dance. "This was also in Howard Mason's journal. A fireplace rimmed with the skulls of English nobility."

"The nobility part is suspect," Chase says behind me, "since a lot of these skulls were found through local grave robbing."

I shy away from the fireplace and sit in the first pew. "And Howard Mason?"

Chase glances in my direction. "What about him?"

"First the renovations, then the trivia of your skeleton hellmouth over there. You're chock full of information. You must know what happened to him." I search his face for clues of knowledge and if he knows who our headmaster really is.

"I'm more concerned with your well-being right now."

"If you're truly worried about me, you'll tell me about Howard Mason."

"Callie, what are you getting at?"

Shoulders tensed, I decide to just get it out. "Headmaster Marron. That's not the last name he was born with. He's Howard Mason."

It's imperceptible, microscopic, but Chase's entire body stiffens in front of the fireplace. "How did you find that out?"

"By accident. He called me into his office this morning." I explain what Marron said and how my reaction tipped over a few pictures.

Chase curses, a blasphemous echo seeping into the hollowed-out eyes of the skulls.

"You knew, didn't you?" My accusation doesn't reach nearly as far. "This whole time—when you threw that journal at me in your father's study, disguising it as something else, something *important*."

Chase's response is quiet. Monotone. "I told you, when you first came here, I was under strict instruction to lead you astray."

"And you were so good at it, too." Now, oh now, my voice reaches echoing levels. "Dumping garbage on me, harassing me in the dining hall, encouraging the bullies—Piper—to do their worst. And then stripping me naked and sleeping with me." I swipe at the sudden dampness under my eyes. "I could've handled a quick fuck. It wouldn't have split my heart open. You could've turned me into an entertaining story for your buddies the next morning, and it would've sucked for me, but I understand some guys are just rotten. And I would've gotten over you."

The barest wind flutters through Chase's lashes, and I tell myself it's coming from the fireplace. It can't be from a flinch of hurt.

"Instead, you used me in all the ways you could. Mentally. Physically. Emotionally. *Verbally*, the way you tossed around 'soulmate' like it meant something. When now, here we are, and you've kept another piece of the society to yourself. Marron was a teacher when my mom went here. Another key to my past you refused to give. Why? Because you want to control me? Just like Sabine?"

Chase jerks like he's been slapped. "Don't you fucking come at me like that."

"Why not?" I stand, my voice reaching a terrible, gut-wrenching level when I do. "Why do I have to peel you like a goddamn onion in order to get the answers I need? What kind of hold do the Nobles have on you that you want to betray them one minute, then protect them the next? Choose a fucking side, Chase!"

"*I choose you!*" he roars, and I shrink at the decibel. "I chose you. I made a promise that I wouldn't keep anything else from you, and I—Headmaster Marron *is* Howard Mason, but I—there's not—I didn't want you to—*ARGH!*" Chase digs his hands into his hair and spins away. His shoulders hunch over, and his voice shreds when he screams, "FUCK. THIS!"

Adrenaline leaks into my bones, the joints of my fingers trembling, my teeth chattering with invigorated fear, but I force myself to be strong. "I've learned a lot since coming to this godforsaken place. About this school, the people here. But I'm noticing a common thread, and it starts with my mother."

Chase says nothing, so I continue, "I learned the hard way that mistakes don't define a person. Their choices do. She left Briarcliff behind when she became pregnant with me. Meredith Ryan ran from the place that tried to hold her prisoner because she couldn't stand still and let the Harringtons kill me or recruit me. My mom *chose* me. And Piper? Piper helped Emma, even though it was to her detriment —even if she put her family's legacy at stake by discovering Rose Briar's hidden bloodline, buried by her ancestors. That was *her* choice. Then there's Ivy, who defied Sabine despite the great risk that *her* family would be forever indebted to the cruelty of the Nobles and Virtues."

When Chase *still* doesn't react, I spit, "Hell, while I'm at it, my stepfather found out about my mom's affair and confronted her, slapped her, and she ended up dead that night before they were ever able to forgive each other. And you? You bowed to your father's mysterious instruction to distract the new girl while they figured out whether I was worth saving. Do you see where I'm going here?"

Chase, breathing heavy, lifts his head enough to peer at me through his fallen strands of blond hair. At last, his lips move. "Yes. We've all been defined by our choices."

"I thought so, too, at first. This whole time, I thought my mother's death was mutually exclusive from this academy—from *me*. Until Sabine forced me to figure out perspective. A person's actions ... they can be seen as choices *or* mistakes. So, I'm asking you here, now, *please*, how I am supposed to interpret yours..."

Chase eats up the space between us, his hands clamping on my upper arms and yanking me against him. His hot breath sweeps over my cheeks, his sweet, minty smell nearly buckling me to the ground. I don't—*can't*—let the impact of his proximity show on my face.

"Listening to my father without question was a mistake," he whispers harshly, his eyes burning against mine. "It's ingrained in me, to emulate him. I nearly lost my sister because of it, and it was with her in mind that I targeted you. But you changed me, in the moment, at the end, fuck, with your first steps into this school. You were traumatized innocence, and I couldn't make sense of you or of the reasons why my father wanted such a delicate, bruised, wide-eyed thing under his watch. But I listened—to you, to him, and I learned. And when you and I slept together, that wasn't part of his plan—that was my *choice*. Opening myself up to the true origins of the Nobles and Virtues was my choice. Deciding to protect you instead of manipulate you was my choice." He slides his hands to my shoulders. "Standing with you, in this room, in direct opposition to the shitstorm going on upstairs, is my choice. You, Callie, are what defines me these days, and that is why I decided to keep Headmaster Marron's true identity from you."

His face is blurred into a faded, bleak watercolor, and he uses his thumbs to wipe the teardrops from under my eyes. I start to say—

"I'm not finished," he says, tilting his head as he searches my face. "I get to say my piece, too. Your accusations against your stepdad were a mistake. And you not being at the apartment to meet your mother for dinner when you were supposed to was a mistake. Your friend's overdose came from the choice *she* made to shoot up and wasn't the result of your decision to go to that party. Piper is not your fault. Ivy is not your fault. Your mom—no, Callie, look at me."

I dove down in defense, my chin digging into my chest, my shirt dampening with my tears. Chase lifts my head by curling a finger under my jaw, urging my gaze to his.

"Your mom," he continues through my soft sobs, "isn't dead because of anything you did. So, now I'm going to pose the same kind of question to you: Are you going to let other people's choices and mistakes define you?"

"Stop," I say, pushing against his chest. It's too hot in his space. Too real. "You're not—that's not—"

"The point you were trying to make?" Chase offers a small smile. "Next time, don't spar with me thinking you have an automatic win."

"I'm damaged," I croak. "These deaths, the destruction that comes in my wake, it's because of my DNA, the blood in my veins—I'm mentally unstable, unreliable, a loser at making the right decisions. I can't even write a detailed letter and email it to every possible person in Briarcliff existence without it being discredited or erased."

"You are so much more than that."

"Oh yeah? Then why am I hiding out in the basement with a guy who thinks keeping me blind and isolated is the best way to protect me?"

Chase's expression goes stiff, his fists clenching as they rest on my shoulders, his internal war made starkly apparent with the forced calm he's etched into his face. He stares at me, looks away, then stares at me again.

"Chase, what—?"

He crushes his lips to mine.

Callie

CHASE USES a distraction tactic as old as time—sex, feelings, touch—and I'm a slave to it, craving the euphoria of pleasure, the ease of forgetting, every time his tongue slides over mine.

"I need you." Chase's breathes into my lips, searing them with vicious, demanding fire no hearth could ever match. "I need you so bad right now."

"Chase, we're not ... this isn't the..."

His lips skim to my neck, while his fingers travel to the hem of my skirt.

I grab his waist in automatic reaction, but I'm not pushing him off.

And so, I give in.

My fingers claw. My nails dig into his skin. They work together to rip his shirt out from his pants. With his hot exhales coating my exposed cleavage, and his trailing touch on my inner thighs, it's hard to imagine a time I'd ever say no to him, unfathomable that I'd ever tell him to stop.

I try to pull away, to separate our mouths, but each time I do, my arms yank him closer, my body molded to his.

I wrench at his collar and his shirt rips open, buttons scattering to the floor. As soon as his gorgeous, firelit chest is exposed, I lick between his pecs.

Chase groans, his fingers tangling at the back of my head, ushering me down until my lips are at his belt, and I make quick work of removing that, too.

He kicks his pants off, and in those freeze-frame seconds, I realize my shirt and blazer have somehow been pulled off as well. A black lace bra, plaid skirt, and tights are all that remain between us, but I find I'm not cold.

I'm not chilled at all.

I grip his dick in my hands, familiar, hot silk sliding against my palm, and when his tip beads with pearlescent shine, my tongue darts out and catches it like a dewdrop.

"Fu..." Chase can't even get the full curse out.

His eyes turn into burnished flames as he looks on, urging me with his hips to take him all in. When I do, his upper lip curls in satisfaction before his head falls back, and he groans to the ceiling.

I'm desperate for more warmth, more soft fire. My other hand massages his balls, pulling gently, and I dip down for an experimental lick.

"Callie ... I can't..." Chase's voice is nothing but a twinkle at the back of my mind, so focused am I on the now, the him, the physical instead of the pain.

"I want you," I say between sucks. "Only you. Just this. I don't want to think about anything else or remember even five minutes ago—"

Chase clasps the back of my neck, tilting my head back as he comes to his knees. His body follows his push until I'm prone on the ground, and his naked, hard body covers mine. "Don't even put the thought of it into existence. We're here, and you're mine. Let me take you."

I nod, my tongue poking between my lips to taste what remains of him on my lips.

His eyes flare. He reaches under my skirt and yanks at my tights until they're around my ankles.

"Chase!" I yelp when he pushes then holds my legs straight to the ceiling. I have a thong on, but I've never felt so exposed, lying on the hard ground in the middle of a forbidden, forgotten room.

"There's no time to be precious with you. I need your pussy *now*." He palms his dick, his eyes never leaving my center.

In one sweeping motion, he's gripping both my ankles in one hand while scooting my panties to the side with the other.

My hands smack into the ground on either side of me when he plunges his fingers deep into my folds.

"So wet. So fucking wet," he rasps, pumping his four fingers, in and out. "I could see it through your G-string, and I'm feeling it now. *Fuck*, I want to taste you, but if I eat you out..." He bares his teeth and slides his tongue over the top row, his stare anchored to mine. "I'll come all over this goddamn room."

My eyes roll to the ceiling, pure bliss settling at my core, then spreading. "Then fuck me," I grit out, "before I come all over your fingers."

He repositions, growls, then slams all the way in.

I cry out, cupping and squeezing my breasts in an automatic will to spread the pleasure, my ankles still held up high by the bulging muscles of his arm and the athletic stability of his hand.

I've never been fucked with my thighs clenched together, and now I'm wondering why I ever left that kind of sex as a question and not a fact.

I can feel every inch of him, sliding in and out, thrusting, every curve of his dick branded on my skin, in my folds, hitting my G-spot with target expertise.

Chase experiences the same ecstasy, a barely contained loss of control lining his face as he plunges, harder and faster, then moves to hold my thighs, keeping my legs clenched together and my knees falling to my chest as soon as he changes the angle and...

HOLY.

"*Chase*," I wheeze through scattered breaths, my fingers curling against the gritty stone floor.

"You're so tight." He groans. Pauses. The sound of my shoes leaving my feet then hitting the wall registers in my ears, then Chase tears off my tights. "Wrap your legs around me. Now."

Legs quaking, I do as instructed, and somehow, though it seems impossible, pull him deeper.

"Come on my cock," he says, rocking his hips, but his restraint is loosening, the imminent unleashing bright in his eyes.

One more thrust and the smallest tilt of my hips is all it takes for my thoughts to explode and my vision to coat with an inner swirl of color.

Chase yells, then collapses on top of me, his breath exploding in short bursts on my breasts, then my neck, until he holds on and kisses my lips.

"I needed this," he says as he lifts his head, drinking me in with a starry haze. "I needed you."

I thread my fingers around his nape. Touching his lips with gentle, velvet kisses, I whisper, "That was a choice?"

I feel his lips curve as an exhausted chuckle leaves his lips. "That will *never* be a mistake."

Chase

I COULD LAY on a dirt-cold stone ground with Callie for decades, taking the aches and pains as a natural consequence to her warmth, but our circumstances could never allow for such an escape.

Even hidden behind walls and down secret staircases, we can't avoid danger.

"Is this why you brought me down here?" she murmurs as she plays with pieces of my hair.

I kiss the top of her head, her vanilla scent a welcome substitute to the dirt and grime of Noble deeds. "No, but it came as a welcome surprise."

She's molded to my side with the artistry of a Renaissance painting, her milk-white thigh curving over my tanned skin, and her hair luscious and streaming across age-old floors.

If anyone deserves an imperial title, it's her. *And she has it.*

"Will anyone walk in on us?" she asks. "I hear this is a place James likes to frequent."

My lip quirks. Yet another detail she's uncovered on her own. "James hasn't convinced a girl to descend to his level in quite some time." I roll until I'm on top of her, nuzzling her nose. "And you're never to use yourself in the same sentence as that fucktard again."

"He's your friend."

"Allegedly."

Sadly, the sparkling amnesia of sex fades. There's nothing quite like the mention of James to give me a flaccid cock.

I push up, then flop into a sit beside her, my forearms resting on my knees.

It's almost non-existent, but I catch the stiffening of her joints as she senses the growing distance between us.

"Chase, have I done something?"

"Nah." I rub my hand across my mouth, staring at the back wall. "It's me that's the bad guy."

"How do you mean?"

Callie doesn't ask the question with surprise, likely because I've proven many times over that I'm not the hero of her story.

But I've yet to explain just how much of a villain I have to become.

She rises to her elbows, her tits covered with black, sexy lace. I'm itching to squeeze them, pinching her nipples through the scant fabric and soaking the peaks with my tongue. It's a much better vision than the future I'm about to give her.

"I brought you down here so we could find the privacy we lack above ground."

"Okay." She sits cautiously.

I stare at my hands, dangling as uselessly as the fucker I feel like I am. "You know we can't do this anymore."

"I'm aware." She tucks a strand of hair behind her ear, a surprisingly enticing movement that I follow. "I'm having issues resisting you, though."

She tries to curve her lips, but her smile hasn't reached her eyes in a long time.

I put my hand to good use and touch her too-soft skin, scraping my thumb down her cheek. "Baby, I couldn't resist you the second I saw you. It's why what I'm going to say next is so hard."

"Tell me." She holds my wrist, pausing my movements. "Just get it over with."

I hate being responsible for capturing the light in her eyes between my fingers and snuffing it out. "I'm no good for you. Look at me, I've taken advantage of you when your friend just died. In front of us. Murdered."

Callie closes her eyes. "You gave me a burst of happiness in an otherwise awful existence. I can't regret something like that, especially when the force of her loss came back the minute we finished." She presses her free hand to her heart. "I feel emptiness, right here, all the time." She lowers her eyes, then whispers, "Except when you fill me."

I stare hard at the top of her head. "Say that again."

She blinks, those wide eyes of hers traveling back up. "I said ... I don't know if I'll ever feel full."

This is the point where I'm supposed to argue with her—grab her by the shoulders and shake the truth out of her. That currently, she can't live without me. A strange, foreign flutter of yearning at the center of my ribs tells me I should.

I don't.

"Do you recall the moment you came up to me and asked me to be cruel to you?"

Callie drags her thighs against her chest, wrapping her arms around her legs. "I guess. Yes. I asked you because Sabine was growing suspicious of us meeting up with each other when she ordered me not to."

"And did we?"

"Fool her?" Callie raises a brow at the same time she rests her chin on her knees. "What do our current events tell you?"

"Mm. Which is why I'm coming to you now and asking you the same thing."

"For me to be cruel to you?" Her voice doesn't carry any intrigue or acceptance. More like the monotone of a girl who knows the opposite is true.

Twisting, I find my shirt nearby and pull it on, but I don't stand. I don't shuffle

619

away from her. The subtle breeze of her sweet cream smell every time she exhales is all that keeps me intact as I share the news that I intend to destroy her.

"I'm warning you this time," I say, knowing full well Callie understands where this conversation is going, "that I will not stop at one event. Or two. Or nine. Sabine intends to implode my life if I don't do what she wants, and that is to separate myself from you."

Callie's fixated on something over my shoulder, but it's with the attention of a woman who's looking so inward, nothing on the outside matters. "So, it's true, then. Everything I've done up until this point is worth nothing. My uncovering of the societies. My attempts to solve Piper's murder. My hope to shield Emma and Eden from more pain and humiliation." Her eyelids lower to half-mast. "To avenge Ivy. You're no longer on my side, are you?"

"Don't put words in my mouth."

"My reputation is gone, too. Any opponent could point to my breakdown after my mom died. Without you backing me up, that transcript has all the merit it needs to erase my side of the story."

"I'm not too worried about your reputation when I'm focused on saving your *life*." It comes out sharper than intended, and I bite my tongue, sending the heat of temper into my eyes instead of through my lips.

Callie lifts her chin from her knees, the gold of her irises growing heated with a glassmaker's perfection. "My reputation is what's holding my life *together*. Without it, I'm unstable. Obsessive. Crazy. And *Sabine* is the sane one."

"I'm not questioning your sanity, but I can't risk Sabine doing to you what she did to Ivy."

"So, you'll make me miserable instead?"

"With or without your permission." I force myself to stand. It should feel exceptional, staring down at her as she's splayed at my feet, but all I cling to is the numbing belief that this is for her own good. "It's not only you I have to protect. It's my sister, my brothers, my society. Sabine is crushing all three—four, including you—between her fists, and I can't sit back and watch my father gift her a kingdom of ruin. We used to stand for something. The Nobles were remarkable, apex humans who could flip the world over with one flick of their finger. This room?" I sweep my arm out. "It has harbored riches you wouldn't believe. Minds that would blow you away. We encouraged capitalism, free-thinking, revolution, and innovation. Astronauts stood where I am. Presidents and bio-scientists. And our sisters, the Virtues, were encouraged to do the same. We operated as one, Callie, and if I don't find a way to bring them together again, I represent nothing. Was raised by nothing. I am *not* nothing."

I say it through clenched teeth, but low thunder accompanies my words. One with erratic lightning.

Callie flinches, but she unfolds and pushes to her feet. Her plaid skirt covers her sweet spot as she rises, and her hair conceals her nipples when she straightens.

Creating a shield of her own sort.

And when her eyes flick to mine, they display a burning, inner core.

"You are so far from zero," she says. "I wish you'd see that. Instead, you're pushing me away. Intending me to suffer."

A sharp rebuttal forms against my lips, but I temper it into a sneer. "I'm sorry you see it that way, because all I'm aiming for is the sacrifice of one chick in order to gift my secret society the limitless power they lost."

She gnaws on her lower lip, a faraway look cresting over her face. "Will you stop Sabine from trafficking girls?"

My gut clenches at her sharp swing into acceptance. I eye her suspiciously because of it. "I said 'reform,' didn't I?"

Callie doesn't wince at the callousness. "With your plans in play, no one will believe I'm the descendent of Rose Briar. My ravings will be solidified by your aggression toward me. I'll become the nothing Sabine wants."

I'd rather you become nothing than lose you.

The words tickle the back of my mind, but don't dare come forward. Instead, I hold her stare, this half-dressed, tousled, prep school reject in a way I can't hold her with my hands. "It's the only way to bring Sabine to my side without destroying the societies."

Callie steps back, and with slow, stilted movements, she gets dressed. I watch her in silence until her last shred of clothing is slipped on, then follow suit.

"I want them destroyed. You want them reformed," she says as I'm fixing my jacket at the collar. "Maybe you're right. We can't be together with such opposite goals in mind."

"We can't be together for a lot of reasons. I'll admit I'm hot for you and have trouble keeping my dick in my pants every time I see your tits, but it stops there. I can control myself for the greater good."

I brace for Callie's reaction, knowing I've hurt her. As expected, her inner flame flickers out, yet I wonder, while her heart turns to cinders, if any embers of protest remain, like how I lost myself in her heat, or the way her strokes create tremors across my skin, and she makes me see stars.

Perhaps it would mean something to her if she knew no one else has ever been so successful in my undoing.

I sling my bag onto my shoulder. "I assume you know the way out. See you around, possum."

Then I turn my back on her.

Unfortunately for both of us, I'll never be the one to confess.

CHASE'S abrupt departure allows me to make it to my English Lit exam with one minute to spare.

I huff into my seat, still smelling like him, the tips of my hair carrying his cologne and my body lingering with the sweat of our sex as I fish through my bag for a pencil.

As the professor hands out exams, floating through aisles with the flutter of paper and the expected, monotone speech about the consequences of cheating, my heart sits like a spade at the bottom of my stomach, its sharp edge spearing me with every fidget, every thought, every frown, involving Chase.

He wants to make my life hell from here on out. Little does he know, I've been living in that fiery pit since my mother was killed.

What will a few more rumors do? Or heightened forms of harassment? Christmas break is coming up. I'll escape, regroup, and find the calm I need to *slit Sabine's fucking throat.*

I tell myself this as the exam is slipped onto my desk. Simple essay questions meant to revolve around our reading assignments for this semester, but all I see is, *You might be able to handle more Briarcliff trash thrown at your face, but what about Chase's cold, soulless stare? How will you handle the facets of his smile as it transforms into a sneer, or the blackening of his heart the longer he tortures you? Explain these points as thoroughly and with as much detail as you can in the section below.*

For bonus points, elaborate about your dead best friend and how it feels having her dried blood on your soul.

The pencil snaps in my hand.

"Here."

The soft, wispy voice comes from my left, accompanied by a manicured hand dangling a spare pencil.

I follow the thin fingers to the delicate, pale wrist, all the way up to bottle-clear, gray eyes fringed with black lashes.

My lips part on a scoff. "I don't want your lead poisoning."

Falyn flicks the pencil with a perfect arc of her fingers and falls back into her chair. "Suit yourself, possum. I was only trying to be nice to my new sister."

Hate fills my body so fast, it leaks venom through my teeth. "You talk about sisters like it means something, when the blood of one of them is still wet on your marble floor—"

"Ladies!" the professor barks from her desk, the lenses of her glasses flashing white with her sharp look. "One warning. That's it."

Falyn's lower lip juts out, feigning proper chastisement, and she goes back to her exam.

I no longer have anything to write with, and we're not allowed to go through our bag once the exam starts. There's no sense of panic in my chest, since leaving an exam blank is the least of my problems. I bury my head in my hands instead.

When the bell goes off, I pry my eyes open, away from the soothing black, and return to the overly bright, obnoxiously loud classroom, the remaining students popping out of their seats or feverishly scribbling the last of their desperate attempts onto their papers.

"Pencils and pens down!" the professor calls, while students jostle each other and scuttle from their seats.

My limp hands lay on my exam, palms open and empty.

"Nice try, possum," Falyn says as she passes, her perfume singeing my nostrils. "Can't blame you, though. It must be hard to focus after the trauma you experienced."

Red coats my vision, turning my papers scarlet and my nails into ruby talons. I rip my gaze up and into Falyn. "You're a cold-hearted bitch. Do you even mourn her? Did she mean anything to you?"

"Who?" Falyn arches a brow. "Ivy? Of course, I feel bad for her. She's in Philly nursing her mom back to health. Or waiting it out until her mom croaks. Whichever. Either way, her vacant spot has to be filled." Falyn shrugs. "She left it up to me to bring our sisters together, which I'm trying to do with you, if you weren't so bitchy about it."

My entire body goes cold. "Falyn." I rise from my seat. "It's all a lie. Ivy's dead, and you can't take her place."

For a brief moment, Falyn's stare turns unsure, but a fast coating of disdain erases the fracture. "There's no guarantee Ivy will make it back next semester. Somebody has to become captain of crew, and I'm next in line."

I grab Falyn's wrist. Cling to it. "You don't want it. Tell Sabine no."

"*Ow.*" Falyn tries to yank her wrist from my grip. "Let *go*, psycho vermin."

"I will if you promise not to be the next princess—I mean, captain." I glance around at the lingering students, some whose attention we caught. "I can't explain right now, but being a captain is so much worse than you think—"

"Get your claws off her, possum," a deep voice comes from the doorway.

My body responds automatically. I release Falyn, but a sickening dread prevents me from looking toward the door.

"Falyn," Chase says. "With me."

Falyn purses her lips, throwing a pert, "It is *so* obvious why you don't want me to be the next captain, Callie. And pathetic," before she sidles over to Chase ... and Tempest, and Rio, the three of them waiting for her in the doorway.

I swallow, collecting my things as if I don't feel Chase's assessing, dead-eyed stare on the body he ravished not two hours ago. "Touch her again, possum, and I'll have to make you pay."

Glancing at him through my lashes, I pull my bag tighter to my chest. "Tell me, is this Prince Charming coming to protect his new princess, or am I staring at the evil sorcerer about to lay the same curse on Falyn that fell on Ivy?"

Chase's jaw tics, but otherwise, he's stone. His family name. His future. "You and your fairytales. Wake the fuck up. Your life would be so much simpler."

"I'm wide awake," I retort, my eyes growing hot. "And you are not taking me down. Do whatever you want, protect the assholes, defend the bullies." I point at Falyn. "They break so much easier than the underdogs. If Ivy couldn't fight it, there's no way Falyn can take the weight of the title. Don't put her in that position."

"Briarcliff has enough saints lording over us," Chase says with his infallible stare. "Do I need to cut you into the glass windows, too? Stay out of it. I've warned you once."

I search for the boy laying in my arms on a stone floor, draped in Briarcliff colors but heated by my kisses alone. I really do. Not one flicker of inner pain mars his perfect face. I'm met with calculated hate. He's nocked his poisoned arrow, and he's aiming for my jugular.

"You have no one, Callie," Chase continues quietly. Falyn floats to his side.

He throws his arm around her shoulders. Falyn's cheeks flush with surprised delight, and she loops an arm around the front of his torso, tipping her chin up at him, then leveling me with a triumphant look.

I pretend like my heart isn't already dust. I respond, through numbed lips, "I certainly don't have you."

Chase tips his head in acknowledgement, then swivels around, dragging a lopsided Falyn with him as she tries to keep up with his strides.

Tempest salutes me, his eyes betraying nothing as he follows Chase into the halls.

Rio, damn him, grins at me with his teeth and says as his parting shot, "When I talk to Ivy tonight, I'll give her your best, you fucking freak."

Callie

BIOLOGY IS JUST as big a mess as English Lit, and calculus before that.

I risk being kicked out before my last semester even begins, but I can't find the inner turmoil necessary to kick my ass into high gear.

Maybe leaving is for the best.

By staying on, I'm putting myself in danger.

If I leave, my Briar legacy won't matter, Sabine will live on as a vindictive queen, Falyn will become a porcelain plaything like she's always wanted, and Chase will...

Chase will...

Ivy won't...

My mom will never...

I shove into my dorm, my winter coat puddling to my feet as I storm into the kitchenette, throwing open cupboards and searching for the bottle of vodka I know Emma stashes here somewhere.

Emma's quiet voice sounds at my back. "I'd ask you what was wrong, but that'd be a stupid question."

The top cupboards don't provide me with anything, so I bend down and pillage the bottom shelves. "Where's your—" *Goddammit. Why must everything be so hidden all the time?* "I need—" *There.* My hand scrapes across a frosted, cylindrical surface. It's in the corner cupboard, behind the lazy Susan. I twist off the cap, fall onto my haunches, and chug on my knees.

"Are you sure getting drunk is the best way to handle this?"

The burn of room temperature vodka at my throat is my answer.

"Oh, Callie." Emma shuffles closer. She crouches to my level and puts her hands on my shoulders.

I meet her eyes through a blurred haze. Vodka dribbles from the corners of my mouth. My cheeks are hot, warm and sticky like the vodka dripping from my chin, but my head's not tipped back that far. There shouldn't be vodka on my cheeks.

625

It's because I'm crying.

My cheeks are wet because I'm crying.

A wet hiccup leaves my mouth, and I pull the bottle from my lips and gag. Then I sob, the half empty bottle leaving my lifeless fingers, clanging to the floor beside me, spilling clear fluid across our floors, spreading like blood.

Emma's forehead crumples, and she pulls me into her chest. "Let it out."

My lips rip apart, my teeth going dry from the sudden suck of air, and I wail.

I howl in her arms, my nails digging into her flesh, and I weep for my mom. For Ivy. For Chase.

For me.

Callie

I'M MEANT to be thankful on Fridays.

TGIF, right?

It's the last day of school before Christmas break, and my final exam before I can exit these halls and find relief in New York City for two weeks. All I have to do is make it through three more hours, then by lunch time, I'm on a train back to meet my new baby sister.

I hold onto that flash of goodness as I roll onto my back but hit something soft on the way.

"Oomf," Emma moans, frowning as she pushes me off her.

"Oh. Sorry." I sit up, pushing my hair out of my face and taking stock of my surroundings.

Emma's shelves stare back at me, barren of pictures but full of knick-knacks like vintage My Little Ponies and various POP figurines of Disney villains.

It hits me at the same time I tuck my hair behind my ears and cock my head at a miniature Darth Vader. I've never been in Emma's room before.

And yet here I sit, in her bed where she comforted me for hours last night as I drained the last of her smuggled alcohol and tore out my heart for the third time.

The headache hits me next.

"Ugh," I moan, leaning my forehead into my hand as I struggle to stand.

"Good. Alcohol poisoning didn't take you like I thought it might." Emma sits up, her blonde hair a scraggly mess on top of her head.

"I'll deal," I groan, then stumble out of her bed, cutting through our central area and into my room.

We don't talk much as we get ready, Emma showering first while I funnel Tylenol and find a piece of bread to line my stomach. Neither of us mention last night or the way Emma patted my back and stroked my hair, offering comfort where her brother couldn't—or wouldn't.

It's not in Emma's nature to rehash her sincerity, and I don't expect it from her as we finish putting on our uniforms and head out the door.

She was there for me, like she always is, in my worst moments.

Emma's glued to her phone as we wander down the hallway, glowering so hard at it, I'm surprised the screen isn't forming cracks under her glare.

"Do you have plans for the holidays?" I ask her as we wait for the elevators. The look on her face instantly makes me feel dumb for asking it, but what am I supposed to do? Ask her how she'll handle Ivy's murder and Sabine's revenge over the break in a public hallway?

A few girls cluster behind us, instantly putting hands to mouths as they whisper to each other and slide glances at me, but I ignore them.

"I'm going to my mom's in LA," she answers, but twists her lips. "It's been a while since I've seen her."

"Is Chase going, too?" I ask, then frown as the girls' giggles get louder.

The elevator dings open, and we step in. The three girls follow.

"He usually hangs back with our father. They're Scrooges on Christmas day, but they go to the Harringtons on Christmas Eve. Father and Sabine might go on a couples' vacation. My brother might just be the Grinch this year, alone in our lake house, instead of Scrooge."

"How nice." My voice comes out hoarse. "I'm sure it'll be extra special for everyone this year."

"*She wishes he was the baby daddy, just like Piper did.*"

I turn sharply to the voice. One girl catches her breath in surprise, then grins. "Can I help you?"

"What did you just say?" I ask.

Emma pockets her phone and grabs my arm. "Leave it. Let's get through the morning."

The girl responds anyway. "I didn't say anything, you furry whore."

My brows jump. "Excuse me?"

"Do you even wax down there?"

Another, braver girl asks, "Or is that what Dr. Luke liked so much about you?"

"He's hot, sure, but he's so fucking old. He probably enjoys a full bush," the last one adds.

I gape at them. "What the hell?"

The elevator slides open, and Emma latches onto me so hard, I trip over my feet as we exit. Emma wears a look of such determination as she pushes through the front doors, I'm forced to ask, "What are they talking about?"

"Another dumb rumor," is all she says before I stumble out of the building and into the blinding white of day.

Emma leaves me in the West Wing, wishing me an aloof "good luck" before she heads off to her Global Studies exam.

It's with the listless trail of a ghost that I make it to biology and take my seat, aiming to be just as invisible.

I'm amazed I've made it this far, considering the trauma that keeps replaying behind my eyes, the dulled, vodka-induced headache acting like a macabre music track replaying over Ivy's dying body and Chase's coldblooded dismissal.

Is this all that's left of me? I wonder as I stare at the black laminate of my desk. *Am I nothing but a vessel of death and loneliness?*

"Baby killer."

I jolt at the hiss at my back, then turn.

The guy meets my confused look with a morbid grin, adding, "Teacher fucker."

Pointing to my chest, I ask, "Are you referring to me?"

"Ain't no other chick I know that gets herself an abortion on a teacher's salary." He licks his top row of teeth.

"Huh?" My vision grows smaller with all the brow-furrowing I'm doing.

A *slam* makes me jump in my seat. Falyn's dropped her books on her lab desk and slithers onto her stool across from me. "Secret's out, possum. Might as well own up to your hideousness."

I shake my head, but only a confused fugue follows. My email about Ivy's murder goes unnoticed, yet what Emma dubbed "another stupid rumor" gets the spotlight?

"What now, Falyn?" I ask, but I'm conscious of the growing stares, and the curious, car-accident attention that's directed my way as more students filter into the classroom and take their seats.

"At least Piper still had the kid in her belly when she died," someone in the back mutters, but it's loud enough for the entire room to hear.

"Yeah, this one decided to have her womb scraped out instead of 'fess up to fucking Dr. Luke, too," his friend responds.

My palms slam against my desk as I stand. "The hell?"

Falyn pipes up. "Admit it, you got an abortion in a desperate move to hide your sluttiness before you went after Chase."

"I did no such thing!"

"Oh, no?" The tip of Falyn's tongue pokes out between her smirk. "Prove it ... 'cause the whole school's talking about you fucking Dr. Luke the second Piper was out of the way. Does the man just not use a condom?" She cackles. "Or do his gray-haired pubes just taste that good?"

This has Chase written all over it is the first thought to sink into my brain as my knees turn to gel, and I fall into my seat. *He swore it'd be worse this time.*

"All right, class!" The professor wanders in, clapping his hands for attention. "Are we ready for our final exam before our highly anticipated break?" He scans the classroom, his hands clasped in front of him. "Who's excited for Santa?"

The class groans in response.

"No? Your teenaged years have jaded you all, sadly. Well, here's your first sack of coal. Grab an exam from the top of the pile and pass it back."

Falyn cuts one last gleeful look my way before turning to the front.

I work hard to focus on the questions, do the experiments, and write down the answers, but whispers and fake coughs keep getting in the way.

Possum probably used tweezers...

So pathetic...
Like Chase would ever want her saggy pussy now...
Loser.
Fugly Piper wannabe.
But it's the last one. Oh, the last one. That gets me.
Murderer.

I fly out of my seat, my stool toppling onto its side. It skids across the floor with a metallic shriek.

Heads pop up from papers, most mouths agape. Falyn props her chin in her hand, watching me with a hungry menace.

I ignore them all and storm to the front of the room, tossing my unfinished exam on the professor's desk.

"Miss Ryan, what on Earth...?"

"I don't feel well," I mumble, then careen out of the classroom before the redness creeps from my cheeks into the whites of my eyes.

The hallway's deserted, the usual proctors either completing their own exams or hooking up in custodial closets and empty classrooms.

Briarcliff Academy's lack of supervision was always obvious, but now I'm disgusted by it. My steps echo through the hallway, and a cold draft follows my every move. None of it dissipates the heating of my bones or boiling of my blood.

Ivy's dead. Piper's dead. Both murdered, and all they can talk about is a malicious rumor about a fake baby I had while fake-fucking a fired professor.

My coat's in my locker, so I brace myself for the long walk ahead of me to get to the opposite wing before the clocktower tolls, signaling the rush of students out of classrooms and the start of winter holidays. I don't want to be caught up in the tide. My shoes squeak against the flawlessly polished floors as I hurry my steps, but the vicious energy sparking against my joints doesn't subside.

"Dipping out early, huh, possum?"

My rubber soles shriek on my abrupt halt in the middle of the hallway.

"Probably a good idea, considering what's leaked to the student body," the deep voice—the *familiar* baritone—continues.

I don't turn around. Counting the tiles at the tips of my shoes, I whisper, "Leave me alone."

"I won't."

With a slow, aching arc, I swivel to the voice.

Chase's smooth, undeterred features stare back at me.

My expression is probably war-torn and famished compared to his, lost in a battlefield where neither side won. He sees it, he must, but there's no reaction in that untarnished expression of his.

"Did none of what we had mean anything to you?" My voice, though low, curls around the thick stone columns and wisps its way into Chase's ear. "Or did it mean so much, you have to eviscerate me in order to separate yourself from any sort of warmth whatsoever?"

I search for a flinch of understanding, a tic of emotion, but he gives me nothing. "I'm doing what I have to."

"No." My heart thumps, filling in the spaces between our breaths.

"You don't see the value in it?" Chase angles his head, resembling a beautiful demon he'd kept so well hidden until now.

"How can I see value in filthy rumors and disgusting gossip?"

"The worse I torture you, the better it is for both of us."

"Says the guy who comes out a king for it."

"Callie." He steps forward.

I skitter back. "Don't you dare come near me."

"I told you what would come next. We talked about this. If your dignity is more important than your life, then I'm sorry to say—"

"It's *erasing* Ivy!" My shout bounces off the walls, the portraits of alumni in their gold-framed paintings seeming to hurl my words right back into the heart of me.

And there it is. The flinch I was waiting for. Yet, instead of being satiated by it, I'm starving for more. More hurt. More humiliation. More pain.

I rake him from head to foot, this golden boy with eyes drenched in liquid bronze, who blinded me and freed me all at the same time.

I'm desperate to stride right up to him and throw him against the wall. Toss him across the floor. My mind begs to break his heart the way he's shattered mine.

One foot steps forward. Then the next.

Chase doesn't react, preferring to observe my performance with cold disdain.

My eyes skate to the side where a large trash bin is nestled beneath an old painting of some benefactor or another. Chase follows the movement and arches a brow of careful disinterest.

That's all it takes for me to storm to the bin, throw off the lid, pick it up, and hurl the contents at Chase.

Crumbled paper scatters across the floor.

Half-empty coffee cups splatter against his shirt and pants.

An open ketchup packet hits him in the chin, leaving a trail of red under his lip.

The empty bin makes a hollow, clanging sound as it hits the floor at my feet, followed by my heaving breaths.

Chase doesn't move. Doesn't twitch.

As the trash floats, then settles around him, the clocktower bell clangs some distance away.

We remain in a brutal lock of eyes, his smoldering, mine alight with rage.

Doors crash open as students sprint out of classrooms, their first taste of freedom since the semester began, but shoes skid to a stop almost instantly. Cries and hollers die out in favor of ogling the Briarcliff prince covered in trash. Some search for hidden phones in their bags and blazers.

A few dare to come closer.

I expect Chase to unleash. To unhinge his jaw and punish me for daring to malign his perfectly pressed appearance. Or at the very least, to drag his hand through his hair and shake off the used tissues and cold noodles dangling there.

He does none of those things.

Just looks at me coldly. Brutal and haunted.

Haunted?

No way. I have to be hallucinating the fragments of misery in his eyes. Misery he caused. Happiness he refuses to consider.

We can beat this together ... I tried to will his way in the Nobles' crypt, but Chase refused, considering me a weakness, an unnecessary accessory to his plans to overthrow his father.

I've never wanted to punch someone yet wrap my arms around them at the same time. The ache is real, and it sits right at the base of my ribs.

Chase parts his lips, his tongue coming dangerously close to the stains I put on his face when it darts out to suck on one of his canines. "You will come to regret this day, possum."

"Do your worst," I retort. "I guarantee it'll never be as bad as watching the guy you loved bow to a woman who brutalizes and kills."

This time, I step all the way up to him, raising my chin one notch. Then two. "All because he's scared."

Chase's mouth twists into a snarl, but I don't wait around for the mushroom cloud of consequence. I turn my back on him and stride down the hall, my quaking limbs for once shrouded and protected by a Briarcliff uniform.

Callie

I **TOLD** him I loved him.

What the *fuck* is wrong with me?

Sitting back in my seat on the train, I watch the afternoon swirl into greens and blues as we chug toward the city, my duffel squished between me and the window as I pretend not to smell the pastrami sandwich a businessman eats beside me.

My stomach rumbles in protest. I mentally remind it that these vicious swings between nausea and starvation can't be good for it, so could it kindly shut up?

The snack cart comes by, and my stomach shows no signs of quieting down. I cave and buy a bag of mini pretzels. As soon as the salt hits my tastebuds, my stomach revolts.

See? Told you.

And now I'm arguing with an organ.

"*Argh,*" I moan in frustration, smacking against my headrest. The guy beside me doesn't flinch at my strange behavior, instead licking remnants of mustard off his fingers before settling in with his tablet.

I'd lost it on Chase, very publicly and with a lot of witnesses. My heart was all-in, but not in the way I'd fantasized. Dreaming of Chase's public declaration of protection, his claiming of *me*, crept into all corners of my mind most nights. Never did I envision a scenario where I'd make *him* the possum with garbage clinging to his body the way his tailored uniform usually did.

He must hate me now. Possibly he always did. Maybe, there was never any love to be lost between us. Just sex and pleasure. Either way, it's all gone now, dust and ash I've left behind at Briarcliff, a two-week reprieve where I don't have to breathe the fumes.

I should be relieved, but I'm worried instead.

Anxious over Sabine. There hasn't been a whisper or a flash of movement since … since...

I shut my eyes tight as images of Ivy splayed across the temple floor flash forward.

My body's thrown in the darkness, and my eyes pop wide at the train's sudden stop. Pulse beating like a drum in my ears, I cling to the window, allowing its cold to seep into the heat of the moment and dissipate the horror.

"You okay, sweetheart?" the businessman asks with a thick Queens accent.

After a single gulp, I nod, unable to yet turn my head. A brownish stain colors the back of the headrest in front me, serving as a stark reminder of my final words to Chase.

All because you're scared.

It's becoming awfully clear who that statement was really meant for.

"This your stop?" the man tries again. He's moved—standing above me and grabbing his overhead luggage. "'cause I think you have about five seconds before this sucker moves again."

Nodding, I shuffle out of my corner, hugging my duffel to my chest as the man steps aside and allows me through first.

I land on the platform in a dusty fugue, blinking fast and searching for my bearings before anyone I know sees me and asks me the dreaded question I wish to avoid the entire holiday: *What's wrong?*

It's impossible to put into words what haunts me, or even words that make sense. I tried with Ahmar and failed. The entire academy backs Sabine's story of Ivy's sudden departure ... not death. Chase makes clear his willingness to sacrifice himself to save the Nobles, and all *I* want to do is nuke the Virtues and take the Nobles down with them as collateral damage.

At the same time my thoughts circle, I'm scanning the crowd for a familiar face, taking tentative steps forward as I enter my old world.

I spot Ahmar after the second sweep, my footsteps picking up, my duffel swinging on its strap against my shoulder as I release it and start to run.

He glances up from his phone at the sudden blur of movement, then stretches his arms wide.

I fly into them with an *oomph*, clutching Ahmar close and smelling his familiar woodsy cologne as I bury my face in his chest.

"That's the kind of welcome I was waiting for!" he says, his chin digging into the top of my head.

I resist the urge to bawl, knotting my fingers in the fabric of his jacket instead. Ahmar's warm. Safe. He's home.

"Ah, Calla." His arms wrap tighter once he realizes I'm not letting go. "I gotcha, kiddo."

Sniffling, I untangle my hands from his coat, stepping back and swiping under my eyes. I take a few deep breaths, too, clinging to normalcy instead of another breakdown.

"Come on." Ahmar throws his arm around my shoulders and directs us to the exit. I'm thankful he doesn't press for more information or ask how I've been doing since our last, frantic phone call. "Pete and Lynda are waiting for you. I'll drop you off there."

"Sure."

In another time, I would've asked him to stop at our usual diner—*our* being his, Mom's and mine—for coffee and pancakes, but as my stomach insists, I can't keep up an act for very long. I'd rather have the distraction of my new sister, the flurry of newborn attention, than searching eyes across the table, cataloguing my every twitch and wondering if it's time for a longer stretch at a facility.

Ahmar takes us to his double-parked car on 42nd Street, opening the passenger door on his unmarked police vehicle so I can slide in.

It hasn't yet snowed in NYC, but the brisk, icy weather turns into condensation on my cheeks as soon as I get into the heated car. Ahmar hops into the driver's side, and in seconds, we're merged into congested city traffic and honking with the rest of them.

I allow Ahmar's curses at pedestrians and derby-bound taxis to settle around me like a comforting blanket, happy to make the ride in the city's version of a quiet evening.

When he pulls up to Meyer House, I straighten out of my relaxed flop against the passenger door.

"Here you are, kiddo."

"Aren't you coming in?"

"Nah. Not today. This is a moment you should enjoy with Pete and Lynda."

I ask, while reaching through the middle console for my duffel, "Have you met Blair yet?"

"Sure have. She's a cutie." Ahmar winks. "But you'll always be my baby girl."

The endearment pulls at the leaden chain in my chest. "Thanks, Ahmar. For the pickup, for the ride, for the…"

"Lack of interrogation?" Another wink. "You deserve a breather. Enjoy your time with your new baby sister. We'll meet up for coffee in a few days."

I'm not so mixed up that I can't sense the promise in the question. *We'll be having a serious talk* is all but scrolling in blinking red lights under his brows.

I nod, leaning over to kiss his cheek. "Got it."

Ahmar hasn't shaved in a few days, his scruff grating against my lips more than usual. I pull back, inspecting him and noticing the purple crescents under his eyes. "Are you sleeping okay?"

"Child, leave." He shoves me affectionately on the shoulder. "We'll have our mutual *come to Jesus* moments when I pick you up for pancakes. I'll text you."

"Okay," I say, but I leave him behind with great reluctance. It's not often I witness Ahmar appearing less than put-together. He uses his tailored appearance as somewhat of a shield to the murder and mayhem he witnesses constantly, taking his time grooming and making weekly barber appointments to counteract the ugliness of other humans.

I've seen him scruffy and unkempt in only one other situation, and I prefer not to dwell on it as I step up to Meyer House's stoop and watch his headlights disappear into the evening haze.

I take the rest of the stairs on a sigh, then stop, hovering near the door. Three months of residency doesn't give me the confidence to saunter in, nor am I considered just a visitor.

My fingers curl over the iron knocker, and I swing it against the door a few times before turning the knob and pushing in—falling somewhere in between.

"Hello?" I call, sliding my bag off my shoulders.

No answer.

Leaving my bag in the foyer, I take the curving staircase, my palm brushing against the cold, solid brass of the railing. "Anyone home?"

The lights are dimmed but not shut off. They have to be around here somewhere.

When the second floor gives me nothing, I make my way to the third, and that's where I find them.

"Hi—"

"*Shh!*" Dad shushes me, though it's seemingly not enough because he also elbow-wrestles me out of the nursery. "We just got her to sleep."

"Oh, sorry," I say in a much softer voice, but peer over his shoulder.

"You want to see her?" he whispers, then nudges me forward. "Go on. But *carefully*. And with *no footsteps*."

Cautiously, I creep into the room, the white trim of the curtains and bassinet framing the shadows with lace.

Blair's face comes into view as I stop beside Lynda, a slip of white cheek peering out of the blanket wrapped tightly around the tiny form.

Impossibly small fingers appear under Blair's neck, sneaking out of her wrapping as she spreads them wide, then clenches them closed again. She coos, her eyes crescents of slumber, and does a little wiggle in her pink cocoon.

"She's like a dancing burrito," I murmur, but the smile crossing my face is warm, real, and wide.

Lynda adjusts one of her nightgown's straps as she straightens and notices me. "Callie! You're here!"

My eyes widen at her excited shout at the same time Dad's face pales.

"Relax, Pete," Lynda says as she envelopes me in a fragrant hug filled with baby powder and ... something sewer-like I can't identify. Baby poop? "Blair rivals an alcohol-induced fraternity hazing once she's down. It's so good to see you, honey."

"You, too," I say, squished against her suddenly voluminous breasts. Our relationship, while cloudy, seems to have cleared into a light fog since Blair was born, and I accept her embrace.

Her Briarcliff roots don't escape my thoughts, nor her high school connection to my mother, but mustering the strength to confront her while she's in day-old pajamas with her normally sleek blonde hair in a sagging top-knot doesn't seem like the best time to create stormy skies again.

Plus, I'm fucking exhausted. Like traumatically, face-down-in-the-dirt, knocked out.

Lynda must sense the direction of my thoughts. "You look so piqued, honey. Long day? You can meet Blair when she's awake in the morning. Or in two hours. How was your last exam this morning? Oh—there's dinner waiting for you downstairs. A crown roast of some sort. Lamb? Help me out here, Pete."

"We've now reached the time of night where my wife is inexplicably ripe—with energy." Pete smiles tightly, his eyes a little wild as he rests his attention on her. "I mean *blooming* with energy. She's filled with chatter. Might I leave you two to it?"

"Sure, Dad." I give him the exit he so desperately needs. "I'll hang with Lynda for a while."

"But not too long," he admonishes. "Lynda's right—you look as tired as we do."

"Exams were ... a lot."

"I bet. Briarcliff doesn't pride itself on poor test-taking. Glad you survived. I'll see you in a few."

His word-choice beats against my skull. *Survived.*

Barely, Dad.

As my dad escapes to the fourth floor of the brownstone to face-plant somewhere, Lynda latches onto my hand and drags me down to the first, where the dining room and a re-heated crown roast await.

"Are you hungry? I'm *starving*." Lynda hops a few steps in front of me. "I'll eat the whole lamb if they let me. They don't teach you in breastfeeding school how dang starved you become."

"Breastfeeding school?"

"Oh yeah. I made Pete attend three of them with me. And swaddling, baby massage, pregnancy yoga..."

As she prattles on, my lips pull into what I hope is a smile as I follow her into the expansive, nineteenth-century dining area, with gold-trimmed panel walls and priceless murals dating back to Lynda's ancestors.

I take a seat next to her at the head of the table, Sophia bursting in just as we sit down.

"Calla Lily! You've arrived!"

Another full-bosomed hug encases me, but as Sophia's heartbeat thrums in my ears, I think this is the closest I've ever come to *home* since Mom.

"Let me get the roast and all the veggies. Good Lord." Sophie pinches my arm as she draws back, clucking. "What are you, an emo hipster? You need meat on these bones."

Sophia heads through the doors to collect our plates. To give myself something to do, I grab the intricately folded napkin from the place setting and smooth it across my lap.

"A little lost?"

I glance up at Lynda's quiet question, surprised to see her red-rimmed but bright blue gaze on me. "I mean no offense—I always feel out of place in crazy-rich rooms."

"Does that discomfort include Briarcliff's classrooms?" she asks.

My hands still on my napkin.

"I realize I'm in a newborn bubble, but I haven't forgotten our phone conversation." Lynda reaches toward me, then lays her hand on the table, palm up.

I stare at her open hand. Watch as her fingers slowly close over her empty palm, a space I was supposed to fill.

"Callie, I don't think I've ever told you how sorry I am about your mother."

"Probably because I didn't give you the chance." I have to stare at the ceiling for this, blinking back the swell of emotion.

"We had a rough start, didn't we? And I don't think I made it any better by keeping my connection to Meredith from you."

My chin falls, and I worry the corner of my napkin. "You told the police. And you hadn't even reunited with my dad yet. That's all that matters."

"No, honey, it doesn't. I should've told you, too, the instant Pete and I grew serious. Now I might be too late. An apology seems so banal, especially considering your worries over your mom's connection to Briarcliff and her..."

"Murder. You can say it." For me at least, it's rolling off my tongue with disturbing ease.

"Yes. Murder. I didn't know her very well, but no one deserves to be treated like that in the end."

I worry the inside of my cheek, glancing at the swinging door Sophia left through. "You said you didn't know Sabine Harrington that well, either."

Lynda murmurs her agreement, then settles against her chair. "She was part of the popular clique. I wasn't." Now it's Lynda's turn to glance at the door. "It was only through the Virtues she really spoke to me, and that was mostly to offer up instructions or chastise my propriety and all the smallest errors I needed to correct if I wanted to keep my membership in the society." Lynda adds quietly, "Even now, she does it."

I lean forward, my better half warning me away from this line of discussion. Lynda's anxious over Blair's safety. She has a new family to think about and a husband who truly doesn't grasp the consequences of Briarcliff secret societies. I should back off, allow her to live a cushioned life where Virtuous membership simply means more perks, better parties, and called-in favors like instructing Lynda to send her newest stepchild to Briarcliff Academy for her senior year. But I can't stop. "Were you ever introduced to older men when you were at Briarcliff?"

A tiny line forms between Lynda's brows. "Such as alumni? Maybe. Possibly. At our underground balls and such."

I risk adding more detail with the next question. "Did you ever notice a Virtue quieter than the others? Standing off to the side at these balls or not contributing much to the meetings, but seemingly protected by Sabine or the current queen?"

"There were always girls like those. The sweet and kind ones who were beautiful inside and out."

The opening is there, but my throat prematurely burns with the consequences. I ask, through thickened tissue, "Was my mother one of them?"

"Meredith?" Lynda cocks a smile. "Not a chance, honey."

My lungs deflate in relief.

"Meredith was outspoken and didn't hesitate to criticize how Sabine was taking on the role of queen before it was earned. I doubt those two ever got along, but in the Society, it was especially tense. In fact, your mom often sought out the girls you're speaking of and made them feel welcome. Experience has taught me that the quiet ones are either the most nervous, or the most diabolical. I think Meredith knew that, too." She gives a closed-mouth chuckle, shaking her head. "Meredith had a knack for befriending the prickly ones, too, but she could never get through to Sabine. Strange, considering the two were matched in every aspect. Academics, sports..."

Not Briar blood, I interject silently. *The trait Sabine covets the most.*

"...boyfriends. Lord, they were cats when it came to boys."

The Meredith she talks about still doesn't connect in my mind. I can't picture

Mom as a high-schooler, jealous over boys. I *can* picture Mom seeking out the outcasts and loners and making them her friends. But how much did she know? Was Sabine's future grandmother-in-law in the midst of grooming them for her new, iniquitous project?

I open my mouth to ask Lynda to elaborate, but Sophia chooses that time to come in with dinner, plated on a silver platter.

"Apologies," she says as she sets the professionally garnished platter in the middle. "It's been so long since we've hosted, and I wanted to make this special on Callie's first day home."

"I love it," I say, and pull Sophia into a side-hug as she stands between us. "It smells freaking divine."

Lies, my stomach grumbles, swaying dramatically. I swallow a ball of saliva, determined to eat a few bites and acknowledge Sophia's hard work.

Sophia squeezes my shoulder with her usual affectionate death grip, then goes about carving the roast and plating. I sit back, allowing the fuss, but desperate to get back to the conversation. Dad could come in at any second, effectively ruining any opening I had with Lynda.

Let Lynda be, he'd say. *She's had a game-changing few weeks and is only now finding her feet.*

Studying the fresh treads of crow's feet around Lynda's eyes and the exhausted sag of her usually expertly filled-in lips, I can agree with him.

But my mother's death matters more.

Sophia finishes, and as soon as the door swings shut behind her, I ask, "Which guy did Mom and Sabine fight over?"

Lynda pauses with her fork in mid-air, the silver sparkling under the chandelier. She hasn't taken her first bite yet. "Honey, it was a long time ago. I can't remember."

"She was eighteen when she got pregnant with me."

Lynda's knife scrapes across porcelain. Her wide-set eyes flick up to mine. "Oh. Oh, sweetie. Here I am being so cavalier when the whole time, you're thinking I know … oh, gosh, that I might know who your father is?"

Her shock resembles my own. I didn't expect her to say something like that. I only wanted to dig up more dirt about Sabine and Mom's history. With Ivy's brutal killing, my mom's murder, and my alliance with Chase morphing into a rivalry, I don't have the capacity to handle my missing baby daddy baggage.

So why is my stupid mind bringing it up?

"How are two of my favorite girls doing?" Dad breezes in, ruffling the top of my head and kissing Lynda's before taking a seat across from me. "I'm surprised half this lamb isn't gone by now."

Lynda's attention doesn't stray. I freeze in my seat, internally begging her not to bring it up while Dad's here.

She blinks, then breaks our stare and turns to Dad. "Give me time, babe. This meat is *mine*."

Releasing a *whoosh* of breath, I paste on a smile, cutting into my dinner, then chewing and swallowing just like they are.

None of us bring up my haggard phone call for the rest of the meal. The few seconds of weighted study Dad gives me every time he looks up from his dinner is couched with a smile and a wink.

We pretend we're fine.

That Briarcliff isn't strung between us on a butcher's hook.

We're not.

Callie

CHRISTMAS EVE in New York City is snowless, blinding with the sunlit shine of skyscrapers, and colorful with determined workaholics, fascinated tourists, and expertly hung Christmas lights.

The day is mild for winter, and I offered to take Blair on a stroll down Madison Avenue to see the decorated storefront windows. Dad hedged around the offer, blinking rapidly and wringing his hands. It felt awful, watching his trust crumbling away from me like the side of an abandoned building when we'd vowed to try and make it better. I bit back the urge to reason with him that I'd never, for one second, consider harming a *baby* for crying out loud, but my history isn't a shining one, and our relationship is so, so tenuous.

Lynda ended up saving us both. Considering her view of the Virtues, and my valid suspicions over being lied to by my mother's membership, she urged me to take Blair out for fresh air. That, and the purple overtaking the red in her eyes clearly begged for quiet solitude away from the baby, which I was only too happy to give.

Lynda's driver, Clifton, drove us to Midtown, parking in a nearby side-street and unfolding the stroller before hanging back a few blocks and watching my every step.

I don't mind Dad's not-so-subtle instructions to their driver to keep an eye on me. Sabine's odd silence causes a queasiness that has me glancing in every alleyway, hesitating under any scaffolding, and biting down on the back of my tongue every time Blair's stroller hits a pothole in the sidewalk. Sabine must be biding her time—or enjoying her vacation—after so successfully killing my best friend and getting away with it. It's her mind games at work: Sabine's well-aware of her power over me and how small I am compared to her. She doesn't need to end my life to show how easy it is to implode it.

Breathing in cold air, I set my shoulders and push the stroller faster, determined to enjoy this small slice of time with my new sister, even as a dark cloud hovers over my head.

It's not likely a two-week-old will have any interest in the beauty of retail celebration, but my spirits are lifted as I park the stroller in front of each window and admire the view. Blair's bundled tight and slumbers through most of it. I'm thankful for it, since I have no idea what to do with a screaming baby, other than to shove a bottle in her mouth. Every so often I get a text from Lynda making sure Blair's okay, but otherwise, I'm deep in the Christmas drift of Midtown, pushing the stroller slow and steady through the dense foot traffic of admirers and commuters alike.

A flash of blond strikes my vision just as I pull up to an intersection and wait by the lights. My heart kicks up, beating into my throat, but it couldn't be.

Chase is in Rhode Island.

Another gust of wind ruffles familiar, thick blond hair, and I watch, mystified, as the guy crosses Madison, his gray peacoat flapping behind him.

I shake my head, dislodging the image as the tall blond merges with other, well-tailored, suited men in various shades of black.

"Lady? You gonna walk or you gonna keep fairy-footin' around?" someone barks behind me.

I turn around and glare at the man before Blair and I travel into the intersection.

A screech of brakes jolts me alive, and I fly back with the stroller right before a car blows through us.

"Jesus Christ!" I screech, then point to the pedestrian walk sign at the same time the driver flips me off. "Are you *blind*?"

He rolls down his window, his elbow spearing through as he replies, "Fuckin' use your eyeballs, bitch!"

"I have a *baby*, you turd!"

Something bumps my shoulder—the rude guy waiting behind me. "You fuckin' spunk tissue, that's a *motha* you nearly ran over! A *motha*! What's wrong with you? You got a problem with a lady trying to walk her child across the road? You wanna go? *You wanna go with me?*"

And just like that, an asshole becomes my savior. Typical New York. I scamper away with an oblivious Blair, appreciative of the Brooklyn man for coming to my rescue, but schooled in the art of disappearing in the midst of a driver-pedestrian throwdown in the city.

The smell of freshly roasted coffee attracts my sense of smell as the men's voices fade into the background. A hot chocolate sounds like the perfect ending to my stroll with Blair, even if it comes at a mere $12 a pop. She bounces along with my picked-up speed, happily dreaming with pursed, rosebud lips, and I wrestle the door open into the warm interior, the sudden burst of lighting and belting of Christmas music doing nothing to disturb her sleep.

I think I like newborns.

The line isn't that long, and I take my place, putting one hand to my hip as the other rests on the stroller, and stare out the storefront window.

There.

Another burst of hair the color of dry sand popping up among sharp grays, serious blacks, and hopeful whites of NYC fashion.

It's not possible. I can't be wishing for Chase's presence on Christmas Eve. Not after what he's done and what I allowed myself to do *with* him. Too much has come between us. Avenging Ivy. Finding justice for my mother. Nuking Sabine. This holiday reprieve with the Meyer-Spencers is nice, but every time I glance down at my sister, I'm reminded of innocence and how easily it can be smothered by evil.

So much more important than *love*.

There it is again: that stupid feeling that creeps into my mind at the most unwanted times. I don't love Chase Stone. I don't care about him. I *don't*.

Disgusted with myself, I swivel to the front.

"Callie?"

I blink at the girl in front of me, dressed in a boyfriend blazer and pleather leggings, her shins hugged by gray, sheepskin boots with a criss-cross of endless laces. Her features solidify, familiarize, and I swallow a small gasp. "Sylvie?"

"My God, I thought it was you, but the stroller threw me." Sylvie tucks a long, mermaid-length strand of silvery blonde hair behind her ear as she stares down at Blair, her stack of gold bracelets jangling. "She's gorgeous."

"Yeah," I say, latching on to the wonderful distraction of Blair rather than ponder the impact of seeing Sylvie for the first time since her overdose. "She is."

Sylvia giggles when she reaches down to tickle one of Blair's exposed palms and Blair clamps around her finger. "She has your lips for sure."

"Oh—Jesus, no." I laugh too loudly. "She's not mine. She's, uh ... she's my sister."

Sylvie's eyes, anime-large on a normal day, stretch wide when she meets mine again. "Wow. A sister?"

"Yeah. Dad remarried." Shit, this is awkward. I wish for the line to go faster, but this is an artisan coffee shop on Madison Ave. On Christmas Eve. Even their drip coffee is a crazy pour-over method requiring at least ten minutes.

Why did I choose to come here again? Oh, right. Nearly being hit by a car and seeing the Ghost of Chase Present everywhere.

Next thing you know, I'll be seeing Sabine's malicious reflection in mirrors.

The thought of her face haunting me on Christmas Eve, with Blair mere inches away, causes a deep-seated shudder to crawl from the base of my spine. My grip clenches on the stroller.

"You okay?"

"Totally great." I rub my temple, smearing Sabine's image and looking for a pressure-point that could ease my headache. "You? What are you doing on Madison? This doesn't seem like your—I mean, I'm not trying to presume. Maybe you love coming here now, shopping at Saks and sampling rare hot chocolate beans..."

I'm rambling. And I'm *also* here. With a baby snoozing lavishly in the latest $1000 stroller.

Sylvie tucks her hair behind her ear again, a nervous habit she must have picked up after we stopped talking to each other. "Matt and I were looking at the window decorations, and like the little girl he is, he had to pee after we walked five blocks. So, you're still hanging out with Pete as your dad, huh?"

Since I don't know Sylvie well enough anymore to understand if that's a jibe, I respond, "Yep. We've reached a sort of understanding. He's tried to be there for me." It feels like a well-versed script on my tongue, but I keep my expression controlled. Solid.

Sylvie raises her brows. "It's really cool, you know. I love how you still call him

'Dad,' even after..." Sylvie trails off, chewing her lower lip but keeping her focus pinned on me. "I totally thought after losing your mom, you'd want nothing to do with him anymore."

"It surprised me, too," I say honestly. "But he's all I had left."

Sylvie's brown eyes shutter. Her hand drops from her hair.

"That's not what I—it's been a rough few months, and it's shocking, but Dad's been a steady source throughout it all." I take a breath. Sort my thoughts. Sylvie has no idea about Mom's hidden history, secret societies, and Briarcliff. She's a reflection of last year's life, when I mourned and partied and lost myself in swirls of meaningless, bottomless, blinding glitter.

And she nearly lost her life because of it.

Before I can add anything to this train wreck of a conversation, she says, "But here you are with a baby! It's great that you call her your sister even though you're not related. I'm sure Pete's beside himself with pride that he was finally able to have a daughter of his own. And you don't feel left out? That's loyalty right there."

I literally feel my throat bob as I try to keep my head high. "The opposite, actually. My family feels full."

Shockingly, I mean it. There will always be a Mom-sized hole in my heart, and maybe it takes confronting my past in the form of a former best friend to realize it, but it's Christmas Eve, and I'm actually looking forward to dinner with Dad, Lynda, and Blair.

"Forget it." She sighs, pulling on a hank of hair—a habit I recognize, and I'm wondering where I went wrong in the conversation. "Matt should be out of the bathroom soon. I'm planning to have our coffees before closing." She glances at the register, where one person stands between her and that promise. "If this lady moves her ass."

The woman hears, and peers over her shoulder to glare at Sylvie and ask where her Christmas spirit is. Sylvie quips, "It's at the bottom of the fucking cup of coffee I'd like to order."

I shuffle uncomfortably beside the stroller.

Sylvie ignores the lady as she huffs and turns back to me. "We were such shits back then, weren't we? Getting into all sorts of trouble. I'm glad to see you looking so great."

I cover my surprise at her perspective of me. "You too, Syl. You look..." *Fantastic. Bright. Flushed, full, and happy.* Yet the words don't come. Instead, I croak out, "I'm sorry. I'm sorry for everything."

Space opens up in front of the register, but Sylvie doesn't move. Just stares at me. Finally, she says, "You never called."

"I was forbidden. And I ... I didn't know if you even wanted to talk to me."

"If you'd tried, you would've figured out I was desperate to talk to you."

"God, Sylvie, I—your parents were threatening to sue. Lawyers told me to stay away. Cops warned me not to go near you." I stop, studying my old friend, a girl so waifish and sallow the last time I saw her, now brimming with health and unfeigned joy as soon as she mentioned Matt.

Ivy. In her I see Ivy, and I falter, my death-grip on the stroller's handle the only thing keeping me upright. The cruel irony isn't lost on me, how a friend I nearly killed picked herself up and righted her life, and the friend who *was* killed had her goodness snuffed out.

I am a magnet of misfortune, that much is clear. I look to Blair and choke back a sob. "I never wanted it to be like this."

"Me neither." Sylvie's soft voice drifts closer as she puts a hand on my shoulder and squeezes.

The register opens, but we remain in a stasis of distant comfort. Sylvie's hand on my shoulder. My eyes to the ground while my arm hangs limply between her squeeze and Blair's stroller handle.

Grumbling sounds at my back. Sylvie looks over my shoulder, blows the impatient patron a kiss, then drops her hand from my shoulder and steps up to the cashier.

She places her order for two coffees. "You?" she asks me.

"Oh—peppermint white mocha."

Sylvie smiles, saying to the barista, "If she hasn't changed since last Christmas, she'd also like whipped cream and candy cane sprinkles."

I smile wanly. "...'tis the season."

Sylvia waves away my offer to pay, and there's too many people behind me to argue the point, so I allow it, shuffling with her to the other side of the counter to wait for our drinks and finagle the stroller to fit between us.

"I forgive you," Sylvie says.

I glance up from Blair—still snoozing, always oblivious.

"Most of all," Sylvie continues, "I forgive myself. It took a long time for me to do that."

Shaking my head, I say, "It was my fault. I pressured you to experiment with me. I hated reality so much, yet I didn't want to enter a forced dreamland on my own—and I pushed you into a nightmare. I'm sorry, Sylvie. Every time I say it, *think* it, it doesn't seem enough, but I can't find other words. The thought of you on that floor..."

Sylvie shushes me by covering her hand on my own. "I take it you haven't forgiven yourself yet."

"How could I?"

"Because we were young and stupid. Still are. My brain is my own, though. I've owned up to my decision to stick junk in my veins. Matt helped me through it, sure —I dunno if I could've gotten through it without him. And yeah, I was mad at you. Ravenously furious, actually. But therapy, and Matt, and rehab, told me a different story where you weren't the villain. You were merely the rabbit hole I chose to fall into. You had your own demons, too. With your mom and being orphaned. Having a stepdad who you were totally sure killed her ... Callie, you were wrung out, too. And we got strung out, together. But we're out of it now. Right? We've moved on." She squeezes my hand. "I want to move on."

I squeeze back. "I want that, too. God, I ache for that."

"Then let yourself."

"I don't know if I ... there's so much I haven't told you."

Another blond flash changes the filter of my viewpoint, and my head snaps up, following the weave of gold through the crowded shop.

And closer to us.

As he approaches, the twinkling aura of my filter disappears. His angles change, a sharper chin emerging from a heart-shaped face. Sandy hair flopping against a forehead rather than a textural sweep across.

"Babe!" Sylvie wraps an arm around Matt's—Matt, *not* Chase—waist, tilting her head and accepting his kiss. "Look who I found! And she has a baby!"

Matt's mental flash-carding of memories can literally be seen scrolling across his face, his eyes popping wide when he puts a name to who I am and hears the word *baby*.

"Not mine," I say, the lighthearted chuckle that follows coming naturally. It ends on a choke the minute I realize how soothing and familiar it was coming out of my throat. "My sister."

"Shit. Callie. Congrats. Uh..." He looks to Sylvie, probably in an attempt to gauge how our conversation is going.

"We were catching up," Sylvie says. "Mainly it was me explaining to Callie that I don't blame her for almost dying anymore."

"Oh." Matt's brows jump, despite being well-versed in Sylvie's bluntness. "Well. Good."

I study him for signs—tics or flashes of anger, any clue of unshed blame directed at me for putting his girlfriend in a situation where she could've been killed.

My knees nearly buckle when I find none. Nothing except open curiosity as he gets a good look at me after almost a year of silence.

Could Sylvie be right? Am I deserving of forgiveness from these two? From *anyone*?

Our coffees come, and I swipe mine up with new fervor, itching to remove myself from the happy couple ... except, the urge to flee doesn't feel natural. Sylvie's question of forgiveness gnaws at the back of my head, shockingly drawing me closer instead of leaping for an escape.

"Sit with us," Sylvie says to me. She gives me the once-over, reading my body language. "Don't leave yet."

"Syl, maybe she—"

Sylvie cuts Matt off. "I won't interrogate you ... I swear. I'd like to catch up for real. See what you've been up to."

Ivy's loss clouds my vision. Chase's unexpected cruelty squeezes my throat. My mom's hidden bloodline stiffens my back, and I'm positive my anguish from the last few months is reflected in my eyes.

Sylvie zeroes in on my expression. "Don't tell me it's gotten worse for you since we last saw each other. How much bad luck can one person have?"

Blair gurgles from her luxurious recline, and grabbing at the opening, I search the attached diaper bag for a bottle. "I should feed her."

"Excellent. You'll do it while hanging out with us." Sylvie pulls me in the direction of a recently vacated table. "Because you've been through a ton of shit, including a dead mom."

Matt, sending me a sympathetic glance, helps Sylvie by nudging Blair's stroller forward.

Sylvie continues, "You deserve to dedicate some time to inane conversation where I regale you with our pointless semester at school and the lame friends I've tried to replace you with. Especially on Christmas Eve, of all nights. This is your second year without her, right? Your mom?"

My heart wrenches open. "I..."

"Sit your ass down, Ryan." Sylvie shoves me into a seat.

Sylvie may have forced me into a chair, but I stay where she put me, delicately nudging Blair's lips open with the bottle until she's sucking contentedly.

And I listen. Hang out. And catch up with old friends as if my mom is waiting for me at home, ordering in our favorite Italian and attempting to make hot chocolate on the stove—this time without burning it and covering up the faux pas with a mountain of marshmallows.

While it feels like I'm tugging on an old sweater a little too small for me, I appreciate the softness, the warmth. Moreover, I accept Sylvie's smile and Matt's deep laugh as they tell me about my old high school. And I study Sylvie's complexion, rosy and vibrant, as her hands whip around with emphasis. She resembles the girl I met in elementary school, brimming with mischief and unafraid of the future.

And I wonder if this is what it looks like when someone embraces all the bad they've done. And forgives themselves.

Callie

THE GLOW of my phone is the only light in the kitchen where I'm plopped on a stool, gaping at the letters scrolling across the screen.

As if I've already formed the habit, my free hand moves to brush against the pendant at my neck while I squint at my phone. It's a piece of jewelry I'd found when I trekked into the attic where Dad said he'd stored Mom's more precious items. It was difficult, almost impossible, to open the first box, then the second, and go through what's left of her. Mom's favorite purple dress was at the top of the pile, and after delicately setting it aside, I found her most loved (but never used) cookbooks, and the one pair of Jimmy Choo's she'd purchased for herself. Her old, ratty t-shirts were next, ones she often wore around the house. They still smelled like her.

Thank you, Dad, for not throwing these away, I think as I run my hand along the softened seams of one. It used to be blue but had faded to the color of an afternoon sky, and I lifted it to my nose. Flashbacks whirled at the scent, Mom enveloping me in a hug, the way she danced in the kitchen, and that time I broke curfew and she'd screamed at me in this shirt and sweats, her hair in a sideways bun and her eyes sparking flames.

The memories broke me and soaked her shirt.

Sniffling, I pulled it away from my face and started rolling it up. Something clanged to the floor, falling out of the single front pocket, and I scooped up the gold, shiny item on a delicate chain, inspecting it closer.

Oh my God.

The raven's crest flashed up at me, so blinding and invasive.

I couldn't put it down.

Without thinking, I clasped it around my neck and tucked it into my shirt, then scooped up Mom's box and tore out of the attic, my heart pounding.

A few hours later, I've calmed down enough that the gold doesn't burn against my skin anymore. I've pulled it out now, rubbing the pendant between my thumb and index finger, immersed the email on my phone and wondering whether I've been hacked.

The under-cabinet lights flicker on. I jump, then scream and fall off my stool at the sudden movement in the doorway.

The shadow screams back.

"Christ on a cracker, Callie!" Lynda cries, clutching the collar of her nightgown as she bends over to catch her breath.

"I—Jesus on a biscuit, Lynda!" I retort, tucking the necklace back inside my shirt.

"You scared the life out of me." She puts her hands on her hips, then arches her back until she's exhaling toward the ceiling. "Usually I'm alone when I'm wandering the halls late at night."

"Sorry." I resume my position on the stool. "Couldn't sleep."

"Don't tell me you're waiting up for Santa?"

I huff out a laugh, but hunch over my phone again. "I wish."

"Blair has me up at such odd hours, my stomach's starting to adapt to midnight snacks. Want to join me for some hot chocolate?"

"Sure. That'd be nice."

Lynda opens the upper cabinet, pulling out two mugs. "Tell me what's going on, honey."

"Nothing. I..."

"Those are your final grades for the semester, aren't they?"

I peer up from my phone, straightening in my seat. "How'd you know?"

"Oh, please, I'm hardly psychic." Lynda chuckles at my expression. "Your Dad was emailed them a few hours ago."

Grades must've come in while I was out with Blair. After the incident at the traffic light, I was reluctant to add another distraction and look at my phone until I got home. Then, Christmas Eve dinner happened, and it was only an hour ago that I'd thought to check my email. That stopped any slim chances of catching any sleep.

"You don't look happy," Lynda observes as she sets a pot on the stove. "If I were you, I'd be ecstatic at those grades. Your dad and I are so proud of you."

I stare back down at my phone, the letters growing blurry the longer I forget to blink. "They're not mine."

"Don't be silly. Of course they are. Briarcliff doesn't make those kinds of mistakes."

Her words hit me in the exact opposite way she intended. My hand clenches around my phone as I glance between the screen and her.

"Lynda."

I use her name forcefully, so she'll stop puttering around the stove and turn to look in my direction.

She does, her long, satin nightgown flowing with her movements. "Cal? What is it?"

"Did Briarcliff falsify my grades because I'm a Virtue initiate?"

Lynda's brows disappear into her blonde highlights. "Goodness, you don't mince words, now do you?"

"That's what they did." I flip the phone so she can see the screen. "There's no *way*

I managed a 4.0 GPA. I daydreamed through half my exams and scribbled nonsense on the rest."

"Honey." Lynda's soft voice floats closer. "I'm sure that's not what happened. You're an intelligent girl who's finally been given a chance at a top tier school, and you've excelled."

"I don't deserve these grades, because they're not *mine*."

"But they are." Lynda points to the top of the screen. "Isn't that your student number?"

"It is, but I ran into my friend Sylvie today. Remember what I said at dinner? She looked amazing. Happy and healthy. And it got me thinking, why can't I turn over a new leaf? She's forgiven herself, and I want to try to do the same. I want to forgive myself for what happened between us, and what I did to Dad. I really think going back to school here in the city would—"

"Then those are your grades." Lynda spins back to the stove as if I just answered her question and hadn't poured out my insecurities. "Don't question their origins past tonight."

"But—I'm really happy with you, and Dad, and Blair."

"Callie." Lynda lifts a wooden spoon, keeping her back to me. "Do what they want. Accept the perks and keep attending Briarcliff."

Lynda's shoulder blades spear out of her back as she deliberately sets out to stir the milk and chocolate with awful, jerky movements.

"Lynda," I whisper, "The Virtues' perks come with awful consequences. I don't want to be a part of it anymore."

It's the closest I've come to confessing about Ivy, and my throat swells with the effort.

"Refusing them comes at an even greater cost," Lynda replies, her voice invoking an eerie calm.

My hackles rise. "I'm beginning to think they just do whatever the fuck they want, regardless of whether or not you bend to their will."

"I know you're confused." *Stir, stir, stir.* "Angry, even. But coming at them the way you have isn't going to work out the way you think it will."

"Oh, really? Is someone I know going to get hurt? Newsflash, that's already—"

The wooden spoon slams against the countertop. Hot milk splashes with Lynda's arc, but she doesn't react to the boiling liquid hitting her skin.

"Please." Her voice breaks. Placing her palms on the edge of the counter, she sags forward over the stove, exhausted. "No more. Don't put this family through more struggles."

I slide off my stool, clutching my phone to my chest, and step up behind Lynda. Afraid to touch her. "I'm not trying to put you or Blair in more danger..."

"But you are." Lynda straightens, but she still doesn't turn around. "I'm aware of their abuse of power. How well they manipulate and extort. I learned early that it's better to just do as they ask than fight against the inevitable." Abruptly, Lynda spins, then clutches my face between her hands. Her pressure stings. "Honey, there isn't any fairness in it, but it keeps us safe. You're about to become a Virtue, whether you like it or not. Accept the good. The privilege that comes with it. You're primed to attend any Ivy League you want. *Any.* So few students get that kind of chance. And if you do that, if you listen to the Virtues and do as they say, they'll leave you alone. Let you live a life of comfort and wealth in peace. It's really the only way to survive them."

The pot gurgles and hisses behind her, but Lynda doesn't move.

My eyes dart to the bubbling steam spilling over the edges, then back to Lynda. "I don't—I can't do that."

Her eyes well. Lynda's so close, I feel the heat of her breath. Smell the sweetness of milk on her skin. Her fingers dig into the fat in my cheeks, my teeth aching with her applied pressure.

"You know what your mother endured," she whispers.

I swallow, quelling the need to jerk out of her hold and scream.

"It's because she didn't like their rules and went against them. She was forced to run, then live a life as an office cleaner and single mother. She had everything, *everything*, at her fingertips, and they stripped it all from her. Do *not* be your mother."

They killed her just like they killed Ivy.

The accusation is silent on my lips. Lynda looks upon me with such need, I can't voice the truth because I'm certain she won't listen.

"I'm not a Virtue," I say instead.

Lynda blinks. Her arms drop from my face, then she breaks into a smile. "Well, have you had your robing ceremony?"

I shake my head, eyeing her warily as she goes back to the overboiling pot and turns down the dial.

"Then you're right. You're not one of them, yet. However, if they've..." She gestures to my phone dangling in my hand. "It's clearly still in their plans to accept you."

I'm desperate to get through to her and end up deploying the last weapon in my arsenal. "Ahmar's looking into them. If he finds any proof of their history of trafficking, bribery, lies, and murder—"

"Oh, honey, Ahmar will be blocked at every turn. And if you keep pushing him, he will be the only one that loses. You can't tell me part of you doesn't know that."

Lynda lifts the pot from the stove—there's no way that milk isn't burned—and pours the brown liquid into the two mugs. Once finished, she carries them over to me at the opposite counter.

"It's in his best interest for you to stop feeding him information," she says as she hands me a steaming mug.

I stare at her in horror. "Whose side are you on?"

"The one that's gotten me through decades of living untouched by them," Lynda says sharply. "Now, go on. Drink."

I do, wincing as the scalded liquid hits my tongue.

A faint squeal carries down the hallway. Lynda jerks her chin to the sound, tilting her head. "Damn. Blair's up again. You should get some sleep, Cal. We have a big day tomorrow, now that we also get to celebrate your first semester at Briarcliff." She beams, then sets down the mug. "I'm not lying when I say we're so proud of you. You're so strong, and you're doing great."

Lynda kisses my cheek, her lips cold despite her recent sip of hot chocolate. She sweeps out of the room, dimming the lights as she goes, until I'm left in a room of shadows.

I sag into a stool, staring into nothing.

It was such a stupid idea, thinking I could be happy with Dad and Lynda, that I belonged and had their love. The Virtues will never let me. They've seeped into Lynda's soul, altering her and poisoning her to levels where she can't see clearly enough to know she's tearing me apart with her wish for me to just fall in line.

But, perhaps it's the only way. As a Virtue, I'll gain power. I can claim the status of the Missing Heir.

It could give me the leverage I need to cut Sabine down with the very knife used on Ivy. A blade that could've been used on my mother, too.

The only people who have ever loved me are dead. Anyone alive pretends to care about me to serve themselves.

Glimpsing Sylvie's new life was nice while it lasted.

I know my place now.

The sharp wings of the pendant pierces my thumb through my shirt's fabric.

The only way to end the Virtues...

Is to finish becoming one.

Chase

NO MUSIC PLAYS.

The clink of silverware and Tempest's loud sips of wine are the sole distractions in this expansive, *stifling* dining room.

Nobody has even decorated it for Christmas, never mind Christmas Eve dinner.

Emma and I were largely forced to my father and Sabine's penthouse in Manhattan through fear of impending doom. The happy couple was supposed to be bound for the tropics, but instead changed their plans last minute to attend all the Christmas parties the Manhattan elite offered, leaving me extremely suspicious of their motives. With Callie too close to Sabine for comfort, I cajoled Emma to come with me to the empty luxury of the five-bedroom apartment, instead of to our mother's in California. I guilted my sister, manipulated her, and told her that if something happened to Callie in the city, she'd never forgive herself.

I didn't give much thought that this would be the first time Emma sat at dinner with the woman who had auctioned her off, then tried to burn her alive when she'd rebelled. The most I offered was to bring Tempest along for the ride, since he never has family around the holidays.

I can be a rat bastard, especially after having trash thrown at my face, but now that we're here, my plan borders on fucking dumb.

My knife screeches against the priceless, gold-embossed plate as I cut into my steak.

"Problem, dearest?"

My attention hovers over my plate, my eyes scraping in much the same way my knife did as I look across the table and meet Sabine's question with a direct stare. "None whatsoever."

Sabine responds with a closed-mouthed smile, returning to her dinner with dainty, calculated bites.

She doesn't take her eyes off me.

A sharp jab to my thigh severs the animosity holding me taut. To further enunciate his point, Tempest clears his throat and shifts his ass in his seat, as if I can't catch his thoroughly subtle way of telling me to stop trying to eviscerate Sabine with my stare.

"I assume exams went well?" my father asks, seated beside Sabine and looking to anyone else who bothers to duck into the dining room that he's enjoying dinner with his family.

"Fine," I bite out.

Even if they didn't, the Noble King would never let his son fail on paper. My exams are likely being doctored as we speak.

"They went okay," Emma murmurs beside me.

I stiffen at her voice. She hasn't spoken since we were forced into the penthouse and asked to sit down for a fake-ass family dinner. And unlike me, her exams won't be forged. She's left with whatever she worked hard enough to achieve—a notion I doubt will ever resonate with dear Dad.

Yet here she is, seated in front of the woman who tried to end her life and pretending like school matters. What Emma went through —what she *hid* from me —boils my blood to demon spawn levels, but rather than directing my barely contained ire at my sister, I'd rather fuse it into my father. He's marrying a murderess. Binding himself to a woman who spites his own children, yet he doesn't bat an eye.

I eviscerate whatever food's left in my mouth, then shove my plate away. "Are we finished with this charade?"

"Son," Father intones. "Try to keep your temper at a minimum. We have guests."

"You mean your fiancée?" The title sits gluttonous, slippery with fat, on my tongue. "Or the dude who's spent every Christmas with us since he was in diapers?"

"Are you calling me a mooch, fucktard?" Tempest asks, cocking his head with a smarmy grin. I know what he's doing, but I refuse to let him defuse the situation before I fuck it up royally.

"I'm not doing this," I grind out. "Pretending all is well when—"

"Chase." Emma's hand clamps down on my wrist, keeping me from rising.

Her nails bite into my skin, but I welcome the pain and her sincere reminder that I shouldn't storm from the table, earning a pissy lecture from my father later, and more importantly, signaling to Sabine that I'm anything but defeated.

Protect Callie won't leave my head. I can't very well do that if I don't have my eye on Sabine at all times during the academy's break. Even during an innocuous holiday dinner, Sabine could be laying a foundation with my father or concocting future plans involving Callie's demise. The bitch never rests, and neither should I.

"Perhaps we should change the subject," Sabine says. "How was everyone's day?"

My lips twist at the same time Tempest says, "Tolerable. Christmas cheer usually makes me sociopathic." Tempest pauses. Grins subtly. Sabine doesn't react, keeping her expression remote while she angles her head with pretend interest. Tempest continues, "But I controlled myself this year and joined Emma to see the tree at Rockefeller."

"Interesting. You all must've seen it millions of times before." Sabine picks up her fork, but before she bites down, she pins me with a look and asks, "Did you all go?"

She's searching for a tell. Any indication that I nearly broke my frozen balls off ducking and diving into blind spots and traffic every time Callie looked over her shoulder, rather than join the masses of tourists in snapping pictures of a giant tree with a bunch of lightbulbs on it.

"We did," Emma says, her voice barely above a whisper. A worm of guilt inches its way into one of the many holes in my heart. Here is my sister whose every minute is strangled the longer she's forced to dine with Sabine, and I was about to smash my plate to pieces and leave her here.

"Aren't you aware, Sabine?" I ask. "It's a different tree every year. Thus, I'd argue a new experience every time we go."

"Indeed," Sabine says. She draws in another bite, chewing thoughtfully.

I take that as a sign this inane conversation is finished, thank fuck, but she draws my attention as she sucks on the tines of the fork. "I wonder if Callie took the time to see the tourist spectacle today as well?"

My father stiffens beside her. "Darling," he chastises. "Not today."

Emma audibly swallows beside me. I wonder if her twin sense is attuned to the lightning bolt shooting down my spine as I ask, "Why not, Father? You two have won, haven't you? She's no longer a threat to the societies."

My father's hooded gaze meets mine in warning. "And no longer of interest to you, either, so I suggest we move on from Calla Lily Ryan."

"Oh, I'm far from interested." My fork lands on my plate with a clink, and I lean back in my seat. "I've shunned, humiliated, lied, and cheated her. Have I missed anything, Em?"

Emma shakes her head without looking at me. I notice the trembling of her hand as it hovers over her dinner, her silverware held uselessly in her grip. She hasn't eaten a bite, but I refuse to take the blame.

"I believe you accomplished all those on her last day of exams," Tempest pipes in, then mutters, "and she, you."

I nail him with a glare, which he ignores.

"Should we invite her to our New Year's party, then?" Sabine asks.

My gaze flies to hers. She smiles coldly. "Perhaps she's willing to accept her position now that she's been ... thoroughly convinced."

I take a breath. A cleansing one. A damned centering one. "I doubt she'd have any desire."

"Mm," Sabine murmurs as she brings her wine to her lips. "Too bad. She'd make such a breathtaking Virtuous princess, if only she'd accept our rules."

The tablecloth wrinkles in my death grip. I can't bite down on the instinct enough to quip, "Like Emma was?"

"*Son*," Father spits, the same time Emma's head whips toward me.

She begs, "Chase, don't—"

The temptation to lay out all Sabine's done and how far she's gone—killing Ivy—while dart-boarding a butter knife to her forehead is so strong it's almost irresistible, but I hold myself back.

"Emma made her choice." A vein pulses in my father's forehead. "She decided to forsake her duty as a Virtue princess and betray us by collecting secrets to sell to the highest bidder. Though I doubt we need to rehash this, do we, Emma?"

Emma's jaw locks. She literally can't speak, and my own teeth gnash at the thought of what I've done to her, making her sit here and endure this when she's already become a ghost of her former self.

"Are you really so dense, Father?" I ask.

I stare at him a long time in the tense, frozen silence.

No, my father is a lot of things, but he's not clueless. If he was aware of Sabine's auctioning of Emma, of the reasons she was trapped in a fire of her own making, then he damn well knows what Sabine did to Ivy. The question is whether he understands that Ivy was a spontaneous Plan B, and that his son and only heir was the A-game.

I break our stare, instead grabbing the tongs for a second portion of steak. Tempest mutters his approval of my backing down, and Emma's shoulders sag in relief. Satisfied with my cease and desist, Father asks Sabine how she's enjoying her dinner. She answers that it's delicious.

Idly spinning my fork, I ask, "How far do you think your future wife's willing to go to keep her reign over the Virtues? Besides just marrying you, I mean."

I expect dishes to scatter. Wineglasses topple over as Father hurls himself from his seat, his rage smashing against the table.

Icy derision meets me over the crystal centerpiece. "Are you quite finished, son?"

I smile. "Not in the least."

Tempest throws his napkin on his unfinished dinner with an aggravated, "Shit."

"Do you know what this woman has been through these past few months? This is her first Christmas without her daughters." My father speaks in a silky monotone. If he had a bone to pick his teeth with, he would. "One of which, had she not died tragically, was your soulmate. A wonderful girl, murdered not three months ago, and here you are, shaming her name and humiliating yourself, simply out of jealousy."

"*Jealousy*?" I sputter, but collect myself before my jaw unhinges.

Father folds his hand over his fiancée's. "Sabine is to be my future wife, and she is to have the same respect you gave to Marilee, if not more. This woman has gone through hell, and I refuse to sit here and allow you to disparage her further."

"A hell of her own making," I quip.

"Daniel, it's all right," Sabine says as Father peels his lips back mid-snarl. "He's not wrong. Addisyn murdered Piper. It's awful, and I don't think I'll ever recover from the thought that my girls could've come to that point unless I did something to push them in that direction. A mother's guilt knows no bounds." Sabine raises her demure eyes to me. "I will live with that for the rest of my life. But I plan to change and help the girls I still can, my Virtues, attain the values and positive futures that I can only look back on as an unrealized dream for my daughters."

"Is your simpering supposed to affect me?" I ask her, honestly curious, then turn to my father. "Her daughter was killed by her *other* daughter, Father." I snort. "And if that's not proof enough of her fucked-up mothering, the way she treats her Virtues is by far the worst. Look what she's done to Emma—"

Emma gasps.

"*Get out.*"

If ice could've taken over the walls and cracked into jagged fractures, it would've had the same effect as Father's voice.

"Sadly, I am so far from done." I push my palms into the edge of the table, tipping my chair on its two back legs. If my father can don an arctic veneer, I'll counter it with the blasé attitude of an asshole son. "We've yet to cover Meredith Ryan. Tell me, Sabbie, did you orchestrate that, too?"

Tempest raises his eyes skyward at the same time Emma swivels in her seat, her eyes stretched to their whites.

"How *dare* you?" my father's whisper snaps across the table. "It's amazing to me that the heir to a fortune and to the governing of a powerful, world-wielding secret society can act with such idiocy. Everything we do, boy, is for *you*. Meredith's inheritance—excuse me, Calla Lily's inheritance—could take that all away from you. Do you understand? *I* am protecting you. Sabine is protecting you. Your sister sits here with us because she knows the truth of our influence. She's paid for her rebellion in the worst possible way, and for that I am devastated—"

"That you can no longer sell off your prized stock?"

"*Chase*." Emma's whisper is more of a tremulous gasp. She palms the table, much like I do, but squeezes until her knuckles pop through her skin. "Stop this."

My father goes mute. His lips thin to a needlepoint thread. It is through a very small pocket of air that he says, "I do believe you've overstayed your welcome."

"Oh, have I?" I retort, pushing to my feet. Tossing my napkin on the table, I say, "As always, it's been a pleasure, Father," before whirling for the exit.

He says to my back, "Regardless of your prostrating, I trust you haven't said one word to our girl about the little secret we keep, now have you?"

My shoulders level. My feet stop. But I don't turn around.

"Ah." I hear Father's smile. "I'm delighted to know your loyalty remains bound to the Nobles. If Calla Lily were ever to find out you've known who her real father is this entire time ... well..."

Sabine hums in agreement. "Just when we thought such betrayals were finished with. The poor girl would be devastated."

My hands clench at my sides, the skin growing purple with endless, swirling blood.

Another hand comes to my lower back. Words murmur, "Let's blow this place."

After a curt nod, I allow Tempest to push me out of the dining room. We don't stop until we reach my bedroom on the other side of the penthouse, *far* away from the bruises I'm aching to inflict on someone else. Anyone else.

A speck of clarity remains within the red of my vision, and Tempest steps inside it. "Calm down."

"*Fuck* this." I yank out of his hold. "My sister's back there. We have to get her."

Tempest clamps down on my shoulder and shoves me away from the door. "No, we don't."

I bare my teeth. "Who the fuck are you to tell me what to do? You did nothing back there. Didn't have my back because my best friend is suddenly a mute-ass motherfucker—"

"Emma didn't want to leave."

I choke on my own insults. "What?"

He shrugs. "I asked her. She said she'd like to finish her steak."

"That—doesn't make sense." I rake a hand through my hair.

"You tell me. She's your sister."

"Her tormentor's sitting with her. *Both* of them. And we're not there anymore."

"Need I remind you ... she was also a mute-ass motherfucker during your shit-storm. Considering the numbers are against you, I'm thinking that was the better way to handle it."

"Oh, come on."

"What were you trying to accomplish?"

I wave him off, choosing to scowl out the window.

"Can't say I enjoy Christmas any more than I did before that remarkable dinner," Tempest muses.

He searches through my desk drawer, humming in excitement when he finds what he's looking for and holds up the blunt.

I grunt my assent. He pulls a lighter from his pocket and fires it up. We sit at my two gaming chairs, spinning them until we're looking out over the Manhattan skyline. A few moments pass, and then ten, before a needed weightlessness overtakes my body.

My smoke ring floats up, widening and embracing my second smoke ring before both dissipate near the ceiling.

"Better, friend?" Tempest asks beside me, reclined in much the same way I am.

I pass him the blunt. "Far from it."

A small nudge at the base of my skull keeps reminding me that Sabine might not have concocted Ivy's—or my—death on her own. I lost my cool tonight because Father might know of my goals to usurp him and might not have objected to Sabine's attempts to get rid of me, or Callie, for good. How could I sit across the table from that man, saying nothing? Ivy was an effective warning but a poor substitute for the real thing. I keep waiting for the final thunderclap. Maybe I was even asking for it tonight.

Giving me an excuse to crush both of them before they get to Callie.

Callie, who I hurt and belittled with a dismissive smile. A girl who deserves better, yet thinks that *better* is me.

I glance at Tempest, idly blowing smoke through his nose—a dragon contemplating the art of burning the village below. "This is the part where I'm going to admit being glad I didn't go to Dubai to spend Christmas with my parents and their crew. You're more entertaining than a multi-mil superhero movie."

I gift him with a bold smile that doesn't reach the essential organ I'm told smiles come from. "I'm glad you were beside me tonight, even though you didn't do shit."

"It's not my job to stir up your childhood traumas with your father. It's my duty to keep you in check. We're not winning over the Nobles by having a temper tantrum at the kids' table."

I drop the ash from the blunt into the tray between us. "Sabine's the one who brought up Callie."

"Dude, I can't keep track of all your trigger words."

The bedroom door bursts open, both of us swiveling to the sound. The only light in the room comes from the surrounding buildings, so it takes a moment for my eyes to adjust to the hallway light rimming the form stomping into my territory.

It's not my father or Sabine, that's for sure. I narrow my eyes at the surprise intruder, who, once out of the shadows, turns out to be my sister.

She snarls. "You're an *asshole*, you know that?"

"Yes."

"Don't be glib with me." She halts in the middle of the room and plants her hands on her hips. "Did you think you were funny in there? Brave? A hero?"

I suppose I have to stand up for this. Pushing on the armrests, I rise, unwittingly towering over her. "Did you really expect me to sit through dinner without mentioning a word after what we've been through?"

"You've been through? *You've* been through?" Emma's outrage riddles her cheeks and creates hollows under her eyes. "What about the past two years I've endured under our father's hand?"

"I understand your pain, but—"

"You *don't.* Ivy's dead, and I'm sick over that—over what you and Callie had to witness, how horrible it must be to carry that around when no one's brought to justice for it, but you know what? Same here. I have your rage. I possess your hunger for justice. I've been harboring this shit for years, and the cravings only get worse. But unlike you, I've had time to cultivate. To deliberate. And therefore, to put together a patient, cutting plan that puts your flashbang revenge scheme to shame." Emma takes a deep breath. "I was able to get Callie on my side before you. I had *Piper* helping me before you even knew what the fuck was going on. Though clearly, my efforts mean shit-all to you. You should've given me respect in there or acknowledged my pain and allowed me to speak up when I wanted. And in that dining room, you took away my choice."

I stare at her hard. My jaw clamps shut.

Emma snatches at my silence. "You think you bear all the responsibility, that leadership and reformation fall on you. They don't. *I* am a legacy. *I* am a fallen Virtue. If anybody gets a say in how Sabine's taken down, it's me." She slams her palm against her heaving chest.

"You're right," I say in a low voice, my blood simmering. "I should've handled it better in there."

Emma snorts. "I suppose that's an apology coming from you."

"I mean it."

She looks to Tempest. "Anything to add?"

He raises his hands, palms facing her. "Your argument is sound."

Emma's brows relax. "When we get back to Briarcliff, we're working together. And you're going to let me decide if whatever you're concocting in your vengeful head is the right move. Everything that happens to us starts and ends at Briarcliff. We're not going to decide Callie's fate over Christmas dinner, in a Manhattan high-rise, with anger and spite as our muse. Is that clear?"

Tempest purses his lips. "Crystal, Your Most Respectful Legacy."

Emma cuts him a look.

"Yes," I say, but I'm thinking about Callie on the New York City streets. Vulnerable and exposed, with secrets, lies, and betrayals shadowing her every step.

Emma's wrong on one point—what happens to us doesn't stay at Briarcliff. It can't.

"Now that we've cleared that up," Tempest says, at last rising from his lupine position on the chair. "Anybody going to 'fess up on who Callie's dad is?"

"No," Emma and I bark at the same time. I jolt, then send her a confused brow raise.

"It'll only serve to distract her," Emma says, meeting my stare with a flat one of her own. "I know more than you think, dear brother. Like I said: I've earned your respect."

"Duly noted," I murmur, then watch her as she pivots and exits the room, shutting the door with a punctuated smack.

"Well, that's no fun," Tempest pouts, but reaches for the blunt and takes in a satisfied inhale. "I only enjoy secrets when I'm in on them."

"I'll keep you busy," I say, still staring at the door. "Emma may think she's been biding her time without notice, but she won't protect Callie the way she protects herself. Callie's in incredible danger, and if Callie returns to school"—which, sadly, I know she will—"we have to hunt down Sabine's traps before she falls into one. At the same time, we fuck with her, isolate her, and make her regret ever setting foot in Briarcliff Academy."

Tempest angles his head thoughtfully. "Okay. I'll bite. That sounds fun."

"This isn't for your amusement. Girls are dying on my watch, and I don't want any more blood on my hands."

Callie's, especially. Just thinking of her slack form in my arms, her chin tipped to the sky, her eyes milky with death, causes an unfamiliar, aching shudder starting at the base of my spine and ending with my stomach plummeting through the Earth.

My lips pull down. I don't like this feeling *at all*.

"Relax, Prince. Callie isn't in immediate danger. Sabine won't kill her on sight." Tempest flicks the end of the blunt into the ashtray. "The whole point of having prey is so you can toy with them first."

Callie

EVERY STEP closer to Briarcliff Academy makes me shudder.

I force myself to the top, then through the doors, refusing to tip my chin up to the Wolf's Den, in case Chase is up there, lording over the underclassmen as we all return from winter break.

Someone jostles my shoulder. "Did you keep it or scrape it out with a coat hanger?" flies against my ears.

Grimacing, I push forward, ignoring the sneers and judgmental stares.

Chase. Chase did this.

Amid the societal backstabbing, the scandal, and the *murders*, he decided it was a good time to continue the cruelty, giving a forbidden pregnancy a go, since it worked so well with Piper.

The gall of him. The absolute deplorable nature he would've had to reach for to make this happen and keep it going well after the holidays ... my upper lip curls.

I have to remember what it was like to see Sylvie, and what forgiving yourself for all your mistakes can mean. It doesn't all have to be bad. Good things and happy endings can still happen when we're at our worst.

I don't have to keep being this way.

Turning into my locker area, I'm jostled again. "So, what's it like?"

Without glancing up from my padlock, I snap, "Being pregnant with a disgraced teacher's baby? I dunno ... what's it like embracing yet another unoriginal rumor because your big, bad prince told you to—" I stop as soon as I whip around. "Oh. Hey, Eden."

Her brows jump. "Hey yourself. I just wanted to know what it was like meeting your new sister, but hey, if you've got baggage to unload, I'm your luggage carrier."

Sighing, I lean my shoulder against the locker beside mine. "You haven't heard?"

"That you're preggo? Nope." She cocks her head. "Are you? Because that'd be a twist."

"No," I snap, then draw back my whip. "It's another of the Nobles' rumors, meant to make me run from Briarcliff with my tail between my legs and never come back."

Eden scoffs. "If seeing your best friend murdered in front of you didn't make you want to hightail it out of here, how could they think ... sorry. Too soon."

I pull my mouth out of the frown, peering closer at Eden. She may be talking about Ivy off-the-cuff, but the sheen of loss in her eyes tells me differently. "Did I miss anything while I was away?"

"Nothing to report." Eden shrugs, falling into step beside me as I shut my locker and make my way to class. "The place was deserted, though, which was a nice change. No student ... or Virtue ... in sight." She adds under her breath as we enter the crowded hallway, "No secret meetings, either. I'm guessing it's because Daniel Stone and Sabine stayed in New York for the holidays and couldn't be bothered planning a coup long distance."

I jerk to a stop, grabbing Eden's elbow to halt along with me. "I thought they went on some fancy, tropical vacation together?"

"My sources tell me otherwise," Eden says easily. "They holed up in their luxury penthouse in Manhattan. Chase and Emma were there, too. And that creepy-hot Tempest guy."

"But..." I think back to my rare, but necessary, public outings with Blair. In particular, Christmas Eve, when I saw Chase everywhere, but nowhere, at the same time. I didn't see his ghost at all after that, instead focusing on finishing my break on a high note and spending all my time with Lynda, Dad, and Blair. Lynda never mentioned her hot cocoa meltdown again, and I didn't bring it up, either. Perhaps I'm just as guilty as her, pretending everything's fine when it isn't, but I wasn't sure when I'd see them again. Or if. I *needed* us to be okay when I left.

Eden jolts, her eyes widening in sudden realization. "Shit, your parents run in the same circles as them. You didn't run into those assholes, did you?"

I shake my head. "We kept to ourselves, getting to know the baby as a family instead. Dad and Lynda went to some New Years' ball, but I stayed behind to watch Blair. They might've crossed paths then."

My eyes flit to the side as I work to recall New Years' Eve. Blair was asleep in her bassinet next to me as I watched the ball drop in Times Square from the comfort of the den's couch. I must've fallen asleep, because I don't remember said ball actually dropping and woke up to the sound of footsteps—Dad and Lynda wandering in well after midnight.

"How was it?" I'd mumbled, rubbing sleep from my eyes. Infomercials had replaced the live coverage of the revelry thirty blocks away.

"Good," Dad said at the same time Lynda trilled, "Great! Only one boob decided to leak. The other stayed painful and swollen but, oh my God, to be back in socialization again. I practically forgot it wasn't highbrow to whip a breast out in the middle of the dance floor and squeeze it for relief."

"She's had champagne," my dad said as explanation for her outburst, but I smiled, patting the couch next to me for Lynda to sit down.

"Squeeze away. I won't judge."

I try to remember if there was strain around Dad's eyes, or if Lynda's voice was higher than normal. Wouldn't a surprise confrontation with the Stones send them home stiff-backed and concerned? They don't know about Ivy, but they're well aware of the threat the Virtues pose. Lynda, especially.

I can't recall any tense moments when they got home. Just Lynda sagging in relief beside me and Dad making some dad joke about how badly I want him to order the new omelet maker on television.

After searching my face, Eden grows serious. "Do you think they're in any real danger?"

"I didn't think Ivy was in any danger," I say honestly.

Eden's lips press together.

"How lovely, the stank possum and her skank are back in business."

Rather than turn toward Falyn's familiar, grating voice, I say to Eden, "Let's go."

"Was last semester not enough for you?" Falyn's voice follows us down the halls. "Do you have some sort of sick craving to be humiliated and tossed aside by every guy at Briarcliff? So pathetic, Callie. Why couldn't you have taken the warning and gone back to your gutter?"

I whip around so fast and so hard, Falyn has to skid to a stop before barreling into me. She rights herself, smoothing her skirt, but can't smooth the tic of surprise in her expression when she meets my eye again.

"You were saying?" I say softly. When her chin trembles and she doesn't respond, I add, "Go on."

Falyn lifts her upper lip. "I was saying what a skank you were—"

My arm flies out and slams her against the wall, my forearm pressing against her throat. Gasps sound out, a few footsteps scampering back.

Falyn gurgles, her hands scrabbling against my arm. I say, "I'd appreciate it, as a fellow sister, if you'd shut up about my slut status."

"I'm not your sister," she spits out, her voice strained.

I press harder. Violet yelps, and Willow steps forward, but one scathing look from me and Willow freezes.

"Callie 2.0 in the house," Eden sings under her breath, backing away, but her stare locks on me in fascination.

There must be something different in my eyes, I think offhand. *Enough to make these bitches step back.* Then I add idly, *I wonder what it could be?*

My gaze slides back to a squirming Falyn. "I beg to differ. Not only am I your sister, but I'm next in line for the throne." Falyn starts a garbled protest, but I press harder, adding loud enough for our audience to hear, "But I think you knew that. With that in mind, I'd appreciate you backing off Eden, Emma, and *me*. Understood?"

Falyn's nails, sharpened into manicured talons, dig into my skin, drawing blood. "You can't possibly still want to be with us."

I tip my head. "But I do."

"After ... after everything that's happened?"

A glint forms in Falyn's eyes—a shard of metal, a sharpened, cunning blade.

She knows the truth about Ivy.

Heat travels into my throat, and I snarl into her face, "I'm not going anywhere, you *fucking* bitch."

Heavy, unhurried footsteps sound out, amplified in a hall shocked into silence, until they stop at the base of my heels.

Breath skitters against my nape, goosebumps firing along my jaw. I know without looking that if I spear my elbow back, I'll hit nothing but rock-solid abs.

"Screw off," I say through my teeth, though my focus remains on Falyn.

"I might, if she's worth it," Chase muses at my back. "Is she?"

Heat crackles at the base of my spine. Chase isn't close enough to touch, but he's near enough to awaken the atoms between us, rippling the air as they electrify and pop with every exhale he makes.

If he breathes extra-hard, he'll flutter pieces of my hair.

I keep my inhales steady. My eyes facing forward. "I don't need any *prince*, and neither does she."

Falyn cringes when I press my forearm harder into her neck.

Chase's arm crosses my vision, his gold cufflink shimmering as he grabs my wrist and pulls me off Falyn. I don't have time to cry out my indignation before he sends me into a twirl that has my back crashing against the wall, where Falyn's once was.

He boxes me in, his bronze stare bearing down. Falyn gasps and sputters beside us, clutching her neck and running to her friends for cover. He doesn't spare her a look.

"Causing quite the spectacle on your first day back," he says.

"So what?" I push at his barrel of a chest, but he doesn't move. "I'm sick of being pushed around by assholes like you."

His eyes narrow. "Looks like you can add pissing me off to your first day to-do list as well."

"It's clear you'd rather I cower, or run, or cry whenever I come near you, but you know what? Winter break taught me the opposite."

"And how's that?"

"You can't stay away from me."

A chilled waft of air hits me when he straightens. "Come again?"

"I saw you," I whisper through stiff lips. "Watching me. Stalking me. Unable to stay *away* from me in New York."

Something flickers in Chase's eyes, but he checks it, his nostrils flaring. "Are those paranoid delusions bothering you again, sweet possum?"

I ignore the internal blade slicing through my chest. "You lied to me. Your dad wasn't on some island vacation with Sabine. They were right here. In *my* city, likely watching me as much as you were."

"Is it somehow my fault you can't fly under the radar?"

"Stop it," I hiss. "Don't pretend you're not concerned for me. You wouldn't have tracked me down on Christmas Eve if you didn't still have feelings—"

Chase draws away, pouting as his eyelids give a derisive twitch. "Hmm. Poor thing. I hoped you would've figured out your place while on break, if you decided to come back here, that is. Hasn't enough been done to you? Run back to your fake uncle, or better yet, go live with your fake parents. Or, hey." He points to my stomach. "Go have a fake baby. A little thing like that might actually love you back."

My mouth trembles with the need to hurl insults. My eyes sear into his with the desperation to hurt him as much as he's killing me. I say in a low, unrecognizable voice, while keeping my eyes on him, "I chose the wrong person to save."

A muscle tics in Chase's cheek, yet his stare doesn't waver.

But I know I've hurt him. I know it, and I can't control it once it starts. "You're the last person to dole out love advice. Your mother wants nothing to do with you. Your sister despises you. Your father uses you like an object and can't wait to discard you once you've proven your worth. You're trying to tell me blood means family? None of them have affection for you. I can't even call it goodwill." Chase's lashes flutter close to a flinch. My stomach pitches at how hard he's working not to show emotion, but I forge through the nausea. "Look down on me and my lack of a blood relative all you want, but that only means I have people with no obligation to me who care anyway. You have no idea what that's like, and you never will."

I press my hand to my abdomen, noting the flutter there—butterfly wings of sentiment. *I mean what I'm saying.* Dad, Lynda, Ahmar, Blair ... they may not be tied to me through DNA, but we're something. We could be a family, if I at last opened that door instead of staying in the locked compartment of my mind with my dead mother.

But I can't leave her behind.

Brave hollers and applause echo to the arched ceilings. We've drawn even more of a crowd than I thought, but Chase doesn't acknowledge them. He simply stares in silence, assessing the few feet between us.

"Big words for a discarded orphan. You were shipped back here as soon as they could."

So much blood has collected in my cheeks that my ears ring. But I raise my chin. "I don't need your acceptance to keep going to this school. I certainly don't need it to claim my rightful place."

Chase's lips twitch. His eyes narrow. "If you do that, you'll be making a terrible mistake."

"Too late." I point to Falyn, now part of the audience, the murderous gleam of her teeth visible from here. "I've already sent in my request. It's done."

Chase scans the crowd. He can disparage me all he wants, but the Nobles' long-reaching gag order strangles him from voicing any displeasure at my continued role in the Virtues.

I latch onto that weakness and stand tall. "You tried to scare me away last semester and failed. I'm not going anywhere, Chase Stone. The only difference being, now I'm here for blood."

Spinning on my heel, I push to the exit, finding Eden in the outskirts of the still-forming crowd and pull her along with me.

"Holy shit, what's gotten into you?" she breathes out as she tries to keep up with my steps.

I don't trust myself to speak until we're well away and turning into the South Wing. Facing down Chase is too much. My heart is crumbling in my hands.

I hide it all when I say, "I've decided to no longer take any bullshit."

"Hey, I'm down with you beating up Falyn and putting Chase in his place—that was baller, by the way—but what was that whole thing with Falyn? Are you really—I mean, do you seriously still want to be a Virtue?"

"It's the only way," I say as we wander deeper into the South Wing. New semester, new classes. Philosophy is my first of the day.

"To show Sabine you're not afraid?"

"Not quite." We're approaching my classroom door, first period having started ten minutes ago, and I slow my steps. "To prove she killed my mother."

"Shit. Okay."

"Find Emma after first period and meet me in the gym bathrooms. We all need to talk."

"You don't say?" Eden says dryly, then splits off from me.

I watch her until she disappears into her classroom, then push into mine, beginning my morning of pretending to be a normal teenager in an average high school, starting my last semester of senior year, fresh-faced and filled with revenge.

Callie

NORMALLY, I'd be calling an emergency meeting with Ivy, popping open a bottle of wine, both of us sitting on my bed while I asked her to tell me everything about the Virtue robing ceremony and what I should expect.

She'd hug me with reassurance—I know that. Insist on standing beside me in support. And she'd do everything in her power to help me avoid any surprises ... except for that time she revealed herself as a Virtuous princess after I almost drowned, and then decimated our plans to break into the temple and steal Sabine's files...

On second thought, Ivy would be terrible to doomsday prep with, but the ache between my ribs every time I think about her makes me want her here more than ever.

I miss you, Ivy.

"Okay, so let's get back to the part where your mom was murdered because you're Rose Briar's missing great-great-great-grandchild and stand to inherit the entire fucking society."

It also means I'm left with Emma as my ride-or-die.

"How didn't you know I'm a Briar descendant?" I ask her as we crowd into the handicap stall at the end of the girls' bathroom. After checking that all other stalls are vacant, Eden comes in and locks the door behind us.

"Ivy knew," I continue. "Chase was made aware God knows how long ago." I flick a hand in Eden's direction. "Eden's the one who clued me in. I thought I was the last to figure it out."

"It was obvious there was something special about you," Emma says, "considering how much Father and Sabine were focused on your every move, but no, I was never given that information."

I study Emma quizzically. It's safe to say that out of everyone, I expected her to possess the most information about me—well, her and Chase.

He pops into my mind without permission, and I squeeze my eyes shut to rid myself of the image. I don't need him now. I can't have him.

"If you're robed," Emma says, "that makes it official. You can show your copy of the birth certificate the Nobles have kept hidden and claim your position. Here, send it to me." She pulls out her phone at the same time I do, and I airdrop the photo to Emma and Eden. Safety in numbers, after all. Tempest can't rob all three of us without one of us finding out before he's finished. I've never proven it was him who stole all my evidence, but process of elimination isn't difficult.

"There's also this," I say, and pull the pendant of the raven's crest out from my collar.

Emma gasps.

Eden asks, "Where did you get *that?*"

"It was my mother's. Don't all the Virtues get one?"

Emma shakes her head, her attention locked on the pendant dangling softly from my fingers. "They stopped handing those out years ago. It prompted too many questions from outsiders, especially with the rise of social media and camera phones. Sabine's—I mean, Sabine and your mom's—class was probably the last to receive it. That's really special, Callie, but no one should see you wearing it."

Lifting the pendant to my eyeline, I say somberly, "My mom managed to keep this from me for sixteen years. I can do the same. I'm not taking it off."

"If you're sure." But Emma doesn't sound convinced.

It's because of her tone I don't mention the moment when I first saw the iron raven crest, hidden in the trophy case beside the headmaster's office. The secret society marker was familiar somehow, meaning I must've seen this necklace hanging from my mother's neck at some point. I just can't—*won't*—remember.

Eden cuts into my thoughts. "That's cool and all, but we should probably get back to why Sabine let you get this far. She's not the type to just *allow* you to become a Virtue with this kind of power over her."

"Sabine's the one who tapped Callie as an initiate in the first place," Emma counters.

"So she could control her and show Callie who's boss," Eden says. "Callie coming back from break despite Ivy being killed pretty much splatters that whole plan."

Emma pushes her lips to the side, conceding Eden's point.

"You're quiet, Callie," Emma says after giving me the once-over. "Why?"

The bathroom door pushes open, brisk footsteps following suit. We clamp our mouths shut and freeze, all of us well aware that if whoever's in here so much as glances down, she'll see three pairs of feet and get curious.

But the girl goes about her business, the toilet flushing, then the faucet running, as she finishes up. I relax, remembering that this is Briarcliff Academy—three girls conducting a hush-hush meeting in the bathroom isn't exactly prime time news.

Her footsteps don't slow as she passes our stall and the main door shuts behind her.

"We better hurry," Eden mumbles. "There's three minutes before second period starts. The caffeine addicts are gonna need to pee before class."

"Well?" Emma asks me. "What's wrong with flashing the birth certificate around once you're robed?"

"I can't prove it," I say. Emma's chin jerks back. Eden makes a sound of unfortunate agreement. "Not until I have Sabine's files and prove she killed my mom to end the Briar line."

"She left you alive, though," Emma says. "The Briar line didn't end with your mom."

"Could've been an accident," Eden says. "Contrary to movies, it's difficult to order a hit and get away with it. You said you were supposed to be there for dinner, right?" Eden asks. I nod. "But you were late, and after all that planning, the hit had to go through—it's better to get one than none."

"And knowing Sabine," Emma adds, warming to Eden's argument, "she'd adapt immediately. Instead of killing you another time, which would look suspicious after your mom was just killed, she invited you to Briarcliff Academy, thinking it was better to have her enemy close than not at all."

I should shudder at such matter-of-fact talk regarding Mom's horrible death, but the truth is, I've been thinking the same thing. Maybe I wasn't meant to survive that night. Perhaps, despite Mom's best efforts, I was never meant to live my life free of Briarcliff.

But I can rip from the chains.

"I've always been told what to do, who to be," I say, drawing both of their attention. "I've felt out of control since Mom died, and now I'm finally getting answers. It's time for me to take charge and take away Sabine's power. If I can get back into the temple and into the princess's bedroom, I can get those files. Sabine's vain—if she succeeded in killing my mom, she'll have something to remember that by. I know it."

Emma nods. "We can start there."

"I'm not finished," I say.

Eden perks up. "I like this new Callie."

"I need both of you to go to the public library and steal some of Rose Briar's DNA."

"Excuse me?" Emma asks, at the same time Eden pumps her fist excitedly.

"Oh, come on," Eden says to her. "You willingly took a baseball bat to the face. You can open a compartment in an underfunded library and pocket a hairbrush."

Emma gives me a pointed look. I raise my hands, saying, "I didn't tell her."

"I'm not stupid," Eden says before Emma can respond. "In fact, I'm incredibly observant. It doesn't take a genius to connect the dots between Piper, you, and Callie."

"Actually, it does," Emma says, but her expression softens into one of respect. Maybe, after all this time, it's nice to be acknowledged for all the suffering she endured.

Eden shrugs it off. "I don't think those DNA kits online do these kinds of samples. Is there a way we can trace Rose's descendants?"

I say, "We can try, if we can find her baby, Delilah, and determine the children she had. I'll also call Ahmar, see if he can call in a favor to this forensics lady he used to date."

Emma raises her brows. "Do you think Ahmar would help you with this? You said he was ... concerned ... for your well-being after you confided in him."

I nod tightly. "He will." I hesitate. "If I lie and tell him it's related to finding my real father, he will. Ahmar wouldn't say no to something like that."

"Okay. Good," Emma says, and thankfully, leaves it at that.

"That'll take time, too. It's why I'll focus on pinning Sabine for Mom, first."

Both girls nod in agreement.

"So, we good?" Emma asks, hands on her hips.

"One other thing," I say.

They pause, waiting for me to continue.

"I, uh, I need you to teach me how to swim, Eden."

Eden crosses her arms and glances to the side. "I don't know if..."

"You have to," Emma cuts in, moving to stand next to me. "Callie nearly bit the dust once, and we don't know if that was a fluke or whether Sabine knew Callie couldn't swim. We can't let that happen again."

"Eden," I say softly, blinking away the image of Ivy wrestling me to the surface and saving my life. "I'm sorry. I'm asking you for a tall order, but out of everyone, you could teach me the fastest. You're a champion swimmer."

"Used to be," Eden says, working her jaw.

"You still are," I say.

"Besides, Callie would owe you one."

I cut a sharp look to Emma, who shrugs. "What? Eden does better with quid pro quos."

Sighing, I agree. "I would."

"Fine," Eden says, but directs her statement to the ground.

"Eden, if it's too much—" I start.

"I said fine. Meet me in the mornings at the indoor pool in the rec center. 4 AM." Eden flicks her eyes up. "I don't want anyone seeing us."

The early timing doesn't even register, and I'm not about to push the issue with Eden. "Cool. Thanks."

"Great," Emma says. "We've all got our assignments. But Callie ... there isn't anyone on the inside to protect you anymore. If you do the robing ceremony..."

"I'm on my own," I finish for her, but my voice is strong. "I'm good with that."

Eden angles her head, studying me carefully. "You don't seem the type to *want* to be alone, though."

"I do now."

My statement quiets both of them. After a beat of silence where it's clear I'm not backing down, Emma unlocks the stall, and we head to the exit.

"Hey," Emma says before we split off in the hallway. She squeezes my shoulder. "Good luck."

"You, too," I say. "And thank you."

Emma shakes her head. "You don't have to thank me. I'm finally getting justice, too."

"And me," Eden pipes in.

I smile at both of them, but it's wane and doesn't stretch into my cheeks. To cover it up, I stick my hand out, palm up. "Off with her head."

Both catch on and place their palms on top of mine.

"Off with her head," they echo, before our hands break apart.

Chase

"SHE'S *FUCKING* DOING the robing ceremony," I spit, pacing around my room. "Is she *fucking* out of her mind? Does this chick want to *fucking* die?"

Tempest shrugs. "I doubt emphasizing 'fuck' with every question will get Callie to change her mind."

I run through all the possible reasons Callie has for continuing to step into a viper's nest. She's desperate to solve her mom's murder. Determined to avenge Ivy. Most of all, she wants to decimate the very thing that destroyed her mom: The Virtues.

But at the cost of her life?

"I did this to her."

"Quit jerking off to yourself." Tempest reclines on my bed, propping his hands under his head as he contemplates the ceiling. "Callie's making her decisions with or without your dick."

"No, I pushed her too far. She has no one now. Nothing to lose."

"What about her detective? Her stepparents? Her step*baby*?"

"She'll isolate them." I rub my index finger over my mouth as I contemplate. "Keep them out of it. And Ivy's dead. Now I've left her."

"Your sister hasn't. And that quiet one with the kind of hair that'll come out of an ancient hellhole and strangle you."

"Emma and Eden can only do so much. They're not allowed on societal grounds."

"Okay, then there's her fath—"

"Don't."

Tempest sighs. "It's not like I know his identity, but circumstances tell me it could be *quite* the important clue to help her."

"It won't."

"Whatever. So, what are you saying then?"

I point at him. "You."

"Me, what?"

"You're going to figure out why Sabine would allow Callie to be robed in the first place."

"How am I supposed to do that? She won't say shit to me."

"James might, if you talk to him. He's her latest lackey." I mull over the memory of that jackass tossing a pillowcase over my head, then clamping his hand over my fabric-covered mouth. My heart jackknifed into my throat. My lungs swelled until they squeezed my heart. I couldn't breathe. Couldn't. Breathe.

And one of my supposed best buddies was using my phobia against me. For *her*.

"Or torture it out of him," I growl. "I don't care."

Undeterred by the ominous death-wish in my voice, Tempest says, "It's common knowledge I'm your second-in-command. What makes you think—"

"Then go through Rio, I don't give a shit. Just get it done." I nail him with a look. "I'm ordering you as my second-in-command."

"Jesus. Fine." Tempest sits up. "And what about you? You're not gonna be able to stand back and let other people do your dirty work, despite your vow to keep Callie at arm's length."

My brows lower, shadowing my vision. "I'm going to the source. Sabine may have her reasons for allowing Callie into the Virtues, but my father's priority will always be the Nobles. He doesn't want them destroyed any more than I do."

"Ah." Tempest leans back. "And if Sabine has already conned him to her side?"

"I have another option," I answer. "If Callie tries to claim her rightful place, I'll stop her. Simple as that."

"Uh-huh. You're the boss."

"I am." Stopping in front of the mirror by the door, I take a good look at myself, arming my expression for what it will take to protect the new Nobles from whatever fuckery Callie's planning.

The Noble alumni may be far from her reach, but the initiates aren't. Briarcliff Academy isn't.

But Sabine can't win. She'll have to get through me if she wants to so much as flick a finger against Callie's nose. I have to somehow stop the Virtuous Queen from harming Callie, and yet I also have to stop Callie from reaching her truth and finding justice.

I have to save her and sabotage her, all at the same time.

The lake house is dim and deserted when I pull up the drive and shut off the engine. I slide out, my shoes crunching against the gravel, the noise amplified in the quiet, surrounding forest. It's so cold and blustery, not even the owls hoot.

Ice crackles in my periphery. I glance over on instinct, but it's the brittle tree branches weighed down by snow melted by the sun, then hardened by the moon.

Unlocking the door, I step into the warmth, our lake house kept at a warm 75 degrees despite the lack of residency most of the winter.

My father: the environmentalist.

I don't waste time on the main floor, though my stomach growls at the lack of sustenance I've given it since returning to Briarcliff. My crew practice suffers for it, my 2k completions on the erg becoming longer and longer stretches of time, but I can't bring myself to give a fuck.

Not when Sabine's treating the Virtues as a brothel, with my sister as a victim and Callie's revenge on ultimate nuke level.

The Nobles are redeemable, I think on a determined frown as I take the stairs to the basement level. I wish Callie would simply focus on the destruction of the Virtues, but no, she wants all of us.

I was on her side until she admitted the Nobles had to suffer, too. Now we're at odds, and I've come to believe the rumbling in my stomach isn't solely due to hunger for food.

It's starvation for *her.*

I'm unable to fill myself on her scent, sink into her warmth, find gluttony in nipping and licking her skin. It's sent me into a spiral, where all I can see is her smile, such a rare thing, yet it's settled in my mind's eye as a soft-focus filter whenever I think of her.

I can't. She's the enemy now.

Because of this bullshit, instead of running my hands all over her naked body, she has me going through Father's things, proving her wrong, *showing* Callie there comes good with her Missing Heir status, not simply murder and mayhem.

Sabine has to go—I'll help her with that. But my brothers? *My* heir status? *No.*

I step back after punching in the code at Father's bookshelf, waiting impatiently for the hidden door to slide open, so I can access the Noble files.

There has to be something here to prove to Callie that the Nobles can be saved. A document, a hidden relic from the founders, *anything* to showcase their lack of support in Sabine's disgusting plans, or failing that, my ability to turn them around, *even* while they're still under my father's guidance.

Callie says—my *sister* proves—certain Noble alumni are signing forbidden agreements with Sabine to take advantage of Virtues enrolled at Briarcliff Academy. If I can find those men, kick their asses out, and hell, provide their names to Callie's NYPD detective, I can begin the cleansing process.

But if Father is part of those men? Not necessarily partaking in underage girls, but sanctioning it?

I step into the panic room, scanning the sterile area and the wall of gray cabinets, resembling more of a morgue than a Noble King's workspace.

... then I'll kick his ass out, too, and start my kingship early.

That has to be enough to convince Callie to leave us alone. Her focus can remain on dethroning Sabine. Then she can do whatever the fuck she wants with the Virtue society.

Something chews on the back of my mind as I pull open the nearest drawer, flicking through folders with the expertise of a person who's been locked in here and forced to study Noble rites and rituals for almost a decade.

Why is Sabine allowing Callie to get this far?

It doesn't sit easy with me. I'm in my father's study to sift through all known documents and records of the Nobles, pulling out folder after folder of members, adherence rules, rituals, prohibitions, but it's only now coming to light just how little I've learned of the Virtues.

Was it deliberate? It's unclear what my father was taught, and his grandfather before him, though it makes sense that I learned the same.

Casting through my memories, I touch upon the Virtues' origins. Rose Briar created them soon after her husband established the Nobles, in an effort to educate women and provide them with benefits befitting a privileged woman at the time. Education, a perfect marriage match, a lifetime of wealth. When Rose committed suicide, Thorne Briar allowed the Virtues to continue under the auspices that they would always be second to the Nobles and, if ever overridden, to capitulate to the mens' demands. That was about the time the Harringtons took over.

Add in my self-imposed research of the Virtues and...

Sabine Moriarty became pregnant and married Paul Harrington not for wealth, as she didn't need it, or education, as she was already on track for Harvard, but to inherit the presumptive Harrington throne in the Virtues.

Paul didn't have any sisters. He was an only child. His mother—what was her name? Prudence, yes. The Virtue Queen, Prudence Harrington, was expected to hold the throne until Paul had daughters, otherwise—

Otherwise....

Frowning, I turn back to the files. What would've happened if Prudence Harrington died before Paul had any daughters, if he had any at all? That kind of loophole practically begs for a more cunning, opportune Virtue to step in.

Piper did say her grandmother and Sabine were close. Like true mother and daughter. I wonder if that relationship prospered before Paul came into the picture, and how much Prudence supported Sabine not only getting pregnant but marrying her son.

That would take away any fears of losing the throne to a...

I frown again. To a what? A challenger?

My mind fires on all cylinders, and I flick through the files faster, desperation coating my fingertips. Incident reports, initiation prospects, background checks—all related to the Nobles.

Where are the Virtues? Is there anything in the Virtue handbook about challenges to the queen?

My hands freeze. I straighten, my stare boring into the opposite wall.

Fuck, how about challenges to the king? In all this time, since the Nobles' and Virtues' inception, there's never been a challenger. Thorne passed, and he bequeathed the society to his brother, Theodore. Theodore died, and without heirs or any remaining brothers, he performed the rite to pass it on to his best friend, my great-great-grandfather, Montague Stone.

It's been carte blanche ever since. No ripples, no waves, no angry rebellions...

Until Callie.

The last time I was in here, Callie and I discovered a hidden birth certificate of a child born to Rose Briar. Beside that single piece of paper were decades old records of Virtuous members. But *besides* that, there is nothing in here on the Virtues.

Growling, I slap the tops of the files and step back. How could I not see it before?

I could search through every folder in this place and come up with the same questions I did when I broke in here.

A deliberate veil covers the Virtues, and I'm pretty fucking sure it's been in place since the first Harrington.

"What are you doing in here, boy?"

I don't jump. Any jolt of surprise I feel is pushed down into the dark place I reserve specifically for my father.

I slam the cabinet shut. The metal rattles under the vicious energy. "Searching for answers."

Father stands at the open archway, the eerie blue-black light of his office framing the backs of his shoulders despite the glaring halogens I stand under.

"Nonsense. You've read through these papers and gone through my computer since you were a young boy. There are no surprises in here."

"My point exactly."

Father crosses his arms. "Explain yourself."

"Where do we keep our checks on the Virtues?"

"Pardon?" He arches a brow.

"According to my teachings, thanks to you, Father, the Virtues are allowed to assemble, provided they report to us. Their meetings, their minutes, their prospects and *initiates* ... where are all those records?"

Father chuckles, the sound grating against my spine. A muscle pulls at my jaw, but I keep myself in check.

He says, "Even you can admit times have changed since the nineteenth century. We don't require their every twitch and thought these days."

"Why not?" I counter. "We've preserved every single rule from the beginning—it's our law. Or so I thought."

"Are you saying you prefer your women subservient?" Father's lips pull into a thin smile. "It's lovely to see that my lessons continue to hold. If only you could put them into practice with Calla Lily Ryan."

I play to his assumption rather than give into my boiling rage. "I believe you like to call them accessories. So why give them independence? Free reign? Do you have any idea what my future stepmom is up to?"

"Please, boy." Father scoffs. "There is a reason I keep her near."

"So you know." It's my turn to cross my arms. "You know the truth about Ivara Alling."

Father tips his head, neither acknowledging nor denying.

"And Callie's bloodline." I let my father's controlled expression finish the rest of my explanation.

His lower eyelid tics. He sets his jaw. But he does nothing else.

I come toward him but fall back enough not to grab for his throat. "Tell me the truth, Father. What's Sabine playing at? What are you helping her hide?"

"It's none of your concern."

"Emma was made into a sex slave for Sabine," I deadpan. "How is that not my business?"

Father's eyes spark, flat gray rocks rubbing up against mine. "Get ahold of yourself, boy, before I have to do it for you."

His hands twitch at his sides, aching, I'm sure, for the times when he could put me in a stranglehold, and I'd stay there.

"Don't tell me you're in such denial, Father," I spit. "Your flesh and blood was used, torn open, her soul *eviscerated*, and you stand here before me like it's nothing."

"It isn't," my father snarls.

My cheeks go numb. Any blood anchored in my face is pulled to my fists, swelling them to levels where I need my knuckles to *burst* on my father's skin. "You are pathetic. Sad. A waste of a man who hides behind a woman's skirts while she does your dirty work. You hate us so much, why go through the pretenses of raising us, when we both know you'll never give up your leader status, because that's all you have, you fucking soulless bastard—"

The back of my head slams into a cabinet handle on my father's roar, his maneuver catching me by enough surprise that the sharp corner sinks into my nape and sets my neck on fire.

Father pushes his face into mine, gripping my lapels, spittle hanging onto his stubble as he snarls and spits like a rabid animal. "I don't give a damn about her because *she isn't mine!*"

Shock has me halting my struggle. Father takes advantage of it and swings for my face. I duck, and his fist crashes into the cabinet behind me.

Cursing, he stumbles back, holding his injured fist like he just lost a bar fight and didn't just go head-to-head with non-sentient metal.

"What did you just say?" I whisper while circling him, my breaths haggard.

He glares at me.

"*Answer me!*"

"Emma Loughrey is not mine," he repeats, holding steady. "Why do you think I was more than happy to allow her to take your mother's last name? She is the product of Marilee's weak heart."

"The fuck is that supposed to mean?" I respond, still whispering, still barely breathing.

"She's adopted. When you were two years old, your mother came across a young girl during her charity work. Lovely Marilee decided it was better to work in a homeless teen counseling center than go to college after marrying me—the heir to an empire who put a four-carat diamond on her finger. One of her female Cretans had an unwanted toddler—malnourished, dirty vermin. I blame it on the goddamn hormones, but Marilee wanted this child. She hemorrhaged after having you and was told she couldn't have another. She was desperate for you to have a sibling, and at the time, I wasn't around much—"

"Already fucking Sabine, I bet." But the words have no passion. I'm numb. Sucked dry.

"Watch your mouth, boy. I allowed it, didn't I? You got yourself a sister, Marilee decided to make you two twins, and I was blessed with two assholes instead of one."

"Father of the Year," I say through gritted teeth.

"I care about you," Father says in defense as he rises out of his hunch. "Educated you, taught you, made you the prince to all this." He sweeps his arm out. "Don't you dare be disrespectful in the house you stand in solely because of *my* efforts."

"How about the basement you kept Emma in, when all she wanted to do was escape you? Why didn't you let her? If you wanted nothing to do with her, why keep her after she tried so desperately to leave? All I'm hearing is that Emma was trash to you, so you allowed Sabine to do what she wanted with her. You *sanctioned* young Virtues to be made into pets for your Noble alumni. You betrayed your daughter—because yes, she is your daughter, legally and in all the ways that matter—you never told her she was unwanted, just made her believe it. We're nothing but objects to you, are we, Father? Profits and gains."

"There is nothing profitable about you," Father spits through a trembling jaw. "Your grandfather practically sewed into me the importance of preserving the Stone line, so much so, I impregnated a girl at the neighboring Dover Shores, so he'd shut the hell up. And when that girl found out she was having a boy? I'll admit, I aimed high when it came to my only son. Married her, accepted her goddamn bleeding heart of a baby girl, but here *you* are, flipping through old files instead of solidifying your rightful place as prince and taking control of our initiates, still trying to save Calla Lily. But now I'll say, go ahead." He waves at me in dismissal, but his lips twist into a sneer. "I can't do anything with a child who focuses so hard on saving other people because he's too broken to fix himself."

It takes a severe amount of effort to stay calm through his ruthlessness. It always has. "Doing what is right does not make me flawed."

"Thinking I needed a son to maintain my power over the Nobles is the flaw I'm most ashamed of," Father retorts. "Sabine has taught me just how unnecessary you are, as well as your sister and *Calla Lily*. You were meant to be my mirror image. Instead, you reflect the worst parts of me. You and Emma may not be blood-related, but you were raised as twins. You've inherited her knack for self-mutilation. Get out of here, boy, before I remind you what true anger looks like."

Shaking with wrath, I step toward the door.

Then shoot my arm out and go for his throat.

Father catches me mid-swipe, twisting my arm behind my back until I fold over, my throat clogged with pain.

"Try that again, son," Father mutters near my ear, "and your athletic status will be sorely wanting as you await your sports scholarship from Princeton."

"*Fuck* you," I hiss through the searing tendons gripping my shoulder, my neck, my jaw.

"Indeed."

Father releases his hold, and I stumble forward, my cheeks pulsing with indignation and rebellion.

When I jerk toward him, he throws up a hand. "As for the curiosity that brought you here, allow me to squash that as well."

He moves toward a lower cabinet. I eye him, holding my shoulder, as he pulls open a drawer, takes out the files, and lifts a false bottom, revealing a thick, brown leather book.

"The Virtues' original handbook. Written by Rose Briar, I believe, and revised by Prudence Harrington. Should be some quiet reading for you."

My stare pings from the drawer, to the book, to my father. "Why have you hidden it?"

"For the same reasons we kept the baby Briar birth certificate in my vault all these years, before you and your weak spot decided to weaponize it." He jerks his chin toward the door. "You'll soon discover where you fall, son. Until then, I highly recommend you allow Sabine to do as she pleases when it comes to Calla Lily Ryan."

"Never," I say, but Father shoves the book at me and stalks past me without another word.

I stay where I am, digging my fingers into my wounded shoulder while my slack hand holds onto the book, trying make sense of his revelations.

Twisting my world.

And forcing my hand when it comes to Callie.

Callie

THE LETTER STRIKES me as unceremonious.

You'd think, with all I've endured up to this point, the final communication from the Virtues would be accompanied by an obvious, robed Falyn, or heck, delivered by a live raven or the queen herself.

But no. A single piece of paper is propped in a standing fold on my desk, unimposing, the expensive cream stock a normal occurrence at this point, the white rose accompanying it expected.

I'm predicting the script on the inside flap before my backpack hits the floor and head toward my desk. My damp hair drips the last of the pool's rivulets down my shoulders, Eden's first swim lesson mainly consisting of me bobbing in the shallow end, the water hitting just above my chin.

My swim failure aside, I figure this note contains something along the lines of, *Your ritual rites are complete; thus, you shall be robed. That is, if you're prepared for a Virtuous future* or some other ominous language.

What I'm not prepared for is the addition of a black rose beside it.

Fingering the white satin ribbon, I lift the rose, bringing the ink-dipped petals to my nose and inhaling the sweet, slightly chemical scent. I haven't received one of these in so long, I'd forgotten they were a thing—but they must be how the Nobles communicate, too. I received a black rose when new furniture arrived in my dorm, along with an undamaged uniform. Another appeared on my bed after a particularly haggard day. These petals made an appearance whenever I needed a right amid such wrongs. Part of me assumed—okay, *hoped*—they were from Chase, his secret Noble communication assuring me he had my back, though he had never confirmed it.

But it couldn't be him, not this time. He's made his feelings on me becoming a Virtue clear. This must be their official acceptance of my robing, meaning they'll probably be attending as well.

Chase will be there.

The realization skitters along the edges of my skull, spreading goosebumps and inciting angst. He'll be watching me, and I'm positive I'll feel his disapproval all the way to my toes.

But it's not about him anymore, or us. This is about my mother and all the other girls who've been hurt, maimed, and killed by this so-called society of Virtuous women.

After carefully setting down the rose, I ignore the white one and move to the letter, opening its crisp fold and reading the perfect calligraphy.

Dearest Initiate,

As you receive this letter, you've been granted the highest honor. Passing our trials is no small feat, and congratulations are in order. Please join us at our temple on the eve of Friday the 16th, where it will be my greatest pleasure to lay a Virtuous robe upon your shoulders.

- Your Queen

"Wow," I say under my breath as I close the letter. She actually signed it this time.

"So, it's official, then."

I turn to see Emma hovering in my doorway.

"Sabine's accepted you," she finishes.

Nodding, I set the letter back on the desk. "Am I supposed to pretend that you didn't read this while I was with Eden?"

"Nope, I totally snooped." Emma steps inside my room, then sits on the side of my bed. "Missed the drop-off, though."

"Everyone always does," I muse, then slide off my jacket and perch on the desk chair. "For all we know, there are secret corridors into all the dorm rooms, too."

Emma shudders. "Don't put that into the universe."

I respond with a commiserating grunt. "I can't stand the thought of Falyn watching me while I sleep, either."

"Are you ready for what's next?" she asks.

"As I'll ever be. Unless you have some last-minute wisdom to impart...?"

Emma pushes her lower lip out in thought. "I don't know much about robing a senior. We're usually initiated freshman year, and it always occurs in the forest near Lover's Leap. The fact you're asked to come to the temple is already unusual."

"Yeah." Emma's words bring me back to my first day at Briarcliff when I stumbled blindly behind Richardson House and almost tripped over a Noble and Virtue initiate ceremony. Back then, I was stupid, thinking it was a creepy, witchy extracurricular rich kids enjoyed dabbling in.

Now, there's a body count.

"We cast our invitations into the bonfire," Emma continues, "reciting the motto for our societies. Then, the Viscounts and Viscountesses—that's Headmaster Marron and Miss Lacey, by the way—

"Miss *Lacey* has been a Cloak this whole time?" I cut in, thinking of our small, innocent calculus teacher with a brain the size of Arkansas, and who Chase jokingly said he was screwing. I frown, a lick of jealousy gliding across my gut.

"They like to keep the mentors, or viscounts and countesses, in the faculty, since they're always around."

"I've never had a mentor, other than Ivy, maybe."

Emma gives me the side-eye. "You're a unique case."

"Fair enough. Go on."

"Okay, so, they ask us to pledge our loyalty, to put the societies above all else. We take an oath, sealing it with a blood vow—"

"Excuse me, blood?"

Emma heaves out an exasperated sigh at my constant interruptions. "With Thorne Briar's personal blade, yep."

My vision goes dark as I remember the opulent knife that killed Ivy. Could it be the same one? It was intricate enough. Old, precious, special. If I have to hold it, if I have to place it against my skin the way it pierced hers...

"Callie? You've gone pale. You okay?"

"Uh-huh." I nod, swallowing audibly. "Keep going."

"We hold our wrists over the fire, our blood mixing into the flames. Then, we recite the maxim again, line up in front of the queen and king, accept our robe, then go party in the Nobles' room. That's where our first introduction into the life of a secret society is—drugs, booze, served by almost-naked men and women. And you can take any of them to bed." Emma shrugs, as if throwing this in front of a fourteen-year-old is standard practice at Briarcliff. "Those who overindulge are taken in by Sabine or Daniel and cared for until they can come back to school."

"I'm not sure whether to find that unoriginal, creepy, or downright terrifying," I say, then nod as I come to a conclusion. "It's all of it."

"Yes. It starts off stereotypical. Six figures drop in a bank account they open especially for you, to be accessed when you turn eighteen, earning interest and being invested on your behalf until then. Your wardrobe is updated when you get back to your room. A concierge number is put into your phone, who you can call and ask for anything. A pick-up, a clean-up, a cover-up. Your grades are suddenly switched to the higher tiers—except, to be one of them, you'd already have to excel in something, whether it be athletics, debate, English Lit ... They help you with your weaker subjects."

I prop my chin in my hands, fascinated. "Ivy didn't tell me any of this."

Emma exhales from the side of her mouth. "I said it starts off like that. Then you're asked to do things for them, small favors like allowing a fellow Virtue to cheat off your exam, or cleaning up small, undetermined blood splatters in certain classrooms. After that ... it becomes different from the Nobles. Sabine asks you to attend outside events, like hotel ballrooms with small orchestras, or attending box seats at the Metropolitan Opera one night, before being introduced to her 'friends.' This is probably why Ivy didn't tell you. She showcases her new initiates to her clientele. Sabine selects the girl with the most interest and begins the grooming process for the next princess."

"That's what gets me," I say, giving Emma a needed break. "Do you really think

Sabine stops at just one girl? If she's as greedy and vain as I assume, I'd think she'd have a few, just in case one didn't work out."

I hate talking about my peers like this, girls who could be me, but it's necessary to get into Sabine's head. Think like her, before I confront her.

"It takes a lot of effort to turn a girl," Emma answers, then adds softly, "I should know. Sabine focuses all her energy on you. And it's kind, gentle, alluring. She becomes like a mother, and with many of us being so far away from home ... a yearning starts, right here." She points to her chest. "Suddenly you're confessing all your insecurities to her, and she's bringing you tea and listening intently, offering advice and comfort. You start going to her more and more ... she's the queen, after all. She's given you all these gifts, so many privileges. The least you could do is meet with her and confide all your sins and discomforts until she sees you as perfect and deserving of the Virtue title." Emma pauses, staring unblinkingly at the floor. Her lashes don't flutter. "Until the final time, when, after you finish your tea, you get tired. Heavy. Clumsy. Sabine's beautiful, concerned expression blurs in and out. It goes black. And you wake up in a strange room, on a strange bed, with an undressed man on top—" Emma chokes.

I rush over, grabbing her hand, pressing her head to my clavicle as I stand over her, shroud her. "You can stop. It's okay. It's over."

Her hair tangles in my fingers as she shakes her head back and forth. "That's the problem. It's only just beginning."

My lips turn hard and grim above the crown of her head as I stare off across from us. *This* is why I'm being robed. Precisely the reason I'm staying on the inside instead of skirting the edges and trying to destroy Sabine and the Virtues from afar. I wish, so badly, for Chase to understand that.

The Nobles are a part of this demonic underworld. Riches and unlimited power have turned these high school teens into rabid, unaccountable adults. Girls are destroyed. Rose's message is all but erased.

These societies *have* to go.

"I'm ending this," I say through my clenched jaw, so quietly I'm not sure Emma hears.

"I'll be nearby," Emma says, patting my arm and dragging me back into the present. "I've outlined the standard ceremonial robing process. That doesn't mean I have any idea how Sabine plans to approach yours."

I find a smile and aim it at her as I withdraw. "Sabine won't harm me in front of everyone. It'd ruin her whole image she has going. I think she enjoys being so clandestine and one-upping the Nobles without them even realizing she's pulling all the strings. She wouldn't be so blatant."

"While I agree, Eden and I will still stay close. You never know."

I press my lips together, knowing she's right. We *don't* know what Sabine will do next, even after I'm officially a Virtue. She has yet to even acknowledge my buried secret—my legacy—let alone act on it. Is she allowing me in because she has no other choice? Keeping me close because she killed my mother? To deny me entry would be to admit I *did* have power, enough for her to wantonly keep me out after being the person to ask me in. It would look confusing to her Virtues, maybe suspicious. After all, I don't have proof, merely a picture of an old birth certificate. There's nothing I can point to when it comes to my mother, either, other than conjecture. And she must be aware of that.

Keep playing her game, so you can start your own.

"When are you and Eden headed to town?" I ask.

"We both have a free period after lunch. We'll go then."

"Good."

"Have you called Ahmar about comparing old DNA to yours?"

Preferring to pick at my sweater's sleeve, I answer, "Not yet. I will."

Emma doesn't push it. "Okay. Well, I gotta go. Meeting Chase for breakfast."

"Oh, yeah?"

She hits me with a droll look as she rises. "Wanna come?"

"No."

"That was too quick an answer to be real. You sure you don't want me to tell him what we're doing? You two may be at odds now, but if he knows you're mainly after proving Sabine murdered your mother—"

"He already knows that. Chase'll be at the robing ceremony, anyway, so I have to prepare."

"Fair enough. Want me to figure out his plans for fucking up your ceremony instead?"

A genuine smile crosses my lips. "If you can. The guy's a vault."

"Tell me about it." Emma crosses the room to the door.

"Must be a genetic thing," I say wryly.

She responds with a closed-mouthed grin. "That's the one talent we don't regret inheriting from our father," she responds, then leaves my room.

I wait until she shuts the door, then stand and focus on keeping up pretenses by getting ready for another day at Briarcliff Academy.

Surprisingly, the week whizzes by, my mornings spent in swim lessons, and my evenings focused on homework assignments to the point where I don't have time to stress about the robing ceremony, except to idly wonder if I fail to hand in my homework, if I'll get an A anyway.

Do I even have to apply for colleges, or will the Virtues do that for me, too?

Despite my thoughts lingering on the question, I'm fairly certain the answer to that doesn't have worth, since I don't plan to stay a Virtue past this semester, thus, my studies remain with me.

None of that should be clogging up my mind right now, as I'm gazing at my closet, chewing on my thumbnail, and contemplating the best outfit to wear to tonight's ceremony.

Emma said first years wore something similar—and as important—to a prom dress, but the only gown I have of that nature was gifted by Sabine, and considering what happened the last time I wore it...

No. I won't be wearing that atrocity tonight.

This evening, I get to own my power, striding through the temple doors with the knowledge that I *own* the Virtues. Even if I can't claim it immediately, that hidden diamond glimmers within my soul, just waiting to be cut from the earth and unveiled to the societies.

I have to be smart, though. Sabine's nothing if not scrupulous with her multiple fail-safes, should her original plan falter. If I want to beat her, I have to think like her, and collecting evidence against her, silently and willfully, is the first step in succeeding.

Eden and Emma managed to snag—literally—strands from an old hairbrush of Rose Briar's, on display with other items from her bedroom vanity, carefully protected from the elements in a velvet box when not positioned for tourist's eyes, not that many frequent Briarcliff, never mind the library. Eden parroted that fact while attempting to dunk me in the swimming pool and push me into a front stroke, stating that Darla was only too eager to chat Eden's ear off about the Briarcliff items, while Emma subtly lifted the top of the display case, tweezered a few pieces of Rose's hair from the bristles, and placed it in a plastic baggie before they sat with Darla for another twenty minutes and listened to the founder brothers' scandals.

Once safely ensconced in my room, we put our heads together and searched on my phone whether 200-year-old hair could be viable for a DNA sample. Turns out, it can, since scientists have identified remains of a Woolly Mammoth by ancient pieces of hair. Even better if the hair follicle is attached. We squinted into the baggie, decided there were indeed clear bulbs attached to the ends of some pieces, and then it was up to me to call Ahmar and explain to him *why* I'd like 200-year-old hair DNA tested against mine.

It was an awkward conversation, both in my bringing up the mystery of my child-hood (thinking I'd found Mom's great-great-grandma and how it would be an amazing history project to have my genealogy traced against all these other rich kids with vast resources at their fingertips) and his failed relationship with a forensic anthropologist. He'd also brought up that I'd not seen him for coffee when I was in town, and I was forced to use the baby card, stating I'd fallen in love with Blair and had wanted to spend as much time as I could with her before I went back to school.

It wasn't entirely a lie.

Fifteen minutes later, Ahmar reluctantly agreed, not that he believed shit. *An ancient grandma?* Ahmar had said. *Kid, please.* But I knew he felt guilty for the wedge that's transpired between us, and it didn't take long for him to give in, consid-ering it wasn't doing any harm *and* gave him an excuse to converse with his ex again.

He warned it would take some time—maybe a long time, what with convincing his former lady love to do him a solid and get the results, but I wasn't in a rush. Not on this.

Lynda warned me to keep Ahmar out of society business, and I was. Sort of. I'm not asking him to investigate the societies and Mom's murder anymore. She can be content knowing he's helping me ace a so-called "history assignment."

With those ducks lined up, I could move on to more precarious items on my to-do list ... like choosing an outfit for the first time I'm seeing Sabine since Ivy died.

Ivy's name incites a swell of rage. I rip my thumb from my mouth and grab for the nearest dress, a deep-V black mini Ivy made me wear to Chase's party at his fami-ly's lake house.

It seems fitting that I'd wear this to a ceremony Ivy can't attend. It'll remind me of her, and I'll be the only one to know the tangible memories that float under my newly donned gold cloak.

As I'm pulling off my uniform, I glance out my bedroom doorway, searching for Emma. She's not back from class yet, but I figure I'll cook us a quick dinner before I head out, considering neither of us enjoy dining hall festivities.

I half-expect Chase to be traveling with her, though I know it's a fruitless thought. She hasn't seen him since their breakfast meeting a few days ago, and she told me he was distracted, subdued, and curt enough that she wasn't eager to meet up with him again.

Doesn't matter, anyway. Chase wouldn't be much help, even if he decided to communicate with multiple syllables. He chose his side, and I chose mine.

Now it's time to see who's won.

Callie

IT'S SO cold that a layer of ice has sealed in the mounds of snow, and each time I slip and stumble off the path, despite my winter boots, it cracks under my weight and into the night.

My breath makes opaque shapes in front of me as I trudge on, my fur-lined hood pulled up to protect my face, but my bare knees knock together like a plastic skeleton prop each time I take a shaking step.

A cocktail dress might've been the wrong choice. Snow pants would've been better, whether or not they looked good under a golden cloak.

At last, small beams of light skimming the rooftop of the M.B.S. Library of Studies float into view, and I scurry the rest of the way, slipping only twice on the unsalted sections as I take the gradual hill to the front of the building.

I don't see any other Virtues or Nobles taking the path ahead of or behind me, but as Emma assured at dinner, they would've arrived early in anticipation of getting a prime spot for the rare robing of a senior.

And what a senior I am. A Briar heiress. The Missing Heiress.

Just the thought of throwing that title in Sabine's face makes me flash my teeth into the cold night.

Not yet, my mother's voice reasons. *You don't have enough to prove your legacy. Stay patient, Calla. Stay smart.*

The automatic doors smoothly open as soon as I step up to them, the library black with shadows on the other side.

I take one breath. Two.

Then step over the threshold, alone.

A silent Cloak, head covered in gold fabric and bowed, stands at the secret entrance into the Virtue Temple.

Once I'm close enough, I stop and clear my throat, but the person doesn't move, save for the hem of her Virtue cloak swaying at her ankles.

Unable to stand the silence in such a dark space, I say, "Um. Am I early for—?"

I'm cut off by a whisper. "Do you accept your elevated status, Initiate?"

"Yes," I draw out, clenching and unclenching my fingers as they tingle from the invasive warmth of the library. "It's why I've come."

"I'm tasked to remind you: this is your last chance to turn around."

This time, the whisper is familiar. I peer into the darkness of the hood. "Willow?"

The gold fabric jerks as the head beneath it swivels in my direction. "You are *forbidden* to refer to us by name until you are fully enrobed as a Virtue Baroness. One more mistake, *Calla*, and you'll pay dearly."

Her reference to my endearing nickname, used only by my mother and Ahmar, gives me invisible, painful hives.

"I've already paid the worst price in order to be here tonight," I say through cracked lips.

If Willow reacts, I can't see it. "Take off your jacket."

Deciding not to argue, I unzip my coat and pass it to her. Willow drapes it over one arm, my padded security blanket slumping uselessly in her grip.

I shiver, goosebumps pimpling my exposed arms and legs, colder now than I was outside.

Willow's golden cloak sweeps the floor as she spins, using her credentials to unlock the hidden door.

I wondered about that—if, in killing Ivy, Sabine also scrubbed my clearance into the temple until she deemed my access necessary again.

Denial into the temple would be a petty cherry to her vapid sundae, but I can't put anything past Sabine, from the simplest insults to the vilest deeds.

For you, Ivy, I think as I follow behind Willow. *And you, Mom.*

The circular temple is dark and cavernous, our hollow footsteps absorbing most of the noise. The sconces rimming the main arena create dimmed ovals of illumination on the walls, but they do nothing to highlight the figures I'm sure stand above me, staring down from the rafters as I take up position in the center.

"No one's on your side this time, possum," Willow mutters before she retreats, merging into the shadows.

Like I don't already know that.

With Willow's disappearance goes the only noise, other than my hitched, tentative breaths.

I count to one hundred in my head, refusing to be the first to speak. The chill of such an empty space seeps into my bones, crowding my thoughts, and I'm blinking rapidly even though I don't mean to.

Folding my arms into my chest, I squint into the shadows, searching for vague outlines, desperate for a certain one.

Chase is here. He must be. Where are you?

The darkness is overwhelming, disconcerting. I've spun in place, but I don't know if I've stopped where Willow originally left me.

Disorientation is so much worse when you know at least twenty people are watching you struggle.

"I did not assume you'd get this far, Initiate," comes a sinuous, beckoning voice.

Sabine.

I whip toward the sound. "Then your expectations were wrong."

"Clearly."

A sconce flares to life beside her, fire flickering against her flawless, sharp cheekbones. Her eyes remain eclipsed in shadow.

My heart lurches at the sight of her—my first glimpse since Ivy. She's regal, standing high, so confident she's untouchable as she regards me from her balcony.

Her lips pull at my study, my incendiary wrath likely obvious with each scathing breath I take as I keep my eyes on her.

"You are not afraid?" she asks. "If I were to judge on your current behavior alone, I'd say you were terrified."

"I'm not frightened. I'm cold."

Sabine chuckles. Her cloak ripples with the movement. Something glints under the velvet, and my breaths pause.

The knife. Thorne's blade. Ivy's death.

Sabine casts her gaze up, her arms spreading to her sides. "You stand here before your prospective brothers and sisters, mentors, and rulers."

The second story sconces gleam alive, each one lighting before the next, until all the hoods—both light and dark, black and gold, their outlines taking shape with fiery auras until I'm surrounded by a circle of them on the upper level.

Their faces are unidentifiably black, but experience has taught me they stand according to their ranks. Next to Sabine, the tall man in a purplish-black robe—the sign of a royal—has to be Daniel Stone.

On the other side of Sabine would be the next princess. I squint. Falyn ... or Violet? I can't tell.

Dragging my gaze in the opposite direction, a magnet pulling at the same time it's repelling ... I know who I'll find next to Daniel. The prince.

The purest Noble.

Chase Stone.

My chest sinks with an exhale, almost as if my lungs deflate of all oxygen when I set my eyes upon him. It hurts, just seeing his outline, blurry and obscured by a heavy velvet cloak.

It *burns.*

Swallowing, I tear my gaze away, skimming the red cloaks on either side of the monarchs—cloaks I noticed the older men wear during the Noble initiate's underground ceremony, like Headmaster Marron. They must be the viscounts. Including Miss Lacey, a teacher who could barely suppress her gag reflex at the sight of a used tampon on the ground of her classroom, now positioned ruthlessly beside her underground queen.

The marquis are next. Chase's buddies, Falyn's cronies. Then the rest of the barons and baronesses, because no one is an initiate now. Just me.

It's funny and a little sad how I'm coming to understand the rules of these societies so much clearer at the moment I must ruin them.

"Accept these men and women, boys and girls, into your fold, dearest Initiate," Sabine continues, "for they will be all you have once this night is over."

Hairs spike at the back of my neck. "Touch my family, touch one inch of them, and I'll kill you."

"Oh, my." Sabine feigns shock as she palms her chest. "We would never take it that far, dear one. You are our daughter now, but that does not mean your family will suffer. They will merely become second, for your priority now lies with me. Your every decision shall come up against my permission. Your clothing, your grades, your choice of university. All made with your best interests in mind, of course." Sabine defers to Daniel for a moment when a rumble emits from his hood. "But you are no longer independent, not until we deem it so. We are here to mold you into your better self, and you are to do as we ask with no question."

I clear my throat. Her speech is *mighty* different than the one Emma prepared me for, but all I have to do is remember Ivy, bleeding out on the very floor where I'm standing. And Mom with her throat slit all because of a hidden bloodline of which she had no interest in claiming.

All because of *this* bitch.

"I'm curious why you've allowed me to reenter your temple when I've proven, on multiple occasions, how unstable I am."

"Why, that only makes you a prime candidate," Sabine answers. "It's been so long since I've had the pleasure of breaking in an initiate. They all come so eager to please."

I don't expect even a rumble of discontent or insult to flow through the circle. When it comes to Sabine, no one ever protests.

Sabine continues, "I can understand how this might be difficult for you, but you are here. Capitulating before us despite my continuous reminders that you are no longer the girl who first entered Briarcliff Academy, and you never will be again."

"You took Ivy," I whisper, my lips puckered as I whisper the curse. "You took my mother. But I will take you before you ever get to me."

"What's that, Initiate?"

I jump at Daniel's booming voice, glancing up from the floor.

"I'm ... going over my options," I answer.

A snort comes from Daniel's right. Chase. Daniel's hood jerks at the sound, a profanity spat out.

"It's rather clear you're out of options, since you've shown up to become one of us, rather than heed any warnings, from me or my future stepmother," Chase's voice rings out. He lowers his hood, as if he knows his impact on me is better seen than heard.

His blond hair shimmers in the low light, his brown eyes darkened to black, held in place by chiseled, flawless skin and bone.

I hold my ground, notching my chin and meeting him breath for breath.

"You know why I'm here," I seethe, then blink myself out of the instant anger he sparks in me. "This is a privilege unlike any other."

Chase's mouth starts to move. Maybe one last warning or threat. Dare I think it could be a plea. He's so far into the shadows, it's difficult to make out his expressions, but his jaw appears sharper than normal, his cloak shimmering more than the others with his unseen twitches and tics of stress or frustration. With me? With the world?

I'm not supposed to care anymore.

"Then you will agree to my terms," Sabine cuts in. "You *will* stay quiet, now that you're aware how much authority I hold."

The hidden message is obvious, but only to me. Ivy's quiet whimpers, the sounds of her drowning in her own blood, echo in my ears.

"You claim to be a legacy of this society, but that has yet to be proven, if ever," she says. "I have centuries of history behind my reign, and I've allowed you into this temple and order you to get on your knees, because by now you understand the depth of my abilities to mold you or erase you. I am here to be your queen, Calla Lily Ryan." She shifts, and her eyes come into the light, gleaming. "And I do so look forward to ruling you. On your *knees*, Initiate," Sabine repeats.

Every limb of mine rebels at the forced supplication, but I'm staring past Sabine, through the wall behind her and into her office, into the princess bedroom, and at the red binder.

Mine.

My mother's murder is in there. I'm sure of it. Accessing that evidence is more important to me than satisfying Sabine's hard-on at witnessing me kneel before her. Thinking she's won.

My knees bend—

"Wait," Chase says.

I freeze. Sabine frowns. Daniel throws back his hood. "Son, if you so much as—"

"As her chosen soulmate, I'm the one meant to go down there and take her blood vow," Chase says.

"Why, yes," Sabine answers. "Although you're referencing quite an old rule of the Virtues. Remind me, dear," Sabine says to Daniel. "Something along the lines of a Noble *choosing* a woman to become a Virtue through the soulmate rite. Hmm." She puts a finger to her mouth, innocent enough, yet I brace for impact. "That doesn't apply here, now does it? Callie was tapped before you two got together."

"Wrong, *Mom*," Chase answers. "Father asked me to get close to Callie well before she reached this school. And as prince, it is my right to withdraw any Noble attachment I've given to her. And I'm withdrawing it now."

I angle my head, my stomach swaying at what Chase's outburst could mean.

Chase looks down at me and doesn't speak until I raise my chin and lock eyes with him. "I refuse her as my soulmate."

Sabine freezes. Daniel glowers, and the rest of the Cloaks murmur their shock.

"Come again?" Sabine asks, those two words so stilted and spaced out, it's clear she's making every effort to remain calm.

"I'm rescinding her soulmate status. And as an unbound female who was not initiated as a child..."

"Oh, now you're *really* digging deep into outdated Virtuous rules."

Chase raises a brow at Sabine. "Yet they're still in effect."

"Daniel," Sabine hisses. "*Do* something."

"Son, it's much too late for this unrequited love business. Callie has made it through her three trials, and she's accepted her Virtuous status despite the multiple challenges laid out before her. There is nothing more you can do."

"An elder initiate with her soulmate status revoked can no longer become a Virtue. It's made clear, in black and white, in Rose's original rulebook."

Chase pulls out a tattered leather handbook from beneath his cloak.

Something crushes against my chest like a vise. My ribs move with my breaths, but they're coming ever closer to spearing my heart. "Chase..."

I can't retaliate by arguing my rightful position. I have no evidence of my legacy. Not yet. And I can't retrieve proof relating to Sabine's duplicity without becoming a Virtue.

What is he doing?

What has Chase *done* to me?

He's putting his promise into action.

Chase doesn't blink, the rest of his expression an ambivalent marble carving showing no sorrow or shame. "Callie, as an initiate claiming a Noble soulmate, can't finalize her robing without her soulmate's approval."

He can't do this. I wasn't ignorant enough to believe he'd let this ceremony go on without a fight, but revoking his attachment to me? So officially and publicly? This is worse than being covered in garbage, than enduring public humiliation.

This is final.

"Then I claim another soulmate!" I shout.

Fabric rustles as everyone spins back to me.

Daniel says through downturned lips, "Well. I don't think you can." He turns to Sabine. "Can she?"

Sabine meets my eye with a wicked grin. I recoil, repulsed at the prospect of having something in common with her. Her reasons for keeping me a Virtue can't possibly be as important as mine, yet we're one with this goal, and it makes me sick inside.

Chase's eyes incorporate the flames of the sconces. "That's not possible."

"Isn't it?" Sabine asks sweetly. "I don't believe Rose's handbook touches on that subject. My great-great-grandmother-in-law's, however, does. The Harringtons are about empowering women, not stifling them. Callie may have begun her trials bound to you, but she may choose another eligible Noble at her robing ceremony to assist her in her Virtuous transformation. If you need proof, dear boy, you may go into my study and read through the dusty chapters. The rest of us will see this exciting ceremony through."

"There aren't any *eligible* Nobles left," Chase forces out. His exposed hands clench into vengeful fists. "Our barons have chosen their soulmates. The upperclassmen have theirs. Callie's finished here. There's—" Chase cuts himself off. His eyes widen, his gaze swings to mine, the realization in them as obvious to me as shooting stars in a pitch-black sky.

I narrow my eyes and grin, emitting none of the shrieking pain in my heart. "Tempest," I say, the name echoing in the silent chamber. "I choose Tempest as my soulmate."

Chase

SO FEW WORDS come out of my mouth, yet the curses filling my head would make an undertaker hand over his scythe and slowly back away.

My palms slam against the stone railing, my grip begging for the rock to crumble as I match Callie's defiant stare and try not to strangle her with my mind alone.

The light in here is so dim, shadows claim it as their docile pet, but the scarlet color of her lips manages to cut through the gloom. They're swollen—she's been gnawing at them, chewing out her thoughts until she reached this moment, pitting me against her and the society.

"Tempest?" I ask her. His name cuts against my tongue in ways that make me uncomfortable.

"Yes," she responds. No hesitation. No shame.

My chest tightens, inhales and exhales shrinking into pinpricks of air. Blood rushes into my neck, heating my ears. Tendons harden where my skin should be soft, and I'm having trouble restraining myself where my best buddy is concerned.

"You've been summoned, Tempest Callahan." My father's rough voice lingers in my ears, overtaking the shuffling of his steps and rustle of his robe. "How do you answer?"

"Simple. He doesn't," I bite out.

A heavy hand hits my shoulder and digs under the bone in warning. "It's no longer your call, son."

"It's always my call!"

I'm aware I sound like a spoiled jackass, but see if I fucking care. This is Callie. She can't be one of us. There wasn't supposed to be any chance of her succeeding in becoming a Virtue. I'm protecting the Nobles by exiling her. Ensuring the Stone legacy. Why can't Father *see* this?

Because he's built his empire on lies. Callie isn't yours to direct any more than you believed Emma was your sister.

692

I growl at the unbidden retort, made by my own brain. This is in my control. It's all for the greater good.

Confusion over why Father gave me Rose's handbook in the first place, when he's seemingly taking his fiancée's side, shouldn't take up so much headspace. I invoked my privilege, cast Callie off as insignificant, yet she remains confident and unaffected at naming my most trusted friend as her Plan B.

A black hood slithering off ebony hair catches my attention, Tempest's light eyes, both in hue and in humor, reaching mine before drifting over to Callie. "I'm not sure I have a say in this, brother."

His assessment of her fuses my bones into weapons of destruction.

"You're my second-in-command," I growl, my throat growing hotter the longer I keep focus on a guy who's enjoying this way too much. "Which means, you *do* as I command."

"It's Callie's right as a Virtuous prospect," Sabine adds, capping her statement off with a coquettish wink. "Seeing as her initial soulmate rescinded."

Throwing Sabine off this balcony and breaking her neck in her own temple would be all too kind. Callie may be so blinded by hate, she doesn't see the danger in enfolding herself as a Virtue under Sabine's direction, but I do.

"I believe we've been forced into this conversation because of you, son," Father says. I lock my jaw against his constraining glare. *You're the one who gave me the option, Dad.* "We'd be well on our way to a celebratory party if it weren't for these added shenanigans."

Callie's annoyingly sweet, headstrong voice cuts through our tension. "Then allow me to expedite this part. Tempest? Would you mind?"

Tempest pushes off the railing.

I storm behind the half-circle of Nobles and Virtues and fly in front of him before he hits the stairs. "If you take so much as another goddamned step—"

"You'll what?" Tempest asks dryly but keeps his voice low. "Implode your entire scheme to preserve the Nobles and dropkick your dad and Sabine out the secret door? Let this happen, man." He grabs my wrist before I can cock my fist. "Callie won this round. It doesn't mean she's beat you. So she turns into an insipid Virtue. Who cares? She has no evidence. There's no one on her side to believe her story of legacy and matricide, save for a few unreliable outcasts." He pauses, as if taking time to watch the simmering blood rise from my neck and into my face. "If you'll stop sucking your own balls for a minute, you'd see Callie's in less danger by going along with Sabine's wishes." He gives me a light push. "So, back off. You, me, and Callie are *alllll* aware who the true soulmate is."

"That's not—" I sputter. "Callie's not—I'm not pissed because you're her soulmate instead of me. This is about the brotherhood, and her coming between—"

"Uh-huh. Bye-bye now."

Tempest disappears down the stairs.

Rather than watch him descend, I whirl, then stalk toward the railing, but I'm stopped by a thin, boney hand—deceptively strong and sharp with manicured nails.

"You told me she wouldn't make it this far," Falyn whispers through her over-sized, golden hood.

"I was wrong," I clip out, then glare down at her hand in a gesture of what I think as a polite way to say *get your fucking hand off me.*

"You're admitting played this wrong?" Falyn squeaks, then tempers her voice at my growl of warning. "What's wrong with you? She can't be a Virtue. Sabine won't choose me as the next princess if Callie—"

I yank out of her hold so abruptly, she stumbles forward, but I don't catch her. I leave Falyn to right herself.

Back at the railing, I press my forearms into the cold stone and lean forward, pissed I've missed even seconds of Callie and Tempest's blood union.

Because that's what I'm allowing, aren't I? It should be *me* standing with her, cutting my wrist and pressing it to hers, then slipping the blade through the stain of my blood on her skin and mixing hers with mine.

Tempest is not the one for her. Whether in farce or for the preservation of my goal, he *is not the one for her.*

"Easy, son," my father murmurs beside me while staring ahead.

"You did this," I snarl through my clenched jaw. Tremors collect down my arms, in my thighs, desperate to launch my body over the balcony and drag Callie, kicking and screaming, through the temple doors. "According to Rose Briar's original rules, my revocation should've made Callie's ascension null and void. Yet here I stand, watching another guy claim *my* right—"

"That you revoked. Yes. I can't have you attached to her, boy, in any way, moving forward. She is unstable, volatile, and entirely Sabine's responsibility. We know enough about Calla Lily Ryan now. You're no longer needed as our messenger."

"You knew I'd choose this," I whisper harshly, my stare burning into the two people below. "An official, societal vow to separate myself from Callie was your final blow. That's why you gave me the original handbook."

"It's for your own good."

I whip in his direction. "Just like Emma? You seem to enjoy alternating your mindfucks between us. What's next for her?"

Father doesn't bother to shift in my direction. "My boy. Haven't you learned? I'm leaving that entirely up to you."

I prepare to leap. "You son of a—"

"Are you ready for the blade?" Sabine's melodious voice cuts in.

In the midst of our private, vicious conversation, a stone column rose from the floor between Callie and Tempest, high enough to become a table of sorts.

Or an altar.

Sabine reaches into her robe—

The knife flashing, arcing toward my chest—Callie leaping for Ivy—no, for me— the dagger sinking into Ivy's neck—

Closing my eyes, breathing deep, I dislodge the image.

The dagger shines as it did that night, cleaned and sharpened. Sabine tosses it over the railing, but I don't gasp like the rest of my brothers and sisters. I'm fully aware of Tempest's ability to catch sharp things and come out unscathed.

His hand whips up and catches the blade at its hilt. Callie's eyes widen, impressed, a hot exhale building in my mouth as I watch.

"Let the ritual commence," Sabine coos, ensuring one last look at me, smiling, before she continues conducting the robing ceremony of the Virtues' Missing Heir.

And Tempest's new soulmate.

Callie

WHEN THE LUSH, gold cloak hits my shoulders, I don't smile.

The weight of the heavy fabric anchors my shaking legs, and as Tempest moves to my front, tying the heavy rope at my neck, my throat hits his deft fingers as I swallow.

The balcony applauds as Sabine introduces me as the newest Virtue in her ranks.

"Relax, possum," Tempest says, his eyes lowered to the knot. "This is what you wanted, isn't it?"

"Yes," I whisper, but no amount of licking my lips will keep them moistened.

My wrist burns with his cut, the thin layer of Tempest's blood on the delicate area already stiffening my skin as it dries.

Droplets of my blood and his stain the circular stone table that sinks back into the ground at the same time Tempest pulls up my hood.

My gaze flicks up—unbidden, yet necessary—to Chase, the movement of the table reminding me all too much of his time in the underground cage.

It's just a stupid ceremony, meaning nothing to me. Mixing Tempest's blood with my own—while unsanitary—doesn't say anything about how I feel or to whom my heart belongs.

And the dagger used to slice my flesh may have been used on Ivy, but it's nothing but steel. It doesn't contain Ivy's lost soul, nor is it responsible for her death. Sabine is. She always will be.

So why do I feel so desolate rather than smug? I got what I wanted. I'm a Virtue.

"We shall reconvene in the Nobles' ritual room to celebrate," Sabine continues, her teeth flashing as she pulls up her hood. "You are dismissed, my children. Viscounts and countesses, please come with us."

The elder members retreat from the railing, Sabine and Daniel leading the way until their forms disappear behind the stone carving of a sleeping raven—Sabine's study.

My vision sharpens on their backs, wishing I could run through them and steal Sabine's binder. Now. *Right now.*

"Ready to party?" Tempest asks beside me.

"I'm ready to hurt something."

"Already learning the decorum of a Virtue, I see." Tempest offers me his arm. "Allow me to escort you, *soulmate.*"

I wince but take his arm.

"You know, if you were any other girl, I'd be highly insulted by how clearly it pains you to put your hands on me."

"Why aren't I any other girl?" I ask, but it's distracted and without much feeling. I'm too busy spying Chase, his eyes, a glittering onyx, disappearing as his form merges with the other cloaks and he leaves the balcony.

"Simple. Because you're Chase's."

I turn to him sharply. "Not anymore, I'm not."

He chuckles. "That's what you think."

The temple's underground tunnels take us to the Nobles' ritual room without having to deal with the frigid air outside. Before losing signal, I sent a message to Emma and Eden, telling them it was done. I'm a Virtue.

Eden replied with a thumb's up emoji, and Emma's answer popped up as dancing dots, then disappeared, nothing left in its wake.

I shove my phone in my jacket, the coat being proffered to me by a reluctant Willow as soon as the members started dispersing. Tempest pushes open the final heavy, wooden door and accepts a flute of champagne from a tray and offers it to me, calling me the "martyr of honor." I recall the last time I accepted a glass of champagne within these walls, during the Societal Ball when Chase was buried even deeper in Briarcliff's underground than I am.

He's not helpless this time, instead making it here before me, his shoulders hunched as he feigns interest in what a crowd of Nobles around him are saying as they swig their liquor and stand pretty in their privileged status. He's shed his robe, an expertly cut, two-piece charcoal suit taking its place, and he holds his champagne as if he's drinking it, but I know him well enough that he won't take a sip.

"These peeps are all here for you," Tempest muses, "to celebrate your induction. Try to smile, pretty possum, since all attention's on you."

"I have to figure out a way to get back to the temple."

"Come again?"

I jolt, not realizing I said it out loud. Covering up my blunder by bringing the flute to my lips doesn't do much to sway Tempest's interest. He cocks a brow, regarding me idly. "Whatever could you want to go back there for? To clean up our blood?"

To avenge Ivy's blood is the retort at the tip of my tongue, but I swallow it.

"My, what a murderous look you have," Tempest observes, then squeezes my hand as he draws me deeper into the crowd. "Try not to make it so obvious, not among this crowd of opportunists and savages."

"And what are you?" I ask, submitting to his tug and feeling less like a faulty beacon as I enter the fray of other cocktail dresses, gowns, and suits, now that everyone has shed their cloaks. "An opportunist or a savage?"

"A survivor," Tempest quips before withdrawing his hand, sending a wink—not my way, but behind me, before he meanders away.

Spinning, I nearly smack into the Chase's unforgiving chest.

"Excuse me," I say, side-stepping.

He clasps me by the waist, stalling my movements. "Happy now?" he growls.

I lift my chin to meet his eyes. "Not in the least."

"Good. Neither am I."

"*Good.*" The word comes out more emotional than scathing, but I use that energy to rip out of his hold and stalk around him.

I can't have him so near, hurt and want swirling so close to my heart they threaten to stop its beats. Chase can't be my distraction when I've come so far. My mother's justice is within reach, if only I stick to what's important, and that's *not* Chase Stone.

Music starts, at first mellow in tone, then picks up haunting beats as the DJ, set up under the carving of the Nobles' crest, spins his dials and flicks on otherworldly, neon lights.

The younger members cheer, lifting their drinks up high as they undulate with the admittedly addictive notes, twirling and hopping, twisting and writhing, until they've created a makeshift dance floor, and I'm desperate for escape.

They say it's for me, this celebration of a new member, but it's not difficult to grasp how distant my importance has become with the endless champagne, the private DJ, and the permission to act without boundaries underneath the constraints of Briarcliff Academy.

Falyn separates herself from Willow and Violet, her arms raised as she trots into the fray, her hair wild and her kaleidoscope dress strikingly familiar to the one Sabine gifted me for Winter Formal. When she catches my eye, her carefree smile drops from her face and her arms smack against her sides. She parts her lips and mouths something, but I don't need a translator to understand it's a message along the lines of, "*You don't belong here. Fuck off out of my party.*"

I send her a wink in answer, letting her know I'm just as aware of my place in the Virtues as she is.

"Callie, there you are."

The voice tickles at my nape, spiking the hairs there, sending ice picks under my skin.

Reluctantly, I turn. "Sabine."

"I believe, as a Virtue, you are to refer to me as your queen." She steps up beside me, pretending as much interest in the figures on the dance floor as I am. "I wonder if I could speak with you in private for a moment."

"Not on your life."

"That's fair." Sabine's lips quirk. "Perhaps you'll be willing to join me on the fringes instead. There's much we have to discuss."

"I don't negotiate with murderers."

"Aren't you curious as to why I've allowed you to come this far?"

"*Allowed*," I echo. Unable to contain myself, I turn to her. "What's that supposed to mean? That you could've killed me at any time up until this moment?"

"Well, yes." Sabine smiles, her eyes lighting up with the malicious intent behind her grin. "But that's not what I'm referring to. I'll ask you one more time. Join me."

She tips her head, motioning toward the far wall. I debate for a few seconds, well aware of my penchant for needing answers, then follow her to the far reaches of the room.

I look over my shoulder just once, in time to catch Chase clocking my movements. His focus makes me feel better, knowing, despite our differences, he cares about my outcome.

Or merely waits for another chance to sabotage me.

"There now," Sabine says once we've settled against the wall. Both of us hold flutes of champagne. Neither of us drink from them. "I trust you enjoyed the robing ceremony."

I stare at the shallow cut on my wrist, sliced diagonally and now clotted with dried blood. It still smarts. "I wouldn't call it a happy experience."

"You would have preferred Chase to be the one to welcome you," Sabine surmises, a confident curve to her mouth. "Alas, he is of his own mind and is determined to prevent you from reaching your full potential."

Frowning, I spin the flute's stem between my fingers. "And you *want* me to be at my fullest potential?"

"Indeed, I do. I realize how unconvincing that may seem, what with Ivy's short life so fresh in your mind."

She speaks of ending Ivy's life like she'd ask for a second glass of champagne, and I'm reminded of how dangerous she is, even while in public, mingling with her own kind. There's nothing to stop her from unsheathing the same dagger and stabbing me between the ribs, in front of everyone, their coveted membership to the Nobles and Virtues swearing them into painful silence.

But how excruciating would it be for them? The benefits of the Cloaks are extraordinary. Surreal. Limitless and empowering.

My life—Ivy's life—seems paltry compared to all that.

Shit, what am I doing?

"You may also be wondering why I haven't harmed you," Sabine continues, choosing to run her finger along the rim of her glass rather than look at me. "It's simple, really. I feel like you and I can still reach an agreement. I'd rather have enemies on my side rather than just dispose of them."

My grip tightens dangerously around the crystal stem. "I'll never team up with you for anything. Ever."

"Think wisely, my dear. You have the bloodline to run the Virtues, but no clue how to invoke that right. There's no family tree to point to, no physical evidence to showcase in front of our members."

That's what you think. Give me time, bitch.

"In any case, there's your pesky medical history, which discredits anything you might bring to the table."

I stiffen.

"I want to work with you, Callie. Ivy was a warning, it's true, and Chase would've been a better lesson, but with my hold over the Nobles tiring, new blood needs to step in and keep up the strength of the Virtues. We're better than the Nobles. Quieter, deadlier, smarter. If only you could see that and understand that all I wanted from your mother, from *you*, is cooperation to keep our strength going."

"Strength and power don't include rape," I spit. "Which is exactly what you're doing to your so-called princesses. Harming them, fucking up their psyches, and for what? Money?"

"No, dear. It's true we've only known each other a short while, but surely I've left enough of a powerful impression for you to realize my true nature."

"Manipulation. Extortion. Blackmail."

"Quite right." Sabine brightens. "The girls I choose realize the importance of their position, for it is because of them I'm able to call in favors, for these men who visit them show their weakness, their penchant for the forbidden. Take Ivy, for instance. She was desperate to give her father back his stellar reputation. Once she became princess, we were able to do that, for the Noble who visited her was the CEO of her father's company, and he received a promotion soon after."

I scrunch my eyes shut at the image of what Ivy was forced to do in order to save her family in the only way she thought possible. I can't believe I'm talking to the woman responsible for Ivy's suffering, holding a conversation with her like we would at a reception. "And the princess before that?"

"Emma?" Sabine leans against the wall, pursing her lips in thought. "Before she rebelled, the man I chose for her would've opened the kinds of doors for her that she needed. Finding her father and knowing her mother, for one."

My lips pucker in minor confusion, but I keep on track. "I'm not talking about her. I'm referring to Piper."

Sabine meets my gaze. "Piper wasn't a popular choice when it came to the Nobles who frequent our territory."

"Why? Because she's your daughter, and you can play favorites like that? Use the poor girls, the desperate ones who need something, to do your bidding instead of your own blood?"

Sabine laughs, the champagne flute catching the light as her movements reflect her mirth. "No, child. Piper couldn't be trusted to keep her mouth shut. She was willful, that girl, but when Emma ceded her position—quite permanently, as you know —I was forced to put my daughter in her place before the Nobles started asking questions about Emma's demise. You and I both know my preference would've been Violet, but the amount of trust and grooming it takes to create the ideal princess ... well, there simply wasn't time. To keep up appearances, I chose my daughter, but with that decision came the consequence of losing business."

Business. She calls sex trafficking a business. I'm going to be sick.

"Then I guess her dying opened you up for business again," I deadpan.

I expect Sabine's quiet laughter in response, but shadows cross over her expression instead. "She was never meant do die. And my youngest was never meant to be her killer."

"I guess that's what happens when they get a mother like you."

Sabine's eyes sharpen, then drill into mine. "My girls were strong. Intelligent.

And in one case, lethal. I may not be proud of their actions, but I'll always honor their spirits. Unlike your mother, who couldn't stomach the idea of being pregnant with you. She wanted to abort you; do you know that?"

I ignore the jab, but it's difficult. "Is that why you killed her?"

Sabine lifts her chin, the neon lights from the dance floor cresting over her cheeks. "Meredith ran from greatness. Avoided her potential and squirreled you away in a janitor's closet. She was a coward."

"She *saved* me." I peel my lips back on a snarl.

Sabine doesn't twitch. "Did she? You're here, aren't you? Despite her better efforts."

"I'm here to—" *destroy you*, but I don't allow myself to get that far. Just as Sabine wants me under her wing to gain a closer watch on me, so do I want to keep her at a distance to maintain the element of surprise. "I'm here to claim my rightful place. The Virtues are mine, not yours."

"You can't have them without me, just as I can't keep them without you. Do you finally understand why you're still alive, dear child? We need each other. Keep in mind, do you really want me to stop considering you necessary? Reflect on what happened to your dear friend..."

A slithering, sickening feeling uncoils in my gut, realization mixed with stubborn refusal. I can't resist the next words that peel out of my mouth, "I don't need *you* to take this entire institution down."

"Oh, my, is that why you and that boy are at such odds?" Sabine squints against her new perception. "Sweet child, *now* I understand why you're both so bull-headed about each other. Chase Stone will never allow you to hurt us. His entire life revolves around these societies." Sabine pauses, pushing her lips to the side as she feigns contemplation. "I'd wager he'd rather see *you* destroyed than his brotherhood."

"You overestimate my feelings for him. He doesn't influence my decisions, and I don't affect his." I push off the wall, done with this conversation.

"I'd rather think I've hit them spot on," Sabine murmurs at my back, but I hear the arrogance, the certainty that she can't be wrong.

"Don't forget your first dance with Tempest!" she calls soon after, but I'm pushing through the crowd, searching for the nearest exit. "Your most recent decision notwithstanding of course."

My exposed skin tingles as I pass through the dance floor, the too-tight dress constricting my movements at the same time it's putting them on display. My eyes skim over heads until I land on the second source of my unease.

Chase stands at the opposite wall, his chin lowered, his drink dangling at his side. Yet, in all his languidness, his stare is fervent and on fire, as if he's eager to incinerate me on the spot.

He watches me mumble to Tempest that I'm not feeling well and need to leave. Stares me down as I take the stairs up and out of the Nobles' hidden room.

And I feel him long after I exit into the Wolf's Den and creep along Briarcliff Academy's pathways, searching for warmth.

Callie

EMMA'S WAITING up for me when I step into our room, the under-cabinet lights in our kitchen slinking across her hunched form as she perches on a stool near our countertop.

"Glad you made it," she says, straightening as I shut the door softly behind me.

"There were a few unexpected twists."

"I figured, since a senior's—"

"Never been initiated before. I know," I finish for her on a sigh.

Emma responds with a laugh that surprises me. "You're done. I get it. Go rest, and we'll talk about next steps tomorrow."

She shocks me again when her heavy arm lands on my shoulder. She gives a squeeze so minute I have to concentrate to feel it, then drops it to her side. "Well done, Callie. You did great."

I offer her a slanted smile, then slide my jacket off my shoulders, kick off my shoes, then drag my beaten ass to bed.

"Wait." Emma catches me by the wrist—my wounded one. "This is deeper than normal."

I respond dryly, "Ever heard of a *soulmate* blood vow?"

"The mixing of blood? Shit," Emma hisses. "That kind of thing hasn't been used since, like, the Dark Ages. I can't believe my idiot brother agreed to this."

"He didn't."

"Huh?"

I'm reluctant to get into it, but this is Emma, one of the only friends I've kept. "Tempest did the blood oath with me."

"You did *what* with *who*?" Emma's eyes pop wide.

"Remember a few seconds ago when you said we'd get into the next steps tomorrow? I'd like to play that card again..."

"Nuh-*uh*, Callie Ryan. Explain to me how Tempest is now your soulmate and my brother is not."

I do it in a rush, unwilling to dwell on the devastating moment Chase officially scorned me, yet Emma's astonishment won't fade. "What's the big deal? It's not like we're in a forced marriage or anything. In fact, I'd argue Tempest is the best soulmate to have. He's the human equivalent of a cold-hearted vampire. He has no feelings and doesn't give a damn what I do. I can still break into the temple and get the binder."

"Assuming it's still there."

My lips tighten at Emma's decision to voice what I've been afraid to dwell on. "If it isn't, we'll find out where she put it and grab it from there. I *will* avenge my mother, Emma."

"If you're looking for someone to understand your passion," Emma says softly, "you know I'm your girl. But don't disregard their rules. Sabine will make good on the debt you've created with Tempest. Some way, she will."

"There's nothing more she can do to me that could break me."

Emma gives a sad, slow shake of her head. "Don't be so sure. I mutilated myself to get away from their rules. Think about that."

I open my mouth—

"And there's always my brother."

My jaw hangs silent, caught in the grip of her argument, before I clamp it shut.

"We won't have to worry about him." I shake my head resolutely. "By the time I'm done, there won't be enough Virtues or Nobles remaining to make good on a blood vow *or* a threat to a prince."

"I hope you're right."

"I am." It comes out more clipped than intended, but I can't take it back.

Emma and I war with our eyes for a few more seconds, until her shoulders slope and she motions in the direction of my room. "Go on, then. Catch some sleep."

I nod grimly, tempted to crush her into a sudden, meaningful hug. *We're on the same side. We can do this.*

But we don't do that kind of thing. I wave good night and step into my room, shutting the door.

Then choke on a scream as I'm backed into the wall.

Callie

A FAMILIAR FRESHWATER scent envelops me, even as I squirm and bare my teeth.

The room is dark—pitch black—yet Chase's opaque outline, darker than shadows, more languid than shade, overtakes what little vision I have.

The backs of my hands hit the wall behind me, his unyielding grip on my wrists driving them hard into the plaster.

"The *fuck* do you think you're doing?" he snarls, his teeth snapping near my nose.

I don't flinch. "I'd be quiet if I were you. Your sister's one scream away."

Chase growls in answer. My wrists flop onto the top of my head at his sudden release, his footsteps clomping away.

He flings my door open, the shaft of light caressing his twisted, aggravated features.

"Emma!" he barks. "Go to the lake house."

"What?" comes her addled reply. I don't think she expected him here anymore than I did. The fridge door shuts. "Why?"

"Because I said so. Now."

"You're not my keeper, Chase."

"If you don't leave in the next minute, all you'll hear is Callie's constant orgasms and my pounding—"

"*Ew!* Don't go any further!"

"Uh, how about don't do it at all?" I cut in.

Chase whips his head toward me, his finger cutting through the air as he points. "If I were you, I'd shut the fuck up at this moment. I can't promise I'll be a gentleman any more than you can promise not to betray me."

My mouth drops open. "That's not—"

"Callie. Fucking zip it. Emma, get the fuck out."

Chase's entire body tightens at each jerky move he throws out, gesturing to his sister, pointing at me. His thighs bulge in his pants, primed to leap, while his torso ripples beneath his thin white shirt, begging for release.

I'm not sure what concerns me more. The fact that he's cursing at us like he's *never* done before, or that he looks about to explode, *or* that Chase has been here long enough to strip down to his undershirt and slacks without Emma or I noticing.

I squint at him. This can't possibly all be due to Tempest, can it? "Chase, what's going on?"

He doesn't bother to look my way. "Go," he says to his sister through the doorway. "Unless you want me to make you."

"You had me at 'pounding,' dear brother. I'm outta here."

I push off the wall. "Emma, wait—" but, my voice cuts off as soon as I note Chase's flinch at Emma's use of "brother," the lamplight bathing his expression in golden pain.

"Unless," Emma quantifies, "Callie wants me to stay. Do you, Callie?"

My palms press into the wall in an automatic retreat to Chase's expression. He glares at me under his brows, allowing my response, but his nostrils flare impatiently.

"It's okay," I say, keeping my eyes on Chase. "I'll be fine."

"Good," I hear Emma mumble as her footsteps near the front door. "It's about time you two figure your shit out."

I don't respond, instead licking my lips as I wait for the apartment door to shut. My lips part. "I—"

Chase rounds on me, cutting off anything I was about to say—what *was* I about to say? I can't think clearly when he's this close. Can't form enough obstinance to rip my forearm out of his hand when he lifts my arm and brings my cut into the light.

Chase's nostrils, still flaring, don't compare to the utter, vengeful twist to his lips. "You let him brand you."

I test my strength against his, yanking my arm. It doesn't budge from his hold.

Fine. Plan B. "What did you expect me to do?" I hiss. "After you publicly disavowed me to the entire society?"

His eyes slide from my inner wrist to my face, the action seeming to pain him. "I expected you to walk out of the temple and never look back, like I've asked you to do repeatedly."

"Then you should invest in a better crystal ball," I retort, "if you can't even predict I'd throw your commands back in your *face*."

My back presses against the wall when he steps forward, his forehead almost touching mine as his exhale billows out, spearmint mixing with rage.

"I only wish I'd had a trashcan to toss at you, too," I risk continuing. "And maybe a used tampon or two."

He snarls, slamming my wounded arm back into the wall. "When are you going to figure out what you're dealing with?"

"Depends what you're referring to." I press forward, the front of my body molding to his so well, I can feel his heartbeats against my own. "Are you talking about your possessive, asshole self, or the Nobles and Virtues?"

His voice lowers to a growl. "All of it. You won't get what you want if you continue to walk your insolent ass onto their turf, thinking you have the upper hand. Binding yourself to Tempest hasn't given you any advantages. It only deepens your obligations to them and enters you into a contract you have no hope of escaping."

"I'm not alone," I reply, deeply affected by the flare to his eyes but refusing to show it. "I have Eden helping me. And your sister."

Again, he winces.

"What is that?" I ask. "Your reaction to Emma's name. I noticed it before, too."

Chase lowers his head, and against my better judgment, I lift my free hand and risk tracing a finger along his jaw. "Chase? Talk to me."

His shoulders rise and fall. Chase fixes his gaze to the floor, and I swear, despite the death grip he has on my wrist, he's about to confide in me.

Until his eyes flick up and his snarl reaches my lips, his mouth brushing over mine while his eyes bore rivulets of fire into my gaze.

"You're *mine*," he breathes into my mouth. "Do you understand me?"

"I'm not anybody's—"

He smothers my urge to rebel by yanking my arm forward and forcing my wrist between us. "This means *nothing*. Tempest may cut into you, you may have recited overdone, emotionless, and bloody vows, but this skin is mine. Your body is mine. Your soul?" He angles his head. "Mine."

"*Fuck* you," I spit, trying to wrestle out of his hold. "What makes you think you can come in here and lay a claim on me when you've spent the last few weeks doing everything in your power to push me away? I'm *not* yours. I'll never *be* yours. You lost that chance."

"Everything I do is to protect you."

I roll my eyes, until I'm jerked to a stop with his fingers digging into my cheeks. His fervent stare captures mine, fearless yet exposed, drilling into me with a depth that's almost crazed.

"I kept my distance to prevent Sabine and my father taking further interest in you. I've kept secrets for them involving you not for their benefit, but for yours. You can't know how much they've fucked with you, and how much more they will. I'm acting like your buffer, keeping you away from the worst. But how can I do that when you claim my best friend as your soulmate? Your Noble protector? How can I push at my parents and push at you, thinking I won't fucking snap in two? No. It ends here." He shakes his head. "You aren't anyone else's. I'm staying with you, and I *refuse* to let you do more stupid things."

"Stupid?" I guffaw, uselessly shoving at his chest again. "I've gotten myself this far, no thanks to you. Learned about my mom, kept my promise to Ivy, and I *will* avenge them both, whether or not you decide to be my fair-weather boyfriend. So, go on, come in here and piss on my furniture all you want, but my mind will always belong to *me*."

I expect him to snarl, bark, maybe even spit and swipe, considering he's acting like an animal. What I don't expect is for him to pull my inner wrist up to his lips and bite down hard around my wound.

"*Jeez*—what? Ow! *Ow!*" I scream.

He releases my arm. I inspect the teeth marks around the cut—just indents, he didn't break skin—then hold it close to my chest. "What the hell is wrong with you?"

"Everything. Everything is wrong with me."

"You need to leave."

"Well, I'm not going to."

"Chase, I've had it. With you, with these societies, with this goddamned *school*. Leave me the hell alone and let me—"

He walls me in, his hands slamming on either side of my head. "Mine."

"You don't—"

"What?" he pauses, reading my expression. "I don't know what it's like? To have someone ripped away like they didn't have meaning in your life? All because someone *else* decided to make them disappear just because they could? I know what it's like, Callie. It may not be the same, but that burning inside you because something vital was torn out of your skin..." His voice tightens. "It's been taken from me, too. *I know what it's like.*"

I search his eyes, finding nothing but a shimmering onyx reflecting back at me. "Who?" I manage to whisper. "Who was taken from you?"

Chase glances at the open doorway, then cuts to me. After a few seconds, he growls. "My teeth marks surround Tempest's cut. But if that's not enough for you, I'll use another blade to erase his mark, too."

Breathing heavy, though I've taken no steps, I retort, "You've lost your mind."

"How nice of you to notice."

"Tell me what's going on. Why you're acting like this. You've never been so possessive. Territorial and ... frightening. Tempest and I aren't anything to be jealous of."

Chase's face comes close to mine. "Don't ever use him and you in the same sentence again."

I exhale a loud sigh. "Chase, I'm not about to become some sort of property dispute between you and your friend."

"Then agree with me."

"No."

"Admit you're with me."

"Never."

"You can keep your mind. Save your soul, even. But confess that your heart belongs to a Stone, and I'll let you go."

"N—" I falter. Damn him, he has it. He's always had it, since the moment I walked into Briarcliff, glanced up into the Wolf's Den, and found his eyes clashing with mine.

A distracting flicker of pleasure resonates in my brain, shockwaves of it coming from my core. I glance down in the small space between us, noticing his hand grazing my thigh and moving under my dress.

"Chase—"

His fingers push my underwear aside, and he slips into my folds, his thumb pressing down on my clit. Circling. Massaging. Coaxing.

Moaning.

"Chase, I mean it..."

His nose grazes my jawline when I lift my chin, the back of my head clonking against the wall. Chase nips at my chin, then draws my lower lip into his mouth, sucking on it then biting down.

He catches my yelp of pain, groaning as he savors it and pulls me into a deeper kiss. I sink into his commands as his expert fingers play along my clit, pinching and tugging, creating zips of pleasure that tighten my body as I await delicious release.

My hips take up his rhythm, moving in his circles, angling for his fingers to go deeper, curl more, flick often.

He must hear my wishes, because his fingers do just that.

I lift my leg and curve it over his, widening my pleasure center and forcing his own hand to brush against his bulging erection as well as become soaked in my juices.

Chase groans, angling our kiss until his tongue dances in my mouth, my jaw relaxing at the same time I'm coiling for a salacious orgasm.

"Just ... just..." I pant, breaking off our kiss to better angle myself for his hand. I grip his wrist in much the same way he grabbed mine, but push his hand deeper, his fingers sinking into my folds, first one, then two, three, four....

My head falls back, the tips of my hair tangling in his other hand as he holds the small of my back.

He starts pumping, his thumb still managing to massage my clit as he pushes in roughly, retreating only half a second before diving deep again.

The movements are possessive, mirroring his current, concerning attitude, but my mind merely flits against the similarity, then flutters away, because he's spreading me wide and pushing as much of his hand to the point that I feel stretched and full.

I have to use both hands now to hold his wrist as I ride him, the one leg I have around his torso digging into his back once I reach my climax and...

Oh.

Oh.

OH.

A hand shouldn't be able to do this. His fingers can't produce as much ecstasy as his dick, but here I am, holding onto his arm like a rodeo cowgirl and flying into the air like he's just bucked me.

Spent, I flop into his arms. Chase catches me effortlessly, and instead of wiping my juices on his slacks or doing anything to clean us up, he shifts me against his chest then carries me to bed.

I expect to be laid down, and he does just that, but then he starts pushing my tight mini-dress up my hips, then to my stomach—out of the way.

"You better still have energy for my cock," he says, his gaze meeting mine briefly before he goes back to taking his fill of my half-naked body. "Because I'm two seconds away from creaming my pants, and I'd rather be fucking you while I come."

"Yes," I say, still panting. I glance down, realizing one breast has escaped the deep V of my dress, but I don't bother fixing myself.

I like looking messy.

I love looking roughed up from sex because of *him.*

The whys can be sorted out later. Right now, all I want is his naked body and big, thick dick. I'm swollen for him, aching for his fill, and I hope that's all in my eyes when I look at him and bite down on my lip.

"Ah, fuck me," he whispers, then tears off his shirt and pants.

Chase

"WHAT DID YOU LOSE?" Callie murmurs beside me.

"Hmm?" I let my head fall to the side, catching her in a midnight glow, the moon passing pale white beams across her skin from her window.

I buried myself inside her, losing myself and giving into her heat, her skin, *her*, but the afterglow is wearing thin, and I'm starting to realize I revealed too much when I confronted her.

Tempest's touch upon her body blinded me to the consequences, his nearness and ownership of her, in front of both societies, instantly became too much. I lost control, refusing to believe that on top of having my sister taken away, I have to lose her, too...

I've ended up in Callie's dorm without quite knowing how I got here. The red was too blinding, the possession too complete, for me to realize that I could be hurting Callie more than I was saving her by being here and branding her.

Because that's what I did, didn't I? I bit into her skin just as easily as Tempest's blade, marking her as he did, but not stopping there. No, I had to fuck her, show my weakness, explain that she was mine and mine alone, and in doing so...

I offered her my hurt.

God*dammit*, I can't hurt. Emma's heritage isn't my concern, the Nobles' future is. Emma's adoption, Callie's bloodline—they can't take up my thoughts like this and pulverize my brain, when I have to put all focus on my father and his operations. I *have* to inherit the Nobles.

"Who was it?" she repeats, her voice a note above a whisper.

Callie rolls to her side, her hand sliding over my naked torso, her pinky brushing against my nipple and sending a *zing* of renewed vigor.

Perhaps if I fuck her again...

"No one," I answer, but it comes out guttural, unsure.

"You can try to fool me, but you'll fail." Callie rises up on her elbow, her long hair flipped over one side and cascading down her arm.

The urge to bury my face in it, throw her on her back, and lose myself in her is almost unbearable.

"I recognized it in your voice," she continues. "The rawness. The pain. What has Sabine done to you?"

"It wasn't Sabine." My answer is out before I can control it.

Callie scrunches her brows. "Then who?" When I don't answer right away, her forehead smooths. "Your father."

Her eyes, so liquid they melt into gold when they're on me, won't leave my face. I reach up, tucking errant strands behind her ear, then cup her jaw, tracing the line there. "It's about Emma."

I'm not sure what makes me say it. Perhaps it's her undivided attention, or her soft voice, or the simple understanding of what it's like to live a lie.

"What about her?"

"She's not really my sister."

I leave the bomb between us, unwilling to trigger it further by admitting, *she's not my real twin*. The idea Emma and I don't share the same birthday, never mind the same womb, remains so mind-boggling and heart-wrenching, I can't stand to give it voice.

Callie's hand curls against my chest, her nails scraping my skin. "Wait, what?"

"My father admitted it to me a few nights ago. Emma was some charity case of my mother's, an unwanted pregnancy ... I don't know all the details, but I'm starting to think I don't need to. She's not my blood. She's an imposter and doesn't even know it."

"My god. Chase." Callie sits up. "This will *kill* her. Is this for real?"

I catch Callie's wrist before she lifts it from my chest. "You're not telling her. You can't."

She jerks her chin to me, her eyes widening. "I can't keep something like this to myself! She's my friend, Chase. My best—"

"And I'm her twin." I cut her off, cursing at the easy use of a title that's not mine anymore. Rising, I catch Callie's chin between my fingers. "Think of what you're trying to do. If you admit this to her, you're right, it will kill her. You won't have a comrade anymore. Emma will turn into herself, run, escape, fly back to our mother. In essence, she'll leave you. Us."

"She'd have every right to. You're telling me everything she knows is a lie."

"You know what that's like." I level Callie with a look. "As do I. Your plans to take down Sabine will be null and void."

"I can't..." Callie shakes her head, then digs her fingers into her hair. "So, I use Emma to get Sabine's binder, squeeze her dry until Sabine's named for Ivy's murder and my mother's, and then I tell her? I'm not going to keep this from Emma until she stops being useful to me. I *can't*."

"What's more important to you?"

I ask her the question knowing the answer and hate myself for the added knowledge that it's killing her. All Callie wants is to prove that her mother was a good woman who was wrongfully killed, and Ivy an innocent caught in the crossfire. This additional information about Emma? It's an aggravating twist, a serrated knife to an already too-deep wound. I know it and must use it against her.

"What about you? Why don't you want to tell her?" Callie asks. The sheets have fallen from her chest, her breasts heaving with her aggravated breaths, but I can't bring myself to admire the sheer beauty of her while so much turmoil surrounds us. I shouldn't have taken advantage of her in the first place.

But she's *mine*, damnit.

"Because she's my twin," I say after a beat. "She'll always be my twin, blood or not. And I can't rip something like this away from her—rip *me* from her—when so much hangs in the balance already. She wants Sabine to pay for her sins as much as you do. Wants the Virtues destroyed as desperately as you. To hear this on top of it all ... Emma's been through enough these past few years. I would reduce her to insanity if I told her this without giving her anything in return, like Sabine's head on a platter."

Callie takes a breath, her focus shifting to the wall across from us. "But you want to save the Virtues and the Nobles. You don't want to risk their safety by telling Emma the truth, do you?"

I study her, Callie Ryan, my weakness and my strength. "What would you do if I said my priorities have changed?"

Her stare whips to mine. "Not possible."

"My father can't be saved. The Virtues created under his idleness and Sabine's rule are unsalvageable. What he's done to my *sister*—" I hiss out a breath, collecting myself. "I'll help you with the Virtues and Sabine. But the Nobles? You leave them to me."

Callie stares back silently, her plush lips a hairsbreadth away from gawking. "I can't keep up with your mood swings."

"You don't have to if you simply accept that you're my girl, the Virtues are yours to fuck with, and I retain control of the Nobles." I rest my forearms on my raised knees. "Does that sound good to you?"

To my surprise, Callie breaks out into a genuine smile. She rushes me with her arms, crashing us back to the bed. "You have no idea how much I've wanted you to ... to..."

"Simply be there for you?" I murmur into her ear. "Calla Lily Ryan, it killed me to be away from you."

She finds my lips, sucking them between her teeth, then flicking out her tongue and making that adorable purr I can't resist. Unfortunately, she pulls away soon after. "I wish this could be the end of our fairy tale. But your sister. And Sabine..."

"Are you sure you want that binder?"

Callie nods fervently, her small body pressed against mine.

"You've tried once and failed," I add, my brows weighing heavy above my eyes. "And it's so explicit. Sabine's shown us her knack for predicting our next move." I angle my head and peer at Callie. "What if we approach it from a different angle instead? Like, a more psychological one, and beat Sabine at her own game?"

Callie pulls in her lower lip, sucking on it thoughtfully. In the shadows and moonlight, she looks like a tentative goddess. "If we could somehow make her question the amount of power she has over the girls, plant seeds of doubt..."

"Exactly." I wrap my arms around the small of her back, delighted she's catching my wave of thought. "The way to push Sabine off-balance is to go after her insecurities, and that lies with her false claim as the true queen of the Virtues."

Callie responds, "I don't know if... what if it's not enough? Mom's murder won't be solved. Ivy's death won't have closure..."

I grunt, acknowledging her worry. Sabine and my father always seem to plan for all contingencies, my poor sister included. There must be a reason Father revealed Emma's adoption to me, same as the reasons Sabine allowed Callie to find her hidden folders on Meredith Ryan in the first place. I just haven't figured out why yet.

"We need more believers," I say.

Callie raises her brows.

"The Nobles." I clarify, "The younger initiates, you could probably talk them onto your side, especially with your claim to the Virtue throne. And through that, we could tell them about Sabine's treatment of the princesses. Enough games. No more behind the scenes. We could tell them the truth." I move my gaze to the ceiling. "I'm sick of all the lies."

"Me, too." Callie shifts with me. "Sabine's gotten away with so much because she's kept so many people ignorant. Maybe, if we had numbers on our side. But ... all I have is my word."

I run my finger along her cheek, thinking of my father gleefully admitting my twin is not my twin. Or Sabine, allowing Callie into the Virtues for dangerous reasons that escape me. "Maybe that's enough."

Callie thinks for a moment. "With you beside me, I can try." She raises her eyes to mine. "Will you be? On my side?"

"Sweet possum," I say, "Yes. You're the only good thing I have left."

Callie

IT DOESN'T TAKE LONG for Chase to fall into dreams, but I can't seem to catch up with him.

I love watching him sleep. It's like my favorite parts of him float up to the surface of his skin. Chase's relaxed brows, his soft lips, his thick lashes becoming crescents against his golden skin. It all points to his hidden sweetness, that section of him he works so hard to bury and keep at bay.

I run a hand through his thick, unkempt hair, and he purrs in his sleep, angling toward the touch.

If you were to ask Chase, he'd say he's weakened in slumber, all his vulnerabilities exposed to any enemies creeping closer. He's too soft, he'd argue. His lips would never tilt so serenely, his body would never become so relaxed and floppy if he were awake. But I'd argue he's at peace.

Reluctant to rouse him any further, I withdraw my hand and slide out of bed, in need of a hot coffee so I can sit and think.

Chase gave me a lot of himself tonight—more than he's ever allowed. Now I carry his secrets, and my stomach turns at the thought of what I must keep from Emma.

Darkness eats away at all of us, but I had no idea how it infiltrates even those who think they've overcome it.

My door doesn't creak as I open it, and I close it with just as much silence, aware that the slightest *snick* of sound would wake Chase and ruin any dream state he finds calm in.

That plan is nearly derailed when I catch sight of a shadow in front of me and choke on a scream.

I fumble for the light switch, then release the gasp when I realize it's Emma. "You scared the shit out of me," I say. "I thought you were gone."

Emma doesn't shift or flinch at the sudden glare of light. That should've been my first clue. "I never left."

713

My hand falls from the switch. "What are you doing standing here in the dark?"

"I left the lake house keys here. I came back to get them."

"Then..." I check her empty hands, dangling near her sides. "Where are they?"

"I stopped mid-grab," she answers tonelessly. "Since they were on our coffee table. Right near your door."

Her lower lip trembles, and she blinks rapidly against shining, welling eyes.

"Emma." I don't think I've ever seen her cry before, and I rush to her.

She pushes against my arms as soon as I raise them for comfort. "Get *away* from me!"

Stumbling back, I glance toward my shut door, conscious of Chase's nearby presence. "Emma, what's wrong? What can I do?"

"Were you really going to keep it from me?" she asks, her voice raw and broken.

I stall on the question of what she could be talking about, because I know. *Oh God, I know.*

Emma mistakes my frozen silence as an answer. "So you were. You and my brother weren't going to tell me—" Her voice falters as she meets my eyes with the most crestfallen, defeated expression. "But he's not my brother, is he?"

"Emma, I can explain."

"No. You can't. You were supposed to be my *friend*, Callie!"

"I am! I've only just learned the truth about your family." Even as I say it, I'm aware of how terrible an excuse it is. My heart sinks. "I came out here to process it, to figure out what to do. I didn't want to keep it from you any more than Chase would."

"Don't defend him." Emma sneers, but she's too heartbroken to give it any force. "How long has he known about this? How *long* has he known I'm an unwanted *mistake*?"

"That's not true," I whisper. "You're not a—"

"Four days."

The roughened voice comes from behind me, and I twist to Chase, hovering in my doorframe.

His dark stare rises from the floor to Emma. "I've known for four days."

"And how long were you going to keep this to yourself? Wait—stupid me. You confided in Callie. *She* was more important than enlightening me, whose life has been fucked over for years! *Years!*" Emma cries. "And for so long I wondered why! Why was it always me being punished? Why didn't Father ever compliment me for my good grades, or make our birthday parties equal instead of always defer to your preference for a theme? Why, when we turned sixteen, did you get the fancy car when you failed your driving test and I passed? Why why *why*? And now I know." Tears streak down Emma's face, the rivulets curving and pooling against her scars. "Even when I was hurt, mutilated, *raped*, beaten, and lost, Father still wouldn't come to me."

"I did," Chase cuts in, his voice a rasp as he peels from the doorframe and approaches his sister. "I cared. I was there for you. Good grades? I made sure you got the same credit as me and gave you half of whatever Father awarded. Birthdays? I made sure to choose some godawful theme that was neutral for both of us. Pirates and princesses, donuts and sprinkles, goddamned fairy dust and gun powder, whatever the fuck. And that fancy car?

You can drive it whenever you want, use my things, stay in my room, sleep in my bed when you were too afraid of your shadow. But it's not enough," he adds as Emma opens her mouth to argue. "I'm aware it'll never be enough, not after what you endured, what Father put you through—what he *locked* you in to change you back into a good, supplicant, docile Virtue. I'm sorry. I'm so sorry and that won't change the truth, either, but Emma..." He lets out an explosive breath. "I didn't want to keep hurting you. I kept this from you because I couldn't be responsible for breaking you, too."

"I'm not a doll who rips or shatters," Emma says, her eyes on fire. "I'd prefer my real story over the hell my life has been any day. You don't get to make that choice for me, Chase. Or Callie, for that matter, who should know what it's like to be protected and shrouded when all you want to do is rebel." She shifts her glare to me. "Yet the people closest to you, the ones who supposedly care about you the most, won't let you."

I step forward. "Emma, I—"

"No. You don't get to change your ways now that I've discovered this secret before you were ready to 'process' it. This is *my* life. *My* choices. *My* family and friendships on the line. And you know what? I don't need either of you."

"Emma, wait," I say.

"Waiting is the worst advice I can take," she bites out. "Just look how far it's gotten you."

I reel back, but Chase storms forward. "Emma, sit down. I love you. I'll always love you regardless of what blood is in your veins. You're my sister. My *twin.*"

"I'm not any of those things," she whispers fiercely, her cheeks rising with color. "And it's high time I find out who I am without you, or Father, or the cursed Virtues."

She spins, and I catch Chase's arm before he tries to run her down and keep her here.

He whirls on me, ready for a fight.

"Let her go," I say.

"Never," he snarls.

"Let. Her. Go." My grip tightens on his inner elbow, well aware that if he wanted to rip from my hold, he would've shaken me off like a horsefly by now. "She needs time. We all do."

"This has gone too far." Chase pulls away, raking his hand through his hair and pacing the room. "Murder. Sex. Blackmail. Stolen privilege. Broken families. Callie, I'm fucking done."

I stay where I am, watching him carefully. "So am I."

"We need to do something. Emma's right—waiting is the worst thing we could do right now."

"Biding our time is never a mistake, especially when it comes to Sabine and your father."

"Then our moments of pondering are finished as of now."

"I agree."

Chase pauses in his movements, eyeing me suspiciously. "You never agree with me."

"Maybe that's the problem." I sigh, bone-weary and desolate. "Everyone around me always gets hurt. Destroyed. Killed. I want it to end, too."

Chase checks his watch, but I don't need the time to understand the pinkish gray skies in the window behind him. He looks up and says, "I'll set up a meeting with the Nobles tonight. We'll finish this."

"We'll get your sister back."

He nods resolutely. "And cause enough questions and instability in the ranks to fracture the societies."

"Are you sure that's what you want?" I study him, aware of the Noble Chase simmering under his skin, the one that's desperate to save a society he wants redeemed.

Chase's shoulders rise and fall with deep, angry breaths. "They've involved my family. My sister. I made a promise to her years ago, when she was recovering from her injuries: she would never be fucked with again. And if she was, I would bring down Hell to protect her. Never again would she be hurt on my watch." His black stare lands on mine. "I refuse to fail a second time. When it comes to choosing between my family and the societies, my family wins every time."

My lips pull into a tentative smile. "I'm glad to hear that."

"Callie. My sweet, misdirected possum." Chase comes up to me, his hands landing on my shoulders and pulling me into a deep, heartfelt kiss. He pulls away, but his lingering study keeps the warmth from the kiss. "That includes you, too."

Emma doesn't return before classes, and I don't expect her to.

Chase left shortly after the confrontation, hoping to catch her at the lake house and succeed in the heart-to-heart I don't think either of them ever allowed themselves to have in all these years of forced distance and inequality.

It's what I hope for, and I check my phone constantly for a text from him, but the only *ping* I get is from Eden, reminding me of our 4:30 AM swim lesson at the rec center, which, if I'm already up and zinging with adrenaline, would be a shame to miss.

I pull on a simple black one-piece bathing suit, then dress in Briarcliff sweats. After burrowing into my winter coat, I shove my uniform into my duffel and leave the silent apartment behind, taking the stairs to the bottom floor, the eerie, red, EXIT lights the only source of illumination for my trip down.

I don't mind, since this type of lighting better reflects my thoughts.

The trek to Briarcliff Academy's recreational center goes by fast, mostly because I'm immersed in Chase's and my conversation, and the student pathways are deserted. It's chilly, though, frigid and windy, and I'm thankful to hit the heated confines of one of Briarcliff's more modern buildings on the other side of campus.

Motion lights flash on as I head through the single hallway, making me think Eden either got here much earlier than me or hasn't made it yet. I'm not concerned as I push into the girls' locker room, finding the nearest bench and dumping my bag on it before I strip off my coat.

"What's up, sister?"

My hands freeze at my zipper.

Falyn chills at the end of the row of gym lockers, her arms crossed and her smile wide.

"What are you doing here?" is out before I can tell myself not to ask the obvious question.

"Enjoying the thought of you splashing around like a belly-flopping fish while you try to learn how to swim."

"What makes you think I'm here for that?" I unfreeze, casually stripping my jacket.

"Nice try, possum. Eden and I had a lovely chat." Falyn uncrosses her arms and strides forward. "She mentioned your ... disability. It all makes sense now, that whole Marco Polo thing you and Ivy had going at the lake when I—"

"—pushed me?"

"I was going to say expedited your initiation. You should thank me. If it weren't for that, we wouldn't be here. Aren't you *proud* of being here?"

Falyn strolls ever closer until she's in my personal space, taking up my viewpoint and assaulting my nose with her powdery, fragrant scent. "Why are you taking swimming lessons, possum? Afraid of another drowning?"

"Ivy was killed in front of my face, so yeah, I'm preparing myself."

Falyn laughs, tucking her hair behind her ear as she draws back. "It's amazing how hard you work to cover your ass, when our princess is dead because of you."

I ignore the jab and respond with a croak, "Ivy didn't deserve to die."

"Your avoidance skills need work. You might as well admit blame."

"Maybe I do," I say hoarsely, "but so should you and every other Virtue who stood by or enabled Sabine to gain so much power over you. You're nothing but a pawn, Falyn, just like I am, and Ivy was. The only difference between you and me is that I know it."

Falyn's eyes grow small. "You think you're so much better? It's because of *you* we're all in this position. You've forced your way into a membership, killed people, *hurt* your closest friends, trash Chase, and yet you're standing here trying to tell me you're the good one? All you do is take and take and *take*. You don't care what happens to me, Violet, Willow, the rest of the Virtues, or even Eden and Emma. All you care about is *you*. You're fine with destroying our livelihoods so long as your dead mom gets some justice. So what? She's a rotten carcass, Callie. She doesn't give a shit what you—"

The slap rings out in the empty locker room.

I stare at my hand, appalled, until I tear my gaze away and notice the blooming red stain on Falyn's cheek. Narrowing my eyes, I close the distance between us. "Don't you talk about my mother."

"You fucking mad bitch!" Falyn spits, holding her cheek and stumbling into the wall of lockers. She keeps her back pressed to the maroon metal, hissing, "You deserve everything that comes your way. And *I* deserve everything I've worked for. I'm not going to let you steal it the way you stole Ivy's life or Chase's future. I'm the princess. *I'm* the future of the Virtues. And when Sabine retires and gives the crown to *me* and not you, I'll make sure you pay for every single mistake you've made by coming here."

I stare at her aghast. "You really believe all this, don't you? That Sabine has your back."

"More so than anybody on *your* side, Callie. Say, why don't you go check on Eden. She might need your help."

I stop my stalk toward her and veer to the entrance of the indoor pool, drowning Falyn's laughter with my heavy, panicked breaths. "Don't ever forget who has the upper hand, Calla Lily Ryan! Sabine will always choose me!"

Bursting through the doors, I scan for Eden, my mind concocting images of her floating face-down in the pool, her black hair twisting and twirling with the mirage of life as her body doesn't breathe.

"Eden?" I call. "*Eden!*"

"I'm here," comes the quiet reply.

I race to the shadowed corner of the rectangular room, the pool's lights reflecting soft ripples across the walls and Eden's slumped form at the bottom of the bleachers.

"Thank God," I breathe when I reach her, plop down next to her. "Are you hurt? Did Falyn do something to you?"

"No." Eden won't turn to me. She hides between the curtains of her hair. "We just talked."

"About what? What did she say, Eden? She's as ambitious as Sabine. I can already tell you anything she said is a lie, a power-play designed to mislead you—"

"Did you really choose Tempest as your soulmate?"

I wasn't expecting that. Pushing my brows together, I answer, "Yeah, but—"

"Really?" Eden raises her head and stares at me head-on. "Chase wasn't enough for you? Getting the most popular guy in school to notice you and ... and have *sex* with you wasn't what you wanted? You had to take him, too?"

"Eden, what are you talking about. I didn't take Tempest, and Chase's attention has hardly been wanted or kind..."

"But it turned you on enough to fuck him. Made *him* interested enough to drop every other girl and pledge himself to you, even when he was pretending to hate you —everyone knew it was a lie, including me. *Especially* me. You know why? Because I notice things. Observing is my special skill, and I can tell when you're depressed, or Emma's anxious, or Ivy is—was—upset. I can read you so well because you're my friend and you've been kind to me when no one else was. But it was all an act, wasn't it? To avenge your mom and now Ivy, to ruin the Virtues ... have you ever really wanted to be my friend?"

"Of course, Eden!" Shock and hurt reverberates in my tone, but Eden doesn't take notice.

"You're lying. If you really were my friend, you'd be able to read me, too. Like when every time Tempest entered the room, I'd freeze and duck my head because I had to hide the blood rushing to my cheeks. Or how overly thankful I was that he deleted all traces of my naked photo. Or that every time you mentioned his name, my breaths would come faster, and I latched onto every word you said about him."

"Eden," I whisper, reaching for her hands, but she pulls them from her lap. "I didn't know. I had no idea you had a crush on him."

"*Crush.*" Eden laughs tonelessly. "Is that what you and Chase have? How you define it? I'm in love with him, Callie, and you didn't even notice!"

Straightening, I try to bring feeling back into my face, but it's so numbed, so devoid of blood, I can't tell it to move. *How could I have missed this?* "What I did at the ritual, it means nothing. Chase revoked his soulmate claim in order to sabotage my admission. The only way I could salvage it was to claim another soulmate, and Tempest doesn't have one."

"Neither does James. Why didn't you call out his name?"

I aim for a smile, because that idea is ludicrous. "James is a masochist who gets off on pain. I couldn't tie myself to someone like that."

"So, you tied yourself to the one guy who's ever been nice to me in the entire school. The *only* guy I've ever noticed and have been working so hard to get him to notice me. How can I do that when he has you now? You don't see it, Callie, but you're beautiful. You're ... you're everything I'm not and you could have anything you wanted, even being a part of Falyn and her crew. Instead, you shackled yourself to me and Emma, the outsiders, the loners. It's starting to come together, now. Why you did that. You were using us."

"No," I practically shout. "You've got it wrong. I love you two. You've been there and helped me, and we've all become closer, because we *like* each other, Eden. I'd never use you and I'd never do this to you on purpose."

"You chose Tempest!" Eden screams. "When I wanted him! He's all I want. That's it. Nothing else. Why would you take that away?"

"Because I didn't know!"

"You never asked!"

I take a breath, trying not to flinch under her fury. I say, softer, "His was the first name that popped into my head, so I spoke it. But that's it, Eden. I swear. There's *nothing* going on between us."

Eden's silent for a time, and I allow the pregnant pause, understanding that the more I try to pry, the further I'll push her away. Because I *do* know her. She *is* my friend, and while I've neglected her in favor of gutting Sabine, I would never take her for granted.

I'm about to tell her that, but she speaks first.

"There's nothing going on between you and me, either."

"Wh ... Eden." I reach for her when she stands but miss. "Please. I don't want you to leave. I am your friend. We need to talk about this."

"Try floating without the pool noodle this time," she barks as she storms barefoot back to the locker room. "With any luck, you'll sink to the bottom."

"Eden!" I cry, horrified, but she's already walked into the locker room and shut the door on our friendship.

Callie

"THEY SHOULD BE HERE SOON," Chase says as he finishes helping me button my shirt. His is a lost cause and he's thrown his blazer over his open white shirt.

It's the next evening, and while Chase and I waited in the Nobles' crypt, we couldn't take our hands off each other. It was a nice reprieve, as selfish as it was, to lose myself in him and pretend my friendships weren't hanging on by a thread.

I'm not a complete asshole, however, and I asked Chase about Emma before he distracted me with his scent and prowess, but he refused to say much, and Emma won't answer my texts or calls. I'm determined to speak to both her *and* Eden tonight, and asked them to meet us at the lake house after this meeting. I need them, and not simply because Chase and I are implementing a new plan. I also miss them. I love them.

Chase strokes my hair back from my face. "While I can appreciate the brain fog I've given you, the Nobles are meeting us here any minute. You might want to find your underwear."

"How many?" I ask as I duck under the pews, spotting my pink thong in the cobwebs. I dig it out.

"The initiates and our barons. As well as Tempest, James, and Rio."

The mention of Tempest makes me flinch, but Chase doesn't see it as I shimmy my underwear back on.

"Don't shake your ass," Chase warns on a growl, "unless you want me to part it and slam into you again."

"Such a Romeo," I mumble, but my core sparks with joy. I manage to temper it with the reminder of how screwed up my life and the life of the people around me have become.

"There's not enough time to approach this gently," I say, turning to face him. "While we wait, Sabine and your father have figured out a thousand different ways to defy us. It's better to amass an army *now*, outnumbering the king and queen and ultimately, outvoting them. They can't kill them all, and even if they tried for ruin, my email is still relevant and out there."

Chase voices his agreement. "The Viscounts don't know about this meeting. The Nobles that are coming, they can be reasoned with. Informed. Their minds changed."

The implications sink in. "How confident are you that they won't betray us?"

"Callie." Chase places his hands on my cheeks. "Your email blast didn't work because you weren't writing to the people who could handle that kind of warped reality, especially if nobody but an anonymous sender was behind it. These new Nobles? They'll listen to you. Hear what you have to say. And then we can decide what to do about Sabine and how best to protect you."

I search his eyes. "I can't ask for something like that. You could lose your position in the society because of this. A society that, if you're not around, won't see how damaged and ignorant they've become."

"Seriously? Callie, what's going on with you? You were so confident the other night."

"That was before..." I close my eyes. "I'm realizing how selfish I've become, asking people to sacrifice so much for me. They shouldn't have to. *You* shouldn't have to."

"Crazy-talk," he says, stroking my cheek. "What other choice do we have, other than you breaking into the temple and finding the binder, Sabine's supposed murder book? Or waiting weeks for DNA results? If I'm not mistaken, these require wide enough gaps of time while we research and wait that could epically fuck us over."

I frown at his opinion so expertly tossed in my face, but his point sticks. "You win. We'll give it a shot. But I'd like you to come with me to your lake house after where I'm meeting Emma and Eden. We all need to talk."

"Hashing out our differences." He squeezes my shoulder with a pained expression. "How grand. Emma still wants to kill us, you know."

"I know," I say on a forlorn exhale.

Shuffling turns our attention to the small corridor leading into the room, and Tempest appears first. He nods at Chase, but I brace for when his eyes shift to me, unsure of what I'll find there.

Those unwavering, sharp green eyes of his pin me to the floor, but they're steadying. Encouraging. "'Sup, soulmate," he says before draping over one of the pews, both legs spread, and his hands folded between them expectantly.

I flick a glance up at Chase, rigid and immobile beside me. His stare could melt volcanoes, but Tempest isn't affected. I wonder if he has any idea about Eden's feelings for him and what he'd do about it if he did. As much as Eden thinks I wouldn't, I'd shove his balls into his throat if he hurt her.

Chase moves to greet each boy who follows by name. James is next, then Riordan, and a handful of others whose names I don't catch, because of my fixation on Riordan.

His brown eyes don't contain the mysterious depths of Chase's. No, he shows emotion as easily as dropping a towel from his naked form. And he's glaring at me.

My focus skitters to the side as I try to sort through the reasons he would want to throw so much hate at me.

"Gentlemen," Chase says once everybody's seated. Nobody chatted or slapped each other's backs on their way in. And not one commented on Chase's unbuttoned shirt. "I assume you all know why we're here."

"Where's our king?" someone calls from the last pew.

Tempest slams a fist against the wood and stands. "Your prince is here, the king's legacy. That should be enough."

"And what about *her*?" the guy retorts. "Your ex and Tempest's sloppy seconds. Do you have the same explanation for this chick entering our sacred crypt?"

"In any other circumstance," I say before Chase can decapitate anyone, "it'd be both hilarious and eye-rolling to listen to a freshman whine over cooties in his secret clubhouse, but the fact that you have a flaccid dick and I don't doesn't really help you out here."

A few guys hoot at my gall. I kind of enjoy clapping back. But I still shiver in front of these boys—tapped and initiated to become manipulative, powerful men— and it takes a lot of will-power not to shuffle behind Chase's back and peer around his protective form.

"There's no need for the king to be here," Chase adds, giving me an encouraging smile, "because what we have to say doesn't involve the Nobles of the past."

A few boys tap their feet. Some cross their arms. Chase isn't winning over the room, which is a disconcerting turn of events considering his charismatic air usually commands any space he steps into.

"Get on with it then," someone else says.

Chase's jawline juts out. He narrows his eyes at the idiot who dared to speak, and I wonder if I'm about to witness a vicious Noble punishment.

No. Chase wants to change things.

"I wrote the email," I pipe up, shifting a tiny bit forward, away from the hearth of skulls and towards some very alive, gnashing teeth.

"We know," James drawls. "It wasn't too difficult to put two-and-two together, possum. We didn't come down here for that big reveal. What we're truly interested in is *why* you fucking outed us to the entire school, and everyone associated with it, and now expect us to listen to your cunty mouth—"

"Then you might be surprised to know I was standing behind her the entire time she wrote it," Chase says, but it's a whisper. A purred warning for James to close his mouth before Chase fists it closed.

James shuts up.

I give a small, meaningful smile to Chase, then turn back to the room. "Chase shouldn't have to defend me. You've all read the email, and yeah, you're pissed I gave a public name to all the inexplicable *shit* that goes on at Briarcliff. I'll tell you my reasons. These secrets have turned some of you into accomplices. Ignorant bystanders. Killers. Your counterparts, these soulmates of yours, are being abused under—"

"You said she's dead, you fucking liar."

My speech shrivels in my throat. It doesn't take me long to locate the source of the spiteful voice. Riordan.

Chase raises his hand to his friend. "Let her speak."

Riordan stands, shoving his hands into his slacks' pockets, but it does nothing to relax his posture. "How am I supposed to sit here and listen to you parrot the same lies you wrote when I know for a fact Ivy isn't dead?"

"Riordan," I plead. "She is. I saw it."

"We saw it," Chase adds quietly. "I'm sorry, buddy. She died in Callie's arms."

"*Not true*," Riordan spits. He pulls out his phone. "I have a message from her last night. She went home because her mom's sick, and you assholes are standing up there with this propaganda *bull*shit because you want the society for yourselves." Riordan focuses on Chase. "It's easy to read the room when you saunter in, bro. You despise your father, laugh at our rules, and defy our nature like you're some kind of lost rebel here to expose the relics of this membership. *We* are not artifacts. The Noble maxim isn't some lost language you have to re-translate and sell to new members. I don't want to listen to you spout off about changing our brand when, you know what? It's really fucking awesome already. I'm graduating with Ivy. I'm marrying my soulmate and taking the position the king has offered me as soon as I finish at Yale, which I'm gonna fucking sail through, too. Using the tools the Nobles have given me—"

"Like advanced copies to the exams?" I cut in, unable to listen to his false tirade. "Fake grades? A doctored GPA? How very deserving you are."

Riordan loudly blows air through his nose. "Leave, bitch, before I—"

"Touch her, and I'll smack your head against that bench and taxidermy it for our fireplace over there while you're still fucking screaming at me to stop."

A few boys nearby gulp. I, for one, hold steady, but I don't enjoy the look on Chase's face that accompanies his statement. This is getting way out of control.

I rest a hand on Chase's arm, and say softly into the silent room, "Ivy's dead, Riordan. Sabine killed her. Everything I wrote in that email is true. And if you don't believe me, believe Chase. He's never lied to you, has he?"

"I have her voicemail," Riordan defends instead of answering. But his voice grates. His chin trembles.

"Then you hear the fear in her when she talked about her mom," I say. "Her voice shook, didn't it? Her sentences trailed off, her words turned to whispers ... the Ivy I know bursts with sound and talks so fast, she has trouble catching her breath. She speaks before thinking and shares information because she genuinely thinks she's doing Briarcliff a favor when she gives in to gossip and spreads the latest."

Riordan's brows shadow his eyes, but he doesn't interrupt.

"And when it comes to her family, she confides to her closest friends. And before me, there was you. She was forced to keep a lot from me because of the societies, but she'd never keep anything from you. Would she?"

"She said she'd just heard the news about her mom," Riordan says, his tone rough. "In her voicemail. She said she was surprised by it."

"Then you should find her message suspicious, because when she's truly upset, when something *really* shakes her up and takes her by surprise, she swears. She cusses like a goddamned sailor." My voice shakes. My hands tremble at my sides. "She didn't do any of that in her message to you, did she? Riordan, she was coerced into saying those lies to you."

A deep line forms between Riordan's brows. His mouth drops open, then goes slack before his keening roar disrupts the room.

"Jesus!" James shouts before he grabs his friend, helping him sit down. "C'mon man, you can't honestly believe the possum. Sack up. Ivy's chilling with her parents. These are more lies crafted by a bored prince who doesn't want to be a prince anymore."

"James," Chase grinds out. "What the fuck are you doing?"

James lifts his head. "Putting it out there that you have your own motives in play and don't give a fuck about the rest of us."

"You're a fucking douchebag. You know how much I've sacrificed to stand where I am today."

"Yeah? And I know the spoiled legacy living inside you that loves to create nonsense and chaos—"

"I believe him," Riordan chokes out.

All eyes turn to him.

"I believe Chase. Our prince. My friend. And I believe the possum. Ivy liked her. Trusted her."

"I'm with him, too," another boy pipes in.

"Me, too," says another.

"Oh, yeah." Tempest raises a wry hand, as if his opinion was ever in question. "Then there's me. The soulmate."

"Guys." James drifts away from Riordan and appeals to the room. "Come on. You're taking the word of some chick who hasn't been here two semesters over my suspicions?"

"About that," I say, and this time, my step forward is sure. "One thing I left out in the email, and a fact I'm positive your *suspicious nature* will be interested in. Sabine isn't the true heir of the Virtues. None of the Harringtons are ... or were." I arch a brow. "But I bet you knew that, didn't you?"

James rears back and sneers, "I don't care to know shit about you, possum."

"Listen to her, cocksucker," Chase warns, then gestures for me to continue.

"You're looking at your true queen." I keep walking, my steps loud among the new, shocked hush befalling the room, until I'm all the way in James's face. "My murdered mother was the last descendent of Rose Briar before I came along. Then, when she was nineteen, well, I *came along*. I'm the last living bloodline of the original Virtue queen, so how about you sit the fuck down and listen to your future royals?"

"That was exhilarating," I say as we tumble into the lake house. "Do you think we swayed enough of them?"

He strips off his coat, tossing it on the couch, his open shirttails fluttering with his movements as he strides into the kitchen.

"We've introduced important questions," he says. "Next time Sabine and my father address them, the subject of her legitimacy will come up. The key is not giving her enough time to formulate a plan. When she meets with the Virtues tomorrow, I'll have the Nobles that are with us accompany them. We'll out her. No more secrets. The new generation will want answers."

As he heads to the coffee maker, I ask, "The rules of monarchy are steadfast in the Nobles, but I don't think they ever were in the Virtues. Maybe at face value, to keep the Nobles in the dark, but that's it. Are questions enough to kick her out?" I gesture absently. "We're waiting on DNA results, but that could take a while, and until I can prove Mom's murder..."

"Sabine's ensured a mindfuck kind of loyalty from her Virtues," Chase agrees, "who were left out of this meeting for a reason. But my Nobles still have influence. They can convince a few girls."

"That's looking way too far in the future," I counter, then collapse on the couch.

Chase tips his face to the ceiling, showcasing the purple hollows under his eyes. "All we want right now is uncertainty. Like any unrest, there will be factions—those for you and those for Sabine, but that's where Ivy becomes the tipping point in this war."

"Her death shouldn't be like this." Changing my mind, I push of the couch and go to him. "Used as a wager. Are you sure I can't just steal the binder, involve the police, and arrest Sabine for murder? We *saw* her do it, Chase."

"Your hospital transcripts." Chase lays a hand on my arm when I reach him, but thankfully doesn't expand on the matter. He doesn't have to. I'm the least credible eyewitness there is, and Chase has proven his bias when it comes to me. "The societies have operated underground for centuries. Let me try to fuck her over underground, too. It might cause Sabine to make a public mistake."

I fold my hand on his. "Us. Let *us* try."

"Yes." He squeezes. "Together."

"We did all we could in there," I say. Chase places two steaming mugs in our hands before we head into the den. "I gave them my version of events. Did you see their faces when I told them about Noble alumni sneaking onto the academy—a *high school*—to have sex with the Virtuous princesses and countless other girls? They didn't know. I can't *believe* none of them knew."

Chase goes rigid beside me. His teeth must be cracking under the pressure, but by some miracle, he restrains himself from lashing out with what he must understand is a pointless, too-late temper. He sits.

I nestle closer, holding my mug with two hands while I attempt to soften him with my presence and a reminder that it's in the past. "We won't allow Sabine to hurt Emma anymore," I say to Chase. "When Emma gets here, we'll lay it all out. We haven't been communicating well with our friends, you and me. It's taken too long to realize that. It has to be rectified tonight." I sip my coffee, my teeth clanking against the ceramic. "I won't let them leave until we work through this."

Chase barely blinks in response.

"This is why," I say, moving to squeeze his free hand. When I find it unresponsive, I repeat, "*This* is why we need the new generation of Nobles on our side. I'm hoping we did that tonight, and the next time Sabine tries to walk into a room with them, they'll confront her. Throw Baby Briar's birth certificate in her face. Demand she give them reasons. Maybe even tonight, they'll go to their Virtue soulmates and tell them everything they've learned."

"It's a damn good start," Chase grits out. "And farther than I've ever gotten in changing their views. Listening to you..." Chase rasps but stares vacantly at a spot in front of him. "Hearing it from your lips, it was an entirely new level. And Father ... Father *knowing* about this and marrying the bitch anyway, I—fuck, I need to hit something. Kill something. If this scheme we've started doesn't work, I'll strangle her myself. She's not collecting any more girls. She's not touching my sister again."

I believe him. I'm so confident in his vow, my grip on his wrist turns solid. "There's been enough murder. Let's see where tonight goes, first. And the press could still get involved. My email was opened by enough outsiders that it could get things rolling, too. We haven't given it a whole lot of time. Sabine could be fucked already, inside and out. Can't we pour some whiskey in these coffees to celebrate?" I smile, though it's tight at the edges. "I think I saw a bar cart in your dad's study."

Chase raises his mug in a dry salute and pushes off the couch.

I stand with him. "You said it yourself. Confronting her doesn't work. And Sabine plans for betrayal too much to ever take her by surprise. But creating uncertainty? Having the future Noble society turn against her and demand she abdicate? That's something. They know about the trafficking now, the prostitution and grooming of little girls—that besmirches every single value even Thorne Briar originally created."

I follow Chase down the stairs, ruminating on my words and well aware I've started to ramble. I'm too nervous about Emma and Eden to sit and wait for them to arrive. "Sabine's one true fear is losing control of the Virtues. Each drop of uncertainty counts."

"We've planted seeds of doubt," Chase says, and I stare at a spot between his coiled shoulder blades as we descend. "But there might not be enough time to let it fester."

We reach the bottom, and Chase spins and takes me by surprise when I'm enveloped in a crushing embrace. "I don't know if what we did will keep you safe."

"Sabine wouldn't touch me. Not with the email, and now the Nobles. The old men in that brotherhood have a lot to answer for, too."

"You're staying at the lake house until I'm sure Sabine will stand down."

I lift my head. "Don't you think that's overkill? Sabine hasn't touched me since ... since Ivy. She's even made me a Virtue."

He sighs, then kisses my forehead. "It makes me all the more suspicious. I hate that you have to suffer."

I squeeze his waist. "You and your sister have been suffering under her rule long before I came along."

Chase turns his head to stare down the long, dark hallway. Curious, I follow his gaze. "What's down there?"

"Nothing important," he murmurs, then takes my hand. "Come on."

We step into Daniel Stone's office, that eerie, blue aquarium light traveling over my skin the farther he draws me in. Bottles rattle as Chase sorts through the bar cart, but I can't take my eyes off those white, lethal specks traveling silently through ultraviolet water.

"Got it." An amber bottle catches the preternatural shine as he holds it up. He turns, saying, "Father's best Macallan."

I tear my gaze off the floating creatures in time to see Chase's eyes sharpen. He shoots forward. "*Callie—!*"

Rough, thick fabric covers my head. Air goes stagnant in my mouth before I can scream.

Callie

BLINDED, I can only feel it when arms wrap around me, so tight it's like being squeezed by a python. I gasp, but only manage to suck in cloth.

I choke on Chase's name.

"Get your *fucking* hands off her!" Chase roars.

Ethereal, purple light flickers through the bag—no, it's soft and thick like a cloak—thrown over my head. Daniel Stone's office barely gave me enough light when I had 20/20 vision. Now, I'm certifiably blind.

But I can struggle.

I throw a leg back, aiming for a crotch, but my captor pitches me to the side, and I slam into the wall with a *thump* of impact.

"*You motherfucker*!" Chase yells. A rip of fabric follows. The smack of a fist on skin. A yelp of pain. "You want to take her? I dare you."

"Follow the rules, you asshole!"

James?

My vision's scattered, but my hearing's on point when I sit, my hands immediately going to the cloak wrapped around my face.

A cold, boney vise stops me.

I work up to a scream—

"One sound," a voice whispers into my ear. *Falyn.* "Just one, and I won't hesitate to toss you into the lake again."

I stiffen under her hold on both my wrists, but don't so much as whimper when she pulls me to stand, the blinding cloak still in place.

The fight continues somewhere to my right, Chase and James, arguing, cursing, slamming each other into furniture.

"It was you!" Chase roars.

Scant light, then ripples of shadow, seep into the fabric over my eyes as Chase shouts, "You knocked me out, dragged me from my room, and brought me to

Sabine. Why? Did you know she was going to kill Ivy that night? You want to betray me, fine. But Rio? The guy you love like a fucking *brother*? You let his soulmate *die*."

"Sabine has the right idea," James retorts. A muffled grunt follows his words, buffered by another swipe from Chase. "She learns weaknesses and exploits them until her chicks do whatever she says. Then, she deploys her little dollies out into the world, willing to do her every bidding. Why wouldn't I want to support that? I wish the Nobles would follow suit. They were, actually, until you decided to find a voice and side with that bitch possum over there. Do you have any idea what we could've accomplished?"

"And what do you think Sabine's succeeded in?" Chase's response comes out as a dangerous whisper.

"A First Lady, for one," James spits. "When Sabine calls, that chick does whatever Sabine wants."

"Because she was probably abused, molested, and blackmailed for years, you son of a bitch."

"Sabine has these girls tying themselves to men of influence, and those men turn into their asshole goons. So, we either gotta join her, or become the puppets to her dolls. And I ain't turning into one of those. I'm giving you one last chance, bro."

"She left my sister to die! She murdered Ivy, and had Callie's mom killed!" Chase shouts. "Sabine is a fucking psychopath. We need to stop her, not join her!"

"Suit yourself," James says, and a sickening, wet *crunch* follows.

"What was that?" I cry out, stepping forward, but Falyn holds me back. "Chase? *Chase?*"

James says offhand, "Knock the bitch out, too."

I don't hear the *thwack* when it comes to the side of my head.

But I do see the black.

I'm enveloped in a dark, warm, velvet blanket, and a gentle caress brushes my cheek.

I smile.

"Chase?" I murmur, arching toward the tickle of sweetness.

A gentle lapping drifts into my ears, its lulling tune allowing me to drift away into a relaxing, calming dream, where I do nothing but float...

Wait, float?

I'm floating.

My eyes pop wide, and I spear up, but the motion sends the surface I'm lying on tipping violently to the left, then to the right, every sharp dive causing a dangerous wetness to creep into the hollows of the—boat.

"*Oh my God.*"

My desperate whisper doesn't reach the shore.

I lift my head, scanning and blinking wildly, but any small movement unbalances the boat in a way that makes my heart thump, thud, *crash* into my ears.

And my hands are tied behind my back.

My legs shoot straight out, stuck in a type of foot harness that keeps rowers stable.

Rowers. I'm in a scull. It's nothing but a thin strip of white in the black of the lake, and I bob helplessly along with it, my butt fitted into the rower's seat with tiny wheels underneath that move with my every tremble.

I'm not stable. I'm not safe.

True fear grips my insides.

"There you are. Our newest Virtue. Over here!"

Sabine's voice floats from the docks of the boathouse, and my eyes dart toward the sound. She's not far, maybe two yards away, but for a person who's had only a handful of swimming lessons?

It's an impossible distance.

Her smile under the single lamplight crosses the space between us, seeping into my very airways. "How was your nap, darling?"

Every movement in my expression brings a shot of pain to my right temple. A feeling like dry, cracked paint sticks to every pore.

The dried blood cracks into a million tiny fractures on my face when I voice a guttural, angry scream at her in response.

"Now, now," Sabine trills, her long, golden cloak sparking against the night like a beacon I will never drift toward. "Don't lose your voice so early on in our game."

"Murderer!" I scream, my voice echoing through the quiet bank of trees. "You can kill me, drown me if you want to, but that won't change what I've already done. Everyone knows, Sabine," I bluff. "You tried to make me a Virtue to silence me, but the Virtues who broke from your rule won't stand for your deceit. The Nobles you haven't managed to stick in your pockets will talk to their parents and friends. Then those parents and friends will talk to the *press.* The police. You'll make national news by the weekend."

Sabine chuckles. "Please. You think I'm worried about your little team of avengers and your pathetic attempts at out-maneuvering me? Both Emma and Eden tried before and failed. Dear Emma was willing to lose her life, and her family, for her cause. What makes you think you'll succeed in her place?"

"Because I have the blood you're desperate for," I seethe. "And the legacy prince who will lead the Nobles. You may have manipulated his father, but you failed at bringing him to your side."

"On that, you and I agree." Sabine lifts a hand, gesturing behind her to the boat bay. "James, dear, can you bring out our second problem? I believe Callie needs a slight push in the right direction."

Sabine turns back to me, her face an expressionless mask, her beauty both wasted and wanton as she stands on the Briarcliff dock in the dead of winter as she guides the teenagers she's worked years to coerce into her waiting hands.

"You killed my best friend," I continue. "For *nothing.* I'll never bend to your wishes or do your bidding. Ever!"

"Hold that thought, dear." Sabine clucks her tongue into the shadows, as if calling her most trustful canine, and in a way, she is.

James comes out of the darkness, dragging a furious, struggling Chase down to the end of the dock.

My heart hurls itself into my throat when Chase comes under the paltry light, his black, Noble cloak billowing behind him. A breeze hits the hem, throwing it up into the air, and I notice his hands bound behind his back, just like me.

But unlike me, he's gagged. As he comes closer, I make out the Briarcliff colors on the tie shoved between his teeth.

His eyes are frantic when they land on mine. Stretched and urgent.

Violent shivers overtake my body, as if the fear upon seeing him adds to the cold of being left out at sea, but I keep my back straight. My hands clenched.

I'm confident if Chase is pushed into the lake as some kind of threat to me, he'll untie himself. He'll hold his breath and break the surface easily.

This is his lake. He has to.

"I'm feeling rather benevolent after losing another princess so suddenly," Sabine says, her voice soft but her gaze hard as she follows Chase's reluctant path to the edge. "I'm giving you one last opening, Calla Lily. You're one of us now, so you have a rare choice. Stand by my side. Join me in my efforts to continue my Virtue reign, or..." Sabine glances at the water surrounding me. She shrugs.

"You wouldn't," I say.

Sabine smiles. "Are you still underestimating me, child? I'm fully aware you can't swim."

I keep the shock from rippling across my face. "You can't hurt me—my accusations are too public. If anything happens to me, it'll all point to you."

"Yes, well, you're very distraught, dear girl. After writing an unsubstantiated email of that nature, then being threatened with expulsion by your headmaster, goodness. You've about reached the end of your rope. And with your past... do you know I have a camera recording of you in a New York City intersection with Lynda Meyer's newborn? You rushed into traffic, Calla Lily. You tried to *kill* that baby. If it weren't for that man behind you..." Sabine *tsks*. "There were so many warnings, yet the guardians in your life refused to see them. They wanted you to be good. They were desperate for you to be okay. You'd suffered so much already, what with walking in on your dead mother. Yet, they really should've known you were a danger to Blair. I have eye-witness accounts, too."

"I never tried to hurt Blair! You'll answer for my mother!" I scream, jerking forward, her accusations swirling into a wrathful tornado in my head, my words collapsing into fragments, the people I love breaking to pieces.

The boat tips dangerously, and I freeze.

My mind tells me it's over—I'm restrained in a boat, and Chase is slammed to his knees by his supposed friend. Sabine's won. I'll die here tonight as the villain, the source for all the wrong seeping into Briarcliff Academy, yet it will fester long after I'm gone.

Except, my heart won't concede.

"You need me!" I shout, my voice amplified by the lake. "You can't let me die."

"I killed your mother, didn't I? Blood heirs didn't matter to me then. Why should it matter now? Falyn, dear, go out and assist our poor Callie."

Falyn appears from the second boat bay, her tall, honed body clad in Briarcliff's unisuit. Her rower's knee socks pad silently while holding a scull above her shoulders, its shadow above her head doing nothing to obscure the enticement in her eyes as she locks them with mine.

"Think about this," I say to her, aiming for calm. "Falyn, think about what you're about to do."

Falyn replies, "You're not the queen of the Virtues. I'm here to ensure you never will be."

Chase moans something under his gag, guttural and violent. Falyn tosses a smile James's way but ignores the struggling beast she restrains.

The scull lands in the water. Falyn sets up her oars, then slips in. She pushes off the dock with a silent, deadly curve. Aiming for me.

My eyes dart from her to Sabine. "You can't! You won't. There's no one left for you. If you end my bloodline, you'll end yours, too. Piper's dead. Addisyn isn't eligible to inherit the society because of her crime against her sister. You're left vulnerable, aren't you? You need me. You need me on your side to keep your influence!"

Sabine stills, the water lapping underneath the dock amplifying in the silence.

"The societies follow monarchy rules," I continue. "As much as you've tried to break them. You're out in the open, without daughters, without heirs. Without me, you'll have no claim to the Virtues. *None.*"

Sabine's lips part on my last sentence. "My Virtuous girls will never go against me."

"It doesn't matter what they do." I break off to track Falyn's oars swishing into the water, gaining on me. I go back to Sabine. "The Virtues didn't write the original oaths. The Nobles did. *They* will take control once they find out what you've done to me and their prince. And they'll dispose of you as easily as Daniel Stone will."

"My dear, have you not been listening? It isn't *me* who will end the Noble legacy." She tips her head and smiles. "It's you."

My face grows stiff. Stone cold. I whisper, through numbed lips, "No."

Sabine lowers her chin. Falyn's scull knocks against mine. She takes hold of my hull.

"Don't do this—" I plead with Falyn, but a sharp movement brings my attention back to the dock.

Sabine laughs. "You're beside yourself. I can understand, after what your broken mind has made you endure. Ranting about secret societies. Scaring the children with the myth of a sex ring on school grounds. Traumatizing parents with your hallucinations. This time, it's not merely your stepfather you've made suffer. Your delusions have become too much. You're *hurting* people, dear child. Blair. Sylvie. Ivy. You've experienced so much grief, have ruined too many lives, and you're desperate to end your time here on Earth and join your mother. However..." She pauses. "Your selfish nature won't let you die alone, now will it? You'd never leave Chase, your true soulmate, behind."

My breaths stutter out of my mouth. Tempest. *Where's Tempest?* And Eden and Emma? They could've been upstairs in the lake house when Chase and I were taken...

"Where are my friends? What did you do to Eden and Emma?"

My frantic exhales are the only sound in this cold, quiet lake. Even Falyn is motionless, her spindly fingers curled against my scull in wait.

"You kill the poor boy first," Sabine continues, ignoring my question. "Then, you row out to the middle of the lake and capsize your boat." Sabine's eyes widen. "That's the kind of news that will overshadow a fragile, broken girl's paranoid rambling, don't you agree?"

My breathing turns into hyperventilating. "Ivy's pretend vacation will have to end soon. When she doesn't show—"

"Oh, you killed her, too, and buried her body in the woods. A sad little text message from your phone will admit to all that."

"Monster," I whisper, but Sabine hears, because she slowly, methodically, grins.

Sabine reaches into her cloak, and a silver shine catches against the moonlight. She holds the dagger high. "I believe your DNA is already on this."

"*NO!*" My terrorized yell grows in sound, shattering like moonlit shards across the rippling lake.

A sickening hurricane builds in my chest, ready to burst out of my lungs—

"Callie!"

My terrified gaze turns to Chase. He's wrestled out of the gag, the tie hanging around his neck like a noose. "Howard Mason! Howard Mason is your father!"

Sabine freezes mid-arc.

"Wh-wh—?" I try to respond, but I'm absorbing the winter cold, my words coming out in shivers of sound.

"Security's bound to check the boathouse soon." Sabine jerks her chin at Falyn. "Tip her over, and the title of princess is yours, along with Tempest Callahan as your new soulmate. You'll be the most idolized couple on campus and beyond, sweet girl."

Falyn reaches behind me and pulls the knot holding my wrists, then pulls my feet from the shoes.

"Don't do this—she's manipulating you!" I gasp, wrestling my arms free to try and grab Falyn. She ducks, and I'm too off balance to try again. "She did it to Ivy, to Emma, to her own daughter, and she's disposed of them all. What makes you think you aren't disposable, too? Falyn, please. Please! *Don't*—"

Nothing else I want to say matters, because the last thing I see is the swing of Sabine's knife into Chase's chest before lake water drowns my screams.

Callie

LET *yourself sink a little lower into the water, Callie. Then spread out your arms, your legs. That's it. Relax...*

Float.

Float up....

Eden's wry, unhurried teachings whistle in my ears as my eyes bulge open, searching my watery grave.

Her voice comes back. *There's no time to schedule you in for a second drowning. So, hold on to that boat and KICK.*

My arms shoot up and swipe for the capsized scull, my knuckles knocking against the moving seat on the way back down. I only have time for a second attempt before I sink too deep, and I put all my effort, all my frantic kicks, into stretching my body and curling my hands around the wooden seat inside the hull.

Then, in one death-defying, most important push-up of my life, my face breaks through the water, but beneath the upturned boat.

Holding onto the seat pulls the scull in deeper and it slams against my head. In a desperate maneuver, I change my grip to the outer edges of the boat, my feet flailing.

I'm cold. It feels like my blood is solidifying under my skin.

This isn't like my Thanksgiving dunk. This is so, so, *so* much worse.

It's impossible to last very long in these temperatures. Yet, somehow, I have to move.

Kick. Kick. KICK, Eden screams in my head.

I do.

My iced-over legs spear out and in, but I have no idea if I'm moving. I have to get out from under. I have to get to Chase.

No. I have to stay where I am until I'm sure Sabine, Falyn, and James are gone.

A trembling whimper leaves my throat, but I count to five, then ten. After that, I convince myself that dunking my head one more time—just *one more time*

734

—won't be so bad. I'll hold my breath and come out on the other side. It's that easy.

Eden, Ivy, Emma, please be with me.

I take a deep breath and sink.

My fingers slip against the scull, screeching against the fiberglass. I cry out underwater when I have to loosen a hand, then splash through the surface on a gasping breath that escapes my mouth in clouds.

But there can only be clouds where there's air.

I've made it! I'm on the other side!

I start curving my arms around the smooth curve of the boat before scanning for Sabine. I slip twice, lose my grip once, but at last, I crawl up enough so only a third of my body is still in the water.

And I stare straight ahead.

The dock is deserted, the tall lamps at the end casting fading, golden halos over a slumped, still form.

"Chase," I whisper, then, "CHASE!"

I paddle furiously, using numbed, stiff fingers that no longer listen to commands, but my arms sure do. I kick uselessly, then finally find the clumsy rhythm Eden had me practice with a pool noodle that gets me moving in the direction I need, with the help of the lake's gentle current.

I have no sense of time but know that I'm cold. Covered in winter water. Growing snowflakes that give off frostbitten sparkles under the sleepy, lowering moon, but Chase is dying.

Dying. Not dead. He can't be dead.

"Chase!" I try again, but he doesn't twitch or make a sound.

I kick up enough water that it arcs over my body and into my eyes, but I get closer. Time ticks down, but picturing Chase's blood spilling onto the wood acts as the perfect impetus to keep my exhausted limbs submerged and kicking.

When the scull bumps against the dock, I slide back into the water, clinging to the dock and shuffling to the ladder with a shaking, trembling grip.

The instant I'm on the dock, I launch myself at Chase and drop to my knees beside him.

"Chase," I whisper through bloodless, frozen lips. "Can you hear me?"

He doesn't respond. I don't waste time searching his face, instead looking for the wound. My hands are white—too white—and I can't feel anything. I have to squint. My jaw slams shut with the amount of effort I'm putting into moving him onto his back, lifting fabric and probing skin.

Move. *Move, damn it!*

Blood seeps through the gaps between my fingers when I reach his stomach. Gasping, crying, I press into it, staunching the flow.

"What the...?"

I whip my head to the sound. *"Call 9-1-1!"*

The boy, dressed in his rowing training gear, gapes from the boat house.

"Move, damn it!" I scream. "Call an ambulance, or I will throw this oar like a javelin into your face!"

His duffel drops to his feet. He scampers into the boathouse.

I turn back to Chase, droplets from the tips of my hair becoming teardrops on his pale, bloodless face. "You're okay. We're going to be okay."

My jaw won't stop shaking. My body won't stop shivering.

But I won't stop.

I bend my forehead to his, and I hold on.

Callie

SOFT *BEEPS* FOLLOW the tread of footsteps and gentle hands lift my arm, turn it, then set it delicately on my stomach.

My eyes slowly open, a burst of white solidifying into walls, a door, and someone snoozing in a chair.

I cough at the sudden dryness in my throat and attempt to lift onto my elbows.

The person—Eden—cracks an eye open, then shoots awake and rushes to my side.

"You're okay." I mumble. "I thought Sabine..."

Eden rolls her eyes as she grabs my hand. "Willow and Violet make awful bodyguards, and are even worse at researching their victims. They shoved us into this basement room in the lake house that Emma is all-too-familiar with. She showed me the key she'd hidden away when she was ... stuck there ... to sneak out."

While relief sinks wonderfully into my bones at the news that Emma's okay, too, my short-term memory warps into a nightmare, and my heart picks up an erratic, panicked beat.

"Where...?" I succumb to another fit of coughs.

A plastic cup with a straw appears in front of me. "Drink this. But slowly."

Grateful, I clutch at the cup and bring it to my lips but pause after the first sip.

Tubes hang out of my left hand, and I stare at them in confusion.

"You're in the hospital," Eden explains. "EMTs found you and Chase at the boathouse docks unconscious. You were severely hypothermic. Any longer and..." Eden drags her gaze from mine. "Anyway, you're gonna be okay. You just need to rest."

Eden's explanation brings vivid snapshots of Chase lying at the end of the dock, blood pooling at his middle. Of me, bending over him, screaming.

I lift my hands, looking for his blood on my fingers, dried into my cuticles, but there's none. "What—is he—is Chase—?" I can't say it. I can't.

"He's here." But Eden chews on her lower lip and doesn't elaborate.

I push the water cup at Eden, then fumble for my sheets.

"Nope. No way, Callie. You're staying here." She presses a hand against my shoulder, keeping me down.

"I need to see him."

"I know, but you can't."

"I'm *going* to see him." My voice scratches against the vowels, but I want to be by Chase's side more than I want water.

"You can't, Callie."

"I *will*."

"They won't let you!" Eden cries, using both hands to pin me down. Her face is inches from mine. "Emma said she'd come up to see you as soon as you were awake. I'll go get her. You can ask her about Chase."

"But—"

"I mean it, Callie. Keep your ass in that bed or else I'll explain your hysterics to the nurses and have you restrained."

My eyes widen.

"I'm sorry," Eden says, softer. "But it's for your own good. You can't be with him."

Eden steps back from the bed, her form fading as she moves to the door, but I don't think it's from distance. My blinks are heavier, the periods of blindness longer, and soon, I succumb to a medically induced sleep.

"Callie? Can you wake up for me?"

I stir at the soft, masculine tone, turning my head toward the sound. Ahmar's kind brown eyes flicker through my slitted vision.

"Hey, kiddo. Nice to see you," he says, slipping his hand under mine and squeezing.

I smack my lips together, trying to speak.

Ahmar's answer is to shove a straw between my lips, and I suck in the cool water on instinct. Then I shove the straw out with my tongue. "Chase."

"He's alive," he supplies. "Not doing well but breathing. His family is with him now."

"Sabine ... she can't—don't let her see him."

Ahmar's lips turn down. "She's not with them. She didn't think it'd be proper, under the ... circumstances."

Though my mind is foggy with cotton clouds, I don't miss the undercurrent in his tone. "Does everyone think it was me? That I hurt him?"

He gives a tight nod. "Sabine and Daniel Stone have given statements that your obsession with Sabine after her daughter was killed rose to concerning levels. You accused her of—being a queen of the Virtues? Do I have that right? And tried to take away her title by ... killing her future stepson? Calla, is any of this resonating with you?"

"Fuck," I whisper, my eyes going damp. My restraints don't let me wipe the building tears away.

Ahmar stares so hard at me, I can feel his desperate study within the deep trenches of my heart. As if the answers for what happened last night are written on my skin.

He hesitates, then says, "I'm gonna say this quick, because I—it's difficult. There was a note in your room, written by you, explaining how your obsession was too much for you to bear, and you couldn't handle it anymore. The same people who got to your mom were coming for you. Secret societies want to murder you just like they killed your mom. Headmaster Marron is one of their leaders, in cahoots with Sabine Harrington and Daniel Stone, and they all want you dead. You also drew a map where police could find Ivy's unmarked grave. You killed her to spare her suffering at the hands of the same society that's torturing you—"

"Stop," I whisper.

"I can't." Ahmar's voice cracks. "The police are outside waiting for you to be lucid enough for questioning. Your father and I are doing everything we can to explain you'd never write such a thing, never mind hurt your best friend, but they have all this evidence, all this documentation, proving you're mentally unsound. And this Daniel Stone guy is hellbent on pinning his son's attack on you. He's involved every top official he can think of to bring you down. I ... Jesus, Callie. He's leveraging his kid's near-death to give his accusations extra ammo. It's sickening."

"It'll be okay. When Chase wakes up, he'll explain—"

"*If*, Callie. It's a very real *if*." Ahmar's eyes go damp. He squeezes my hand.

"I tried to stop it," I choke out. "I couldn't—I tried to swim to him in time, but I was so scared. I hid under the boat for too long. He's bleeding out on the docks, and I'm floating three feet away, and I *still* couldn't get there—"

"Sweetie. Shh." Ahmar rests his forearms on the bed, cupping my hand in both of his.

I blink. "This isn't making sense to you, is it? I'm trying to explain, but I'm frightening you."

"This whole fucking thing is frightening to me, which is why this is how it's gonna go: I'll go out there and tell the cops you're still out of it. I have a lawyer friend on her way, and your dad and Lynda are coming, too."

I lift my head from the pillow. "Dad? Lynda? That's good! They know all about the Nobles and Virtues. They can help explain."

"They've already told me everything."

My neck strains as I try to raise myself higher, but my hands and feet are tied securely. "They have? You know?"

Ahmar offers another squeeze. He says somberly, "I do. Yes."

"Then the police can stop looking at me. They can turn to Sabine and Daniel instead. There's an entire underground worth of lies and deceit—I can give you names. I'll give you all of them, if it means—"

"Baby girl." I'm suddenly subjected to Ahmar's sorrowful, defeated gaze. "Lynda won't go on the record. She and Pete confessed to me because I was out of my mind. I thought you'd lost it, that this was the end for you. And I didn't do enough to help you, to stop this. That I failed your momma."

I try to rise again. "Ahmar, no."

"I'm educated, now." Ahmar sniffs hard, swallowing his emotion. "About this place and the players. And once you're given the physical okay, you're coming home with me and I'm going to fight for you until the Stones' Armageddon ends. Kiddo, I believe you. I believe you, and I'm sorry that we can't do more to prove it."

"They're pinning Ivy's murder on me."

Ahmar bows his head. "They're doing a lot more than that, sweetie."

"Then Dad has to speak the truth. He won't let me rot in prison. He can't. I'm—"

When Ahmar angles his head to meet my stare, my words die in my throat.

There's me, and then there's Blair and Lynda.

And the small detail of me accusing him and allowing *him* to rot in prison.

The squeamishness returns, the nausea and slime of not being blood-related to any of them. Of not being needed.

Except, there's Ahmar. No blood exists between us, yet he's my uncle, no question.

At the thought of him, an idea pops into my head regarding the blood I *do* share. "Check my DNA."

Ahmar frowns. "Huh?"

"My DNA," I repeat. "Check it against Headmaster Marron's."

"What are you talking about...?" Realization hits, his forehead smoothing. "No fucking way."

"He was a teacher when Mom went here. They had an affair. I..." I take a breath, weighing my options. "Last night, at the boathouse, the final words Chase spoke were that Howard Mason was my real father. That's Headmaster Marron. I was confused when he shouted it. It was so unexpected that *that* was what he chose to say when Sabine was holding a knife to his throat, but—now I understand why. There's no evidence left. Everything I've learned, all I've collected, was taken by the societies." I look down at my inner elbow, where an IV drips steady fluids into my body. "All except for this. Me."

"I'm ... I think I'm following you, but I need more information."

"Marron is my real father. Is that enough evidence to show some credibility that what I'm saying is true? Marron is a high-ranking official of the Nobles. He works for Daniel Stone. And he's aware of everything Sabine's done for the Virtues. He sanctions it. I have no idea if he knows I exist, but being his secret love child while he was a teacher..." I think of Dr. Luke. "It would disgrace him. He might do anything to keep it from coming out. Including turning into a credible witness for me, explaining to police that I'm not a killer and admitting to them the society exists and Sabine's been trafficking girls. He'd be heralded as a hero if Sabine goes down, can take all the credit for all I care. This could work. It's not much, but it's something."

Ahmar slow-blinks. Licks his lips. "Calla. You're scaring me. Think this through. If this is your father, can you be okay using him this way? It would ruin any chance you have to get to know someone you thought you'd never meet."

I shake my head, my mouth thinning. "He's not my father. He lost that right when he left my mother to fend for herself. He's my sperm donor, nothing more."

"Kiddo."

"I mean it, Ahmar."

"Okay. I won't push it." Ahmar pauses, studying my heart monitor, then comes back to me. "So, this boy. This Chase. You trust what he has to say?"

Marron being my father is yet another secret Chase kept hidden, and while it's crushing, it makes a sick kind of sense that Chase held it back. It's not the proud moment of finding my real father I'd always envisioned. It's a sickening blow of news against my head, and if Marron knew, all this time, yet sicced his actual daughter and her friends on me anyway ... Willow. *My half-sister.*

"Yes," I say. "I believe Chase."

"Jesus, fuck." Ahmar rubs the top of his balding head. "Meredith never said a word."

"Just that he was a random one-night stand," I supply. "I received the same story."

"I gotta believe, with all my heart, she was protecting you." Ahmar leans back. "Considering what you've said, what Pete's told me..."

"She was. Mom didn't want me to know my father, or for me to be at Briarcliff, because I'm a threat to what Sabine and Daniel have built. Tell Detective Haskins. He may not believe it, coming from me. But he might respect your opinion."

Ahmar shakes his head. "I'm trying, kiddo. This whole business about a secret bloodline and you being some kind of rightful heir, though ... it's a hard sell."

"Don't forget sex-trafficking, rigged exams and grades, and tax evasion." I smile wanly.

"Uh-huh." Ahmar sets his jaw, thinking. "Haskins is suspicious, but he's a good man. A smart one, too. These families see him as a small town bumfuck who can be buried alive with enough Benjamins, but—not to get your hopes up—there was a sparkle in his eye when I explained this Noble and Virtue business that Pete threw on me. Haskins wasn't surprised. I'll give him this info about Marron. Testing your DNA against his will take a much shorter time than whatever hair you had me pass over to my ex, but Callie..."

"Be prepared for the worst. I know."

"And I hate that you do."

Ahmar leans down and kisses me on the forehead. "I'm going back out there. And I'll make sure Haskins is the only cop that comes in here to question you. We'll get to the bottom of this, baby girl."

When he pulls back, I read between the lines in his face. Determination and resolve creep into the cracks, but grief remains the deepest crevice.

Frustration at losing my mother. Not being able to save her.

Desperation to save me, instead.

"I love you, Ahmar."

"Ah." Ahmar swipes the back of his hand against his eyes. "Don't do this to me. I'll see you in a few hours. I'll be back *after* I become a goddamned tick on Haskins's back and never leave him alone."

I lift my restrained wrists as much as I can. A light clink of the belt loops follows. "I'll be here."

He stares at the leather cuffs. "I'm sorry."

"Me too," I whisper, and I don't close my eyes until Ahmar disappears from view.

Callie

"UP AND AT 'EM, NIGHT POSSUM!"

The voice, too lighthearted to be real, tinkles against my ear, and I swat at it like a mosquito.

"I'm asking nicely, but seriously. I'm not a nice guy. Wake the fuck up."

I pry my eyes open, heavy with a drugged, gritty sleep the nurses keep forcing on me. But once I focus on the form looming above me, I croak out, "Tempest?"

"Yes, your beard is here to save the day."

"My what?"

"Your fake soulmate. You know, the disguise you wear to cover up all your smushy feely feels for Chasey-poo."

"Whatever." My roll to my side is halted by his rude grip on my wrists.

"Let go!" I complain.

"I'm not touching you."

I glance down and give a small grunt when I notice the shackles on my wrist through the greenish light of my room.

A hospital room. With beeps and blips of machines chugging along softly beside me.

It all comes back in a *whoosh*.

"Chase!" I fight against my restraints. "I need to see him."

"Do *not* fight, scream, or flail, or else I'll be forced to gag you with a latex glove." He waggles his brows. "And I do love my foreplay."

"Are you joking? Your best friend is in critical condition, and you're here making fun of me."

"I'm not kidding around. I'm merely passing the time it's taking for you to have a breakthrough moment where you figure out I'm here to bust you through those doors and take you on a mad escape spree through the halls."

I stare at him.

742

"Well, why didn't you just say so?" I jangle my chains as permission.

Tempest glides to one side of my bed but pauses with his hands hovering over my arm. He arches a brow. "This is gonna hurt."

"What?—*fuck,* Tempest!" My whispered, wet curses fall on deaf ears as Tempest yanks at my IVs and pulls the needles out of my skin without so much as a testing pull.

Tempest moves to unlock the belts at my hands and ankles with surprising dexterity, then helps me sit up until my feet dangle over the bed. But my fingers tangle in the sheets, stopping him from lifting me to a stand.

"What is it?" he asks.

"My hospital gown. I'm..."

"No need to be modest. You have an excellent ass. For a rodent, anyway. And," he adds when I fumble to close my gown at the back, "there's not much time, so grab your shit and let's hustle."

"I need clothes. Did Ahmar...?" I scan the small, private room for any kind of bag, and find a small sports duffel on the single visitor's chair.

I stumble over to it on weak legs, pretending Tempest isn't judging my body as I turn my back to him, my gown puddling to the floor, then throw on a long-sleeve shirt, jeans, and a winter coat.

His silent presence tells me that's exactly what he's doing.

I spin to the clear, plastic bag beside the duffel, containing my soaked clothes. Ripping it open, I search for one item in particular. When a sharp point hits my fingers, I smile.

Tempest is still too quiet, so I distract him while clasping the raven necklace around my neck by saying, "Ahmar has this under control. He believes us and is willing to help reveal the truth to Haskins."

"Oh, yeah? And what happened the last time you trusted the process, little possum?"

I drop the pendant underneath my shirt, zip up my jacket, and turn. "Tell me another option, then, because after becoming a popsicle in a lake while I watched Chase bleed out in front of me, I'm out of ideas."

"There's your problem." Tempest points at me. "You're a no optimism possum."

He hooks my arm and pulls me to the door, using his other hand to put a finger to his mouth.

"Police are stationed at my door," I whisper. "I sure hope you have a plan other than to tip-toe out of here."

Tempest cracks the door open, peers through, then, seemingly satisfied, pushes it all the way open. "The nurses are changing shifts. We'll cut through the hallway and slip through the exit over there. And we're talking small-town cops, babe, not super-duper detectives." After he ushers us all the way out, he gestures to the slumped over cop on the chair. "Slipped him some of James's Ambien in his decaf. He's out."

I study Tempest for some sort of reaction after mentioning a friend who so utterly betrayed him by offering Chase up to Sabine on a platter, but Tempest's face is predictably blank as he scoots me past the snoring guard and through the exit.

He grabs my hand to pull me downstairs, but I hold onto the banister to stop the descent.

Tempest's shoulders slump on a sigh. "Have I not reasonably explained the dire need to run at this point of our escape plan?"

"I thought you were bringing me to Chase."

His lips pop on another exhale. "Babe, I hate to tell ya, but he's the least of your worries."

"Ahmar's dealing with the police. He'll add enough doubt that Haskins'll look at more than just me when it comes to Ivy or Chase's attack."

Another sardonic brow arch. "How is any of this relevant to me right now?"

"You don't have to break me out of the hospital. I trust my uncle. He's the *only* person I'm certain has my back."

"Shit." Tempest tucks his hands in his pockets, then tilts against the wall to better see me. "You're assuming your uncle got out of this hospital unscathed, aren't you?"

Every part of me goes cold. "Why wouldn't he? He has nothing to do with secret societies or Briarcliff. He's an outsider."

"He's yours." Tempest eyes me steadily. "And he's important to you and willing to hear your opinion. All things Sabine doesn't enjoy hanging out in the open."

My chapped lips peel apart. "Sabine has Ahmar?"

Tempest's mouth turns grim. "No, she has Ahmar, Emma, and Eden."

Callie

"HOW AM I supposed to believe what you're saying?" I ask Tempest, but my tone wobbles. My question is frantic. "You're one of them. You could be leading me right into Sabine's clutches."

"Well, I *am* leading you to her, but not for her dinner *appertif.* Chase is my boy." Tempest pushes off the wall. "My ride-or-die. I played no part in what happened tonight, and I fucking wish I did."

Tempest halts at the step below mine. We're almost eye-to-eye, and there, right there, is the emotion I was searching for when it came to discovering one of your best friends is a traitor.

"If I'd known, I would've told Chase not to go near you. If I'd had any *inkling* of what runs in your blood, I would've done everything in my power to harass you, terrify you, get you to quit and have you running back to your uncle-daddy with your tail between your possum pussy—and I promise you, while I might've fucked you like Chase, I wouldn't have left you whole the way he has."

I swallow against the vicious, streaming sentences, but hold his stare. "My mother did her damnedest to keep me away from this hellhole. If *I'd* had any inkling, I would've gladly gone through life without ever going to this school, seeing your face, knowing my real father, and figuring out that all secret societies are good for is protecting murderers and pedophiles."

Tempest tilts his head, a modicum of respect flashing in his eyes. "Not all of us. It's why I find myself in this position, where my boy can't. Chase wants all that shit to end, and so do I. We may be seniors at Briarcliff Academy, but we hold a lot of fucking clout within our Noble circle.

"Sabine's presenting your uncle, Emma, and Eden to the entire societal member-ship. That's right," he says when he registers my wince. "Every. Single. One. She's there to solidify her position as well as your garbage dump of a reputation. She's likely blackmailed, coerced, and threatened your only remaining allies into backing up her

745

story and will have them announce to her entire audience that you are no longer eligible to run the Virtues, even if your DNA results come back and you have Rose Briar's blood. Of course, her speech was meant to occur while you were cuffed, interrogated, and arrested in the nearby hospital, except now I've arrived to seriously fuck her shit up. No bitch who tries to kill my buddy will earn herself a centuries-old society for her efforts." He pauses, then angles his head at me. "So, are you in, or do you want me to assist in buckling you back into your hospital bed and leaving you there to trust your *process*?"

I match his unflinching stare. "I'm in."

"Good." He whips around and flies down the stairs. With my heart beating in my ears, I rush to catch up to him.

Tempest roars through the small town of Briarcliff with the smooth rumbling of a sleek luxury car, and I brace for his abrupt turns with a clenched, whitened grip against the door.

We don't speak during the trip back to the academy, Tempest's foreboding last words as he pushed me into his vehicle being, "By the time the nurses figure out you're gone, we'll be buried underground," before whipping out of the hospital parking garage.

He pulls up to the M.B.S. Library of Studies, and I push my door open without hesitation. Tempest meets me at the front of the car, then takes some of my weight as we stride to the doors, my breaths a lot harsher than his.

"Should I have given you a Gatorade or something?" he asks, side-eyeing me as I hunch into him. "Basic care of another person isn't my strong suit. Chase was better at that shit."

"Is better," I correct.

Tempest holds the door open for me and studies me through the glass.

"*Is*," I repeat. "He's going to be fine, and when I'm done with that cunt in there, I'm going to tell him so myself."

Tempest makes an approving sound at my back. "I kept wondering why Chase decided to keep you instead of scare you off. Now I'm getting it."

We reach the back wall, and when I make noises that my fingerprints may not work anymore—last night's events pretty much exiled me—Tempest waves me off. He bends to the floor, his fingers bringing up a strange screen on the touchpad, then working furiously. After a few minutes, a soft *beep* sounds, and the hidden door slides open.

Callie

I PROBABLY SHOULD'VE BRACED for the moment when the hidden door would slide open to reveal Sabine, standing at the center of the circular room brimming with hooded Nobles and Virtues.

Her mouth is open mid-speech, and when she turns toward the sudden disturbance, her red-rimmed lips part further.

"Are we late to the party?" Tempest calls as he saunters in, hauling me against his side. "Apologies. My plus one had such a complex about coming to a soiree straight out of a hospital bed."

Pure, vile fury runs through Sabine's expression, paling it to such a degree that her lips turn into swatches of fresh blood. Her hateful stare burrows into my skin, my veins popping and thriving with her putrid death wishes, but just as quickly, she covers her surprise behind a serene, confident mask.

"Just as well," she simpers, then glances up to include the rows of Nobles and Virtues. "You're now able to match a face to the girl who's put our societies at so much risk. She writes about us in a mass email to parents, students, and faculty. And if that's not enough..." Sabine chuckles under her breath. "She accuses us of *murder*. This child has gone so far as to accuse us of tracking down her mother and killing her in cold blood. She's gathered so much hatred, so much misdirected anger, that Calla Lily Ryan can no longer tell reality from fiction." Sabine eyes me dryly. "Her very public accusations of her stepfather and resulting psychosis proves that."

I peel my lips from my teeth. "You sociopathic bitch."

"Callie is so traumatized, so unstable, she almost overdoses an innocent girl. But, largely due to her connections in the NYPD, she's able to escape accountability and came to Briarcliff with no charges, no soul. Her lack of empathy—or her succumbing to her demons, however you choose to see it, my lords—coupled with her lax supervision, allowed her to come onto our soil, desecrate our traditions, and *kill* our

Virtuous Princess through a misguided sense of protecting the princess from me, her queen."

Sabine's mask falls when she includes me, her eyes stretching so wide that hollows deepen around them, giving her the face of a skull with stripped-back skin. "You rancid street rat, you have *forsaken* the Virtues." She twists, her scarlet dress billowing with her movements. "Bring them out!"

Noise hits my left ear, and I'm forced to watch my friends, my *uncle*, being dragged out of the same corridor I'd used to follow Chase into an unbearable darkness.

Though their hands are untied and their footsteps free, Emma, Eden, and Ahmar's faces all tell me an emotionless story.

I frantically scan their forms for injuries or torture, but all walk with a natural, albeit hesitant, gait. And none of them look in my direction.

"How has this become a tribunal? I'm not the one needing to face judgment!" I cry out to the crowd.

Even Ahmar. *Even Ahmar* takes his place in the light like he's part of a police line-up. My breath hitches at what they could've done to make this born-and-raised Bronx man so placid. "Sabine's desperate to keep a throne where everything in her life has disintegrated. Yes, she has Daniel Stone, but he's just as colluding as she is. And when he finds out what she did to his son, I very much doubt he'll stick by her side."

I say this loud enough for the entire room to hear. My voice echoes throughout the hushed temple, but the thickened atmosphere, the stone-cold quiet, indicates I have much further to go before any of these people believe me.

"If you're quite done," Sabine quips, "allow your pseudo-uncle to speak. Ahmar Kazmi, is it?"

Ahmar lifts his head, but his eyes are so hollow, his warm brown skin so gray, that my stomach sinks before he utters a word.

"My beloved niece needs help," he croaks out. "She hasn't been right since Mer— my friend's death, and her recent escape from the hospital proves it." Ahmar turns in my direction but keeps his focus on the floor. "These people only wanted to help, honey. You're ruining lives. You've already destroyed so many. Don't bring anyone else down with you."

Tears brim at the edges of my vision. "You don't mean that."

"Emma?" Sabine croons. "How about you, dear?"

"My brother wanted nothing but the best for you." Emma's dulled voice carries across the attentive room. "And you stabbed him for it."

"Eden?" Sabine asks. "Anything to add?"

Eden's quiet voice comes through her curtain of hair. "You sent naked pictures of me to the entire school after I confided in you how much pictures like that destroyed me in ninth grade."

"I don't—Eden, I would never," I say. "Whatever Sabine's done to you ... it can't account for Ivy's death. Sabine *killed* her." My voice breaks. "Please remember that. And she put Chase in critical condition."

"No, dear, *you* did all that."

"No." But it comes out hoarse. "I didn't."

"Oh, but you did. I've called this emergency meeting precisely because you are a danger to our societies, our school, and yourself. Your uncle has kindly offered to put you into psychiatric care as soon as you recover from your ... failed attempt at suicide, which, since you're here, I assume you have."

I find Ahmar through the haze, and he lifts his head without hesitation. The skin around his eyes tightens, as if in a desperate effort to drill his thoughts into mine. I can practically hear them through his closed, tense mouth. *Do as she says, kiddo. Let's escape in one piece, all right? We'll deal with them when we're long gone.*

Or is that even what he's saying? I can't tell anymore. What he said aloud doesn't match these internal thoughts. He stated I was ruining lives. That I'd already hurt my dad. Sylvie.

Did I hurt Ivy and Chase, too?

My hands go to my head, my knuckles digging into my temples.

"Ahmar," I cry, scrunching my eyes shut.

"He can't help you anymore, child." Sabine's heels click against the marble. "In my opinion, he's helped you too much. Falyn? Come down here, please."

Falyn appears after taking the hidden stairs, her golden cloak floating around her ankles as she walks. She smiles when she spies me, then digs into a side pocket of her cloak and pulls out a sheaf of papers she then gives to Sabine.

"No!" Ahmar cries out. Then, his brows draw in. His back goes up. "Lady, I've done everything you've asked. That was the deal. You promised you wouldn't show her."

"What, this old report?" Sabine calls, with a look over her shoulder. "I'll keep my promise. I won't show her. But I *will* tell her."

Ahmar roars, stampeding forward, but is held back by a taller, broader Cloak— the type of stature I didn't think existed above Ahmar, gifted with height and breadth.

But I don't tell the Cloak to release him. I'm too fixated on what Sabine holds in her hands. "What is that?"

"It's a police report, darling, on your mother's death. Oh—I stand corrected," she adds when Ahmar lets loose a string of threats. "A *forged* police report. One your uncle worked very hard to legitimize. And it would've worked, too, had I not done the digging necessary to unveil the true document he buried."

My stomach pitches. "That's not—Ahmar?"

He trembles beneath the Cloak's solid grip, muscles bulging from his neck, his cheeks, and a bulbous vein trailing along his forehead. "Baby girl, don't listen to what comes next."

"Why shouldn't she?" Sabine asks, gesturing to the balcony above. "Everyone else gets to."

Cloaks, a black and gold chessboard of iniquity, lean over the railings, their hoods dangling eagerly.

"Damn it, lady, *no*—"

Sabine turns to me and smiles, her teeth gleaming. She doesn't need fangs. She harbors so much dark energy her grin might as well contain venom dripping from her canines. "Calla Lily, I regret to inform you that it was you who held the knife. Your killing spree didn't begin with Ivara Alling. It began with your mother. *You* murdered her."

Callie

THE MARBLED flooring lurches beneath my feet. My vision shrinks to a pinprick, Sabine's face at the helm. Chills pass along my skin, ants marching in single file until they reach their hill, apexed at the core of my heart.

"You had your mother's blood on your hands when Mr. Kazmi found you that night," Sabine continues, her voice a soft lullaby trailing across the hard stone walls. "Along with bruises around your neck, consistent with your mother defending herself. Your uncle covered it up as best he could—even allowed you to accuse your stepfather of your crime."

Breath lies ragged in my throat. "That's not true!"

"Mr. Kazmi?" This time, Sabine cuts her attention in his direction. "Care to provide some background information?"

Ahmar's throat bobs. He finds me in the small crowd, where even Tempest takes a step back, his brows arched in surprise.

Ahmar rasps, "Kiddo..."

"Oh my God," I whisper. My legs ache to run, but there's nowhere to hide. I'm blocked in, by marble and stone, by people, by guilt. "I refuse to believe it. I won't!"

"He'd do anything for you, that man," Sabine says, clucking her tongue. "You were the last remnant of Meredith Ryan, a woman he was terribly in love with."

"Don't," I say, but my eyes *ping* to Ahmar's, and they won't leave.

She continues, the pain in my plea fueling her next words. "He saved you because he loved you like a daughter. Couldn't bear to see you rotting away in prison. It's not something Meredith would've wanted. Knowing that idiot whore, she likely would want you free, despite you slitting her throat. Because you're sick, darling. Your delusions started well before your mother's untimely demise."

"I tried to help you, Calla," Ahmar says. The words seem like they're choking him. "I convinced your dad to put you in a psychiatric hold. I'd hoped they'd diagnose you and work with you to get you better, but all they did was release you. And I couldn't ... I didn't..."

"Ahmar, I didn't kill her!" I'm so resolute, my voice strikes through the room like a whip. "I'd remember something like that. I'd *know* if I hurt her. She was my best friend. My favorite person. My *mom*." Shaking my head, I retreat, uncaring if my back hits the wall. It would feel more solid than the ground right now.

Ahmar drags his eyes to the report, still clenched between Sabine's long, taloned fingers. "It's all there, baby girl. I did everything I could to stop this from happening, but this place, these people ... they dredge up the worst in us."

"Our lies all have to catch up with us sometime," Sabine says. "And time is up for you. If you leave this temple, I will send this report directly to the NYPD. You will be arrested, and so will your uncle. Therefore, it's in your best interest to remain Virtu-ous. Stay by my side, do as I say, and this evidence will never leave the lips of a member." She looks up to the rafters. "Are we in agreement?"

A chorus of voices ring out, "*altum volare in tenebris.*"

Fly high in the dark.

Sabine lowers her stare to mine. "You see, child, we live off the dark collateral of others. It's how we keep everyone in such pristine alignment."

My mind pendulums through the possibilities—*did I really kill her, or am I making up the image of cornering my mother in her bedroom, wielding a chef's knife in my hands, and piercing her skin?*—

My shoulder slams into the wall, and I slide down into a crouch, covering my face, moaning the denial even as remembered rivulets of blood seep between my fingers, staining my clothes and puddling at my feet.

Sabine's faraway voice circles my head like a vise. "I think I've proven my point, my noblemen. My dear Virtues, even if she is who she claims to be and has the Briar bloodline..."

This is what they do. They use your greatest fear against you.

An inner voice speaks over Sabine, poking at my conscience, prodding me awake. Chase's cadence echoes into my soul, the very words he used when trapped in a dark cage coming into the light of my eyes.

I blink.

Sabine's using what I'm most afraid of. My fear of madness.

Because *I did not kill my mother.*

The certainty is etched into my bones.

Slowly, I stand. Push off the wall and stalk to the center of the temple, where Sabine, with her back turned, continues her propaganda.

"You're the elite!" I scream at the balcony, cutting her off. "Faculty. Senators. CEOs. *Parents.* And you allow this woman to use your children for the sexual plea-sure of men who are standing right *next* to you. My own father—Headmaster Marron—seduced my mother when she was a student and he was a teacher. This club of yours isn't about rising high, it's about using sex and getting away with scandal, and allowing your children to suffer at the hands of your so-called members. You're all twisted and sick, the way you let her get away with this."

"You're forgetting an important piece of the truth you're building," Tempest adds, striding up next to me. He'd walked deeper into the temple but hadn't donned his robe. Nor has the fire died out in his otherworldly green eyes. "Calla Lily Ryan is a descendent of Rose Briar."

A rush of voices hit the air at Tempest's endorsement. Hoods bow together, arms gesticulate, and my chin notches higher. I step farther into the room. Closer to *her*.

"Don't believe me?" Tempest continues. "Ask your queen. Her family has hidden the birth certificate of the baby born from Rose Briar and *Theodore* Briar for well over a century. That's a decent piece of history she's kept from Noble discovery, and all because the Harringtons wanted the throne. Fuck, her eldest daughter dies and the other is arrested for murder—leaving *no chick* to inherit, and the bitch *still* won't admit that she's kept the true heir from you all this time."

Hoods murmur, but Sabine seethes. "Shut your mouth, boy, and join your ranks. You betray everything you've worked for, all you've earned, by defending this girl and helping to spread her lies."

"Am I a fibber?" Tempest looks up at the balcony, spreading his arms. "Guys? Am I known to have my pants on fire—ah, shit. *Fire.* Right." Tempest wags his index finger at Sabine. "You trapped a Virtue princess and the Noble legacy who rushed to save her in a fire and left them to die. Let's take bets on who's been a bad girl, 'cause I don't think it's Callie."

Sabine lashes out her arm and screams, "Take him! Tempest Callahan has no proof other than the word of a girl too mute with hallucinations to lend credence to a single word in her defense."

"I'm not suffering from anything," I say, "other than your lethal attempts to ruin me so you can continue your reign of terror on these girls. You traffic them. You make them have sex." I glance up at the balcony, shouting, "Too many of you know this to be true, because you're the ones who trap these girls in white sheets and pretend they want you to take their purity."

"Here we are, gentlemen," Sabine says through the increased mutterings, "solidified proof that this girl succumbs to nothing but her own fancies."

"Your Noble prince knew the truth!" I yell. "And Sabine stabbed him for it!"

"Lies!" a male voice cries.

A litany of "here, here," agreements follow.

"Then ask him," I counter. "When Chase Stone wakes up, hear it from his mouth. He doesn't suffer from 'hallucinations.' His credibility is tied to your reputations. You wouldn't dare go against—"

"*If* he wakes up," Sabine cuts in, "and indeed, agrees with your statements, it is only because you seduced him." Sabine's lips peel back in a grin. "The same way your mother seduced all the boys when she was here. Meredith Ryan was nothing but a slut, and you've inherited the same genes."

"I've inherited the Virtues!" I yell, stepping closer.

Sabine, not expecting the outburst, hobbles back in her heels but quickly composes herself.

I add in a softer voice, "Say what you want about me, but utter another word about my mother, and I will not regret putting real blood on your lips."

"My, my. Is that the guilt talking?"

My chest heaves. My vision skews with fury, but I don't look away from her. "You're a liar, a killer, and a terrible mother. Rot in hell."

Sabine's chest concaves, her clavicles poking out like weapons forged from bone. "Do not force me to teach you another lesson."

I bare my teeth at her, but say to the room, "If you're all so proud, so willing to be a part of her madness, *show your faces!* Look upon your queen as your true selves and study your neighbors, while asking yourself if they've touched your daughter."

Voices pitch in horror, and to my amazement, some draw back their hoods. Others grab the shoulders of their neighbors and demand they reveal themselves.

Tempest sidles up to me, a smile plastered across his face. "My boy would be proud of you."

"Stop! All of you!" Sabine howls. Veins pulse as she strains her neck. "The girl is delusional! I have a *report!*" She smacks her hand on the abused paper, then flaps it around.

"And they have a birth certificate," a female voice calls down. "Tempest Callahan backs her up. I can't discount that."

"You very well *will,* Alexandra," Sabine spits. "*My* word is final, not a child's."

"Virtues!" I cry. "Speak up. Please. Tell these people what you've endured." I search the upper floor, aiming for a face, one that will, if pushed, speak the truth. She has to.

"Violet!" I call out, but I can't find her. So, I plead with her instead. "Please. I know you hate what the Virtues have become. You shied away every time I was beaten, or humiliated, or harassed. You've come to hate what the Virtues represent. You didn't accept their invitation to watch your friends be charmed, manipulated, then coerced. You've lost Piper. Addisyn is gone. And Ivy—Ivy was cast aside in an unmarked grave, all because Sabine covets power over human lives. Come out here and tell your story. I know you have one." My voice lowers. "You're the only one left who can speak the truth."

I hear a whispered *yes* behind me. I whirl, thinking Violet's appeared from the shadows, but it was Emma who spoke, her side resting against Eden's as they raise their bowed heads and give me an affirming nod.

"Our stories were told and ignored," Emma says. "Spun by Sabine into necessary lies. My torture, my burns, my *life,* couldn't fall on her, because she's not the one who lit the match or swung the bat. But she didn't have to. Her intimidations start when we're young. Her promises ingrained in us before we hit puberty. She hides the truth about as well as Piper hid her true self from her mother. So, if you can't listen to me—if you refuse to read my scars—then listen to a present Virtue. Violet, I'm begging you, give me, Eden, Piper, Ivy, and Callie, a voice."

Tears frame my vision. I give Emma a resolute nod in return.

"You sorry girls, I warned you of the consequences of rebelling in this temple. Emma Loughrey, the fake, adopted, *unwanted* child of Daniel Stone and false sister of Chase." Sabine says, only loud enough for us to hear, as she stalks toward me. Emma winces. "And Eden, an overweight, pathetic, useless vision of the swim champion she used to be. You swore to represent me, not Callie, in exchange for my assistance in giving you back everything you'd lost. Yet here you are, betraying not me, but yourselves."

"That's your problem," Eden says. "You're so up your own ass, you can't believe we'd choose a friend over vanity. An orphaned girl over a queen."

"It's so impossible for you to fathom I'd prefer being an adopted Loughrey over a Stone," Emma chimes in, then looks at me. "We would never let it get so far, Callie. We just had to play the game to get in here. But we're on your side. Thanks for the signal, Tempest. And for getting her here like you promised."

Tempest nods, crossing his arms on a grin. I narrow my eyes at him, wondering just what my Scooby crew had gotten up to while I was unconscious.

"Violet is not like any of you liars," Sabine sputters, her eyes glancing over Tempest, Eden, Emma, me. She's counting the growing number against her. "She is the loveliest of my Virtues. She would never, *ever*—"

"I'm here," a small voice says.

The scuffling, the accusations, the robe-tearing, halts at those two, whispered words.

Violet pushes past Falyn and ignores Willow's imploring hand as she moves to stand by my side.

She lowers her arm, catches my hand in hers, and squeezes. "Callie speaks the truth."

I jolt at the volume, unused to Violet emitting such echoing certainty. "Piper admitted her involvement in Emma's beating, in the fire, before she died. I was too afraid to say anything. I ... I couldn't believe it. She spoke of her mother like our queen was a monster. She told me what Emma was forced to do ... with you, Senator Bachman."

The entire temple gasps. Mine might've joined them.

"And you, Mr. Torrence, Mr. Andrews, Dr. Hoffman. Piper named you all." Violet bows her head, her fingers digging into my hand, but she pivots to Emma. "I'm so sorry. You endured the worst the society had to offer. You went to Piper for help, and she tried and failed. It should've landed on me next. But I was too scared. Too much of a cowardly mouse to ever be considered commanding." She looks at her friends, Willow, and Falyn. "Not anymore. I mentioned my worries to you guys, but you brushed me off. You acted like I was mistaken. And you put me up as the next princess after Ivy." Violet tilts her head. "You knew what that meant for me."

Willow looks to the side, her gaze skating across mine but never landing. I study her expression, searching for our similarities, but I find none. Not inside, or out.

Falyn glares at Violet, insolence twisting her lips.

Shifting my balance, I squeeze Violet's shoulder. She's not alone when it comes to being a recipient of Willow and Falyn's ire.

"This is all your fault."

I jerk my gaze to Falyn's.

"No. It's yours," Violet says, either not realizing Falyn's speaking to me or deciding she doesn't care. "You stand by Sabine and do her bidding like what she demands isn't despicable and belittling."

"Shut up, Vi. I'm talking to your pet possum—or should I say, everybody's pest. You refuse to be put down, Callie, instead involving our entire *school*, thinking you're doing them a favor, when all you've accomplished is ruin. For them. For *us*."

I part my lips. "That's big talk for a girl who's never been forced to fuck one of those men up there to fill Sabine's pockets."

"*Enough!*" Sabine screeches. She prowls over to me, wraps her cold, bony hand around my wrist, and holds it high. "Is this your new princess? Your future *queen*? She is as my Marquess says. A rodent. A pest. A delusional *imbecile*."

The crowd above murmurs among each other, so low in tone, it's difficult to tell which way they're leaning.

I struggle against Sabine, but she holds fast. "Allow me to put it to a vote," she says. "I'll admit to concealing Rose Briar's surviving lineage, but it was for the best interests of the Society. Rose was not well before she disappeared. Manic, untrustworthy, and mourning her multiple miscarriages and stillbirths." Sabine slants her gaze to me. "Hereditary, I'm sure. My great-great grandmother understood this and deduced that the Virtues could not endure if they were to wait for Rose's secret child to come of age. The Harringtons took over, if only to keep our women strong. To maintain their educations and discover the top girls, grooming them for successful futures—"

"Did you start back then?" I sneer. "Selling your girls to maintain your authority over the Nobles?"

"Shut up," she hisses, her nails biting into my skin. "Your credibility has long since soured, you useless, vile cunt."

My eyes widen at her open vindictiveness, my hand going slack in her hold.

But nobody saw or heard it.

"Yes, put it to a vote." Tempest saunters to center stage.

Sabine's lower lip trembles with the intense need to shut him up, but a part of her must know she can't, not if she wants to continue her charade.

"Vote with the full knowledge that I'm with Callie, as is Emma Loughrey, a legacy of the Nobles and a former Virtue Princess, adopted or not. And Eden Yurman, a recipient of the Virtue's torture." Tempest notches up his chin. "And the current Noble Prince, Chase Stone, who's authorized me as his emissary and wishes for Sabine Harrington to step down."

A rush of voices meets his statement, but one person manages to talk over him. "And the king?"

"The king stands with his queen." Tempest shrugs.

"The king should be here. As should Viscount Marron," another deep, masculine voice pipes in. "Why aren't they here representing themselves?"

"Ask your queen," Tempest answers. "She's sneaky. While we wait, let's all consider how this is looking to that NYPD guy over there, and what he might do once he's released." Tempest's forehead wrinkles. "Unless we're supposed to dispose of him? I dunno, Queen, do you want to graduate to serial killer status so soon?"

Sabine drops my hand. "You little prick."

She moves so fast, her billowing skirts are a blur until the *slap* rings out.

Tempest's head jerks to the side, the tanned skin on his cheek blooming with red.

My jaw drops open. Violet whispers, "Oh my God."

Both of us are so glued to the action in anticipation of Tempest's response, I don't see Falyn coming in time.

Until the flash of silver.

The glint of her teeth.

And the roughened edges of her scream.

Callie

FALYN'S SCREAM echoes above the rafters, ricochets off the walls, and tunnels into my ears with such murderous accuracy that my body responds before my mind figures out I'm about to be disemboweled in an effort to save Tempest.

I duck, the blade whistling above my head, and tackle Falyn at the waist until we both tumble to the ground.

Shouts and hollers follow, the heavy clomps of footsteps and the high-pitched decibels of screams, but Falyn spins me to my back, covering my face with her robe and pressing down so hard, I don't have to hear my nose crack under the pressure—I *feel* it.

The fabric quickly becomes soaked with my saliva and blood as my mouth gapes and I fight against her suffocation, the random acts and heightened ruckus becoming quieter as my sole focus turns to survival.

The knife—where's the knife?

I have the keen sense she'll be swinging it down at any moment, and I won't be joining Chase in the hospital after. It'll be the morgue.

Falyn straddles me, howling triumph over the outbreak in the temple. My arms start to tire. My vision dots with darker stars, but all I can think is: *Fight.*

I raise my knees. Blindly bring my legs forward in an attempt to cross them at the front of her chest and throw her down to the ground.

The pretzel idea works—as soon as Falyn feels my shins at her face, her arms lift and she pushes at them, but thigh muscles are *so* much stronger than arms. Bunching my abs and arching my back, I smack her onto the ground and rise to a seated position, scrambling to get the cloak off my face.

And open my eyes to a violent melee.

Cloaks stream down the back stairwells onto the main floor, some trying to stop the cluster of fights, but most starting them.

Tempest's A-list actor father stands in front of his son, screaming obscenities at whoever tries to come near them and attempting to push Tempest to the exit.

Tempest cuts his eyes to me and smirks. As Willow beelines over to me and Falyn on the ground, he kicks out his foot and she belly-flops.

Sabine? Where's Sabine?

Frantic, I search the room, but Falyn is fast recovering. I peel off her and stand, dodging her hands and running into the fray, but not before collecting the knife on the way.

It's heavy with quality. Ornate with silver. Wet with invisible blood—Ivy's blood. Chase's blood. Tempest's and mine.

My grip tightens around the hilt. I wrestle my way into the middle of the temple, pausing. Then scream: "*Sabine!*"

As I do, my eyes travel up. I spot her on the balcony, alone, looking down. When she catches my eye, she curls a beckoning finger.

I don't hesitate. Sprinting to the nearest staircase, I take the steps two at a time, the knife sharp and heavy at my side.

I burst onto the balcony, the shouts and pummels down below somehow echoing louder up here, but I force the distraction away, centering all my senses on Sabine.

She reclines against the railing, her arms spread, her red dress lifting at every silky, invisible movement. The French twist in her hair is intact, and she's as regal as ever as she stands above the chaos she's caused.

"Your mother cried while she was dying," she purrs.

My feet turn to rocks. Immobile with the weight of the Earth.

"She did," Sabine assures, her hands trailing across the top of the railing. "And her last words were, '*Don't hurt my daughter.*' Oh, my." Sabine mock frowns as she watches me process her words. "Tough, isn't it? To realize the very nightmares you had over how she died were probably correct."

"You ... *monster.*"

"Did you think I hired a hitman, or manipulated one of my impressionable Virtues, or even James, that dear, malleable boy, to do my bidding? No, Calla Lily. I wanted your mother for myself. Our time together at Briarcliff was wrought with conflict. She had everything at her fingertips—her heritage was known by my future grandmother-in-law at that point. In fact, Prudence Harrington was grooming her for the succession, proud of Meredith's rise from nothing, and many accomplishments, despite her buried upbringing no high Noble or Virtue wanted to admit to. But then something changed." Sabine arcs her stare up to the elaborate ceiling, pondering her words as though pure chaos isn't exploding around her. "I believe she realized that if she accepted the role, she'd have to confess all her sins, including her illegal affair with a teacher. I do believe her mind started backtracking when she realized she was pregnant with you, sweet child, and she finally understood that once you enter succession, all your heirs are automatically obligated to enter the process, too. She didn't want that for you. At that point, she'd noticed the foulness, understood the dark nature that one had to possess to truly rule the Virtues. You see, she walked in on a princess and a Noble doing ... well, you're aware. Hmm. Now that I think of it, it was our newest Senator, dragging the girl's thighs toward him and positioning her to best accept his cock."

I wince, the dagger shaking by my side. "That's enough."

"Is it, my dear? Don't you want to hear how I found your mother after she ran, kept apprised of your upbringing, and waited for the perfect moment to kill both of you so there would never be a question as to my rule? Or would you rather we skipped that part and go straight to the crime scene I orchestrated when you were annoyingly late to your weekly dinner plans, and I had to MacGyver a scene of destruction *you* were responsible for."

My brain screams at me to remain standing when my knees buckle. I right myself, but my vision's blurred. My lips seize.

"How was I supposed to know you had an impressionable detective in your pocket? As an aside, you do have a knack for convincing men you're so small, fragile, and innocent. I wish you'd use that talent, but sadly, here we are. Ahmar Kazmi covered up everything I planted, forged a police report, and put his job and future on the line. All for ... you."

"Because Ahmar *loves* me." The wet whisper coats my lips. "An emotion you'll never come to understand. He believed in me so much, he couldn't let me fall for something I did not—would *never*—do. That's what you can't fathom, you witch. The idea that men love me for me, not for gain, or indecent motive, or blackmail. Ahmar loves me." I take a step. "Dad loves me." Another step. "*Chase* loves me." One more. "*My mother loved me.*"

Sabine's eyelids twitch, her lips thinning in fury. "I'm well aware of what love is, you pitiful trash. I loved my daughter! Piper was everything to me, and your meddlesome cunt took her from this world! Chase was hers. If he were hers that night, she would never have fallen."

"She was pushed by your other forgotten, neglected daughter," I retort. "Playing favorites doesn't really work when it ends in murder, does it, you felon-of-the-year?"

Sabine's face twists into haggard rage. "You wasted, undeserving slut of a girl! You're nothing! You will become nothing! I'll never give you this throne. I'd rather take your life just as I took your mother's."

"It's over, Sabine. Look around you. This chaos is yours. You're done—"

Sabine's hands wrap around my neck. She squeezes so tightly, my muscles shrink, tendons pop, and I gag on my own insides.

"Callie!" I hear Ahmar scream, and my bulbous eyes move past the railing to down below, where Ahmar is frozen between two fighting cloaks, his neck arched as he spots me and attempts to separate himself and get to me.

A red cloak swoops in just as he disentangles himself, the hood falling back and revealing Headmaster Marron, grabbing Ahmar by the arms and pulling him back. He came late to the party, but he's making his statement known.

Marron wants me to die? floats through my addled mind, but the black stars bouncing into my vision prevent me from dwelling on it.

Watching Ahmar be wrestled to the ground sends me into a fit of panic, and in a feat of pure desperation, I lift the dagger and shove it into Sabine's side.

Sabine gasps with a shocked kind of pain, her eyes widening, but she doesn't release me.

Worse, she glances down behind her at the floor below. Then she looks back at me and smiles. "Do you want to know how my daughter felt?"

"N—N—" I garble, dropping the knife as my hands flail and scratch against her forearms.

We grapple on the balcony, Sabine using her full, rage-filled force to bend me over the railing.

She doesn't resemble the groomed, sleek woman she's presented herself as all this time. Large, streaked blood vessels pop red in her eyes, the tip of her nose is a vicious scarlet, and her ruby lipstick is smeared across her too-white teeth, her canines shining with saliva.

"Piper will finally be avenged, and you'll die knowing your mother's murder will never be solved," she whispers hoarsely. "And my Virtues? They'll live *long* after you."

My side strains against the stone, my legs screaming for me to relent, but my lack of breath prevents any sort of failsafe. I'm being forced over the rail, Sabine's stick-thin arms growing the strength of ten vengeful men...

Fight, Callie. Fight!

A chorus of voices shoot forward, silently chanting.

Chase. Ivy. Mom.

You're strong. You will be missed if you go. You don't have to come to us yet.

As if summoned, Eden and Emma appear at the top of the stairs, rushing toward me.

They're here. They're not mad, anymore.

Their faces flash in and out of a black void as they come closer. *I'm dying. When they get here, it'll be too late. I'll pass out, and Sabine will—*

NO.

A bolt of energy soars through me at the image of my friends, desperate to save me. And Ahmar down below, fighting to get to the balcony.

My hands form into a prayer at my stomach. Sabine sees the motion and smiles. "That's right, dear girl. Succumb to my inevitable triumph."

Her face wavers, in and out, and I realize it's not my blinking that's making me see black, then reality, then black.

Pressed together, my hands shoot up, between her strangling arms. Sabine doesn't expect the move and stiffens her grip, but with enough force, I pull my hands apart and break her hold.

Sabine stumbles at the unexpected show of self-defense. I give her no time to recover.

I glance at her bleeding stomach. "That was for Chase."

Then I twist her until her back smacks against the railing. "This is for Ivy."

I push her.

Her face warps with enraged panic and she swipes for my neck, but her balance is too far over the rail. Sabine's fingers hook my necklace instead, the chain ripping free and tangling into tarnished gold treasure in her palm as she falls.

Eden and Emma reach me, their palms smacking against the stone as they bend forward over the rail.

"And that?" I say dully as Sabine's scream is abruptly cut off. "That was for my mom."

Callie

TWO WEEKS LATER

"SWEETHEART? You can go in and see him now."

The nurse pads quietly away after notifying me in the hospital's waiting room, and I stand, smoothing my shirt and casually wiping drool from the side of my mouth from when I tipped my head back to count the ceiling tiles, then never lowered my chin.

I'm not sure how long I slept in the chair, but my neck aches with a crick, and I massage it as I follow the nurse's footsteps into the corridor. It gives me something to do rather than focus on the nervous beats of my heart or the swarm of butterflies in my stomach.

The nurse didn't have to tell me what room he's in—I've known the number since the moment he was taken out of ICU and put in a private room. I've counted the days since he opened his eyes, the hours since he's been taken off a breathing tube, and added up every day I wasn't allowed to see him.

After a whirlwind of police, press, and parents, I've at last been granted permission from Chase's team of doctors to see him.

Creeping past the other rooms, all silent and dark save for the soft green glow of machines, I find Chase's with his door slightly ajar.

My breaths come out shaky. Phone calls with Ahmar and Dad have prepared me for this moment—a section of time where Chase may not look like himself or speak much at all, but instead of being scared, all I want to do is run to his hospital bed and grab his hand, then hold it to my cheek.

Because even through all the surgeries, a new reality to wake up to, and his recovery, he'd still be warm, and I need that assurance more than anything.

The large window is dark with night, but silhouetted with lights from neighboring city buildings. Those white lights crest over the still form in the bed, machines beeping softly beside him.

"I'm not Frankenstein's monster," comes a gristly, hoarse voice. "Unless that means you want to be my Bridezilla."

Smiling, I step through the reflection of lights across the floor and to his bedside, where I can get a closer look.

"Chase," I whisper.

His head falls to the side at my voice, his onyx eyes shimmering through the shadows. He blinks. "Hey, sweet possum."

"How are you ... I mean, do you feel okay? Can I get you anything?"

Amazing, how after weeks of mental preparation and all the make-believe conversations I had with him in my head, *that's* what I come up with.

"Nurse just gave me my meal." He clears his throat, grimacing when his body moves with the gesture. "Wouldn't say no to a sponge bath, though."

"I'll give you all the sponge baths you want if it means you'll be okay." I'm not surprised at the break in my voice. I only wish I'd held it in longer—I don't want to fall apart in front of him so soon. "I'm sorry. You've gone through the most harrowing injury of your life, and here I am blubbering over you."

"Hey, I like a good hot chick blubber." His voice comes out soft. "C'mere."

I shuffle closer, finding that hand I was so desperate to hold, but reluctant to put it to my cheek, now wet with a mixture of terrified and relieved tears.

"More than that, sweet possum. Get up here."

"But I could hurt you."

"No more than I already am, baby."

I hesitate, but my mind's already at his side. The mattress dips when I put a knee to it, and Chase flinches again. "Maybe this isn't—"

His arm shoots out, and he pulls me the rest of the way in, nestling me into his uninjured side.

The smell of him—a mixture of hospital and forest and *him*, has me relaxing against him as easily as if we were in my dorm room.

"I missed this," he murmurs against my hair as he strokes it away from my face.

"I missed you," I counter. "I thought you were—when I got to the dock, I thought it was too late."

"Never. Well, maybe a few seconds longer and I might've been." He keeps stroking, and my eyelids fall heavy like a cat's. "Tempest told me what you did. How you fought the water and almost died of hypothermia to get to me."

"I'd do it again."

I feel his chin pull with a smile. "Sweet possum, you did. Isn't that the second time you almost drowned? I gotta start calling you Lady of the Lake."

"No way. I don't want to ever see that placid, bullshit water ever again."

His hand moves from my temple to my shoulder and squeezes. "Does that mean you're out?"

"Out of what?"

"Briarcliff. The academy. Tempest also gave me the low-down on the temple, and the societies, and..."

"Sabine," I finish for him.

"Yeah."

I rise up on my elbow, wanting to see him and not just feel him. "Somebody called the police. Actually, a bunch of people did, once it was clear Sabine was losing ground and was obviously going to resort to violence to keep it. They came in right as she fell, swarming the temple. I've never seen Cloaks scatter so fast, and I thought I'd witnessed them at their sneakiest."

"I heard it was a clusterfuck."

"A lot of Cloaks had left before it got out of control—the ones called out by Violet, the powerful, older men and women. All that remained was ... us. The kids. I keep trying to imagine what it was like to be one of the Briarcliff PD, walking in to a bunch of rumpled high schoolers in fancy, torn velvet robes, surrounding a woman bleeding out in the middle of the floor."

"The three of you were on the upper balcony looking down." Chase shifts to get more comfortable. "You, my sister, and Eden."

"Wow, Tempest didn't leave anything out, did he? I thought we weren't supposed to upset you in your..."

"Tempest is a fucking choirboy right now who refuses to tell me shit. I've been reading the news on a tablet Rio snuck in here under a Big Mac. *Both* were very much appreciated."

The mention of his friends causes me to think about all the arrests. "I'm sorry about James."

"Stop apologizing, Calla."

My eyes tighten at the use of my nickname, previously only used by Mom and Ahmar. But as fast as they narrow, they soften. I don't correct him. I want to hear it more from him.

He says, "You're the one who endured the worst. Sabine was gonna kill you—I read the Article."

Chase refers to the Briarcliff Patch local newspaper, written by one librarian named Darla Dumphries, outlining the events of the temple showdown in scarily accurate detail. She wasn't there, but enough shellshocked new initiates spoke in detail about the allegations of trafficking against Sabine Harrington and all those in cahoots with her. Darla wasn't afraid to name names or explain how Sabine strangled an unnamed high school senior, and the two were wrestling for enough time for the girl to be forced into using self-defense before she was tossed over the railing by a very angry, very unhinged alumnus and formally respected member of Briarcliff Academy.

I have a lot to thank Darla for. It's because of her all those men and women who escaped were now being dragged in for police interviews. Lawyered up to their necks, of course, but the media prints their names in block letters across the nation every time another one is rounded up. Daniel Stone and Headmaster Marron are a few such individuals, brought in to explain their actions and how a club so egregious, so despicably vile, could possibly be allowed to function on private school grounds. The indictments should come any day now.

"The Nobles and Virtues are no more," Chase says, drawing me back to the present.

"This isn't what I wanted," I respond quietly. "Not like this, anyway."

"Please. This is perfect for you. The societies are dismantled, press is all over the scandal, and my father is so fucking infamous, he can't even hire drivers without them either attempting to pass on any information about him for money or refusing to go near him. It's amazing."

I lift my head. "But all you wanted was to save them, and I imploded that goal into dust."

"Yeah, you fucked it up real good, but I'm glad you did, because otherwise you'd be dead."

Chase says it so simply, but I sense his burning stare in the gloom.

"It didn't go as planned," I say.

"No shit. Nothing ever does. My psycho stepmom stabs me in the stomach—I lose my fucking gall bladder for it—and what does Father do? Stays at my bedside like a good little daddy, all the while aware of a temple ceremony where Sabine railroads you and solidifies their positions as kings and queens for fucking world domination. We can't make this shit up, and I was a fool to think a malignant society could cure itself."

"You were right about the new pledges, though. They're the ones who stood up to this mess and made it public."

"No, Calla, *you* did." He finds my hand in the tangled sheets and holds it firm. "The news about you is scarce, but I got the gist that you held your ground with Sabine in front of all the people who wanted to either destroy you, or bury you, or both. You got balls, kid."

I smile at the reference, similar to what Ahmar said to me once we both recovered enough from the all-night interviews and interrogations, and he tucked me under his emergency blanket, where we sat at the back of an ambulance and just stared out at the mess. He wasn't able to discuss the forged police report or his belief that I could actually hurt Mom. I'd searched for his hand and squeezed hard, letting him know I forgave him. All his actions after that report told me how sorry he was and how much he wanted to protect Meredith's only child. We have a lot to work out, but I'm thankful we're both alive to do it.

"Marron didn't do anything but hold Ahmar back from saving me," I say now. "He arrived near the end but didn't say anything in my defense."

"I'm not surprised."

"Do you think he knows about me? Or believes it? He hasn't said anything since he resigned. He's only speaking through his lawyers, and he hasn't bothered to get in contact with me."

"Does that upset you?"

I think about it. The first thing I saw as dawn crept up over all the flashing police lights was my parents tumbling out of their car as it screeched to a halt in front of yellow crime scene tape. Lynda's arms were flailing, and Dad was screaming at whoever was unfortunate enough to be loitering nearby. But like a boat searching for a lighthouse, they found me through the chaos. I've never seen Dad sprint so fast, or heard such an echoing, keening sob come from Lynda. They found me, they held me, and they cried until they finally believed I was safe.

"No," I answer Chase. "He's not my father. Never will be."

"I wish, in the midst of all this crazy, you could've found justice for your mom."

My gaze slides over to him. "But I did."

"Oh, yeah?"

"Sabine admitted everything and told me how she killed Mom. I've given all those details to the NYPD, but I don't know if they have enough evidence to pursue it. But you know what? I'm okay with that. I have my answers, and Sabine's getting her punishment. Perhaps she was suffering already, what with Piper's betrayal and then death. Not even Addisyn's willingness to act just like her mother was enough to convince Sabine to be satisfied with what she's gotten away with. It was always more. Just *more*. She wasn't going to stop."

Chase is silent for a moment. He changes our grip, lacing his fingers through mine. "You good?"

"About as good as you," I say.

He grumbles in agreement. "I mean about the whole self-defense thing."

"You mean my attempted murder."

"Don't call it that." A rough edge overtakes his voice. "It'll never be that. She was close to killing you."

I shrug it off, but Chase reads me better than that.

"C'mon, sweet possum, talk to me."

"It's terrible," I say eventually. "I hate thinking about it. I have nightmares, sometimes even when I'm awake. The way her face contorted and the crunch of her ... her skull. It's always here in my head. But my fear of the police not believing me because of my past—that's over now. There are enough witnesses, and Sabine made her motives clear when she screamed she wanted to kill me."

"The Article mentioned something like Eden and Emma tried to get Sabine's hands off you, and in the struggle, Sabine fell. But that's not what happened, is it?"

This is for Chase. Ivy. My Mom.

"No," I admit. "Do you think differently of me now? Now that..." *you know what I'm capable of?*

Chase speaks through my flashback. "I'm thinking what I've always thought. That you're a gorgeous, perplexing, frustrating, addictive girl who I never want to let out of my sight again."

I study him, wondering how two such screwed up people could still find happiness amid all this horror.

As if in answer, Chase shuffles to make room for me to snuggle closer. "Get back here. I'm cold."

This time, I don't hesitate.

"I love you," I whisper into his skin. "Don't ever leave me again."

He tips my chin up and kisses me, slow and light, breathy and sweet. "Remind me never to push you into a lake."

I smile, then at his goofy, lopsided grin, start laughing.

Soon, we're both shaking with painful, needed laughter, our hearts entwined with our voices as we unconsciously wish for better, lighter things to come.

Epilogue

CHASE

GRADUATION - 4 MONTHS LATER

"ARE YOU READY YET? I feel like you should be ready by now," I say as I twirl my tie between my fingers, wearing a path in Callie and my sister's wood flooring.

"Almost!" comes Callie's faint call through her door.

There's a faint twinge in my gut as I move, my skin tight, uncomfortable, and itchy over the ache. I absentmindedly brush a thumb over the scar tissue.

Callie flings her door open. "We just have to—oh."

She gives an appreciative sweep from my feet to my head. I'm in a pantsuit, shirtless, swinging a tie around, and she looks like she wants to lick me from top to bottom.

"Like what you see?" I ask, summoning my arrogance instead of shrinking and covering the nasty mark on my abs like instinct tells me to.

"Very much." She bites her lower lip.

My pants tighten at the groin because of it.

A blush creeps across her cheekbones, and she glances behind her. "Um. Emma? You almost ready?"

Aaaaand shrinkage. Nothing like the mention of my sister to deflate the moment.

"Yeah. Hang on," Emma says, her voice faint.

I perk up, angling my head to better see into Callie's room. Callie steps aside, the deep puirple of her floor-length gown flowing across her legs as she walks. It sets off the subtle red in her hair—a copper fire I always knew was in her but never took the time to spot outside her.

My sister steps into the doorframe in a pale blue gown, her hair combed to one side and flowing over her shoulder. She chose to have her hair styled on her right to mask the scars on her cheek and neck, but I want her to wear them proudly.

As if summoned, my healing stab wound throbs a reminder that physical differences can sometimes make one shy.

Emma raises her eyes to mine. I'm about to say, "You look extravag—"

"Put a shirt on, you social media whore."

I bark out a laugh. "I'm only holding out my phone so I can constantly check the time while I wait for you angels." I peer behind her. "Is Eden ready, or am I still waiting to put on my shirt?"

"She's ready," Callie says, and I can't help but look to her and smile.

Her voice remains quiet, tentative and unsure. After the events that transpired, and my long hospital stay, she's approached these last months as she would a viper. Cautious, suspicious, and threatened.

Especially considering Sabine is still in a coma. My hope is she'll never wake up.

The temple's showdown was told to me in spurts as I regained consciousness and how the society lost control of some members, many were hurt, and one severely injured when she was stabbed in self-defense, then folded over the second-story barrier.

That was the first story given to me by Detective Haskins. The truth was whispered in my ear, Callie curled against me and explaining how she pushed—*she* pushed—Sabine headfirst into a marble floor.

She admitted to killing my mother, Callie said. *And was unashamed about Ivy, unrepentant about all the girls she'd had molested and raped. All she cared about was Piper, a girl she could never get back. She didn't give a shit about anybody living. It's like the rage of every person wronged by her swept through me. I couldn't stop it if I tried.*

Did you try? I asked, but it wasn't with judgment.

Her hair brushed under my jaw as she shook her head in answer. *I didn't want to be a good person then. I wanted to be as bad as her.*

I kissed her head. *You'll never be like her. I love you, Callie.*

After one beat. Two. Three. *I love you, too.*

I said them. After years of refusing love, I've finally accepted it. It's with those words in mind I tilt my head back to get a better, full-on view of her as she passes me and heads to the kitchen for a trillionth cup of coffee. Callie catches on to my attention, covering her mouth with her fingers as she quiets a soft huff of embarrassment. "Stop looking at me like that. Your sister is right there." She motions to the bedroom, a place I wish *we* were frequenting right about now.

The mention of Emma sobers me. Again. "She handling everything okay?"

Callie shrugs. "Graduation day? Sure. It's nothing compared to the level of torture she endured at the hands of your father, being told she was adopted, then witnessing Sabine plunge off a balcony."

"Fair point," I muse, but I'm not convinced.

Emma and I hashed things out as much as we could with only a four-month time period between Hell and Earth. It took a lot of coaxing, but I'm pretty confident I've convinced her she'll always be my twin, no matter fucking what.

It was important to me that Emma and Callie work their shit out, too, and while it's still in progress, the fact that these three misfits are getting ready together for our final day at Briarcliff Academy is a big win.

"Do you regret staying at Briarcliff?" I ask her as she fiddles with the coffee machine. Emma and Eden stay in the bedroom, bickering about some sort of salmon sash—whatever the hell that means.

Callie answers with zero hesitation, "No." She stops what she's doing and looks up. "Because that would've meant leaving you."

My girl.

My girl blew the case wide open when she did what she did that day. I wish I could tell her daily how proud of her I am, how *strong* she is, but the words always die on my lips when those haunted eyes of hers meet mine. They're burnished now, those golden greens. Torn and spent with wear.

But I love them. And I love her about as much as I can love anybody—with every fiber I possess.

"You guys ready?" Callie calls, sliding a mug over to me.

I take the shot of espresso, wishing it were tequila.

"Yes, yes, we're coming!" Eden answers and soon, the two of them shuffle out of Callie's bedroom, so uncomfortable in their fancy-ass frocks I want to bust out with belly laughter. Not wanting to lose my balls so soon after recovery, I amend by saying, "You girls look great."

"Awesome. Let's get this over with so I can find my sweatpants," Eden says.

They head to the door, attempting to corral Callie on the way.

"Hang on," I say to them. All three heads turn.

Damn. It's eerie how much these girls mirror each other's movements now. Is this what death and trauma does to a group?

"What?" my sister barks when I'm momentarily speechless.

"Callie stays with me for a minute. We'll meet you guys downstairs."

"What happened to the crankasaurus who wanted us in our finest so we could get this shit over with?" Eden asks.

"He needs a minute," I retort, and leave it at that.

"Go," Callie says to the girls. "We'll be right down."

They're not happy about it, and I'm confident I hear "topless hypocrite" muttered from one of their mouths, but they leave.

"What?" Callie asks. She moves her hands to her hips. "Dad, Lynda, and Blair are waiting. If we want to make the ceremony, we should—"

"Take the dress off."

Callie's mouth falls open. Before she can question me, I prowl toward her, reaching around for her zipper, or buttons, or whatever holds this royal purple *fuck me* gown in place.

"Chase, don't! We have to—" Her words are cut off with a kiss, one her lips instantly go supple for.

She groans, batting at my bare chest but not putting much effort into it.

Our tongues dance and grind, but instead of giving into the bliss, I pop one eye open and continue wrestling with the back of her dress. Goddamnit. I can't—it won't—

Fuck this.

I break off the kiss, lift her skirts, and place her thong-clad ass on the kitchen counter.

"Chase!" she cries. Mugs rattle on their tree.

I give her one last, searing, biting kiss, then coax her until she's lying flat. "I want your pussy, and I want it now. Oh, and I'm thirsty."

Callie struggles onto her elbows. "What? Oh, g—" Her head falls back, that incredible hair cascading, as soon as I push my tongue into her folds and play with the hood of her clit.

"Mm," I say into her sweetness, then lick for more.

She cries out, her legs swinging up and pretzeling around my neck, her fingers tangling into my hair to bring me deeper. I do as she requests, diving and twirling my tongue, using my fingers to spread and stroke her, until she writhes against my mouth, each moan and mewl escaping those pert lips sending my cock higher and higher.

There's not much more I can take. I push off, though I'm still parched and starving for her, to undo my belt and pants. Tossing them somewhere, I then palm my dick, aligning it to her perfectly.

She spreads her legs, as if my cock isn't a magnet to her pussy and couldn't find her anywhere.

"Are you wet for me?" I say, though her folds shine with both my saliva and her juice. I just want to hear her say it.

"Yes." When I don't move, she growls, "Goddammit, *yes*, Chase, now fuck me like you promised you would, or I'll just get myself off while you watch!"

"Don't you dare," I growl, then sink into her.

Callie's palms smack against the granite as she spreads her arms wide and tilts her chin to the ceiling, accepting my dick like a sex goddess in benediction.

It turns me on so much that I have to reel in the tingling warning at my balls, the tightening in my shaft. I want to draw this out. It's been too long, and I'm not about to play the game of delicacy when she looks so damn hot spread out on the counter.

I start hard, but I won't finish fast. Our skin smacks together. My tie hangs open at my bare neck and at each thrust, the Briarcliff colors bounce.

"More," Callie whispers through her cries, her hands scrabbling for my pecs as she arches and pulls me closer. "More, more, *more.*"

"Always," I groan near her ear, then sit her up so she's draping over me, and I clutch her thighs and pound.

The edge is near, that placid sparkling surface below begging for me to make waves.

"You with me?" I ask her between thrusts, surprisingly breathless.

I could blame it on my recovery, but...

It's her.

She's done this to me.

"Yes," she whispers back, just as starved for oxygen.

"Then come," I order, gripping the back of her neck, her hair tangling against my fingers. "Come with me."

"Yes," she says, her back arching as the first wave hits her, then the next.

I take some pleasure for my own, my lips peeling back at the first fractal impact, my vision blacking out right about the time my entire being comes alive.

When it's over, we collapse against each other, breathing heavy, the fabric of her dress curling and tickling my ass cheeks.

I take my time leaving her, since she feels so good and right, but I also don't want to take away the moment she's been waiting for—the moment we all want.

Graduation out of this motherfucking school.

I kiss her before I draw away, her lips swollen and reddened with my scruff. I love that I've left my mark on her and that when she accepts her diploma from the acting headmaster, our sex will be all over her.

Callie pops down from the counter, smoothing her hair. "I should probably straighten up."

"You look perfect."

"Sure." She scoffs. "If you like the whole scruffy possum look."

"I *love* the scruffy possum look."

She catches my stare and smiles.

In that moment, I'm lost.

I'm hers.

"Fine, but only because we're a million minutes late," she says, then helps me dress, especially as I can't bend down so well anymore.

Callie fixes my tie around my collar in between stolen kisses, then scrapes back my hair from my face and laughs when it pops right back into the tousled position as soon as she lets go.

"I think we're as ready as we'll ever be," she says.

"Agreed. Let's go."

She takes my hand, but as we stroll to the door, something through her open door and under her bed catches my eye.

A green stem.

"Hang on a minute, would you?" I say as soon as she steps into the hallway.

"Really? Again?"

"Not for sex," I say on a huff, though when I give her the once-over, I can't promise anything. "Be right back."

I jog into her room while she waits, grab the stem, white petals escaping with my pull. I stare at the fresh bloom.

"Chase? Everything okay?"

"Yeah," I call, then break the stem in half. I stroll into the bathroom like nothing's amiss, then flush the white rose down the toilet.

"You ready?" I ask as I step into the hallway and shut the door.

"Isn't that what I should be asking you, Mr. There's Always Time For Sex?"

"I'm golden," I say with a grin, then take her warm, welcoming hand and lead us into our society-free future.

Can't get enough of the Nobles and Virtues? Read the latest spin-off, THORNE! Don't miss out on Ketley's darkest romance yet.
    The moment I stepped into Winthorpe High, I was branded as the new girl who stole somebody else's life, and he hates me for it...

Sneak Peek of Thorne

THE THORNE OF WINTHORPE HIGH, BOOK ONE

I PULL at the thin gold chain around my neck, dragging it across the pad of my thumb until it burns.

"We're almost there," he says.

I call him *he* because ... I don't know what to call him yet. His thick blond hair flows back from his face, the silver highlights catching in the meager sun when it decides to show itself as we drive through the low-hanging gray clouds. Crow's feet line his striking blue eyes, and the stubble on his jaw sparkles with the same silver threads, framing his full lips.

Staring, studying, I look for similarities in his face but find none.

He notices my attention, his eyes darting to mine before going back to the road, but thankfully, he does nothing except clutch the wheel tighter.

When I first met him two months ago, I didn't have the wherewithal to search for a ring on those long, slender fingers. I do now. His left hand is bare, the only adornment an expensive matte metallic watch wrapped around his wrist. It peeks out through the cuffs of his blazer—the man picked me up in a *suit*—along with a thin, black threaded bracelet knotted so tightly, its frayed ends puff out as if strangled.

I wrinkle my nose at the time-worn band. The rest of him is so put-together, like his handsomeness is his brand, but I can't think of him as good-looking. I don't want to think of him at all.

The view out the passenger window offers enough of an escape, and I stare out at the cliffs and the white spray of the ocean crashing against the rocks below. The winding seaside road carries us to the top, driving into bottomless clouds, only to come out of the fog and do it again. I'm protected by the car's cabin, but the salty mist seems to have crusted against my skin regardless. I drift a finger down my cheek, wondering if my flesh has turned to granules the incoming storm will lift to the sky.

"It'll be okay, Ember."

My hand drops from my face.

Are you saying that for yourself or for me? I don't voice a response. Nor do I turn from the window.

"I don't intend to steal you away forever." He clears his throat. "In fact, I was hoping during these past few weeks you would've come to understand the advantages of coming to Raven's Bluff." He pauses. "Do as I say, and you can see them again. One day."

The mention of my parents has me whipping toward him. "I plan to."

In truth, I don't know if I want to see my parents any more than I want to live with this man, but I refuse to offer any reasons to continue this conversation.

A muscle in his cheek clenches, but his attention doesn't stray from the winding asphalt. It can't, considering how narrow and close this road is to the edge of the cliffs. "I'd like to take this opportunity to get to know you as well."

My lashes flutter into my vision as I shut down and go back to the window.

He sighs heavily but doesn't push it.

What he calls advantages, I see as fractures growing and expanding through the life I thought I knew. He came to my home two months ago and ruined everything. I was happy, settled, and eager to start the summer with the knowledge I was at the top of my class after my junior year. Captain of the debate team. Co-president of the coding club.

It was perfectly laid out, all of it, and this man took it all away with a simple snap of his fingers and the question, *Wouldn't you want Winthorpe Preparatory on your college applications?*

Of course, he prefaced it with a hangdog look and the hollowed-out eyes of a man who was just as shocked to see me as I was him. Our background noise was my mother's sobs and my father's sharp growls, demanding proof yet refusing to answer *my* questions, my devastation.

Is it true, Dad? Mom? I'm adopted?

The memories echo inside my skull, not unlike the caves carved into the cliffs by the angry ocean below.

"Are you all right?"

My eyes snap open at his concerned tone, tense anger replacing the grimace tightening my features. He doesn't have the right to be worried about me. He's neglected me for almost eighteen years of my life. I'd dismissed him entirely, screamed at him to leave, to stop lying in my home, *you are not my father*, to which he responded with his own hoarse cry. *I never knew I had a daughter!*

You would think neither one of us would want a relationship after that.

Yet ... he knew how to reel me in with promises of a position at a prestigious, impossibly attainable school, an academy in his hometown where he was an alumnus. If I agreed to live with him for my senior year, he would get me in.

To a school where the entire graduating class made it into the Ivies.

A place where the academic brainpower of rare, handpicked professors made the other top high schools in the United States seem like kindergarten play.

The one spot that held the most coveted tech internship and scholarship in the country. An award I fantasized about receiving but never actually believed I'd have a chance in hell of qualifying for.

Somehow, *he* understood my weakness and pounced on it. He made it seem like such a sure thing that even my parents couldn't argue once they finally admitted the truth. At least, that was how he made it appear. I doubt he would've given them a choice, but I was too angry with them to argue to stay.

The adoption was illegal, he said. *I never gave my consent. Once I found out, I was determined to meet you.*

That only made my mother sob harder, her shoulders quaking as she confessed how desperate she and Dad were to have a baby. So fraught with emptiness, they were willing to drain their life savings for a baby and never questioned my origins after being told my mother died in childbirth.

The thought makes me sick. And while this man didn't come out and say it, his insinuations that he would file kidnapping charges against my parents if I didn't submit to his wishes were enough to make me feel putrid, wrong, and boxed in.

Then he pretended to give me eight weeks to think about it. My summer break, reeking with the hidden poison under the offer of a bright future.

I've been lied to my entire life, and now the person gaining the most advantage is taking me to his home, all because I can't resist the road to perfection.

I should ask myself again, who is the weaker of us two?

The car slows, redirecting my focus to the front. We turn a hard left to pass through iron gates with the twisted iron cursive of "Weatherby Manor" lining the top. Instead of a long drive leading up to the house, there's a circular driveway. While consumed in my internal rage, I'd missed our turn away from the ocean to a crowded street of mansions, each hidden behind large brush, stone, and iron, sitting five or six yards from the main road.

He slows the car in front of the black double doors, each showcasing identical, elaborate door knockers. At this vantage point, glimmering black twines around the iron circle like snakes, with bumps and ridges like the features of a face resting in the middle.

A *splat* against the window has me jumping back. Then another and another. Soon, Medusa's double heads blur into distorted ink as raindrops start falling in buckets against the car.

"Shit," he mumbles while twisting to reach into the back seat.

I flinch at the close contact, a motion he doesn't miss. For a moment, his brows sag in disappointment, but he quickly smooths his expression as he hands me an umbrella. "Marta and Dash have left for the day, so you'll have to make a break for the door without assistance."

Frowning at his notion of needing help to step out of a car, I open the door. The mansion seems close enough, so I sprint to the house, leaving the unopened umbrella to bounce against my side.

By the time I make it to the entrance, my hair sticks to my temples, and my black tank sags against my torso. Rain droplets fall into my eyes as I turn under the stone awning and watch him step out of the black sedan and head to the trunk —umbrellaless.

Did he give me his only umbrella? My fingers tighten on its handle.

He lifts the trunk, the rain drenching the top of his head and his shoulders, falling so hard it blurs the landscape into white streaks as he pulls out my luggage.

I can't very well stand here and witness him struggle with my things in a storm—

though it's tempting—and I don't have a key. The umbrella *thwicks* open at the press of a button, and I jog back to the car, helping him with my two carriers.

"I got it," he says, ushering me back to the house. His previously coiffed hair falls into his eyes. The blue sky seems to have taken shelter in his irises until the storm passes.

"You're soaked," I say.

"So are you," he counters, "and without a jacket. Wait for me at the doors."

Ignoring his request, I'm about to shove the umbrella into his chest and grab one of my roller bags when movement behind him catches my eye.

The rain seems to lighten as my attention focuses across the street. A figure leans against a stone column, legs crossed at the ankle and eerily still despite the cascading rain, their umbrella tipped just enough to disguise their face. Smoke drifts from underneath the nylon canopy, the pungent smell of weed soon following, even at this distance.

Their eyes are hidden, but I *feel* this person watching my movements.

"Who's that?" I ask, a crash of thunder almost stealing my words.

Lightning flashes, placing the figure in stark relief. The person hasn't moved, as if impervious to the sharp crackle of thunder and deadly spikes of lightning.

"Ignore him."

The man grips the back of my arm and ushers me away, but I can't peel my gaze from the boy across the street—because he is a guy, I can see it now that he's raised the umbrella and his broad shoulders come into view, then his face.

Keys jangle as the front door's unlocked, but my stare remains on the figure. His features are obscured, but his pale skin and dark hair come through the rain in stark relief.

So does the moment when the joint falls from his mouth, his lips part in disbelief, and his eyes lock on mine.

He jerks back, doing a double take, but then blinks out of it, turning rigid. That face—oddly mesmerizing in the blur of the storm—hardens before his mouth turns up into a sneer, and he whirls from the stone column on one side of a curving drive-way, disappearing into the thick foliage beyond.

My brows pinch together. "What's his problem?"

"When I say ignore him," the man says as he pushes open the door, "I'm not kidding around, Ember." He waits for me to step in first, but as I turn my attention to him, I notice the sky has left his eyes. "He's the son of a terrible man. You'd do best to stay away from him."

I sneak a final look across the street before stepping inside, but the boy is long gone.

Terrible man, huh? You mean, he could be an enemy of the guy who upended my life simply out of curiosity and a desire for control?

I think I'd do best knowing everything about him.

Read the latest spin-off, THORNE, now!

About the Author

Ketley Allison has always been a romantic at heart. That passion ignited when she realized she could put her dreams into words and her heart into characters. Ketley was born in Canada, moved to Australia, then to California, and finally to New York City to attend law school, but most of that time was spent in coffee shops thinking about her next book.

Her other passions include wine, coffee, Big Macs, her cat, and her husband, possibly in that order.

If you're wondering about that final rose ... Callie and Chase have their happy ending, but what about those societies?

Not to worry, Tempest's story is coming soon. Until then, keep an eye out for the Briarcliff spin-off series, *The Thorne of Winthorpe Academy* (and OMG this cover).

If you're looking for more books by me, check out my romcom, angsty romances, available on Amazon under Ketley Allison.

Thank you for reading this series all the way to the end! I love my stories, but it always feels so nice and surprising that other people love them, too. If you have the time, I'd be grateful if you left a review on your preferred platform, or tag me on social media to let me know your thoughts. Those golden little stars are what drive me to keep writing.

tiktok.com/ketleyallison

facebook.com/ketleyallison

instagram.com/ketleyallison

bookbub.com/authors/ketleyallison

amazon.com/author/ketleyallison

goodreads.com/ketleyallison

Also by Ketley Allison

all in kindle unlimited

If you want more bullies and secret societies, read:

Rival

Virtue

Fiend

Reign

If you like your bad boys and bullies as standalones (no series, one book, with a happy ending), read:

I'm Not Faking You

I'm Not Craving You

If you like the dark underground princes, read

Underground Prince

Jaded Princess

If you like a grump turned into a softie, read:

I'm Not Dating You

I'm Not Loving You

If you like your playboys with big hearts and bigger secrets, read:

I'm Not Trusting You

I'm Not Daring You

I'm Not Playing You

If you like crime with your romance, read the Vows duet:

Have

Hold

Lightning Source UK Ltd.
Milton Keynes UK
UKHW020306080223
416610UK00016B/1874